[signature]
....
Lucius Shepard

THIS EDITION OF *DAGGER KEY* IS LIMITED TO 200
NUMBERED SLIPCASED HARDCOVER COPIES SIGNED BY LUCIUS
SHEPARD AND CHINA MIÉVILLE, AND 500 NUMBERED
JACKETED HARDCOVER COPIES SIGNED BY LUCIUS SHEPARD.

This is copy 172

DAGGER KEY
And Other Stories

DAGGER KEY
And Other Stories

 Lucius Shepard

INTRODUCTION BY CHINA MIÉVILLE

PS Publishing 2007

Dagger Key And Other Stories / Copyright © 2007 by Lucius Shepard

Introduction / Copyright © 2007 by China Miéville

Cover / Copyright © 2007 by J.K. Potter

Published in September 2007 by PS Publishing Ltd. by arrangement with the author. All rights reserved by the author.

FIRST EDITION

ISBN
978-1-904619-74-1 (Deluxe slipcased hardcover)
978-1-904619-73-4 (Trade hardcover)

This book is a work of fiction. Names, characters, places and incidents either are products of the author's imagination or are used fictitiously. Any resemblance to actual events or locales or persons, living or dead, is entirely coincidental.

"Stars Seen Through Stone" first appeared in *The Magazine of Fantasy & Science Fiction*, July 2007; "Emerald Street Expansions" first appeared on *Sci Fiction*, March 2002; "Limbo" first appeared in *The Dark*, edited by Ellen Datlow (Tor, 2003), and has been revised for its appearance here; "Liar's House" first appeared on *Sci Fiction*, December 2003; "Dead Money" first appeared in *Asimov's*, April 2007; "Dinner at Baldassaro's" first appeared in *Postscripts* 10, Spring 2007; "Abimagique" first appeared on *Sci Fiction*, August 2005, and has been extensively revised for its appearance here; The Lepidopterist" first appeared in *Salon Fantastique*, edited by Ellen Datlow and Terry Windling (Thunder's Mouth, 2006); "Dagger Key" is original to this collection.

Design and layout by Alligator Tree Graphics

Printed and bound in Great Britain by Biddles Ltd

PS Publishing Ltd / Grosvenor House / 1 New Road / Hornsea, HU18 1PG / Great Britain

e-mail: editor@pspublishing.co.uk • *Internet:* http://www.pspublishing.co.uk

CONTENTS

Introduction by China Miéville v
Stars Seen Through Stone 3
Emerald Street Expansions 77
Limbo 115
Liar's House 191
Dead Money 235
Dinner At Baldassaro's 309
Abimagique 341
The Lepidopterist 393
Dagger Key 409
Story Notes 463

INTRODUCTION
Griaule and the Mountains

(warning—spoilers ho.)

*L*overs of the fantastic are special.

We, and especially we, can see through the grubbiness of reality. We, and especially or even only we, are attuned to the marvellous, not bowed down by the grinding tedium of quotidian life. It's no wonder we so love the figure of the special, visionary child who never fits in with her so-boring parents, town and classmates, and who eventually finds her way to the enchanted land she deserves. We are that child. In our passion for the magic behind the everyday, we are an elect.

Yeah.

Right.

Is that a parody of the position? Certainly, a little, but consider the cavalierly nouned adjective "Mundane". It's a common enough term used by some SF/F fans to refer to those who prefer their cultural production "realist" and mainstream. Such an epithet bespeaks the ludicrously aggrandising self-image of some fans of the fantastic. Because if they, everyone else, are "mundane", what are we, but, well . . . special?

Fortunately there have always been countertraditions. There are, for example, the anti-fantasies of M. John Harrison, or Michael Swanwick's astonishing *The Iron Dragon's Daughter*. These are books with an antagonistic, even punitive relationship with the fantastic they express.

And there's Lucius Shepard.

Shepard, too, is too tough, too political to let fantasy believe in its own

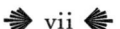

fey daydream of escape. But his strategy is not one of scorching earth. It is a little gentler, no less effective, and altogether fascinating.

It's hard to put your finger on. You read and reread these stories, and know that something strange is going on, but for a while you can't work out what it is.

At last it hits you. In the stories of *Dagger Key*, Lucius Shepard makes the fantastic a bit *low-key*.

Wait, wait. There's no cause for alarm. This is high praise, not criticism. This is at the crux of what makes Shepard so exceptional.

Let's be clear: addicts of the wow-porn we call the Sense of Wonder need not be concerned—*Dagger Key* contains unspeakably alien creatures, body-hopping ghosts, impossible conspiracies, zombies (a rare treat, "Dead Money", a follow-on to the astonishing early novel *Green Eyes*), fallen angels, dimensional portals, lives after deaths, a sex-magic apocalypse, and a story set on and around the flanks of what is perhaps Shepard's most popular and enduring creation, the huge, nebulously malevolent dragon Griaule.

But despite and alongside the traditional vasty strangeness of these concerns, Shepard brilliantly and provocatively pokes the grandiosity of the strange, in his precise delivery, his bewildered protagonists, his refusal of bombastic catharsis or explanation. He *teases* the magic.

Take the book's opening story, "Stars Seen through Stone". It opens with Shepard's usual exceptionally acute dialogue and observations, a study of a loathsome little man. Gradually the scene becomes more uncomfortable, at first in ways that would be familiar in "mainstream" fiction, before the gradual realisation that something else is going on. Some entity from beyond is spreading its influence. It is preparing to feed. The wall between worlds is growing thin. Until, at last, in a vivid and dramatic supernatural culmination, those boundaries are breached, and things from beyond emerge, to feast, to harvest humans.

After which, we learn, "there was a hue and cry about leaving the town, [until] . . . calmer voices prevailed, pointing to the fact that there had been no fatalities".

Wait . . . what?

It's a horror story. What else can it be? That burgeoning foreboding, the creaking of the seams of the world, the maleficent intervention, the breach, the monstrous feeding. But how many horror stories end, in effect, ". . . and then everything was back to normal and no one died."?

The events described weren't the apocalypse they appeared to be. They were just something that happened, and that finished *without that much lasting impact*. It is an absolutely bravura move, that only a writer of supreme confidence and guts could carry off.

Shepard knows well that we have read the same books he has. He knows that we know how that story must end. He withholds, though, because that is not the universe in which his characters live. We may have thought they lived in a story, but actually they are somewhere more real, more *natural* than that.

That is the key. The signs are there: Shepard's dialogue; his descriptions of landscape; his focus on human motivations; his political savvy. He is a naturalist (in a particularly American tradition). All the dragons, zombies, ghosts or otherworldly spirit-harvesters do not alter that a jot. What he's not is a *lumpen* naturalist—the reality he depicts contains more things than are dreamt of in our philosophy. But it's still real, still natural. It is a naturalism invigorated but never overwhelmed by the uncanny.

The most brilliant expression of this comes in "Liar's House", the recounting of one of the dragon Griaule's opaque schemes. There is one throwaway clause, early on, which provides a startling insight into Shepard's project. Describing his sculptures of the great Griaule, the protagonist Hota sees them as "objects that—like their model—appeared to be natural formations that bore a striking resemblance to dragons."

Run though that implicit description of Griaule. What does a miles-long, vastly recumbent dragon look like? It looks like a mountain range that looks like a dragon.

Here is an answer to the conundrum, faced whether they acknowledge it or not by all writers of the fantastic, of how to describe the magically indescribable. All we have for reference is the everyday.

With this extraordinary sentence—which must surely go down as one of the most incisive, radical and rigorous examinations of the fantastic in fantasy—Shepard achieves something remarkable. On the one hand, he undercuts the self-big-up of magic. We cast about for similes, but the magic is, and can be, "like" nothing other than the mental furniture we have to hand, that very unmagic stuff all around us.

At the same time, Shepard honours that everyday too often denigrated. What, the analogy asks, can be more extraordinary than a mountain? After all, they are what *dragons* look like! Dragons, in this radical grammar, aren't their own end; they are referents to help us visualise rocks. What an astonishing thing to do to the fantastic.

But it is astonishing because we know that dragons are astonishing. And we know that, and Shepard knows it, and the analogy knows it too, though it pretends not to.

So this is no crude rebuke or simplistic reversal of priorities: it is a fractal blossoming of reference and counter-reference, a giddying out- and infolding. Shepard does not invert the mawkish privileging of "magic": he undercuts the unequal binary itself. We're too enamoured of hierarchical dyads to give them up *tout court*. Instead, in that elegant and extraordinary comparison, Shepard makes the distinction self-cannibalising, destabilising.

And he points out that we've all been doing this all along. The passage is a canny reversal of one of the most clichéd analogies known to poets of geography: what, after all, does a certain type of mountain range look like but a sleeping dragon? It's a commonplace for us to so "uncover" the never-very-covered-up-anyway magic under the skin of the natural; here is fantasy that lays bare the natural below the magic.

Lucius Shepard has a name for what he does. In the story notes to "Abigmagique", he memorably describes one of his strengths as a writer as "bungling naturalism". Read him and you read a naturalist who bungles, repeatedly and almost seemingly inadvertently straying into the *un*natural, the supernatural. Fantasy here is a kind of systemic, fecund and felicitous writerly mistake, one that vastly invigorates the naturalism Shepard seemed to be angling for.

"Bungling Naturalism" may the best term for serious non-realist literature ever arrived at. It is a great boon to fiction that Shepard strives for the kind of naturalism he does; and it is a great boon to fantasy that he so brilliantly bungles.

China Miéville

FOR
BOB AND KAROL

STARS SEEN THROUGH STONE

I was smoking a joint on the steps of the public library when a cold wind blew in from no cardinal point, but from the top of the night sky, a force of pure perpendicularity that bent the sparsely leaved boughs of the old alder shadowing the steps straight down toward the earth, as if a gigantic someone above were pursing his lips and aiming a long breath directly at the ground. For the duration of that gust, fifteen or twenty seconds, my hair did not flutter but was pressed flat to the crown of my head and the leaves and grass and weeds on the lawn also lay flat. The phenomenon had a distinct border—leaves drifted along the sidewalk, testifying that a less forceful, more fitful wind presided beyond the perimeter of the lawn. No one else appeared to notice. The library, a blunt Nineteenth Century relic of undressed stone, was not a popular point of assembly at any time of day, and the sole potential witness apart from myself was an elderly gentleman who was hurrying toward McGuigan's Tavern at a pace that implied a severe alcohol dependency. This happened seven months prior to the events central to this story, but I offer it to suggest that a good deal of strangeness goes unmarked by the world (at least by the populace of Black William, Pennsylvania), and, when taken in sum, such occurrences may be evidence that strangeness is visited upon us with some regularity and we only notice its extremes.

Ten years ago, following my wife's graduation from Princeton Law, we set forth in our decrepit Volvo, heading for northern California, where we hoped to establish a community of sorts with friends who had moved to that region the previous year. We elected to drive on blue highways for their scenic value and chose a route that ran through Pennsylvania's

Bittersmith Hills, knuckled chunks of coal and granite, forested with leafless oaks and butternut, ash and elder, that—under heavy snow and threatening skies—composed an ominous prelude to the smoking red-brick town nestled in their heart. As we approached Black William, the Volvo began to rattle, the engine died, and we coasted to a stop on a curve overlooking a forbidding vista: row houses the color of dried blood huddled together along the wend of a sluggish, dark river (the Polozny), visible through a pall of gray smoke that settled from the chimneys of a sprawling prisonlike edifice—also of brick—on the opposite shore. The Volvo proved to be a total loss. Since our funds were limited, we had no recourse other than to find temporary housing and take jobs so as to pay for a new car in which to continue our trip. Andrea, whose specialty was labor law, caught on with a firm involved in fighting for the rights of embattled steelworkers. I hired on at the mill, where I encountered three part-time musicians lacking a singer. This led to that, that to this, Andrea and I grew apart in our obsessions, had affairs, divorced, and, before we realized it, the better part of a decade had rolled past. Though initially I felt trapped in an ugly, dying town, over the years I had developed an honest affection for Black William and its citizens, among whom I came to number myself.

After a brief and perhaps illusory flirtation with fame and fortune, my band broke up, but I managed to build a home recording studio during its existence and this became the foundation of a career. I landed a small business grant and began to record local bands on my own label, Soul Kiss Records. Most of the CDs I released did poorly, but in my third year of operation, one of my projects, a metal group calling themselves Meanderthal, achieved a regional celebrity and I sold management rights and the masters for their first two albums to a major label. This success gave me a degree of visibility and my post office box was flooded with demos from bands all over the country. Over the next six years I released a string of minor successes and acquired an industry-wide reputation of having an eye for talent. It had been my immersion in the music business that triggered the events leading to my divorce and, while Andrea was happy for me, I think it galled her that I had exceeded her low expectations. After a cooling-off period, we had become contentious friends and whenever we met for drinks or lunch, she would offer deprecating comments about the social value of my enterprise, and about my girlfriend, Mia, who was nine years younger than I, heavily tattooed, and—in Andrea's words—dressed "like a color-blind dominatrix."

"You've got some work to do, Vernon," she said once. "You know, on the taste thing? It's like you traded me in for a Pinto with flames painted on the hood."

I stopped myself from replying that it wasn't me who had done the trading in. I understood her comments arose from the fact that she had regrets and that she was angry at herself: Andrea was an altruist and the notion that her renewed interest in me might be partially inspired by envy or venality caused her to doubt her moral legitimacy. She was attractive, witty, slender, with auburn hair and patrician features and a forthright poise that caused men in bars, watching her pass, to describe her as "classy." Older and wiser, able by virtue of the self-confidence I had gained, to cope with her sharp tongue, I had my own regrets; but I thought we had moved past the point at which a reconciliation was possible and refrained from giving them voice.

In late summer of the year when the wind blew straight down, I listened to a demo sent me by one Joseph Stanky of Mckeesport, Pennsylvania. Stanky billed himself as Local Profitt Jr. and his music, post-modern deconstructed blues sung in a gravelly, powerful baritone, struck me as having cult potential. I called his house that afternoon and was told by his mother that "Joey's sleeping." That night, around 3 AM, Stanky returned my call. Being accustomed to the tactless ways of musicians, I set aside my annoyance and said I was interested in recording him. In the course of our conversation, Stanky told me he was twenty-six, virtually penniless, and lived in his mother's basement, maintaining throughout a churlish tone that dimmed my enthusiasm. Nevertheless, I offered to pay his bus fare to Black William and to put him up during the recording process. Two days later, when he stepped off a bus at the Trailways station, my enthusiasm dimmed further. A more unprepossessing human would be difficult to imagine. He was short, pudgy, with skin the color of a new potato and so slump-shouldered that for a moment I thought he might be deformed. Stringy brown hair provided an unsightly frame for a doughy face with a bulging forehead and a wispy soul patch. His white T-shirt was spattered with food stains, a Jackson Pollack work-in-progress; the collar of his windbreaker was stiff with grime. Baggy chinos and a trucker wallet completed his ensemble. I knew this gnomish figure must be Stanky, but didn't approach until I saw him claim two guitar cases from the luggage compartment. When I introduced myself, instead of expressing gratitude or pleasure, he put on a pitiful expression and said in a wheedling manner, "Can you spot me some bucks for cigarettes, man? I ran out during the ride."

I advanced him another hundred, with which he purchased two cartons of Camel Lights and a twelve-pack of Coca Cola Classic (these, I learned, were basic components of his nutrition and, along with Quaker Instant Grits, formed the bulk of his diet), and took a roundabout way home, thinking I'd give him a tour of the town where he would spend the next few weeks. Stanky displayed no interest whatsoever in the mill, the Revolutionary Era Lutheran Church, or Garnant House (home of the town's founding father), but reacted more positively to the ziggurat at the rear of Garnant House, a corkscrew of black marble erected in eccentric tribute to the founding father's wife, Ethelyn Garnant, who had died in childbirth; and when we reached the small central park where stands the statue of her son, Stanky said, "Hey, that's decent, man!" and asked me to stop the car.

The statue of William Garnant had been labeled an eyesore by the Heritage Committee, a group of women devoted to preserving our trivial past, yet they were forced to include it in their purview because it was the town's most recognizable symbol—gift shops sold replica statuettes and the image was emblazoned on coffee mugs, post cards, paperweights, on every conceivable type of souvenir. Created in the early 1800s by Gunter Hahn, the statue presented Black William in age-darkened bronze astride a rearing stallion, wearing a loose-fitting shirt and tight trousers, gripping the reins with one hand, pointing toward the library with the other, his body twisted and head turned in the opposite direction, his mouth open in—judging by his corded neck—a cry of alarm, as if he were warning the populace against the dangers of literacy. Hahn did not take his cues from the rather sedentary monuments of his day, but, improbably, appeared to have been influenced by the work of heroic comic book artists such as Jim

Steranko and Neal Adams, and thus the statue had a more fluid dynamic than was customary... or perhaps he was influenced by Black William himself, for it was he who had commissioned the sculpture and overseen its construction. This might explain the figure's most controversial feature, that which had inspired generations of high school students to highlight it when they painted the statue after significant football victories: thanks to an elevated position in the saddle, Black William's crotch is visible, and, whether intended or an inadvertency, an error in the casting process that produced an unwanted rumple in the bronze, it seems that he possessed quite a substantial package. It always gladdened my heart to see the ladies of the Heritage Committee, embarked upon their annual spring clean-up, scrubbing away with soap and rags at Black William's genital pride.

I filled Stanky in on Black William's biography, telling him that he had fought with great valor in the Revolutionary War, but had not been accorded the status of hero, this due to his penchant for executing prisoners summarily, even those who had surrendered under a white flag. Following the war, he returned home in time to watch his father, Alan Garnant, die slowly and in agony. It was widely held that William had poisoned the old man. Alan resented the son for his part in Ethelyn's death and had left him to be raised by his slaves, in particular by an immense African man to whom he had given the name Nero. Little is known of Nero; if more were known, we might have a fuller understanding of young William, who—from the war's end until his death in 1808—established a reputation for savagery, his specialities being murder and rape (both heterosexual and homosexual). By all accounts, he ruled the town and its environs with the brutal excess of a feudal duke. He had a coterie of friends, who served as his loyal protectors, a group of men whose natures he had perverted, several of whom failed to survive his friendship. Accompanied by Nero, they rode roughshod through the countryside, terrorizing and defiling, killing anyone who sought to impede their progress. Other than that, his legacy consisted of the statue, the ziggurat, and a stubby tower of granite block on the bluff overlooking the town, long since crumbled into ruin.

Stanky's interest dwindled as I related these facts, his responses limited to the occasional "Cool," a word he pronounced as if it had two syllables;

but before we went on our way he asked, "If the guy was such a bastard, how come they named the town after him?"

"It was a PR move," I explained. "The town was incorporated as Garnantsburgh. They changed it after World War Two. The city council wanted to attract business to the area and they hoped the name Black William would be more memorable. Church groups and the old lady vote, pretty much all the good Christians, they disapproved of the change, but the millworkers got behind it. The association with a bad guy appealed to their self-image."

"Looks like the business thing didn't work out. This place is deader than Mckeesport." Stanky raised up in the seat to scratch his ass. "Let's go, okay? I couldn't sleep on the bus. I need to catch up on my Zs."

My house was one of the row houses facing the mill, the same Andrea and I had rented when we first arrived. I had since bought the place. The ground floor I used for office space, the second floor for the studio, and I lived on the third. I had fixed up the basement, formerly Andrea's office, into a musician-friendly apartment—refrigerator, stove, TV, et al—and that is where I installed Stanky. The bus ride must have taken a severe toll. He slept for twenty hours.

After three weeks I recognized that Stanky was uncommonly gifted and it was going to take longer to record him than I had presumed—he kept revealing new facets of his talent and I wanted to make sure I understood its full dimension before getting too deep into the process. I also concluded that although musicians do not, in general, adhere to an exacting moral standard, he was, talent aside, the most worthless human being I had ever met. Like many of his profession, he was lazy, irresponsible, untrustworthy, arrogant, slovenly, and his intellectual life consisted of comic books and TV. To this traditional menu of character flaws, I would add "deviant." The first inkling I had of his deviancy was when Sabela, the Dominican woman who cleaned for me twice a week, complained about the state of the basement apartment. Since Sabela never complained, I had a look downstairs. In less than a week, he had trashed the place. The garbage was overflowing and the sink piled high with scummy dishes and pots half-full of congealed grits; the floors covered in places by a slurry of cigarette ash and grease, littered with candy wrappers and crumpled Coke cans. A smell compounded of spoilage, bad hygiene and sex seemed to rise from every surface. The plastic tip of a vibrator peeked out from beneath his grungy sheets. I assured Sabela I'd manage the situation, whereupon she burst into tears. I asked what else was troubling her and she said, "Mister Vernon, I no want him."

My Spanish was poor, Sabela's English almost non-existent, but after a few minutes I divined that Stanky had been hitting on her, going so far as to grab at her breasts. This surprised me—Sabela was in her forties and on the portly side. I told her to finish with the upstairs and then she could go home. Stanky returned from a run to the 7-11 and scuttled down to the basement, roachlike in his avoidance of scrutiny. I found him watching *Star Trek* in the dark, remote in one hand, *TV Guide* (he called it "The Guide") resting on his lap, gnawing on a Butterfingers. Seeing him so at home in his filthy nest turned up the flame under my anger.

"Sabela refuses to clean down here," I said. "I don't blame her."

"I don't care if she cleans," he said with a truculent air.

"Well, I do. You've turned this place into a shithole. I had a metal band down here for a month, it never got this bad. I want you to keep it presentable. No stacks of dirty dishes. No crud on the floor. And put your damn sex toys in a drawer. Understand?"

He glowered at me.

"And don't mess with Sabela," I went on. "When she wants to clean down here, you clear out. Go up to the studio. I hear about you groping her again, you can hump your way back to Mckeesport. I need her one hell of a lot more than I need you."

He muttered something about "another producer."

"You want another producer? Go for it! No doubt major labels are beating down my door this very minute, lusting after your sorry ass."

Stanky fiddled with the remote and lowered his eyes, offering me a look at his infant bald spot. Authority having been established, I thought I'd tell him what I had in mind for the next weeks, knowing that his objections—given the temper of the moment—would be minimal; yet there was something so repellent about him, I still wanted to give him the boot. I had the idea that one of Hell's lesser creatures, a grotesque, impotent toad, banished by the Powers of Darkness, had landed with a foul stink on my sofa. But I've always been a sucker for talent and I felt sorry for him. His past was plain. Branded as a nerd early on and bullied throughout high school, he had retreated into a life of flipping burgers and getting off on a 4-track in his mother's basement. Now he had gravitated to another basement, albeit one with a more hopeful prospect and a better recording system.

"Why did you get into music?" I asked, sitting beside him. "Women, right? It's always women. Hell, I was married to a good-looking woman, smart, sexy, and that was my reason."

He allowed that this had been his reason as well.

"So how's that working out? They're not exactly crawling all over you, huh?"

He cut his eyes toward me and it was as if his furnace door had slid open a crack, a blast of heat and resentment shooting out. "Not great," he said.

"Here's what I'm going to do." I tapped out a cigarette from his pack, rolled it between my fingers. "Next week, I'm bringing in a drummer and a bass player to work with you. I own a part-interest in the Crucible, the alternative club in town. As soon as you get it together, we'll put you in there for a set and showcase you for some people."

Stanky started to speak, but I beat him to the punch. "You follow my lead, you do what I know you can . . ." I said, leaving a significant pause. "I guarantee you won't be going home alone."

He waited to hear more, he wanted to bask in my vision of his future, but I knew I had to use rat psychology; now that I had supplied a hit of his favorite drug, I needed to buzz him with a jolt of electricity.

"First off," I said, "we're going to have to get you into shape. Work off some of those man-tits."

"I'm not much for exercise."

"That doesn't come as a shock," I said. "Don't worry. I'm not going to make a new man out of you, I just want to make you a better act. Eat what I eat for a month or so, do a little cardio. You'll drop ten or fifteen pounds." Falsely convivial, I clapped him on the shoulder and felt a twinge of disgust, as if I had touched a hypo-allergenic cat. "The other thing," I said. "That Local Profitt Junior name won't fly. It sounds too much like a country band."

"I like it," he said defiantly.

"If you want the name back later, that's up to you. For now, I'm billing you as Joe Stanky."

I laid the unlit cigarette on the coffee table and asked what he was watching, thinking that, for the sake of harmony, I'd bond with him a while.

"*Trek* marathon," he said.

We sat silently, staring at the flickering black-and-white picture. My mind sang a song of commitments, duties, other places I could be. Stanky laughed, a cross between a wheeze and a hiccup.

"What's up?" I asked.

"John Colicos sucks, man!"

He pointed to the screen, where a swarthy man with Groucho Marx eyebrows, pointy sideburns, and a holstered ray gun seemed to be undergoing an agonizing inner crisis. "Michael Ansaara's the only real Vulcan," Stanky looked at me as if seeking validation. "At least," he said, anxious lest he offend, "on the original *Trek*."

Absently, I agreed with him. My mind rejoined its song. "Okay," I said, and stood. "I got things to do. We straight about Sabela? About keeping the place . . . you know? Keeping the damage down to normal levels?"

He nodded.

"Okay. Catch you later."

I started for the door, but he called to me, employing that wheedling tone with which I had become all too familiar. "Hey, Vernon?" he said. "Can you get me a trumpet?" This asked with an imploring expression, screwing up his face like a child, as if he were begging me to grant a wish.

"You play the trumpet?"

"Uh-huh."

"If you promise to take care of it. Yeah, I can get hold of one."

Stanky rocked forward on the couch and gave a tight little fist-pump. "Decent!"

I don't know when Stanky and I got married, but it must have been sometime between the incident with Sabela and the night Mia went home to her mother. Certainly my reaction to the latter was more restrained than was my reaction to the former, and I attribute this in part to our union having been joined. It was a typical rock and roll marriage: talent and money making beautiful music together and doomed from the start, on occasion producing episodes in which the relationship seemed to be crystallized, allowing you to see (if you wanted to) the messy bed you had made for yourself.

Late one evening, or maybe it wasn't so late—it was starting to get dark early—Mia came downstairs and stepped into my office and set a smallish suitcase on my desk. She had on a jacket with a fake fur collar and hood, tight jeans, and her nice boots. She'd put a fresh raspberry streak in her black hair and her make-up did a sort of Nefertiti-meets-Liza thing. All I said was, "What did I do this time?"

Mia's lips pursed in a *moue*—it was her favorite expression and she used it at every opportunity, whether appropriate or not. She would become infuriated when I caught her practicing it in the bathroom mirror.

"It's not what you did," she said. "It's that clammy little troll in the basement."

"Stanky?"

"Do you have another troll? Stanky! God, that's the perfect name for him." Another moue. "I'm sick of him rubbing up against me."

Mia had, as she was fond of saying, "been through some stuff," and, if Stanky had done anything truly objectionable, she would have dealt with him. I figured she needed a break or else there was someone in town with whom she wanted to sleep.

"I take it this wasn't consensual rubbing," I said.

"You think you're so funny! He comes up behind me in tight places. Like in the kitchen. And he pretends he has to squeeze past."

"He's in our kitchen?"

"You send him up to use the treadmill, don't you?"

"Oh . . . right."

"And he has to get water from the fridge, doesn't he?"

I leaned back in the chair and clasped my hands behind my head. "You want me to flog him? Cut off a hand?"

"Would that stop it? Give me a call when he's gone, okay?"

"You know I will. Say hi to mom."

A final moue, a moue that conveyed a *soupcon* of regret, but—more pertinently—made plain how much I would miss her spoonful of sugar in my coffee.

After she had gone, I sat thinking non-specific thoughts, vague appreciations of her many virtues, then I handicapped the odds that her intricate make-up signaled an affair and decided just how pissed-off to be at Stanky. I shouted downstairs for him to come join me and dragged him out for a walk into town.

A mile and a quarter along the Polozny, then up a steep hill, would bring you to the park, a triangular section of greenery (orange-and-brownery at that time of year) bordered on the east by the library, on the west by a row of brick buildings containing gentrified shops, and, facing the point of the triangle, by McGuigan's. For me alone, it was a brisk half-hour walk; with Stanky in tow, it took an extra twenty minutes. He was not one to hide his discomfort or displeasure. He panted, he sagged, he limped, he sighed. His breathing grew labored. The next step would be his last. Wasn't it enough I forced him to walk three blocks to the 7-11? If his heart failed, drop his bones in a bucket of molten steel and ship his guitars home to Mckeesport, where his mother would display them, necks crossed, behind the urn on the mantle.

These comments went unvoiced, but they were eloquently stated by his body language. He acted out every nuance of emotion, like a child showing off a new skill. Send him on an errand he considered important and he would give you his best White Rabbit, head down, hustling along on a matter of urgency to the Queen. Chastise him and he would play the penitent altar boy. When ill, he went with a hand clutching his stomach or cheek or lower back, grimacing and listless. His posturing was so pitifully false, it was disturbing to look at him. I had learned to ignore these symptoms, but I recognized the pathology that bred them—I had seen him, thinking himself unwatched, slumped on the couch, clicking the remote, the Guide spread across his lap, mired in the quicksand of depression, yet more arrogant than depressed, a crummy king forsaken by his court, desperate for admirers.

On reaching the library, I sat on a middle step and fingered out a fatty from my jacket pocket. Stanky collapsed beside me, exhausted by the

Polozny Death March he had somehow survived. He flapped a hand toward McGuigan's and said, hopefully, "You want to get a beer?"

"Maybe later."

I fired up the joint.

"Hey!" Stanky said. "We passed a cop car on the hill, man."

"I smoke here all the time. As long as you don't flaunt it, nobody cares."

I handed him the joint. He cupped the fire in his palm, smoking furtively. It occurred to me that I wouldn't drink from the same glass as him—his gums were rotting, his teeth horribly decayed—but sharing a joint? What the hell. The air was nippy and the moon was hidden behind the alder's thick leaves, which had turned but not yet fallen. Under an arc lamp, the statue of Black William gleamed as if fashioned of obsidian.

"Looks like he's pointing right at us, huh?" said Stanky.

When I was good and stoned, once the park had crystallized into a Victorian fantasy of dark green lawns amid crisp shadows and fountaining shrubs, the storefronts beyond hiding their secrets behind black glass, and McGuigan's ornate sign with its ruby coat of arms appearing to occupy an unreal corner in the dimension next door, I said, "Mia went back to her mom's tonight. She's going to be there for a while."

"Bummer." He had squirreled away a can of Coke in his coat pocket, which he now opened.

"It's normal for us. Chances are she'll screw around on me a little and spend most of the time curled up on her mom's sofa, eating Cocoa Puffs out of the box and watching soaps. She'll be back eventually."

He had a swig of Coke and nodded.

"What bothers me," I said, "is the reason she left. Not the real reason, but the excuse she gave. She claims you've been touching her. Rubbing against her and making like it was an accident."

This elicited a flurry of protests and I-swear-to-Gods. I let him run down before I said, "It's not a big deal."

"She's lying, man! I . . ."

"Whatever. Mia can handle herself. You cross the line with her, you'll be picking your balls up off the floor."

I could almost hear the gears grinding as he wondered how close he had come to being deballed.

"I want you to listen," I went on. "No interruptions. Even if you think I'm wrong about something. Deal?"

"Sure . . . yeah."

"Most of what I put out is garbage music. Meanderthal, Big Sissy, The Swimming Holes, Junk Brothers . . ."

"I love the Junk Brothers, man! They're why I sent you my demo."

I gazed at him sternly—he ducked his head and winced by way of apology.

"So rock and roll is garbage," I said. "It's disposable music. But once in a great while, somebody does something perfect. Something that makes the music seem indispensable. I think you can make something perfect. You may not ever get rock star money. I doubt you can be mainstreamed. The best you can hope for, probably, is Tom Waits money. That's plenty, believe me. I think you'll be huge in Europe. You'll be celebrated there. You've got a false bass that reminds me of Blind Willie Johnson. You write tremendous lyrics. That fractured guitar style of yours is unique. It's out there, but it's funky and people are going to love it. You have a natural appeal to punks and art rockers. To rock geeks like me. But there's one thing can stop you—that's your problem with women."

Not even this reference to his difficulties with Sabela and Mia could disrupt his rapt attentiveness.

"You can screw this up very easily," I told him. "You let that inappropriate touching thing of yours get out of hand, you *will* screw it up. You have to learn to let things come. To do that, you have to believe in yourself. I know you've had a shitty life so far, and your self-esteem is low. But you have to break the habit of thinking that you're getting over on people. You don't need to get over on them. You've got something they want. You've got talent. People will cut you a ton of slack because of that talent, but you keep messing up with women, their patience is going to run out. Now I don't know where all that music comes from, but it doesn't sound like it came from a basement. It's a gift. You have to start treating it like one."

I asked him for a cigarette and lit up. Though I'd given variations of the speech dozens of times, I bought into it this time and I was excited.

"Ten days from now you'll be playing for a live audience," I said. "If you put in the work, if you can believe in yourself, you'll get all you want of everything. And that's how you do it, man. By putting in the work and playing a kick-ass set. I'll help any way I can. I'm going to do publicity, T-shirts . . . and I'm going to give them away if I have to. I'm going to get the word out that Joe Stanky is something special. And you know what? Industry people will listen, because I have a track record." I blew a smoke ring and watched it disperse. "These are things I won't usually do for a band until they're farther along, but I believe in you. I believe in your music. But you have to believe in yourself and you have to put in the work."

I'm not sure how much of my speech, which lasted several minutes more, stuck to him. He acted inspired, but I couldn't tell how much of the act was real; I knew on some level he was still running a con. We cut across the park, detouring so he could inspect the statue again. I glanced back at the library and saw two white lights shaped like fuzzy asterisks. At first I thought they were moving across the face of the building, that some people were playing with flashlights; but their brightness was too sharp and erratic, and they appeared to be coming from behind the library, shining through the stone, heading toward us. After ten or fifteen seconds, they faded from sight. Spooked, I noticed that Stanky was staring at the building and I asked if he had seen the lights.

"That was weird, man!" he said. "What was it?"

"Swamp gas. UFOs. Who knows?"

I started walking toward McGuigan's and Stanky fell in alongside me. His limp had returned.

"After we have those beers, you know?" he said.

"Yeah?"

"Can we catch a cab home?" His limp became exaggerated. "I think I really hurt my leg."

*P*art of the speech must have taken, because I didn't have to roust Stanky out of bed the next morning. He woke before me, ate his grits (I allowed him a single bowl each day), knocked back a couple of Diet Cokes (my idea), and sequestered himself in the studio, playing adagio trumpet runs and writing on the Casio. Later, I heard the band thumping away. After practice, I caught Geno, the drummer, on his way out the door, brought him into the office and asked how the music was sounding.

"It doesn't blow," he said.

I asked to him to clarify.

"The guy writes some hard drum parts, but they're tasty, you know. Tight."

Geno appeared to want to tell me more, but spaced and ran a beringed hand through his shoulder-length black hair. He was a handsome kid, if you could look past the ink, the brands, and the multiple piercings. An excellent drummer and reliable. I had learned to be patient with him.

"Overall," I said, "how do you think the band's shaping up?"

He looked puzzled. "You heard us."

"Yes. I know what I think. I'm interested in what you think."

"Oh . . . okay." He scratched the side of his neck, the habitat of a red and black Chinese tiger. "It's very cool. Strong. I never heard nothing like it. I mean, it's got jazz elements, but not enough to where it doesn't rock. The guy sings great. We might go somewhere if he can control his weirdness."

I didn't want to ask how Stanky was being weird, but I did.

"He and Jerry got a conflict," Geno said. "Jerry can't get this one part down, and Stanky's on him about it. I keep telling Stanky to quit ragging him. Leave Jerry alone and he'll stay on it until he can play it backwards. But Stanky, he's relentless and Jerry's getting pissed. He don't love the guy, anyway. Like today, Stanky cracks about we should call the band Stanky and Our Gang."

"No," I said.

"Yeah, right. But it was cute, you know. Kind of funny. Jerry took it personal, though. He like to got into it with Stanky."

"I'll talk to them. Anything else?"

"Naw. Stanky's a geek, but you know me. The music's right and I'm there."

The following day I had lunch scheduled with Andrea. It was also the day that my secretary, Kiwanda, a petite Afro-American woman in her late twenties, came back to work after a leave during which she had been taking care of her grandmother. I needed an afternoon off—I thought I'd visit friends, have a few drinks—so I gave over Stanky into her charge, warning her that he was prone to getting handsy with the ladies.

"I'll keep that in mind," she said, sorting through some new orders. "You go have fun."

Andrea had staked out one of the high-backed booths at the rear of McGuigan's and was drinking a martini. She usually ran late, liked sitting at the front, and drank red wine. She had hung her jacket on the hook at the side of the booth and looked fetching in a cream-colored blouse. I nudged the martini glass and asked what was up with the booze.

"Bad day in court. I had to ask for a continuance. So . . . " She hoisted the martini. "I'm boozing it up."

"Is this that pollution thing?"

"No, it's a pro bono case."

"Thought you weren't going to do any pro bono work for a while."

She shrugged, drank. "What can I say?"

"All that class guilt. It must be tough." I signaled a waitress, pointed to Andrea's martini and held up two fingers. "I suppose I should be grateful. If you weren't carrying around that guilt, you would have married Snuffy Huffington the Third or somebody."

"Let's not banter," Andrea said. "We always banter. Let's just talk. Tell me what's going on with you."

I was good at reading Andrea, but it was strange how well I read her at that moment. Stress showed in her face. Nervousness. Both predictable components. But mainly I saw a profound loneliness and that startled me. I'd never thought of her as being lonely. I told her about Stanky, the good parts, his writing, his musicianship.

"The guy plays everything," I said. "Guitar, flute, sax, trumpet. Little piano, little drums. He's like some kind of mutant they produced in a secret high school band lab. And his voice. It's the Jim Nabors effect. You know, the guy who played Gomer Pyle? Nobody expected a guy looked that goofy could sing, so when he did, they thought he was great, even though he sounded like he had sinus trouble. It's the same with Stanky, except his voice really is great."

"You're always picking up these curious strays," she said. "Remember the high school kid who played bass, the one who fainted every time he was under pressure? Brian Something. You'd come upstairs and say, 'You should see what Brian did,' and tell me he laid a bass on its side and played Mozart riffs on it. And I'd go . . ."

"Bach," I said.

"And I'd go, 'Yeah, but he faints!'" She laughed. "You always think you can fix them."

"You're coming dangerously close to banter," I said.

"You owe me one." She wiggled her forefinger and grinned. "I'm right, aren't I? There's a downside to this guy."

I told her about Stanky's downside and, when I reached the part about Mia leaving, Andrea said, "The circus must be in town."

"Now you owe me one."

"You can't expect me to be reasonable about Mia." She half-sang the name, did a little shimmy, made a *moue*.

"That's two you owe me," I said.

"Sorry." She straightened her smile. "You know she'll come back. She always does."

I liked that she was acting flirty and, though I had no resolution in mind, I didn't want her to stop.

"You don't have to worry about me," she said. "Honest."

"Huh?"

"So how talented is this Stanky? Give me an example."

"What do you mean, I don't have to worry about you?"

"Never mind. Now come on! Give me some Stanky."

"You want me to sing?"

"You were a singer, weren't you? A pretty good one, as I recall."

"Yeah, but I can't do what he does."

She sat expectantly, hands folded on the tabletop.

"All right," I said.

I did a verse of "Devil's Blues," beginning with the lines:

> "There's a grapevine in heaven,
> There's a peavine in hell,
> One don't grow grapes,
> The other don't grow peas as well . . ."

I sailed on through to the chorus, getting into the vocal:

"Devil's Blues!
God owes him . . ."

A bald guy popped his head over the top of an adjacent booth and looked at me, then ducked back down. I heard laughter.

"That's enough," I said to Andrea.

"Interesting," she said. "Not my cup of tea, but I wouldn't mind hearing him."

"He's playing the Crucible next weekend."

"Is that an invitation?"

"Sure. If you'll come."

"I have to see how things develop at the office. Is a tentative yes okay?"

"Way better than a firm no," I said.

We ordered from the grille and, after we had eaten, Andrea called her office and told them she was taking the rest of the day. We switched from martinis to red wine, and we talked, we laughed, we got silly, we got drunk. The sounds of the bar folded around us and I started to remember how it felt to be in love with her. We wobbled out of McGuigan's around four o'clock. The sun was lowering behind the Bittersmiths, but shed a rich golden light; it was still warm enough for people to be sitting in sweaters and shirts on park benches under the orange leaves.

Andrea lived around the corner from the bar, so I walked her home. She was weaving a little and kept bumping into me. "You better take a cab home," she said, and I said, "I'm not the one who's walking funny," which earned me a punch in the arm. When we came to her door, she turned to me, gripping her briefcase with both hands and said, "I'll see you next weekend, maybe."

"That'd be great."

She hovered there a second longer and then she kissed me. Flung her arms about my neck, clocking me with the briefcase, and gave me a one-hundred percent all-Andrea kiss that, if I were a cartoon character, would have rolled my socks up and down and levitated my hat. She buried her face in my neck and said, "Sorry. I'm sorry." I was going to say, For what?, but she pulled away in a hurry, appearing panicked, and fled up the stairs.

I nearly hit a parked car on the drive home, not because I was drunk, but because thinking about the kiss and her reaction afterward impaired my concentration. What was she sorry about? The kiss? Flirting? The divorce? I couldn't work it out, and I couldn't work out, either, what I was feeling. Lust, certainly. Having her body pressed against mine had fully engaged my senses. But there was more. Considerably more. I decided it stood a chance of becoming a mental health issue and did my best to put it from mind.

Kiwanda was busy in the office. She had the computers networking and was going through prehistoric paper files on the floor. I asked what was up and she told me she had devised a more efficient filing system. She had never been much of an innovator, so this unnerved me, but I let it pass and asked if she'd had any problems with my boy Stanky.

"Not so you'd notice," she said tersely.

From this, I deduced that there *had* been a problem, but I let that pass as well and went upstairs to the apartment. Walls papered with flyers and band photographs; a grouping of newish, ultra-functional Swedish furniture—I realized I had liked the apartment better when Andrea did the decorating, this despite the fact that interior design had been one of our bones of contention. The walls, in particular, annoyed me. I was being stared at by young men with shaved heads and flowing locks in arrogant poses, stupid with tattoos, by five or six bands that had tried to stiff me, by a few hundred bad-to-indifferent memories and a dozen good ones. Maybe a dozen. I sat on a leather and chrome couch (it was a showy piece, but uncomfortable) and watched the early news. George Bush, Iraq, the price of gasoline . . . fuck! Restless, I went down to the basement.

Stanky was watching the Comedy Channel. *Mad TV.* Another of his passions. He was slumped on the couch, remote in hand, and had a Coke and a cigarette working, an ice pack clamped to his cheek. I had the idea the ice pack was for my benefit, so I didn't ask about it, but knew it must be connected to Kiwanda's attitude. He barely acknowledged my presence, just sat there and pouted. I took a chair and watched with him. At last he said, "I need a rhythm guitar player."

"I'm not going to hire another musician this late in the game."

He set down the ice pack. His cheek was red, but that might have been from the ice pack itself . . . although I thought I detected a slight puffiness. "I seriously need him," he said.

"Don't push me on this."

"It's important, man! For this one song, anyway."

"What song?"

"A new one."

I waited and then said, "That's all you're going to tell me?"

"It needs a rhythm guitar."

This tubby little madman recumbent on my couch was making demands—it felt good to reject him, but he persisted.

"It's just one song, man," he said in full-on wheedle. "Please! It's a surprise."

"I don't like surprises."

"Come on! You'll like this one, I promise."

I told him I'd see what I could do, had a talk with him about Jerry, and the atmosphere lightened. He sat up straight, chortling at *MadTV*, now and then saying, "Decent!," his ultimate accolade. The skits were funny and I laughed, too.

"I did my horoscope today," he said as the show went to commercial.

"Let me guess," I said. "You're a Cancer."

He didn't like that, but maintained an upbeat air. "I don't mean astrology, man. I use The Guide." He slid the *TV Guide* across the coffee table, pointing out an entry with a grimy finger, a black-rimmed nail. I snatched it up and read:

> "*King Creole:* *** Based on a Harold Robbins novel. A young man (Elvis Presley) with a gang background rises from the streets to become a rock and roll star. Vic Morrow. 1:30."

"Decent, huh!" said Stanky. "You try it. Close your eyes and stick your finger in on a random page and see what you get. I use the movie section in back, but some people use the whole programming section."

"Other people do this? Not just you?"

"Go ahead."

I did as instructed and landed on another movie:

"*A Man and a Woman:* **** A widow and a widower meet on holiday and are attracted to one another, but the woman backs off because memories of her dead husband are still too strong. Marcello Mastroiani, Anouk Aimee. 1:40."

Half-believing, I tried to understand what the entry portended for me and Andrea.

"What did you get?" asked Stanky.

I tossed the *Guide* back to him and said, "It didn't work for me."

I thought about calling Andrea, but business got in the way—I suppose I allowed it to get in the way, due to certain anxieties relating to our divorce. There was publicity to do, Kiwanda's new filing system to master (she kept on tweaking it), recording (we laid down two tracks for Stanky's first EP), and a variety of other duties. And so the days went quickly. Stanky began going to the library after every practice, walking without a limp; he said he was doing research. He didn't have enough money to get into trouble and I had too much else on my plate to stress over it. The night before he played the Crucible, I was in the office, going over everything in my mind, wondering what I had overlooked, thinking I had accomplished an impossible amount of work that week, when the doorbell rang. I opened the door and there on the stoop was Andrea, dressed in jeans and a bulky sweater, cheeks rosy from the night air. An overnight bag rested at her feet. "Hi," she said, and gave a chipper smile, like a tired girl scout determined to keep pimping her cookies.

Taken aback, I said, "Hi," and ushered her in.

She went into the office and sat in the wooden chair beside my desk. I followed her in, hesitated, and took a seat in my swivel chair.

"You look . . . rattled," she said.

"That about covers it. Good rattled. But rattled, nonetheless."

"I am, too. Sorta." She glanced around the office, as if noticing the changes. I could hear every ticking clock, every digital hum, all the discrete noises of the house.

She drew in a breath, exhaled, clasped her hands in her lap. "I thought we could try," she said quietly. "We could do a trial period or something. Some days, a week. See how that goes." She paused. "The last few times I've seen you, I've wanted to be with you. And I think you've wanted to be with me. So . . ." She made a flippy gesture, as if she were trying to shade things toward the casual. "This seemed like an opportunity."

You would have thought, even given the passage of time, after all the recriminations and ugliness of divorce, some measure of negativity would have cropped up in my thoughts; but it did not and I said, "I think you're right."

"Whew!" Andrea pretended to wipe sweat from her brow and grinned.

An awkward silence; the grin flickered and died.

"Could I maybe go upstairs," she asked.

"Oh! Sure. I'm sorry." I had the urge to run up before her and rip down the crapfest on the wall, chuck all the furniture out the window, except for a mattress and candles.

"You're still rattled," she said. "Maybe we should have a drink before anything." She stretched out a hand to me. "Let's get good and drunk."

As it happened, we barely got the drinks poured before we found our groove and got busy. It was like old times, cozy and familiar, and yet it was like we were doing it for the first time, too. Every touch, every sensation, carried that odd *frisson*. We woke late, with the frost almost melted from the panes, golden light chuting through the high east windows, leaving the bed in a bluish shadow. We lay there, too sleepy to make love, playing a little, talking, her telling me how she had plotted her approach, me telling her how I was oblivious until that day at lunch when I noticed her loneliness, and what an idiot I had been not to see what was happening . . . Trivial matters, but they stained a few brain cells, committing those moments to memory and marking them as Important, a red pin on life's map. And then we did make love, as gently as that violence can be made. Afterward, we showered and fixed breakfast. Watching her move about the kitchen in sweats and a T-shirt, I couldn't stop thinking how great this was, and I wanted to stop, to quit footnoting every second. I mentioned this as we ate and she said, "I guess that means you're happy."

"Yeah! Of course."

"Me, too." She stabbed a piece of egg with her fork, tipped her head to the side as if to get a better angle on me. "I don't know when it was I started to be able to read you so well. Not that you were that hard to read to begin with. It just seems there's nothing hidden in your face anymore."

"Maybe it's a case of heightened senses."

"No, really. At times it's like I know what you're about to say."

"You mean I don't have to speak?"

She adopted the manner of a legal professional. "Unfortunately, no. You have to speak. Otherwise, it would be difficult to catch you in a lie."

"Maybe we should test this," I said. "You ask my name, and I'll say, Helmut or Torin."

She shook her head. "I'm an organic machine, not a lie detector. We have different ways. Different needs."

"Organic. So that would make you . . . softer than your basic machine? Possibly more compliant?"

"Very much so," she said.

"You know, I think I may be reading you pretty well myself." I leaned across the table, grabbed a sloppy kiss, and, as I sat back down, I remembered something. "Damn!" I said, and rapped my forehead with my knuckles.

"What is it?"

"I forgot to take Stanky for his haircut."

"Can't he take care of it himself?"

"Probably not. You want to go with us? You might as well meet him. Get it over with."

She popped egg into her mouth and chewed. "Do we have to do it now?"

"No, he won't even be up for a couple of hours."

"Good," she said.

The Crucible, a concrete block structure on the edge of Black William, off beyond the row houses, had once been a dress outlet store. We had put a cafeteria in the front, where we served breakfast and lunch—we did a brisk business because of the mill. Separate from the cafeteria, the back half of the building was given over to a bar with a few ratty booths, rickety chairs and tables. We had turned a high-school artist loose on the walls and she had painted murals that resembled scenes from J.R.R. Tolkien's lost labor-union novel. An immense crucible adorned the wall behind the stage; it appeared, thanks to the artist's inept use of perspective, to be spilling a flood of molten steel down upon an army of orc-like workers.

There was a full house that night, attracted by local legends, The Swimming Holes, a girl band who had migrated to Pittsburgh, achieving a degree of national renown, and I had packed the audience with Friends of Vernon whom I had enjoined to applaud and shout wildly for Stanky. A haze of smoke fogged the stage lights and milling about were fake punks, the odd goth, hippies from Garnant College in Waterford, fifteen miles away: the desperate wanna-be counter-culture of the western Pennsylvania barrens. I went into the dressing rooms, gave each Swimming Hole a welcome-home hug, and checked in on Stanky. Jerry, a skinny guy with buzzcut red hair, was plunking on his bass, and Geno was playing fills on the back of a chair; Ian, the rhythm guitarist, was making a cell call in the head. Stanky was on the couch, smoking a Camel, drinking a Coke, and watching the Sci-Fi Channel. I asked if he felt all right. He said he could use a beer. He seemed calm, supremely confident, which I would not have predicted and did not trust. But it was too late for concern and I left him to God.

I joined Andrea at the bar. She had on an old long-sleeved Ramones shirt, the same that she had worn to gigs back when my band was happening. Despite the shirt, she looked out of place in the Crucible, a swan floating on a cesspool. I ordered a beer to be carried to Stanky, a shot of tequila for myself. Andrea put her mouth to my ear and shouted over the recorded music, "Don't get drunk!," and then something else that was lost in the din. I threw down the shot and led her into the cafeteria, which was serving coffee and soda to a handful of kids, some of whom appeared to be trying to straighten out. I closed the door to the bar, cutting the volume by half.

"What were you saying?" I asked.

"I said not to get drunk, I might have use for you later." She sat at the counter, patted the stool beside her, encouraging me to sit.

"They're about to start," I said, joining her. "I've only got a minute."

"How do you think it'll go?"

"With Stanky? I'm praying it won't be a disaster."

"You know, he didn't seem so bad this afternoon. Not like you described, anyway."

"You just like him because he said you were a babe."

I took a loose cigarette from my shirt pocket, rolled it between my thumb and forefinger, and she asked if I was smoking again.

"Once in a while. Mainly I do this," I said, demonstrating my rolling technique. "Anyway . . . Stanky. You caught him on his best behavior."

"He seemed sad to me." She lifted a pepper shaker as she might a chess piece and set it closer to the salt. "Stunted. He has some adult mannerisms, adult information, but it's like he's still fourteen or fifteen."

"There you go," I said. "Now ask yourself how it would be, being around a twenty-six year old fourteen-year-old on a daily basis."

One of the kids, boys, men . . . there should be, I think, a specific word for someone old enough to die for his country, yet can't grow a proper mustache and is having difficulty focusing because he recently ate some cheap acid cut with crank. One of the guys at the end of the counter, then, came trippingly toward us, wearing an army field jacket decorated with a braid of puke on the breast pocket, like a soggy service ribbon. He stopped to leer at Andrea, gave me the high sign, said something unintelligible, possibly profane, and staggered on into the club.

It had been Andrea's stance, when we were married, that episodes such as this were indicative of the sewer in which she claimed I was deliquescing, AKA the music business. Though I had no grounds to argue the point, I argued nonetheless, angry because I hated the idea that she was smarter than I was—I compensated by telling myself I had more soul. There had been other, less defined reasons for anger, and the basic argument between us had gotten vicious. In this instance, however, she ignored the kid and returned to our conversation, which forced me to consider anew the question of my milieu and the degradation thereof, and to wonder if she had, by ignoring the kid, manipulated me into thinking that she had changed, whereas I had not, and it might be that the music business was to blame, that it had delimited me, warped and stunted my soul. I knew she was still the smart one.

The music cut off mid-song and I heard Rudy Bowen, my friend and partner in the Crucible, on the mike, welcoming people and making announcements. On our way back into the club, Andrea stopped me at the door and said, "I love you, Vernon." She laid a finger on my lips and told me to think about it before responding, leaving me mightily perplexed.

Stanky walked out onto the stage of the Crucible in a baggy white T-shirt, baggy chinos and his trucker wallet. He would have been semi-presentable had he not also been wearing a battered top hat. Somebody hooted derisively, and that did not surprise me. The hat made him look clownish. I wanted to throw a bottle and knock it off his head. He began whispering into the mike. Another hoot, a piercing whistle. Not good. But the whisper evolved into a chant, bits of Latin, Spanish, rock and roll clichés, and nonsense syllables. Half-spoken, half-sung, with an incantatory vibe, scatted in a jump-blues rhythm that the band, coming in underneath the vocal, built into a sold groove, and then Stanky, hitting his mark like a ski jumper getting a lift off a big hill, began to sing:

"I heard the Holy Ghost moan . . .
Stars seen through stone . . ."

Basically, the song consisted of those two lines repeated, but sung differently—made into a gospel plaint, a rock and roll howl, a smooth Motown styling, a jazzy lilt, and so on. There was a break with more lyrics, but the two lines were what mattered. The first time he sang them, in that heavy false bass, a shock ripped through the audience. People looked up, they turned toward the stage, they stopped drinking, their heads twitched, their legs did impromptu dance steps. Stanky held the word "moan" out for three bars, working it like a soul singer, then he picked up the trumpet and broke into a solo that was angry like Miles, but kept a spooky edge. When he set the trumpet down, he went to singing the lyric double time, beating the top hat against his thigh, mangling it. The crowd surged forward, everyone wanting to get next to the stage, dancing in place, this strange, shuffling dance, voodoo zombies from hell, and Stanky strapped on his guitar. I missed much of what happened next, because Andrea dragged me onto the dance floor and started making slinky moves, and I lost my distance from the event. But Stanky's guitar work sent the zombies into a convulsive fever. We bumped into a punk who was jerking like his strings were being yanked; we did a threesome with a college girl whose feet were planted, yet was shaking it like a tribal dancer in a National Geographic Special; we were corralled briefly by two millworkers who were dancing with a goth girl, watching her spasm, her breasts flipping every whichaway. At the end of the song, Jerry and Geno started speaking the lyric into their mikes, adding a counterpoint to Stanky's vocal, cooling things off, bringing it down to the creepy chant again; then the band dropped out of the music and Stanky went a capella for a final repetition of his two lines.

Applause erupted, and it was as idiosyncratic as the dancing had been. This one guy was baying like a hound; a blond girl bounced up and down, clapping gleefully like a six-year-old. I didn't catch much of the set, other than to note the audience's positive response, in particular to the songs "Average Joe" and "Can I Get A Waitress?" and "The Sunset Side of You"—I was working the room, gathering opinions, trying to learn if any of the industry people I'd invited had come, and it wasn't until twenty minutes after the encore that I saw Stanky at the bar, talking to a girl, surrounded by a group of drunken admirers. I heard another girl say how cute he was and that gave me pause to wonder at the terrible power of music. The hooker I had hired to guarantee my guarantee, a long-legged brunette named Carol, dish-faced, but with a spectacular body, was biding her time, waiting for the crowd around Stanky to disperse. He was in competent hands. I felt relief, mental fatigue, the desire to be alone with Andrea. There was no pressing reason to stay. I said a couple of good-byes, accepted congratulations, and we drove home, Andrea and I, along the Polozny.

"He's amazing," she said. "I have to admit, you may be right about him."

"Yep," I said proudly.

"Watch yourself, Sparky. You know you get when these things start to go south."

"What are you talking about?"

"When one of your problem children runs off the tracks, you take it hard. That's all I'm saying." Andrea rubbed my shoulder. "You may want to think about speeding things up with Stanky. Walk him a shorter distance and let someone else deal with him. It might save you some wear and tear."

We drove in silence; the river widened, slowed its race, flowing in under the concrete lees of the mill; the first row house came up on the right. I was tempted to respond as usually I did to her advice, to say it's all good, I've got it under control, but for some reason I listened that night and thought about everything that could go wrong.

Carol was waiting for me in the office when I came downstairs at eight o'clock the following morning. She was sitting in my swivel chair, going through my Rolodex. She looked weary, her hair mussed, and displeased. "That guy's a freak," she said flatly. "I want two hundred more. And in the future, I want to meet the guys you set me up with before I commit."

"What'd he do?" I asked.

"Do you really want to know?"

"I'm kind of curious . . . yeah."

She began to recite a list of Stanky-esque perversions, and I cut her off.

"Okay," I said, and reached for my checkbook. "He didn't get rough, did he?"

"Au contraire." She crossed her legs. "He wanted me to . . ."

"Please," I said. "Enough."

"I don't do that sort of work," she said primly.

I told her I'd written the check for three hundred and she was somewhat mollified. I apologized for Stanky and told her I hadn't realized he was so twisted.

"We're okay," she said. "I've had . . . hi, sweetie!"

She directed this greeting to a point above my shoulder as Andrea, sleepily scratching her head, wearing her sweats, entered the office. "Hi, Carol," she said, bewildered.

Carol hugged her, then turned to me and waved good-bye with my check. "Call me."

"Pretty early for hookers," Andrea said, perching of the edge of the desk.

"Let me guess. You defended her."

"Nope. One of her clients died and left her a little money. I helped her invest. But that begs the question, what was she doing here?"

"I got her for Stanky."

"A reward?"

"Something like that."

She nodded and idly kicked the back of her heel against the side of the desk. "How come you never were interested in the men I dated after we broke up?"

I was used to her sudden conversational U-turns, but I had expected her to interrogate me about Carol and this caught me off-guard. "I don't know. I suppose I didn't want to think about who you were sleeping with."

"Must be a guy thing. I always checked out your girlfriends. Even the ones you had when I was mad at you." She slipped off the desk and padded toward the door. "See you upstairs."

I spent the next two days between the phone and the studio, recording a good take of "The Sunset Side Of You"—it was the closest thing Stanky had to a ballad, and I thought, with its easy, Dr. John-ish feel, it might get some play on college radio:

> "I'm gonna crack open my venetian blind
> and let that last bit of old orange glory shine,
> so I can catch an eyeful
> of my favorite trifle,
> my absolutely perfect point of view . . .
> That's an eastbound look,
> six inches from the crook
> of my little finger,
> at the sunset side of you . . ."

Stanky wasn't happy with me—he was writing a song a day, sometimes two songs, and didn't want to disrupt his creative process by doing something that might actually make money, but I gamed him into cutting the track.

Wednesday morning, I visited Rudy Bowen in his office. Rudy was an architect who yearned to be a cartoonist, but who had never met with much success in the latter pursuit, and the resonance of our creative failures, I believe, helped to cement our friendship. He was also the only person I knew who had caught a fish in the Polozny downstream from the mill. It occupied a place of honor in his office, a hideous thing mounted on a plaque, some sort of mutant trout nourished upon pollution. Whenever I saw it, I would speculate on what else might lurk beneath the surface of the cold, deep pools east of town, imagining telepathic monstrosities plated with armor like fish of the Mesozoic and frail tentacled creatures, their skins having the rainbow sheen of an oil slick, to whom mankind were sacred figures in their dream of life.

Rudy's secretary, a matronly woman named Gwen, told me he had gone out for a latte, and let me wait in his private office. I stepped over to his drafting table, curious about what he was working on. Held in place on the table was a clean sheet of paper, but in a folder beside the table was a batch of new cartoons, a series featuring shadowy figures in a mineshaft who conversed about current events, celebrities, et al, while excavating a vein of pork that twisted through a mountain . . . This gave rise to the title of the strip: *Meat Mountain Stories*. They were silhouettes, really. Given identity by their shapes, eccentric hairstyles, and speech signatures. The strip was contemporary and hilarious. Everything Rudy's usual work was not. In some frames, a cluster of tiny white objects appeared to be floating. Moths, I thought. Lights of some kind. They, too, carried on conversations, but in pictographs. I was still going through them when Rudy came in, a big, blond man with the beginnings of a gut and thick glasses that lent him a baffled look. Every time I saw him, he looked more depressed, more middle-aged.

"These are great, man!" I said. "They're new, right?"

He crossed the room and stood beside me. "I been working on them all week. You like 'em, huh?"

"I love them. You did all this this week? You must not be sleeping." I pointed to the white things. "What're these?"

"Stars. I got the idea from that song Stanky did. 'Stars Seen Through Stone.'"

"So they're seeing them, the people in the mine?"

"Yeah. They don't pay much attention to them, but they're going to start interacting soon."

"It must be going around." I told him about Stanky's burst of writing, Kiwanda's adventures in office management.

"That's odd, you know." He sipped his latte. "It seems like there's been a real rash of creativity in town. Last week, some grunt at the mill came up with an improvement in the cold forming process that everybody says is a huge deal. Jimmy Galvin, that guy who does handyman work? He invented a new gardening tool. Bucky Bucklin's paying his patent fees. He says they're going to make millions. Beth started writing a novel. She never said anything to me about wanting to write, but she's hardly had time for the kids, she's been so busy ripping off the pages. It's not bad."

"Well, I wish I'd catch it," I said. "With me, it's same old same old. Drudgeree, drudgeroo. Except for Andrea's back."

"Andrea? You mean you guys are dating?"

"I mean back as in back in my house. Living with me."

"Damn!" he said. "That's incredible!"

We sat in two chairs like two inverted tents on steel frames, as uncomfortable as my upstairs couch, and I told him about it.

"So it's going okay?" he asked.

"Terrific, I think. But what do I know? She said it was a trial period, so I could get home tonight and she might be gone. I've never been able to figure her out."

"Andrea. Damn! I saw her at the club, but I didn't realize she was with you. I just had time to wave." He leaned across the space between us and high-fived me. "Now maybe you'll stop going around like someone stole your puppy."

"It wasn't like that," I said.

He chuckled. "Naw. Which is why the people of Black William, when asked the date, often reply, 'Six years, a months, and twelve days since the advent of Vernon's Gloom.'"

We moved on to other topics, among them the club, business, and, as I made to leave, I gestured at Rudy's grotesque trophy and said, "While those creative juices are flowing, you ought to design a fishing lure, so I can watch you hook into the Loch Polozny Monster."

Rudy laughed and said, "Maybe if I have a couple of minutes. I'm going to keep working on the comic. Whatever this shit is, it's bound to go away."

I was fooling around in the studio one evening, ostensibly cleaning up the tape we'd rolled the previous weekend at the Crucible, hoping to get a live rendition of "Stars Seen Through Stone" clean enough for the EP, but I was, instead, going over a tape I'd made, trying to find some ounce of true inspiration in it, finding none, wondering why this wave of creativity—if it, indeed, existed—had blessed Rudy's house and not mine. It was after seven, Stanky was likely on his way home from the library, and I was thinking about seeing if Andrea wanted to go out, when she leaned in the doorway and asked if she was interrupting. I told her, no, not at all, and she came into the booth and sat next to me at the board, looking out at the drum kit, the instruments, the serpents' nest of power cords.

"When we were married, I didn't get what you saw in this," she said. "All I saw was the damage, the depravity, the greed. Now I've been practicing, I realize there's more-or-less the same degree of damage and greed and depravity in every enterprise. You can't see it as clearly as you do in the music business, but it's there."

"Tell me what I see that's good."

"The music, the people."

"None of that lasts," I said. "All I am's a yo-yo tester. I test a thousand busted yo-yos, and occasionally I run across one that lights up and squeals when it spins."

"What I do is too depressing to talk about. It's rare when anyone I represent has a good outcome, even if they win. Corporations delay and delay."

"So it's disillusionment that's brought us together again."

"No." She looked at me steadily. "Do you love me?"

"Yeah, I love you. You know I do. I never stopped. There was a gap . . ."

"A big gap!"

"The gap made it more painful, but that's all it did."

She played with dials on the sound board, frowning as if they were refusing to obey her fingers.

"You're messing up my settings," I said.

"Oh . . . sorry."

"What's wrong?"

"Nothing. It's just you don't lie to me anymore. You used to lie all the time, even about trivial things. I'm having trouble adjusting."

I started to deny it, but recognized that I couldn't. "I was angry at you. I can't remember why, exactly. Lying was probably part of it."

"I was angry at you, too." She put her hands back on the board, but twisted no dials. "But I didn't lie to you."

"You stopped telling me the truth," I said. "Same difference."

The phone rang; in reflex, I picked up and said, "Soul Kiss."

It was Stanky. He started babbling, telling me to come downtown quick.

"Whoa!" I said. "If this is about me giving you a ride . . ."

"No, I swear! You gotta see this, man! The stars are back!"

"The stars."

"Like the one we saw at the library. The lights. You better come quick. I'm not sure how long it'll last."

"I'm kind of busy," I said.

"Dude, you have got to see this! I'm not kidding!"

I covered the phone and spoke to Andrea. "Want to ride uptown? Stanky says there's something we should see."

"Maybe afterward we could stop by my place and I could pick up a few things?"

I got back on the phone. "Where are you?"

Five minutes later we were cutting across the park toward the statue of Black William, beside which Stanky and several people were standing in an island of yellow light—I had no time to check them out, other than to observe that one was a woman, because Stanky caught my arm and directed me to look at the library and what I saw made me unmindful of any other sight. The building had been rendered insubstantial, a ghost of itself, and I was staring across a dark plain ranged by a dozen fuzzy white lights, some large, some small, moving toward us at a slow rate of speed, and yet perhaps it was not slow—the perspective seemed infinite, as if I were gazing into a depth by comparison to which, all previously glimpsed perspectives were so limited as to be irrelevant. As the lights approached, they appeared to vanish, passing out of frame, as if the viewing angle we had been afforded was too narrow to encompass the scope of the phenomenon. Within seconds, it began to fade, the library to regain its ordinary solidity, and I thought I heard a distant gabbling, the sound of many voices speaking at once, an army of voices (though I may have manufactured this impression from the wind gusting through the boughs); and then, as that ghostly image winked out of existence, a groaning noise that, in my opinion, issued from no fleshly throat, but may have been produced by some cosmic stress, a rip in the continuum sealing itself or something akin.

Andrea had, at some point, latched onto my arm, and we stood gaping at the library; Stanky and the rest began talking excitedly. There were three boys, teenagers, two of them carrying skateboards. The third was a pale, skinny, haughty kid, bespotted with acne, wearing a black turtleneck sweater, black jeans, black overcoat. They displayed a worshipful attitude toward Stanky, hanging on his every word. The woman might have been the one with whom Stanky had been speaking at the Crucible before Carol made her move. She was tiny, barely five feet tall, Italian-looking, with black hair and olive skin, in her twenties, and betrayed a compete lack of animation until Stanky slipped an arm around her; then she smiled, an expression that revealed her to be moderately attractive.

The skateboarders sped off to, they said, "tell everybody," and this spurred me to take out my cell phone, but I could not think who to call. Rudy, maybe. But no one in authority. The cops would laugh at the report. Stanky introduced us to Liz (the woman lowered her eyes) and Pin (the goth kid looked away and nodded). I asked how long the phenomenon had been going on before we arrived and Stanky said, "Maybe fifteen minutes."

"Have you seen it before?"

"Just that time with you."

I glanced up at Black William and thought that maybe he *had* intended the statue as a warning . . . though it struck me now that he was turning his head back toward the town and laughing.

Andrea hugged herself. "I could use something hot to drink."

McGuigan's was handy, but that would have disincluded Pin, who obviously was underage. I loaded him, Stanky, and Liz into the back of the van and drove to Szechuan Palace, a restaurant on the edge of the business district, which sported a five-foot-tall gilt fiberglass Buddha in the foyer that over the years had come to resemble an ogre with a skin condition, the fiberglass weave showing through in patches, and whose dining room (empty but for a bored wait-staff) was lit like a Macao brothel in lurid shades of red, green, and purple. On the way to the restaurant, I replayed the incident in my head, attempting to understand what I had witnessed not in rational terms, but in terms that would make sense to an ordinary American fool raised on science fiction and horror movies. Nothing seemed to fit. At the restaurant, Andrea and Pin ordered tea, Liz and Stanky gobbled moo shu pork and lemon chicken, and I picked at an egg roll. Pin started talking to Andrea in an adenoidal voice, lecturing her on some matter regarding Black William, and, annoyed because he was treating her like an idiot, I said, "What does Black William have to do with this?"

"Not a thing," Pin said, turning on me a look of disdain that aspired to be the kind of look Truman Capote once fixed upon a reporter from the Lincoln Journal-Star who had asked if he was a homosexual. "Not unless you count the fact that he saw something similar two hundred years ago and it probably killed him."

"Pin's an expert on Black William," Stanky said, wiping a shred of pork from his chin.

"What little there is to know," said Pin grandly, "I know."

It figured that a goth townie would have developed a crush on the local bogeyman. I asked him to enlighten me.

"Well," Pin said, "when Joey told me he'd seen a star floating in front of the library, I knew it *had* to be one of BW's stars. Where the library stands today used to be the edge of Stockton Wood, which had an evil reputation. As did many woods in those days, of course. Stockton Wood is where he saw the stars."

"What did he say about them?"

"He didn't say a thing. Nothing that he committed to paper, anyway. It's his younger cousin, Samuel Garnant, we can thank for the story. He wrote a memoir about BW's escapades under the *nom de plume,* Jonathan Venture. According to Samuel, BW was in the habit of riding in the woods at twilight. 'Tempting the Devil,' he called it. His first sight of the stars was a few mysterious lights—like with you and Joey. He rode out into the wood the next night and many nights thereafter. Samuel's a bit vague on how long it was before BW saw the stars again. I'm guessing a couple of weeks, going by clues in the narrative. But eventually he did see them, and what he saw was a lot like what we just saw." Pin put his hands together, fingertips touching, like a priest preparing to address the Ladies' Auxiliary. "In those days, people feared God and the Devil. When they saw something amazing, they didn't stand around like a bunch of doofuses saying, 'All right!' and taking pictures. BW was terrified. He said he'd seen the Star Wormwood and heard the Holy Ghost moan. He set about changing his life."

Stanky shot me one of his wincing, cutesy, embarrassed smiles—he had told me the song was completely original.

"For almost a year," Pin went on, "BW tried to be a good Christian. He performed charitable works, attended church regularly, but his heart wasn't in it. He lapsed back into his old ways and before long he took to riding in Stockton Woods again, with his manservant Nero walking at his side. He thought that he had missed an opportunity and told Samuel if he was fortunate enough to see the stars again, he would ride straight for them. He'd embrace their evil purpose."

"What you said about standing around like doofuses, taking pictures," Andrea said. "I don't suppose anyone got a picture?"

Pin produced a cell phone and punched up a photograph of the library and the stars. Andrea and I leaned in to see.

"Can you email that to me?" I asked.

Pin said he could and I wrote my address on a napkin.

"So," Pin said. "The next time BW saw the stars was in eighteen-oh-eight. He saw them twice, exactly like the first time. A single star, then an interval of a week or two and a more complex sighting. A month after that, he disappeared while riding with Nero in Stockton Wood and they were never seen again."

Stanky hailed our waitress and asked for more pancakes for his moo shu.

"So you think the stars appeared three times?" said Andrea. "And Black William missed the third appearance on the first go-round, but not on the second?"

"That's what Samuel thought," said Pin.

Stanky fed Liz a bite of lemon chicken.

"You're assuming Black William was killed by the stars, but that doesn't make sense," said Andrea. "For instance, why would there be a longer interval between the second and third sightings? If there *was* a third sighting. It's more likely someone who knew the story killed him and blamed it on the stars."

"Maybe Nero capped him," said Stanky. "So he could gain his freedom."

Pin shrugged. "I only know what I read."

"It might be a wavefront," I said.

On another napkin, I drew a straight line with a small bump in it, then an interval in which the line flattened out, then a bigger bump, then a longer interval and an even bigger bump.

"Like that, maybe," I said. "Some kind of wavefront passing through Black William from God knows where. It's always passing through town, but we get this series of bumps that make it accessible every two hundred years. Or less. Maybe the stars appeared at other times."

"There's no record of it," said Pin. "And I've searched."

The waitress brought Stanky's pancakes and asked if we needed more napkins.

Andrea studied the napkin I'd drawn on. "But what about the first series of sightings? When were they?"

"Seventeen-eighty-nine," said Pin.

"It could be an erratic cycle," I said. "Or could be the cycle consists of two sequences close together, then a lapse of two hundred years. Don't expect a deeper explanation. I cut class a bunch in high school physics."

"The Holy Ghost doesn't obey physical principles," said Stanky pompously.

"I doubt Black William really heard the Holy Ghost," Andrea said. "If he heard what we heard tonight. It sounded more like a door closing to me."

"Whatever," he said. "It'll be cool to see what happens a month from now. Maybe Black William will return from the grave."

"Yeah." I crumpled the napkin and tossed it to the center of the table. "Maybe he'll bring Doctor Doom and the Lone Ranger with him."

Pin affected a shudder and said, "I think I'm busy that day."

*P*in sent me the picture and I emailed it to a gearhead friend, Crazy Ed, who lived in Wilkes-Barre, to see what he could make of it. Though I didn't forget about the stars, I got slammed with business and my consideration of them and the late William Garnant had to be put on the backburner, along with Stanky's career. Against all expectations, Liz had not fled screaming from his bed, crying Pervert, but stayed with him most nights. Except for his time in the studio, I rarely saw him, and then only when his high school fans drove by to pick up him and Liz. An apocryphal story reached my ear, insinuating that she had taken on a carload of teenage boys while Stanky watched. That, if true, explained the relationship in Stanky-esque terms, terms I could understand. I didn't care what they did as long as he fulfilled his band duties and kept out of my hair. I landed him a gig at the Pick and Shovel in Waterford, filling in for a band that had been forced to cancel, and it went well enough that I scored him another gig at Garnant College. After a mere two performances, his reputation was building and I adjusted my timetable accordingly—I would make the college job an EP release party, push out an album soon thereafter and try to sell him to a major label. It was not the way I typically grew my acts, not commercially wise, but Stanky was not a typical act and, despite his prodigious talent, I wanted to have done with this sour-smelling chapter in my life.

Andrea, for all intents and purposes, had moved in, along with a high-energy, seven-month-old Irish Setter named Timber, and was in process of subletting her apartment. We were, doubtless, a disgusting item to everyone who had gotten to know us during our adversarial phase, always hanging on one another, kissing and touching. I had lunch with her every day—they held the back booth for us at McGuigan's—and one afternoon as we were settling in, Mia materialized beside the booth. "Hello," she said and stuck out a hand to Andrea.

Startled, Andrea shook her hand and I, too, was startled—until that moment, Mia had been unrelentingly hostile in her attitude toward my ex, referring to her as "that uppity skank" and in terms less polite. I noticed that she was dressed conservatively and not made up as an odalisque. Instead of being whipped into a punky abstraction, her hair was pulled back into a ponytail. The raspberry streak was gone. She was, in fact, for the first time since I had known her, streakless.

"May I join you?" Mia asked. "I won't take up much of your time."

Andrea scooted closer to the wall and Mia sat next to her.

"I heard you guys were back together," said Mia. "I'm glad."

Thunderstruck, I was incapable of fielding that one. "Thanks," said Andrea, looking to me for guidance.

Mia squared up in the booth, addressing me with a clear eye and a firm voice. "I'm moving to Pittsburgh. I've got a job lined up and I'll be taking night classes at Pitt, then going full-time starting next summer."

Hearing this issue from Mia's mouth was like hearing a cat begin speaking in Spanish while lighting a cheroot. I managed to say, "Yeah, that's . . . Yeah. Good."

"I'm sorry I didn't tell you sooner. I'm leaving tomorrow. But I heard you and Andrea were together, so . . ." She glanced back and forth between Andrea and myself, as if expecting a response.

"No, that's fine," I said. "You know."

"It was a destructive relationship," she said with great sincerity. "We had some fun, but it was bad for both of us. You were holding me back intellectually and I was limiting you emotionally."

"You're right," I said. "Absolutely."

Mia seemed surprised by how smoothly things were going, but she had, apparently, a pre-arranged speech and she by-God intended to give it.

"I understand this is sudden. It must come as a shock . . ."

"Oh, yeah."

". . . but I have to do this. I think it's best for me. I hope we can stay friends. You've been an important part of my growth."

"I hope so, too."

There ensued a short and—on my end, anyway—baffled silence.

"Okay. Well, I . . . I guess that's about it." She got to her feet and stood by the booth, hovering; then—with a sudden movement—she bent and kissed my cheek. "Bye."

Andrea put a hand to her mouth. "Oh my God! Was that Mia?"

"I'm not too sure," I said, watching Mia walk away, noting that there had been a complete absence of *moues*.

"An important part of her growth? She talks like a Doctor Phil soundbyte. What did you do to her?"

"I'm not responsible, I don't think." I pushed around a notion that had occurred to me before, but that I had not had the impetus to consider more fully. "Do you know anyone who's exhibited a sudden burst of intelligence in the past few weeks? I mean someone who's been going along at the same pace for a while and suddenly they're Einstein. Relatively speaking."

She mulled it over. "As a matter of fact, I do. I know two or three people. Why?"

"Tell me."

"Well, there's Jimmy Galvin. Did you hear about him?"

"The gardening tool. Yeah. Who else?"

"This guy in my office. A para-legal. He's a hard worker, but basically a drone. Lately, whenever we ask him to dig up a file or find a reference, he's attached some ideas about the case we're working on. Good ideas. Some of them are great. Case-makers. He's the talk of the office. We've been joking that maybe we should get him to take a drug test. He's going back to law school and we're going to miss . . ." She broke off. "What's this have to do with the new Mia?"

I told her about Rudy's cartoons, Beth's novel, Kiwanda's newfound efficiency, the millworker, Stanky's increased productivity.

"I can't help wondering," I said, "if it's somehow related to the stars. I know it's a harebrained idea. There's probably a better explanation. Stanky . . . he never worked with a band before and that may be what's revving his engines. But that night at the Crucible, he was so polished. It just didn't synch with how I thought he'd react. I thought he'd get through it, but it's like he was an old hand."

Andrea looked distressed.

"And not everybody's affected," I said. "I'm not, for sure. You don't seem to be. It's probably bullshit."

"I know of another instance," she said. "But if I tell you, you have to promise to keep it a secret."

"I can do that."

"Do you know Wanda Lingrove?"

"Wasn't she a friend of yours? A cop? Tall woman? About five years older than us?"

"She's a detective now."

The waitress brought our food. I dug in; Andrea nudged her salad to the side.

"Did you hear about those college girls dying over in Waterford?" she asked.

"No, I haven't been keeping up."

"Two college girls died a few days apart. One in a fire and one in a drowning accident. Wanda asked for a look at the case files. The Waterford police had written them off as accidents, but Wanda had a friend on the force and he slipped her the files and showed her the girls' apartments. They both lived off-campus. It's not that Wanda's any great shakes. She has an undistinguished record. But she had the idea from reading the papers—and they were skimpy articles—a serial killer was involved. Her friend pooh-poohed the idea. There wasn't any signature. But it turned out, Wanda was right. There was a signature, very subtle and very complicated, demonstrating that the killer was highly evolved. Not only did she figure that out, she caught him after two days on the case."

"Aren't serial killers tough to catch?"

"Yes. All that stuff you see about profiling on TV, it's crap. They wouldn't have come close to getting a line on this kid with profiling. He would have had to announce himself, but Wanda doesn't think he would have. She thinks he would have gone on killing, that putting one over on the world was enough for him."

"He was a kid?"

"Fourteen years old. A kid from Black William. What's more, he'd given no sign of being a sociopath. Yet in the space of three weeks, he went from zero to sixty. From playing JV football to being a highly organized serialist. That doesn't happen in the real world."

"So how come Wanda's not famous?"

"The college is trying to keep it quiet. The kid's been bundled off to an institution and the cops have the lid screwed tight." Andrea picked at her salad. "What I'm suggesting, maybe everyone *is* being affected, but not in ways that conform to your model. Wanda catching the kid, that conforms. But the kid himself, the fact that a pathology was brought out in him . . . that suggests that some people may be affected in ways we don't notice. Maybe they just love each other more."

I laid down my fork. "Like with us?"

A doleful nod.

"That's crazy," I said. "You said you'd been plotting for months to make a move."

"Yes, but it was a fantasy!"

"And you don't think you would have acted on it?"

"I don't know. One thing for certain, I never expected anything like this." She cut her volume to a stage whisper. "I want you all the time. It's like when we were nineteen. I'm addicted to you."

"Yeah," I said. "Same here."

"I worry that it'll stop, then I worry that it won't—it's wreaking havoc with my work. I can't stop thinking about you. On a rational level, I know I'm an animal. But there's a place in me that wants to believe love is more than evolutionary biology. And now this thing with the stars. To think that what I'm feeling could be produced by something as random as a wavefront or a supernatural event, or whatever . . . it makes me feel like an experimental animal. Like a rabbit that's been drugged. It scares me."

"Look," I said. "We're probably talking about something that isn't real."

"No, it's real."

"How can you be sure? I only just brought the subject up. We can't have been discussing it more than five minutes."

"You convinced me. Everything you said rings true. I know it here." Andrea touched a hand to her breast. "And you know it, too. Something's happening to us. Something's happening to this town."

We stepped back from that conversation. It was, I suppose, a form of denial, the avoidance of a subject neither of us wished to confront, because it was proof against confrontation, against logic and reason, and so we trivialized it and fell back on our faith, on our mutuality. Sometimes, lying with Andrea, considering the join of her neck and shoulder, the slight convexity of her belly, the compliant curve of a breast compressed into a pouty shape by the weight of her arm, the thousand turns and angles that each seemed the expression of a white simplicity within, I would have the urge to wake her, to drive away from Black William, and thus protect her, protect us, from this infestation of stars; but then I would think that such an action might destroy the thing I hoped to protect, that once away from the stars we might feel differently about one another. And then I'd think how irrational these thoughts were, how ridiculous it was to contemplate uprooting our lives over so flimsy a fear. And, finally, having made this brief rounds of my human potential, I would lapse again into a Praxitelean scrutiny, a sculptor in love with his stone, content to drift in-and-out of a dream in which love, though it had been proved false (like Andrea said, an animal function and nothing more), proved to be eternally false, forever and a day of illusion, of two souls burning brighter and brighter until they appeared to make a single glow, a blazing unity concealed behind robes of aging flesh.

The world beat against our door. Pin's photograph was printed on the third page of the *Black William Gazette,* along with the news that the University of Pittsburgh would be sending a team of observers to measure the phenomenon, should it occur again, as was predicted (by whom, the *Gazette* did not say). There was a sidebar recounting Black William's sordid history and Jonathan Venture's version of BW's involvement with the stars. The body of the article . . . well, it was as if the reporter had been privy to our conversation at the Szechuan Palace. I suspected that he had, if only at second-hand, since my wavefront theory was reproduced in full, attributed to "a local pundit." As a result of this publicity, groups of people, often more than a hundred, mostly the young and the elderly, came to gather in front of the library between the hours of five and nine, thus depriving me of the customary destination of my evening walks.

Stanky, his ego swollen to improbable proportions by two successful performances, by the adulation of his high school fans ("Someone ought to be writing everything Joey says down," said one dreamy-eyed fool), became increasingly temperamental, lashing out at his bandmates, at me, browbeating Liz at every opportunity, and prowling about the house in a sulk, ever with a Coke and cigarette, glaring at all who fell to his gaze, not bothering to speak. In the mornings, he was difficult to wake, keeping Geno and Jerry waiting, wasting valuable time, and one particular morning, my frustration with him peaked and I let Timber into his bedroom and closed the door, listening while the happy pup gamboled across the mattress, licking and drooling, eliciting squeals and curses from the sleepy couple, an action that provoked a confrontation that I won by dint of physical threat and financial dominance, but that firmly established our unspoken enmity and made me anxious about whether I would be able to maneuver him to the point where I could rid myself of him and show a profit.

A gray morning, spitting snow, and I answered the doorbell to find a lugubrious, long-nosed gentleman with a raw, bony face, toting a briefcase and wearing a Sy Sperling wig and a cheap brown suit. A police cruiser was parked at the curb; two uniformed officers stood smoking beside it, casting an indifferent eye toward the Polozny, which rolled on blackly in—as a local DJ was prone to characterize it—"its eternal search for the sea." Since we were only a couple of days from the EP release, I experienced a sinking feeling, one that was borne out when the man produced a card identifying him as Martin Kiggins of Mckeesport, a Friend of the Court. He said he would like to have a word with me about Joseph Stanky.

"How well do you know Joseph?" he asked me once we had settled in the office.

Kiwanda, at her desk in the next room, made a choking noise. I replied that while I had, I thought, an adequate understanding of Joseph as a musician, I was unfamiliar with the details of his life.

"Did you know he has a wife?" Kiggins was too lanky to fit the chair and, throughout our talk, kept scrunching around in it. "And he's got a little boy. Almost two years old, he is."

"No, I didn't know that."

"Poor little guy nearly didn't make it that far. Been sick his whole life." Kiggins' gaze acquired a morose intensity. "Meningitis."

I couldn't get a handle on Kiggins; he acted as if he was trying to sell me something, yet he had arrived on my doorstep with an armed force and the authority of the law.

"I thought meningitis was fatal," I said.

"Not a hundred percent," said Kiggins cheerlessly. "His mother doesn't have insurance, so he didn't get the best of care."

"That's tough."

"She's on welfare. Things aren't likely to improve for the kid or for her. She's not what you'd call an attractive woman."

"Why are we talking about this?" I asked. "It's a sad story, but I'm not involved."

"Not directly, no."

"Not any damn way. I don't understand what you're looking for."

Kiggins seemed disappointed in me. "I'm looking for Joseph. Is he here?"

"I don't know."

"You don't know. Okay." He put his hands on his knees and stood, making a show of peering out the window at his cop buddies.

"I really don't know if he's here," I said. "I've been working, I haven't been downstairs this morning."

"Mind if I take a look down there?"

"You're goddamn right, I mind! What's this about? You've been doing a dance ever since you came in. Why don't you spit it out?"

Kiggins gave me a measuring look, then glanced around the office—I think he was hoping to locate another chair. Failing this, he sat back down.

"You appear to be a responsible guy, Vernon," he said. "Is it okay I call you Vernon?"

"Sure thing, Marty. I don't give a shit what you call me as long as you get to the point."

"You own your home, a business. Pay your taxes . . . far as I can tell without an audit. You're a pretty solid citizen."

The implicit threat of an audit ticked me off, but I let him continue. I began to realize where this might be going.

"I've got the authority to take Joseph back to Mckeesport and throw his butt in jail," said Kiggins. "He's in arrears with his child and spousal support. Now I know Joseph doesn't have any money to speak of, but seeing how you've got an investment in him, I'm hoping we can work out some arrangement."

"Where'd you hear that?" I asked. "About my investment."

"Joseph still has friends in Mckeesport. High school kids, mainly. Truth be told, we think he was supplying them with drugs, but I'm not here about that. They've been spreading it around that you're about to make him a star."

I snorted. "He's a *long* way from being a star. Believe me."

"I believe you. Do you believe me when I tell you I'm here to take him back? Just say the word, I'll give a whistle to those boys out front." Kiggins shifted the chair sideways, so he could stretch out one leg. "I know how you make your money, Vernon. You build a band up, then you sell their contracts. Now you've put in some work with Joseph. Some serious time and money. I should think you'd want to protect your investment."

"Okay." I reached for a cigarette, recalled that I had quit. "What's he owe?"

"Upwards of eleven thousand."

"He's all yours," I said. "Take the stairs in back. Follow the corridor to the front of the house. First door on your right."

"I said I wanted to make an arrangement. I'm not after the entire amount."

And so began our negotiation.

If we had finished the album, I would have handed Stanky over and given Kiggins my blessing, but as things stood, I needed him. Kiggins, on the other hand, wouldn't stand a chance of collecting any money with Stanky in the slam—he likely had a pre-determined figure beneath which he would not move. It infuriated me to haggle with him. Stanky's wife and kid wouldn't see a nickel. They would dock her welfare by whatever amount he extracted from me, deduct administrative and clerical fees, and she would end up worse off than before. Yet I had no choice other than to submit to legal blackmail.

Kiggins wouldn't go below five thousand. That, he said, was his bottom line. He put on a dour poker face and waited for me to decide.

"He's not worth it," I said.

Sadly, Kiggins made for the door; when I did not relent, he turned back and we resumed negotiations, settling on a figure of three thousand and my promise to attach a rider to Stanky's contract stating that a percentage of his earnings would be sent to the court. After he had gone, my check tucked in his briefcase, Kiwanda came to stand by my desk with folded arms.

"I'd give it a minute before you go down," she said. "You got that I'm-gonna-break-his-face look."

"Do you fucking believe this?" I brought my fist down on the desk. "I want to smack that little bitch!"

"Take a breath, Vernon. You don't want to lose any more today than just walked out of here."

I waited, I grew calm, but as I approached the stairs, the image of a wizened toddler and a moping, double-chinned wife cropped up in my brain. With each step I grew angrier and, when I reached Stanky's bedroom, I pushed in without knocking. He and Liz were having sex. I caught a foetid odor and an unwanted glimpse of Liz's sallow hindquarters as she scrambled beneath the covers. I shut the door partway and shouted at Stanky to haul his ass out here. Seconds later, he burst from the room in a T-shirt and pajama bottoms, and stumped into the kitchen with his head down, arms tightly held, like an enraged penguin. He fished a Coke from the refrigerator and made as if to say something; but I let him have it. I briefed him on Kiggins and said, "It's not a question of morality. I already knew you were a piece of crap. But this is a business, man. It's my livelihood, not a playground for degenerates. And when you bring the cops to my door, you put that in jeopardy."

He hung his head, picking at the Coke's pop top. "You don't understand."

"I don't want to understand! Get it? I have absolutely no desire to understand. That's between you and your wife. Between you and whatever scrap of meat loaf shaped like the Virgin Mary you pretend to worship. I don't care. One more screw-up, I'm calling Kiggins and telling him to come get you."

Liz had entered the kitchen, clutching a bathrobe about her; when she heard "wife," she retreated.

I railed at Stanky, telling him he would pay back every penny of the three thousand, telling him further to clean his room of every pot seed and pill, to get his act in order and finish the album; and I kept on railing at him until his body language conveyed that I could expect two or three days of penitence and sucking up. Then I allowed him to slink by me and into the bedroom. When I passed his door, cracked an inch open, I heard him whining to Liz, saying, "She's not *really* my wife."

I took the afternoon off and persuaded Rudy to go fishing. We bundled up against the cold, bought a twelve-pack of Iron City and dropped our lines in Kempton's Pond, a lopsided period stamped into the half-frozen ground a couple of miles east of town, punctuating a mixed stand of birch and hazel—it looked as if a giant with a peg leg had left this impression in the rock, creating a hole thirty feet wide. The clouds had lowered and darkened, their swollen bellies appearing to tatter on the leafless treetops as they slid past; but the snow had quit falling. There was some light accumulation on the banks, which stood eight or nine feet above the black water and gave the pond the look of an old cistern. The water circulated like heavy oil and swallowed our sinkers with barely a splash. This bred the expectation that if we hooked anything, it would be a megalodon or an ichthyosaur, a creature such as would have been trapped in a tar pit. But we had no such expectation.

It takes a certain cast of mind to enjoy fishing with no hope of a catch, or with the faint hope of catching some inedible fishlike thing every few years or so. That kind of fishing is my favorite sport, though I admit I follow the Steelers closely, as do many in Black William. Knowing that nothing will rise from the deep, unless it is something that will astound your eye or pebble your skin with gooseflesh, makes for a rare feeling. Sharing this with Rudy, who had been my friend for ten years, since he was fresh out of grad school at Penn State, enhanced that feeling. In the summer we sat and watched our lines, we chatted, we chased our depressions with beer and cursed the flies; in winter, the best season for our sport, there were no flies. The cold was like ozone to my nostrils, the silence complete, and the denuded woods posed an abstract of slants and perpendiculars, silver and dark, nature as Chinese puzzle. Through frays in the clouds we glimpsed the fat, lordly crests of the Bittersmiths.

I was reaching for another Iron City when I felt a tug on the line. I kept still and felt another tug, then—though I waited the better part of a minute—nothing.

"Something's down in there," I said, peering at the impenetrable surface.

"You get a hit?" Rudy asked.

"Uh-huh."

"How much line you got out?"

"Twenty, twenty-five feet."

"Must have been a current."

"It happened twice."

"Probably a current."

I pictured an enormous grouper-like face with blind milky-blue globes for eyes, moon lanterns, and a pair of weak, underdeveloped hands groping at my line. The Polozny plunges deep underground east of the bridge, welling up into these holes punched through the Pennsylvania rock, sometimes flooding the woods in the spring, and a current was the likely explanation; but I preferred to think that those subterranean chambers were the uppermost tiers of a secret world and that now and again some piscine Columbus, fleeing the fabulous madness of his civilization, palaces illumined by schools of electric eels controlled by the thoughts of freshwater octopi, limestone streets patrolled by gangs of river crocs, grand avenues crowded with giant-snail busses and pedestrian trout, sought to breach the final barrier and find in the world above a more peaceful prospect.

"You have no imagination," I said.

Rudy grunted. "Fishing doesn't require an imagination. That's what makes it fun."

Motionless, he was a bearish figure muffled in a down parka and a wool cap, his face reddened by the cold, breath steaming. He seemed down at the mouth and, thinking it might cheer him up, I asked how he was coming with the comic strip.

"I quit working on it," he said.

"Why the hell'd you do that? It was your best thing ever."

"It was giving me nightmares."

I absorbed this, gave it due consideration. "Didn't strike me as nightmare material. It's kind of bleak. Black comedy. But nothing to freak over."

"It changed." He flicked his wrist, flicking his line sideways. "The veins of pork . . . you remember them?"

"Yeah, sure."

"They started growing, twisting all through the mountain. The mineworkers were happy. Delirious. They were going to be rich, and they threw a big party to celebrate. A pork festival. Actually, that part was pretty funny. I'll show it to you. They made this enormous pork sculpture and were all wearing pork pie hats. They had a beauty contest to name Miss Pork. The winner . . . I used Mia for a model."

"You're a sick bastard, you know that?"

Again, Rudy grunted, this time in amusement. "Then the stars began eating the pork. The mineworkers would open a new vein and the stars would pour in and choff it down. They were ravenous. Nothing could stop them. The mineworkers were starving. That's when I started having nightmares. There was something gruesome about the way I had them eating. I tried to change it, but I couldn't make it work any other way."

I said it still didn't sound like the stuff of nightmares, and Rudy said, "You had to be there."

We fell to talking about other things. The Steelers, could they repeat? Stanky. I asked Rudy if he was coming to the EP release and he said he wouldn't miss it. "He's a genius guitar player," he said. "Too bad he's such a creep."

"Goes with the territory," I said. "Like with Robert Frost beating his wife. Stanky's a creep, he's a perv. A moral dwarf. But he is for sure talented. And you know me. I'll put up with perversity if someone's talented." I clapped Rudy on the shoulder. "That's why I put up with you. You better finish that strip or I'll dump your ass and start hanging with a better class of people."

"Forget the strip," he said glumly. "I'm too busy designing equipment sheds and stables."

We got into a discussion about Celebrity Wifebeaters, enumerating the most recent additions to the list, and this led us—by loose association only—to the subject of Andrea. I told him about our conversation at McGuigan's and what she had said about the outbreak of creativity, about love.

"Maybe she's got a point," Rudy said. "You two have always carried a torch, but you burned each other so badly in the divorce, I never would have thought you'd get back together." He cracked open a beer, handed it to me, and opened one for himself. "You hear about Colvin Jacobs?"

"You mean something besides he's a sleazeball?"

"He's come up with a plan to reduce the county's tax burden by half. Everybody says it's the real quill."

"I'm surprised he found the time, what with all those congressional junkets."

"And Judy Trickle, you hear about her?"

"Now you're scaring me."

"I know. Ol' Juggs 'R Us Judy."

"She should have been your model for Miss Pork, not Mia. What'd she do? Design a newfangled bra?"

"Lifts *and* separates."

"You mean that's it?"

"You nailed it."

"No way!"

"She's been wearing a prototype on the show the last few days. There's a noticeable change." He did a whispery voiceover voice. "The curves are softer, more natural."

"Bullshit!"

"I'm serious. Check her out."

"I got better things to do than watch *AM Waterford*."

"I remember the time when you were a devoted fan."

"That was post-Andrea . . . and pre-Andrea." I chuckled. "Remember the show when she demonstrated the rowing machine? Leotards aren't built to handle that sort of stress."

"I knew the guy who produced her back then. He said they gave her stuff like that to do, because they were hoping for a Wardrobe Incident. They weren't prepared for the reaction."

"Janet Jackson's no Judy Trickle. It was like a dam bursting. Like . . . help me out here, man."

"Like the birth of twin zeppelins."

"Like the embodiment of the yang, like the Aquarian dawn."

Rudy jiggled his line. "This is beginning to border on the absurd."

"You're the one brought her up."

"I'm not talking about Judy, I'm talking about the whole thing. The outbreak."

"Oh, okay. Yeah, we're way past absurd if Miz Trickle's involved. We're heading toward surreal."

"I've heard of five or six more people who've had . . . breakthroughs, I suppose you'd call them."

"How come I don't hear about these people except from you? Do you sit in your office all day, collecting odd facts about Black William?"

"I get more traffic than you do, and people are talking about it now."

"What are they saying?"

"What you'd expect. Isn't it weird? It must be the water, the pollution. I've even heard civic pride expressed. Someone coined the phrase, 'Black William, Pennsylvania's Brain Capital.'"

"That's taking it a bit far." I had a slug of Iron City. "So nobody's panicking? Saying head for the hills?"

"Who said that?"

"Andrea. She was a little disturbed. She didn't exactly say it, but she seemed to think this thing might not be all good."

He tightened his lips and produced a series of squeaking noises. "I think Andrea's right. Not about head for the hills. I don't know about that. But I think whatever this is, it's affecting people in different ways. Some of them emotionally."

"Why's that?"

"I . . ." He tipped back his head, stared at the clouds. "I don't want to talk anymore, man. Okay? Let's just fish."

It began to snow again, tiny flakes, the kind that presage a big fall, but we kept fishing, jiggling our lines in the dead water, drinking Iron City. Something was troubling Rudy, but I didn't press him. I thought about Andrea. She planned to get off early and we were going to dinner in Waterford and maybe catch a movie. I was anticipating kissing her, touching her in the dark, while the new James Bond blew stuff up or (this was more likely) Kenneth Branagh destroyed *As You Like It,* when a tremor ran across the surface of the pond. Both Rudy and I sat up straight and peered. "T-Rex is coming," I said. An instant later, the pond was lashed into a turbulence that sent waves slopping in all directions, as if a large swimmer had drawn near the surface, then made a sudden turn, propelling itself down toward its customary haunts with a flick of its tail. Yet we saw nothing. Nary a fin nor scale nor section of plated armor. We waited, breathless, for the beast to return.

"Definitely not a current," said Rudy.

*E*xcept for the fact that Rudy didn't show, the EP release went well. The music was great, the audience responsive, we sold lots of CDs and souvenirs, including Average Joe dogtags and a Joe Stanky's Army khaki T-shirt, with the pear-shaped (less so after diets and death marches) one's silhouette in white beneath the arc of the lettering. This despite Stanky's obvious displeasure with everyone involved. He was angry at me because I had stolen his top hat and refused to push back the time of the performance to 10 o'clock so he could join the crowd in front of the library waiting for the return of Black William (their number had swelled to more than three hundred since the arrival of the science team from Pitt, led by a youngish professor who, with his rugged build and mustache and plaid wool shirts, might have stepped out of an ad for trail mix). He was angry at Geno and Jerry for the usual reasons—they were incompetent clowns, they didn't understand the music, and they had spurned the opportunity to watch TV with him and Liz. Throughout the hour and a quarter show, he sulked and spoke not a word to the audience, and then grew angry at them when a group of frat boys initiated a chant of "Skanky, Skanky, Skanky . . ." Yet the vast majority were blown away and my night was made when I spotted an A&R man from Atlantic sneaking around.

I was in my office the next morning, reading the *Gazette,* which had come late to the party (as usual) and was running a light-hearted feature on "Pennsylvania's Brain Capital," heavy on Colvin Mason quotes, when I received a call from Crazy Ed in Wilkes-Barre, saying that he'd emailed me a couple of enhancements of Pin's photograph. I opened the emails and the attachments, then asked what I was looking at.

"Beats me," said Ed. "The first is up close on one of those white dealies. You can get an idea of the shape. Sort of like a sea urchin. A globe with spines . . . except there's so many spines, you can't make out the globe. You see it?"

"Yeah. You can't tell me what it is?"

"I don't have a clue." Ed made a buzzing noise, something he did whenever he was stumped. "I assumed the image was fake, that the kid had run two images together, because there's a shift in perspective between the library and the white dealies. They look like they're coming from a long way off. But then I realized the perspective was totally fucked up. It's like part of the photo was taken though a depth of water, or something that's shifting like water. Different sections appear to be at different distances all through the image. Did you notice a rippling effect . . . or anything like that?"

"I only saw it for a couple of seconds. I didn't have time to get much more than a glimpse."

"Okay." Ed made the buzzing noise again. "Have you opened the second attachment?"

"Yep."

"Once I figured out I couldn't determine distances, I started looking at the black stuff, the field or whatever. I didn't get anywhere with that. It's just black. Undifferentiated. Then I took a look at the horizon line. That's how it appeared to you, right? A black field stretching to a horizon? Well, if that was the case, you'd think you'd see something at the front edge, but the only thing I picked up was those bumps on the horizon."

I studied the bumps.

"Kinda look like the tops of heads, don't they?" said Ed.

The bumps could have been heads; they could also have been bushes, animals, or a hundred other things; but his suggestion gave me an uneasy feeling. He said he would fool around with the picture some more and get back to me. I listened to demos. Food of the Gods (King Crimson redux). Corpus Christy (a transsexual front man who couldn't sing, but the name grew on me). The Land Mines (middling roots rock). Gopher Lad (a heroin band from Minnesota). A band called Topless Coroner intrigued me, but I passed after realizing all their songs were about car parts. Around eleven-thirty I took a call from a secretary at Dreamworks who asked if I would hold for William Wine. I couldn't place the name, but said that I would hold and leafed through the Roll-o-dex, trying to find him.

"Vernon!" said an enthusiastic voice from the other side of creation. "Bill Wine. I'm calling for David Geffen. I believe you had drinks with him at the Plug Awards last year. You made quite an impression on David."

The Plugs were the Oscars of the indie business—Geffen had an ongoing interest in indie rock and had put in an appearance. I recalled being in a group gathered around him at the bar, but I did not recall making an impression.

"He made a heck of an impression on me," I said.

Pleasant laughter, so perfect it sounded canned. "David sends his regards," said Wine. "He's sorry he couldn't contact you personally, but he's going to be tied up all day."

"What can I do for you?"

"David listened to that new artist of yours. Joe Stanky? In all the years I've known him, I've never heard him react like he did this morning."

"He liked it?"

"He didn't like it . . . " Wine paused for dramatic effect. "He was knocked out."

I wondered how Geffen had gotten hold of the EP. Mine not to reason why, I figured.

Wine told me that Geffen wanted to hear more. Did I have any other recorded material?

"I've got nine songs on tape," I said. "But some of them are raw."

"David likes raw. Can we get a dupe?"

"You know . . . I usually prefer to push out an album or two before I look for a deal."

"Listen, Vernon. We're not going to let you go to the poorhouse on this."

"That's a relief."

"In fact, David wanted me to sound you out about our bringing you in under the Dreamworks umbrella."

Stunned, I said, "In what capacity?"

"I'll let David tell you about that. He'll call you in a day or two. He's had his eye on you for some time."

I envisioned Sauron spying from his dark tower. I had a dim view of corporate life and I wasn't as overwhelmed by this news as Wine had likely presumed I would be. After the call ended, however, I felt as if I had modeled for Michelangelo's Sistine Chapel mural, the man about to be touched by God's billionaire-ish finger. My impulse was to tell Stanky, but I didn't want his ego to grow more swollen. I called Andrea and learned she would be in court until mid-afternoon. I started to call Rudy, then thought it would be too easy for him to refuse me over the phone. Better to yank him out of his cave and buy him lunch. I wanted to bust his chops about missing the EP release and I needed to talk with someone face-to-face, to analyze this thing that was happening around Stanky. Had the buzz I'd generated about him taken wings on a magical current? The idea that David Geffen was planning to call seemed preposterous. Was Stanky that good? Was I? What, if anything, did Geffen have in mind? Rudy, who enjoyed playing Yoda to my Luke, would help place these questions in coherent perspective.

When I reached Rudy's office, I found Gwen on the phone. Her make-up, usually perfect, was in need of repair; it appeared that she had been crying. "I don't know," she said with strain in her voice. "You'll have to . . . no. I really don't know."

I pointed to the inner office and mouthed, Is he in?

She signaled me to wait.

"I've got someone here," she said into the phone. "I'll have to . . . yes. Yes, I will let you know. All right. Yes. Goodbye." She hung up and, her chin quivering, tried several times to speak, finally blurting out, "I'm so sorry. He's dead. Rudy's dead."

I think I may have laughed—I made some sort of noise, some expression of denial, yet I knew it was true. My face flooded with heat and I went back a step, as if the words had thrown me off-balance.

Gwen said that Rudy had committed suicide early that morning. He had—according to his wife—worked in the office until after midnight, then driven home and taken some pills. The phone rang again. I left Gwen to deal with it and stepped into the inner office to call Beth. I sat at Rudy's desk, but that felt wrong, so I walked around with the phone for a while. Rudy had been a depressed guy, but hell everyone in Black William was depressed about something. I thought that I had been way more depressed than Rudy. He seemed to have it together. Nice wife, healthy income, kids. Sure, he was a for-shit architect in a for-shit town, and not doing the work he wanted, but that was no reason to kill yourself.

Standing by the drafting table, I saw his waste basket was crammed with torn paper. A crawly sensation rippled the skin between my shoulder blades. I dumped the shreds onto the table. Rudy had done a compulsive job of tearing them up, but I could tell they were pieces of his comic strip. Painstakingly, I sorted through them and managed to reassemble most of a frame. In it, a pair of black hands (presumably belonging to a mineworker) were holding a gobbet of pork, as though in offering; above it floated a spiky white ball. The ball had extruded a longish spike to penetrate the pork and the image gave the impression that the ball was sucking meat through a straw. I stared at the frame, trying to interpret it, to tie the image in with everything that had happened, but I felt a vibration pass through my body, like the heavy, impersonal signal of Rudy's death, and I imagined him on the bathroom floor, foam on his mouth, and I had to sit back down.

Beth, when I called her, didn't feel like talking. I asked if there was anything I could do, and she said if I could find out when the police were going to release the body, she would appreciate it. She said she would let me know about the funeral, sounding—as had Gwen—like someone who was barely holding it together. Hearing that in her voice caused me to leak a few tears and, when she heard me start to cry, she quickly got off the phone, as if she didn't want my lesser grief to pollute her own, as if Rudy dying had broken whatever bond there was between us. I thought this might be true.

I called the police and, after speaking to a functionary, reached a detective whom I knew, Ross Peloblanco, who asked my connection to the deceased.

"Friend of the family," I said. "I'm calling for his wife."

"Huh," said Peloblanco, his attention distracted by something in his office.

"So when are you going to release him?"

"I think they already done the autopsy. There's been a bunch of suicides lately and the ME put a rush on this one."

"How many's a bunch?"

"Oops! Did I say that? Don't worry about it. The ME's a whack job. He's batshit about conspiracy theories."

"So . . . can I tell the funeral home to come now?"

Peloblanco sneezed, said, "Shit!," and then went on: "Bowen did some work for my mom. She said he was a real gentleman. You never know what's going on with people, do ya?" He blew his nose. "I guess you can come pick him up whenever."

✥

The waters of the Polozny never freeze. No matter how cold it gets or how long the cold lasts, they are kept warm by a cocktail of pollutants and, though the river may flow more sluggishly in winter, it continues on its course, black and gelid. There is something statutory about its poisonous constancy. It seems less river than regulation, a divine remark rendered daily into law, engraving itself upon the world year after year until its long meander has eaten a crack that runs the length and breadth of creation, and its acids and oxides drain into the void.

Between the viewing and the funeral, in among the various consoling talks and offerings of condolence, I spent a great deal of time gazing at the Polozny, sitting on the stoop and smoking, enduring the cold wind, brooding over half-baked profundities. The muted roaring of the mill surrounded me, as did dull thuds and clunks and distant car horns that seemed to issue from the gray sky, the sounds of business as usual, the muffled engine of commerce. Black William must be, I thought, situated on the ass-end of Purgatory, the place where all those overlooked by God were kept. The dead river dividing a dying landscape, a dingy accumulation of snow melting into slush on its banks; the mill, a Hell of red brick with its chimney smoke of souls; the scatters of crows winging away from leafless trees; old Mrs. Gables two doors down, tottering out to the sidewalk, peering along the street for the mail, for a glimpse of her son's maroon Honda Civic, for some hopeful thing, then, her hopes dashed, laboriously climbing her stairs and going inside to sit alone and count the ticks of her clock: these were evidences of God's fabulous absence, His careless abandonment of a destiny-less town to its several griefs. I scoffed at those who professed to understand grief, who deemed it a simple matter, a painful yet comprehensible transition, and partitioned the process into stages (my trivial imagination made them into gaudy stagecoaches painted different colors) in order to enable its victims to adapt more readily to the house rules. After the initial shock of Rudy's suicide had waned, grief overran me like a virus, it swarmed, breeding pockets of weakness and fever, eventually receding at its own pace, on its own terms, and though it may have been subject to an easy compartmentalization—Anger, Denial, et al—that kind of analysis did not address its nuances and could not remedy the thousand small bitternesses that grief inflames and encysts. On the morning of the funeral, when I voiced one such bitterness, complaining about how Beth had treated me since Rudy died, mentioning the phone call, pointing out other incidences of her intolerance, her rudeness in pushing me away, Andrea—who had joined me on the stoop—set me straight.

"She's not angry at you," Andrea said. "She's jealous. You and Rudy . . . that was a part of him she never shared, and when she sees you, she doesn't know how to handle it."

"You think?"

"I used to feel that way."

"About me and Rudy?"

She nodded. "And about the business. I don't feel that way now. I guess I'm older. I understand you and Rudy had a guy thing and I didn't need to know everything about it. But Beth's dealing with a lot right now. She's oversensitive and she feels . . . jilted. She feels that Rudy abandoned her for you. A little, anyway. So she's jilting you. She'll get over it, or she won't. People are funny like that. Sometimes resentments are all that hold them together. You shouldn't take it personally."

I refitted my gaze to the Polozny, more-or-less satisfied by what she had said. "We live on the banks of the River Styx," I said after a while. "At least it has a Styx-ian gravitas."

"Stygian," she said.

I turned to her, inquiring.

"That's the word you wanted. Stygian."

"Oh. . . right."

A silence marked by the passing of a mail truck, its tire chains grinding the asphalt and spitting slush; the driver waved.

"I think I know why Rudy did it," I said, and told her what I had found in the office waste basket. "More than anything he wanted to do creative work. When he finally did, it gave him nightmares. It messed with his head. He must have built it into this huge thing and . . . " I tapped out a cigarette, stuck it in my mouth. "It doesn't sound like much of a reason, but I can relate. That's why it bites my ass to see guys like Stanky who do something creative every time they take a piss. *I* want to write those songs. *I* want to have the acclaim. It gets me thinking, someday I might wind up like Rudy."

"That's not you. You said it yourself—you get pissed off. You find someplace else to put your energy." She rumpled my hair. "Buck up, Sparky. You're going to live a long time and have lots worse problems."

It crossed my mind to suggest that the stars might have played some mysterious part in Rudy's death, and to mention the rash of suicides (five, I had learned); but all that seemed unimportant, dwarfed by the death itself.

At one juncture during that weekend, Stanky ventured forth from TV-land to offer his sympathies. He may have been sincere, but I didn't trust his sincerity—it had an obsequious quality and I believed he was currying favor, paving the way so he might hit me up for another advance. Pale and shivering, hunched against the cold; the greasy collar of his jacket turned up; holding a Camel in two nicotine-stained fingers; his doughy features cinched in an expression of exaggerated dolor: I hated him at that moment and told him I was taking some days off, that he could work on the album or go play with his high school sycophants. "It's up to you," I said. "Just don't bother me about it." He made no reply, but the front door slamming informed me that he had not taken it well.

On Wednesday, Patty Prole (nee Patricia Hand), the leader of the Swimming Holes, a mutual friend of mine and Rudy's who had come down from Pittsburgh for the funeral, joined me and Andrea for dinner at McGuigan's, and, as we strolled past the park, I recalled that more than a month—thirty-four days, to be exact—had elapsed since I had last seen the stars. The crowd had dwindled to about a hundred-and-fifty (Stanky and Liz among them). They stood in clumps around the statue, clinging to the hope that Black William would appear; though judging by their general listlessness, the edge of their anticipation had been blunted and they were gathered there because they had nothing better to do. The van belonging to the science people from Pitt remained parked at the southeast corner of the library, but I had heard they were going to pull up stakes if nothing happened in the next day or two.

McGuigan's was a bubble of heat and light and happy conversation. A Joe Henry song played in the background; Pitt basketball was on every TV. I had not thought the whole town dressed in mourning, but the jolly, bustling atmosphere came as something of a shock. They had saved the back booth for us and, after drinking for a half-hour or so, I found myself enjoying the evening. Patty was a slight, pretty, blue-eyed blond in her late twenties, dressed in a black leather jacket and jeans. To accommodate the sober purpose of this trip home, she had removed her visible piercings. With the majority of her tattoos covered by the jacket, she looked like an ordinary girl from western Pennsylvania and nothing like the exotic, pantherine creature she became on stage. When talk turned to Rudy, Andrea and I embraced the subject, offering humorous anecdotes and fond reminiscence, but Patty, though she laughed, was subdued. She toyed with her fork, idly stabbing holes in the label on her beer bottle, and at length revealed the reason for her moodiness.

"Did Rudy ever tell you we had a thing?" she asked.

"He alluded to it," I said. "But well after the fact. Years."

"I bet you guys talked all about it when you're up at Kempton's Pond. He said you used to talk about the local talent when you're up there sometimes."

Andrea elbowed me, not too sharply, in mock reproof.

"As I remember, the conversation went like this," I said. "We were talking about bands, the Swimming Holes came up, and he mentioned he'd had an affair with you. And I said, 'Oh, yeah?' And Rudy said, 'Yeah.' Then after a minute he said, "Patty's a great girl.'"

"That's what he said? We had an affair? That's the word he used?"

"I believe so."

"He didn't say he was banging me or like that?"

"No."

"And that's all he said?" Patty stared at me sidelong, as if trying to penetrate layers of deception.

"That's all I remember."

"I bet you tried to get more out of him. I know you. You were hungering for details."

"I can't promise I wasn't," I said. "I just don't remember. You know Rudy. He was a private guy. You could beat on him with a shovel and not get a thing out of him. I'm surprised he told me that much."

She held my gaze a moment longer. "Shit! I can't tell if you're lying."

"He's not," said Andrea.

"You got him scoped, huh? He's dead to rights." Patty grinned and leaned against the wall, putting one fashionably booted foot up on the bench. "Rudy and me . . . it was a couple weeks right before the band left town. It was probably stupid. Sometimes I regret it, but sometimes I don't."

Andrea asked how it happened, and Patty, who obviously wanted to talk about it, said, "You know. Like always. We started hanging out, talking. Finally I asked him straight out, 'Where's this going, Rudy?' Because we only had a couple of weeks and I wanted to know if it was all in my head. He got this peculiar look on his face and kissed me. Like I said, it didn't last long, but it was deep, you know. That's why I'm glad Rudy didn't tell everyone how it was in the sack. It's a dumb thing to worry about, but . . . " Her voice had developed a tremor. "I guess that's what I'm down to."

"You loved him," said Andrea.

"Yeah. I did." Patty shook off the blues and sat up. "There wasn't anywhere for it to go. He'd never leave his kids and I was going off to Pittsburgh. I hated his wife for a while. I didn't feel guilty about it. But now I look at her . . . She was never part of our scene. With Vernon and Rudy and the bands. She lived off to the side of it all. It wasn't like that with you, Andrea. You had your law thing going, but when you were around, you were into it. You were one of the girls. But Beth was so totally not into it. She still can't stand us. And now it feels like I stole something from her. That really sucks."

Platitudes occurred to me, but I kept quiet. Andrea stirred at my side.

"Sometimes it pays to be stupid," Patty said gloomily.

I had a moment when the light and happy babble of the bar were thrust aside by the gonging thought that my friend was dead, and I didn't entirely understand what she meant, but I knew she was right.

Patty snagged a passing waitress. "Can I get a couple of eggs over?" she asked. "I know you're not serving breakfast, but that's all I eat is breakfast." She winked broadly at the waitress. "Most important meal of the day, so I make every meal breakfast."

The waitress began to explain why eggs were impossible, but Patty cut in, saying, "You don't want me to starve, do ya? You must have a couple of eggs back there. Some fries and bacon. Toast. We're huge tippers, I swear."

Exasperated, the waitress said she'd see if the cook would do it.

"I know you can work him, honey," Patty said. "Tell him to make the eggs dippy, okay?"

We left McGuigan's shortly after eight, heading for Corky's, a workingman's bar where we could do some serious drinking, but as we came abreast of the statue, Patty said, "Hey, let's go talk to Stanky." Stanky and Liz were sitting on the base of the statue; Pin and the other boys were cross-legged at their feet, like students attending their master. The crowd had thinned and was down, I'd guess, to about a hundred and twenty; a third of that number were clustered around the science van and the head scientist, who was hunched over a piece of equipment set up on the edge of the library lawn. I lagged behind as we walked over and noticed Liz stiffen at the sight of Patty. The boys gazed adoringly at her. Stanky cast me a spiteful glance.

"I heard your EP, man," Patty said. "Very cool."

Stanky muttered, "Yeah, thanks," and stared at her breasts.

Like me, Patty was a sucker for talent, used to the ways of musicians, and she ignored this ungracious response. She tried to draw him out about the music, but Stanky had a bug up his ass about something and wouldn't give her much. The statue loomed above, throwing a shadow across us; the horse's head, with its rolling eyes and mouth jerked open by the reins, had been rendered more faithfully than had Black William's face . . . or else he was a man whose inner crudeness had coarsened and simplified his features. In either case, he was one ugly mother, his shoulder-length hair framing a maniacal mask. Seeing him anew, I would not have described his expression as laughing or alarmed, but might have said it possessed a ferocious exultancy.

Patty began talking to the boys about the Swimming Holes' upcoming tour, and Andrea was speaking with Pin. Stanky oozed over to me, Liz at his shoulder, and said, "We laid down a new song this afternoon."

"Oh, yeah?" I said.

"It's decent. 'Misery Loves Company.'"

In context, it wasn't clear, until Stanky explained it, that this was a title.

"A guy from Dreamworks called," he said. "William Wine."

"Yeah, a few days back. Did Kiwanda tell you about it?"

"No, he called today. Kiwanda was on her break and I talked to him."

"What'd he say?"

"He said they loved the tape and David Geffen's going to call." He squinched up his face, as if summoning a mighty effort. "How come you didn't tell me about the tape? About him calling before?"

This, I understood, was the thing that had been bothering him. "Because it's business," I said. "I'm not going to tell you about every tickle we get. Every phone call."

He squinted at me meanly. "Why not?"

"Do you realize how much of this just goes away? These people are like flies. They buzz around, but they hardly ever land. Now the guy's called twice, that makes it a little more interesting. I'll give it a day or two, and call him back."

Ordinarily, Stanky would have retreated from confrontation, but with Liz bearing witness (I inferred by her determined look that she was his partner in this, that she had egged him on), his macho was at stake. "I ought to know everything that's going on," he said.

"Nothing's going on. When something happens, I'll tell you."

"It's my career," he said in a tone that conveyed petulance, defiance, and the notion that he had been wronged. "I want to be in on it, you know."

"Your career." I felt suddenly liberated from all restraint. "Your career consists of my efforts on your behalf and three hours on-stage in Nowhere, Pennsylvania. I've fed you, I've given you shelter, money, a band. And now you want me to cater to your stupid whims? To run downstairs and give you an update on every little piece of Stanky gossip because it'll gratify your ego? So you can tell your minions here how great you are? Fuck you! You don't like how I'm handling things, clear the hell out of my house!"

I walked off several paces and stood on the curb, facing the library. That rough cube of Pennsylvania granite accurately reflected my mood. Patches of snow dappled the lawn. There was a minor hubbub near the science truck, but I was enraged and paid it no mind. Andrea came up next to me and took my arm. "Easy, big fella," she said.

"That asshole's been under my roof for what? Two months? It feels like two years. His stink permeates every corner of my life. It's like living with a goat!"

"I know," she said. "But it's business."

I wondered if she was hammering home an old point, but her face gave no sign of any such intent; in fact, her neutral expression dissolved into one of befuddlement. She was staring at the library, and when I turned in that direction, I saw the library had vanished. An immense rectangle—a window with uneven edges—had been chopped out of the wall of the world, out of the night, its limits demarked by trees, lawn, and sky, and through it poured a flood of blackness, thicker and more sluggish than the Polozny. Thick like molasses or hot tar. It seemed to splash down, to crest in a wave, and hold in that shape. Along the top of the crest, I could see lesser, half-defined shapes, vaguely human, and I had the thought that the wave was extruding an army from its substance, producing a host of creatures who appeared to be men. The temperature had dropped sharply. There was a chill, chemical odor and, close above our heads (five feet, I'd estimate), the stars were coasting. That was how they moved. They glided as though following an unseen track, then were shunted sideways or diagonally or backward. Their altitude never changed, and I suspect now that they were prevented from changing it by some physical limitation. They did not resemble stars as much as they did Crazy Ed's enhancement: ten or twelve globes studded with longish white spines, the largest some eight feet in diameter, glowing brightly enough to illumine the faces of the people beneath them. I could not determine if they were made of flesh or metal or something less knowable. They gave forth high-frequency squeaks that reminded me, in their static quality, of the pictographs in Rudy's cartoons, the language of the stars.

I'm not sure how long we stood there, but it could not have been more than seconds before I realized that the wave crest was not holding, it was inching toward us across the lawn. I caught Andrea's hand and tried to run. She screamed (a yelp, really), and others screamed and tried to run. But the wave flowed around us, moving now like black quicksilver, in an instant transforming the center of town into a flood plain, marooning people on islands of solid ground bounded by a waist-high flood that was coursing swiftly past. As Andrea and I clung together, I saw Stanky and Liz, Pin and

Patty, the rest of the kids, isolated beside the statue—there were dozens of such groupings throughout the park. It seemed a black net of an extremely coarse weave had been thrown over us all and we were standing up among its strands. We stared at each other, uncertain of our danger; some called for help. Then something rose from the blackness directly in front of me and Andrea. A man, I think, and fully seven feet tall. An African negro by the scarifications on his face. His image not quite real—it appeared to be both embedded in the tarry stuff and shifting over its surface, as if he had been rotoscoped. At the same time, a star came to hover over us, so that my terror was divided. I had from it an impression of eagerness—the feeling washed down upon me; I was drenched in it—and then, abruptly, of disinterest, as if it found Andrea and me unworthy of its attention. With the onset of that disinterest, the black man melted away into the tar and the star passed on to another group of stranded souls.

The largest groups were those two clustered about the science van. Figures began to sprout from the tar around them, and not all of these were men. Some were spindly as eels, others squat and malformed, but they were too far away for me to assign them a more particular identity. Stars hovered above the two groups, and the black figures lifted people one by one, kicking and screaming (screams now issued from every corner of the park), and held them up to the stars. These did not, as in Rudy's cartoons, suck in the meat through one of their spikes; they never touched their victims. A livid arc, fiery black in color, leaped between star and human, visible for a split-second, and then the figure that had lifted the man or woman, dropped him or her carelessly to the ground and melted back into the flood, and the star moved on. Andrea buried her face in my shoulder, but I could not turn away, transfixed by the scene. And as I watched these actions repeated again and again—the figure melting up, lifting someone to a star, and then discarding him, the victim still alive, rolling over, clutching an injured knee or back, apparently not much the worse for wear—I realized the stars were grazing, that this was their harvest, a reaping of seed sown. They were harvesting our genius, a genius they had stimulated, and they were attracted to a specific yield that manifested in an arc of fiery black. The juice of the poet, the canniness of the inventor, the guile of a villain. They failed to harvest the entire crop, only that gathered in the park.

The remainder of those affected would go on to create more garden tools and foundation garments and tax plans, and the stars would continue on their way, a path that now and again led them through the center of Black William. I must confess that, amid the sense of relief accompanying this revelation, I felt an odd twinge of envy when I realized that the genius of love was not to their taste.

How did I know these things? I think when the star hovered above us, it initiated some preliminary process, one incidental to the feelings of eagerness and disinterest it projected, and, as it prepared to take its nutrient, its treasure (I haven't a clue as to why they harvested us, whether we were for them a commodity or sustenance or something else entire), we shared a brief communion. As proof, I can only say that Andrea holds this same view and there is a similar consensus, albeit with slight variances, among all those who stood beneath the stars that night. But at the moment the question was not paramount. I turned toward the statue. The storefronts beyond were obscured by a black rectangle, like the one that had eclipsed the library, and this gave me to believe that the flood was pouring off into an unguessable dimension, though it still ran deep around us. Stanky and Liz had climbed onto the statue and were clinging to Black William's leg and saddlehorn respectively. Patty was leaning against the base, appearing dazed. Pin stood beside her, taking photographs with his cell phone. One of the kids was crying, and his friends were busy consoling him. I called out, asking if everyone was all right. Stanky waved and then the statue's double reared from the flood—it rose up slowly, the image of a horse and a rider with flowing hair, blacker than the age-darkened bronze of its likeness. They were so equal in size and posture and stillness, it was as if I were looking at the statue and its living shadow. Its back was to me, and I cannot say if it was laughing. And then the shadow extended an arm and snatched Stanky from his perch. Plucked him by the collar and held him high, so that a star could extract its due, a flash of black energy. And when that was done, it did not let him fall, but began to sink back into the flood, Stanky still in its grasp. I thought it would take him under the tar, that they would both be swallowed and Stanky's future was to be that of a dread figure rising blackly to terrify the indigenes in another sector of the plenum. But Black William—or the agency that controlled him—must have had a change of heart and, at the last second, just as Stanky's feet were about to merge with that tarry surface, dropped him clear of the flood, leaving him inert upon the pavement.

The harvest continued several minutes more (the event lasted twenty-seven minutes in all) and then the flood receded, again with quicksilver speed, to form itself into a wave that was poised to splash down somewhere on the far side of that black window. And when the window winked out, when the storefronts snapped back into view, the groaning that ensued was much louder and more articulated than that we'd heard a month previously. Not a sound of holy woe, but of systemic stress, as if the atoms that composed the park and its surround were complaining about the insult they had incurred. All across the park, people ran to tend the injured. Andrea went to Liz, who had fallen from the statue and tearfully declared her ankle broken. Patty said she was dizzy and had a headache, and asked to be left alone. I knelt beside Stanky and asked if he was okay. He lay propped on his elbows, gazing at the sky.

"I wanted to see," he said vacantly. "They said . . ."

"They?" I said. "You mean the stars?"

He blinked, put a hand to his brow. As ever, his emotions were writ large, yet I don't believe the look of shame that washed over his face was an attempt to curry favor or promote any agenda. I believe his shame was informed by a rejection such as Andrea and I experienced, but of a deeper kind, more explicit and relating to an opportunity lost.

I made to help him up, intending to question him further; but he shook me off. He had remembered who he was, or at least who he had been pretending to be. Stanky the Great. A man of delicate sensibilities whom I had offended by my casual usage and gross maltreatment. His face hardened, becoming toadlike as he summoned every ounce of his Lilliputian rage. He rolled up to his knees, then got to his feet. Without another word to me, he arranged his features into a look of abiding concern and hurried to give comfort to his Liz.

*I*n the wider world, Black William has come to be known as "that town full of whackos" or "the place where they had that hallucination," for as with all inexplicable things, the stars and our interaction with them have been dismissed by the reasonable and responsible among us, relegated to the status of an aberration, irrelevant to the big picture, to the roar of practical matters with which we are daily assailed. I myself, to an extent, have dismissed it, yet my big picture has been enlarged somewhat. Of an evening, I will sit upon the library steps and cast my mind out along the path of the stars and wonder if they were metaphoric or literal presences, nomads or machines, farmers or a guerilla force, and I will question what use that black flash had for them, and I will ponder whether they were themselves evil or recruited evil men to assist them in their purpose simply because they were suited to the task. I subscribe to the latter view; otherwise, I doubt Stanky would have wanted to go with them . . . unless they offered a pleasurable reward, unless they embodied for him the promise of a sublime perversion in exchange for his service, an eternal tour of duty with his brothers-in-arms, dreaming in that tarry flood. And what of their rejection of him? Was it because he was insufficiently evil? Too petty in his cruelty? Or could it have been he lacked the necessary store of some brain chemical? The universe is all whys and maybes. All meanings coincide, all answers are condensed to one or none. Nothing yields to logic.

Since the coming of the stars, Black William has undergone a great renewal. Although in the immediate aftermath there was a hue and cry about fleeing the town, shutting it down, calmer voices prevailed, pointing to the fact that there had been no fatalities, unless one counted the suicides, and but a single disappearance (Colvin Jacobs, who was strolling through the park that fateful night), and it could be better understood, some maintained, in light of certain impending charges against him (embezzlement, fraud, solicitation). Stay calm, said the voices. A few scrapes and bruises, a smattering of nervous breakdowns—that's no reason to fling up your hands. Let's think this over. Colvin's a canny sort, not one to let an opportunity pass. At this very moment he may be developing a skin cancer on Varadero Beach or Ipanema (though it is my belief that he may be sojourning in a more unlikely place). And while the town thought it over, the tourists began to arrive by the busload. Drawn by Pin's photographs, which had been published around the world, and later by his best-selling book (co-authored by the editor of the *Gazette*), they came from Japan, from Europe, from Punxsutawney and Tuckhannock, from every quarter of the globe, a flood of tourists that resolved into a steady flow and demanded to be housed, fed, T-shirted, souvenired, and swindled. They needed theories upon which to hang their faith, so theory-making became a cottage industry and theories abounded, both supernatural and quasi-scientific, each having their own battery of proponents and debunkers. A proposal was floated in the city council that a second statue be erected to commemorate Black William's visitation, but the ladies of the Heritage Committee fought tooth and nail to preserve the integrity of the original, and now can be seen twice a year lavishing upon him a vigorous scrubbing.

Businesses thrived, mine included—this due to the minor celebrity I achieved and the sale of Stanky and his album to Warner Brothers (David Geffen never called). The album did well and the single, "Misery Loves Company," climbed to No. 44 on the Billboard charts. I have no direct contact with Stanky, but learned from Liz, who came to the house six months later to pick up her clothes (those abandoned when Stanky fled my house in a huff), that he was writing incidental music for the movies, a job that requires no genius. She carried tales, too, of their nasty break-up, of Stanky's increasing vileness, his masturbatory displays of ego. He has not written a single song since he left Black William—the stars may have drained more from him than that which they bred, and perhaps the fact that he was almost taken has something to do with his creative slump. Whatever his story, I think he has found his true medium and is becoming a minor obscenity slithering among the larger obscenities that serve a different kind of star, anonymous beneath the black flood of the Hollywood sewer.

The following March, I went fishing with Andrea at Kempton Pond. She was reluctant to join me, assuming that I intended to make her a stand-in for Rudy, but I assured her this was not the case and told her she might enjoy an afternoon out of the office, some quiet time together. It was a clear day, and cold. Pockets of snow lay in the folds and crinkles of the Bittersmiths, but the crests were bare, and there was a deeper accumulation on the banks than when Rudy and I had fished the pond in November. We had to clear ourselves a spot on which to sit. The sun gilded the birch trunks, but the waters of the pond were as Stygian and mysterious as ever.

We cast out our lines and chatted about doings in her office, my latest projects—Lesion (black metal) and a post-rock band I had convinced to call themselves Same Difference. I told her about some loser tapes that had come my way, notably a gay Christian rap outfit with a song entitled "Cruisin' For Christ (While Searching For The Heavenly City)." Then we fell silent. Staring into the pond, at the dark rock walls and oily water, I did not populate the depths with fantasies, but thought instead of Rudy. They were memorial thoughts untainted by grief, memories of things said and done. I had such a profound sense of him, I imagined if I turned quickly enough, I would have a glimpse of a bulky figure in a parka, wool cap jammed low on his brow, red-cheeked and puffing steam; yet when I did turn, the figure in the parka and wool cap was more clearly defined, ivory pale and slender, her face a living cameo. I brushed a loose curl from her eyes. Touching her cheek warmed my fingertip. "This is kind of nice," she said, and smiled. "It's so quiet."

"Told you you'd like it," I said.

"I do."

She jiggled her line.

"You'll never catch anything that way." I demonstrated proper technique. "Twitch the line side-to-side."

Amused, she said, "I really doubt I'm going to catch anything. What were you and Rudy batting? One for a thousand?"

"Yeah, but you never know."

"I don't think I want to catch anything if it resembles that thing he had mounted."

"You should let out more line, too."

She glanced at me wryly, but did as I suggested.

A cloud darkened the bank and I pictured how the two of us would appear to God, if God were in His office, playing with His Gameboy: tiny animated fisher folk hunched over their lines, shoulder-to-shoulder, waiting for a tiny monster to breach, unmindful of any menace from above. Another cloud shadowed us. A ripple moved across the pond, passing so slowly, it made me think that the waters of the Polozny, when upthrust into these holes, were squeezed into a sludgy distillate. Bare twigs clattered in a gust of wind.

"All these years," Andrea said. "All the years and now five months . . ."

"Yeah?"

"Everyday, there'll be two or three times when I see you, like just now, when I look up and see you, and it's like a blow . . . a physical blow that leaves me all ga-ga. I want to drop everything and curl up with you."

"Me, too," I said.

She hesitated. "It just worries me."

"We've had this conversation," I said. "I don't mind having it again, but we're not going to resolve anything. We'll never figure it out."

"I know." She jiggled her line, forgetting to twitch it. "I keep thinking I'll find a new angle, but all I come up with is more stupidity. I was thinking the other day, it was like a fairy tale. How falling back in love protected us, like a charm." She heel-kicked the bank. "It's frustrating when everything you think seems absurd and true all at once."

"It's a mystery."

"Right."

"I go there myself sometimes," I said. "I worry about whether we'll fall out of love . . . if what we feel is unnatural. Then I worry if worrying about it's unnatural. Because, you know, it's such a weird thing to be worried about. Then I think, hey, it's perfectly natural to worry over something you care about, whether it's weird or not. Round and round. We might as well go with the flow. No doubt we'll still be worrying about it when we're too old to screw."

"That's pretty old."

"Yep," I said. "Ancient."

"Maybe it's good we worry." Then after a pause, she said, "Maybe we didn't worry enough the first time."

A second ripple edged the surface, like a miniature slow tsunami. The light faded and dimmed. A degree of tension seemed to leave Andrea's body.

"You want to go to Russia?" she asked. "I've got this conference in late May. I have to give a paper and be on some panels. It's only four days, but I could take some vacation."

I thought about it. "Kiwanda's pretty much in control of things. Would we have to stay in Russia?"

"Don't you want to go clubbing in Moscow? Meet new people? I'll wear a slutty dress and act friendly with strangers. You can save me from the white slavers—I'm sure I'll attract white slavers."

"I'll do my best," I said. "But some of those slavers are tough."

"You can take 'em!" She rubbed the side of her nose. "Why? Where do you want to go?"

"Bucharest."

"Why there?"

"Lots of reasons. Potential for vampires. Cheap. But reason number one—nobody goes there."

"Good point. We get enough of crowds around here."

We fell silent again. The eastern slopes of the Bittersmiths were drowning in shadow, acquiring a simplified look, as of worn black teeth that still bore traces of enamel. But the light had richened, the tree trunks appeared to have been dipped in old gold. Andrea straightened and peered down into the hole.

"I had a nibble," she said excitedly.

I watched the surface. The water remained undisturbed, lifeless and listless, but I felt a presence lurking beneath, a wise and deliberate fish, a grotesque, yet beautiful in the fact of its survival, and more than a murky promise—it would rise to us this day or some other. Perhaps it would speak a single word, perhaps merely die. Andrea leaned against me, eager to hook it, and asked what she should do.

"It's probably just a current," I said, but advised her to let out more line.

EMERALD STREET EXPANSIONS

I went down to Emerald Street in search of something new, an attitude with keener claws, a sniper's calm and distant eye, a thief's immersion in the night. I wanted some red and unreasonable religion to supplant the conventionality I believed was suffocating my spirit . . . though I was less dissatisfied by conventionality itself than by my lack of dissatisfaction with it. That I had embraced the cautious and the conservative so readily seemed to reflect a grayness of soul. I thought adding a spare room to my mind, a space with a stained-glass window through which I could perceive the holy colors of the world, would allow me to feel content within my limitations.

It was a gloomy Seattle morning with misty rain falling and a cloud like a roll of silvery dough being squeezed up from the horizon and flattened out over the Sound. The shop, to which I had been directed by friends—satisfied customers all, successful young men and women of commerce who once had suffered from maladies similar to mine—was a glass storefront sandwiched between a diner and a surgical arcade. A hand-painted sign above the door depicted a green crystalline flash such as might be produced by a magical detonation, with the name—EMERALD STREET EXPANSIONS—superimposed. As I drew near, two neutral-looking, well-tailored men in their thirties, not so different from myself, emerged from the shop. The idea that I might be typical of its patrons diminished my enthusiasm. But recognizing that the mental climate that bred this sort of hesitancy was precisely my problem, I pushed in through the door.

The interior of the shop was furnished like a living room and all in green. The color of the carpet was a pale Pomona, the grouped chairs and couches a ripe persimmon, and the attendant was a woman of approximately my own age, wearing a parrot-green dress with a mandarin collar and a tight skirt. Her features were too strong for beauty, her cheekbones too sharp. Yet she was striking, impressive in her poise, perched alertly on the edge of a chair, and I had the thought that this was not a considered pose, that she must always sit this way, prepared to launch herself at some helpless prey. Her skin had a faint olive cast, testifying to a Latin heritage, and a coil of hair lay across her shoulder and breast like the tail of a black serpent. She glanced down at her hand, at a tiny palm console that—assuming the doorway was functioning—revealed my personal information. She smiled and indicated that I should sit beside her.

"Hello, David," she said. "My name is Amorise. How may I help? Something to brighten the overcast, perhaps? Or are you interested in a more functional expansion?"

I explained my requirements in general terms.

"I assume you've read our brochure," she said, and when I said I had, she went on: "We provide you with a perceptual program that you'll access by means of a key phrase. It's the usual process. The difference is that we only do custom work. We expand what is inborn rather than add an entirely new facet to the personality." She glanced down at the palm console. "I see you design weapons. For the military?"

"Personal protection devices. Home-defense."

"David LeGary . . ." She tapped her chin with a forefinger. "Wasn't there a piece about you on the news? Murderous appliances, windows that kill . . . that sort of thing."

"They sensationalized my work. Not all my designs are lethal."

We talked for fifteen or twenty minutes. As Amorise spoke she touched my hand with a frequency that appeared to signal more than simple assurance; yet I did not believe she was teasing me—there was a mannered quality to her gestures that led me to suspect they were an element of formal behavior. Her eyes, of course, were green. Lenses, I assumed. I doubted such a brilliant shade was found in life.

"I was going to pass you off to another therapist," she said. "But I'd like to treat you myself . . . if that's all right." She rested a hand on my forearm. "Do you want to hear what I have in mind?"

"Sure."

"A poet," she said.

My face may have betrayed disappointment, because she said hurriedly, "Not an ordinary poet, but a *poet maudit*. A lover, a thief, a man who shed the blood of a priest. He lived six hundred years ago in France. Like your own ancestors, David."

"You can provide elements from a specific personality? I didn't know that was possible."

She passed my comment off with a wave. "The man's name was Francois Villon. Have you heard of him?"

I said, "No," and Amorise said, "Well, it's not an age for poetry, is it?" She looked down at her hands, as if dismayed by the thought. "Villon was a cynic, but passionate. Sensitive, yet callous. A drunkard and an ascetic."

"I don't believe any of those qualities are inborn in me."

"I'm certain that they are. Though the world has done its best to murder them."

I recognized that people in her line of work were gifted with intuition, capable of quick character judgments, but this intimation that she had some innate understanding of me, a knowledge that ran so contrary to my own—it seemed ridiculous. A silence shouldered between us, and then she said, "Let me ask you something, David. If you had the opportunity to create something miraculous, something that would ensure the continuance of a great tradition, but to achieve it you would have to risk everything you've worked for . . . What would you decide?"

"It's too general a question," I said.

"Is it? I think it's the basic question you're asking yourself, the one you're trying to answer by coming here. But if you want specifics, let's imagine you're Francois Villon, and that if you surrender your soul to a woman, you will achieve immortality as a poet. What would you do?"

"I don't believe in souls," I told her.

"Of course you don't. That's why I phrased my original question as I did."

"I suppose," I said after a moment's consideration, "that I would like to feel comfortable with taking that kind of risk."

"Taking that kind of risk never bestows comfort," said Amorise.

"But I'll consider that a 'yes.'" She got to her feet and offered me her hand. "Are you ready?"

A dozen questions sprang to mind, but they all illustrated a tiresome conventionality, and I left them unasked. I filled out a form, essentially a disclaimer, paid the fee, and Amorise ushered me into a small room in the back containing a surgical chair with arm and leg restraints. Once I had taken a seat, she handed me a cup half-filled with a bright green liquid, saying that it would put me to sleep. After I drank down the sweetish mixture, she leaned across me to secure the restraint on my left arm, her breast pressing my shoulder. She did not draw back immediately, but remained looking down at me.

"Are you afraid?" she asked. The unreal clarity of her brilliant eyes—they made me think of the painted eyes on signs outside psychics' doors.

I was afraid, a little, but I said, "No."

She caressed my cheek. "You surrender your power so easily . . . like a child."

Before I could analyze this obscure comment, she kissed me on the mouth. A deep, probing kiss to which, dizzied by the potion I had swallowed, I could not help responding. It was such a potent kiss, I can't be sure whether it or the liquid caused me to lose consciousness. When I woke, light-headed and groggy, I found the restraints had been removed and I discovered in my hand a business card advertising a club called the Martinique in South Seattle. On the back of the card Amorise had written the following:

> These are your codes. The first accesses Francois, the second is to exit.
> *"Je t'aime, Amorise."*
> *"Je te deteste, Amorise."*

Those phrases, when I put them together with the kiss . . . they unsettled me. I suspected that Amorise had done something to harm me, or at least something that I might regret. I pocketed the card and stepped into the corridor. It was empty, as was the anteroom. I went back into the corridor and called loudly for Amorise. A petite blond woman poked her head out from another door and hushed me. In a calmer voice, I said, "I'm looking for Amorise."

"She's with a client . . . Oh, wait!" She put a hand to her cheek. "I believe she had an emergency."

"I need to talk to her."

"Well, I'm sure she'll be back." The woman glanced at her watch. "No . . . maybe not. It's late. She might not come in again until tomorrow. I'm sorry."

She started back into the room from which she had emerged. Inside, a woman was lying in a chair like the one in which I had been treated, different only in that a cylindrical machine mounted on the ceiling had been lowered to fit over the woman's head.

"The machine," I said. "That provides the therapy?"

"Yes." The woman pushed me gently away. "Now please . . . I have work to do."

"There was no machine in my room! I think she did something to me . . . I don't know. It doesn't feel right."

The woman closed the door on her patient and said firmly, "All the rooms have machines."

"Not the room I was in!"

She let out an impatient sigh. "Which room was it?"

I pointed. "There."

She preceded me into the room.

"You see?" I said, triumphant.

She pushed a button on the wall; a section of ceiling slid back, and a machine like the one I had seen in the other room lowered to a point directly above the surgical chair.

"She didn't use the machine," I said. "I have no memory of it."

"I have to see to my client." The woman retracted the machine. "But I'm sure you'll be happy with the work. Amorise is extremely capable."

"You don't understand!" I said. "I think . . ."

"Have you tried out what she did?"

"No, I . . ."

"Give it a try," she said. "If you're not satisfied, call and we'll set up another appointment. You can ask for me. My name is Jane Eisley. Now, please . . . I do have to get back to my client."

The earthquake of '19 had leveled downtown Seattle, and from the windows of my apartment I could see out across the rebuilt city, the skyscrapers replaced by green domes of glass silicate whose facets winked like emeralds, nested among gardens and stands of firs. The Emerald City. Perhaps it had been a foolish conceit on the part of the city fathers to remodel the business district after the nickname applied by an advertising agency, but I enjoyed the view it afforded. However, after pronouncing the phrase, *"Je t'aime, Amorise,"* I found the prospect trivial. Jewels like fat green bugs and not the subtle traps and trickeries of light that true gems embody. I wanted to stand in the sky above them and piss down the purest of criticisms. The century, I thought, aspired to be its own ornament, a bauble floating upon the bloody river of history.

I had a thirst, but there was no wine in the apartment. I called Spirits, an environment of black leather booths and chrome ornaments in the subterranean levels beneath my complex that pretended to be a bar, and ordered a case of wine sent up. Shortly after I received it, while sitting by my window and trying to discover the characteristics of whatever it was that Amorise had done, my message wall bonged and the larger-than-life image of my ex-girlfriend Angelica Korn snapped into view. I had not talked with her for several weeks, and I saw that she had lost weight, her skin drawn taut from cheekbone to jaw. She had always struck me as somewhat clownish in appearance. Coarsely, commonly pretty, with her thick eyebrows and an overly generous mouth. But there was nothing clownish about her at that moment. Her body language, formerly a vocabulary of exuberant head-tosses and giddy gestures, was restrained, elegant, and her steady gaze unnerved me. Instead of offering pleasantries, she said, "You've been down to Emerald Street. How was it?"

"I'm not sure yet," I said. "I didn't tell you I was going, did I?"

"You need to explore it," said an off-screen voice.

Carl McQuiddy stepped into view behind Angelica. A slim dark man whose goatee and receding hairline lent him a vulpine look. He was one of those who had recommended Emerald Street Expansions as a cure for my malaise. Yet had it been his recommendation alone, I would have paid it no mind. I didn't care for him, and I had assumed Angelica felt the same. If the Devil were to need a lawyer, McQuiddy would be a perfect choice. His black eyes were cold and inexpressive. If anything, they seemed more so than usual that day.

"Perhaps you should get out of the apartment," he suggested. "Go someplace that will bring it out."

"Bring what out?" I asked.

"The effect."

"Are you afraid?" The corners of Angelica's mouth lifted in a half-smile, causing me to believe that her repetition of Amorise's words was no coincidence. It angered me to think that she might be playing games, that she and McQuiddy were baiting me.

"Afraid of what?" I said.

"Whatever it is you're afraid of," she said. "Take my advice. You won't remember much. Just scraps. So don't waste time trying."

"Tacque Thibault," Carl said. "Do you recall the name?"

"No." The name did sound a murky resonance, but I had no wish to say anything affirmative to him.

He smiled thinly. "Yet your name is familiar to me."

"Are you trying to trip me out?" I asked. "That's pitiful."

Carl turned his back. "See you tonight," said Angelica, and the wall was restored to its normal white blankness.

The call put me in a foul temper, yet I was delighted by the richness of my anger, a far cry from my usual pallid incarnation of the mood. For a time I drank and experimented with the two key phrases, saying them in succession, over and over, like a child playing with a light switch. Whenever I said, *"Je t'aime, Amorise,"* the apartment with its metal furniture and white walls and stainless steel workbench seemed a cross between a morgue and a dentist's office, annoying in its spotless minimalism. When I said, *"Je te deteste, Amorise,"* it became charming, functional, comfortable. Yet as I continued to alternate between these states, I came to see the place in a generally unfavorable light, as if the perceptual lens I had acquired was infecting all my orderliness.

Troubled by this, I accessed Francois Villon on the computer and learned that the surname was a *nom de plume*, taken in honor of his benefactor Guillaume du Villon. His given name had been Francois Montcorbier. Born in poverty in Paris in 1431, educated at the University of Paris. Convicted of the murder of a priest, the sentence of death dropped when he was found to have acted in self-defense. Always a martyr to love, he had been especially stricken by a woman named Martha Laurens. In 1453 he had been condemned to death a second time for fighting in the streets, the sentence commuted to banishment from Paris, a term during which he had written his most famous work, "The Testament," at the age of thirty—my age exactly—whereupon he vanished from history. It was believed that he had begun the poem while in prison, and it was assumed that he died shortly after completing it, probably from syphilis.

Nothing of this shadowy life was familiar. Yet when I began to read "The Testament," a poem constructed in the form of a will that enumerated dozens of bequests, the bulk of them ironic . . . as I read the poem, the names of his beneficiaries resonated in me. Noel Jolis, Fat Margot, Guillaume Charruau, Jeahn Cornu, Jeanneton the Bonnet-Maker, Tacque Thibault—the name McQuiddy had mentioned. Villon's jailer and torturer. There were ninety-two names (ninety-three if I counted Villon), and I could have sworn I remembered every one, yet I could not call the people they signified to mind. They seemed to be standing just beyond a locked door in my memory, and the poem itself . . . the words latched onto my mind as if slotting into spaces already created for them. After two readings I could quote sections by heart.

On occasion Villon was given to stitching his name and those of others down the left-hand side of his poems, forming acrostics, and toward the end of "The Testament," written in this exact way, was the name Amorise DeLore. This discovery aroused conflicting emotions in me. Paranoia, due to my suspicion that Amorise, perhaps obsessed with Villon, was using me to further some insanity; and frustration stemming from the fact that I remembered nothing of her namesake, Amorise DeLore. Acting out my frustration, I threw a wine bottle at the wall and stood admiring the purple stain it created. It served me as a kind of divination—staring at it, I realized that if I wanted to gain a better grasp of the situation, I had no choice other than to visit the club in South Seattle. I fingered out the business card and noted that the address was located in a high crime area. On my workbench lay a variety of psychotropic sprays, macrowebs, and other sophisticated devices designed for personal defense, but without a thought for these weapons, I chose a flick knife that I used to trim wire—it seemed perfectly suited to my anger.

South Seattle had not been rebuilt in such grand fashion as the downtown. Most of the buildings were one or two stories, spun by genetically engineered beetles out of cellulose, but there were a smattering of stores and homes that pre-dated the quake, the building that housed the Martinique among them—a low cement block affair with a facade rising above roof level. I must confess that by the time I reached the club, I was not certain which of my key phrases I had most recently uttered. However, I do know that I had come to detest Amorise—I was convinced she had performed an illegal manipulation—and this may indicate that I was under the spell of *"Je t'aime, Amorise,"* for hate was something I had never before indulged. Though like everyone I had experienced bouts of temper, rancor, and so forth, my life until that day had been undisturbed by obsessive emotion.

A straight-down rain was falling when I emerged from the cab, and I stood beneath the overhang of a Vietnamese restaurant across the street from the club, watching the neon script letters on its facade come greenly alight one after another. The initial T was shaped like a coconut palm. My thoughts proceeded in a curious fashion, entirely unlike my usual process. On spotting a whore sheltering in a doorway next to the club, arms folded, a white thigh gleaming through the slit in her skirt, I imagined her face to be an undertaker's dream of lust, a corpse prettified by sooty eyes and spots of rouge. In a moment she would step forward, open her mouth to the black wine spilling from God's table, and be renewed. The passage of a car, puddled rainwater slashing up from its tires, bred the image of a razor slicing translucent flesh, and two drunken shadows walking away from the club, laughing and stumbling, implied a revel of shades within. I crossed the street, anxious to join them.

Inside, the smoky brown gloom seemed like an exhaust generated by the babble of voices. Perhaps a hundred patrons were gathered about tables and along the bar. On the walls were murals depicting scenes of voluptuous women with fanciful headdresses dancing in jungles. Spotlighted on the stage, visible above the heads of the crowd, a tall black man cried through a golden saxophone, backed by a bass and drum. His cheeks bulged hugely, and he glowed with sweat; his sidemen were all but invisible in the shadows. The melody he played was slow and lugubrious, but the rhythms beneath it were those of a drunken waltz, and this lent the music a rollicking air, making it seem that the idea of sadness was being mocked. I felt the tune tugging at some ghost of memory, but could not put a name to it. However, I recognized the man to be a street musician who played in the fish market and had once cursed me for not tossing money into his instrument case.

I located an unoccupied barstool and ordered a glass of wine. Most of the patrons were of an age with me, fashionably dressed, and as I glanced about, I realized I knew everyone that I had thus far seen, either as business associates or chance acquaintances. Just down the counter was Joan Gwynne, a lovely dark-haired woman who had catered several of my dinner parties before I was forced to let her go due to our unfortunate romantic entanglement, one toward which she had since expressed great bitterness. She had on a parrot-green dress identical to that Amorise had worn, and her drink shone with the same hue and intensity as the neon letters on the facade. Though all about me other women were being clutched and pawed, no one was bothering Joan. A space had been cleared around her, and she sat without speaking, her viridian eyes flicking side to side. Behind the bar was a long mirror so unclouded it appeared to form an adjunct to the club. In its reflection I saw Carl McQuiddy and Angelica Korn conversing together, separated from me by at least a dozen people. They were dressed in matching gray suits and black shirts. A large golden pin nested in Angelica's hair. I had no urge to join them.

I drank several glasses of wine and continued to stare at Joan. Something about her made my thoughts bend like a field of wheat impressed by a force of wind. I might have approached her, but her eerie solitude restrained me, and when the saxophonist completed his song to scattered applause, she downed her drink and moved off into the crowd. I was oddly distressed by her departure. Someone jostled my elbow. I spun about and confronted John Wooten, my lawyer for the last few years—he had recently successfully defended me in a civil suit brought by the families of two clients who had been killed when they misused one of my devices. Thick-waisted and jovial, with shoulder-length chestnut hair, clothed in a blue suit. He looked down at my hand and said with wry amusement, "Quick to anger as ever, Francois."

I discovered that without my notice, as if obeying some old barfighter reflex, I had put knife to his belly; but this did not concern me as much as the fact that he had called me Francois.

"Guillaume de Villon," said the man I knew as John, inclining his head. "I was your friend, Francois. Of course I have no memory of that time. We have only your words and fragments of history to tell us who we were. Nonetheless, I'd know you anywhere." He clapped me on the shoulder. "Put your knife away, man. Things have always been unclear. Our task is to make as much light as we can in the darkness of life. Let us enjoy this night."

He raised his glass in a toast, and responding to what must have been a vestigial trace of camaraderie, I followed suit.

"What's happening here?" I asked.

"I confess that my understanding is incomplete," he said. "But from what I can gather, Amorise has brought us all forward from the fourteenth century to enact a certain rite that will allow us—and her—to continue."

I stared at him, rejecting this preposterous notion . . . and yet something would not allow me to completely reject it.

"Of course," he went on, "I'm merely repeating the consensus view. I haven't spoken to anyone who claims to know anything for certain."

"Are you saying she carried our essences inside her? Our . . ."

"Our souls," he said. "Her sinecure at Emerald Street afforded her the means to effect the transfers."

I wanted to inquire further, but at that moment a woman's voice sounded from the stage, asking for our full attention. It was Amorise. She posed as if embracing the spotlight, her arms outspread, wearing a simple white dress whose hem grazed the floor. Beside her, Joan Gwynne stood swaying, her eyes closed. The crowd grew still. It was so quiet I could hear the rain beating down on the roof. Amorise took Joan in her arms and kissed her deeply. Just as she had kissed me back at the shop. The kiss lasted nearly a minute, I reckoned, and for its duration no one spoke. Amorise's cheeks filled then hollowed, as if she were breathing into Joan's mouth. The expulsion of breath appeared to be causing her difficulty, for she soon began to tremble. At last she broke from the kiss. Two men jumped onto the bandstand to support Joan by the elbows, or else she might have fallen. Amorise steadied herself and then, flinging up her arms, she proclaimed, "The sublime act has begun!" She gestured at Joan. "I wish to present she who was last Martha Laurens! Our beautiful friend, Joan Gwynne!"

Martha Laurens.

The woman who, according to "The Testament," had metaphorically buried Francois Villon's heart in a little casket.

Shaken, I stared at Joan as the crowd applauded, seeing another woman, or rather seeing in her the force of another, one toward whom I felt both an intense longing and an intense aversion. Moved by no act of will or conscious desire, merely drawn to her, I pushed toward the stage. By the time I reached it, she had regained her senses and—to a degree— marshaled her composure. She looked as I imagined I must have when I woke from my kiss. Ruffled and disoriented. But there was no alarm in her face, and it occurred to me, thinking about her green dress, her solitude at the bar, that she had been prepared for whatever had happened. When she noticed me, the corners of her mouth lifted in a smile. She extended a hand so I could help her down from the stage, and then led me toward the bar, glancing at me with shy anxiety as we proceeded. We sat on stools near the end of the bar and considered one another.

"I don't know what to call you," she said.

It was as if another face were melting up from beneath the pallor of her familiar face, thus making her doubly familiar. Though disguised by bright green lenses, the shape of her eyes fit a shape in my brain that seemed to have been waiting for this sight. As did the fullness of her mouth, the concavities of her cheeks, her graceful neck and smooth forehead, every part of her.

"Aren't you going to say anything?" she asked.

"No," I said. "I don't think so."

She laughed, letting her head drop and glancing away, and the delicacy of that movement enraptured me. This was wrong, I told myself. I didn't want to feel what I was feeling. I wanted the comfort and security of David LeGary's blighted yet well-tended mental garden. *Je te deteste, Amorise.* I said it beneath my breath, but to no effect.

Joan, Martha, this creature whom I sat before, nervous and eager as a dog hoping for a treat, she looked at me, and that look became a heated environment, an absolute immersion—I had no idea why. Martha Laurens was to me no more than a name that caused a bloom of heat beneath the ice of my soul, and Joan Gwynne was an attractive, personable, yet rather *soi disant* woman who, according to other of my business associates, had—following our brief fling—seen the light of the White Goddess and was now an avowed lesbian with a live-in lover. Yet blended together, cooked in the same flesh (this, if I were to believe the improbable scenario related by John/Guillaume), they became a third person whose luminous specificity enlivened and bewildered me. If what I had been told was truly happening, *why* was it happening?

A rite, Guillaume had said. To allow our continuance. But for what reason did we continue . . . and what was "the sublime act?"

The saxophone man was back on stage, executing a mournful ballad. The people who milled about us were all, like Joan, doubly familiar, as if two identities had been combined within their bodies. I did not believe in souls. So I had told Amorise. Yet feeling what I felt, having witnessed what I had, how could I not believe that the kiss had effected a transference, that Amorise had breathed some essence into me, into all assembled, and now into Joan?

"What are you thinking?" Joan asked, taking my hand.

That simple touch caused my head to swim. I saw that she had removed her green lenses; her eyes were still brilliant, live wheels of agate. The tip of her tongue flicked the underside of her upper lip. I was overwhelmed by sensory detail. The push of her breasts against green silk, the long sweep of her thigh . . .

"I'm trying to make sense of this," I said.

Joan leaned close, kissed my cheek, then—briefly—my mouth. "How does one make sense of a kiss?"

Her comment distanced me, seeming to imply a perspective on the situation that I had not yet achieved. I asked her if she cared for a drink, signaled the bartender and ordered two glasses of wine. A soul, I thought. A scrap of energy to which only trace memories attached and yet which sustained emotions such as love. A force that could be transferred from one mouth to another. My thoughts, pure contraries, ideological oppositions, began to strangle one another before they could fully establish themselves.

The wine came, and we drank. Everywhere I cast my eye I saw someone I knew and whom I sensed that I had also known half a millennium ago. Thomas Hamada who, until his incompetence cost me a large sum of money, had served as my accountant. Diana Semple, a former patron. Several old lovers. There were, as I've stated, about a hundred people in the Martinique that night, and I suspected that if I were to introduce myself to each and every one, I would discover there were exactly ninety-two, and that their names would be those Villon had mentioned in "The Testament." The poem, I decided, was likely central to the rite that Guillaume had mentioned. And since I was ostensibly the poet, I must also be central to it, trapped in its unclear heart like a flaw in the depths of an emerald.

"I want to be alone with you," Joan said.

I wanted to be alone with her, too, though I was not entirely certain why. Something was being orchestrated here, some music of action and word I was supposed to perform. The thought that I was being manipulated infuriated me, and I felt a more profound rage as well, one emblematized by a section of "The Testament" that then surfaced from my mind:

> I renounce and reject love
> And defy it in blood and fire
> With such women death hustles me off
> And they couldn't give a damn . . .

Ignoring Joan's startled cry, I stood and walked briskly away, intent upon returning home and getting to the bottom of whatever was going on; but as I made for the door, Carl McQuiddy and Amorise emerged from the crowd to block my path. She had changed out of her robe into a black cocktail dress with a short skirt and low-cut bodice—her weapons in full

Emerald Street Expansions

view, she seemed even more the predator. "Where are you going, David?" she asked.

That she dared to ask this or any question of me, it was like gasoline thrown on a fire. I lunged at her, but McQuiddy stepped between us. I shoved him back and drew my knife. "Stand aside," I told him.

"A knife," said McQuiddy. "That's so fifteenth century!"

He gave a flick of his left hand—an almost imperceptible shadow briefly occupied the air between us. I felt the skeins of the macroweb settling over me, flowing down my face and shoulders in a heartbeat, growing and tightening, rendering the upper part of my body immobile. I knew that to strain against it would cause the web to tighten further, and I stood without twitching.

"What do you want of me?" I asked Amorise.

"I want you to enact the laws of your nature," she said.

"I was about to do that very thing," I said. "Dissolve the web—I'll be happy to oblige."

The web began to tighten. McQuiddy was standing beside me. I could not turn my head to see him, but I knew he was controlling the web, because I had not stirred. The mesh cinched about my throat and chest—I had difficulty drawing breath.

"Carl!" Amorise frowned at him. The web loosened slightly, and McQuiddy whispered in my ear, "Just like old times . . . eh, Francois?"

Amorise moved closer, so that her startling green eyes were inches from my own. Perhaps, I thought, they were not lenses.

"If you let your soul speak," she said, "you will know what I want."

"My soul? Are you referring to the thing you breathed into me, or the one whose place it usurped?"

"There's no difference between the two now. But don't be alarmed, David. You worked in machines instead of words, but you always had the soul of a *poet maudit*. I've done very little to you. I've simply given you the chance to fulfill your destiny." Then, to McQuiddy, she said, "I'm through here. Take his knife and release him."

Grudgingly, McQuiddy did as instructed.

As the web dissolved, a more protracted process than it had been to ensnare me, Amorise studied my face. What she saw there must have pleased her, for she smiled and allowed herself a laugh, a mere spoonful of sound.

"I've chosen well," she said. "You will create a beautiful text."

Je te deteste . . .
Je te deteste . . .
Je te deteste, Amorise . . .

Had they not been given me to say, I would have said those words on my own, repeated them a thousand times as I did that night and into the morning, for I hated Amorise. Whenever I said them I hated her more, for no change followed upon them. Whether Villon or a transformed David LeGary, or a syncretic being comprised of the two, I was trapped in the role Amorise had designed for me, thanks to her witchery . . . and what else could this be but the product of witchery? Science did not rely on kisses for an empirical result. My thoughts were iron flails demanding a target. I strode about my apartment, lashing out at end tables, framed photographs, sculptures, and chairs, wrecking the accumulation of a life to which I had ceased to relate. At one point, giving in to a longing I was unable to suppress, I called Joan Gwynne's office; but she had not yet come in to work and I couldn't pry her home number out of the secretary. I flung myself onto a couch and scribbled down some thoughts and then realized that what I had written formed the first few verses of a bitter poem concerning my previous relationship with Joan. I crumpled the paper, tossed it into a corner, and continued to drink, to destroy the artifacts of David LeGary's trite existence, and then drank some more. And when morning came dull and drizzly, like an old gray widow hobbling out from the dark, her cold tears freckling the sidewalks, in all my drunkenness and disarray, I went down to Emerald Street to seek my satisfaction.

"Mister LeGary," said the blond woman, Jane Eisley, who had dealt with me the previous afternoon. "We've been trying to call you."

Something about her seemed familiar, in the way that the individual members of the crowd the night previous had seemed familiar, but this resonance did not interest me. "I broke my phone," I said grimly. "Where is Amorise?"

"I'm afraid she no longer works here," Jane Eisley said. "But I have good news. We checked the machine she used to treat you. It was inoperable. The power leads were burned out. She could have done nothing to you. That's why we had to let her go. She received payment for work she didn't do. I have your refund here."

She held out a slip of paper that I supposed was a record of a transfer to my credit line. I knocked her hand away. "Where is Amorise?"

"You've no reason to act this way!" She fell back a step. "Take the refund. She didn't do anything to you."

"The hell she didn't! She doesn't need a fucking machine. Give me the address!"

When Jane Eisley refused to cooperate, I pushed past her and went along the corridor searching for the office. At the very back lay a room with a desk atop which a computer was up and running. I searched the files for Amorise's address. It was listed under the name Amorise LeDore, and I recognized it to be a house on Vashon Island whose defense system I had installed six weeks before. I recalled that I had not dealt with the owner, but her lawyer, who had referred to her merely as "my client."

The lawyer had been Carl McQuiddy.

Just off the office was a room containing a number of lockers. The name "LeDore" was written on the third one I came to. The door was loose, and I managed to pry it open. Inside were a pair of athletic shoes, cosmetics, and a slim leather-bound volume that I assumed to be an address book. I pocketed it and went out into the corridor. Jane Eisley was at the front of the shop, talking on the phone. I tore the phone from her grasp and said, "Don't cause me any trouble, or my lawyer will smother you." She made a shrill response that I, in my anger and haste, failed to register. I slammed the door behind me with such force, it called after me in a fruity computerized voice that I would be charged for any damage that had been incurred.

On returning to my apartment, I found that the leather-bound volume I had taken from Amorise's locker was no address book, but rather a compendium of arcana entitled *Against Nature,* authored by someone who called themselves Novallis. I asked the computer to search for information relating to the author—it could supply none, but informed me that in Europe during the Middle Ages, dabblers in the black arts often adopted Latinate *noms de plume*. The book itself was of ancient vintage—the pages waterspotted and brittle, the leather cracked. A strip of green silk served as a bookmark, lying across the opening of a section called "The Sublime Act." It was written in archaic French, but thanks to my knowledge of the modern language, I understood that it described some sort of complex magical operation, one involving the manipulation of a large number of people in order to produce what Novallis referred to as "the Text." Once the Text had been created, those involved in the operation would live out their natural spans (unless taken prematurely by act of God or man), but their essence (*"elan vital"*) would be collected by "The Host", who would convey them through the years, keeping them safe for a period of time Novallis termed "the Interval," at which point the Sublime Act would need to be performed again in order to ensure the rebirth and survival of its participants. There was a great deal of stress laid upon the consideration that the subjects must be perfectly suited to their roles, and finally a good bit of nonsense about the Many becoming Three, the Three becoming One, and the One becoming Zero. Also a long section whose essential theme I failed to comprehend, though the word "retribution" was frequently used.

Having deciphered this much, I tossed the book aside, went to my workbench, and called up my designs for Amorise's house on my computer. If I were, indeed, infected by the soul of a dead poet, one spat into my body by a centuries-old witch—and it seemed such was the case—I refused to be her pawn. I did not intend to produce a text, and more, I resolved to put an end to the Sublime Act, and to Amorise herself. It was not merely anger that inspired me. As I examined the plans, determining what I might need to neutralize my defensive system, I experienced a feeling of revulsion in reaction to the Sublime Act, an apprehension of sacrilege, of unholy practice—I thought this might well be Villon's reaction and not LeGary's.

The message wall bonged, and John Wooten appeared. Sitting in his study, wearing a black dressing gown. He looked worried, and his first words to me were, "David, we have problems."

"What are they?" I asked, returning my attention to the plans.

"I had a call from an attorney representing the Villanueva family. They're planning to refile on the basis of new evidence."

"The suit was dismissed," I said.

"Yes, but not with prejudice. They have the right to refile." He leaned back, lowered his chin to his chest so that his jowls flattened out like a fleshy ruff framing the lower portion of his face. "They're also urging the district attorney to institute criminal charges. Negligent homicide. Reckless endangerment."

"That's ludicrous!"

"Perhaps. But it's a problem nonetheless." Wooten folded his hands on his belly. "What new evidence could they have, David?"

"You know, John," I said, my temper fraying. "This is not my concern. You're the lawyer. Find out what they have."

"I'm trying to do just that. It would help if I knew what there was to find."

"Nothing!" I slapped the palm of my hand hard against the workbench. "These fucking people! They could have heat sensors, motion detectors . . . but normal security isn't enough. It doesn't satisfy their urge to be trendy. So they hire me to devise clever little toys they can show off to their friends . . ."

"Calm down, David."

"House pet assassins! Robotic freaks! Then when two Mexican rich kids don't bother to read the manuals and zap themselves, I'm to blame for what happens? It's bullshit!"

"I agree," Wooten said. "But you're the standard of the industry, David. I doubt the Villanuevas can win in court. They've already lost once. But you have to expect to be the target of litigation now and then."

"You know what I expect?" I said. "I expect you to handle the Villanuevas. You're the fucking lawyer. I don't want to be bothered. If you can't do it without calling me every five goddamn minutes, I'll get someone else."

"It would be unprofessional of me—if not unethical—to fail to consult you."

"All right. You've consulted me. What else?"

Wooten appeared puzzled.

"You said there were *problems*," I said. "Give me the rest of it."

He was silent for a short count, then he said, "Francois . . ."

I looked up at him, calmer, as if he had spoken to some deeper part of me, though I was still angry at his intrusion. "What?" I said gruffly.

"Nothing . . . Never mind." He broke the connection.

I continued my preparations for breaking into Amorise's house, but my anger had cooled somewhat, and by mid-afternoon another passion had taken its place. Everywhere I aimed my thought I met with the image of Joan Gwynne and the ghost of Martha Laurens. I saw Joan's long legs, those amazing eyes, the lush curvature of her lips. I tried to suppress these yearnings, but they surrounded me like perfume, and finally I called her office again, intending to threaten the secretary. But this time she put me through without hesitation. Joan was sitting at her desk, dressed in a dark blue business suit. She smiled on seeing me, but it was a troubled smile.

"I was going to call you," she said.

"After the way I broke up with you . . . and then last night, I don't know why you would," I said. "I was rude. I . . ."

"I understand. It's all so new . . . so strange."

"Can we meet somewhere? I want to make it up to you."

Her expression grew more distressed. "I don't know."

"Dinner," I said. "We can go anywhere you like."

She put her head down a second. "I have . . ." She sighed, as if arriving at a decision, and glanced up at me. "I'm involved with someone, David. I don't know what to do about it. I want to see you, but I'm not sure what's right here."

"Are we not involved?" I asked, recalling what I had heard about her lesbian lover.

"So it would seem. But I . . ." She shook her head, signifying her bewilderment. "You have to give me time to sort things out."

"How long?"

"A day or two. I'll call you."

Try as I might, I could not sway her. I ended the call and paced about the apartment, feeling like a fool for being so besotted by a woman with whom

I'd had only fleeting intimacy in the present, no matter how deep our relationship in the past. But I no longer wanted to deny the connection, and I decided to send her flowers. As it was late in the afternoon, I thought I would send them to her home. If it aroused the suspicions of her lover, then so much the better. Once again I called the office and asked the secretary for her address. At first she refused to provide it, but when I told her my purpose she relented. She read it to me, and I did not have to write it down. The address was on Vashon Island.

Joan lived with Amorise.

I was, for several seconds, absolutely blank, and the thoughts and feelings that rushed in to fill the blankness, though framed by an overarching anger, were touched with admiration at the neatness of the web in which I had become stuck. Every strand led to Amorise, and I realized she was inviting me to come to her. She had contrived her design so that everything I wanted was under her control.

Close upon this recognition came a powerful sense of loss and a comprehension that—although I had walked away from Joan the night before, and no matter the source of the attraction—those feelings were as sharp in me as the touch of fire. I could not, for several minutes, compose myself, realizing that Amorise had placed Joan beyond my grasp. This recognition overwhelmed any logic that might deny or ameliorate its truth. My brain had turned to iron, penetrated by a single white-hot thought that had no voice or means of expression . . . at least not at first. For as I sat at my desk, unable to move or even to contemplate movement, words came to me, almost without any awareness on my part, and I found myself scribbling on the sides of a circuit diagram:

> The black dog who carries my heart in its jaws
> Firmly so as not to drop it into puddles or pissholes
> Having been marked by God for this special task
> To remind me that Love is such a caring beast . . . .

I wrote dozens of lines, perhaps eighty or ninety all told, an entire poem of such acid and fulminant bitterness, I felt drained from having given it birth, and when this fever of creativity lifted, I had the fleeting impression that I was not sitting in my apartment but rather at a wooden table sticky with spilled food and drink, and above me were smoke-darkened beams, and on every side was the brightness of human activity, people laughing and conversing. Even after this brief confusion fled and I recognized myself to be seated at my workbench, it seemed that I could perceive a variant architecture of thought inside my head, gothic arches of compulsion and buttresses of emotion whose antiquated sweep and form were different from yet somehow akin to my own. It was the clearest sense yet I'd had of the spirit wedded to me by the Sublime Act, and as it faded, submerged once again into the turbulent soul we were together, my hatred for Amorise swelled to monstrous proportions, increased by the knowledge of what she had done not only to me, but to Villon.

I began to study the plans of the security system I had designed for her. It was likely that she had made modifications, but I doubted she would have had time to install an entirely new system. Once inside I could lock the house and prevent her from escaping, but she would then retreat into the panic room and call the police. Of course I could cut her lines, jam her outside communications, and I could override her alarms and counterfeit an all-is-well signal to the private cops that patrolled the neighborhood. That would leave us in a stalemate—Amorise in the panic room and me standing by the door. But a stalemate might be all that was required. My actions might convince her that I would not do her bidding... not this time around. Afterward I could take a short vacation, or a long one, and let Wooten handle the fallout. One way or another, though, I intended to make a statement with Amorise.

The house was a twenty-eight-room structure of gabled gray stone facing the water—in the moonlight it had an air of somber opulence, like a hotel for vampires. Amorise had not tricked up the external security, and I was able to penetrate the grounds without difficulty. It was after one in the morning, and I watched the house from amid a stand of old-growth firs, dressed in burglar black, my breath smoking in the cold damp air. In my pockets were a freon spray, a scrambler, a laser torch, and an ultrasonic whistle. I had coated my skin and clothing with an agent that would dissolve macrowebs on contact—I had set several booby traps utilizing such webs and I could not be certain that Amorise had not altered their locations. There were a couple of lights on downstairs, but I believed that was for show. I doubted anyone was awake. Keeping to the shadows, I made my way to a side window. When lifted by an intruder, the bottom of the window would, once weight was placed upon the sill, extrude a hidden blade and slam down with the force of a guillotine. It was exactly as I had created it, not modified at all. I deactivated the mechanism, and after I had climbed inside, I overrode the alarms with my palm console and locked the house down. This all seemed far too easy. I switched on my penlight, bringing bulky sofas, a pool table, and an oriental carpet up from the shadows, and scanned the immediate area for electronic activity, finding none.

I had made my entrance into a smallish game room, but the living room beyond was as big as the lobby of a grand hotel, with a marble fireplace, five groupings of chairs and sofas ranging its more than one-hundred-foot length. The air was scented by a half-burned cedar log in the hearth, and the area was filled with security devices, all coded so as to prevent remote disabling, each keyed to ignore those people whom its detectors registered as familiar. I moved into the room and a cleaning robot—a flat black shape capable of prospecting for dust beneath the furniture—came trundling across the carpet toward me, spitting blue tongues of electricity. I jumped aside and immobilized it with a freon spray. As I went forward, I was attacked by a lamp cord of so-called "intelligent plastic" that tried to garrote me, whipping up into the air like a flying snake. I immobilized it as well. Most of the security devices in the room were centered about a vault set in the left-hand wall—I gave it a wide berth and continued on cautiously, a scanner in one hand, laser torch in the other, searching for any potential threat. I managed to negotiate the room without further incident, but as I stepped out into the main entryway, at the foot of a curving marble staircase, one of the larger cleaning units, a domed white shape the size of a wastebasket, hurtled at me, visible in the moonlight spilling through the windows flanking the front door. I eluded its rush, and as it turned back toward me, I swung the laser torch over the top of the dome, where the control package was housed, burning a seam along the right quadrant. It kept coming. I held the torch steady, burning smoking lines across the entirety of the machine, but in the instant I disabled it, it succeeded in brushing against my leg, transmitting a shock that threw me onto my back and left me stunned. I lay for a moment, gathering myself. Apparently Amorise had been able to make more significant changes than I had believed possible. I wondered why I wasn't dead—the unit I had just disabled carried a lethal voltage. Then I had a revelation: Amorise must have reduced the charge. She could not afford to kill me. Not, at any rate, until I produced the Text. I felt suddenly foolish. What was I doing here? I could thwart Amorise's intentions simply by leaving town. It was only my anger—Villon's anger, I thought—that had brought me to the house.

I struggled to my feet, still woozy, and started for the front door. But every step I took caused a resurgence of anger, and my desire to harm Amorise was reinvigorated. I stood for a moment, revising my plans. If she had not been roused by the incident with the cleaning unit, and I presumed this to be the case, for I had given no outcry, then I might be able to get to her before she succeeded in locking herself in the panic room. I was not certain what I would do to her if I were able to head her off, but I was willing to let that decision await the moment. But if she had locked herself away, well, the panic room was on the second floor, and I remembered now that I had suggested to McQuiddy that I install a reinforced framework to support the room; he had rejected the idea due to budgetary concerns. It might be possible to set a fire that would eat away the supports beneath it, and the steel box with Amorise inside would come hurtling down—at the very least she would be injured.

I was about to head upstairs to find Amorise's bedroom when from the various rooms and corridors that opened off the entryway there poured an army of household appliances and robots. More than a hundred, by my estimate. I darted back toward the living room, but that avenue of escape was blocked by a green gardening robot, headless yet taller than a man, armed with several pairs of snapping foot-long shears. Chittering and beeping, the machines formed into a semi-circle, forcing me back against the front door. The sight was both frightening and absurd. At their forefront was a twelve-slice toaster that I had made mobile by the addition of six black humanoid feet. It was a conversation piece, a status item intended to evoke laughter. But now, waddling about and lashing its non-functional plug like a maddened tail, the general of a force composed of various cleaners and scrubbers, centipedelike air purifiers, and saucer-sized spider-like ceiling sweeps, there was little humorous about it. I'd been prepared to deal with the machines individually—*en masse* they presented a problem. I fumbled out my scrambler and punched in an emergency override. The gardening robot became inactive, but the rest remained jittering, trembling, leaking a high-pitched electronic babble, the moonlight polishing their sleek surfaces.

Deciding that I had a better chance on the move than standing my ground, I leaped over half the force, landing amidst a cluster of sweeps. Several of them clung to my leg as I jumped again, clearing the edge of the marshaled machines, and ran full tilt along a darkened corridor. I managed to scrape the sweeps off my leg, crushing one of them against the wall—I could hear the rest of the machines beeping and squeaking behind me. I pushed through swinging doors into the kitchen, a large cluttered space bright with moonlight. Something rushed at my ankles—I kicked at it and it let out a yelp. It was only a dog, and a smallish one at that. I heard it whimper, its paws clittering on the linoleum as it slunk away. The next instant something bit into my shoulder and buried itself into the wall beside me. An electric knife. It tried to wrench itself free, but I grabbed the hilt and broke off the blade. Blood was trickling down my arm from the point of my shoulder. I wrangled a refrigerator in front of the door, blocking it, and stood for a second, breathing hard. Slants of bone-white light, alternated by zones of deep shadow, fell across the center island and hanging copperware, an enormous range, and a counter lined with bins and appliances. The kitchen was a dangerous place, but I liked my chances there better than out in the corridor. I crawled up on top of the center island just in time to avoid a buzzing object that thudded into the base of the island. I was safe for the moment, but I knew I could not stay there long and I decided to try for the pantry, which opened onto another corridor—this led, after a turn or two, back to the entryway. I walked cautiously across the top of the island, torching a food processor that had been lurking behind a colander, pretending to be an ordinary appliance—half its circuits fused, it lunged forward on stilt-like legs in a futile attempt to maim me, then fell on its side. I stopped with a foot in the air, remembering the microwave, in front of which I was just about to pass. I eased back a step, stood one-footed and removed a shoe. I took a couple of warm-ups and then slung the shoe at the door of the oven. A beam of ruby light speared it, causing it to burst into flame. I skipped to the other end of the island before the oven's laser could reset. I sat on the edge of the island, holding the laser torch at the ready, and stretched my foot down. A toy truck rolled out of the shadows and tried to impale my foot with the electrified spike extruded from its grille—I hit it with a swing of the torch and it expired with a tinny rattle.

The pantry door, a flat white rectangle with a recessed square, looking rather like an invitation blank that had not yet been printed upon, lay twenty feet from the island. I did not believe there were any other mobile units left in the kitchen, but adrenalized as I was, I couldn't be sure. I stretched out my foot again, and when nothing attacked it, I leaped down and dived through the door. The air inside the pantry was sweet, musty. I flattened myself against the shelves and scanned the area. No sign of activity. I went to the opposite end of the room and thought what to do. A mad dash seemed to be the best solution—if I remained in the pantry, sooner or later the little army of machines would break through the kitchen door and push on in. The narrow windows that flanked the front door were of ordinary glass. If I could reach the entryway, I thought, I might be able to smash one of the windows and squeeze through it. I shrugged off my jacket and wrapped it about my right forearm. I cracked the pantry door, scanned. Then, one-shoed, I raced along the corridor. But on rounding a corner, I caught sight of a large indistinct shape hovering in the air, silhouetted against the light of the entryway. I put on the brakes. It was a moth, a gray death's-head moth with a ten-inch wingspan. Beyond it, also hovering, were a number of smaller moths. Twelve in all. I had manufactured them for McQuiddy, but he'd told me the client had rejected them as being too dangerous and that they would be returned. Each powered by a microscopic chip; a brush of their wings, coated with a contact poison, would cause a painful death. Amorise must have taken them to another craftsman and had them activated. The ultrasonic whistle, which I'd brought to counter a machine guarding her bedroom, would keep the moths away if I played the correct tones, but I had designed the moths to be difficult to control—the tones would have to be exact, and because I had not thought of them in some time, I was less than certain in my memory. Nevertheless, I had no choice. It was barely conceivable that Amorise had rendered them non-lethal, but I could not trust that she had. The fibers of the wings had been saturated with poison, and to minimize the effect would require painstaking work of which very few people were capable.

With trembling fingers, I took the whistle from the inside pocket of my jacket and set it to my lips. If I were to gasp, if my breath were to falter to the least degree as I played the pattern of notes, the moths would attack me. I moved forward, one careful step at a time, playing the progression that, I believed, would keep me safe. The largest moth drifted to within inches of my face, so close I could see every detail of the ghostly patterns on its carapace and read the words I had imprinted as a macabre joke half-hidden in the patterns—Death Courtesy of David LeGary. The tip of its wing fluttered past my cheek and then slid away without touching me. I had the urge to let out a sigh of relief, but I held firm and continued my inaudible tootling. Two more moths flittered near, and though my chest muscles tightened, I managed to keep my throat relaxed and played my way past them. A group of four, the smallest of the bunch, darted at me, dancing on air like gray leaves in a storm. I swallowed in reflex, but thankfully this occurred during an interval. I thought I heard my heart slugging against my chest wall. The five remaining moths formed into a picket line across the corridor. I mustered my resolve and went forward, my cheeks puffed, trying not to blink, watchful of their every flutter, and they parted before me, fluttering up toward the ceiling. Once past them I kept playing for a few steps, and then, my breath sobbing out, I ran.

As I came into the entryway, my feet skidded on the marble floor, but I righted myself and pushed hard toward the window to the right of the front door, showing like a narrow box of moonlight. Upon reaching it, I slammed my elbow against the glass, splintering it. But as I knocked aside the shards that remained stuck in the frame, I heard an electric gabbling at my back, and on turning, saw the army of household machines wobbling, whirring, vibrating, scuttling toward me. This time they did not hesitate. The toaster waddled forward, leading a group charge. I kicked at the thing and sent it flying, but it delivered a painful jolt to my ankle with its plug. A ceiling sweep bunched its silvery legs and propelled itself into a feathery leap that left it clinging to my shirtfront—I hurled it against the wall before it could sting me with its wire molding brushes. For the next two or three minutes, like Gulliver among the Lilliputians, I engaged in battle with this cartoonish troop, swinging the torch in wild arcs, brushing the sweeps off my clothing, crushing the littlest ones underfoot. But I received countless shocks, and at last one of the sweeps managed to scale the back of my trousers and shirt and deliver a jolt to my neck that knocked me flat.

I must have lost consciousness for a time, because when next I looked about, the army had withdrawn, leaving behind their scorched and crumpled casualties. Painfully, I struggled to my feet, and as I leaned against the door, trying to get my bearings, to decipher the patterns of moonlight and shadow that lay across the entryway, the lights went on, confusing me for an instant. Standing at the top of the stairs were Amorise and Joan Gwynne, both dressed in nightgowns. At the bottom of the stair, his back to the banister, was Carl McQuiddy, wearing black slacks and turtleneck. He offered me an amused smile. Amorise, too, smiled, but it was an expression of pure triumph. Joan appeared upset.

"That was epic, David," said Amorise. "Truly entertaining."

The workings of my mind were clumsy, impaired, and I could only stare at the three of them, though I felt anger pressing against the fogginess that hampered my thoughts, like a dome of heat bulging up from some buried molten turbulence. Then Amorise drew Joan into a kiss, one almost as deep as that she had given her on stage at the Martinique, and the anger broke through, not clearing my head but seeming to irradiate the fog.

"And, of course, your machines are delightful," Amorise said, breaking from the kiss. "Such a wonderful imagery. I imagine it must be strange for you to be attacked by them. Rather like old friends turning traitor."

I tried to speak, but succeeded only in making a strangled noise. McQuiddy chuckled and said to Amorise, "I don't think he's up to a conversation."

"Fuck you!" I said.

"Well, we don't really have much to say to one another, anyway." Amorise took Joan's hand and they descended partway down the stairs. "David knows what he has to do . . . don't you, David?"

"I'm not going to do anything for you," I told her. "And there's nothing you can do to make me."

"I don't know," Amorise said. "I might find a way. You tried to assault me at the club. You stole from my locker at Emerald Street. Now you've broken into my home and destroyed considerable of my property. Those are serious charges. What will you say in your defense? That I've kissed the soul of a poet dead these six hundred years into your body? That won't gain you much credence."

"I have a witness who'll back me up," I said. "John Wooten."

"Oh, I don't think you can count on John," McQuiddy said. "He was extremely distressed by the way you spoke to him earlier today."

That they had been privy to my private communications did not surprise me, but McQuiddy's assured demeanor was unnerving.

"You don't have any friends, David," Amorise said. "You offend everyone who tries to befriend you. No one cares about you. In fact, they'd love to see you fall."

I was beginning to regain control of my body, to be more aware of my surroundings. The chandelier that lit the entryway applied a high gloss to McQuiddy's forehead and put glittering points in the eyes of the two women.

"You did this!" I said to Amorise. "It's not me."

"Did I?" Amorise laughed. "The anger, the disdain for others . . . they've always been part of you. You were the perfect subject."

"Actually," McQuiddy said, "I think it's a distinct improvement. At least the bastard will serve some purpose now."

His smile acted on me like a goad, and I sprinted toward him. He flicked out a macroweb, but the strands dissolved as they touched me, and I knocked him off-balance with a glancing blow to the cheek. He recovered quickly and reached into his trouser pocket—for another weapon, I assumed. Before he could withdraw his hand, I struck him hard in the neck with my fist, and then again flush on the jaw. He fell backward, cracking his head on the banister, and went down. I stood over him, waiting for him to stand. His eyes were open, lips parted. Dark blood was pooling beneath his head, spreading across the marble floor. I knew he was dead, but I hunkered down beside him anyway and touched my fingers to his throat, hoping to detect a pulse. Yet at the same time I exulted in the death of my old tormentor, Tacque Thibault.

"Oh, David! What will you do now?"

Amorise was pointing a small caliber automatic with a chrome finish at me. Joan stood at her shoulder, her expression horrified.

"You can wait for the police here if you like," said Amorise. "Or if you prefer, you can make a run for it. But I can guarantee that the authorities will meet you at the ferry dock."

I wiped my fingers on my slacks to clean them of McQuiddy's blood and glared hatefully at her.

"There's something you may want to factor in to your decision," said Amorise, descending the stair—she gestured at me to move away from McQuiddy and I complied, retreating to the door. "Running will certainly lend the appearance of guilt. If you stay, you might be able to justify a plea of self-defense. Of course the validity of such a plea will depend upon my testimony. And I'm certain I'll be too distraught for several days to be clear on the details of what has happened here. Perhaps in the interim, you'll consider how you might influence *my* decision."

Once again I was astonished by the neatness of her scheme. I recalled Villon's fragmentary history, how he had been charged with murder and released once it was established that he had acted in self-defense. Had he begun writing "The Testament" while incarcerated, and changed his mind after his release? So I suspected, and I suspected further that Amorise had been instrumental in obtaining that release, and that when he had failed to complete the Text, she had subsequently managed to have him indicted for another capital crime, which she then managed to have commuted. She was duplicating those events to a nicety. The Sublime Act was halfway to being complete.

"For example," Amorise went on, "I might testify that I'd been having difficulty with your machines and called you here to make some adjustments. I might say that poor Carl had tampered with the machines with the idea of killing you. He has a history of enmity with you. You caught him in the act of sabotage. He attacked you and you defended yourself. Who knows what his specific motives might have been? An emotional entanglement, perhaps. It's well known that he was attracted to Joan."

I tried to catch Joan's eye. Concern was written in her face, but she refused to look at me. I believed she wanted to help me, but could not, being under Amorise's thrall.

Amorise kneeled beside McQuiddy and to my surprise, still pointing the gun at me, she kissed him on the mouth. She closed her eyes, as if savoring the kiss, and then smiled as if enjoying a subtle aftertaste. The kiss had been brief, not at all like the one she had given me at Emerald Street. I imagined the soul must quit the body more readily than it entered, and that McQuiddy's sour scrap of vitality now was lodged in some secret cavity within Amorise's flesh.

"It may cross your mind to try and take the gun from me," she said. "Let me assure you, I'm an excellent shot. I won't kill you, but I will happily cripple you. It'll make your self-defense plea slightly more difficult to justify. But I can always say I was confused—I thought you had attacked Carl and realized too late what the actual circumstances were."

I did not hesitate in making a decision, for in truth there was no decision to be made. She had walled me off from every possibility but one.

"I'll wait for the police," I said.

All the events of this world are liable to a variety of interpretations. I have always understood this, but only lately have I come to recognize the absolute rule of this truism, and the corresponding impossibility of penetrating to the heart of any action. Either there is no heart, no immutable center, or else the ultimate nature of the universe is a profound ambiguity that will not admit to certainty. I believe the nature of the Sublime Act reflects that essential imprecision, that core deceptiveness. Evidence of this may or may not have been presented me on the third day of my incarceration in the King County Jail, when I received a visit from Amorise LeDore.

The guard ushered me into a closed-in metal booth equipped with a telephone and scored with graffiti, most of it obscene in character. Seated opposite me, separated by a divider of scarred, clear plastic, Amorise was wearing a green silk blouse adorned with delicate silver accents. Her long black hair was loose about her shoulders, and her hawkish face was made up to seem softer and more feminine. She picked up her receiver and asked, with no apparent irony, how I was doing.

"Is that a formality?" I asked. "Or do you really care?"

"Of course I care, David. You're dear to me . . . as you know."

Though I despised her, I had become acclimated to hate—it was an environment in which I dwelled, and I felt I could speak to her without losing my temper.

"Then you'll be glad to hear I've been writing," I said, and held up several sheets of paper that I had brought with me from my cell.

"May I see?"

One after the other I pressed the pages against the plastic so she could read them. When she had done she said, "It's good . . . but not up to standard. You'll have to do better."

"I might be more highly motivated if you were to recover your memories of the crime of which I've been accused."

Her brow furrowed, expressing a transparently insincere degree of concern. "I'm working very hard in therapy. I'm sure I'll have a breakthrough soon." She brightened. "But I do have something to tell you. Whether you perceive it as an encouragement . . . that's entirely up to you."

I signaled that she should continue.

"Joan Gwynne, as you recall, came to embody the soul of Villon's lost love, Martha Laurens. Carl was Tacque Thibault. John Wooten . . . Guillaume du Villon. But have you ever asked yourself who embodies the soul of Amorise LeDore, and why, of all those people gathered in the Martinique to celebrate the inception of the Sublime Act, she is the only one with whom you have no apparent previous connection?"

"Is that important?"

"Everything is important, David." A note of venom crept into her voice. "Surely as a craftsman, a devisor of murderous machines, you realize the importance of details?"

"Very well," I said. "Who are you?"

"Let us suppose that this woman, the woman whom you know as Amorise LeDore, is also named Allison Villanueva. And that her brother Erik and her sister-in-law Carmen were murdered by one of your security devices." She gave these last two words a loathing emphasis. "Let us further suppose that in her grief Allison came to recognize that if the courts would not punish you, she must seek her own vengeance, and after the lawsuit against you was dismissed, she traveled from her home in Merida to do that very thing."

Astonished, I jumped to my feet and the guard stationed behind Amorise gestured at me with his baton. I sat back down. "What are you telling me!"

"What I'm telling you," she went on, "is what I am telling you. Make of it what you will." She reached into her purse and withdrew the book I had taken from her locker at Emerald Street Expansions. "Novallis. Did you notice, David, that by rearranging the letters you can also spell out the name Allison V? It's not a difficult chore to forge an antique, and Allison may have taken pains to do so. Or she may not. Did you verify the book's age?"

"No," I said in a tight voice. "I did not."

"Well, if you had, you might have discovered that the book, if a forgery, is a very good forgery. I doubt any expert would claim that it is inauthentic. Be that as it may . . ." She restored the book to her purse.

"I don't believe you!"

"What is it you don't believe? That I'm Allison, or that I'm Amorise? Perhaps both are true. That would suit the subtle character of the Sublime Act, would it not? The subjects must be suitable, and Allison is perfect for Amorise. But then, too, Amorise is precisely what Allison needed."

"You fucking witch!" I said. "Don't try to con me!"

"Why not, Francois? You're a natural-born mark."

"I know who you are . . . and I know who I am."

"Let's examine who you are," said Amorise. "I must confess I've deceived you to an extent. We did do a little something to you at Emerald Street."

"That's crap!" I said. "The woman there . . . the blonde. She told me the machine didn't work. The leads were burned out."

"Jane Eisley. She's a friend. Actually, you know her, too. You dated her sister at Stanford. There was some slight unpleasantness involved. A pregnancy, I believe. An abortion, a broken heart. And a very long time ago, you may have known her as Fat Margot, a Parisian prostitute."

I was at a loss, capable only of staring at her.

"We didn't have to do much," she said. "It's as I told you the other night, you were perfect for Francois. Well . . . almost perfect. I needed you to fall in love with Joan, so we tweaked your emotional depth a bit. The rest of it . . . the anger, the violence, the disdain. You supplied all that. But love was needed to make you fully inhabit those qualities, to bring them to flower." She fixed me with her disturbing green eyes. "Do you understand me, David? I wove the web, but you flew into it with passion, abandon, arrogance. All those qualities you thought you lacked and wanted to explore. From the moment we met, you surrendered yourself to me. You desired what I have given you . . . and what I have given you is yourself."

"What do you want?" I pressed my palms hard against the plastic barrier, hoping for a miraculous collapse that would allow my hands to close about her throat.

"No more than what I told you at the club. I want you to enact the laws of your nature. So far you're doing a splendid job." She settled back in her chair, folded her arms and regarded me coolly. "I'd like you to consider the possibilities. On the one hand, it's possible that this is no more than an ornate Latina cruelty. That Allison Villanueva has manipulated you through completely ordinary means in order to avenge her brother and her sister-in-law. That utilizing your suggestibility, your gullibility, your penchant for the macabre and your underused yet nonetheless potent imagination, she has persuaded you that a witch has come from the fifteenth century to implant the soul of Francois Villon into your body for some arcane purpose—something she may have done many times before. And now she's telling you that the entire scenario may be a fraud. That would be the logical conclusion . . . at least if we are to accept the logic of the age. On the other hand, it's conceivable that the story of the witch is true. Or, a third possibility, both stories are true. This speaks to the beautiful symmetry of the Sublime Act. It begins with a multitude of options, but eventually reduces those choices to three. Ultimately those three become indistinguishable."

It took all my strength to restrain anger—I wanted to yell at her, to revile her; but if I did the guards would return me to my cell, and I wanted to stay, to hear everything she had to say.

"Next," she said, "consider the character of the Sublime Act. I believe Guillaume du Villon told you that it was 'to ensure our continuance.' Were those not his words?"

I nodded.

"For the sake of argument, let's say that our continuation is simply the mechanism by which the Sublime Act is effected. Its character may well be something other than mere immortality. Why would a woman, a witch, wish to drag the same ninety-three souls forward in time, skipping like a stone across the centuries, causing the same event to be re-enacted over and over? What purpose could this painful form of immortality serve . . . if not vengeance? Do you see the correspondence, David? Why the subjects must be suitable? A crime, a terrible crime committed millennia ago, is redressed endlessly by conforming to a contemporary crime and thus achieves the most terrible of vengeances. The kind that never ends. An eternity of punishment. A hell that the object of vengeance creates for himself by enacting the laws of his nature. The Sublime Act. Sublime because the witch achieves sublimity through her creation. She is an artist, and vengeance is the canvas upon which she paints variations on a theme."

"What crime," I asked shakily, "could merit such a punishment?"

"Perhaps I've already told you. Perhaps someday I will tell you. Perhaps I'll never tell you. So many questions, David. Were some or all of your acquaintances in the Martinique acting, or were they, like you, manipulated by science or witchery or both? Is Joan Martha, and will you ever have her again? Or is she just another person whom you have wronged and who hates you with sufficient passion to be my complicitor? Could she have a connection to that ancient and possibly fraudulent crime? You will never answer any of these questions . . . unless you create the Text. Then you may discover the truth, or you may not. The thing you must accept is that whoever I am—Amorise or Allison or both—I own you. I control you. I may testify in such a way that you will be set free, but I will still control you. I'll continue to cause you pain. I've surrounded you with a circumstance you cannot escape. You may come to think that you can injure me, but you can't. My wealth and power insulate me. I swear you will never be happy in this life or any other. Not until I decide enough is enough. If, that is, I ever do."

She closed her purse and stood looking down at me. "There is one way out. But to take it you must go contrary to your nature. You can disobey me and not create the Text. Then I'll testify that you murdered Carl McQuiddy, and you will die. That's your choice, the only one I offer. To die now, or to create the Text and die after long years of suffering. What will you do, David . . . Francois? You can't believe a thing I've told you, and yet you cannot disbelieve me. The stuff of your being has been transmuted from confidence to doubt. Logic is no longer a tool that will work for you."

"I wouldn't be here," I said, "if I hadn't killed McQuiddy. It was an accident. You couldn't have predicted it."

"You always kill, Francois," she said. "A priest, a lawyer . . . Are not lawyers the true priests of our time? You're drawn to detest such authority as they represent. If you hadn't attacked McQuiddy, he would have attacked you. I own him as well." She let out a trickle of laughter, a sound of sly delight. "So many questions. And the answers are all so insubstantial. What *will* you do?"

She walked away and my anger faded, as if my soul had been kindled brightly by her presence, and now, deprived of her torments, I had sunk back into a less vital state of being. At the door she turned and looked at me, and for an instant it seemed I was gazing through her eyes at a man diminished by harsh light and plastic into a kind of shabby exhibit. Then she was gone, leaving me at the bottom of the world. I perceived my life to be a tunnel with a round opening at the far end lit like a glowing zero.

I let the guard lead me back to my cell. For a long time I sat puzzling over the conversation. A hundred plans occurred to me, a hundred clever outcomes, but each one foundered and was dissolved in the nets of Amorise's gauzy logic. Eventually a buzzer sounded, announcing lockdown. The gates of the cells slammed shut, the lights dimmed. Everything inside me seemed to dim. A man on the tier above began to sing, and someone threatened him with death unless he shut up. This initiated a chorus of shouted curses, screams, howls of pain. They seemed orchestrated into a perverse and chaotic opera, a terrible beauty, and I recalled a line from "The Testament" that read: ". . . only in horrid noises are there melodies . . ." I wondered what Villon had been thinking when he reached this point in the Act, what kind of man he had been before meeting Amorise. If, indeed, any of that had happened. For an instant, I felt a powerful assurance that the Act was a fraud, a mere device in the intricate design of Allison Villanueva's vengeance; but then this sense of assurance dissolved in a flurry of doubt. It would never be clear. Only one kind of clarity was available to me now.

From beneath my pillow I removed the stub of a candle I'd bought from a trustee. I lit it, dripped wax onto the rail of my iron bunk and stood the stub upright in the congealing puddle I had made, and as I did I seemed briefly to see an ancient prison, begrimed stone walls weeping with dampness, a grating of black iron centering a door of age-stained wood, a moldy blanket and straw for bedding. I slipped a writing tablet from beneath my mattress, thin and smelly as an old man's lust. I opened the tablet and set it upon my knee. It made no difference whether the woman who had done this to me was Allison or Amorise. Either version of reality provided the same sublime motivation. I felt words breaking off from the frozen cliffs of my soul and scattering like ice chips into plainspoken verse, the ironic speech of a failed heart. Then, in the midst of that modern medieval place, with the cries of the damned and the deranged and the condemned raining down about me, I began:

> Villain and victim, both by choice and by chance
> I hereby declare void all previous Testaments
> Legal or otherwise, whether sealed by magistrate
> Locked away in the rusty store of memory
> Or scribbled drunkenly upon a bathroom wall
> Not knowing whether it is I, LeGary, who writes . . .

LIMBO

> *. . . limbo, limbo, limbo like me . . .*
> —Traditional

The first week in September, Detroit started feeling like a bad fit to Shellane. It was as if the city had tightened around him, as if the streets of the drab working-class suburb that had afforded him anonymity for nearly two years had become irritated by the presence of a foreign body in their midst. There was no change he could point to, no sudden rash of hostile stares, no outbreak of snarling dogs, merely a sense that something had turned. A similar feeling had often come over him when he lived back east, and he had learned to recognize it for a portent of trouble; but he wasn't sure he could trust it now. He suspected it might be a flashback of sorts, a mental spasm produced by boredom and spiritual disquiet. Nevertheless he chose to play it safe, checked into a motel and staked-out his apartment. When he noticed a Lincoln Town Car across the street from the apartment, he trained his binoculars on it. In the driver's seat was a young man with short black hair and a pugilist's flattened nose. Beside him sat an enormous, sour-looking man with bushy gray sideburns and a bald scalp, his face vaguely fishlike. Thick lips and popped eyes. Marty Gerbasi. Shellane had no doubt as to what had brought Gerbasi to Detroit. A half-hour later, after doing some banking, he picked up a green Toyota that had been purchased under a different name and kept parked in a downtown garage for the past twenty-nine months, and drove north toward the Upper Peninsula.

At forty-six, Shellane was a thick-chested slab of a man with muscular forearms, large hands, and a squarish homely face. His whitish blond hair had gone gray at the temples, and his blue eyes were surprisingly vital by contrast to the seamed country in which they were the only ornament. He customarily dressed in jeans and windbreakers, a wardrobe designed to reinforce the impression that he might be a retired cop or military man—he had learned that this pretense served to keep strangers at bay. His gestures were carefully managed, restrained, all in keeping with his methodical approach to life, and he did not rattle easily. Realizing that assassins had found him in Detroit merely caused him to make an adjustment and set in motion a contingency plan that he had prepared for just such an occasion.

When he reached the Upper Peninsula, he headed west toward Iron Mountain, intending to catch a ferry across to Canada; but an hour out of Marquette, just past the little town of Champion, he came to a dirt road leading away into an evergreen forest, and a sign that read: Lakeside Cabins—Off-Season Rates. On impulse he swung the Toyota onto the road and went swerving along a winding track between ranks of spruce. The day was sunny and cool, and the lake, an elongated oval of dark mineral blue, reminded Shellane of an antique lapis lazuli brooch that had belonged to his mother. It was surrounded by forested hills and bordered by rocky banks and narrow stretches of brownish-gray sand. Under the cloudless sky, the place generated a soothing stillness. A quarter-mile in from the highway stood a fishing cabin with a screen porch, peeling white paint, a tarpaper roof, and a phone line—it had an air of cozy dilapidation that spoke of evenings around a table with cards and whiskey, children lying awake in bunk beds listening for splashes and the cries of loons. Several other cabins were scattered along the shore, the closest about a hundred yards distant. Shellane walked in the woods, enjoying the crisp, resin-scented air, scuffing the fallen needles, thinking he could stand it there a couple of weeks. It would take that long to set up a new identity. This time he intended to bury himself. Asia, maybe.

A placard on the cabin door instructed anyone interested in renting to contact Avery Broillard at the Gas 'n Guzzle in Champion. Through a window Shellane saw throw rugs on a stained spruce floor. Wood stove (there was a cord of wood stacked out back); a funky-looking refrigerator speckled with decals; sofa covered with a Mexican blanket. A wooden table and chairs. Bare bones, but it suited both his needs and his notion of comfort.

The Gas 'n Guzzle proved to be a log cabin with pumps out front and a grocery inside. Hand-lettered signs in the windows declared that fishing licenses were for sale within, also home-baked pies and bait, testifying by their humorous misspellings to a cutesy self-effacing attitude on the part of ownership. The manager, Avery Broillard, was lanky, thirtyish, with shoulder-length black hair and rockabilly sideburns; he had one of those long, faintly dish-shaped Cajun faces with features so prominent, they seemed caricatures of good looks. He said the cabin had been cleaned, the phone line was functional, and quoted a reasonable weekly rate. When Shellane paid for two weeks, cash in advance, Avery peered at him suspiciously.

"You prefer plastic?" Shellane asked, hauling out his wallet. "I don't like using it, but some people won't deal with cash."

"Cash is good." Avery folded the bills and tucked them in his shirt pocket.

Shellane grabbed a shopping basket and stocked up on cold cuts, frozen meat and vegetables, soup, bread, cooking and cleaning necessities, and at the last moment, a home-baked apple pie that must have weighed close to four pounds. He promised himself to eat no more than one small slice a day and be faithful with his push-ups.

"Get these pies made special," Avery said as he shoveled it into a plastic bag. "They're real tasty."

Shellane smiled politely.

"Might as well give you one of these here." Avery handed him a leaflet advertising the fact that the Endless Blue Stars were playing each and every weekend at Roscoe's Tavern.

"That's my band," Avery said. "Endless Blue Stars."

"Rock and roll?"

"Yeah." Then, defensively, "We got quite a following around here. You oughta drop in and give a listen. There ain't a helluva lot else to do."

Shellane forked over three twenties and said he would be sure to drop in.

"If you're looking to fish," said Avery, continuing to bag the groceries, "they taking some pike outta the lake. I can show you the good spots."

"I'm no fisherman," Shellane told him. "I came up here to work on a book."

"You a writer, huh? Anything I might of read?"

Shellane resisted an impulse to say something sarcastic. Broillard's manner, now turned ingratiating, was patently false. There was a sly undertone to every word he spoke, and Shellane had the impression that he considered himself a superior being, that the Gas 'n Guzzle was to his mind a pit stop on the road to world domination, and as a consequence he affected a *faux*-yokelish manner toward his patrons that failed to mask a fundamental condescension. He had bad luck eyes. Watered-down blue; irises marked by hairline darknesses, like fractures in a glaze.

"This one's my first," said Shellane. "I just retired. Did my twenty, and I always wanted to try a book. So . . ."

"What's it about," Avery asked. "Your book."

"Crime," said Shellane, and tried to put an edge on his smile. "Like they say—write what you know."

It took him until after dark to settle into the cabin, to order an Internet hook-up, to prepare and eat his dinner. Once he'd finished with dessert, he poured a fresh cup of coffee, switched on his laptop and sent an email that prevented a file from being sent to the U.S. Justice Department. The file contained a history of Shellane's twenty years as a thief, details of robberies perpetrated and murders witnessed and various other details whose revelation might result in the indictment of several prominent members of Boston's criminal society. It was not that effective an insurance policy. The men who wanted to kill him were too arrogant to believe that he could bring them down, and perhaps their judgment was accurate; but knowing about the file had slowed their reactions sufficiently to allow his escape. He was confident that he would continue to stay ahead of them. However, this confidence did not afford him the satisfaction that once it had. It had been many years since Shellane had derived much pleasure from life. Survival had become less a passion than a game he was adept at playing. Lately the game had lost its savor. Apart from the desire to thwart his pursuers, he was no longer certain why he persevered.

He was about to shut down the computer when he heard a noise outside. He went into the bedroom, took the nine-millimeter from his suitcase, and holding it behind him, went out onto the porch and nudged open the screen door. A slim figure, silhouetted against the moonstruck surface of the water, was moving briskly away from the cabin. Shellane called out, and the figure stopped short.

"I'm sorry," a woman's voice said. "I was out for a walk. The lights . . . I didn't know the cabin was rented."

"It's okay." Shellane stuck the gun into his belt behind his back and pulled his sweater down over it. "I thought it was an animal or something."

"Aren't many animals around anymore," said the woman as she came into the light. "Just squirrels and raccoons. People say we've still got a few wolverines in the woods, but I've never seen one."

She was slender and tall, most of her height in her legs, with long red hair gathered in a ponytail, wearing jeans and a plaid wool jacket. Early thirties, he guessed. A pale country Irish face, with a pointy chin and wide cheekbones. Pretty as a morning prayer. Faint laugh lines showed at the corners of her olive green eyes. Yet she had a subdued air, and he suspected that she had not laughed in a while.

"I'm Grace," she said.

"Michael," said Shellane, remembering to use his temporary identity. "Guess you're my neighbor, huh?"

She gestured toward the lake. "Three cabins down."

Being accustomed to city paranoia, it surprised him that an attractive woman—any woman, for that matter, would tell a stranger where she lived. He had assumed that following the introduction she would retreat, but she stood there, smiling nervously.

"How about some coffee?" he asked. "I was going to make another pot."

Once again she surprised him by accepting the invitation. As he fixed the coffee, she moved about the cabin, keeping away from the center of the room, touching things and stopping suddenly, like a cat exploring new territory. Now and then she would glance at him and flash a nervous smile, as if to assure him she meant no harm. She possessed a jittery vitality that drew his eye, alerted him to her every gesture. He set a cup of coffee on the table and she sat on the edge of her chair, ready to take flight.

"I didn't really want coffee," she said. "It's just living out here, I don't get to meet many people."

"You're not renting, then?"

"No, I . . . no."

Her mouth thinned, as if she was keeping something back.

"What are you doing up here?" she asked. "Vacation?"

He told his retirement story. Her attention wandered, and he had the idea that she knew he was lying. He asked what she did.

"I . . . Nothing, really. I take a lot of walks." She came to her feet. "I should go."

Maybe, he thought, paranoia just took a while to develop in the Upper Peninsula. He followed her to the door, watched her start toward the lake. She turned, walking backwards, and said brightly, "I'm sure we'll run into each other again."

"Hope so," he said.

He stood in the doorway until she was out of sight, sorting through his impressions of her, trying to distinguish the real from the imagined. "Trouble," he said, addressing himself to the shadows along the shore, and went back inside.

That night Shellane had an unusual dream. Unusual both as to its particulars, which bore no obvious relation to the materials of his life, and to the fact that he rarely remembered dreams. He was walking in a roiling gray fog so thick it seemed like flimsy tissue, scraps of the stuff clinging to his clothing. Visibility was severely limited and he was afraid, yet determined. As if on an important errand. Soon a rambling building with a gabled second story partially materialized from the fog. It was fashioned of black boards and had a look of false antiquity redolent of the Gas 'n Guzzle, suggesting that it, too, was a quaint facade housing some less savory enterprise than might be expected. The windows were shuttered; no light escaped from within, and yet there was light enough to see. Except for the weeds that sprang up here and there, the surrounding land was devoid of vegetation. Jutting from the side of the house was an architectural feature he couldn't quite make out, but seemed curious in some way . . . At this point the dream had faded. He recalled fragments. Shapes in the fog. Someone running. And that was all.

As though the dream were made of the same clingy stuff as the fog, its imagery stayed with him all the following day, as did his brief encounter with Grace. She had, he believed, been interested in him. Because he was interested in her, he questioned whether he might be flattering himself; but he was not given to assuming that every woman with whom he spoke was attracted to him. He trusted his instincts. She had to be fifteen years younger than he. It would be foolish to get involved with her—under the best of circumstances she would be a problem, and these were far from the best of circumstances.

That evening, however, he went for a walk along the dirt road that followed the shore, half in hopes of running into her. Her cabin, set among the trees high on the bank, was more a house than cabin. A deck out back. Satellite dish on the roof. Light sprayed from a picture window, and Grace was standing at it, wearing jeans and a cable-knit white sweater. Curious about her, wanting to get closer, he climbed the bank to the right of the window. Her head was down, arms folded. She looked miserable. He had an urge to knock, to say he was passing by and had spotted her, but before he could debate the wisdom of obeying this urge, headlights slashed across the front of the house. Rattling and grumbling, a big blue Cadillac at least thirty-five years old pulled up beside the house and the reason—Shellane suspected—for Grace's misery climbed out. Avery Broillard. He clumped to the door, knocked his boots clean, and went inside. Grace had apparently retreated into the rear of the house. Broillard stood in the front room, hands on hips. "Fuck!" he shouted, and made a flailing gesture. Then he stomped off along a corridor.

As Shellane headed for home a bank of fog moved toward him across the lake, like the ghost of a crumbling city melting up from the past. He was furious with himself. That he had been on the verge of coming between husband and wife, boyfriend-girlfriend, whatever . . . it spoke to a breakdown in judgment. All it would take to bring the cops nosing around was some asshole like Broillard getting his wind up, and though Shellane could handle the cops, it would be wiser to avoid them. Agitated, unable to calm down, he drove into town, thinking he would eat at a diner; but when he saw the lights of Roscoe's, a low concrete building with a neon sign that sketched the green image of a snub-nosed pistol above the door, he turned into the parking lot. Inside, he grabbed a seat at the bar and ordered a cheeseburger plate. At the far end of the room was a stage furnished with amps and mike stands and a PA, backed by a sequined curtain. A bearded roadie was engaged in setting up the mikes. All the tables were occupied, and it appeared that more than half the crowd were women. The babble of laughter and talk outvoiced the jukebox, which was playing "Wheel in the Sky," a song emblematic to Shellane's mind of the most pernicious form of jingle rock. He nursed a draft, watching the place fill beyond its seating capacity. Apparently Broillard did have a following. People had packed in along the walls and were standing two-deep at the bar.

He had intended to leave before the live music started, but when the lights dimmed and a cheer went up, people massing closer to the stage, jamming the dance floor like a festival audience, curiosity got the better of him. Five shadows moved out from the wings. A spot pinned the central mike stand, where Broillard was strapping on a Telecaster with glittery blue stars dappling its black finish. He flashed a boyish grin and said, "How 'bout somebody bringing me a beer. I feel a thirst coming on." Then he turned his back on the crowd and the band kicked in.

At best Shellane expected to hear uninspired songs about beer and dangerous roadhouses and wild, wild women played with a rough, energetic competence; because of his distaste for the band's front man, he hoped for worse. But the Endless Blue Stars had a lyrical sound that was way too big for Roscoe's, their style falling into a spectrum somewhere between Dire Straits and early Cream. Retro, yet carrying a gloss of millennial cynicism. The first song featured a long intro during which Broillard laid down sweetly melodic guitar lines over a 4/4 with a Brazilian feel that built gradually into a rock tempo. When he stepped to the mike, the crowd waved their arms and shouted.

> "Walked out tonight, a frozen blue,
> the moon was dark and shooting stars were dying . . ."

The bassist and drummer added harmony on the next line:

"... with a cold white fire..."

Then Broillard's throaty baritone soared over the background:

"... things ain't been the same
since I fell in love with you,
I've been so hypnotized..."

The mood cast by the song—by all the song—was irresistibly romantic, an invitation to join in a soothing blue dream of love and mystery, and Broillard's Byronic stage persona was so persuasive, Shellane wondered if he might have misjudged him. But when the band went on break and Broillard came swaggering over to the bar, dispensing largesse to well-wishers, his arm about a pretty albeit slightly overstuffed brunette, caressing the underside of her right breast, Shellane decided this was the thing that made music—all art, for that matter—fundamentally suspect: that assholes could become proficient at it.

Broillard spotted him, dragged the girl over, and said, "Needed a break from all that peace and quiet, eh?"

Shellane said, "Yeah, you were right," and then, though he was tempted to dishonesty, complimented him on the set.

"I didn't figure you for a music lover," said Broillard.

"That song, the one that went into a seven-four break after the second verse..."

"'Three Fates.'" Broillard looked at him with renewed interest. "You play?"

"Used to," Shellane said. "I liked that song."

"Yeah, well," said Broillard dismissively. "Cool." He gave the brunette a squeeze. "Annie, this is..."

"Michael," Shellane said when Broillard couldn't dredge up the name.

"Right. Mister Michaels is a writer. Crime novels."

Annie blinked vacantly up at Shellane, too blitzed to say Hi.

Somebody caught Broillard's shoulder, claiming his attention. As he turned away, he smirked and said to Shellane, "Stick around, man. It gets better."

Over the next two days Shellane was kept busy in detailing a new passport, setting up bank accounts on-line. Twice he caught sight of Grace walking along the shingle and considered calling to her, but her air of distraction reinforced his belief that she was a woman with time on her hands. Such women had a need for drama in order to give weight to their lives—he did not intend to become the co-star in her therapy. But he continued to speculate about who she was. He remembered no wedding ring, yet she displayed a kind of cloistered unhappiness that reminded him of married women he had known. Perhaps she removed the ring to give herself the illusion of freedom.

Around noon on the third day, he took a couple of beers, a sandwich, the new James Lee Burke novel, and went down to the shore and sat with his back against a boulder that emerged from the bank, a granite stump scoured smooth by glaciers and warm from the sun. He read only ten or fifteen minutes before laying the book aside. If he had done crime in Louisiana, he thought he might have stayed with it. The players there were more interesting than the Southie ratboys he'd crewed with in Boston . . . at least if he were to trust the novel. Burke might be exaggerating. Crews were likely the same all over, just different accents. He stared out across the sunstruck lake, watched a motor boat cutting a white wake, too far away for the engine noise to carry over the sighing wind and the slop of the water. He half-believed nothing bad could happen here. That was ridiculous, he knew. Yet he felt serene, secure. It seemed the landscape had adjusted to him, reordered itself to accommodate his two hundred and twenty-six pounds, and settled around him with the perfection of a tailored coat. No way he could hack it here for three years as he had in Detroit. But the fit felt better than it had in Detroit, and he could not understand why this was. He stuck out in Champion. There was no cover, no disguise he could successfully adopt.

He finished one beer, ate half the sandwich, and went back to the book, but his attention wandered. Wind ruffled the long reach of the water, raising wavelets that each caught a spoonful of dazzle, making it appear that a myriad diamond lives were surfacing from the depths. The trees stirred in dark green unison. The shingle was decorated with arrangements of twigs, matted feathers and bones, polished stones. Mysteries and signs. Shellane closed his eyes.

"Hello," said Grace, and his heart broke rhythm. He let out a squawk and sat up, knocking over his freshly opened beer.

"I'm sorry!" Her chin was quivering, hands upheld in a posture of alarm.

"I didn't hear you come up," he said.

She relaxed a little, but still seemed wary, and he had the idea that she was used to being frightened.

"It's okay," he said. "No big deal."

She had on jeans, the plaid jacket, and a T-shirt underneath—black with sequined blue stars. Her hair, loose about her shoulders, shined a coppery red under the sun. All her being was luminous, he thought. It was as if a klieg light were trapped in her body.

"Did you eat yet? I've got half a sandwich going to waste." He held out the baggie containing the sandwich.

She stared at it hungrily, but shook her head. The wind lifted the ends of her hair, fluttered the collar of her jacket

The depth of her timidity astonished him. Broillard, he figured, had a lot to answer for.

"What are you reading?" she asked.

He showed her the book.

"I don't know him," she said.

"It's detective fiction, but the writing's great."

She cast an anxious glance behind her, then sank to her knees beside him. "I mostly read short stories. That's what I wanted to write . . . short stories."

"*Wanted* to write'?"

"I just . . . he . . . I couldn't . . . I . . . "

She stalled out, and Shellane resisted the impulse to touch her hand.

"I wasn't very good," she said.

"Who told you that?" he asked.

As he spoke he recognized that he was casting aside his resolve and making a choice that could imperil him. Something about Grace, and it was not just her apparent hopelessness, pulled at him, made him want to take the risk. Her face serially mapped her emotions: surprise and alarm and fretfulness. Green eyes crystalled with reflected light.

"Your husband," Shellane said. "Right?"

"It's not . . . " She broke off, and glanced off along the shore road. The blue Cadillac was slewing toward them from the direction of Broillard's cabin. Grace scooted behind the boulder. As the car turned onto the access road, Shellane saw that the brunette from the tavern occupied the passenger seat. The Cadillac skidded in the gravel, then sped off among the evergreens.

"Did he see me?" Grace emerged from behind the boulder. "I don't *think* he did."

He ignored the question. "He brings 'em home? His fucking bimbos? You're there, and he just brings 'em home?"

Her nod was almost imperceptible, hardly more than a tucking in of the chin.

"Why do you put up with it? What does he do? Does he hit you?"

"He never . . . No. Not for a long time."

"Not for a long time? Terrific!"

She opened her mouth, but only shook her head again. Finally she said, "It's not entirely his fault."

"Sure, I can see that."

"You don't understand! He's very talented, and he's been so frustrated. He . . ."

"So he takes his frustrations out on you. He makes you feel bad about yourself. He tells you you're worthless. He blames you for his failings."

Shellane reached for her hand. She looked startled when he touched her wrist, but let him pull her down onto her knees. "If that's how it is," he said, "you should leave him."

The boat that had been racing around at the far end of the lake swung close in along the shore, the sound of its engine carving a gash in the stillness. The driver and the woman with him waved. Neither Shellane nor Grace responded.

"He doesn't deserve you," Shellane said.

"You don't know me . . . and you don't know him."

"Twenty-five years ago I used to *be* him."

"I doubt that. Avery's one of a kind."

"No he's not. I had a girlfriend . . . a lot like you. Sweet, pretty. She loved me, but I couldn't get it together. I was too damn lazy. I thought because I was smart, the world was going to fall at my feet. Eventually she left me. But before that happened, I did my best to make her feel as bad about herself as I felt about myself."

She was silent a few beats. "Did you ever get it together?"

"I got by, but I never did what I wanted."

"What was that?"

"It's a bit of a coincidence, actually. I wanted to be a musician. I wrote songs . . . or tried to. Screwed around in a garage band. But I settled for the next best thing."

She looked at him expectantly.

"Maybe I'll tell you about it sometime," he said.

They sat without speaking for a minute. Shellane told himself it was time to pull back. The pause was an opportunity to quit this foolishness. But instead he said, "Have dinner with me tonight. We can drive into Marquette."

"I can't."

"Why not? He'll be playing tonight."

"He plays every night."

"Then why not have dinner? You afraid someone will see us?"

She gave no reply, and he said, "Come over to the cabin, then. I'll cook up some steaks."

"I might have to eat at home." She flattened her palms against her thighs. "I could come over after . . . maybe."

"Okay," he said.

"I don't want you to think . . . that . . ."

"I promise not to think."

That brought a wan smile. "We can just talk, if that's all right."

"Talk would be good."

She appeared to be growing uncomfortable and, watching her hands wrestle with one another, her eyes darting toward the lake, he timed her and said to himself, the instant before she spoke the same words, I should go.

Late that afternoon it seemed deep November arrived at the lake in all its dank and gray displeasure, a cold wind pushing in a pewter overcast and spatterings of rain. As the dusk turned to dark, a fog rolled in, ghost-dressing the trees in whitish rags that clung to the boughs like relics of an ancient festival. Shellane, who had gone for a walk just as the fog began to accumulate, was forced to grope his way along, guided by the muffled slap of the waves. He had brought a flashlight, but all the beam illuminated was churning walls of fog. He must have been within a hundred yards of the cabin when he realized he could no longer hear the water. He kept going in what he assumed to be the direction of the shoreline, but after ten minutes, he was still on solid ground. He must have gotten turned around, he thought. He shined the flashlight ahead. A momentary thinning of the mist, and he made out a building. If anyone was at home, he could ask directions. The visibility was so poor, he couldn't see much until he was right up next to the wall. The boards were knotty and badly carpentered, set at irregular slants and coated with pitch. He ran his right hand against one and picked up a splinter.

"Shit!" He examined his palm. Blood welled from a gouge, and a toothpick-sized sliver of wood was visible beneath the skin. He shook his hand to ease the hurt and happened to glance upward. Protruding from the wall some twenty feet overhead was a huge black fist, perfectly articulated and twice the circumference of an oil drum. From its clenched fingers hung a shred of rotting rope.

Shellane's heart seemed itself to close into a fist. Swirling fog hid the thing from view, but he could have sworn it was not affixed to the wall, but rather emerged from it, the boards flowing out into the shape, as if the building were angry and had extruded this symptom of its mood.

He heard movement behind him and spun about, caught his heel and fell. Knocked loose on impact, the flashlight rolled away, becoming a mound of yellowish radiance off in the fog. Panicked, he scrambled up, breathing hard. He could no longer see much of the building, just the partial outline of a roof.

A guttural noise; pounding footsteps.

"Hey!" Shellane called.

More footsteps, and another voice, maybe the same one.

"Quit screwing around!" he shouted. The hairs on his neck prickled. Who the fuck would own such a place? Some pissant Goths. Rich kids who'd never gotten over The Cure. Movement on his right. Something heavy and ungainly.

Fuck directions, he told himself.

He started away from the building, walking fast, holding his arms out like Frankenstein's monster to ward off obstructions. Less than ten seconds later, he hit a drop-off and staggered into cold ankle-deep water. He overbalanced and toppled onto his side, raising a splash. He pushed up from the silty bottom, found his way to shore, and stood shivering. Listening for voices. The only sound was that of the water dripping from his clothes onto the sand. He felt foolish at having been spooked by, probably, a bunch of twits who wore eyeliner and drank wine out of silver cups and thought they were unique.

That fist, though. What a freakshow!

If things were different, he thought, he'd give them a lesson in reality. Blow a couple of nine-millimeter holes in their point of view. But his annoyance faded quickly, and after squeezing and shaking the excess water from his clothes, he trudged off along the shore.

*H*e doubted that Grace would show that evening, and truth be told, he wasn't sure he wanted her to. His experience in the fog had rekindled his caution, and he thought it might be best for them both if she blew him off. He could be no help to her, and she would only endanger him. At nine o'clock he switched on the laptop and called up his crime file. Seeing Marty Gerbasi in Detroit had made him realize it was time to add a more personal reminiscence. He'd been having a beer in the Antrim back in Southie, the winter of '83, when Marty had come in with Donnie Doyle, a pale twist of a kid with peroxided hair and a rabbity look who occasionally hooked on with a crew as a driver. Stupid as a stopped clock. They'd sat down next to Shellane and all three of them had tried to drink the bar out of Bushmills. Marty was buying, playing the grand fellow, laughing at Donnie's stories, most of them lies about his gambling prowess, and winking broadly at Shellane as if to say he knew the kid was bullshit. Around 1 AM they staggered out of the bar—at least Donnie had staggered. Marty and Shellane had handled their liquor. No one ever saw

Donnie Doyle after that night, and Shellane understood that having Marty buy you drinks was not a good thing. Like so many of Shellane's associates, he lacked the necessary inch of conscience to qualify as human. Over the years, Shellane's recognition that he was involved with a company of affable sociopaths had grown more poignant, eventually causing him to rethink his future, to realize that sooner or later Marty would offer to buy him drinks. He never found out what Donnie Doyle had done to deserve his night out with good ol' Roy Shellane and the guinea angel of death, but he figured it was nothing more than some unfortunate behavior, maybe a tendency toward loquaciousness or . . .

A knock on the door. Ignoring his determination that he was better off without her, he jumped up to let Grace in. The plaid jacket and jeans again. Ponytail.

"Sorry I'm late," she said as he stood aside to allow her to pass.

"I didn't know if you'd make it at all, what with the fog."

She sat at the table, shrugged out of the jacket; she had on a green turtleneck underneath. "It's nice and warm in here," she said, then pointed to his hand, which he had bandaged after removing the splinter. "What happened?"

Her eyes widened when he told her about the black house.

"You know who owns the place?" he asked.

A shake of her head. "It's really old. Lots of people stay there."

"Have you met any of them?"

"They don't talk to me."

Shellane went into the kitchen and poured two fingers of bourbon. He glanced at her inquiringly, held up the bottle, expecting her to refuse.

"I'll try it," she said.

He poured, set the glass in front of her. She touched the rim with her forefinger, closed her hand around it, then had a sip. She sipped again and smiled. "It's good!"

She was easier around him than before, and this both elated and distressed him. What he felt for her, when he tried to isolate it, was less defined than what he felt toward her husband. He was attracted, but the basis of the attraction confounded him. True, she was sexy, with her green eyes and expressive mouth and strong, slender body. Her vulnerability made him feel protective, and this enhanced the other feelings. But he could not help thinking that a large part of his attraction was due to the danger she posed. For several years he had limited his contact with women to those he met through outcall services; now, alone with her in this secluded place, he wondered if he was not toying with fate, pretending there was something for them other than the moment. She finished her drink and asked for a refill. He doubted she was much of a drinker and thought this might be her way of signaling that she was ready to take a step. He did not believe her capable of discretion. Her spirit was so damaged, if Broillard were to get a whiff of another man and pressured her, she might confess everything. Broillard might no longer care about he . . . rthough in Shellane's experience, men who abused their women were extremely possessive of them.

She asked what he used the laptop for, and he told her the lie about his book. She pressed him on the subject, inquiring as to his feelings about his work, and he fended off her questions by saying he didn't know enough about writing yet to be able to talk about it with any intelligence.

"But you were a songwriter," she said.

"I was a wanna-be. That doesn't qualify me to speak about it."

"That's not true. If you want to do something, you think about it. Even if it's not conscious, you come to understand things about it. Techniques . . . strategies."

"Sounds like you should be telling me about *your* work," he said. When she demurred, he asked what she would write about if she regained her confidence.

"It's not my confidence that's the problem."

"Sure it is," he said. "Having enough confidence to fail is most of everything. So tell me. What would you write about?"

"The lake." She tugged at a strand of hair that had come loose from the ponytail, stretched it down beside her ear so as to contrive a sideburn. "It's all I know. My father and I lived here from the time I was four. My mother died when I was a baby."

"It's your father's house you're in now?"

She nodded. "After he died, Avery came along. He helped me with the business."

"The Gas 'n Guzzle?"

"Avery renamed it," she said. "It used to be Malloy's. I wanted to keep the name, but . . ." She gave another of those glum gestures that Shellane was beginning to interpret as redolent of her attitude toward an entire spectrum of defeats.

"So Avery moved right in, did he?"

"I guess." She held out her empty glass again and he poured a stiffer drink.

"Looks like I'm going to have to call you a cab," he said

She giggled, lifted the glass and touched the liquid with the tip of her tongue. It was the first sign of happiness she had shown him, and it was so pure a thing, evocative of a girlish sweetness, that Shellane, himself a little drunk, was moved to touch her cheek.

Alarmed, she pulled away. He started to apologize, but she said, "No, it's okay. Really!" But she appeared flustered. At any minute, he thought, he would hear her say she had to go.

She stared into her glass for such a long time, Shellane grew uncomfortable. Then, her tone suddenly forceful, she said, "I could write a hundred stories about the lake. Every day it has a different mood. I never wanted to live anywhere else." She looked up at him. "You like it here too, don't you?"

"Yeah, but I couldn't live here."

"Why not?"

"It's complicated," he said after a pause.

She laid her palms flat on the table and appeared to study their shapes against the dark wood; then she pushed up to her feet. "May I use your restroom?"

She was so long in the bathroom, Shellane began to worry. The water had been running ever since she went in. What could she be doing? Effecting an ornate suicide? Praying? Changing into animal form? He considered asking if she was okay, but decided this was too much solicitude.

Wind jiggled the door latch, and a bough scraped the roof. He stretched out his legs, let his eyelids droop. He pictured Grace with the glass raised to her pale lips, the tawny whiskey and the coppery color of her hair blended by lamplight. He did not notice the sound of the bathroom door opening, but heard her soft step behind him. Her face was freshly scrubbed and shining. She was holding a bath towel in front of her, but let it drop to the side. Her breasts were high and small, strawberry-tipped; the pearly arcs of her hips centered by a tuft of coppery flame. Her eyes locked onto his.

"I'd like to stay," she said.

*T*here came a point during the night, with the wind sharking through the trees, rattling the cabin as if it were a sackful of bones, knifing through the boards to sting Shellane's skin with cold . . . there came a point when he recognized that he understood nothing, either of the world or the ways of women, not even the workings of his own heart. Or maybe understanding was not the key he had thought it was. Maybe it only functioned up to a point, maybe it explained everything except the important things, and they were in themselves like the underside of a cloud, part of an overarching surface that was impossible to quantify from a human perspective. Maybe everything was that simple and that complex. Whatever the architecture and rule of life, whatever chemistry was in play, whatever rituals of pain and loneliness had nourished the moment, it was clear they were not just fucking, they were making love. Grace was a river running through his arms, supple and easy, moving with a sinewy eagerness, as if new to each bend and passage of their course. The wind drove away the clouds, the fog. Moonlight slipped between the curtains, and she burned pale against the sheets, announcing her pleasure with musical breaths. Coming astride him, she appeared to hover in the dimness, lifting high and then her hips twisting cleverly down to conjoin them, face hidden by the fall of her hair. At times she spoke in a whisper so faint and diffuse, it seemed a ghostly sibilance arising from her skin. She would say his name, the name she thought was his, and he would want to tell her his true name, to reveal his secrets; but instead he buried his mouth in her flesh, whispering endearments and promises that, though he meant them, he could never keep. At last, near dawn, she fell asleep, and he lay drifting, so exhausted he felt his soul was floating half out of his body, points of light flaring behind his lids, the afterimages of his intoxication.

He must have slept a while, for the next he recalled she was stirring in his arms. The sun sliced through the curtains, painting a golden slant across the shadow of her face. Her eyelids fluttered, and she made a small indefinite noise.

"Morning," he said.

Anxiety surfaced in her sleepy face, but lived only a moment. "I wasn't sure . . ." she murmured.

"Sure about what?"

"Nothing." After a second or two she sat up, holding the sheet to her breasts, looking about the room in bewilderment, as if amazed to find herself there.

"You all right?" he asked.

She nodded, settled back onto the pillow. Her eyes, lit by the sun, were weirdly bright, like glowing coins. He turned her to face him, laying a hand on her hip. A tear formed at the corner of her left eye.

"What's this?" he asked, wiping it away.

Her expression was almost clownishly dolorous. She took his hand and placed it between her legs so he could feel the moistness there, then pushed into his fingers, letting him open her.

"Holy Jesus," he said. "You'll be the death of me."

After she had gone, making another of her sudden exits, leaving before he could determine what she wanted or be assured as to what she felt, Shellane went down to the shore and rested against the old glacial boulder. His thoughts were images of Grace. Her face close to his. How she had looked above him, her hair flipped all to one side in violent toss, like the flag of her pleasure, head turned and back arched as she came. A presentiment of trouble, of Broillard and what he might do, called for his attention, but he was not ready to consider that question. He believed he could handle Broillard—he had handled far worse. The Mitsubishi warehouse in Brooklyn. The New Haven bank job. He recalled a mansion they'd broken into in upstate New York, going after an art collection. An old Nathaniel Hawthorne sort of house with secret rooms and hidden passages. A billionaire's antique toy. The security system had not been a problem, but the house had been full of 18th-century perils they could never have anticipated, the most daunting of which was a subterranean maze. One man had been skewered by a booby trap, but Shellane had succeeded in unraveling the logic of the maze, and they managed to escape with the art. If he could deal with all of that, he could take care of Mister Endless Fucking Blue Stars.

He chuckled at the brutal character of his nostalgia.

Memories.

He had been hoping Grace would return, but several hours passed and she did not. Around noon, the blue Cadillac roared past the cabin on its way toward Champion, Broillard off to spend the afternoon at the Gas 'n Guzzle, and Shellane headed along the shore toward Grace's house. He stood on the beach below the place for several minutes, uncertain about approaching. At length he climbed the slope and peeked through the picture window. She was sitting on the carpet with her back toward him, legs drawn up beneath her. Her shoulders were shaking, as with heavy sobs. He had not taken notice of the furniture before—ratty, second-hand stuff in worse shape than the pieces in his cabin. Clothing strewn on the floor. A plate of dried pasta balanced on the arm of the sofa. Piles of compact discs and magazines. Empty pizza boxes, McDonald's cartons, condom wrappers. Your basic rock and roll decor. He went to the door and knocked. No answer. He pushed on in. She did not look up.

"It's me," he said.

She sat staring straight ahead, strands of coppery hair stuck to her damp cheeks.

"Come on," he said, extending a hand. "Let's get out of here."

She did not move; her expression did not change.

He dropped to his knees. "What's he say to you?' he asked. "That you're ugly . . . stupid? That you don't have a clue? You can't believe that."

A damp heat of despondency radiated from her. It was as if she were steeped in the emotion, submerged beneath it, like a statue beneath a transparent lake.

"You're beautiful," he said. "You know things with your heart most people don't have names for. I can tell that of you . . . even after just one night." Though he believed this of her, though belief in her had been born in him, what he said rang false to his ears, as if it were a line he had learned to recite and had chosen to believe.

She began to cry again, silently, her shoulders heaving. Shellane felt incompetent in the face of her despair. He wanted to put an arm around her, but sensed she wouldn't want to be touched.

"Is it guilt you're feeling?" he asked. "About last night?"

He might not have been there, for all the attention she gave to him. He remained kneeling beside her for a short while and then asked if she wanted him to go.

It seemed that she nodded.

"All right." He got to his feet. "I'll be at the cabin." He crossed to the door, hesitated. "We can get past this, Grace."

Once outside, he recognized the idiocy of that statement. She was not going to leave with him—he knew that in his bones. Even if she would, he had no desire to drag her along through the shooting gallery of his life. Anger at Broillard grew large in him. Back at the cabin, he paced back and forth, then flung himself into the Toyota and drove toward town at an excessive rate of speed. He parked in the Gas 'n Guzzle lot and sat with his hands clamped to the wheel, telling himself that if he let go he would charge into the place and play an endless blue tune on Broillard's head. Yet as he continued to sit there, he recognized that his battle to maintain control was pure bullshit. He was conning himself. Playing at being human. If he let go of the wheel, he would do nothing. He might wish that he would act, that he would lose it and go roaring into the Gas 'n Guzzle and drop the hammer on Broillard in the name of love and honor. But he would never risk it. Twenty years in the cold ditches of the underworld had left him at a remove from the natural demands and fevers of the heart. He supposed he had become, like his old crime partners, an affable sociopath who stood with one foot outside the world, a man whose emotions were smaller than the norm. And this being the case, wasn't what he felt for Grace equally bullshit?

His anger dimmed and, without ever having left the car, he drove back to the cabin and sat on the steps, practicing calm, gazing out at the tranquil blue surface of the lake, the evergreens standing sentinel along the shadowy avenues leading off among them. Still as a postcard image. Soothing in its simple shapes and colors. He recalled how Grace had talked about it. He believed her view of the place to be romantic delusion, but wished he could share in it. The idea of sharing anything, after the years of solitude, filled him with yearning. But he knew he was incapable of it. Those shadows of Hiroshima burned onto stone, those parings of lives. That was him. A thin dark urgency was all that remained.

Mid-afternoon, and Grace had not appeared. Shellane started toward her house, but thought better of it and took himself in the opposite direction, hoping to walk off his gloom. The sun had sunk to the level of the treeline and, though a rich golden light spread throughout the air, the glaze of mid-day warmth had dissipated. His breath smoked; a chill cut through his windbreaker and hurried his step. He kept his eyes down, kicking at stones, at whatever minor obstructions came to view, manufacturing small goals such as kicking a fish head without breaking stride. He had gone almost a mile when he saw a figure standing among the trees about a hundred feet away. A naked man. Not wearing a stitch. Skinny and tall and pale. Judging by the man's stillness, Shellane thought he must be waiting for someone. His second impression, based on no clear evidence, was that the man was waiting for *him*. A pinprick of cold blossomed at the center of his chest and he peered at the man, trying to make out his particulars. He felt as if a channel had opened between them, a clear tunnel in the air, and that along it flowed a palpable menace.

This, he thought, was a sign of how shaky the thing with Grace had made him. There were no grounds for fear. Yet he kept on his guard, uncertain whether to turn back or go forward, and, when the man started toward him, moving with a purposeful stride, he felt a sting of panic that sent him scrambling up the shadowed, needle-covered slopes, in among the trees. After perhaps twenty or thirty seconds, he was overtaken by embarrassment—he did not consider himself the sort to panic for any reason, let alone the appearance of a skinny naked stranger whom he could surely snap in two. He stopped and looked around, but saw no one. He adjusted the windbreaker about his hips and shoulders. Drew a steadying breath and rested a palm against the trunk of a spruce; his palm came away sticky, smeared with reddish resin. He studied the marks—like a little hexagram of tacky blood—and wiped it clean on his trousers.

"Fucking Christ," he said, and stepped out of hiding.

The man was standing no more than twenty-five feet away, his bony ass was turned to Shellane, and he was staring down at the lake. He was bald, his skull was knobbly, almost bean-shaped, and his skin was bleached and grayish. Shellane eased behind the spruce trunk and turned sideways so as to be completely hidden. The wind built a faltering rush from the boughs, like the amplified issuance of a final breath. His heart felt hot and huge, less beating than pulsing rapidly. A scraping noise caused him to stiffen. The idea that he had nothing to fear wouldn't stick in his mind—he was terribly afraid, and for no reason he could fathom. Then the man came stalking past Shellane's hiding place, and a reason became apparent: his face had the glaring eyes and gashed mouth and mad fixity of a jack o'lantern. Outsized features carved into the gray skin. He paused, no more than a dozen feet away, his head tilted. Shellane noticed a ruff of flesh at the base of his neck . . . maybe it wasn't flesh. Rubber. The son-of-a-bitch must be wearing one of those rubber Halloween masks. But if it was a mask, Shellane wasn't eager to learn what lay beneath. He held still, not allowing himself to breathe until the man's ground-eating stride carried him out of sight.

On his way home he remembered the black house and thought that the man in the mask must be one of the freaks who lived there. The thing to do would be to check the house out . . . No. That wasn't it. The wise thing to do, the rational thing, would be to put the lake in his rear view. This place was punching holes in him. Or maybe it wasn't the place. Maybe the years had worn him down to zero, and he just happened to be here when it all started to fall apart, a sudden erosion like that of a man who'd been granted an extra century of life and on the day the term expired, he turned to dust? What if he was only walking around in his head, and in reality he was no more than two piles of gray dust in a pair of empty shoes?

Bullshit, he said to himself, and picked up the pace. To be that way, to be the dust of a dead spell . . . he should be so lucky.

✤✤✤✤✤✤

By the time Shellane reached the cabin, his desire to leave the lake had been subsumed by concern for Grace and a generalized depression that blunted the sharpness of his fears and muddied his thoughts. Feeling at loose ends, his energy low, he sat at his laptop playing solitaire. The darkness that soon began to gather seemed to compress the space around him, and he saw himself isolated in a little cube of brightness adrift in boundless night. A man holding digital aces, cards made of light, haunted by freaks and old crimes and a weeping woman. It was all bullshit, he realized. This poetry of self-pity leaking from him. He remembered the ridged and bloody hole in Donnie Doyle's forehead, and he remembered a few seconds before the hole had appeared, Marty Gerbasi handing him the gun and saying, "You do it, Roy." And he had said, "What?", as if he didn't know what Marty meant. But he knew, he knew this was how he bought into the big game, this was the soul price of his profession. Gerbasi said. "I like you, Roy. But that don't mean shit. You need to do this now, understand?" He understood everything. The moral choices, the consequences attending each choice. And so he took the gun and wrote a song on Donnie Doyle's forehead, the only important song he had ever authored, a hole punched through the bone . . .

The door latch rattled at Grace's knock, so light it might have been a puff of wind. He felt the pressure of her gloom brushing against his own, like two rain clouds merging. He let her in and sank to his knees before her, his face to her belly, the clean smell of wool soaking up and stilling the tumble of his thoughts. When he stood, his hands following the curve of her hips, slipping beneath the sweater to cup her breasts, he felt his fingers were stained white by her flesh, that whiteness was spreading through him. Her lips grazed his ear and she said, "He hit me. In the stomach where it wouldn't show. He told me I was ignorant. A fat Irish cow." She went on and on, cataloguing Broillard's attacks upon her, all in a husky tone doubtless influenced by Shellane's gentler assault, and yet the list of her husband's sins had an erotic value of its own, informing and encouraging his gentleness. Rage and desire partnered in his mind, and as he removed her clothing, it seemed he was removing as well the baffles that kept his anger contained, so that when they fell into the bed and made the mattress springs creak in a symphony of strain, it was as if anger were riding between his shoulder blades, spurring his exertions, inspiring him to pin her to the bed like a broken insect and fabricate a chorus of moans and cries. Though joined to her, part of his mind listened with almost critical acuteness as she whispered all manner of breathy endearments. Wind dance, meaningless love garbage. Garbled expressions of comic book word balloon passion, sounding one moment like she was strangling on oatmeal, the next emitting pretty snatches of hummed melody. She bucked and plunged, heels hooked behind his calves, the tendon strings of her thighs corded like wires. They were both fucking to win, he thought. To injure, to defile. Love . . . love . . . love . . . love. The chant of galley slaves stoking his mean-spirited rhythm. When he came, a cry spewing from his throat, he was aware of its rawness, its ugly finality, like that of man gutted by a single stroke, shocked and beginning to die.

She left him with her usual suddenness in the morning, returning, he assumed, to the befouled emptiness of her home. Scatters of rain tap-danced on the roof, and he stood by the bed, staring down at the wet spot on the sheet, which had dried into a shape reminiscent of a gray bird on the wing. The violence of their passion, its patina of furious artificiality, all inspired by her relation of Broillard's abuse—it unsettled him. He was still angry. Angry at her for trying to use him. That was what she had been doing, he believed. Trying to rouse his anger. And she had succeeded. He was angry at Broillard for having caused her to hate so powerfully, so obsessively, that she would use him, Shellane, as a means of wreaking vengeance. But he didn't care if that was her intent. He was ready to be used.

He drove into town and parked off to the side of the Gas 'n Guzzle, then walked toward the entrance, moved by an almost casual animus, as if of a mind merely to offer a stern warning. It was no act of self-deception—not this time; it was a mask he wore to hide from others a dangerous mood. Thanks to Grace, he had at least reclaimed something of his old self, the purity of his anger. He pushed the door inward, jingling the bell atop it. A girl in a hooded gray sweatshirt was at the counter, buying cigarettes from

Limbo 141

Broillard, who offered him a careless one-fingered wave. Shellane ambled along the aisles, picking up a can of soup, spaghetti, a bottle of virgin olive oil. When the girl left, he waited at the counter while Broillard rang up the sale.

"Little pasta tonight, eh?" said Broillard, checking the price of the spaghetti. "How's it going out there?"

"Real great," Shellane said. "I'm fucking your wife."

The words released a cold chemical, sent it flooding through him. His hands were like ice. Broillard gaped at him, an expression that—with his long hair and sideburns—lent him a hayseed look.

"I know how you treat her," Shellane went on. "But you lay a hand on her, you say an unkind word, I will take you into the deep woods and leave you for the beasts. My word on it."

"You nuts, man?" Broillard made a grab for something on the shelf beneath the counter, but Shellane caught his wrist and squeezed until the bones ground together. With his free hand, he fumbled about on the shelf. His fingers curled around a wooden shaft—a sawed-off baseball bat. He rapped Broillard with it on the side of his head, hard enough to provoke an outcry.

"Supposing I smash your fingers with this little guy," Shellane said. "There goes the ol' career, eh?"

He rapped Broillard again, harder this time, sending him to his knees, hands upheld to stave off another blow.

"I don't know who it is you're doing," Broillard said with whiny outrage, "but it ain't my wife!"

"Nice-looking redhead name of Grace. Beautiful green eyes, perky tits. Ass round as a teapot. Sound familiar?"

Broillard pushed himself into a corner, as far from Shellane as possible, and his voice unsteady, shrilled, "Get the fuck outta here!"

"Oh, I'll be going. Soon as I'm certain you understand that I'm your daddy. From this point on, you don't even whimper unless I give you a kick."

Broillard summoned breath and shouted, "Help!"

Shellane leaned across the counter and clubbed him on the kneecap. While Broillard was busy absorbing the pain, he went to the door, locked it, and turned the Closed sign outward. He shut the blinds, throwing the interior of the store into a gray twilight.

"Now we can be intimate," he said, coming back over to the counter. "Now we can communicate."

"I swear to God," Broillard said. "If you . . ."

Shellane shouted, an inarticulate roar that caused Broillard to flatten himself against the wall.

"Grace told me a great deal about you," Shellane said. "But she didn't let on what a big pussy you are."

"I don't know what the fuck you want, man! This is crazy!"

"Crazy is hitting her in the stomach so it won't show. Telling her she's a fat cow and she fucks like a sick fish. Like a cat with the heaves. That was very inventive, Avery . . . that last. It has the feel of hateful observance."

Looking stricken, Broillard came to one knee. "Who told you?"

"Grace. She gave me chapter and verse on your sorry ass."

"She's dead." Broillard said it with bewilderment, then more vehemently: "She's dead! Somebody's feeding you a bunch of shit!"

Shellane left a pause. "What do you mean she's dead?"

"She's dead . . . she died! Two years ago!" Broillard's expression gave no indication that he was lying. "She's dead," he repeated with an air of maudlin distraction. "I . . . You can't . . ."

"Don't play with me."

"I'm not playing. It's the truth!" Broillard put his hands to his head, as if fearful it might explode. "This is too weird, man. What're you trying to do?"

Shellane wondered if he had been tricked. "You have a picture of her?"

Broillard blinked at him. "Yeah . . . I think. Yeah."

"Let me see it!"

"I gotta . . ." Broillard pointed to the cash register.

"Get it!" Shellane told him.

Broillard reached with two fingers between the cash register and a display case, extracted a dusty photograph with curled edges, and handed it to Shellane. In the picture Broillard was standing in front of the blue Caddy, his arm around Grace, who was shielding her eyes against the sun. He was thinner. The shape of one sideburn barely sketched on his cheek. Grace looked the same as she had that morning. Both wore Endless Blue Stars T-shirts.

"That's not her," Broillard said with weak assurance. "She's not the woman you're banging, right?"

Shellane had a moment's dizziness, as if he'd stood up too quickly. He stared at the photograph, unable to gather his emotions, aware only of dread and hopelessness.

"She's dead!" Broillard said with desperate insistence. "Go out to the cemetery and look, you don't believe me."

Shellane let the picture fall onto the counter. "We'll both go," he said.

*T*he local boneyard was quiet and neatly landscaped and, as they passed among the ranked stones, a few drops of rain still falling, Shellane was annoyed by the impacted piety of grandfather trees and green lawns and had the thought that death was quiet enough in its own right and he would prefer to wind up in a Third World cemetery, some place with a feeling of community, kids drooling taco juice on your plot, balloon salesmen, noisy families picnicking in front of a loved one's crypt. Grace's stone was a modest chunk of gray marble in a corner of graveyard, close by an elderly maple, its crown of yellow leaves half denuded. What looked to be her college yearbook photo, a waist-up shot of a smiling girl in a dark blue sweater, a gold locket on a chain, was recessed in the marble beneath a transparent plastic square. Her legend read:

GRACE BROILLARD
1971-2000
BELOVED WIFE

No flowers were in evidence. The smell of leaf mold and a damp, darker odor.

Numb, uncomprehending, Shellane asked, "How did she die?"

"Natural causes," Broillard said.

"The hell does that mean? What's natural about the death of a twenty-nine-year-old woman?"

"She passed out," said Broillard with a quaver. "Some kinda trouble with her heart. We thought she drowned, 'cause she fell over at the edge of the lake. But the doctor told us her heart just stopped. She didn't have any water in her lungs."

Looking off at the sky, Shellane felt that his emotions had been eclipsed by a gray sun. "Lie down," he said. Broillard tried to dart away, but Shellane caught his arm. "I want you to lie down on the grave."

When Broillard refused, Shellane swept his legs from beneath him, and he went sprawling atop the grave. He propped himself up on his elbows.

"Lie flat," Shellane told him. "Get familiar with the pose."

Reluctantly, Broillard obeyed. "What you gonna do?"

"I know how she died. You drained the life out of her. You beat her down inch by fucking inch. You had her trapped. You took over her home, her business and, for her kindness, you hammered on her until she didn't care enough to live."

"You didn't know her! She was a liar! Anything she wanted she'd lie to get it! She . . ."

Shellane kicked him in the side; Broillard gasped, clutching the injured area.

"You didn't know her, man," he said again.

"If she lied, it was because you tormented her. You gave her no reason to be truthful." He nudged Broillard's leg. "Come on, Avery. Confess your sins. Cleanse your soul before you come face to face with the Creator."

Broillard's eyes were squeezed shut. "Please . . . Please don't."

Shellane wanted to hurt him, but each time he contemplated doing so, he lost focus. The sky above had the look of a flat gray lid; a maple leaf skated sideways back and forth on the breeze before settling to the ground. "Grace," he said, testing the truth of the name, finding that it provoked not dread but desolation.

"I'm sorry . . . I . . ." Broillard began to weep, his words fractured by sobs.

"Shut up," Shellane told him.

"I didn't want her to die!" Broillard said. "I was all fucked up, I just . . ."

Shellane put his foot on Broillard's stomach, a light pressure, and Broillard tensed, sucked in his breath.

"I want you to lie there for an hour," Shellane said. "One full hour. Maybe she'll come to you."

"No, man. I . . ."

Shellane pressed down harder with his foot.

"Maybe she'll want something from you. Tell her you were fucked up. Stoned. Drunk. Stressed out. Tell her you were crazy. That your creative spirit was suffocating. Buried under a rock of circumstance. And as you struggled to liberate your essence, you accidentally kicked her in the heart ten thousand times. I know she'll be merciful." He knelt beside Broillard. "A full hour. You leave before the hour's up, I'll find out. Do you know how?"

Eyes still shut, Broillard shook his head.

Shellane put his mouth close to the man's ear and whispered very softly, "She'll tell me."

Of course he had his doubts. Doubts assailed him as he drove back to the cabin. There must be an explanation other than the obvious. A twin sister, an actress hired to play a part. Something. But that was ludicrous, soap opera-ish. The idea of a ghost was much more logical, and what did that say about the world? That the occult could seem more rational than the mundane. Yet he suspected that he must not believe it. If he did he would be more frightened of returning to the lake; he would want to run into the cabin, scoop up his belongings and be gone. Or was it that he was half a ghost himself? So diminished and deadened by his sins, he was accessible to death's creatures, immune to their terrors. This struck him with the force of truth, and he tried to dredge up some awful fear hidden momentarily from sight, a mortal terror that would humanize him. He conjured new images of Grace. Imagined himself in bed with a corpse, a skull filled with maggots, a mummified tongue. But she was none of those things. Whatever the physics of her substance, it was akin to his own. When he saw her, he thought, maybe then he'd be afraid. Now it was all speculative, but when he saw her . . . that would be the test of his humanity. Then he'd know if she was too real for him, or if he was sufficiently unreal to be real for her.

The lake had gone a deep ocean blue under the prison sky, sluggish waves piling in to scour the shingle, and the boughs of the evergreens lifted with the hallucinatory slowness of undersea life. The cabin looked forlorn, a shabby relic. Grace was standing among the trees behind it, watching the road as he pulled up. Like a tiny figure placed in the corner of a landscape to lend perspective and a drop of color. He sat in the car, waiting for her to call out, but she remained silent. He climbed halfway out, one foot on the ground, one on the floorboards, and stared at her across the roof of the car. In her jeans and plaid jacket, she looked entirely ordinary. He wanted her to be real. Whether ghost or flesh-and-blood, it made no difference so long as she was real. As he walked toward her, she folded her arms and ducked her head. He stopped a few feet away, thinking that he would see death in her; but she was only herself. Mouth held tightly. Eyelids lowered. He started to frame a question, but could not come up with one that didn't sound absurd. Finally he said, "I know what happened to you."

"Do you?" She gave an unhappy laugh. "I'm not sure I do." Coppery strands of hair drifted across her face—she did not bother to brush them aside.

"You died," he said. "Two years ago." Unable to speak for a second, he put a hand to his brow—his fingers trembled. "How's it possible . . . for you and me . . . ?"

"I'm not an expert on the subject," she said with irritation. "I've only done it the once."

"But we can touch each other. That's . . . It doesn't make sense."

"I don't understand how it happened. When you put your hand on me, the first time, down by the water . . . I felt it. That's all I know." She shrugged. "I'm amazed you can even see me. No one else does, I don't think."

"You were worried about Broillard seeing you. The other day on the beach."

"That's how I react to him. I don't go, 'Oh, he can't see me.' I just react."

The wind poured through the trees, drowning out every other sound, and Shellane turned up the collar of his jacket. He found himself considering Grace's edges, hoping to determine if they wavered or flickered or displayed any other sign of the uncanny. Which they did not.

And yet there was something about her. That luminous quality he had first observed down by the water. With the gray sky above and trouble in the air, she should have looked pale and drawn; but she still had that glow, that eerie vitality, and he thought now this must be a symptom of her unnatural state. The desolation he'd felt beside the grave returned. He had an impulse to hurry back to the car, but his feet were rooted.

"Avery told me," he said. "I had a talk with him about the way he treated you, and he told me."

"You must have frightened him. For all his bullying, Avery's a very frightened man."

"I was tempted to kill the son-of-a-bitch."

She let out a dismayed sigh. "I wanted you to. That's why I told you that stuff about him. For a long time, getting back at him was all I thought about."

Some ducks that had been floating by the margin of the shore flapped up from their rest and beat against the wind toward the far end of the lake. Grace watched them go. "I'm sorry," she said. "I hated him so much."

"And now you don't?"

"No, I still hate him. But it doesn't seem as important."

She held out her hand and he drew back, both a fearful rejection and one of embittered practicality. If she was a ghost—and what else could she be?—he was not relating to her as such, but rather as he might to a woman with a problem he did not want to get involved in. Like a girlfriend with a drug habit. Fear nibbled at the edges of his awareness, an old Catholic reflex serving to remind him that she was an abomination, a foulness, a scrap of metaphysics. But he could not turn away.

"Why'd you think I'd kill Avery?" he asked.

"I knew things about you from the first moment. It was so weird. I knew who you were. Not your name or anything, but I had a sense of your character. I could tell you'd done violent things."

"My name's Roy Shellane."

She repeated it. "I didn't think you looked like a Michael."

The wind came again, and she hugged herself.

"I feel alive," she said wonderingly. "Ever since you got here, it's like I'm back in the world. I've never felt so alive."

He studied her face, trying to discern some taint of death, and she asked what was wrong.

"I keep expecting things to be different now I know," he said. "That you'll turn sideways and vanish. Something like that."

"Maybe I will."

"And I keep thinking I'm going to be afraid."

"Are you?"

"Just that you'll vanish," he said. "And I guess it frightens me that I'm not more afraid."

The way she was looking at him, he knew she wanted him to reassure her. With only the slightest hesitancy, he stepped forward, half-expecting his arms to pass through her, but she nestled against him, warm and vivid in her reality. He felt a stirring in his groin, the beginnings of arousal, and this caused him to question himself again, to speculate about what he had become.

"Roy," she said, as if the name were a comfort.

He rested his chin on the top of her head and gazed out over the lake, at the heavy chop, the foot-high waves trundling toward shore, and felt a sudden brilliant carelessness regarding all his old compulsions.

"I know you can't stay," she said. "But a little while . . . maybe that would be all right."

During the days that followed, it occurred to Shellane that theirs was a pure romance, free of biological imperatives, divorced from all natural considerations, and yet it seemed natural in all its particulars. They made love, they slept, they talked, they were at peace. Even knowing their time together would be brief, that was not so different from the sadness of more conventional lovers whose term of intimacy had been prescribed. Yet Grace's abrupt departures continued to trouble him. For one thing, he was never certain she would return, and for another, he could not think where she went or into what condition she might have been reduced. If he asked, he believed she would tell him—if she herself knew—but he was afraid to hear the answer, imagining some horrid dissolution. Sometimes when he left her sleeping and was busy at his laptop or puttering in the kitchen, he would have the feeling that in his absence she ceased to exist and sprang back into being whenever he peeked in at her. But these were minor discords in the music of those days. The most difficult thing for Shellane was an increasingly acute feeling that his ability to interact with her hinted at either madness or the imminence of some black onrushing fate. The similarity of his youthful behavior to that of Broillard seemed to tilt the scales of possibility toward the latter, to hint at a karmic synchronicity. Yet he was not prepared to give her up. Whenever he considered leaving, this thought would be pushed aside by more immediate concerns, and though he realized he would soon have to leave, he was unable to confront the fact.

Two days after he had learned the truth about her, while she lay sleeping, Broillard knocked at the door. He was in bad shape. Bloodshot eyes; disheveled; coked up, his sinuses mapped by hectic blotches. Like a vampire beginning to decompose in the strong sun. He wiped his nose and twitched, yet attempted to present a manly appearance by speaking in a stern voice and holding his shoulders square.

"You'n me need to work shit out," he said.

"Not a good time," Shellane told him. "I'm occupied."

"Yeah? Me, too. I'm occupied in figuring out why I shouldn't call the cops on your ass."

"Perhaps what stays your hand is the thought that you don't want them sniffing around your place, looking for drugs."

"You think I won't go to the cops? I'll call 'em right now."

"I'll wait inside, shall I? We'll have a chat when they get here."

Shellane started to close the door, but Broillard shouldered it open. Abandoning the tactics of machismo, he said with unvarnished desperation, "C'mon! I need to talk to you!"

"It'll have to be another time."

"If you're fucking with me, that's cool. I don't care. I just wanna know!"

"I'm not fucking with you," said Shellane. "Grace is with me now."

Broillard stood on tiptoes, trying to see past Shellane into the cabin. "Where is she?"

Shellane flirted with the notion that this might all be a hustle involving a fake grave and a pretend ghost, a variation on the Hooker with an Outraged Husband. "Seems I'm the only one who can see her," he said.

"Oh, sure . . . yeah." Confidence soaring on chemical wings, Broillard made as though to push inside, but Shellane elbowed him back.

"You're more than a little thick, Avery. Where else do you think I learned the sordid facts of your life?"

"She mighta called you . . . or written you a letter. Like maybe you're a relative or something."

"Of course she did. 'Dear Uncle, the other night Avery sent me to the outlet store to buy him a pair of cashmere socks. He prefers to masturbate in cashmere. We haven't made love in four months—he says I'm too fat. But he's gone through dozens of socks.' Exactly the sort of thing she'd disclose to a relative."

Broillard gaped at him.

"We're all sad animals." Shellane gave him a gentler shove, moving him back from the door. "Some of us manage to rise above the state."

"You think she's such a saint? Maybe it *was* me fucked her up, but she wasn't never a saint, man. She wanted something, she'd do whatever she needed to get it." Broillard bunched his fists. "This is my fucking property, and I got a right to inspect it. I'm coming in."

Shellane was about to repeat his original response, but then, thinking that Broillard might become a problem, he said, "All right. But you won't be able to see her."

Once inside, Broillard stood in the center of the room, turning his head this way and that. "Is she here?" He fixed Shellane with a terrified look. "Where is she?"

Shellane pointed to the refrigerator, and Broillard stared at it. "Grace?" he said; then, to Shellane: "What's she doing?"

"Watching. She doesn't appear to be overjoyed at your presence."

Doubt and fear contended for control of Broillard's expression. He sat heavily in a straight-backed chair beside the table. "Can she hear me?"

Shellane sat opposite him, facing away from the refrigerator. "Give it a try."

Broillard made an effort to compose his face. "Grace," he said. "I'm so sorry, baby. I was . . ."

"She doesn't like you calling her 'baby,'" Shellane said. "She never liked it."

Broillard nodded, swallowed hard. "I didn't want to hurt you, ba . . . Grace. It's like I was watching someone else do the things I did. I don't know what the fuck was going on." His voice cracked and he covered his eyes with his right hand. "I'm so sorry!"

Shellane glanced at the refrigerator. Grace was standing next to it, wearing only panties. Tears cut down her cheeks. A cold pressure pushed upward from the base of Shellane's spine and he had the feeling that something very bad was about to happen.

Broillard's tone was urgent. "What's she doing?"

"Crying," Shellane said.

"Aw, Christ . . . Grace! I know I can't make things right. But I'm . . ." Broillard fumbled in his trouser pocket, pulled forth several folded sheets of notebook paper. "I wrote something. About you . . . about everything. You want to hear it?"

He looked to Shellane for guidance, and Shellane shrugged, as if communicating Grace's indifference.

"I don't know how to talk to you, Grace," Broillard said in a plaintive voice. "This is the only way I got."

Her face empty, Grace had come halfway across the room and was standing to his left as he addressed himself to the refrigerator, reading from the sheets of paper, singing the words in a muted but obviously practiced delivery intended to convey anguish:

"Never thought it could happen,
never saw the storm comin',
never once had a clue about
how much you were sufferin' . . .
It all was so damn easy,
I took love for nothin',
What I thought was us livin'
was the heart of your dyin',
and now all I remember is
Grace Under Pressure . . ."

As he reached the chorus, Broillard built his reading to the level of a performance, half-shouting the words. Shellane could not decide whether his loathing was colored by pity, or if what he felt was embarrassment at seeing another man act with such unabashed stupidity and arrogance.

> "... forever and ever,
> Grace Under Pressure...
> It's all I can think of,
> the way you just sat there,
> with everything broken...
> Grace Under Pressure...
> Grace Under Pressure...
> Grace Under Pressure..."

He began a second verse, and Grace stepped behind him, gazing at the back of his head with dispassion.

> "Aw, I wish I could breathe you
> straight through until mornin',
> where a white dream arises
> from the bright flash of being..."

Grace trailed her fingers across his neck, and Broillard broke off, stared at Shellane. "What just happened? She do something to me?"

"Did you feel something?"

"What'd she do? I got all cold and shit."

Grace appeared to have lost interest in Broillard. She was weeping again, her shoulders hunched and shaking, and Shellane recalled how she had acted the afternoon when he had come to her house. Silent; tearful; unmindful of him. He wondered why her fingers never left him cold. "She touched you," he said.

Broillard scraped back his chair and stood, hands braced on the table. He seemed poised to run, but unable to take the first step. His eyes were bugged, and he breathed through his mouth.

"I don't think she liked your song," said Shellane mildly.

"Is she close? Where the fuck is she?"

"I wouldn't move if I were you," said Shellane, though Grace had wandered back toward the refrigerator. "You'll bump into her."

He took Broillard by the elbow. "Let's go." He opened the door to the porch, admitting a glare of the lowering sun, and guided him through it. "You wouldn't want to piss her off. She gets pissed off, she does all that *Exorcist* shit."

Broillard shook free of Shellane's grasp. "You're fucking with me, man. You got my imagination playing tricks, but I know you're fucking with me. I'm calling the cops."

He started for the outer door, but stopped dead. The door stood open, and framed there, barely visible against the light, a glowing silhouette had materialized. It was as if an invisible presence were drawing the light in order to shape a rippling golden figure with the swelling hips and breasts of a woman, limned by a paler corona that crumbled and reformed like superheated plasma. The figure was so faint, it seemed a trick of the light, similar to an eddy on the surface of a pond that briefly resembles a face. But it brightened, acquiring the wavering substantiality of a mirage, and Shellane saw that the light within the outline was flowing outward in all directions, a brisk tide radiating from some central source.

Broillard made a squeaky noise in his throat.

"Grace?" Shellane said.

With a womanly shriek, Broillard sprang for the door and burst through the figure, briefly absorbed by its golden surface. He went sprawling over the bottom step, rolled up to his knees, and ran. The figure, its brightness diminishing, billowed like a curtain belling in a breeze, then winked out.

Shaken, unable to relate this apparition to what he knew of Grace, Shellane went back inside. The sheets of paper on which Broillard had scribbled his song lay on the floor. He picked them up and stood at the table, unable to think or even to choose a direction for thought. Finally he crossed to the bedroom door and opened it. Grace was still asleep, lying on her side, one pale shoulder exposed. He touched her hip and was so relieved by her solidity, he felt light-headed and sat down on the edge of the bed. She turned to face him, reached out with her eyes closed, groping until her fingers brushed his thigh.

"Grace?"

"I'm here," she said muzzily.

"Avery's gone."

"Avery?"

"Don't you remember? He was here . . . a minute ago."

"I'm glad you didn't wake me." She stretched, twisted onto her back, and looked up at him. "What did he want?"

"He wrote you a song."

"Oh, God!"

"It really sucked." Shellane crumpled the pages in his hand. "You don't remember him being here?"

"I was asleep." Her brow furrowed. "What's the matter?"

He told her how she'd acted with Avery, how she acted the afternoon he had come inside her house—another occasion she did not recall—and about the apparition. She listened without speaking, sitting with her knees drawn up, and when he had done she rested her head on her knees, so he could not see her face, and asked him if he loved her; then, before he could answer, she said, "I realize that's a difficult question, since it's not altogether clear what I am."

"It's not a difficult question," he said.

"Then why don't you answer it?"

"Every minute I stay here, I know I'm in danger. You probably don't understand that . . ."

"I do!"

"Not all of it, you don't. The fact remains I'm in danger and yet I feel at home. Easy with this place and with you. That frightens me. You frighten me. What you might mean frightens me."

Her injured expression hardened, but she continued to look at him.

"There's an old Catholic taint in me wants to deny it," he said. "It's telling me this is unnatural. Against God. But I love you. I just don't know what's to come of it."

She said nothing, fingering an imperfection in the blanket.

"And you?" he asked.

She shrugged, as if it were trivial. "Of course. But I wonder if I'd love you if you weren't my only option."

His face tightened as he parsed meaning from the words.

"See how we hurt each other," she said. "We must be in love."

The light dimmed, clouds moving in from the south to shadow the lake. They started to speak at the same time. Shellane gestured for her to go on, but she said, "No . . . you."

"Where do you go when you leave?" he asked. "What happens to you?"

"Limbo," she said.

The word had the sound of a stone dropped into a puddle. "That's where unshriven infants go after they die . . . right?"

"'Unshriven.'" She laughed palely. "You're way too Catholic, Roy. Limbo's just what I call it. I don't know what it is." She touched the place on his palm where he had picked up the splinter. "You were there. You saw it."

"I did?"

"The black house. The one you asked me about."

He took this in. "You're saying the afterlife's a house on the lake?"

"Not on the lake. You could walk around the entire lake, you wouldn't find it."

"I found it," he said.

"You weren't walking anywhere near the lake."

All the half-formed suspicions he'd entertained regarding his fate seemed to mist up inside his head, merging into a dark shape. "Then where was I?"

"I'll tell you what I know . . . if you want." She slid down in the bed, curled up in the way of a child getting cozy. "It was night when I died. Avery was off playing somewhere, and I wasn't feeling well. My chest hurt . . . but I had an ache in my chest all the time, so I didn't think it was anything. I went outside to get some air and I was walking along the shore when I had a feeling of weakness. It came on so suddenly! I could tell something was really wrong, and I tried to call for help, but I was too weak. I thought I'd fainted because the next I knew I was sitting up and a fog had gathered. I wasn't in pain anymore, but I felt . . . odd. Disoriented. I kept walking and before long I came to the house. I was terrified, but there was nowhere else to go, so I went inside."

"What it's like in the house?" Shellane asked.

"When I'm there I feel kind of how I did with Avery. Dejected. Faded.

I'm always getting lost. The people there . . . Nobody talks much to anyone. Maybe I'm projecting, but I get the idea everyone's like me. They're people who gave up and now they're just moping about. There are some others, though. Tall . . . and really ugly. That's what I call them. The uglies. I don't think they're human. There aren't very many of them. Maybe twenty. They chase after us—it seems like it's a game for them. They can't kill us, of course. But they hurt us . . . and they use us. Men, women. It doesn't matter."

"They use you sexually?" he asked.

A nod. "They act like animals. They're strong, but incredibly stupid. But they know how to move around in the house without getting lost."

Shellane recalled the naked man who had pursued him in the woods. "You ever see them around the lake?"

"The uglies? Sometimes they follow me out, but they won't go far from the house. They only follow a little ways."

"Why's it so difficult to get around inside the house?"

"It's not difficult, it's just you never know where the doors will take you. The house changes. You go through a door and it kind of sucks you in. Like . . . *whoosh!*, and you're somewhere else. But you can't retrace your steps. If you go back through the same door, you won't wind up in the room you left. I try to figure it out, but it seems I never have enough energy. Or I'm too busy hiding from the uglies."

"But you return here," he said. "You learned how to do that."

"That's different. It's not like I understand what I'm doing. I get a strong feeling that I have to leave, so I head for the nearest door, and when I step through I'm back at the lake. I think it's the same for the others. At least I've been in rooms when people suddenly space out. They get a blank expression and then they take off."

She tugged at him, drew him down beside her. He lay on his back, studying the water stains on the ceiling, appearing to map a rippled white country with a sketchily rendered brownish-orange coastline. His arm went about her, but his thoughts were elsewhere.

"What are you doing?" she asked.

"Thinking about the house?"

"It doesn't do any good."

"Maybe not."

"But you're going to do it anyway?"

"I'm good with problems. It's what I did for a living."

"I thought you were a thief."

"I wasn't a snatch-and-grab artist. I stole things that were hard to steal."

A gust of wind shuddered the bedroom window, and coming out of nowhere, a hard rain slanted against the panes.

"When you pass through the doors," he said, "you say it feels as if you're being sucked in. Does anything else happen?"

"I get lights in my eyes. Like the sort that come when you're hit in the head. And right after that, I'll get a glimpse of other places. Just a flash. I can't always tell what it is I'm seeing, but they don't seem part of the house."

"What makes you think the ugly ones know how to get around in the house?"

"Because whenever they take me with them, we always go the same places. They don't display any uncertainty. They know exactly where they're headed."

"Do they do anything to the doors before opening them? Do they touch anything . . . maybe turn something, push something?"

She closed her eyes. "When I'm with them, I'm afraid. I don't notice much."

"You said there are about twenty of them?"

"Uh-huh."

"What about the rest of you . . . How many?"

"The house is so big, it's impossible to tell. A lot, though. I hardly ever see anyone I've seen before."

"It doesn't look all that big."

"When you're standing outside," she said, "you don't really get the picture."

Shellane worried the problem, turning it this way and that, not trying to reach a conclusion, just familiarizing himself with it, as if he were getting accustomed to the weight and balance of a stone he was about to throw. He heard a rustling, saw that Grace had picked up the sheets of paper on which Broillard had scrawled his lyrics and was reading them.

"God, this is . . ." She made a disparaging sound. "Delusional."

"He's better when he writes about feelings he doesn't have," said Shellane. "Grandiose, beautiful feelings. He's got no talent for honesty."

"Not many do," said Grace.

When she left that afternoon, he did not follow her, though he intended to follow her soon. That was the one path available to him if he was to help her, and helping her was all he wanted now. He sat at his computer and accessed treatises on the afterlife written from a variety of religious perspectives. He made notes and organized them into thematic sections. Then he wrote lists, the way he did before every score he'd ever planned. Not coherent lists, merely a random assortment of things he knew about the situation. Avenues worth exploring. Under the word "Grace" he wrote:

—becomes a real woman in my company
—can taste things, drink, but doesn't eat
—lapses into ghostly state around others (once with me alone)
—endures a state of half-life at the house
—feels that there is something she's supposed to do
—"knows" I can help her

He tapped the pen against the table, then added:

—is she telling me everything?
—if not, why?
—Duplicity? Fear? Something else?

It was not that he sensed duplicity in her, but her situation was of a kind that bred duplicity. Just like a convict, wouldn't she be looking to play any angle in order to improve her lot? And wouldn't that breed other forms of duplicity? It was not inconceivable that she might love him and at the same time be playing him.

Under the word "House" he wrote:

>   —In my Father's house, many mansions . . .
>   —Philosophical speculations—particularized form of afterlife? For people who've given up. Who, failing to overcome problems, surrender to death. (Look up Limbo in Catholic dictionary)
>   —The uglies (men?). Demons. Instruments of God's justice. Forget Christianity. What if the afterlife is an anarchy? Lots of feudal groups controlled by a variety of beings who can cross back and forth between planes of existence.

Science fiction, he thought; but then so was Jesus.

>   —A maze. Hallucination?
>   —Mutable reality?
>   —The doors. Core of the problem? Can they be manipulated?

He made several more notations under "House," then began a new list under the heading "Me."

>   —Have passed over into the afterlife once, maybe, twice if dream can be counted. Why?

He circled the word "Why"—it was an omnibus question. Why had he turned off the highway toward the lake? A whim? Had he been led? Was some ineffable force at work? Why had he, after years of caution, been moved to such drastic incaution? He wrote the word "Love" and then crossed it out. Love was the bait that had lured him, but he believed the hook was something else again.

The lists were skimpy. His preliminary lists for taking down a shopping mall bank had been far more substantial. This would be, he thought, very much like the job in upstate New York, the house with the subterranean maze. He'd have to case the place while attempting to survive it . . . if survival was possible. And maybe that was the answer to all the "Whys?". He could feel his body preparing for danger, cooking up a fresh batch of adrenaline, putting an edge on his senses. It was the kick he'd always been a chump for, the thrill that writing songs could not provide, the seasoning he needed to become involved in the moment. He had caught the scent of danger, followed the scent to the lake, and there had taken it in his arms. Like Grace, for the first time in a very long while, he felt alive.

After waking, Grace liked to have a shower. It was not a cleanliness thing—at least so Shellane thought—as much as a retreat. He assumed that she must have taken a lot of showers when she was in the world, hiding from Broillard behind the spray, deriving comfort from her warm solitude. Shellane usually let her shower alone, but the next afternoon, he joined her and they made love with soapy abandon, her heels hooked behind his thighs, back pressed up against the thin metal wall, whose surface dimpled and popped when he thrust her against it. As they clung together afterward, he watched rivulets of water running over her shoulderblades toward the pale voluptuous curves of her ass, gleaming with a film of soap, dappled with bubbles. He saw nothing unusual to begin with—he wasn't looking for anything. But then he realized that the streams of water were not flowing true, they were curving away from the small of her back, as if repelled by a force emanating from that spot. Curving away and then scattering into separate drops, and the drops skittering off around the swells of her hips. Fear brushed his mind with a feathery touch, a lover's touch. Instead of recoiling, however, he moved his hand to cover the place that the water avoided, pressing his fingertips against the skin, and imagined that he felt a deep, slow pulse. This was the thing he most wanted, he thought. The seat of what he loved.

"I'm drowning," Grace said, and pushed him away. "There was a waterfall coming off your shoulder. I couldn't breathe."

Her smile lost wattage, and he knew she must have understood the irony of her complaint. He cleared wet strands of hair from her face and kissed her forehead.

"This must be so awful for you," she said. "To feel comfortable with someone. Almost like normal. And to know it's anything but." Soapy water trickled into her left eye and she rubbed it. "It does feel like that sometimes, doesn't it?"

"Normal? Yeah, more-or-less."

She seemed disappointed by his response.

He put his hands on her waist. "All the craziness that goes on between men and women, 'normal' isn't the word I'd use to describe any relationship."

She slid past him out of the shower and began to dry herself. He had the feeling that she was upset.

"You okay?" he asked.

"I'm cold," she said in a clipped tone, and briskly toweled her hair. Then, her voice muffled: "Are you always so analytical?"

"I try to be. Does it bother you?"

She left off drying and held the towel bunched in front of her breasts. "God knows it shouldn't. I do understand how hard this . . ." She broke off and started drying her hair again, less vigorously.

Shellane turned off the water, stepped out of the shower. The linoleum was sticky beneath his feet; his skin pebbled in the cool air. The back of his neck tingled, and he had the feeling they were not alone, that an invisible presence was crammed into the bathroom with them.

"It's almost over, you know," Grace said. "One of these times soon, I won't come back. Or else you'll leave."

"We've got a while yet."

"You don't know that. You don't know anything about what's happening."

A noise came from the front of the house—a door closing. He threw open the bathroom door and peered out. Nobody in sight.

"Who is it?" asked Grace from behind him.

"Maybe the wind."

He wrapped a towel about his waist and went out into the living room. On the table next to his laptop was an envelope and a portable cassette recorder. The envelope was addressed to Grace. She came up beside him, wearing his bathrobe, and he offered the letter to her. She shook her head. He tore open the envelope and read from the enclosed sheet of paper.

"Once again Avery offers his apologies," he said. "He regrets everything." He read further. "He claims he wouldn't have treated you so badly if you weren't unfaithful."

"He never changes!" Grace folded her arms and scowled at the letter as if it were a live thing and could register disapproval. "He was unfaithful to me every day . . . with footwear! And then when I . . ." She made a spiteful sound. "We hardly ever made love after we got married. I was just so desperate . . ."

"You don't have to explain," he said.

"It's habit. I used to have to explain it to Avery all the time. He liked hearing me explain it."

Shellane set the letter on the table and pressed the play button on the recorder. Avery's voice, tinny and diminished, issued forth over a strummed guitar:

> "Beauty, where do you sleep tonight?
> In whose avid arms, do you conspire . . . ?"

"Our boy's waxing Keatsian," said Shellane.
"Turn it off."

> ". . . beauty is everywhere they say,
> but I just can't find a beauty like thine . . ."

"Please!" said Grace.

Shellane switched off the recorder. "Sure sounds like he loves you."

"I believe he did once. But you can't tell with Avery. He's adept at mimicry."

They stood without speaking for a time, then Grace pressed herself against him. "I shouldn't have pulled you into this," she said.

He wanted to reassure her, to tell her that he would not have foregone the experience of being with her. But though he believed this to be true, he no longer was certain of it. That he could accept her to the point that he could dismiss, even dote upon, the symptoms of her strangeness—this fact had, almost without his notice, so shredded the fabric of his emotions, it had grown difficult for him to separate hope from desire.

After she had gone into the bedroom, to become whatever she became without him, he dressed and sat at the table, studying his lists. They revealed no pattern, no truth other than the nonsensical and menacing truth that he was in love with a dead woman. In love, also, with her deathly condition, with her odd glow and the curious behavior of water on her skin. It was a splendid absurdity worthy of an Irish ballad. The trouble with such tunes, though, they tended to neglect the ordinary heart of things, things such as the commonplace mutuality that had developed between them, and that was the matter truly worth commemorating in song. Nobody sat around scratching their ass or discussing the character of an ex-husband in an Irish ballad. They were all grand sadness and exquisite pain. Of course, sadness and pain were likely headed his way, and he had little doubt they would be grand and exquisite. As if anticipation were itself an affliction, his thoughts spun out of control, images and fragments of emotions whirling up and away, prelude to a despair so profound it left him hunched over the table, eyes fixed on the lists, like a troll turned to stone by an enchantment he had been tricked into reading.

The last of the gray light blended with the mist forming above the lake. Shellane stirred himself, went to the stove and heated a can of soup. He leaned against the counter, watching steam rise from the saucepan, remembering an interview he'd seen with a man who had directed a horror movie—the man said his film was optimistic because, though its view of the afterlife was gruesome, that it lent any credence whatsoever to the afterlife was hopeful. Shellane supposed this would be a healthy attitude for him to adopt. But the prospect was so completely daft . . . It had been a long while since his Catholic schooldays, and the concepts associated with religion—virgin birth, the Assumption, the hierarchies of angels, and so forth—had lost their hold on him. Now he was being forced to confront a concept even less logical, one concerning which his knowledge was so fragmentary, any conjecture he made about it had the feeling of wild speculation.

Once his soup was hot, he went on the Internet, accessed a Roman Catholic dictionary, and looked up Limbo. According to doctrine, Limbo referred to a place in which unbaptized children, souls born before the advent of Christ, and prudent virgins awaited the Second Coming, at which point they would be assumed into Heaven. Grace did not appear to fit any of these categories; thus it followed that the Church was a bit off-base in its comprehension of the afterlife. No surprise there. Yet the idea of a halfway house, an interim place where souls were parked for the duration, for some term pertinent to their lives—this accorded with what Grace had told him. The black house, however, seemed to incorporate an element of punishment, to be less a limbo than a state of purgatory. A kind of boutique hell targeting a select clientele? "Fuck," he said, switching off the laptop, and stared at his uneaten soup.

Grace, fully dressed, came out of the bedroom. "I have to go," she said absently as she crossed the room. He watched her leave, sat a moment longer, then once again said, "Fuck," heaved up to his feet, grabbed his jacket off the peg beside the porch door, and followed.

He moved cautiously through the fog, listening, peering ahead, and thus he noticed the point at which he crossed over from the lakeshore into whatever plane it was that Grace had made her home. The wind suddenly died, the sounds of the spruce boughs swaying were sheared away, and his anxiety spiked. Despite the cold, a drop of sweat trickled down his back; he felt a pulse in his neck. Each step he took seemed the step of a condemned criminal walking toward the death chamber. Legs weak, mind bright with fear. When he came in sight of the black house, its gabled second story lifting from the murk, he did not think he could go on. Even without the motive force of the wind, the fog boiled around him, as if alive, and the notion that it might be a form of ectoplasmic life, tendrils and feelers plucking at his clothes, trailing across his skin, wanting to touch him . . . that got him moving again.

He paused at the door. The knob was of black iron and had the shape of an open hand. He would have to give it a shake in order to enter, and the dire symbolism inherent in this made him less eager to proceed. He had a memory of himself as an altar boy, kneeling, striking the bell as the priest intoned the litany, gazing up at the great gold cross mounted against crimson drapes, participating in the medieval magic of the mass. Whatever he had believed then, he wished he could believe it now. He wished he could take the power that had inspired his awe, all that glorious myth and promise, into his shaking heart. But if the house proved anything, it was that God was far more perverse than the Church had ever dreamed. He imagined the fingers of the fog traipsing across the back of his neck, and the fingers of the iron hand seemed to press into his wrist, trying to feel the hits of his heart. Before further doubts could assail him, he clasped it firmly and gave it a turn.

White lights stabbed into his eyes. It was precisely as Grace had described—like the actinic flashes caused by a blow to the head. And then he was drawn deep inside the house, hurtling forward as if on a walkway that was moving much too fast for safety's sake. For an instant he thought he had been transported to the ground floor of a parking garage. A dark, musty space with a strip of brilliant light to his left. Then either his vision steadied or the house settled on a form, and he realized that he was facing a row of large round holes—perhaps forty or fifty in sum—piercing a wall of black boards, yellow radiance spilling from them. He strained his ears, listening for signs of life. Hearing none, he came closer. The holes were of equal dimension, six feet wide and high, each opening onto a small cell, unfurnished except for a bowl set in the floor. These bowls were the radiant source, light spraying up from them. The first cell he came to held no prisoner and was littered with dried wastes. Shreds of a slick transparent membrane adhered to the edges of the hole. As far as he could tell, the membrane had not been affixed to the wall, but had been extruded from it, as though it were, like the great fist outside, a natural production of the wood. The second hole was also empty, the membrane shredded. Shellane reached in to learn if the bowl could be lifted out and used to light his way. The radiance burned him, provoking a prickly, crawly sensation like that deriving from an inflamed rash. In the third cell sat a figure that appeared to be made of dull, tarnished gold. It had the bulbous shape and pudgy face of an infant, but was the size of a man. Swaddled head to foot in a golden robe that seemed of a piece with its flesh and left only the face exposed beneath a tightly fitted cowl. Its features had an Asiatic cast, and Shellane recalled photographs of Chinese babies clothed in similar fashion. He was so certain it was a statue, when the creature twitched its head toward him, mouth open in what appeared to be a full-throated scream (though he heard nothing), he fell back a step. He punched at the membrane, which was stretched tight across the entrance to the cell. The blow had no effect; the shreds hanging from the entrances of the first two cells were flimsy, the surface of the intact membrane was hard and rubbery. The huge baby lowered its head and, with a chubby hand that emerged from the sleeve of its robe, pawed in apparent agony at its face and gave another silent scream.

Five more cells were occupied, three by normal men, all naked. The other prisoners were two extremely tall men, also naked, with grayish skin and deformed faces, similar in every regard to the man who had chased Shellane along the margin of the lake . . . except that their deformities were not as severe as his had been. Sunken eyes; their mouths gashes with thin, ragged lips; flat noses, elongated skulls; ruffs of flesh at the back of their necks. This last caused Shellane to realize that his pursuer had not been wearing a mask and to speculate that, due to his fear, he must have exaggerated the man's deformities. The chests of the two gray-skinned men displayed a peculiar articulation, as if they had too many bones. Their genital areas were hairless and their eyes so deeply recessed, shadowed by prominent ridges, they gave back not a glimmer of light. On seeing him, they reacted in fright, scrambling back against the rears of their cells and gaping. One of the ordinary-seeming men—scrawny, with a careworn face and stringy gray hair—was initially disinterested in him, but after Shellane had been standing in front of his cell for a minute or so, he pushed himself up against the membrane, pleading with his eyes, mouthing words that Shellane could not understand.

Beyond the cells lay a door taller and wider than the first; the doorknob was a clenched fist of black iron. Shellane was still afraid, but he was operating efficiently now. Fear had become a resource, an energy he could tap into, a means of refining judgment—he did not necessarily heed its promptings, but remained aware of them. He inspected the frame and the wall beside it for projections, a declivity that might conceal a control, a switch. At about eye level he found a patch of wormy ridges in the surface of the boards, like a cross between circuitry and varicose veins. He tried pushing at them and felt some give; he pushed harder but achieved no result. At length he opened the door and was swept forward into a space full of shattering light. Like hundreds of flashbulbs being set off. For a second, he seemed to be in a place that was all bright movement and crystalline geometry, and then he found himself on a balcony guarded by a sway-backed railing, overlooking a confusing perspective of other balconies and windows and doors and stairways, above and below and beyond, every structure fashioned of black wood. The scene was confusing partly because of the lack of variation in color, and partly because the architecture had such a uniform character, an Escher-esque repetitiveness of form. It reminded him, in sum, of old wooden tenements in New Orleans with their courtyards and step-through windows and rickety stairs. These structures, with their sagging balconies and cockeyed doors and unevenly set windows, had the same louche aura and arthritic crookedness, the same apparent degree of age and disrepair. But unlike New Orleans, there were no planter boxes, no music, no bright curtains, no brightness of any kind apart from the white glare in which everything was bathed. Instead of a sky, the space was roofed with boards and massive beams, but it was unclear if what he saw was a single enormous building or many separate ones. About a dozen people were in sight and, whether on balconies, in the various rooms, or passing along the street of boards below, they went slowly, hesitantly, their movements suggesting that they were on medication. He wasn't close enough to see their faces, but they appeared to be of ordinary human dimension.

A stairway led down from the balcony on which he stood, and he descended it, passing empty rooms, crossing other balconies. Three floors down, he encountered a pretty black-haired woman leaning against a railing. Her pale blue eyes flicked toward him—they matched the background color of her flowered summer dress. Though she was young, no more than eighteen or nineteen, a consequential term of disappointment was clearly written in her kittenish face.

"I'm looking for a woman named Grace Broillard," he said.

"Good luck."

"You know her? Red hair, green eyes. About thirty."

She refitted her gaze to the crooked black distance. "Goodbye."

He was silent a moment. "I need some help, okay?"

"Help? That's a concept I'm not familiar with."

He rested a hand on the railing next to hers. "What's wrong with you? I'm not asking you to do anything except answer . . ."

"I don't want to talk," she said. "I don't want to share your pain. I don't want to hear about your pitiful life. I've . . ."

"I'd like to ask you some questions, that's all."

"I've got my own pitiful life to think about. So fuck off."

He put a hand on her arm, and she looked up angrily; but anger faded, replaced by shock.

"Shit, man!" She placed a hand on his chest as though to feel his heartbeat.

"What?" he asked. "What is it?"

"You're alive." This was voiced in an astonished tone, reminding him of how Grace had behaved toward him on the beach that first day.

"You didn't notice?" he asked after a pause.

"Un-uh." She touched his hair. "You're going to be very popular here . . . as long as you stay alive."

"Why's that?

"Because of how you make me feel. I'm assuming the effect isn't specific to me." She smiled. "It's okay if it is."

"What did you see just now that made you aware I was alive?"

"I don't know. I didn't notice, I guess. Life's not something you expect to find here."

Shellane thought about the gray-haired man in the cell. He had ascribed his delayed reaction to his presence to the fact of his being in pain; but that might not be the case. He had stopped only briefly in front of the other occupied cells.

"Maybe you can help me," she said. "And maybe I can help you find your friend. I bet the jerks have got her."

"The jerks?"

"Do you even know where you are? The freaks, the creeps. The tall, geeky fucks." She disengaged from him and retreated along the railing. "If you can't find her, she's probably with them."

"I don't follow," he said. "She could be anywhere. Why would you think she's with them?"

"That's how it works here. If you know someone from outside the house, you never stray far from them inside it. So if you can't find her, she's probably with the jerks." She went back to staring out at the black tenements. "You're not going to help me, are you?"

Her shift in mood had the same abruptness as Grace's withdrawals, the same switched-off quality, and he wondered if this was a condition of the place or if the people who gravitated here were all prone to similar behavior.

"I don't know if I can help," he said. "But I need to find this woman before . . ."

"Yeah, I know. Grace. The love of your life or some shit. Gotta find her." She walked off several paces. "Keep going through the doors. You'll hook up eventually."

"You want to come with me?" he asked. "I don't know what's going to happen, but if you want to come . . ."

He eased up behind her, trying to see her face. She was weeping and appeared no longer to recognize that he was there.

Shellane abandoned the stairs, passing through a number of rooms in rapid succession. One contained several items of furniture, notably a dusty standing mirror in which he glimpsed a haggard, rumpled version of himself, and in three of them he found a single person, two women and a man. They treated him much as had the black-haired woman. They did not recognize immediately that he was alive and, once they did, they answered a few questions, asked for his help, then lost interest. Based on their reactions and what they told him, he constructed a hypothesis.

Religious perspectives on the afterlife were, of course, inaccurate; but it might be that none of them were completely inaccurate. Perhaps the afterlife consisted of many planes, and these planes—or rather a misapprehension of their nature—had given rise to the various religions. Might it not be possible, then, that one such plane had been appropriated by a sub-order of creatures whose power was slight, and who were capable of capturing a certain type of enfeebled soul? Perhaps they were themselves enfeebled—creatures perceived as terrifying by the earthbound, but to those who were familiar with them, those whose fear was colored with contempt, they were jerks, creeps, geeks. The uglies. Metaphysical lowlifes. It seemed a ludicrous proposition until he compared it to the ludicrous propositions of the major religions. The salient difference between those propositions and his own was that his was based to a degree on personal observation.

Beside each door were small patches of ridges in the wood similar to that he had found beside the second door he'd tried. He pushed at them in sequence, two at a time, all to no avail. But then he gave the knob of one door a quarter turn, not sufficient to disengage the lock, and the seams beside the door pulsed as if some charge or fluid were passing through them. He was elated to find that some orderly process was involved. There must be a sequence—many sequences—of constrictions that affected the doors, causing them to take you to different quarters of the house. Either he was not strong enough to manipulate the ridges or else there was some other factor involved that he did not understand.

The last door he tried delivered him into a tunnel with walls of black boards . . . though at first glance they had the irregular, roughened look of wood in a natural state, making it appear that he was walking along inside a huge hollow limb. Like the fist that protruded from the exterior of the house, the boards here were warped into shapes that simulated nature. Thin gaps between them glowed whitely, effecting a dim lighting. The other parts of the house he had investigated—despite the people he'd encountered—had seemed sterile. Lifeless. But here he caught a vibe of animal presence, and as he proceeded along the tunnel he smelled a fecal odor and observed signs of rough occupancy. Gashes and indentations in the wood; boards that had been pried loose. Evidences, he thought, of rage or frustration or some allied emotion. Or perhaps of a vandal's idiot frenzy. The tunnel wound downward at a steep angle for approximately forty feet, then straightened and narrowed to the point that he could touch both walls at once; after a stretch of about sixty feet it widened by half and, as he rounded a bend, he spotted Grace standing a few yards ahead, her back pressed against the wall. When he called out, she turned her head and stared at him with an aggrieved expression. Drawing near, he saw that she was imprisoned by bands of black wood that encircled her waist and neck, leaving her arms free.

"Roy!" She strained toward him, then slumped in her restraints. "Get away from here."

Shellane tugged at the bands. There was no visible lock, no catch. They looked to have grown around her.

"They'll be back soon." Grace tried to push him away. "You have to go!"

He studied the wall beside her.

"They'll kill you," Grace said.

"Be quiet," he told her. "I'm working."

"If they see you, they'll know. I won't be able to come to you anymore. Please!"

Next to one end of the band encircling her waist was a single raised seam, barely an inch long. Close by it, a board had been worked loose, leaving a half-inch aperture aglow with white radiance.

"You can't help. This is just going to make things worse for me," she said. "I want you to leave now!"

He unbuckled his belt, whipped it off, and pried with the buckle at the loose board.

"What're you doing?"

"Trying to understand this."

He managed to pry the board up sufficiently that he could grip it with the tips of his fingers. He pulled it back farther and put an eye close to the gap he had made. A flash of light, and he saw an unfamiliar night sky with too many stars and a glowing red cloud occupying its southern quadrant. Hovering at an unguessable distance between him and the cloud was a dark wormlike structure. He had the impression he was looking at something of immense size.

Another flash of light, then another, and another yet . . .

In the intervals between flashes, he was afforded glimpses of different vistas. Many he was unable to quantify, their geography too vast and bewildering to be comprehensible. Those that he was able to comprehend all possessed the quality of immensity. Great reaches containing strangely proportioned structures. By the time he pressed the board back into place, he thought he understood the house. A sketchy understanding, but the basic picture was clear. The doors were programmed (he could think of no better term) to admit you to different portions of the house; but before you settled into the room to which you had been directed, you saw the place through which you transited, or perhaps it was simply another place that you might have transited to. A place removed from or perhaps inclusive of the house. There was much he was unsure of, but he was sure of one thing—the doors could be reprogrammed.

Grace continued to warn him away, but he refused to listen. Wishing it were sharper, he pushed the tongue of the belt buckle against the seam beside her neck, denting it slightly. He pushed harder, lodging the point in the dent and jamming it down with both hands. The seam writhed and suddenly deflated; the bands holding her retracted without a sound, appearing to flow back into the boards behind her. She let out a gasp and staggered away from the wall.

"The doors," he said. "They can be adjusted . . . calibrated to take you away from the house. I'm not sure what this place is, but it embodies physical principles. Mechanical principles. Maybe . . ."

Grace planted both hands on his chest and sent him reeling backward. "You're not hearing me!"

"I'm telling you how to escape," he said.

She tried to shove him again, but he caught her hands.

"You're not hearing *me*," he said angrily. "I'm trying to help you. The uglies . . . they manipulate the house. And they're stupid, right? Everyone I've talked to says that. So if they can do it, the chances are you can manage it, too."

Grace twisted away from him. "You don't know! You've only been here a little while. No time at all. Most of us have been here for years."

"But you haven't tried, have you? All you've done is mope about. Why don't you take a moment and . . ."

"Do you want to die? That's what's going to happen."

"Just listen and I'll go."

"I heard what you told me, all right? I'll check the doors!"

"And watch the uglies," he said. "When you're with them, watch what they do with the doors."

She started to speak, but instead stared past him, looking at something over his shoulder with fierce concentration. There was no sign of fear in her face, though fear, Shellane understood upon turning, must be responsible for her intensity of focus.

Three of the uglies had come into view around a bend and were crouched as if in preparation for an attack, squeezed together by a narrowing of the walls. Two of them resembled the men imprisoned in the cells, but the third, the biggest, was identical to the man who had pursued Shellane through the woods. Severely deformed. Jagged orbits shadowing his eyes, a darkly crimson mouth visible behind a toothy jack o'lantern grimace. Shellane braced himself for a fight. Despite Grace's assertion that they were strong, they looked spindly and frail, and he believed he could do some damage. But rather than charging at him, they began to whimper like a chorus of terrified children, gaspy and quavering. The one on the right lifted its head to the ceiling, as if seeking divine assistance, and gave forth with a feeble ululation. Urine dribbled down its leg. The others hid their eyes, but continued to peek at him, as if not daring to turn away from the cause of their terror.

They were afraid of him, Shellane realized. No other explanation satisfied. He took a step toward them—their whimpers rose in pitch and volume. Definitely afraid. He caught Grace's hand, tried to pull her away. If they could get clear, he thought, he would have time to come up with a plan. But she yanked her hand free and dropped to her knees, then sank into a reclining position, her eyes averted, like a child who sees the inevitable, some terrible punishment, and seeks refuge in collapse.

The uglies still seemed afraid, but Shellane's confidence had been weakened by Grace's surrender. Nevertheless, he steeled himself and ran at them, waving his arms, shouting, hoping to drive them off. They scuttled away, yet when he stopped his advance, they, too, stopped, huddling together, plucking and clutching at one another like fretful monkeys. He made a second menacing run. Once again they fell back, but not so far this time. A touch of curiosity showed in their crudely drawn faces and one of them growled, bassy and articulated, a bleakly mechanical noise, like the idling of some beastly machine. Two lesser yet equally chilling growls joined in guttural disharmony with the first, and he lifted hands in a defensive posture, knowing now that he would be forced to fight.

But it was no fight.

In a few shambling strides they were on him, a wave of bony edges and jagged, blunt teeth that carried him down, enveloping him in a bitter stench. He managed to land a single punch, striking the chest of the tallest. Like hitting a wall of granite. Then he was tossed, kicked, slammed into the boards, worried, scratched, bitten, and kicked again until he lost consciousness. When he woke, once he managed to unscramble his senses, he found he was being dragged along by the feet. Head bumping, arms flopping. He heard Grace scream and struggled to wrench free, but the hands gripping his ankles were irresistible. He twisted about, trying to find her. Caught a glimpse of her being carried aloft, held by the collar of her jacket in one long-fingered gray hand. Bile flushed into his throat. The effortful grunting breath of the creature dragging him seemed the sound of his panic. He closed his eyes and summoned his reserves, focusing, contriving a central place in his mind from which he could observe and judge what, if anything, might be done.

They came to a door. The creature released one of his ankles; through slitted eyes, Shellane watched it press a forefinger in sequence against the raised seams clumped together on the wall. The door opened and they were sucked inside. Flashing white lights disoriented Shellane and, despite himself, he cried out. His tormentor bent down to him, its insult of a mouth—wide enough to swallow a ham—widened further in a smile, its tongue dark red and thick, like a turtle's. Beneath the ridges of its orbits, its eyes were visible. Gleaming not with reflected light, it seemed, but with the animal sheen of a rotted deliquescence. It slashed at his face with its thumb. A warm wetness spread across his cheek, and he realized it had sliced him with its thumbnail. It seized him by the shirtfront and he was lifted up, dangled over a gulf—it appeared that a boulder had hurtled down from heaven or the heights of whatever place this was, smashing everything in its path, creating a central shaft in one of the tenements, leaving a hole roughly twenty feet in diameter. The shaft its passage had made fell away into shadow, walled by a broken honeycomb of exposed rooms and splintered black boards. Before he could fully absorb the sight, the creature swung him as easily as he himself might swing a cat and let him fly out through the air. A desperate cry tore from his throat. The ruin pinwheeled. The pull of gravity and death took him at the top of his arc. Turning sideways as he fell, he saw a gaping darkness rush up at him, and the next instant he slammed into something that drove wind from his chest and light from his brain. Only after regaining consciousness a second time did he understand that he had been thrown completely across the gap, and that the uglies, bearing Grace with them, had leaped across after him.

They passed through another door. Shellane was too groggy to register much about the room beyond, but he caught sight of a hearth in which a roaring fire had been built, and though he realized he was not the most reliable of witnesses at the moment, he could have sworn he saw tiny homunculi playing in the flames, hopping from log to log. Grace was speaking urgently, the words unintelligible, but he had the impression that she was pleading. Another room. His head had cleared to a degree, but his vision was still impaired—or so he assumed. Then he recognized that the indistinctness of the large shadowy figure sitting cross-legged in a corner was due not to any failure of his eyesight, but rather to the fact that its black substance was in a state of flux. A muffled shouting issued from the figure, and as Shellane was hauled past it, he saw that the whirling black stuff was a filmy shell encasing a human form, and further saw a man's face within the shell, pain contorting his features. At the next door the tallest of the uglies again manipulated a little patch of ridges in the wood. Shellane felt a perverse satisfaction in knowing that he had been right about the doors.

The room into which the creature then dragged him was small, the ceiling so low that the uglies had to walk in a half-crouch, with a gabled roof and a shuttered window that extended up from the floor. Shellane was left to lie beside the window and, when one of the uglies threw the shutters open onto a foggy darkness, he saw a huge black fist jutting from the boards directly below and realized where he must be. He was past fighting. His ribs ached, his left knee throbbed, and his mind worked sluggishly. Even when a rope was placed around his neck, he could not rouse himself, but only wondered how they were going to pass his body through the fist, a question answered when another of the uglies pressed a finger to a ridged patch beside the window and, with terrible slowness, the fist uncurled as if to welcome him. Grace let out a shriek. He turned on his back and spotted her at the door. Two of their captors were fondling her roughly, grabbing her breasts and buttocks. He started to tell her something, but forgot what he had been going to say. It became irrelevant as a foot nudged him out the window.

He dropped only a foot or so, but the rope choked him and his feet kicked against the boards. In reflex, he grabbed the rope, tried to haul himself back up; but he was being lowered and made no progress. Overhead, the uglies were framed by the window, one embracing a still-struggling Grace, whose face was pressed into its chest, and the biggest paying out the rope. It was all chaotic, a delirium. His vision darkened, and he felt a tremendous heat inside his skull. His right foot bumped against the half-curled hand, and then he was inside it, waist-deep in its loose grip. He caught at its upper edge, levering himself up with his elbows, refusing to be lowered any farther. The surface of the uppermost finger was crusted with brownish stains. He puzzled over them, wondering what they might be. That question was answered as the hand began to close into a fist and he understood that some who'd had the misfortune to happen onto the house while alive had chosen to be crushed rather than hanged. Gasping for air, his throat constricted, he looked up to Grace, not seeking help but dimly moved to find her. The figures above were joined in a wobbling dance, pushing one another to gain a better view of the proceedings, communicating in grunts and growls and screams. And then the smallest of the four, the shrillest, flung herself at the tallest, clawing at its eyes. The rope came uncoiling down toward Shellane. He released his grip on the hand, allowing himself to fall, this due to a sympathetic reaction to the rope's fall as much as to his vague comprehension that by doing so he would not hang. His head struck the first joint of the fist's little finger, and he dropped the last few feet, landing on his back with a jolting impact.

He did not black out, and the recognition that he was free penetrated the confused clutter of his thoughts. Gritting his teeth against the pain, he pushed up to a standing position and began a limping retreat. Grace screamed at him to run, and he threw himself forward with his shoulders, dragging his left leg, moving blindly through the fog. He knew she must still be struggling with the uglies, or else they would be on him—his pace was much too slow to outrun them—and this spurred him to limp faster. There was nothing he could do for her, yet this pragmatic view did not sit well with him and every step he took sparked feelings of shame and inadequacy. Wincing whenever he planted his left foot, he kept on going until, after only a little while, he heard the wind sighing in the spruce and water lightly slapping the shore, and realized that he was safe, an infinity removed from certain lesser demons and their rickety black hell, and utterly alone.

Once he had bandaged his wounds, believing that Grace would not return to the cabin, that she was lodged in a cell filled with burning light or enduring some crueler punishment, Shellane spent the remainder of the night hoping he was wrong. Whatever pain she was experiencing, he was to blame—he had insinuated himself into a situation that he had not fully grasped, and as a result he had caused her situation, already bleak, to worsen. Staying at the house would have served no purpose, yet he felt he had breached a bond implicit to the relationship, and he castigated himself for having abandoned her. The hours stretched and he understood once again how frail and attenuated his attachment to life had become. Without Grace, without the renewal of passion she had inspired, he could not conceive of going on as before, preparing a new identity, finding a new hiding place. What could any place offer him apart from the fundamentals of survival? And what good were they without a reason to survive? As it grew increasingly clear that she would not return, he sat at the table breeding a dull fog of thought, illuminated now and then by fits of memory. Her face, her laugh, her moods. Yet those memories did not brighten him. All the ordinary instances of her person that shone so extraordinarily bright in his mind were grayed with doubt. He knew almost nothing about her and he suspected that if he were capable of analysis, he might discover that the things he knew were dross not gold, and that she was not in the least extraordinary. She simply seemed to fit a shape in his brain, to be unreasonably perfect in some essential yet incomprehensible way. Something had been ripped out of him. Some scrap of spirit necessary for existence. Every part of his body labored. Heart slogging, lungs heaving. He felt himself the center of a howling absence.

To distract himself, he wrote lists. Long lists, this time, comprised chiefly of supposition. His knowledge of the house was limited, but he was certain about the doors—the uglies were able, thanks to their strength, to depress the ridged patches on the walls with their fingers and thus program their destination. Though pointless to do so, he could not keep from speculating on the nature of the place and the apparent infinity of locations to which it was, in some unfathomable way, connected. It was hard to accept that the afterlife possessed an instrumentality. Back when he was a believer, his notion of heaven had been diffuse, his vision of hell informed by comic books. Spindly crags and bleak promontories atop which the greater demons perched, peering into the fires where their minions oversaw the barbecue of souls. The house was at odds with both conceptions, but now he had no choice other than to believe that beyond death lay a limitless and intricate plenum whose character was infinitely various, heavens and hells and everything in-between. It was similar to the Tibetan view—souls attracted to destinations that accorded with what they had cherished in life, be it virtuous or injurious. Unlikely, though, that Tibetan cosmology had any analog to the black house. If he found himself trapped in the house, he thought, he'd study the way the uglies manipulated the doors, then devise a mechanism that would allow him to exert more force when pushing . . .

Why had they been afraid of him?

Reason dictated that they'd presumed him to be dead, and had lost their fear after noticing he was alive and mortally vulnerable. As with everyone else he had met in the house, it took them a while to notice his vitality. But that didn't explain why they had been afraid when they believed him dead. Perhaps they saw things that people did not. Different wavelengths. Auras. Perhaps they perceived him as a threat, someone who might be able to manipulate the doors. That was self-flattery, but they could have no other cause to fear him. None of which he was aware. Of course if they did know him for a threat, though they weren't able to kill him, they'd make his life—his afterlife—hell. Punish him. Keep him penned up or too busy to interfere. At least they would try. As primitive as they were, they'd screw up sooner or later and give him an opportunity. But he would have to endure a great deal of torment before the opportunity arose . . . He understood then that he was not thinking in the abstract, but was contemplating his death. He was, after all, a perfect candidate for the house. He didn't give a damn about living anymore and like Grace, who'd had Broillard to finish her off, he had his own killers to hand. They would eventually track him down. All he needed to do was wait.

He rebelled against the thought, tempting himself with the prospect of Asia, of new possibilities, yet he felt the pull of a more powerful temptation. How easy it would be to surrender. What was he giving up? Paranoia and solitude, hookers and barflies, no plans for the future but those of escape. A life without significant challenge or involvement. An emptiness that would feel far emptier without Grace. He kept expecting that he would resist these arguments, yet the longer he sat there, the more seductive they seemed. He tried to weaken them with doubt. His belief that he could learn to manipulate the doors—wouldn't death make of him, as it had of Grace and the rest, a befuddled, energy-less soul incapable of functioning? Then he recalled how he and Grace had interacted inside the house. She had been angry, afraid, but full of vitality. Of life. The two of them together might form a battery that would provide sufficient strength to manage an escape. And what if there were more than two? He had seen—what?—fifty or sixty people in the house, and there had to be more. The energy he and Grace generated might infect the rest. Some of them, anyway. They might be able to overpower the uglies. And if they could do that, together they could determine . . .

That he could entertain these fantasies, a post-mortem revolution, an overthrow of minor-league demons . . . Fuck! Next he'd be accepting Jesus as his personal savior. He went into the bedroom and pulled his suitcases from beneath the bed. Out of here now. That was the only agenda that made sense. He began to pack, though not in his usual painstaking style. Balling up shirts and stuffing them in. But gradually his pace slowed. The sheets smelled of her. She was real. Nothing could change that. She was real, the house was real. And however frail the foundation supporting his guesswork, everything he had seen and done was real. He had followed a trail of intuitive decisions and they had led him to the lake, to Grace, to this moment and to these speculations, which his instinct judged sound, and though the logic of the world prevailed against his judgments, he could not refute them.

Leaving his bags open, he returned to the front room. Trees and shrubs and shoreline were melting up from the half-dark, and as they grew sharper, shadowy branches evolving into distinct sprays of needles, the margin of the lake defining itself in precise gray etchings, the things of the world came to seem increasingly imprecise to Shellane. Their precision a clumsy illusion, a poor reflection of the simpler albeit more daunting order he had detected in the house, as if death were simply a refinement of life. He settled back into the chair. Noon approached. Soon a blue Cadillac would come grumbling along the lake road. Soon he would cook breakfast, take a shower, make a plan, erecting a structure that had no other purpose than to repeat itself. He saw himself as he had once been. Rock and roll days. Girlfriend sobbing in a corner of that dingy, brain-damaged apartment in Medford. Him yelling, shouting, because he had no self-justification that could be spoken in a quiet tone or a reasonable voice. The quick drug hit of a score, adrenaline rushes and gleefully desperate escapes, and afterward sitting in a nondescript bar with nondescript men, laughing madly over drink at the skill, the guts and brains required to risk everything for short money in the service of greater men who watched them like spiders watching trained flies and smiled at their ignorance. Walking like a ghost through Detroit. Brushing past the world, touching it just enough to envy its unreal brilliance. Was that it? A life like so many bits of rusty tin threaded onto a gray string? These days of Grace cancelled out every moment of that dreary, heatless past. He put his hand on the telephone, let it rest there for several minutes before lifting the receiver and dialing, not because he was hesitant, but rather stalled, lost in a fugue from which he emerged diminished and uncaring.

A man's voice spoke in his ear. "Yeah, what?"

"You recording this?" Shellane asked.

A pause. "Who's asking?"

"If you're not recording, start the tape. I don't want to have to repeat myself."

Another pause. "You're on the tape, pal. Go for it."

"This is . . ." Shellane had a thought. A wicked thought, another addition to his Book of Sin. But damned once, damned twice . . . What did it matter?

"You still there?"

"My name is Avery Broillard," Shellane said. "I work at the Gas 'n Guzzle in Champion, Michigan. In the Upper Peninsula, about an hour's drive west of Marquette."

"No shit? How's the weather up there?"

"I can tell you how to find Roy Shellane."

Silence, and then the man said, "That would be extremely helpful, Avery. Why don'tcha go ahead and tell me?"

"It's tricky... the directions. I'll have to show you. I work until seven tonight. Can you have somebody up here by seven?"

"Oh, yeah. We can handle that. But, Avery... whoever the fuck you are. If this is bullshit, I'm gonna be very upset with you."

"Just have someone here by seven."

After hanging up he had a moment's panic, a twinge of fear, an urge toward flight, but these found no purchase in his thoughts. He sat a while longer, then set about making breakfast. Fried eggs and ham, toast, and his last wedge of apple pie.

Shortly after six o'clock that afternoon, a dark green Datsun parked about a hundred feet off along the access road. Shellane pictured Gerbasi crammed into the front seat—the rental car options in Marquette must not have been to his liking. He considered going out to meet them, but though he was eager to have done with it, he was so enervated, worn down by depression, feelings of loss and anxiety, his eagerness did not rise to the level of action. At a quarter to seven the doors of the Datsun opened and two shadows moved toward the cabin, one much bulkier than the other. They vanished behind trees, then reappeared larger, at a different angle to the cabin, like ghosts playing interdimensional tag. Shellane could have picked them off, no problem. He was in an odd mood. So lighthearted that he was tempted to hunt up the nine-millimeter and destroy the men who were intending do what he wanted, just as a prank on himself; but he couldn't recall where he had put the gun. He heard whispers outside. Probably arguing over whether to shoot through the window. Gerbasi wouldn't go for it. He enjoyed the laying on of hands. That was his kink. The fat bag of poison wanted you to commune with him before he did the deed. Over thirty years of murdering people who had not necessarily required it, life had been kind to him, except socially. For some years now he had been in love with a woman who shared a house with a guy who claimed to be a gay political refugee from Cuba, a story that scored him few points in the neighborhood, but lent his bond with the woman an innocence that placated Gerbasi, who remained oblivious to the fact that he was being cheated on in plain view. It was amazing, Shellane thought, what there was to know about people.

The door blew inward and Gerbasi's associate, a light-heavy who must have taken a pounding in the ring—ridges of scar tissue over his eyes—before entering this line of work, posed TV-cop-style with his shiny gun and grunted something that Shellane did not catch but took for an admonition. Then Gerbasi hove into view. Spider veins were thick as jail tattoos on his jowls, and the bags beneath his eyes appeared to have been dipped in grape juice. His breathing was wet and wheezy, and his muted plaid suit had the lumpish aspect of bad upholstery. The lamplight plated his scalp with an orange shine. He waddled three steps into the room and said, "This don't seem like you, Roy. Just sitting here waiting for it."

Shellane, his flame turned low, had no reply.

Gerbasi snapped at his helper, telling him to close the door. "What's going on with you?" he asked of Shellane.

"I surrender," said Shellane.

"The guy Broillard, he claims he didn't call us." Gerbasi's eyes, heavy-lidded, big and brown like calf's eyes, ranged the tabletop. "Know anything about that?"

"Broillard? The Gas 'n Guzzle guy? He called you about me?"

Gerbasi's stogie-sized forefinger prodded Shellane's laptop. "Somebody called. Broillard says it wasn't him."

"Maybe he had a change of heart," suggested Shellane.

"Maybe you set his ass up." Gerbasi gave him a doleful look.

"You didn't hurt him, did you?" Shellane failed to keep the amusement from his voice.

The light-heavy chuckled doltishly. "He ain't hurting no more."

"I figure you set him up," Gerbasi said. "But why would ya do that and still be hanging around?"

"Don't think about it, Marty. You'll just break your brain."

"Maybe he's got cancer," offered the light-heavy.

"Worse," said Shellane.

"What's worse than cancer?"

"Shut the fuck up," Gerbasi said to the light-heavy; he removed a long-barreled .22 from his shoulder holster.

"Truth," Shellane said.

"Y'know, you look way too satisfied for a man's gonna be wearing his brains in a coupla minutes," Gerbasi said. "You waiting for rescue, Roy? That it?"

"Why don't you just do your business."

"Guy's in a hurry," said the light-heavy. "Never seen one be in a hurry."

"Who cut your face?" Gerbasi asked.

"Just do it, you fat fuck!" said Shellane. "I've got places I need to get to."

"Hear that shit?" said the light-heavy. "Motherfucker's crazy."

"Nah, he's got an angle," Gerbasi said. "Man's always got an angle. Don'tcha, Roy?"

Shellane smiled. "I live in certain hope of the Resurrection."

Gerbasi gave his head a dubious shake. "Know what I useta say about you? I'd say Roy Shellane runs the best goddamn crews of anybody in the business, but he's too fucking smart for his own good. One of these days he's gonna outsmart himself." He seemed to be expecting a response; when none came, he said, "I think maybe that day's come."

A bough ticked the side of the cabin; the light-heavy twitched toward the door. Shellane was beginning to understand why Gerbasi enjoyed playing out these scenes—he wanted the fear to grow strong so he could smell it. But though Shellane was not free of fear, it was weak in him, and he thought he must be proving a profound disappointment to Gerbasi.

"You look to me like a man who's holding good cards, but don't know he's in the wrong game," Gerbasi said.

"Do I have to fucking beg you to shoot?" Shellane asked.

"Hey." The light-heavy came up beside Gerbasi. "Maybe he's wearing a wire."

"He was, they'd already be down on our ass 'cause of what'cha said about Broillard. But something ain't kosher." Gerbasi let the gun dangle at his side. "Tell me what's going on, Roy, or I'm gonna hafta give ya some pain."

"I don't give a shit what you do. You understand? I don't give a shit about anything."

Gerbasi said, "No, explain it to me."

"If you had a soul, I wouldn't need to explain it. You'd feel the same as me. You'd be sickened by what you are."

"I told ya the guy's crazy," said the light-heavy.

"You don't shut your goddamn mouth, I swear to Christ I'm gonna put one in ya," Gerbasi told him.

"Jeez!" said the light-heavy. "Fine. Fuck . . . whatever."

"The man's tired of living," Gerbasi went on. "That's all he's saying. Right, Roy?"

"Right."

"Remember Bobby Sheehan? Man just looks at me and says, 'Fuck you, Marty.' Not like he was pissed off. Just weary. Just fed up with it all. I asked, man, I said, 'Fuck's wrong with you, Bobby? This how you wanna go out? Like a fucking sick dog?' And he says, 'A sick dog's got it all over me. A sick dog don't know what's making it sick.' It's kinda like that, ain't it, Roy?"

"Fuck you, Marty."

Gerbasi stepped around behind Shellane, and a weakness spread from the center of Shellane's chest outward, resolving into a chill that coiled the length of his spine. He fixed his eyes on the door, but he seemed to see everything in the room, and he sensed his isolation, the gulf of the surrounding dark with its trillion instances of life. Spiders, beetles, roosting birds, serpents, badgers, moles, fish streaming through the dim forests of the lake bottom. Every least scrap of vitality enviable to him now. Somehow from that darkness he managed to summon the image of Grace's face. The brightness of her olivine eyes struck deep into him, calmed the fluttering thing that was his life, and filled him with acceptance. This was the end to which he had come. This woman, this unstable chair, this badly hung door, this shabby room drenched in orange lamplight. He felt he was falling forward into a dream.

"You wanna say a prayer?" Gerbasi asked. "I'll give you a minute."

Shellane did not answer, absorbed by the particulars of his vision.

"You hear what I said, Roy? Want me to give you a minute?"

"Now would be good," said Shellane.

Limbo

*I*n the beginning there was the memory of pain, a pain so vast and white it seemed less a condition of the mind and body than the country of his birth. But it was only a memory and did not afflict him for long. There followed a period of vagueness and confusion, but as he walked, moving through the dark, fogbound country of his death, he came to think that death had not left him much the worse for wear. He recalled what Grace had said about the process and realized that he, too, was coming to feel stronger, more settled in his head . . . and yet he also felt strangely out-of-sorts, plagued by an ill-defined sense of foreboding. He presumed this feeling would intensify once he reached the black house, and that it contributed to the low energy and aimlessness of the house's residents; but he told himself that none of them had been informed with such clear purpose and determination—he believed this would shield him to an extent from the effect. And when he saw the gabled roof rising from fog and the black fist protruding from the wall, even after he opened the door and was drawn inside, he remained hopeful, focused on his intention to find Grace, to escape with her. Where they might escape to . . . Well, that was not something upon which he had expended a great deal of thought. The potentials of the afterlife undoubtedly incorporated worse places than the house, and should they manage to reach a better one, what would they do then? He recognized there were many things he might have considered before acting. Matters of personal as well as metaphysical consequence. But they involved questions best answered by both him and Grace, and so would have to wait judgment.

It was not a room into which he was admitted upon opening the door, but a corridor that appeared to be endless, an unrelieved perspective of black doors and black walls, black floors and ceiling, the surfaces of the boards shiny like newly exposed veins of coal. He received a distinct impression of menace from each door he passed, and he wondered if his ability to apprehend such a psychic reek had been enhanced by his mortal transition. He walked for what must have been twenty minutes. The black perspective continued to recede. If there was an end to the corridor, he had made no appreciable progress toward it, and he realized that he would have to pick one of the doors and deal with whatever lay behind it. But before he could choose, Grace spoke from close behind him, giving him a start, just as she had their first morning on the beach.

"Hello, Roy," she said.

She was standing no more than fifteen feet away, two of the lanky gray hominids crouched at her side, flanking her like faithful hounds. Her hair was loose about her shoulders, but otherwise she was as always, dressed in jeans and a sweater. Her attitude, however, betrayed no hint of anxiety, and her smile was an act of disdainful aggression. She absently trailed the fingers of her left hand across the scalp of one of the uglies, and it trembled, rolling its sunken eyes toward her.

"Grace . . ." Stunned, unable to match her coolness, her poise, with anything he knew about her, Shellane was at a loss for words.

"Roy!" She spoke his name in a husky mockery of passion and laughed, her laughter lasting a touch long to be the record of any wholesome emotion. That laugh resolved some of his questions. Not in detail, yet it supplied enough of an answer to make him suspect that his view of her was based on a fundamental misconception.

"Thanks for getting rid of Avery," she said. "That was sweet of you." Her tone grew chilly. "All your self-involvement is such a shuck! You're too much of a coward to admit you're a conscienceless bully, so you contrive moral dilemmas to hide the truth from yourself. I knew you'd find a way to kill him. It's who you are." She gave her hair a toss. "Actually, things couldn't have worked out better. I can't have Avery, but I've got someone like him to play with. You'll be much more amusing. Avery wasn't a deep thinker, but you . . . you'll drive yourself crazy trying to understand where you are and what's really happening. Am I merely an unhappy woman who's been empowered by death, or was Grace a facade, a disguise used by a creature beyond your comprehension? You'll drown yourself in that crap."

Shellane remained speechless, unable to believe that he had been so wrong about her. She looked away, as if made uncomfortable by his stare.

"Come on," she said after a while. "You must have known deep down no one could love something like you."

"This . . . us . . . It was all about revenge?"

"You say that as if it were trivial. Revenge is beautiful. I can speak with authority on the subject. Haven't you been hurt by anyone? Didn't you want to fuck her up? Tear her life apart . . . like what she did to you? If you're not feeling that now, you will be soon, I promise. Don't underestimate the value of revenge. I imagine the thought of it is all that's going to keep you sane in the years ahead."

Incredulous, he said, "Why me? How did you lead me here? To the lake?"

"It's nothing I did. *You* did it. You found me, you found the house. All your life you've been looking for a place that fit you perfectly. That's how you saw it, anyway. The truth is, you were looking for a suitable punishment." She tipped her head coquettishly and said, "And here you are!"

"But what did . . . ?"

"No, no, no!" She waggled her forefinger at him. "No more clues. I want you to figure it out for yourself. If you can. I'm not sure *I* understand everything. But understanding's overrated, Roy. Try and stay in the moment."

Maybe, he thought, the desire for revenge had been so strong in her, she had failed to notice what had transpired between them.

"Grace," he said. "Listen, I can still take us out of here."

"I don't want to leave. Don't you get it? I'm the bitch queen of this little slice of heaven. I'm not about to give up what I've won."

The uglies strained forward at her side, craning their necks toward Shellane, making whimpering sounds.

"Know what hell is, Roy? Hell is repetition. Having to repeat what you did in life forever. When I came here, when I saw all these fucked-up, defeated people, I swore I'd break the mold. I was fed up with taking a beating. But what you did in life was run, and I don't see how you're going to change that." She patted the uglies' heads with rough affection. "I think the boys here could use a little exercise. How about it? Want to give them a run?"

His mind burned with questions that she would never answer . . . or that she never *could* answer. And that, he thought, was the crux of the matter. She didn't have all the answers. Perhaps she didn't even have all the questions. If she was the queen of the house, why hadn't the people he questioned on his first visit known her? Perhaps they had been dissembling, afraid to speak of her, but he didn't think so. It might be that Grace was not the only power in the house, that there was still power to be had by anyone resourceful enough to grasp it. And then he wondered, if her contempt for him was as she stated, why had she appeared uncomfortable a moment before? Why had she looked away from him? It was as if she was putting on an act for someone and the act had broken down and she'd had to pull it together.

"That's the spirit!" She tapped her forehead. "I can hear the wheels spinning. If anyone can beat the odds, it's a great big criminal type like you!"

He could have sworn there was a note of urgency in her voice, of pleading. The uglies surged forward—she snapped at them and they heeled.

"Better get going, Roy," she said. "I'd like to give you a head start, but I won't be able to hold them much longer."

He gripped a doorknob shaped like a hand, and the contact sent a cold charge through his emotions. If she wanted a game, he'd give her one. He'd give her all she could handle. But then he turned the knob, heard the uglies growling at his back, and his anger was drowned beneath a tide of terrible recognitions. The hopelessness of his situation, the complexity of the problem he confronted, and, most disabling of all, the appropriateness of the punishment he faced. To run ceaselessly, to hide, to exist—however fractionally—without the consolations that made existence endurable. He wondered where he would return when he returned to the world. Had to be the lake. Where else? He understood why it had seemed such a good fit. It was his resting place, his final worldly destination. He'd spend eternity, if eternity there was, scurrying through the maze of this black sedated house like a rat in a ruin—all that was left to him of heaven—and mooning about the lake where death and love had found him.

He set these considerations aside and opened the door, passing through flickering white lights and into the shadowy space beyond. He thought again of Grace, her clean beauty, the simple virtues he had so desired. She no longer seemed to embody those qualities, and it would have been easy to hate her; but though revenge had motivated her, or so she claimed, hating her was not in his best interests. If he was to win at this, he knew he had to make it a fool's game, he had to play himself as she had played him . . . if she had. If she had been so accomplished an actress that she could counterfeit love in all its frailty, with its self-doubts and confident passions. The longer he considered the question, loping along a black corridor that led everywhere and nowhere, the more certain he became that she was acting now, that her coldness and sarcasm were a show designed to impress some hidden, watchful eye. The real power in the house. And the break in her voice, the momentary lapse in tone . . . it had let her true self come through. She wanted his help, she was depending on him, but had to present a hostile front in order to maintain her position. And if he were wrong, well, what would be the harm in that? Better to be wrong forever than to live without hope.

He hewed to this logic, letting it build an inspiring edifice within him, gothic and noble, with great arches and vaults into which he could pour his faith, a statue of a redheaded Virgin upon its altar, and, hearing the faint sounds of pursuit at his back, with love in his heart, he began to run.

LIAR'S HOUSE

*I*n the eternal instant before the Beginning, before the Word was pronounced in fire, long before the tiny dust of history came to settle from the flames, something whose actions no verb can truly describe seemed to enfold possibility, to surround it in the manner of a cloud or an idea, and everything fashioned from the genesis fire came to express in some way the structure of that fundamental duality. It has been said that of all living creatures, this duality was best perceived in dragons, for they had flown fully formed from out the mouth of the Uncreate, the first of creation's kings, and gone soaring through a conflagration that, eons hence, would coalesce into worlds and stars and all the dream of matter. Thus the relation of their souls to their flesh accurately reflected the constitution of the Creator, enveloping and controlling their material bodies from without rather than, as with the souls of men, coming to be lodged within. And of all their kind, none incarnated this principle more poignantly, more spectacularly, than did the dragon Griaule.

How Griaule came to be paralyzed by a wizard's magical contrivance is a story without witness, but it has been documented that in this deathlike condition he lived on for millennia, continuing to grow, until he measured more than a mile in length, lying athwart and nearly spanning the westernmost section of the Carbonales Valley. Over the years he came to resemble a high hill covered in grass and shrubs and stunted trees, with here and there a portion of scale showing through, and the colossal head entirely emergent, unclothed by vegetation, engaging everything that passed before him with huge, slit-pupiled golden eyes, exerting a malefic influence over the events that flowed around him, twisting them into shapes that conformed to the cruel designs his discarnate intellect delighted in the weaving of, and profited his vengeful will. During his latter days, a considerable city, Teocinte, sprawled away from Griaule's flank over the adjoining hill, but centuries before, when few were willing to approach the dragon, Teocinte was scarcely more than an outsized village enclosed by dense growths of palms and bananas, hemmed in between the eminence of Griaule and a pine-forested hill. Scruffy and unlovely; flyblown; its irregularly laid-out dirt streets lined by hovels with rusting tin roofs; it was lent the status of a town by a scattering of unstable frame structures housing taverns, shops, and a single inn, and was populated by several thousand men and women who, in the main, embodied a debased extreme of the human condition. Murderers and thieves and outlaws of various stamp. Almost to a one, they believed that proximity to the dragon imbued them with a certain potency (as perhaps it did) and refused to concern themselves with the commonly held notion that they had been drawn to Teocinte because their depravity resonated with the dragon's depraved nature, thus making them especially vulnerable to his manipulations. What does it matter whose purpose we serve, they might have asked, so long as it satisfies our own?

By all accounts, the most fearsome of Teocinte's citizens and, at forty-two, its eldest, was Hota Kotieb, a brooding stump of a man with graying, unkempt hair, his cheeks and jaw scarred by knife cuts. His hands were huge, capable of englobing a cantaloupe and squeezing it to a pulp, and his powerful arms and oxlike shoulders had been developed through years of unloading ships at the docks in Port Chantay. Deep-socketed eyes provided the only vital accent in what otherwise seemed the sort of brutish face sometimes produced by the erosion of great stones. Unlike his fellows, who would make lengthy forays out into the world to perpetrate their crimes, then returned to restore themselves by steeping in the dragon's aura, Hota never strayed from the valley. Eleven summers previously, after his wife had been run over in the street by a coach belonging to the harbormaster in Port Chantay, he had forsworn the unreliable processes of justice and forced his way into the man's home. When the harbormaster ordered him ejected, Hota stabbed him, his two sons and several retainers, himself receiving numerous wounds during the skirmish. On realizing that he would be hung were he to remain in the town, he looted the house and fled, killing three policemen who sought to stop him outside the door. Casting aside a lifetime of unobtrusive action and docile labor, he had murdered ten men in the space of less than an hour.

Though he had never attended school and was ignorant of many things, Hota was by no means dull-witted, and when he meditated on these events, his red victory and the grim chaos that preceded it, he was able to place his actions in a rational context. He felt little remorse over the murders of the harbormaster and his sons. They were oppressors and had received an oppressor's due. As for the rest, he regretted their deaths and believed that some would have been spared had he not been enraged to the point of derangement; yet he refused to use derangement as a sop to his conscience and recognized that the potential for extreme violence had always been his. He had not wished his wife to die, but neither had he loved her. Thirteen years of marriage had doused the spark that once leaped between them. Their union had decayed into indifference and sham. They were like two plow horses harnessed together, endlessly tilling a field barren of children and every other promise, yet led to continue their dreary progress by the litany of empty promises they spoke to one another. It seemed her death had less inspired than legitimized a violent release, and that he had been longing to kill someone for quite some time, motivated in this by feelings of impotence bred over years of abject poverty. Now this tendency had made itself known, he supposed it would rise all the more easily to the surface. For this reason, though he was lonely, he kept no one close.

The money and gems he had stolen from the harbormaster enabled Hota to live as comfortably as the rough consolations of Teocinte permitted. He occupied a third-floor room at the rear of Dragonwood House, a weathered, boxlike building with a tin roof and a tavern downstairs and a newer, less ruinous single-story wing attached, where prostitutes were housed. Its ashen gray facade was dressed with a garishly painted sign that depicted a dragon soaring through a fiery heaven. The inn was situated near the edge of town and serviced the steady stream of visitors that came to look at Griaule, offering views of the dragon's side from its front windows. Its owner, Benno Grustark, claimed that the boards employed in its construction were manufactured from trees that had grown atop

Griaule's back, but his patrons, knowing that few dared to set foot upon the dragon, let alone cut timber, referred to the inn as Liar's House.

Having no need to work, Hota passed many of the days at woodcarving, a hobby of his childhood that still pleased him, though he displayed no talent for the work. Since there was little in the town to attract his eye, he took to carving likenesses of Griaule. Dozens of such pieces were crowded together on his shelves, atop the bureau and chairs, and scattered across the floor of his room. On occasion he would give one to a child or to a prostitute who shared his bed, but this made no appreciable dent in the clutter. To avoid further clutter, he began working on a grander scale, walking out into the hills, felling trees, chiseling dragons from the trunks, and leaving the completed figures to the depredations of the rain and the insects. He set no great store by the work, caring only that it distracted him, but was nonetheless pleased that the woods were becoming littered with his sculptures, crude figures weathering into objects that—like their model—appeared to be natural formations that bore a striking resemblance to dragons.

In the early spring, eleven years after his arrival in Teocinte, Hota hired a carter to haul the trunk of a white oak to the crest of a hill from which he had a profile view of Griaule with the valley spreading beyond, an undulant reach of palms and palmettos, figs and aguacastes, threaded by red dirt paths. There he set about his most ambitious project. Previously he had carved the dragon as he might have appeared during more vital days—flying, crouched, or rampant; now he intended to create a sculpture that would depict Griaule as he was: the oddly delicate, birdlike head, jaws half open, tongue and fangs embroidered with lichen, vines depending in loops and snarls from the roof of the mouth; the bluish green folds and struts of the sagittal crest, that same color edging the golden scales; his sinuous body, the haunches, flanks, and back mapped by a forest whose dark green conformation was so similar to the shapes of the hills that lifted higher behind him, it caused Hota to wonder if they, too, might not conceal gigantic dragons. He spent a week in laying out the design and then several days more gathering the details of Griaule's shape in his mind and letting that knowledge flow into his hands.

Toward noon one morning, as Hota was busy carving, he noticed something flying in loops above Griaule's snout, difficult to make out against the strong sun, as tiny in relation to the dragon as a swallow fluttering about a bull's nose. To his astonishment, for Hota had thought Griaule to be the sole survivor of his species, he realized it was another dragon. Thirty to forty feet long, by his estimate. With bronze scales. Enthralled, he watched the creature swoop and soar, maintaining a predictable circuit, as if she (because of her daintiness by contrast to Griaule, Hota thought of the second dragon as she) were tracing the same character over and over, enacting a ritual of some kind. Her wings seemed to ripple rather than to beat against the air, and her long neck glided through its attitudes with the suppleness of a reed borne on a stream, and her tail lashed about with what struck him as a lascivious ferocity. She might be, he surmised, attempting to communicate with Griaule. Or perhaps *he* was communicating with her; perhaps the patterns of her flight gave visual form to the eddies of his thoughts. At length she broke off her circling and settled onto Griaule's broad back, passing out of sight behind his sagittal crest.

Dropping his chisel, Hota hurried down the hill, following a track that merged with one of the red dirt paths criss-crossing the valley, and approached Griaule from the side, heading for the bulge of his foreleg. As the dragon came to loom above him, he felt a surge of terror. The tightly nested scales of the jaw; the gray teeth with their traceries of lichen, like the broken wall of a fortress city; the bulge of an orbital ridge: seen close to hand, the monumental aspect of these things dismayed him, and when he moved into the dragon's shadow, something colder and thicker than air seemed to glove him, as if he were moving in invisible mud. But fascination overbore his fright. The prospect of observing a dragon who was capable of motion excited him. There was nothing of the academic or the artistic in his interest. He simply wanted to see it.

He scrambled up the slope afforded by the brush-covered foreleg, then ascended to the dragon's thicketed shoulder, catching at shrubs to pull himself higher. His breath labored, sweat poured off him. On several occasions he nearly fell. When at last he stood atop Griaule's back, clinging for support to a pine branch, looking down at the valley hundreds of feet below, Teocinte showing as an ugly grayish patch amid the greenery, he understood the foolishness of what he had done. He felt unarmored against the arrows of fate, as if he had violated a taboo and been stripped of all his immunities. Adding to his anxiety was the fact that nearby was a dragon who, upon sensing him, would seek to tear him to pieces . . . unless she had flown away while he was climbing, and he doubted this to be the case. Fear mounted in him once again, but he did not place so much value on his life as once he had—indeed, he often wondered why he had bothered to save himself from the hangman's rope that night in Port Chantay—and his desire to see her remained strong. Planting his feet with care, easing branches aside, he pressed on into the brush and headed for the spot where he supposed the second dragon had landed.

The heat of the day came full and Hota continued to sweat profusely. The needle sprays of stunted pine and the yellowed round leaves of the shrubs that dominated the thicket limited his view to a few yards ahead and stuck to his damp neck and cheeks and arms. After wandering blindly about for a quarter of an hour, he began to speculate that the second dragon had made no landing at all, but merely swooped down behind the sagittal crest and then leveled off and flew away over the hills. He found a bare patch of ground and sat, deliberating whether or not to give up the search. Scutterings issued from the brush and this alarmed him. Rumor had it that many of the animals living in and on Griaule were poisonous. Deciding that he had been foolish enough for one day, Hota stood and headed back the way he had come. After half an hour, when he had not reached the edge of the thicket, he realized with annoyance that he must have gotten turned around and was walking along the spine. He stood on tiptoes, caught sight of the dragon's crest, and, thus oriented, started off parallel to it. Another half hour passed and Hota's annoyance blossomed into panic. Someone— doubtless Griaule himself—was playing a trick on him. Clouding his thoughts, causing him to go in circles. Again he sighted the sagittal crest and beat his way through the brush; but the ground beneath his feet did not slope away as it should have done and when he checked the crest once more, he saw that he had made no progress whatsoever.

After two hours, Hota's panic lapsed into resignation. This, then, was the fate to which his violence had led him. Trapped in a magical circumstance that he could not hope to fathom, he would wander Griaule's back until he grew too weak to walk and died of thirst and exposure. He would, he thought, have preferred to be hung. Yet he could not deny that he was deserving of worse and there was no defiance in him. He kicked broken branches aside, cleaning a spot where he could sit and wait for death; but upon reflection, he kept on walking, deciding it would be best to wear himself out and so hasten the inevitable. He hurried through the thicket, no longer trying to hide his presence, for he assumed that the second dragon had been an illusion, bait in the trap Griaule had set. He swatted boughs aside and shouldered through entangled places, forcing himself whenever possible into a lumbering trot. As he went, he began to feel exhilarated and it occurred to him that this might be because he finally had something meaningful to do. All his years of drinking and inept woodcarving, and all the years prior, the numbing labor, shabby, juiceless days and silent evenings spent staring glumly at his wife . . . it was right they should end here and now. They had profited no one, least of all himself.

The longer he contemplated the prospect of dying, the more eager to have done with life he became. What did he have to look forward to? A few uneventful years followed by the loss of his physical powers? Assaults by younger, stronger men who would rob him and leave him destitute? And that would not be the worst of it. Exhilaration turned to something approaching glee and he increased his pace. Twigs stabbed at him, abrading his skin, but he ignored the pain. He remembered another occasion on which he had felt a similar measure of . . . what? Enthusiasm? Vitality?

Delirium.

That was the word, he thought.

It was a feeling very like the one he had experienced at the harbormaster's house in Port Chantay.

Sobered by an awareness of this connection, he slowed to a walk, mulling it over, wondering if what he felt, then and now, might be an indication of mental infirmity or some physical ailment. He was still considering this notion when he slapped aside a pine bough and stepped into a clearing where stood a slender woman with bronze skin, long black hair falling to the small of her back, and wearing not a stitch of clothing.

The woman was so startling a sight, Hota's initial reaction was one of disbelief. He imagined her to be part of his delirium, or perhaps a further trick of Griaule's. She was half-turned away, a hand to her cheek, as if she had been struck by a remembrance. A pattern of dark irregular lines covered her body. Like, he thought, a sketch of reptilian scales. He first believed the lines to be a tattoo, but then noticed they were growing fainter every second, and he recalled that the scales of the female dragon had been the exact shade of bronze as the woman's skin. On hearing his choked outcry, she glanced at him over her shoulder, displaying no indication of fear such as might be expected of a naked woman alone when surprised by a man of his threatening appearance. She remained motionless, calmly regarding, and Hota, unable to accept what he was tempted to believe—that here stood the dragon he had sought, transformed somehow—was torn between the desire to flee and the need to know more about her. In a matter of seconds the lines on her skin faded utterly and, as if this signaled the completion of a process that had restrained her, she turned to face him and said in a dry, dusty voice, "Hota."

The sound of his name on her lips, freighted with a touch of menace, or so he heard it, spurred him to flight. Unwilling to look away from her, he took a backward step, tried to run, but stumbled, and went sprawling onto his belly. He scrambled to one knee and found her standing above him.

"Are you afraid?" she asked, tipping her head to the side.

Her eyes were dark, the irises large, leaving room for scarcely any white and her face, with its sharp cheekbones and full lips and delicate nose, was too perfect, lifeless, as might be an uninspired artist's rendering. She repeated her question and, like her face, her voice was empty of human temper. The question seemed pragmatic, as if she were unfamiliar with fear and was hoping to identify its symptoms. Though she looked to be a mature woman, not a girl, her breasts and hips and belly betrayed no marks of age or usage.

Hota sank back into a sitting position, dumbstruck.

"There's no reason to fear. We have a road to travel, you and I." A cloud passed across the sun; the woman looked up sharply, scanning the sky, and then said, "I'll need some clothing."

Somewhat reassured, Hota edged away from her and got to his feet. He gave thought again to running, but recalled being lost among the thickets and decided that running would probably do him no good.

"Did you hear?" she asked, and again her words conveyed no sense of impatience or anger. "I need clothing."

Hota framed a question of his own, but was too daunted to speak.

"Your name is Hota, isn't it?" the woman asked.

"Yes." He licked his lips, tried to dredge up the courage to ask his question, failed, and succeeded only in making a confused noise.

"Magali," said the woman, and touched the slope of a breast. "My name is Magali."

He could detect nothing of her mood. It was as if she were hidden inside a beautiful shell, her true self muffled. She waited for him to speak and finally, when he kept silent she said, "You know me. Is that what's troubling you?"

"I've never seen you before," Hota said.

"But you know me. You saw me fly. You saw me while I was yet changing."

This, though it was the answer to his unasked question, only confounded him further and he merely shook his head in response.

"How can you not believe it? You saw what you saw," she said. "You have nothing to fear from me. I'm a woman now. My flesh is as yours." She reached out and took his hand. Her palm was warm. "Do you understand?"

"No . . . I . . ." He shook his head vigorously. "No."

"You will in time." She released his hand. "Now can you bring me some clothing?"

"There are no shops that sell women's clothes in Teocinte."

"Borrow some . . . or bring me some of your own."

By agreeing to do her bidding, Hota thought he would be able to make his escape. "All right. I'll go now," he said.

"You'll come back. Don't think you won't."

"Of course I will."

She laughed at this—it was, he thought, the first purely human thing she had done. "That's not what is in your mind."

"How can you know what's in my mind?"

"It's written on your face," she said. "You can't wait to be gone. Once out of sight, you'll run. That's what you're thinking, anyway. But later you'll tell yourself that if you don't return, I'll come after you. And it's true—I would. And you have deeper reasons for returning as well."

"How can that be?" he asked. "We have no history together, nothing that would furnish a depth of reason."

She moved away a few paces, turning toward the sun, and a pattern of leaf shadow fell across her hip, reminding him of the pattern that had faded from her skin. She arranged her hair so that it trailed across her breasts, dressing herself in the black skeins.

"You'll come back because there's no other direction for you," she said. "Your life until this moment has been empty and you hope I'll offer fulfillment of a kind. You'll come back because you want to. And because the road you and I must travel, we have already set foot upon it."

When Hota and Magali, clad in an unflattering ankle-length dress he had borrowed from a prostitute, arrived at Liar's House that evening, Benno Grustark, portly and short-legged, his round, dark-complected face set in grouchy lines, framed by oily black ringlets, hurried out of his office and admonished Hota that if the woman were to spend the night, he would have to pay extra. However, after taking a closer look at Magali, after she turned her flat stare upon him, his delivery sputtered and he fell silent. When they passed up the stairs, leaving Benno looking up from the dusty lobby, not offering, as was his habit, further admonitions, Hota suspected that the innkeeper was unaccustomed to having so beautiful a woman frequent his establishment.

Ushering her into his room, Hota apologized for its sorry condition, but Magali paid no attention to the disarray and walked over to the wall beside his bed and began to inspect the weathered gray boards, running her forefinger along the black complexities of their grain, appearing to admire them as though they were made of the finest marble. Still daunted to a degree, Hota busied himself by straightening the room, picking up carved dragons and stowing them into drawers, dusting his rude furniture with a shirt. Glancing up from these chores, he saw that Magali had taken a seat on the bed and was picking at the folds of her skirt.

"I'd like a green dress," she said. "Dark green. Do you have a seamstress in the town?"

Hota wadded up the dust-covered shirt and tossed it onto a chair. "I think so . . . yes."

She nodded solemnly as if he had imparted a great wisdom and then swung her legs up and lay back on the bed. "I want to sleep for a while. Perhaps we can have something to eat afterward."

"The tavern downstairs has food, but it's not so good."

She closed her eyes, let out a sigh, and after a minute or two Hota assumed that she had drifted off; but then, with a sudden violent twisting of her body, she turned onto her side and said, her words partially muffled by the pillow, "Just so long as there's meat."

*T*heir first days together passed uncomfortably for Hota. Magali left the room only to visit the bathroom down the hall and spent much of the time sleeping, as if, he thought, she were acclimating to her new form. When awake she would peer at the boards or sit silently on the bed. Their infrequent conversations were functional, pertaining to things she needed, and if he was not off running errands for her, he sat in the chair and waited for her to wake. The town's seamstress delivered two dark green dresses. Magali, without thought for modesty, would change from one to the other in full view of Hota and he would feel stirrings of desire. How could he not? He was not used to this sort of display. His wife had gone to bed each night swaddled in layers of clothing, and even the prostitutes with whom he slept would merely hike up their skirts. With its high, small breasts and sleek flanks and long, graceful legs, Magali's body was a sculptor's dream of unmarred sensuality. But desire would not catch in him. He was still afraid, his mind too full of questions to permit the increase of lust, and he never ventured near her, sleeping on the floor or in a chair. What, he found himself wondering, was the road they were to travel? Was she truly a dragon recast as a woman, or was this all the result of a trick, a conspiracy of event and moment? And, most urgently, why had any of this happened? How could it be happening?

Sitting beside her day after day, week after week, Hota grew discontented with his surroundings and thought this might be because Magali's presence pointed up their shabbiness. He became assiduous in his cleaning, brought in flowers, new cushions for the chairs, and purchased prints to hang on the walls, brightening the long gray space. The footsteps and voices that sounded from the hallway irritated him and to mute them he hung blankets across the door. He dispersed the room's stale odor with cachets he bought in the market. None of these improvements registered with Magali. For no reason he could grasp, she seemed interested only in the boards. Then one night while she slept, as he was pacing about, he noticed that the grain of the planking looked sharper than before, considerably sharper than could be expected to result from his daily dusting. Curious, he examined them in the light of an oil lamp and discovered that the patterns of the grain had, indeed, grown more pronounced, forming intricacies of dark lines in which it was possible to see almost shape. At least this was his initial impression. As he continued to peer at them, certain shapes came to dominate. He saw narrow wings replete with struts and vanes, sinuous scaled bodies, fanged reptilian heads. A multiplicity of dragons. Every plank bore such images, all cunningly devised. And more were emerging all the time, as if they had been buried beneath gray snow that was now thawing. Holding the lamp above his head, he studied them and began to think he was not looking at many dragons, but at countless depictions of one. There were similarities in the architecture of the scales and the birdlike profile, the . . .

"What do you see?"

Given a start, Hota yipped and spun about to face Magali, who had padded up behind him. Her dress was unbuttoned to her navel, exposing the swell of her breasts, and though her hair was tousled from sleep, her usual neutral stare was not in evidence. She looked animated, excited, and this acted to suppress the anxiety her nearness inspired in him. She repeated her question and he said, "Dragons . . . or maybe one dragon. I'm not sure. Is that what you see?"

She ignored the question. "Anything else?"

"No. Is there more?"

"There's no end of things that can be seen."

She stepped up beside him and ran a hand along one of the boards, as if caressing it, then pointed at one of the images. "Here. Do you see the way this fang juts out at an angle? What does it remind you of?"

Uncomprehending, he gazed at the board for the better part of a minute and then he saw it. "Griaule! Is it Griaule?"

"All this"—she made a sweeping gesture, her voice quavering as with strong emotion—"it's his life. Ingrained within the trees that sprouted from his back. The entire inn is a record. All his days are written here."

So, Hota thought, Benno had not lied. It was difficult to believe. In Hota's experience, Benno had never exhibited an ounce of physical bravery, and the idea that he would chop down trees on Griaule's back was laughable. It was equally unlikely that he could have hired anyone to do the cutting for him. Those few who claimed to have set foot upon the dragon spoke of climbing onto the tail—none had trespassed to the degree that Hota himself had. And yet he remembered the way Benno had gaped at Magali. Might that have been a recognition of sorts, evidence that Benno, being more familiar than most with dragons, had sensed her hidden nature?

"Whatever else there is to see . . ." Hota said. "Will I see it?"

"Who knows?" She returned to the bed and as she settled upon it, smoothing out her skirt beneath her, she said, "You've seen what's necessary."

"Why's it necessary for me to see this much and no more? What's the point?"

She reclined upon the bed, braced on an elbow. "So you'll understand the extent of Griaule's dominion. So you'll accept it."

This half-answer irritated him, but he was not sufficiently confident with her to express anger. "Why is that important? I already know he shapes our lives to some extent."

"Knowing a thing is far from accepting it."

"What are you talking about?"

She put an arm across her eyes and said nothing.

"Are you saying I need to make an acknowledgment of some sort? Why? Explain it to me."

She would say no more on the subject and, shortly thereafter, she asked him to bring food from the tavern. Hota did not care to be treated like a child, given answers that suggested there were things he was better off not knowing—that was how he interpreted her responses—and as he waited for Magali's food to be prepared, standing by the kitchen door, gazing through smoke and steam at the hubbub generated by two matronly cooks and several grimy children, he thought contemptuously of her. How could he doubt she was who she claimed to be? For all her good looks, the woman behaved like a lizard. Torpid the day long. Rising only to piss and stare at the boards. And the way she ate! She brought to mind geckos back in Port Chantay, clinging to the walls for hours, motionless, before finally flicking out their tongues to snag a mosquito, lifting their . . . One of the serving boys, carrying a plate of rice and shredded pork into the tavern, brushed against Hota's hip. Hota snapped at him, then felt badly for having frightened the boy. What was he doing here? he asked himself. Cohabiting with a woman who had some mysterious plan for him. Languishing in a room where pictures of dragons manifested upon the walls. He should have done with her. With Teocinte. The next time she asked for food, he should take his bag of gems and cash, and head inland. Make for Caliche or cross the country altogether to Point Horizon. But could he leave? That was the question. Would he wander the valley, confused, unable to find his way out, always winding up back in Teocinte? The answer to this question, he decided, was probably yes. He was still caught in the snare Griaule had set for him the day he met Magali. If he were ever able to escape it, he assumed it would be because the dragon was done with him.

Despite his annoyance, that conversation marked a turning in their relationship. Though she remained less than talkative over the next month, now and then, in addition to asking him for things, she would inquire as to how he felt or, standing at a window, would offer comments on the weather, the unsightliness of the town, or laugh at, say, the misery of a carter whose wheels had gotten stuck in the mud. It appeared she was developing a personality. Mean-spirited, for the most part. Minimal. But a personality nonetheless. She continued her habit of disrobing in front of him and he noticed changes in her body: a faint crease demarking the lower reach of her abdomen; a hint of crowsfeet; the slightest sag to her breasts. Changes that would have been imperceptible to anyone else, but that to a man who had observed her for seven weeks, whose only occupation had been that observation, stood out like mountains on a plain. He wondered if these marks and slackenings signaled the ultimate stage of her transformation and, against the weight of logic, he began to think of her as a woman more often than not. As a consequence, his desire burned hotter, despite an apprehension that such feelings were touched with the perverse.

During the eighth week of her stay at Liar's House, Magali became more active, sleeping less, enjoining Hota in conversations that, albeit brief, served to grow the relationship. One night, rather than sending him for food, she suggested that they eat in the tavern. Her suggestion did not sit easily with Hota. Under the best of circumstances, he preferred solitude. Further, he worried that Magali might not react well to being exposed to a crowd. But when they entered the tavern, a low-ceilinged room with the same gray weathered planking, furnished with long benches and tables, lit by lanterns of fanciful design, each consisting of frosted panes held in place by ironwork dragons, they found only five patrons in the place: two prostitutes and their clients dining together, and a burly blond man with a pink complexion and a pudgy, thick-lipped face who was drinking beer from a clay mug. They stationed themselves well away from the others, close to the wall, and ordered wine and venison. Magali sat without saying a word, taking in the scene, and Hota watched her with more than his usual fixity. The din and angry shouts from the kitchen, the laughter of the prostitutes, all the sounds of the tavern receded from him. It seemed that a heartbeat was buried in the orange glow of the lamps, contriving a pulsing backdrop for the woman opposite him, whose bronze skin was in itself a radiant value. He gazed at her thoughtlessly, or else it was a single formless thought that uncoiled through his mind, imposing an almost ritual attentiveness.

When the food arrived, Magali picked up her venison steak and nibbled a bite, chewed, threw back her head and swallowed. She repeated this process over and over. Hota shoveled down his meal without tasting it, his attention unwavering. Like the icon of some faded gaiety, an old man with wisps of white hair fraying up from his mottled scalp, wearing a ratty purple cloak, entered the tavern and played a whistling music on bamboo pipes; he stopped at the other tables, begging for a coin, but veered away from Hota after receiving a hostile look.

Hota understood that something was wrong. The ordinary grind of his thoughts had been suppressed, damped down, but he had no will to contend against the agent of suppression, whatever it was, so seduced was he by Magali's face and figure. He derived a proprietary pleasure from watching the convulsive working of her throat, the fastidious movements of her fingers and teeth. Like an old man watching a very young girl. Greedy for life, not sex. Lusting after some forbidden essence. Although he perceived this ugliness in himself and wanted to reject it, he could not do so and tracked her every gesture and change in expression. She gave no sign that she noticed the intensity or the character of his vigilance, but the fact that she never once engaged his eyes told him she knew he was looking and that all her actions were part of a show. The inside of his head felt warm, as if his brain, too, were pulsing with soft orange light.

More customers drifted into the tavern. The conversation and laughter outvoiced the kitchen noises, but it seemed quiet where Hota and Magali sat, their isolation unimpaired. Two bulky men in work-stained clothes came to join the blond man at his table. They drank swiftly, draining their mugs in a few gulps, and began casting glances at Magali, who was now devouring her second steak. They put their heads together and whispered and then laughed uproariously. Typically, Hota would have ignored their derision, but anger mounted in him like a liquid heated in a vial. He heaved up from the bench and went over to the men's table and glared down at them. The newcomers appeared to know him, at least by reputation, for one, adopting an air of appeasement, muttered his name, and the other fitted his gaze to the table top. But either the blond man was only recently arrived in Teocinte or else he was immune to fear. He sneered at Hota and asked, "What do you want?"

One of the others made silent speech with his eyes to the blond man, as if encouraging him to be wary, but the man said, "Why are you frightened of this lump of shit? Let's hear what's on his mind."

Through the lens of anger, Hota saw him not as a man, but as a creature you might find clinging to the pitch-coated piling of a dock, an unlovely thing with loathsome urges and appetites, and a pink, rubbery face that was a caricature of the human.

"Can't you talk, then? Very well. I'll talk." Smirking, the blond man settled back against the wall, resting a foot on the bench. "Do you know who I am?"

Hota held his tongue.

"No? It doesn't matter. The thing that most matters is who you are. You're a man who needs no introduction. Useless. Dull. A clod. You might as well carry a sign with those words on it. You announce yourself everywhere you go, in everything you do."

Hota felt as if his skin were a crust that was restraining some molten substance beneath.

"I suppose it would be easiest for you to think of me as your opposite," the blond man continued. "I employ men such as you. I turn them to my purposes. I might be persuaded to employ you . . . if you're as strong as you look. Are you?"

A smile came unbidden to Hota's face.

The blond man chuckled. "Well, strength's not everything, my friend. I've bested many men who were stronger than me. Do you know how?" He tapped the side of his head. "Because I'm strong up here. I could take things from you and you wouldn't be able to stop me. Your woman, for instance. Beautiful! I gave some thought to taking her off your hands. But I've concluded that she'll feel more at home with you." He gave a bemused sniff. "For your sake, I hope she fucks less like a pig than she eats."

As Hota reached for the blond man's leg, the closer of his two companions threw a punch at Hota's forehead. The punch did no damage and Hota struck him in the mouth with an elbow, breaking his teeth and knocking him beneath the adjoining table. He seized the blond man's ankle, yanked him out into the center of the tavern, holding his leg high so he could not get to his feet. The third man came at him, a lack of conviction apparent in the hesitancy of his attack. Hota kicked him in the groin and, taking a one-handed grip on the blond man's throat, lifted him so that his feet dangled several inches above the floor. He clawed at Hota, pried at his fingers. His face empurpled. A froth fumed out between his lips. He fumbled out a dagger and tried to stab Hota, but Hota knocked the dagger to the floor, caught the man's knife hand and squeezed, at the same time relaxing his grip on his throat. The blond man sank to his knees, screaming as the bones in his hand were snapped and ground together.

"Hota!"

Magali was standing by the door that led to the street. Despite the urgency of her shout, she appeared unruffled. Hota released the blond man, who rolled onto his side, cradling his bloody, mangled hand, cursing at Hota. Other men had drawn near, their physical attitudes suggesting that they might be ready to fight. Hota faced them down, squaring his shoulders, and, instead of cautioning them, he roared.

The noise that issued from him was more than the sum of a troubled life, of old angers, of social impotence—it seemed to spring from a vaster source, to be the roar of the turning world, a sound that all creation made in its spin toward oblivion, exultant and defiant even in dismay, a sound that went unheard until, as now, it found a host suitable to give it tongue. Quailed, the men backed toward the kitchen. Recognizing that they no longer posed a threat, his anger emptied, Hota went to Magali's side. Her face was difficult to read, but he felt from her a radiation of contentment. She took his arm—proudly, it seemed—and they stepped out into the town.

*B*y night, Teocinte had an even more derelict aspect than by day, the crooked little shacks, firelight flickering through cracks in the doors and from behind squares of cloth hung over windows. Streets winded and quiet, except for the occasional scream and burst of laughter. A naked infant, untended, splashed in a puddle formed by that afternoon's rain. Above, the silhouette of Griaule's tree-lined back outlined in stars against a purple sky. It had altogether the atmosphere of a tribal place, of people huddled together in frail shelters against the terrors of the dark, dwelling in the very shadow of those terrors.

That night Hota felt estranged from the town and from himself, troubled by the vague presence in his thoughts that had spurred him to violence. But Magali's closeness, her scent and the brush of her hip, the pressure of her breast against his arm, these things prevented him from brooding. They idled along the downslope of the street that fronted Liar's House, moving toward the dragon's head, and as they walked she said, "We should be flying now."

"Flying?" he said. "What do you mean?"

"It's the most wonderful thing, flying together."

He suspected that she was dissembling and knew she did not like being pressed; but he had the itch to press her. She rarely spoke about her life prior to their meeting and, though he was not convinced that she was who she claimed to be, he wanted to believe her. It surprised him that he wanted this. Until that instant he had been uncertain as to what he wanted, but he was clear about it now. He wanted her to be a fabulous creature, for himself to be part of her fabulous design, and, sensing that she might be receptive to him, he asked if she could tell him how it was to fly.

She was silent for such a length of time, he thought she would refuse to answer, but after five or six paces she said, "One day you'll know how it feels."

Puzzled, he said, "I don't understand."

"You can't . . . not yet."

That comment sparked new questions, but he chose to pursue the original one. "You must be able to tell me something about it."

They walked a while longer and then she said, "Each flight is like the first flight, the flight made at the instant of creation. You're in the dark, you're drowsy. Almost not there. And then you wake to some need, some urgency. Your wings crack as you rise up. Like thunder. And then you're into the light, the wind . . . the wind is everything. All your strength and the rush of the wind, the sound of your wings, the light, it's one power, one voice."

As she spoke he seemed to understand her, but when she fell silent the echoes of her words lost energy and were transformed into generalities. He tried to explore them, to recapture some fraction of the feeling her voice had communicated, but failed.

The town ended in a palm hammock, and at the far edge of the hammock, resting among tall grasses, was a squarish boulder nearly twice the height of a man, like a giant's petrified tooth. They climbed atop it and sat gazing at Griaule's head, a hundred yards distant. The sagittal crest was visible in partial silhouette against the sky, but the bulk of the head was a mound of shadow.

"You keep telling me I can't understand things," he said. "It's frustrating. I want to understand something and I don't understand any of it. How is it you can be here with me like this . . . as a woman?"

She lifted her head and closed her eyes as she might if the sun were shining and she wanted to indulge in its warmth, and she told him of the souls of dragons. How, unlike the souls of men, they enclosed the material form rather than being shrouded within it.

"Our souls are not prisoners of the flesh, but its wardens," she said. "We control our shapes in ways you cannot."

"You can be anything you choose? Is that what you mean?"

"Only a dragon or a woman . . . I think. I'm not sure."

He pondered this. "Why can't Griaule change himself into a man?"

"What would be the point? Who would be more inviolate—a paralyzed dragon or a paralyzed man? As a dragon, Griaule lives on. As a man, he would long since have been eaten by lesser beasts. In any case, the change is painful. It's something done only out of great necessity."

"You didn't appear to be in pain . . . when I found you?"

"It had ebbed by the time you reached me."

At first there were too many questions flocking Hota's thoughts for him to single any out, but before long one soared higher than the rest: what great necessity had caused her to change? He was about to ask it of her when she said, "Soon you'll understand all of this. Flying. How the soul can grow larger than the flesh. How it is that I have come to you and why. Be patient."

Moonglow fanned up above the hills to the west and in that faint light she looked calm, emotionless. Yet as he considered her, it struck him that a new element was embodied in her face. Serenity . . . or perhaps it was an absence he perceived, some small increment of anxiety erased.

"Griaule," she said in a half-whisper.

"What of him?" he asked, perplexed by her worshipful tone.

She only shook her head in response.

Something scurried through the grass behind the boulder. A dull gleam emerged from the shadow of Griaule's head, the tip of a fang holding the light. The wind picked up, bringing the still palms alive, swaying their fronds, breeding a sigh that seemed to voice a hushed anticipation. Magali folded her arms across her breasts.

"I'm ready now," she said.

Hota assumed that by those last words, she meant she was ready to return to Liar's House, for after saying them, she hopped down from the boulder and led him back toward the town; but once they closed the door of his room behind them, it became clear she had intended something more. She undressed quickly and stood before him in a silent yet unmistakable invitation, her skin agleam in the unsteady lamplight. Skeins of hair fell across her breasts, like black tributaries on the map of a voluptuous bronze country. Her eyes were cored with orange reflection. She looked to be a magical feminine treasure whose own light devalued that of the lamp. All his flimsy moral proscriptions against intimacy melted away. He took a step toward her and let her bring him down onto the bed.

During the first thirty-one years of his life, Hota had made love to but one woman: his wife. Since then, he had made love to many more and thought himself reasonably knowledgeable as to their ways. Magali's ways, however, enlarged his views on the subject. For the most part she lay quiescent, her eyes half-closed, as if her mind were elsewhere and she were merely allowing herself to be penetrated; yet every so often, abruptly, she would begin to thrash and heave, pushing and clawing at him, breath shrieking out of her, throwing herself about with such apparent desperation, he was nearly unseated. Initially, he took this behavior for rejection and flung himself off her; but she pulled him back between her legs and, once he had entered her, she lay quiet again. This alternation of corpselike stillness and frenzied motion distressed him and he was unable to lose himself in the act, half-listening to the sounds of more commercial passions emanating from adjoining rooms. When he had finished and was lying beside her, sweaty and breathing hard, she demanded that he repeat the performance. And so it went, the second encounter like the first, equally as awkward and emotionally unsatisfying. In her frenzied phase, she seemed even less a complicitor in pleasure than she did when she was still. She took to snapping at his arm, his shoulder, making cawing noises deep in her throat. But their third encounter, one into which Hota had to be vigorously coerced, was different. She drew up her knees and met his thrusts with sinuous abandon and kept her arms locked about his neck, her eyes on his face, until at long last she offered up a shivery cry and clamped her knees to his sides, refusing to let him move.

After he withdrew, pleased, feeling that they had managed actual intimacy, he tried to be tender with her, but she shrank from his touch and would not speak. More confused than ever, he decided that her behavior must be due to a lack of familiarity with her body, and he counseled himself to remain patient. They had come this far and whatever road lay ahead, there would be time to smooth over these problems. Fatigued, his eyes went to the lamp lit ceiling. It looked as if all the dragons imprinted in the grain were quivering, shifting agitatedly, as if preparing to take flight. He watched them, imagining that if he watched long enough he would see one fly, the tiny black sketch of dragon flap up off the boards and make a circuit of the room. Eventually he slept.

The following morning, gray and drizzly, with a touch of chill, he woke to find Magali at the window, which stood half-open. She had on her favorite green dress and was looking out onto the street. He sat up, groggy, rubbing his eyes. The bedsprings squeaked loudly, but she gave no sign of having heard.

"Magali?" he said.

She ignored him. The rain quickened, drumming on the tin roof. Feeling the bite of the cold, Hota swung his legs onto the floor, grabbed his shirt from among the rumpled bedclothes and began to pull it over his head.

"Is something wrong?" he asked.

Without turning, she said glumly, "You've given me a child."

He paused, the shirt tangled about his neck, and started to ask how she could know such a thing, then remembered that she had knowledge inaccessible to him.

"A son," she said dully. "I'm going to have a son."

The idea of fathering children no longer figured into Hota's plans and his immediate reaction was uneasiness over having to shoulder such a responsibility. He tugged the shirt down to cover his belly. "You don't seem happy. Is it you don't want a child?"

"It isn't what I want that's of moment." She paused and then said, "The birth will be painful."

Her attitude, so contrary to what he would have expected, provoked an odd reaction in him—he wondered how it would feel to be a father. "It might not be so bad," he said. "I've known women to have easy births. At the end we'll have our son and perhaps that'll give . . ."

"He's not *your* son," she said. "You fathered him, but he will be Griaule's son."

The rain came harder yet and, amplified by the tin, filled the room with a kind of roaring, a din that made it difficult for Hota to think, to hear his own voice. "That's impossible."

Magali turned from the window. "Haven't you heard a thing I've told you?"

"What have you told me that would explain this?"

She stared at him without expression. "Griaule is the eldest of all who live. Over the centuries, his soul has expanded with the growth of his body. How far it extends, I can't say. Far beyond the valley, though. I know that much. I was flying above the sea when he drew me to him." She dropped into the chair beside the window and rested her hands on her knees. "His soul encloses him like a bubble. For all I know that bubble has grown to enclose the entire world. But I'm certain you live inside its reach. You've lived inside it your entire life. Now he's drawn you to him as well. It's possible he caused the events that drove you from Port Chantay. That would be in keeping with what I understand of his character. With the deviousness and complexity of his mind."

Hota felt the need to offer a denial, but could find no logical framework to support one.

"Don't you see?" she went on. "Griaule desired to father a son. Since he couldn't participate in the act of conception, he contrived a means by which he could father the child of his will. And for this purpose he sought out a man who embodied certain of his own qualities. Someone with a stolid temperament. With great strength and endurance. And great anger. A human equivalent of his nature who fit the shape of his design. Then he chose me to endure the birth."

Rain slanted in through the window. Hota crossed the room and closed it. As he returned to the bed, he said, "You must have known this all along? Why didn't you tell me?"

She clicked her tongue in annoyance. "I didn't know all of it. I still don't know it all. And it's as I've said—these things that have happened to us, they weren't my wish. Even if they were, I'm not like you, Hota. My thoughts are not like yours. My motives are not yours. You asked why I wasn't happy? I'm never happy. My emotions . . . you couldn't grasp them."

"You should have told me," he said sullenly.

"It would have only upset you. There's nothing you could have done."

"Nevertheless, you lied to me. I don't deserve to be kept in the dark about what's going on."

"I haven't lied!" she said. "Have I withheld things from you? Yes. I did what I was compelled to do. But all the things I know, the things I don't know, they may or may not be good for you. And that's what you truly want to know, isn't it? What's going to happen to you? In the end all your questions will be answered and you'll be pleased with that. That's what I think. But I can't be certain. That's the problem, you see? Any answer I can give you is essentially a lie, except for 'I don't know.'"

Her response had the same disorienting effect as the rain—he believed her, but it was like believing in nothing, knowing nothing. He sat with his head down, dull and listless, looking at his fingers, wiggling them for a distraction. "You and me. What about you and me?"

"We'll travel the road together and learn what fate has in store. That's all I can tell you."

"I don't believe you."

"What don't you believe?"

"About your feelings," he said. "I know you were happy last night. For a time, at least."

She leaned toward him and spoke slowly, with exaggerated emphasis, as though to a child. "I lived in the side of a cliff. A sea cave. I was alone, yet I wanted for nothing. I was content with the world I knew." She resettled in her chair. "Last night, that was . . . strange. Now it's done. We're past that turn of the road."

She appeared to lose interest in the conversation, her eyes traveling across the boards. In the rainy light, her beauty was subdued, diminished. "Are you happy?" she asked after a minute.

"Maybe I was, a little." He spotted his pants lying on the floor and stepped into them. "Why would Griaule do this? For what reason does he want a son?"

"I've no idea. Perhaps it's just a game he's playing. You can't know Griaule's intent. Some of his schemes play out over thousands of years. He's unique, as unlike me as I am unlike you. No one can fathom what he intends."

Of a sudden the rain let up and a weak sun broke through the overcast; the wind gusted and a distorted shadow of the window, pale panes and darker divisions, canted out of true, trembled on floor.

"I need food," Magali said.

Though Hota held out some hope that their night together would be the beginning of intimacy, he soon recognized it to have been their peak. Thereafter the relationship settled back into one of functional disengagement. He brought her food, whatever she needed, and kept watch over her with devotional intensity. Their conversations grew less frequent, less far-ranging, as her belly swelled . . . and it swelled much more rapidly than would a typical pregnancy. Four weeks and she had the shape of a woman in late-term. She stayed in bed most of the day. Never again did they visit the tavern or walk out together in the town. Hota sat in a chair, brooding, or stood at the window and did the same. He became familiar with the window much in the way he had become familiar with Magali, noting all its detail: patches of greenish mold on the sill; a splintery centerpiece; areas of wood especially stained and swollen by dampness; rotted inches eaten away by infestation. Its gray dilapidation was, he thought, emblematic not only of the room, but of his life, which was itself a gray, dilapidated region, a space that contained and limited his spirit, stunting its growth.

He recognized, too, that his position in the town had changed. Whereas formerly he had been someone whom people avoided, few had spoken against him; but now when passed in the streets, no one offered a greeting or a salute—instead, men and women would stand closer together, whisper and dart wicked glances in his direction. The reasons for this change remained unclear until one afternoon, as he entered the inn, Benno Grustark accosted him at the door and demanded twice the usual rent.

"I'm losing business, having you here," Benno told him. "You need to compensate me."

Hota pointed out that his was the only place in town where visitors could stay and thus he doubted Benno's claim.

"When people hear about you, some will sleep outside rather than rent my rooms," Benno said.

"When they hear about me?" Hota said, bewildered. "What do they hear?"

Benno, who was that day dressed in his customary brown moleskin trousers and a red tunic that clung to his ample belly, a costume that lent him an inappropriately jolly look, shifted his feet and cut his eyes to the side as if fearing he would be overheard. "Your woman . . . people say she's a witch."

Hota grunted a laugh.

"It's not a joke for me," Benno said. "What do you expect them to think? She's about to give birth and yet she's only been with you a few months!"

"She was pregnant before I brought her here."

"Oh, I see! And where was she before that? Did you keep her in your pocket? Did you make her pregnant at a distance?"

"It's not my child," Hota said, and realized that this, unlike his previous statement, was only partially a lie.

An expression of incredulity on his face, Benno said, "I saw her when she came. She wasn't showing at all. And I've seen her since, in the hallway, no more than a month ago. She wasn't showing then, either."

"All pregnant women show differently. You know that."

Benno started to raise a further point, but Hota cut him off. "Since you're so observant, I have to assume you're the one who has been spreading rumors about her."

Benno popped his eyes and waggled his hands at chest-level in thespian display of denial. "Plenty of people have seen her. Other guests. Some of my girls. Her condition's hardly a secret."

Hota dug coins from his pocket and pressed them into Benno's hand. "Here," he said. "Now leave us alone."

With a plodding tread, he started up the stairs.

Benno followed to the first step and called out, "As soon as she's able to travel, I want the both of you gone! Do you hear me? Not one day longer than necessary!"

"It'll be our pleasure." Hota paused midway up the stairs and gazed down at him. "But take this to heart. Until that day, you would do well to suppress the rumors about her, rather than foster them." Then a thought struck him. "What possessed you to cut the boards of the inn from Griaule's back?"

Benno's defensive manner was swept away by a confounded look, one similar—Hota thought—to the looks he himself often wore these days. "I just did it," Benno said. "I did it because I wanted to."

"Is that another one of your lies?" Hota asked. "Or don't you even know?"

Over the course of the following two weeks, Magali became increasingly irritable, not asking things of Hota so much as giving orders and expressing her displeasure when he was slow to obey. She otherwise maintained a brittle silence. Thrown back onto his own resources, Hota fretted about the child and speculated that it might be some mutant thing, awful in aspect and nature. Burdened with such a monster, where could he take her that people would tolerate them? It was not in him to abandon her. Whether that was a function of his character or of Griaule's, he could not have said and was a question he did not seek to answer. He had accepted that this, for the time being, was his station in life. That being the case, he tried to steel himself against doubt and depression, but doubt and depression circled him like vultures above a wounded dog, and the rain, incessant now, drummed and drummed on the tin roof, echoing in his dreams and filling his waking hours with its muted roar. Out the window, he watched the street turn into a quagmire, people sending up splashes with every step, thatched roofs melting into brownish green decay, drenched pariah dogs curled in misery beneath eaves and stairs. The smell of mildew rose from the wood, from clothing. The world was drowning in gray rain and Hota felt he was drowning in the rain of his own existence.

Then came a morning when the rain all but stopped and Magali's spirits lifted. She seemed calm, not irritable in the least, and she offered apology for her moodiness, then discussed with him what she would require after the child was born. He asked if she thought the birth would be soon.

"Soon enough," she said. "But that's not your worry. Just bring me food. Meat. And make sure no one disturbs me. The rest I'll take care of."

She needed an herb, she told him, that grew on the far side of the dragon's tail. It was most efficacious when picked at the height of the rains and she asked him to go that day and gather all he could find. She described the plant and urged him to hurry—she wanted to begin taking it as quickly as possible. Then she brushed her lips against his cheek, the closest she had ever come to giving him a kiss, and tried to send him on his way. But this diffident affection, so out of character for her, provoked Hota to ask what she felt for him.

She gave an impatient snort. "I told you—my emotions aren't like yours."

"I'm not an idiot. You could try to explain."

She sat on the edge of the bed, gazed at him consideringly. "What do you feel for me?"

"Devoted, I suppose," he said after a pause. "But my devotion changes. I remain dutiful, but there are times when I resent you . . . I fear you. At other times, desire you."

She appeared to be studying the floor, the boards figured by dragons, blackly emerging from the grain of the wood. "Love and desire," she said at last, imbuing the words with a wistful emphasis. "For me . . . " She shook her head in frustration. "I don't know."

"Try!" he insisted.

"This is so important to you?"

"It is."

She firmed her lips. "Inevitability and freedom. That's what I feel. For you, for the situation we're in . . . " She spread her hands, a gesture of helplessness. "That's as near as I can get."

At a loss, Hota asked her to explain further.

"None of this was our idea, yet it was inevitable," she said. "Its inevitability was thrust upon us by Griaule. But that's irrelevant. We have a road to travel and must make the best of it. And so we . . . we've formed an attachment."

"And freedom? What of that?"

"To find your way to freedom in what is inevitable, within the bonds of your fate . . . that, for me, is love. Only when you accept a limitation can you escape it."

Hota nodded as if he understood her, and to a degree he did; but he was unable to apply what he understood to the things he felt or the things he wanted her to feel.

Perhaps she read this in his face, for she said then, "Often I feel other emotions. Strains . . . whispers of them. I think they're akin to those you feel. They trouble me, but I've come to accept them." She beckoned him to come stand beside her and then took his hand. "We'll always be bound together. When you accept that, then you'll find your freedom." She lay back and turned onto her side. "Now, please. Bring me the herb. This is the day it should be picked."

There was no shortcut to the spot where the herb grew, unless you were to climb over Griaule's back. Hota was loath to run that course again and so he went up into the hills behind the town and walked through pine forest along the ridges for an hour until he reached a pass choked by a grassy mound that wound between hills: the dragon's tail. Once across the tail, he walked for half an hour more through scrub palmetto before he came to an undulant stretch of meadow close to the dragon's hind leg, where weeds bearing blue florets sprouted among tall grasses. He worked doggedly, plucking the weeds, cramming them into his sack and tamping them down. When the sack was two-thirds full, he sat beneath a palmetto whose fronds still dripped with rain, facing the massive green slope of the dragon, and unwrapped his lunch of bread and cheese and beer.

The trappings of his life seemed to arrange themselves in orderly ranks as he ate, and he realized that for the first time he had a significant purpose. Aside from momentary impulses, he had never truly wanted anything before Magali appeared atop Griaule's back. Nor, until the day of his wife's death, had he ever acted of his own volition. He had done everything by rote, copying the lives of his father, his uncles, compelled by the circumstance of birth to obey the laws of his class. Of course, it was conceivable . . . no, it was certain, that he had always been the subject of manipulation, that what he had done in Port Chantay and since was not of his own choosing, and he was merely a minor figure in Griaule's design. It was immaterial, he thought, whether the manipulative force were the arcane directives of a dragon or the compulsions of a society. The main distinction, as he saw it, was that his current purpose—that of surrogate father, caretaker, protector of a woman once a dragon—was a duty for which he had been singled out, for which he was best suited of all the available candidates, and that bred in him an emotion he had felt so rarely, he scarcely knew it well enough to name: Pride. It pervaded him now, alleviating both his anxieties and his aversion toward being used in such a bizarre fashion.

An armada of clouds with dark bellies and silvered edges swept up from the south, grazing the sharp crests of the distant hills and thundering, as if their hulls were being ruptured. White lightnings pranced and stabbed. The rain began to pelt down in scatters, big drops that hit like cold shrapnel, and Hota, leaving the remnants of his food for the ants, returned to his task, tearing up fistfuls of weeds and stuffing them into the sack. Soon the thunder was all around, deafening, one peal rolling into the next. Then he heard a low rumble that came from somewhere closer than the sky, an immense, grating voice that seemed to articulate a gloating satiety, a brute pleasure, and lasted far too long to be an ordinary peal. Hota dropped the sack and stared at Griaule, expecting the hill to shake off its cloak of soil and trees, and walk. Expecting also that the head would lift and pin him with a golden eye. Rain matted his hair, poured down his face, and still he stood there, waiting to hear that voice again. When he did not, he became uncertain he had heard it the first time, and yet it resounded in memory, guttural and profound, a voice such as might have risen from the earth, from the throat of a demon pleased by the taste of a freshly digested mortal soul. If he *had* heard it, if it had been Griaule's voice, Griaule who never spoke, Hota could think of only one thing that would have summoned so unique a response. The child. He set about stuffing the sack with renewed vigor, ripping up weeds, unmindful of the rain, and when the sack was full, its girth that of a wagon wheel, he shouldered it and headed back into the hills and along the ridge toward Teocinte.

By the time he began descending through the pine forest, angling for the center of town, Hota was shivering, his clothes soaked though, but his thoughts were of Magali's well-being and not his own. She might have needed the herb in preparation for the birth and suffered greatly for lack of it. The idea that he had failed her plagued him more than the cold. He increased his pace, hustling down the slope with a choppy, sideways step, the sack bumping and rolling against his back. On reaching the lower slope, where the pines thinned out into stands of banana trees and shrubs, he heard voices and caught a glimpse of several men sprinting up the hill. He was too worried about Magali to make a presumption concerning the reason for their haste. Forcing his way through the last of the brush, he burst out onto a dirt street, repositioned the sack, which had slipped from his shoulder. Then he glanced to his left, toward Liar's House.

What he saw rooted him to the spot. Off along the bumpy, muddy street, many-puddled, strafed by slashing rain and lined with shanties that in their crookedness and decrepitude looked like desiccated wooden skulls with tin hats, lay the wreckage of the inn. There appeared to have been an explosion inside the place, the walls and roof blown outward . . . yet not blown far. Just far enough so as to form, of shattered gray boards, crushed furniture, ripped mattresses, and scraps of tin, the semblance of an enormous nest. One corner post with a shard of flooring attached had been left standing, detracting from the effect. Resting at the center of the ruin, her head high and her body curled about a grayish white egg twice the size of Hota's sack, was a dragon with bronze scales. Perhaps forty feet in length, tip to tail. Twists of black smoke fumed from the boards around her and were dispersed by the rain. Smoke also rose from the wreckage of a shack opposite the hotel. She had breathed fire, Hota told himself. He felt a twinge of regret that he had not been present to see it.

No one else was about and Hota could feel the emptiness of the town. Everyone had fled. All the thieves and murderers. Except for him. The men whom he had passed on the outskirts must have been stragglers. His sack grew heavy. He lowered it to the ground, with no thought of running in his mind, and drank in the scene with the greediness of a connoisseur of desolation, savoring every detail, every variation in tint, every fractured angle. Liar's House had been constructed from exactly the right amount of timber to make a nest, enough to provide protection, yet not so much as to interfere with Magali's field of vision as she lay beside the egg. Griaule's design at work, Hota imagined. The boards had fallen perfectly. Those that had been part of the interior rooms had collapsed outward and thus created a wall around the inner nest; those that had been part of the exterior had fallen inward, creating a field of debris that would afford a treacherous footing to anyone who tried to cross.

Hota was still marveling over the rectitude and precision of Griaule's plan, when Magali's neck flexed, her head turned toward him, and she gave a cry that, though absent the chthonic power of the grumbling he had earlier heard, nonetheless owned power sufficient to terrify him. It started as a guttural cawing and narrowed to a violent whistling scream that seemed to skewer his brain with an icy wire. He wanted to run now, but the sight held him. How beautiful and strange she looked at the heart of her ruinous nest, with her child in his glossy shell, smoke rising about them like black incense burnt to celebrate an idol. Her sagittal crest was a darker bronze, a corroded color—some of her scales shaded toward this same hue at the edges. The shape of her head was different from Griaule's. Not birdlike, but serpentine. Her eyes, also dark, set in deep orbits, were flecked with many-colored brightnesses; her folded wings were of an obsidian blackness, the struts wickedly sharp. All in all, like a relic treasure of the orient in her armored gaud. She screamed again and he thought he understood the urgency her voice conveyed.

The herb.

She wanted the herb.

He hoisted the sack onto his shoulder. Got his feet moving. Shuffled toward her, resolute yet weak with fear, his scrotum cold and tightened. He paused at the point where the front steps of the hotel had stood, now smashed to kindling, and imagined the change, the floor giving way beneath her suddenly acquired weight, the walls sundered by lashings of her tail and blows from her head. Even with the heavy odor of the rain and smoke, he could smell her scent of bitter ozone. He opened the sack, preparing to dump the contents on the ground, and she screamed a third time, a blast that nearly deafened him.

Closer.

She wanted him closer.

He knew she could extend her neck and snap him up at this distance— there was no reason for him to be more afraid and yet he was. He reshouldered the sack and picked his way across the outer wreckage, scrambling over broken-backed couches, rain-heavied folds of carpet, barricades of splintered wood, and a litter of items belonging to guests: undergarments, shoes, spectacles, books, tin boxes, satchels, hip flasks, a trove of human accessories, all crushed and rent. As he crawled over the last of these obstacles, he saw a taloned foot ahead. The talons gleaming black, the neat scales into which they merged no larger than his hand. The boards beneath him—those that had fallen so they formed a circular wall about the inner nest—they were alive with the images of dragons. Tiny perfect dragons flowing up from the grain of the wood, changing moment to moment, clearer than previously counterfeiting movement by their flow, as if they were pictographs emanating from Griaule's mind and he was telling a story in that language to his son, the story of a single dragon and how he flew and hunted and ruled. Like, Hota thought, a nursery decoration. Magical in character, yet serving a function similar to that of the fishes he had painted on the ceiling of his own back room in Port Chantay when his wife had informed him she was pregnant. He had painted them over after learning it was a lie told to prevent him from straying.

Standing beneath the arch of Magali's scaled chest and throat, Hota found he could not look up at her. He dumped the weeds from the sack and remained with his head down, appalled by the chuffing engine of her breath, the terrible dimension of her vitality. He shut his eyes and waited to be bitten, chewed, and swallowed. Then a nudge that knocked him sideways. He fetched up against the wall of the nest and fell onto his back. She peered at him with one opaline eye, the great sleek wedge of her head hanging six feet above the ground, snorting gently through ridged nostrils. Her belly rumbled and her head swung in a short arc to face him and he was enveloped in steamy breath. The implausibility of it all bore in upon him. That his seed had been transformed into the stuff of dragons; that he was father to an egg; that the beautiful woman to whom he had made love now loomed above him, costumed in fangs and scales, an icon of fear. His eyes went to the egg, glistening grayly with the rain. Lying beyond it was a sight that harrowed him. The lower portion of a leg, footless, the calf shredded bloodily. Tatters of brown moleskin adhering to the flesh. Benno. It seemed he had paid for his dutiful trespass by becoming Magali's first post-partum meal.

Magali's neck twisted, her head flipping up into the cloudy sky, and she vented a third scream. Once again, Hota understood her needs.

Bring me food, she was saying.

Meat.

How the days passed for them thereafter was very like the passage of all their days. Hota sat, usually on the steps of a shanty across the way, and watched over Magali. Intermittently, she would scream and he would walk to the livery where a number of horses were stabled, left behind by the panic-stricken citizens of Teocinte. He would lead one into the street (he could never manage to get them closer to the inn) and cut its throat; then he would butcher the animal and carry it to her in bloody sections. From time to time he spotted townspeople skulking on the outskirts, returned to reclaim personal possessions or perhaps to gauge when they might expect to reclaim their homes. They cursed at him and threw stones, but fled whenever he attempted to approach. He himself considered fleeing, but he seemed constrained by a mental regulation that enforced inaction and was as steady in its influence as the rain. He assumed that Griaule was its source, but that was of no real consequence. Everywhere you went, everything you did, some regulation turned you to its use. His thoughts ran in tedious circuits. He wondered if Magali had known she would change back into her original form. He believed she had, and he further believed that everything she had said to him was both lie and truth. She had wanted the herb, but she had also sent him to collect it in order to keep him away from the inn, to prevent him from being injured or killed during her transformation. That was the way of life. His life, at any rate. Even the truest of things eventually resolved into their lie. Every shining surface was tarred with blackness. Every light went dark. He speculated absently on what he would do after she left, as he knew she must, and devised infant plans for travel, for work. A job, he decided, might be in order. He had been idle far too long. But he realized this to be a lie he was telling himself—he doubted he would survive her and, though this might also have been a deception, he did not think he cared to survive her.

His habits became desultory. He fell to drinking, rummaging through the wreckage of the tavern for unbroken bottles and then downing them in a sitting. He slept wherever he was when sleep found him. Out in the street; in a shanty; amid the ruins of Liar's House. Not even the hatching of his golden-scaled child could spark his interest. The cracking of the shell started him from a drunken stupor, but he derived no joy from he event. He stared dumbly at the little monster mewling and stumbling at its mother's side, asking its first demanding questions, learning to feed on fresh horsemeat. At one point he attempted to name it, an exercise in self-derision inspired by his mock-paternity. The names that he conjured were insults, the type of names given to goblins in fairytales. Tadwallow. Gruntswipe. Stinkpizzle. When he brought the food, Magali would nudge him with her snout, gestures he took for shows of affection; but he understood that her real concerns lay elsewhere. They always had.

That time was, in essence, an endless gray day striped with sodden nights, a solitude of almost unvarying despondency. Weeks of drinking, slaughtering horses, staring at the sleeping dragon and their reptilian issue. On rare occasions he would rouse himself to a clinical detachment and give thought to the nature of the child. Dragons, so the tradition held, bore litters, and that Magali had borne a single child caused him to suspect that embedded in the little dragon's flesh was a human heart or a human soul or some important human quality that would enable it to cross more easily between shapes and sensibilities than had its mother. Then he would look to Griaule, the mighty green hill with its protruding, lowered head, and to Magali in her nest, and would have a sense of the mystery of their triangular liaison, the complex skein that had been woven and its imponderable potentials, and thereupon he would briefly regain a perspective from which he was able to perceive the dual nature of her beauty, that of the woman and that of the sleek, sculptural beast with lacquered scales, monster and temptress in one.

The rainy season drew toward its close and often he woke to bright sunlight, but his thoughts remained gray and his routine stayed essentially the same. The child had grown half as big as an ox, ever beating its wings in an effort to fly. It required more food. After killing all the horses, Hota found it necessary to go into the hills and hunt wild boar, jumping from branches onto their backs, stabbing them or, failing that, breaking their necks. He felt debased by the brutality of their death struggles. The animal stench; the squeals; the hot blood gushing onto his hands—these things turned something inside him and he began to see himself as a primitive, an apelike creature inhabiting a ruin and pretending to be a man. At night he stumbled through the town carrying an open bottle, singing in an off-key baritone, howling at the night and serenading the tin-hatted wooden skulls, addressing himself by name, offering himself advice or just generally chatting himself up. He refused to believe this was a sign of deterioration. He knew what he was about. It was an indulgence and nothing more. A means of passing the hours. And yet it might be, he thought, the prelude to deterioration. He was not, however, prepared to give up the practice. The sound of his voice distracted him from thinking and frightened off the townspeople, whose incursions had become more frequent, though none would come near Liar's House. Day and night they shouted threats from the hills, where many had taken refuge, and he would respond by singing to them and telling them what he had recently learned—that a man's goals and preoccupations, perhaps his every thought, were the manufacture of a higher power. Whatever agonies they threatened had been promised him since birth.

His dreams acquired a fanciful quality that went contrary to the grain of his waking life, and he came to have a recurring dream that seemed the crystallization of all the rest. He imagined himself running across fields, through woods, tireless and unafraid, in a state of exaltation, running for the joy of it, and when he approached the crest of a hill overlooking a steep drop, instead of halting, he ran faster and faster, leaping from the crest and being borne aloft on a sweep of wind, flying in the zones of the sun, and then seeing Magali, joining her in flight, swooping and curving, together weaving an endless pattern above a mighty green hill, the one from which he had leapt, and the child, too, was flying, albeit lower and less elegantly, testing itself against the air. It must be Griaule's dream, he thought. Though liberating, there was about it the cold touch of a sending. He recalled what Magali had said—that one day he would know how it felt to fly—and he wondered if the recurring dream was a reminder of that promise, or else the keeping of it. Set against all he had endured, it did not weigh out as a suitable reward. But suitable or not, he enjoyed the dream and sleep became the sole thing in his routine to which he looked forward.

One morning he woke lying in the street down from the inn. His joints stiff, eyelids crusted and stuck together, a foetid taste in his mouth. The brightness of the day pained him. Heat was beginning to cook from the abandoned town a reek compounded of rotting flesh and vegetable spoilage. His vision blurry, he looked toward the inn. Magali, crouched in her nest, emitted a scream. In reflex, Hota took a step toward the hills, thinking that she was demanding food. Then she screamed a second time. He stopped and rubbed his eyes and tried to focus on her. Clinging atop her back, between her wings, its diminutive talons hooked into her crest, was the child. Before Hota could put reason to work and understand what he was seeing, Magali unfurled her obsidian wings—each longer than her body—and beat them once, producing a violent cracking sound and a buffet of wind that knocked him off-balance and caused him to fall. She leaped to the edge of the nest and, using her grip on the shattered boards as a boost, vaulted into the air, paper debris from the street whirling up in her wake. Within seconds she was soaring high above and Hota, stupefied by the abruptness of her departure, felt as empty and abandoned as the town.

Magali disappeared behind Griaule's back and Hota regained his feet. He stood a while with his hands at his sides, unable to summon a thought; then he walked over to the inn and clambered across the rubble to the inner nest. What he expected to find, he could not have said. Some token, perhaps. An accidental gift. A scale that had worked loose; a scrap from a green dress. But there were only wastes and bloody bones. The images on the boards had receded into the grain. No dragons were visible upon their surfaces, agitated or otherwise. The silence oppressed him. Irrational though it was, he missed Magali's rumblings, her newborn's trebly growls. Fool, he thought, and struck himself on the chest. To be mooning over a monstrosity, a twisted union that had been arranged by a still greater monstrosity. He picked up a fragment of board and slung it toward the looming green hill, as if his strength, inflamed by anger, could drive it like a missile through scale and flesh and guts to pierce the enormous heart. The plank splashed down into a puddle and he felt even more the fool. He crawled up out of the nest and went into the street and sat beneath the remaining corner post of the inn. If he stayed much longer, he thought, people would drift back into town and there would be trouble. It would be best to leave now. Forego searching for his money, his gems, and walk away. He would find work somewhere. The notion tugged at him, but it refused to take hold. He clasped his hands, hung his head, and waited for another impulse to strike.

And then, as suddenly as she had departed, Magali returned, swooping low above Liar's House, the rush of her passage shattering the silence. She arrowed off over the hills behind the town, but returned again, swooping lower yet. Restored by the sight, Hota sprang to his feet. Watching her dive and loop, he soon recognized that she was repeating a pattern, that her flight was a signal, a ritual thing like the pattern she had flown above Griaule so many months ago. An acknowledgement. Or a farewell. Each time after passing above the street, a streaking of bronze scales, a shadowing of wings, she loosed a scream as she ascended. The guttural quality of her voice was inaudible at that distance, and her call had the sound of an eerie whistling music, three plaintive notes that might have been excerpted from a longer song whose melody played out closer to the sun. For an hour and more she flew above him. Like a scarf drawn through the sky. Entranced, he began to understand the meaning of the design her flight wove in the air. It was a knot, eloquent in its graceful twists, a sketch of the circumstance that had bound them. They had met, entwined into a minor theme that served the purpose of a larger music, one whose structure neither could discern, and now they would part. But only for a while. They would always be bound by that knot. All its loops led inward toward Liar's House. He understood what she had told him on the day he went to gather the herb. He understood the congruence of inevitability and love, fate and desire, and, having accepted this, he was able to take joy in her freedom, to be confident that a like freedom would soon be his.

Even after she had gone, flown beyond the hills, he watched the sky, hoping she would reappear. Yet there was no bitterness or regret in his heart. Though he did not know how it would happen, he believed she would always return to him. They would never be as he might have hoped them to be, but the connection between them was unbreakable. He would go inland, toward Point Horizon, and somewhere he would find a suitable home, a sinecure, and he would await the day of her return. No, he would do more than wait. For the first time in memory, he felt the sap of ambition rising in him. He would soar in his own way. He would not allow himself to settle for mere survival and drudgery.

His mind afire with half-formed plans, with possibility of every sort, Hota turned from the inn, preparing to take a first step along his new road, and saw a group of men approaching along the street. Several dozen men. Filthy and bearded from their exile in the hills. Clad in rags and carrying clubs and knives. A second group, equally proportioned, was approaching from the opposite end of the street. He ducked around the corner of the inn, onto a side street, only to be confronted by a third group. And a fourth group moved toward him from the other end of that street.

They had him boxed.

Hota was frightened, yet fear was not pre-eminent in him. He still brimmed with confidence, with the certainty that the best of life lay ahead, and refused to surrender to panic. The third group, he judged, was the smallest of the four. He drew his boar-killing knife and ran directly at them, hoping to unnerve them with this tactic. The center of the group, toward which he aimed, fell back a step, and, seeing this, Hota let out a hoarse cry and ran harder, slashing the air with his knife. Seconds later, he was among them. Their bearded, hollow-cheeked faces aghast, they clutched at him, tried to stab him, but his momentum was so great, he burst through their ranks without injury, and ran past the last shanties into the palms and bananas and palmettos that fringed the outskirts. Jubilant in the exercise of strength, he zig-zagged through the trees, knocking fronds aside, stumbling now and again over a depression or a bump, yet keeping a good pace, liking the feel of his sweat, his exertions. His muscles felt tireless, as in his recurring dream, and he wondered if the dream had foreshadowed this moment and he would climb the green hill of Griaule's back—he was, he realized, heading in that very direction—and leap from it and fly. But though strong, Hota was not fleet. Soon he heard men running beside and ahead of him. Heard their shouts. And as he passed a large banana tree with tattered yellow fronds, someone lying hidden in the grass reached out a hand and snagged his ankle, sending him sprawling. His knife flew from his hand. He scrambled to his knees, searching for it. Spotted it in the grass a dozen feet away. Before he could retrieve it, someone jumped onto his back, driving him face first into the ground. And before he could deal with whoever it was, other men piled onto him, pressing the air from his lungs, beating him with fists and sticks. A blow to his temple stunned him. They smelled like beasts, grunted like beasts, like the spirits of the boars he had killed come for their vengeance.

There seemed no dividing line between consciousness and unconsciousness, or perhaps Hota never completely blacked out and, instead, sank only a few inches beneath the surface of the waking world, and was, as with someone partially submerged in a stream, still able to hear muted voices and glimpse distorted shapes. It seemed he was borne aloft, jostled and otherwise roughly handled, but he did not fully return to his senses until he stood beneath the remnant corner post of Liar's House, something tight about his neck, surrounded by a crowd of men and women and children, all of whom were shouting at once, cursing, screaming for his blood. He wanted to pluck the tight thing away from his neck and discovered his hands were lashed behind his back. Dazedly, he glanced up and saw that a rope had been slung over the wedge of flooring still attached to the corner post, and that one end of the rope was about his neck. Terrified now, he surged forward, trying to break free, but whoever held the rope pulled it tight, constricting his throat and forcing him to stand quietly. He breathed shallowly, staring at the faces ranged about him. He recognized none of them, yet they were all familiar. It was as if he were looking at cats or dogs or horses, incapable of registering the distinctions among them that they themselves noticed. A woman, her thin face contorted with anger, spat at him. The rest appeared to think this a brilliant idea and those closest to him all began spitting. Their saliva coated his face. It disturbed him to think that he would die with their slime dripping from him. He lifted a shoulder, rubbed some of it off his cheek. Then the blond man whom he had beaten in the tavern stepped forth from the crowd. Hota recognized him not by his pink complexion or pudgy features, but by his mangled right hand, which he held up to Hota's eyes, letting him see the damage he had caused.

The man waved the crowd to silence and said to Hota, "Speak now, if ever you wish to speak again."

Still groggy, Hota said, "None of this is my doing."

Shouts and derisive laughter.

Once more, the man waved them to silence. "Who then should we blame?"

"Griaule," Hota said, and was forced to shout the rest of his statement over the renewed laughter of the crowd. "How could I have brought a dragon here? I'm only a man!"

"Are you?" The blond man caught the front of Hota's shirt with his good hand and brought his face close. "We've been wondering about that."

"Of course I am! I was manipulated! Used! Griaule used me!"

The blond man seemed to give the idea due consideration. "It's possible," he said at length. "In fact, I imagine it's probable."

The crowd at his back muttered unhappily.

"The thing is . . ." said the blond man, and smiled. "We can't hang Griaule, can we? You'll just have to stand in for him."

Hooting and howling their laughter, the crowd shook their fists in the air. Some snatched at Hota, others clawed and slapped at his head. The blond man moved them back. "You've killed our horses, you've stolen from us. You're responsible for that bitch tearing Benno Grustark to pieces. Any of these crimes would merit hanging."

"What could I have done!" Hota cried.

"You could have talked to us. Helped us. Brought us food." The blond man waved his damaged hand toward the hills. "Do you know how many of us died for want of food and shelter?"

"I *didn't* know! If you'd told me, if you hadn't threatened me . . . But I wasn't thinking about you! I couldn't! I had no choice!"

"Lack of choice. A common failing. But not, I think, a legal remedy." The blond man moved the crowd farther back, warning that Hota might kick them as he was being hauled up. He turned to Hota and asked blithely, "Anything else?"

A hundred things occurred to Hota. Pleas and arguments, statements, things about his life, things he had learned that he thought might be worth announcing. But he could muster the will to speak none of them. The rope made his neck itch. His balls were tightened and cold. His knees trembled. His eyes went out along the street, past the drying mud and the crooked shanties and their rust-patched roofs, and he felt a shape inside his head that seemed to have some correspondence with the green mountainous shape that lay beyond, as if Griaule were telling him a secret or offering an assurance or having a laugh at his expense. Impossible to guess which. A desire swelled in him, a great ache for life that grew and grew until he thought he might be able to burst his bonds and escape this old fate he had avoided for so long.

"Hang him," said the blond man. "But not too high. I want to watch his face."

As Hota was yanked off his feet, the crowd's roar ascended with him, and blended into another roar that issued from within his skull. The roar of his life, of his constricted blood. It was as if he had been made buoyant by the sound. His face was forced downward by the rope and his vision reddened. He saw the upturned faces of the crowd, their gaping black mouths and widened eyes, and he also saw his legs spasming. He had kicked off a shoe. The inside of his head grew hot, but slowly, as if death's flame were burning low. Fighting for breath, he flexed the roped muscles of his neck. The heat lessened.

They had set the knot in the noose incorrectly.

Air was coming through.

Barely . . . but enough to sustain him.

That became a problem, then. To breathe, to hold out against fate, or to relax his muscles and let go. Soon the decision would be made for him, but he wanted it to be his.

A terrible new pressure cinched the rope tighter.

Two children had shinnied up his lower legs and were humping themselves up and down. Trying to break his neck, he realized. The little shits were giggling. He squeezed his eyes shut, focusing all his energy and will on maintaining breath.

Fiery pains jolted along his spine. White lights exploded behind his lids. One such flash swelled into a blinding radiance that opened before him, vast and shimmering and deep, a country all its own. He felt a shifting inside him, a strange powerful movement that bloomed outward . . . and then he could see himself! Not just his legs, but his entire bulky figure. The children jiggling up and down, and the crowd; the exhausted town leached of every color but the redness of his dying sight.

Then he lost interest in this phenomenon and in the world, borne outward on that curious expansion. He recalled Magali and he thought that this—here and now—must be the fulfillment of her promise, the beginning of fulfillment, and that his soul was growing large, coming to enclose the material in the way of a dragon's soul . . .

And then a violent crack, like that of a severing lightning stroke or an immense displacement, and a thought came to mind that stilled his fears, or else it was the last of him and there was no fear left . . . the thought that it was all a dream, his dream, how he had run and felt joy, how he had leaped—sprawled, really, but that was close enough—and been borne aloft and now he was soaring, and the crack he had heard was the crack of his wings as they caught the air, and the roaring was the rush of first flight, and the light was the high holy sun, and soon he would see Magali and they would fly together along the pattern of their curving fate, with the child flying below them, above the green hill of their religion, and this was his reward, this transformation, this was the fulfillment of every promise, or else it was the lie of it.

DEAD MONEY

I knew slim-with-sideburns was dead money before Geneva introduced him to the game. Dead money doesn't need an introduction; dead money declares himself by grinning too wide and playing it too cool, pretending to be relaxed while his shoulders are racked with tension, and proceeds to lose all his chips in hurry. Slim-with-sideburns-and-sharp-features-and-a-gimpy-walk showed us the entire menu, plus he was wearing a pair of wraparound shades. Now there are a number of professional poker players who wear sunglasses so as not to give away their tells, but you would mistake none of them for dead money and they would never venture into a major casino looking like some kind of country-and-western spaceman.

"Gentlemen," Geneva said, shaking back her big blonde hair. "This here's Josey Pellerin over from Lafayette."

A couple of the guys said, Hey, and a couple of others introduced themselves, but Mike Morrissey, Mad Mike, who was in the seat next to mine, said, "Not *the* Josie? Of Josie and the Pussycats?"

The table had a laugh at that, but Pellerin didn't crack a smile. He took a chair across from Mike, lowering himself into it carefully, his arms shaking, and started stacking his chips. Muscular dystrophy, I thought. Some wasting disease. I pegged him for about my age, late thirties, and figured he would overplay his first good hand and soon be gone.

Mike, who likes to get under players' skins, said, "Didn't I see you the other night hanging out with 'A Boy Named Sue?'"

In a raspy, southern-fried voice, Pellerin said, "I've watched you on TV,

Mister Morrissey. You're not as entertaining as you think, and you don't have that much game."

Mike pretended to shudder and that brought another laugh. "Let's see what you got, pal," he said. "Then we can talk about my game."

Geneva, a good-looking woman even if she is mostly silicon and botox, washed a fresh deck, spreading the cards across the table, and shuffled them up.

The game was cash only, no-limit Texas Hold 'em. It was held in a side room of Harrah's New Orleans with a table ringed by nine barrel-backed chairs upholstered in red velvet and fake French Colonial stuff—fancy swords, paintings with gilt frames, and such—hanging on walls the color of cocktail sauce. Geneva, who was a friend, let me sit in once in a while to help me maintain the widely held view that I was someone important, whereas I was, in actuality, a typical figment of the Quarter, a man with a few meaningful connections and three really good suits.

It wasn't unusual to have a couple of pros in the game, but the following week Harrah's was sponsoring a tournament with a million dollar first prize and a few big hitters were already filtering into town. Aside from Mad Mike, Avery Holt was at the table, Sammy Jawanda, Deng Ky (aka Denghis Khan), and Annie Marcus. The amateurs in the game were Pellerin, Jeremy LeGros, an investment banker with deep pockets, and myself, Jack Lamb.

Texas Hold 'em is easy to learn, but it will cost you to catch on to the finer points. To begin with, you're dealt two down cards, then you bet; then comes the flop, three up cards in the center of the table that belong to everyone. You bet some more. Then an up card that's called the turn and another round of betting. Then a final up card, the river, and more betting . . . unless everyone has folded to the winner. I expected Pellerin to play tight, but five minutes hadn't passed before he came out firing and pushed in three thousand in chips. Le Gros and Mike went with him to the flop. King of hearts, trey of clubs, heart jack. Pellerin bet six thousand. LeGros folded and Mike peeked at his down cards.

"They didn't change on you, did they?" asked Pellerin.

Mike raised him four thousand. That told me Pellerin had gotten into his head. The smart play would have been either to call or to get super aggressive. A middling raise like four thousand suggested a lack of confidence. Of course with Mad Mike, you never knew when he was setting a trap. Pellerin pushed it again, raising ten K, not enough to make Mike bag the hand automatically. Mike called. The card on the turn was a three of hearts, pairing the board. Pellerin checked and Mike bet twenty.

"You must have yourself a hand," said Pellerin. "But your two pair's not going to cut it. I'm all in."

He had about sixty thousand stacked in front of him and Mike could have covered the bet, but it wasn't a percentage play—losing would have left him with the short chip stack and it was too early in the evening to take the risk. He tried staring a hole through Pellerin, fussed with his chips, and eventually mucked his hand.

"You're not the dumbest son-of-a-bitch who ever stole a pot from me," he said.

"Don't suppose I am," said Pellerin.

As I watched—and that is what I mainly did, push in antes and watch—it occurred to me that once he sat down, Pellerin had stopped acting like dead money, as if all his anxiety had been cured by the touch of green felt and plastic aces. He was one hell of a hold 'em player. He never lost much and it seemed that he took down almost every big pot. Whenever he went head-to-head against somebody, he did about average . . . except when he went up against Mad Mike. Him, he gutted. It was evident that he had gotten a good read on Mike. In less than two hours he had ninety percent of the man's money. He had also developed a palsy in his left hand and was paler than he had been when he entered.

The door opened, the babble of the casino flowed in and a security man ushered a doe-eyed, long-legged brunette wearing a black cocktail dress into the room. She had some age on her—in her mid-thirties, I estimated—and her smile was low wattage, a depressive's smile. Nonetheless, she was an exceptionally beautiful woman with a pale olive complexion and a classically sculpted face, her hair arranged so that it fell all to one side. A shade too much make-up was her only flaw. She came up behind Pellerin, bent down, absently caressing the nape of his neck, and whispered something. He said, "You going to have to excuse me, gentleman. My nurse here's a real hardass. But I'll be glad to take your money again tomorrow night."

He scooted back his chair; the brunette caught his arm and helped him to stand.

Mike, who had taken worse beats in his career, overcame his bad mood and asked, "Where you been keeping yourself, man?"

"Around," said Pellerin. "But I've been inactive 'til recently."

I smelled something wrong about Pellerin. Wrong rose off him like stink off the Ninth Ward. World class poker players don't just show up, they don't materialize out of nowhere and take a hundred large off Mad Mike Morrissey, without acquiring some reputation in card rooms and small casinos. And his success wasn't due to luck. What Pellerin had done to Mike was as clean a gutting as I had ever witnessed. The next two nights, I stayed out of the game and observed. Pellerin won close to half a million, though the longest he played at a single sitting was four hours. The casino offered him a spot in the tournament, but he declined on the grounds of poor health—he was recovering from an injury, he said, and was unable to endure the long hours and stress of tournament play. My sources informed me that, according to the county records, nobody named Josey Pellerin lived in or near Lafayette. That didn't surprise me. I knew a great number of people who had found it useful to adopt another name and place of residence. I did, however, manage to dredge up some interesting background on the brunette.

Jocundra Verret, age forty-two, single, had been employed by Tulane University nearly twenty years before, working for the late Dr. Hideki Ezawa, who had received funding during the 1980s to investigate the possible scientific basis of certain voodoo remedies. She had left the project, as they say, under a cloud. That was as much as I could gather from the redacted document that fell into my hands. After Tulane, she had worked as a private nurse until a year ago; since that time, her paychecks had been signed by the Darden Corporation, an outfit whose primary holdings were in the fields of bioengineering and medical technology. She, Pellerin and another man, Dr. Samuel Crain, had booked a suite at Harrah's on a corporate card, the same card that paid for an adjoining suite occupied by two other men, one of whom had signed the register as D. Vader. They were bulky, efficient sorts, obviously doing duty as bodyguards.

I had no pressing reason to look any deeper, but the mention of voodoo piqued my interest. While I was not myself a devotee, my parents had both been occasional practitioners and those childhood associations of white candles burning in storefront temples played a part in my motivation. That night, when Pellerin sat down at the table, I went searching for Ms. Verret and found her in a bar just off the casino floor, drinking a sparkling water. She had on gray slacks and a cream-colored blouse, and looked quite fetching. The bodyguards were nowhere in sight, but I knew they must be in the vicinity. I dropped onto the stool beside her and introduced myself.

"I'm not in the mood," she said.

"Neither am I, cher. The doctor tells me it's permanent, but when I saw you I felt a flicker of hope."

She ducked her head, hiding a smile. "You really need to go. I'm expecting someone."

"Under different circumstances, I'd be delighted to stick around and let you break my heart. But sad to say, this is a business call. I was wondering how come a bunch like the Darden Corporation is bankrolling a poker player."

Startled, she darted her eyes toward me, but quickly recovered her poise. "The people I work for are going to ask why you were talking to me," she said evenly. "I can tell them you were hitting on me, but if you don't leave in short order, I won't be able to get away with that explanation."

"I assume you're referring in the specific to the two large gentlemen who've got the suite next to yours. Don't you worry. They won't do anything to me."

"It's not what they might do to *you* that's got me worried," she said.

"I see. Okay." I got to my feet. "That being the case, perhaps it'd be best if we talked at a more opportune time. Say tomorrow morning? Around ten in the coffee shop?"

"Please stay away from me," she said. "I'm not going to talk to you."

As I left the bar, I saw the bodyguards playing the dollar slots near the entrance—one glanced at me incuriously, but kept on playing. I walked down the casino steps, exiting onto Canal Street, and had a smoke. It was muggy, the stars dim. High in the west, a sickle moon was encased in an envelope of mist. I looked at the neon signs, the traffic, listened to the chatter and laughter of passers-by with drinks in their hands. Post-Katrina

New Orleans pretending that it was the Big Easy, teetering on the edge of boom or bust. Though Verret had smiled at me, I could think of no easy way to hustle her, and I decided to give Billy Pitch a call and see whether he thought the matter was worth pursuing.

I had to go through three flunkies before I got to Billy. "What you want?" he said. "You know this is *Survivor* night."

"I forgot, Billy. Want me to call back? I can call back."

"This is the two-hour finale, then the reunion show. Won't be over 'til eleven and I'm shutting it down after that. Now you got something for me or don't you?"

I could hear laughter in the background and I hesitated, picturing him hunched over the phone in his den, a skinny, balding white man whom you might mistake for an insurance salesman or a CPA, no doubt clad in one of his neon-colored smoking jackets.

"Jack, you better have something good," Billy said. "Hair's starting to sprout from my palms."

"I'm not sure how good it is, but . . ."

"I'm missing the immunity challenge. The penultimate moment of the entire season. And I got people over, you hear?"

Billy was the only person I knew who could pronounce vowels with a hiss. I gave him the gist of it, trying not to omit any significant details, but speeding it along as best I could.

"Interesting," he said. "Tell me again what she said when you spoke to her."

I repeated the conversation.

"It would seem that Miz Verret's agenda is somewhat different from that of the Darden Corporation," Billy said. "Otherwise, she'd have no compunction about reporting your conversation."

"That was my take."

"Voodoo business," he said musingly.

"I can't be sure it's got anything to do with voodoo."

"Naw, this here is voodoo business. It has a certain taint." Billy made a clicking noise. "I'll get back to you in the morning."

"I was just trying to do you a favor, Billy. I don't need to be involved."

"Honey, I know how it's supposed to work, but you're involved. I got too many eggs in my basket to be dealing with anything else right now. This pans out, I'm putting you in charge."

The last thing I had wanted was to be in business with Billy Pitch. It wasn't that you couldn't make a ton of money with Billy, but he was a supremely dangerous and unpleasant human being, and he tended to be hard on his associates. Often he acted precipitately and there were more than a few widows who had received a boatload of flowers and a card containing Billy's apologies and a fat check designed to compensate for their loss and his lamentable error in judgment. In most cases, this unexpected death benefit served to expunge the ladies' grief, but Alice Delvecchio, the common-law wife of Danny "Little Man" Prideau, accused Billy of killing her man and, shortly after the police investigation hit a dead end, she and her children disappeared. It was rumored that Billy had raised her two sons himself and that, with his guidance, hormone treatments, and the appropriate surgery, they had blossomed into lovely teenage girls, both of whom earned their keep in a brothel catering to oil workers.

Much to my relief, no call came the following morning. I thought that Billy must have checked out Pellerin and Verret, found nothing to benefit him, and hadn't bothered getting back to me. But around ten o'clock that evening, I fielded a call from Huey Rafael, one of Billy's people. He said that Billy wanted me to run on out to an address in Abundance Square and take charge of a situation.

"What's up?" I asked.

"Billy says for you to get your butt over here."

Abundance Square was in the Ninth Ward, a few blocks from the levee, and was, as far as I knew, utterly abandoned. That made me nervous.

"I'm coming," I said. "But I'd like to know something about the situation. So I can prepare for it, you understand."

"You ain't need nothing to prepare you for this." Huey's laugh was a baritone hiccup. "Got some people want watching over. Billy say you the man for the job."

"Who are these people?" I asked, but Huey had ended the call.

I was angry. In the past, Billy had kept a close eye on every strand of his web, but nowadays he tended to delegate authority and spent much of his time indulging his passion for reality TV. He knew more about *The Amazing Race* and *The Runway Project* than he did about his business. Sooner or later, I thought, this practice was going to jump up and bite him in the ass. But as I drove toward the Ninth Ward, my natural paranoia kicked in and I began to question the wisdom of traipsing off into the middle of nowhere to hook up with a violent criminal.

Prior to Katrina, Abundance Square had been a housing project of old-style New Orleans town homes, with courtyards and balconies all painted in pastel shades. It had been completed not long before the hurricane struck. Now it was a waste of boarded-up homes and streets lined with people's possessions. Cars, beds, lamps, bureaus, TV sets, pianos, toys, and so on, every inch of them caked with dried mud. Though I was accustomed to such sights, that night it didn't look real. My headlights threw up bizarre images that made it appear I was driving through a post-apocalyptic version of Claymation Country. I found the address, parked a couple of blocks away, and walked back to the house. A drowned stink clotted my nostrils. In the distance, I heard sirens and industrial noise, but close at hand, it was so quiet you could hear a bug jump.

Huey answered my knock. He was a tall drink of water. Six-five, six-six, with a bluish polish to his black skin, a lean frame, pointy sideburns, and a modish goatee. He wore charcoal slacks and a high-collared camp shirt. Standing in the door, a nickel-plated .45 in hand, he might have been a bouncer at the Devil's strip club. He preceded me toward the rear of the house, to a room lit by a kerosene lantern. At its center, one of Pellerin's bodyguards was tied to a wooden chair. His head was slumped onto his chest, his face and shirt bloody. The air seemed to grow hotter.

I balked at entering and Huey said, "What you scared of, man? Lord Vader there ain't going to harm you. Truth is, he gave it up quick for being a Jedi."

"Where's the other guy?" I asked.

"Man insisted on staying behind," Huey said.

I had a sinking feeling, a vision of the Red House at Angola, guards strapping me down for the injection. "Jesus Christ," I said. "You tell Billy I'm not going down for murder."

Huey caught me by the shoulder as I turned to leave and slammed me up against the wall. He bridged his forearm under my jaw, giving me the full benefit of his lavishly applied cologne, and said, "I didn't say a goddamn thing about murder, now did I?" When I remained silent, he asked me again and I squeezed out a no.

"I got things to take care of," he said, stepping back. "Probably take me two, three hours. Here go." He handed me the .45 and some keys. "You get on upstairs."

"Who's up there?"

"The card player and his woman. Some other guy. A doctor, he say."

"Are they . . ." I searched for a word that would not excite Huey. "Uninjured?"

"Yeah, they fine."

"And I'm supposed to keep watch, right? That's all?"

"Billy say for you to ask some questions."

"What about?"

"About what they up to."

"Well, what did he tell you?" I pointed at the bodyguard. "I need something to go on."

"Lord Vader wasn't too clear on the subject," said Huey. "Guess I worked him a little hard. But he did say the card player ain't a natural man."

Some rooms on the second floor of the townhouse were filled with stacked cots, folding tables and chairs, and with bottled water, canned food, toilet paper, and other supplies. It seemed that Billy was planning for the end times. In a room furnished with a second-hand sofa and easy chairs, I found Verret, Pellerin, and a man in his fifties with mussed gray hair and a hangdog look about the eyes. I assumed him to be Doctor Crain. He was gagged and bound to a chair. Verret and Pellerin were leg-shackled to the sofa. On seeing me, Crain arched his eyebrows and tried to speak. Pellerin glanced up from his hand of solitaire and Verret, dressed in freshly ironed jeans and a white T-shirt, gave me a sorrowful look, as if to suggest she had expected more of me.

"It's the night shift," Pellerin said and went back to turning over cards.

"Can you help us?" asked Verret.

"What's up with him?" I pointed at Crain with the gun.

"He annoyed our previous keeper." Pellerin flipped over an ace and made a satisfied noise. "He's an annoying fellow. You're catching him at his best."

"Can you help us?" Verret asked again, with emphasis.

"Probably not." I pulled a chair around and sat opposite the two of them. "But if you tell me what's going on with you, what's the relationship between the Darden Corporation and Tulane, the Ezawa project . . . I'll try to help."

Pellerin kept dealing, Verret gave no response, and Crain struggled with his bonds.

"Do you know where you are?" I asked. "Let me you clue you in."

I told them who had ordered their kidnapping, mentioning the Alice Delvecchio incident along with a couple of others, then reiterated that I could probably be of no help to them—I was an unwilling participant in the process. I was sorry things had reached this pass, but if I was going to be any help at all, they ought to tell me what was up; otherwise, I couldn't advise them on how to survive Billy Pitch.

Verret looked to Pellerin, who said, "He ain't that damn sorry. Except where his own sorry ass is concerned."

"Is he telling the truth?" she asked.

"More-or-less."

Crain redoubled his efforts to escape, forcing muted shouts through his gag.

"I guess that's why you're so expert at the tables," I said to Pellerin. "You're good at reading people."

"You have no idea, Small Time," he said.

I wiggled the gun. "You're not in a position to be giving me attitude."

"You going to shoot me?" He gave a sneering laugh. "I don't think so. You're about ready to piss yourself just hanging onto that thing."

"Josey!" Verret started to stand, then remembered the shackles. "I'll tell you," she said to me. "But I'd rather do it in private."

Crain threw a conniption fit, heaving himself about in his chair, attempting to spit out his gag.

"You see," she said. "He's going to act like that every time I tell you something. I have to use the restroom, anyway."

I undid the shackles, then I locked Crain and Pellerin in and escorted her down the hall, lagging behind a step so I could check out her butt. When she had finished in the john, we went into one of the storerooms. I set up a couple of folding chairs and we sat facing one another.

"May I have some water," she asked.

"Help yourself."

She had a drink of water, then sat primly with the plastic bottle resting on one knee. I knew I had to watch myself with her—I'd always been a sucker for tall brunettes who had that lady thing going. She must have had a sense of this, because she worked it overtime.

"Here's what I know," I said. "The Ezawa project was investigating voodoo remedies. And Josey Pellerin, according to your bodyguard, is not a natural man. That suggests . . . well, I'm not sure. Why don't you just tell me everything?"

"Everything? That'll take a long time." She screwed the bottle cap on and off. "The project wasn't considered important at the outset. The only reason Ezawa got funding was because he was a golfing buddy of one of the trustees. And he *was* brilliant, so they were willing to give him some leeway. He isolated a bacterium present in the dirt of old slave graveyards. He used dirt from the graveyard at the Myrtles—that old house over in Saint Francisville? The bodies were buried in biodegradable coffins, or no coffins at all, and the micro-organisms in the dirt had interacted with the decomposing tissues."

She left room for me to ask a question, but I had none.

"A DNA extract from datura and other herbs was introduced into the growth medium," she said. "Then the bacteria were induced to take up DNA and chromosomes from the extract, and Ezawa injected the recombinant strain into the cerebellum and temporal lobes of a freshly dead corpse. The bacteria began processing the corpse's genetic complement and eventually the body was revivified."

"Whoa! Revivified?" I said. "You mean, it came back to life?"

She nodded.

"How long were these people dead?" I asked.

"On the average, a little under an hour. The longest was about an hour and a half. The process required a certain amount of time, so the bodies had to be secured quickly."

"Makes you wonder, doesn't it? Getting the paperwork done for releasing a body generally takes more than an hour."

"I don't know," she said.

"Jesus. Ezawa was basically making zombies. High-tech zombies."

She started, I presumed, to object, but I headed her off.

"Don't bullshit me," I said. "I grew up voodoo. Datura's one of the classic ingredients in the old recipe books. I bet he tried goat's rue, too . . . and Angel's trumpet. The man was making zombies."

She frowned. "What I was going to say, the term was appropriate for most of the patients. They were weak. Helpless. They rarely survived longer than a day. But there were a few who lived longer. For months, some of them. We called them 'slow-burners.' We moved them out to a plantation house in bayou country and brought in a clinical psychologist to assess their new personalities. You see, the patients developed personalities markedly different from the ones they originally had. The psychologist, Doctor Edman, he believed these personalities manifested a kind of wish-fulfillment. His theory was that the process changed a portion of the RNA and made it dominant. 'The bioform of their deepest wish,' that's how he put it. The patients manufactured memories. They recalled having different names, different histories. In effect, they were telling us—and themselves—a new life story, one in which they achieved their heart's desire. The amazing thing was, they had abilities commensurate with these stories."

I could have used some of Pellerin's ability to read people. What she had told me had a ring of authenticity, but if I were to accept it as true, I would have to rearrange my notion of what was possible. I started to speak, but I was on shaky ground and wasn't certain which questions to ask.

"It's hard to believe," she said. "But it's the truth." She let some seconds slip past and then, when I remained mute, as if she were trying to keep the conversation going, she went on: "I disagreed with Edman about a great many things. He demanded that we allow the patients to find their own way. He believed we should let their stories come out naturally. But I thought if we prompted them some, if we reminded them of their original identities . . . I don't mean give them every detail, you understand. Just their names and a little background. That would have afforded them a stronger foundation and perhaps we wouldn't have had so many breakdowns among the slow-burners. These people were re-inventing themselves out of whole cloth. They were bound to be unstable. I was hoping Crain would agree with me, but . . ." She made a contemptuous gesture, then seemed to remember where she was. "Do you want to know anything else?"

I still was at a loss for words, but I managed to say, "So I'm guessing Pellerin's a slow-burner."

"Yes. He was born Theodore Rankin. He's forty-three. He believes he's the world's best poker player. And he may well be."

"What was he before?"

"A bartender. He was killed during a robbery. I don't know how the corporation got hold of the body."

"The corporation. I assume they took the project over after it went in the toilet at Tulane."

"That's right. But there was a gap of ten years or so."

"Why're they so interested in a poker player?"

"It's not the poker playing per se that's of interest, it's the patients' underlying abilities. Their potentials go far beyond the life story they construct for themselves. We don't understand what they can do. None of them lived long enough. But with the advances in micro-biology made during the last two decades, Doctor Crain thinks Josey may live for years. He's developing more rapidly than the others, too. That may be a result of improvements in the delivery system. We used a heart pump at Tulane, but now they . . ."

"I don't have to know the gearhead stuff." I mulled over what she had told me. "You were fired from the original project. Why would Darden hire you? Where do you fit in?"

Verret toyed with the bottle cap. "I helped a patient escape. I couldn't go along with what they were doing to him anymore. He developed some astonishing abilities while he was on the run. I'm the only person who's dealt with someone that advanced."

"What sort of abilities we talking about?"

"Perceptual, for the most part. Changes in visual capacity and such."

She said this off-handedly, but I doubted she was being straight with me. I decided not to push it, and I asked what they had been doing at Harrah's.

"At Tulane we kept the patients confined," she said. "But Crain thought Josey would develop more rapidly if we exposed him to an unstructured environment under controlled conditions." She gave a rueful laugh. "Turns out we didn't have much control."

"How much does Pellerin know?"

"He knows he was brought back to life. But he doesn't know about the new personality . . . though he suspects something's wrong there. It's up to me to determine when he's ready to hear the truth. Things go better if we tell them than if we let them piece it together on their own."

"I still don't understand your function. What exactly is it you do?"

"Patients need to bond with someone in order to create a complex personality. They have to be controlled, carefully manipulated. We were trained to instill that bond, to draw out their capabilities."

She folded her arms, compressed her lips. I had the thought that, though none of what she had told me was comedy club material, talking about her role in things distressed her more than the rest.

"If the other therapists are good-looking as you," I said, "I bet that instilling thing goes pretty easily."

That seemed to distress her further.

"Come on, cher," I said. "You going to be just fine. Y'all can be a significant asset for Billy, and that works to your advantage."

She leaned forward, putting a hand on my knee; the touch surprised me. "Mister Lamb," she said, and I said, without intending to, "Jack. You can call me Jack."

"I want to be able to count on you, Jack. Can I count on you?"

"I told you I don't have any control over the situation."

"But can you be a friend? That's all I'm asking. Can we count on you to be a friend?"

Those big brown eyes were doing a job on me, but I resisted them. "I haven't ever been much good as a friend. It's a character flaw, I'm afraid."

"I don't believe that." She sat back, adjusting her T-shirt so it fit more snugly. "You can call me Jo."

I contacted Billy Pitch, though not during prime time, fearing I might interrupt *The Surreal Life* or *Wife Swap*, and I told him what I had learned, omitting any mention of the "remarkable powers" that might soon be Pellerin's, stressing instead his developing visual capacity. I wasn't sure why I did this—perhaps because I thought that Billy, already powerful, needed no further inducement to use his strength intemperately. He professed amazement at what I had to say, then slipped into business mode.

"I got an idea, but it needs to simmer, so I'm going to stash you away for a while," he said. "Get everybody ready to travel tonight."

"By 'everybody,'" I said, "you don't mean me, right? I got deals cooking. I have to . . ."

"I'll handle them for you."

"Billy, some of what I got going requires the personal touch."

"Are you suggesting I can't handle whatever piddly business it is you got?"

"No, that's not it. But there's . . ."

"You're not going to thwart me in this, are you, Jack?"

"No," I said helplessly.

"Good! Call my secretary and tell her what needs doing. I'll see it gets done."

That night we were flown by private jet to an airstrip in South Florida, and then transported by cigarette boat to Billy's estate in the Keys. Absent from our party was Dr. Crain. I never got to know the man. Each time I walked him to the john or gave him food, he railed at me, saying that I didn't know who I was dealing with, I didn't understand what was involved, causing such a ruckus that I found it easier to keep him bound and gagged in a separate room. I warned him that he was doing himself no good acting this way, yet all he did was tell me again I didn't know who I was dealing with and threaten me with corporate reprisals. When it was time to leave, I started to untie him, but Huey dropped a hand onto my shoulder and said, "Billy say to let him be."

"He's a doctor," I said. "He's the only one know's what's going on. What if Pellerin gets sick or something?"

"Billy say let him be."

I tried to call Billy, but was met with a series of rebuffs from men as constricted by the literal limits of their orders as Huey. Their basic message was, "Billy can't be disturbed." Crain's eyes were wide, fixed on me; his nostrils flared above the gag when he tried to speak. I made to remove it, but Huey once again stayed my hand.

"Let him talk," I said. "He might . . ."

"What he going to say, Jack?" Huey's glum, wicked face gazed down at me. "You know there ain't nothing to say?"

He steered me into the corridor, closed the door behind us and leaned against it. "Get a move on," he said. "Ain't nothing you can do, so you might as well not think about it."

Yet I did think about it as I descended the stair and walked along the corridor and out into the drizzly New Orleans night. I thought about Crain waiting in that stuffy little room, about whether or not he knew what was coming, and I thought that if I didn't change the way things were headed, I might soon be enduring a similar wait myself.

Some weeks later I watched a videotape that captured Jo's interaction with one of the short-lived zombies whose passage from death to life and back again she had overseen at Tulane. By then, I had become thoroughly acquainted with Pellerin and the zombie on the tape didn't interest me nearly as much as Jo's performance. She tempted and teased his story out of him with the gestures and movements of a sexier-than-average ballerina, exaggerated so as to make an impression on the man's dim vision, and I came to realize that all of her movements possessed an element of this same controlled grace. Whether she was doing this by design, I had no clue; by that time I had tumbled to the fact that she was a woman who hid much from herself, and I doubted that she would be able to shed light on the matter.

Over the space of a month, Pellerin grew from a man whom I had mistaken for dead money into a formidable presence. He was stronger, more vital in every way, and he began to generate what I can only describe as a certain magnetism—I felt the back of my neck prickle whenever he came near, though the effect diminished over the days and weeks that followed. And then there were his eyes. On the same day I interrogated Jo, I was escorting him to the john when he said, "Hey, check this out!, Small Time." He snatched off his sunglasses and brought his eyes close to mine. I was about to make a sarcastic remark, when I noticed a green flickering in his irises.

"What the fuck!" I said.

Pellerin grinned. "Looks like a little ol' storm back in there, doesn't it?"

I asked him what it was and he told me the flickers, etched in an electric green, signaled the bacteria impinging on the optic nerve.

"They're bioluminescent," he said. "Weird, huh? Jocundra says it's going to get worse before it gets better. People are going to think I'm the goddamn Green Lantern."

Though he had changed considerably since that day, his attitudes toward almost everyone around him remained consistently negative—he was blunt, condescending, an arrogant smart-ass. Yet toward Jo, his basic stance did change. He grew less submissive and often would challenge her authority. She adapted by becoming more compliant, but I could see that she wasn't happy, that his contentiousness was getting to her. She still was able to control him by means of subtle and not-so-subtle manipulation, but how long that control would last was a matter for conjecture.

The island where we were kept was Billy's private preserve. It was shaped roughly like a T, having two thin strips of land extending out in opposite directions from the west end. Billy's compound took up most of the available space. Within a high white brick wall topped by razor wire were a pool, outbuildings (including a gym and eight bungalows), a helicopter pad, and a sprawling Florida-style ranch house that might have been designed by an architect with a Lego fetish—wings diverged off the central structure and off each other at angles such as a child might employ, and I guessed that from the air it must resemble half a crossword puzzle. There were flat screen TVs in every room, even the johns, and all the rooms were decorated in a fashion that I labeled *haute mafia*. The dining room table was fashioned from a fourteenth century monastery door lifted from some

European ruin. The rugs were a motley assortment of modern and antique. Some of the windows were stained glass relics, while others were jalousies; but since heavy drapes were drawn across them, whatever effect had been intended was lost. Every room was home to a variety of antiquities: Egyptian statuary, Greek amphorae, Venetian glassware, German tapestries, and so on. In my bathroom, the toilet was carved from a single block of marble, and mounted on the wall facing it, a section of a Persian bas-relief, was yet another flat screen. It was as if someone with the sensibility of a magpie had looted the world's museums in order to furnish the place, and yet the decor was so uniformly haphazard, I had the impression that Billy was making an anti-fashion statement, sneering at the concept of taste. Elvis would have approved. In fact, had he seen the entirety of Billy's house, he would have returned home to Graceland and redecorated.

Beyond the wall was jungly growth that hid the house completely. The beach was a crescent of tawny sand fringed by palms and hibiscus shrubs and Spanish bayonet, protected by an underwater fence. A bunkerlike guard house stood at the foot of the concrete pier to which the cigarette boat was moored, and a multicultural force (Cuban, white, African-American) patrolled within and without the walls. The guards, along with gardeners and maids, were housed in the bungalows, but they entered the house frequently to check on us. If we stepped outside they would dog us, their weapons shouldered, keeping a distance, alert to our every movement. It was easier to find privacy inside the house. Relative privacy, at any rate. Knowing Billy, I was certain that the rooms were bugged, and I had given up on the idea that I could keep anything from him. Whenever Pellerin and Jo were closeted in their rooms, I would walk along corridors populated by suits of armor and ninja costumes fitted to basketwork men and gilt French chairs that, with their curved legs and positioned between such martial figures, looked poised for an attack. I would poke into rooms, examine their collection of *objets d'art*, uniformly mismatched, yet priceless. Sometimes I would wonder if I dared slip one or two small items into my pocket, but most of my thoughts were less concerned with gain than with my forlorn prospects for survival.

Occasionally in the course of these forays, I would encounter a maid, but never anyone else, and thus I was surprised one afternoon when, upon entering a room in the northernmost wing with a four-poster bed and a fortune in gee-gaws littering the tables and bureaus, I saw Jo standing by the entrance to a walk-in closet, inspecting the dresses within. She gave a start when I spoke her name, then offered a wan smile and said, "Hello."

"What are you doing here?" I said.

"Browsing." She touched the bodice of a green silk dress. "These clothes must have cost hundreds of thousands of dollars. They're all designer originals."

"No, I meant aren't you supposed to be with Pellerin."

"I need breaks from Josey," she said. "His intensity gets to me after a while. And he's getting more independent, he wants time to himself. So . . ." She shrugged. "I like to come here and look at the clothes."

She stepped into the closet and I moved into the room so I could keep her in view.

"He must bring a lot of women here," she said. "He's got every imaginable size."

"It's hard for me to think of Billy as a sexual being."

"Why's that?"

"You'd have to know him. I've never seen him with a woman on his arm, but I suppose he has his moments."

She went deeper into the closet, toyed with the hem of a dress that bore a pattern like a moth's wing, all soft grays and greens, a touch of brown.

I perched on the edge of the bed. "Why don't you try it on?"

"Do you think he'd mind?" she asked.

"Go for it."

She hesitated, then said, "I'll just be a second," and closed the closet door.

The idea that she was getting naked behind the door inspired a salacious thought or two—I was already more than a little smitten. When she came out, she was barefoot. She did a pirouette and struck a fashion magazine pose. I was dumbstruck. The dress was nearly diaphanous, made of some feathery stuff that clung to her hips and flat stomach and breasts, the flared skirt reaching to mid-thigh.

"You like?" she asked. "It's a little short on me."

"I didn't notice."

She laughed delightedly and went for another spin. "I could never afford this. Not that I care all that much about clothes. But if I had a couple of million, I'd probably indulge."

Shortly thereafter she went back inside the closet, re-emerging wearing her jeans and a nondescript top. It seemed that she had exchanged personalities as well as clothes, for she was once again somber and downcast. "I've got to get back," she said.

"So soon?"

She stopped by the door. "I come here most days about this time," she said. "A little earlier, actually." Then, after a pause, she added, "It's nice having someone to wear clothes for."

We started meeting every day in that room. It was plain that she was flirting with me, and I imagine it was equally plain that I was interested, but it went on for over a month and neither one of us made a move. For my part, the fear of rejection didn't enter in. I was used to the man-woman thing being a simple negotiation—you either did the deed or you took a pass—but I thought if I did make a move, I might frighten her off, that she needed to feel in control. If I had been free of constraint, my own agent, I might have given up on her . . . or maybe I wouldn't have. She was the kind of woman who required a period of courtship, who enjoyed the dance as much as the feast, and she caused you to enjoy it as well. Basically an unhappy soul, she gave the impression of being someone who had been toughened by trouble in her life; but whenever she was happy, there was something so frail and girlish about the mood, I believed the least disturbance could shatter it. I grew more entranced by her and more frustrated day-by-day, but I told myself that not getting involved was for the best—I needed to keep clear of emotional entanglements and concentrate on how to stay alive once Billy came back into the picture. That didn't prevent me, however, from exploring certain of her fantasies.

I knew that she had been married when she was a teenager and one morning while we sat on the bed, her cross-legged at the head and me sort of side-saddle at the foot, I asked her about it. She ran a finger along a newel post, tracing the pattern carved into it, and said, "It was jus t. . . foolishness. We thought it would be romantic to get married."

"I take it, it wasn't."

She gave a wan laugh. "No."

"Would you ever do it again?"

"Marry? I don't know. Maybe." She smiled. "Why? Are you asking?"

"Maybe. Tell me what type of man it is you'd marry. Let's see if I fit the bill."

She lay down on her side, her legs drawn up, and considered the question.

"Yeah?" I said.

"You're serious? You want me to do this?"

"Let's hear it, cher. Your ideal man."

"Well . . ." She sat up, fluffed the pillow, and lay down again. "I'd want him to have lots of money, so maybe a financier. Not a banker or anything boring like that. A corporate tiger. Someone who would take over a failing company and reshape it into something vital."

"Money's the most important qualification?"

"Not really, but you asked for my ideal and money makes things easier."

She had on a blouse with a high collar and, as often happened when thinking, she tucked in her chin and nibbled the edge of the collar. I found the habit sexy and, whenever she did it, I wanted to touch her face.

"He'd be a philanthropist," she said. "And not just as a tax dodge. He'd have to be devoted to it. And he'd have an introspective side. I'd want him to know himself. To understand himself."

"A corporate raider with soul. Isn't that a contradiction?"

"It can happen. Wallace Stevens was an insurance executive and a great poet."

"I like to think of myself as an entrepreneur when I'm feeling spunky. That's like a financier, but I'm getting that we're talking about two different animals."

"You've got possibilities," she said, and smiled. "You just need molding."

"How about in the looks department?" I asked. "Something George Clooney-ish? Or Brad Pitt?"

She wrinkled her nose. "Movie stars are too short. Looks aren't important, anyway."

"Women all say that, but it's bullshit."

"It's true! Women have the same kind of daydreams as men, but when it comes to choosing a man they often base their choices on different criteria."

"Like money."

"No! Like how someone makes you feel. It's not quantifiable. I would never have thought I could . . ."

She broke off, thinning her lips.

"You would never have thought what?"

"This is silly," she said. "I should check on Josey."

"You never would have thought you could be attracted to someone you met at gunpoint?"

She sat up, swung her legs off the side of the bed, but said nothing.

"You might as well confess, cher," I said. "You won't be giving away any secrets."

She stiffened, as if she were going to lash out at me, but the tension drained from her body. "It's the Stockholm Syndrome," she said.

"You reckon that's it? We are for sure stuck on this damn island, and there's not a whole lot to distract us. And technically I am an accomplice in your kidnapping. But there's more to it than that."

"You're probably right," she said, coming to her feet. "If we'd met on our own in New Orleans, I'd probably have been attracted to you. But that's neither here nor there."

"Why not? Because Pellerin's your priority?"

She shrugged as if to say, yes.

"Duty won't keep you warm at night," I said.

"Keeping warm has never been my biggest goal in life," she said with brittle precision. "But should that change, I'll be sure to let you know."

I didn't go outside much. The guards made me nervous. When I did it was usually to have a swim, but some nights I went along the shore through a fringe of shrubs and palms to the west end, the crosspiece of the

T, a place from which, if the weather was clear, I could make out the lights on a nearby Key. And on one such night, emerging from dense undergrowth onto a shingle of crushed coral and sand, littered with vegetable debris, I spotted a shadow kneeling on the beach. Wavelets slapping against the shingle covered the sound of my approach and I saw it was Pellerin. I hadn't realized he could walk this far without help. He was holding a hand out above the water, flexing his fingers. It looked as if he were about to snatch something up. Beneath his hand the water seethed and little waves rolled away from shore. It was such a mediocre miracle, I scarcely registered it at first; but then I realized that he must be causing this phenomenon, generating a force that pushed the waves in a contrary direction. He turned his head toward me. The green flickers in his eyes stood out sharply in the darkness. A tendril of fear uncoiled in my backbrain.

"What's shaking, Small Time?" he said.

"Don't call me that. I'm sick of it."

He made a soft, coughing noise that I took for a laugh. "Want me to do like Jocundra and call you Jackie boy?"

"Just don't call me Small Time."

"But it suits you so well."

"You been through a rough time," I said. "And I can appreciate that. But that doesn't give you the right to act like an asshole."

"It doesn't? I could have sworn it did."

He came to his feet, lost his balance. I caught him by the shirtfront and hauled him erect. He tried to break my grip, but he was still weak and I held firm. He had a soapy smell. I wondered if Jo had to help him bathe.

"Let me go," he said.

"I don't believe I will."

"Give me another month or two, I promise I'll tear you down to your shoelaces, boy."

"I'll be waiting."

"Let me go!"

He pawed at my hand and I let loose of the shirt. That electric green danced in his eyes again.

"'Pears you growing a pair. Love must be making you bold." He hitched up his belt. "Yeah, I been catching you looking at Jocundra. She looks at you the same. If I wasn't around, the two of you be going at it like. But I *am* around."

"Maybe not for too long," I said.

"I might surprise you, boy. But whatever. As long as I'm here, Jocundra not going to stray. She's just dying for me to tell her about every new thing I see. She finds it fascinating."

"What do you see?"

"I'm not telling you, pal. I'm saving all of my secrets for sweet cheeks." He took a faltering step toward the house. "How's about we make a little side bet? Bet I nail her before you."

I gave him a shove and he went over onto his back, crying out in shock. A guard stepped from the shadow of the trees—I told him to be cool, I had things covered. I reached down and seized hold of Pellerin's arm, but he wrenched free.

"You want to lie there, fine by me," I said, and started back along the shore.

He called to me, but I kept walking.

"Know what I see in your future, Small Time?" he shouted as I passed into the trees. "I see lilies and a cardboard casket. I see a black dog taking a piss on your grave."

What he said didn't trouble me, but I was troubled nonetheless. When I had reached for his arm, I had brushed the fingers of his right hand, the same hand that he'd been holding above the water. I wouldn't have sworn to it, but it seemed that his fingertips had been hot. Not just warm. Burning hot. As if they'd been dipped into a bowl of fire.

If pressed to do so, I might have acknowledged Jo's right to value her duties, but I was unreasonably angry at her. Angry and petulant. I kept to my room for a day and a half after that night on the beach, lying around in my boxers and doing some serious drinking, contemplating the notion that I was involved in a romantic triangle with a member of the undead. On the morning of the second day, I realized that I was only hurting myself and had a shower, changed my shorts. Still a little drunk, I was debating whether or not to see what was up in the rest of the house, when someone knocked on my door. Without thinking, I said, "Yeah, come in," and Jo walked into the room. I thought about making a grab for my trousers, but I was unsteady on my feet and feared that I'd stumble and fall on my ass; so I sat on the edge of the bed and tried to act nonchalant.

"How are you feeling," she asked.

"Peachy," I said.

She hesitated, then shut the door and took a seat in a carved wooden chair that likely had been some dead king's throne. "You don't look peachy," she said.

I'd cracked the drapes to check on the weather and light fell directly on her—she was the only bright thing in a room full of shadow. "I had a few drinks," I told her. "Drowning my sorrows. But I'm pulling it together."

She nodded, familiar with the condition.

"How come you didn't tell me your boy could do tricks?" I asked.

"Josey? What are you talking about?"

I told her what Pellerin had been doing with the ocean water and she said she hadn't realized he had reached that stage. She hopped up from the chair, saying she had to talk to him.

"Stay," I said. "Come on. You got all day to do with him. Just stay a while, okay?"

Reluctantly, she sat back down.

"So," I said. "You want to tell me what that is he was doing."

"My previous patient developed the ability to manipulate electromagnetic fields. He did some remarkable things. It sounds as if Josey's doing the same."

"You keep saying that. Remarkable how? Give me an example."

"He cured the sick, for one."

"Did he, now?"

"I swear, it's the truth. There was a man with terminal cancer. He cured him. It took him three days and cost him a lot of effort, but afterward the man was cancer-free."

"He cured a guy of cancer by . . . what? Working his electromagnetic fields?"

"I think so. I don't know for sure. Whatever he did, it produced a lot of heat." She crossed her legs, yielding up a sigh. "I wish it had stopped with that."

I asked what had happened.

"It's too long a story to tell, but the upshot was, he built a *veve* . . . Do you know what a *veve* is?"

"The things they draw on the floors of voodoo temples? Little patterns?"

"That's them. They relate to the voodoo gods, the *loas*." She flicked a speck of something off her knee. "Donnell . . . my patient. He built the *veve* of Ogoun Badagris out of copper. Several tons of copper. It was immense. He said it enabled him to focus energy. He used to walk around on top of it and . . . one day there was an explosion." She made a helpless gesture. "I don't understand what happened."

Neither did I understand. I couldn't wrap my brain around the idea that Pellerin might be some kind of green-eyed Jesus; yet I didn't believe she was lying.

"What do think was going on with him?" I asked. "With Pellerin. I mean, what's your theory? You must have a theory."

"You want to hear? I've been told it's pretty out there."

"Yeah, and nothing about this is out there, so your theory's got to be way off base."

She laughed. "Okay. The bacteria we injected into Josey was the same strain we used at Tulane. All the slow-burners have reproduced those designs in one way or another. It's as if they're expressing the various aspects of Ogoun. Doctor Crain's theory was that because the bacteria eventually infested the entire brain, the patients used more of their brains than normal people—this resulted in what seemed to be miraculous powers. And since the bacterial strain was the same, it prevailed upon the host brain to acquire similar characteristics. That makes a certain amount of sense as far as it goes, but Crain was trying to explain voodoo in terms of science, and some of it can't be explained except in voodoo terms."

She paused, as if to gather her thoughts. "Someday we may discover a biochemical factor that makes the patients prone to seeing the *veve* patterns. But we'll never be able to explain away all the mystery surrounding Ezawa's work. I think he discovered the microbiological analogue of possession. In a voodoo ceremony, a possession occurs quickly. The god takes over your body while you're dancing or having a drink. You jerk around as the god acclimates to the flesh, and then you begin acting like that god. With the bacteria, it takes longer and the transition's smoother. You notice a growing awareness in the patients that they're different. Not just because they've come back from the dead. The real difference lies in the things they see and feel. They sense there's something qualitatively different about themselves. They recognize that they have their own agendas. They grow beyond their life stories the way Jesus and Buddha outgrew the parameters of their lives. Things Donnell said . . . they led me to believe that the bacteria allowed them to access their *gro bon ange*. Do you know the term? The immortal portion of the soul? According to voodoo, anyway. And that in turn opened them to the divine. As the bacterial infestation increased, they became more open. The slow-burners all demonstrated behavioral arcs that fit the theory. I guess it sounds crazy, but no one's come up with anything better."

She seemed to be waiting for me to speak.

"You're right," I said. "That's out there."

"Donnell was seeing these peculiar shadows before he died. I think he was seeing peoples' souls. I can't come close to proving it, of course, but there were things he told me . . ." She sighed in exasperation. "I begged Crain to let me work with Josey my way. I thought if I started from a position of intimacy, we could forge a bond strong enough to endure until the end. We'd see the maturation of the new personality. If my theory's right, we'd have a captive god fully integrated with a human personality. Whatever a god is. That might be something we could determine. Who knows what's possible?" The energy drained from her voice and her tone softened. "As things stand I doubt we'll ever get any further than I got with Donnell. He should have been given the space to evolve, but all they did was harass him."

"I'm getting you liked this Donnell," I said.

Her face sharpened. "Yes."

"How about Pellerin?"

"He's not very likeable. Part of it is, he's afraid of everything. Confused. He doesn't know yet who or what he is. He may never know. So he tends to be angry at everyone. That said, he's coarse, he's truculent and difficult to be around." She made a sad face and pushed up from her throne. "I wish I didn't have to go, but I should get back to him."

"Jo?"

"Uh-huh?"

"Remember when you asked if you could count on me as a friend? For what it's worth . . ."

"I know," she said, coming toward me.

"We've been forced onto the same side, but . . ."

She embraced me, pulling my head down onto her shoulder. I breathed in her warm, clean smell, and kissed her neck. She tensed, but I nuzzled her neck, her throat, and she let her head fall back. When I kissed her on the mouth, she kissed me back, fully complicit, and, before long, we were rolling around on the bed. I worked her T-shirt up around her neck and had disengaged the catch of her bra, a hook located under a flare of white lace between the cups, when I realized that, although she was not resisting, neither was she helping out as she had a moment earlier. I slid my hand under the bra, but she remained motionless, reactionless, and I asked what was the matter.

"I can't cope with this. You're the first man I've been attracted to in a long time. A very long time." She adopted an injured expression, like the one a child might display on running up against a rule that denied it a treat. "I want to make love with you, but I can't."

My hand was still on her breast and desire crowded all coherent thought from my head.

"Say something." She shifted, turning on her side, and my hand was no longer happy.

"Does this have anything to do with Pellerin?"

"Partly."

"You're sleeping with him?"

"No, but I might have to. It may be the only way to control him."

"Is that how you controlled Donnell?"

"It wasn't like that! I was in love with him."

"You loved him."

"I know it sounds strange, but I was . . ."

I experienced a flash of anger. "It sounds twisted."

She froze.

"You ever think," I said, "you might have a kink for dead guys?"

She held my eyes for a second, then sat up, rehooked her bra and tugged down her T-shirt.

"Maybe I do," she said. "Maybe I find them a vast improvement."

"I'm sorry," I said. "I didn't mean that. I was just . . ."

"What did you mean?"

"It was frustration talking."

"Don't you think I'm frustrated, too? I could probably find an insult to toss at you if I wanted."

I could have pointed out that she was the cause of her own frustration, but I'd already dug myself a hole and saw no good reason to pull the dirt down on top of me.

"I'm sorry," I said. "I truly am."

"It's not important," she said icily. "I've heard it before."

She flung herself off the bed.

"Jo," I said despairingly.

"Oh," she said, stopping in the doorway. "I nearly forgot. Your employer has a message for you. He'll be arriving in three days. Maybe you'll find his company less perverse than mine."

I wasn't accustomed to viewing myself as an employee, and it took me a hiccup to translate the term "your employer" into the name Billy Pitch. I'd been anticipating his arrival, but the news was a shock nonetheless. My dalliance with Jo, brief and unsatisfying as it was, had placed our time on the island in the context of a courtship, and I needed to reorder my priorities. I knew I had to tell Billy everything—he had likely already heard it and our first conversation would be a test of my loyalty—and I would have to put some distance between Jo and me. You might have thought this would be an easy chore, given the state of the relationship, yet I was down the rabbit hole with her, past the point where longing and desire could be disciplined. Even my most self-involved thoughts were tinged with her colors.

Like advance men for pharaoh, Billy Pitch's retinue arrived before him.

Security people, chef, barber, bed fluffer, and various other functionaries filtered into the compound over the next day and a half. A seaplane brought in Billy the following morning and, after freshening up, accompanied by an enormous bodyguard with the coarse features of an acromegalic giant, he swept into the foyer of the main wing, the most grotesquely decorated room of all, dominated by a fountain transplanted from 19th century Italy, with floors covered by pink and purple linoleum and vinyl furniture to match. It had been over a year since I had seen Billy in the flesh, but I had known him for almost a decade and he had always seemed ageless in a measly, unprepossessing way—I was thus pleased to note a pair of bifocals hanging about his neck and that his fringe of hair was turning gray. He wore a garish cabana set that left his bony knees and skinny forearms bare. The outfit looked ridiculous, but amplified his air of insectile menace. He directed a cursory glance toward Pellerin, sitting on a plum-colored sofa, but his gaze lingered on Jo, who stood behind him.

"My, my! Aren't you the sweet thing?" Billy wagged a forefinger at her. "Who's she remind me of, Clayton?"

The bodyguard, a mighty android in a blue silk T-shirt and white linen jacket, rumbled that he couldn't say, but she did look familiar.

"It'll come to me." He tipped his head pertly to one side and said to me, "Let's talk."

He led me into a room containing a functional modern desk and chairs and one of the ubiquitous flat screens, where I delivered my report. When I had done, he said, "Good job. Very good job." He drummed his fingers on the desk. "Do you believe her? You think that boy is a miracle worker? Or you think maybe that girl in there's gone crazy?"

"It sounds crazy," I said. "But everything I've seen so far backs her up."

He nodded like he wasn't so much agreeing with me, but rather was mulling something over. "Let me show you a piece of tape I landed. Part of the Ezawa project at Tulane. The sound's no good, but the picture speaks volumes."

He switched on the TV and the tape began to play. The original of the tape had been a piece of film. It had an old-fashioned countdown—10, 9, 8, etc.—and then the tape went white, flickered, and settled into a grainy color shot of an orderly removing electrodes from the chest of a man wearing a hospital gown. He appeared to be semi-conscious and was sitting in a wheelchair. Rail-thin, with scraggly dark hair and rawboned hillbilly face. A woman in a nurse's uniform came into view, her back to the camera, and there was a blurt of sound. The legend "Tucker Mayhew" was briefly superimposed over the picture. Another blurt of sound, the woman speaking to the orderly, who left the room. Then the woman moved behind the wheelchair and I saw it was a younger, less buxom Jo, her make-up so liberally applied as to seem almost grotesque.

Billy asked why the heavy make-up and I replied, "She said they don't see very well at first. Must be to help with that."

Jo began to touch the man's shoulders and neck. Initially he was unresponsive, but soon the touches came to act like shocks on him, though he was still out of it. He twitched and stiffened as if being jabbed with needles. His eyelids fluttered open and his eyes showed green flashes, already brighter than Pellerin's.

"The part where she's touching him went on longer," Billy said. "I had it edited down."

The man's eyes opened. Jo left off touching him and moved away. He gaped, glanced around, his face a parody of loss. Jo spoke to him and he located her again. The change in his expression, from woebegone to gratified, was so abrupt as to be laughable. The sound came and went in spurts, and what I could hear was garbled, but I caught enough to know she was teasing out his life story, one he was inventing in order to please her, one that fit the absence in his mind. His eyes tracked her as she performed movements that in their grace and ritual elegance reminded me of Balinese dancers, yet had something as well of the blatant sexuality of bartop strippers you see in clubs on the edge of the Quarter. She passed behind the wheelchair and again touched him on the back of the neck.

Billy paused the tape. "There. Look at that."

The man had his head back and mouth open, searching for Jo, and she was about to touch him again, her long fingers extended toward the nape of his neck. Her smile was, I thought, unreadable, yet the longer I stared at it, the more self-satisfied it seemed. The image trembled slightly.

"Anybody doing that job is going to look bad from time to time," I said.

"But that's the job she does, honey," Billy said. "You can't get around that." He unpaused the tape and muted the sound. "Know what it puts me in mind of? Those women who marry men on death row. It's all about being in control for them. They control the visits, letters . . . everything. They don't have to have sex, yet they have all the emotional content of a real relationship and none of the fuss. And it's got a built-in expiration date. It's a hell of a deal, really. Of course our Miz Verret, she took it farther than most."

A jump in the film, another edit. The man's eyes blazed a fiery green that appeared to overflow his sockets. His coordination had improved, he made coherent gestures and talked non-stop. He struggled to stand and nearly succeeded, and then, after making an obviously impassioned statement, he fell back, dead for the second time. Jo stood beside the body for almost a minute before closing his eyes. A faint radiance shone through the lids. An orderly removed the body as Jo made notes on a clipboard. The screen whited out and another countdown started. Billy switched off the TV.

"Forty-seven minutes," he said. "Scratch one zombie. You got to be careful around that girl."

"Billy, I was . . ."

"I know. You were trying to get a little. But I'd hate to see you screw this up over a piece of ass." His voice acquired a pinched nastiness. "Especially since the bitch is such a freak!" He peered at me over top of his glasses, as if assessing the impact of his words. He sighed. "Let's go have a chat with them, shall we?"

We went back into the living room. Clayton and the other bodyguard stood at ease. Billy took a chair opposite the sofa where Pellerin was sitting and I hovered at his shoulder. Behind Pellerin, Jo tried to make eye contact with me, but I pretended not to notice.

"Mister Pellerin," said Billy. "I have a question for you."

Pellerin looked at me and said, "This dab of cream cheese is the badass you warned us about?"

"Clayton?" said Billy. "Would you mind?"

Two strides carried Clayton to the sofa. He backhanded Pellerin viciously, knocking his sunglasses off. Jo shrieked and Clayton stood poised to deliver another blow.

"In the stomach," Billy said.

Clayton drove his fist into Pellerin's belly, and Billy signaled him to step back. Jo hurried around the couch to minister to Pellerin, who was trying to breathe, bleeding from a cut on his cheek.

"I'm not a very good businessman," said Billy sadly. "I let things get personal. I miss out on a lot of opportunities that way, but I've learned if you can't have fun with an enterprise, it's best to cut your losses. Do you need a moment, Mister Pellerin?"

"You could have killed him!" Jo said, glancing up from Pellerin.

"Precisely." Billy church-and-steepled his fingers. "Your boy there's a valuable commodity, yet because of my intemperate nature I might have done the unthinkable. Do we understand each other? Mister Pellerin?"

Pellerin made a stressed yet affirmative noise.

"Good. Now . . . my question. Is your ability such that you can control the play of seven or eight good card players so as to achieve a specific result?"

With considerable effort, holding his belly, Pellerin sat up. "How specific?"

"I'd like you to arrange it so that you and a certain gentleman outlast all the rest, and that he has a distinct advantage in chips at that point. Let's say a four to one advantage. Then I'd like you to beat him silly. Take all his chips as quickly as you can."

"That's risky," said Pellerin. "The guy could get a run of great cards. It's hard playing heads-up from that far down. You can't bluff effectively. Why do you want me to do it that way? If you let me play my game, I can guarantee a win."

"Because he'll want the game to continue if he thinks you lucked out. He'll offer you a check, but you tell him it's cash or nothing."

"What if he . . ." Pellerin began, and Billy cut him off: "No what-ifs. Yours not to wonder why, yours but to do or die." He looked to Clayton. "Is that Byron?"

"Tennyson," said Clayton. "'The Charge of the Light Brigade.'"

"Yes, of course!" He gave himself a pretend-slap for having forgotten. "Well. Can you do the job, Mister Pellerin?"

"I'll need a little luck, but . . . yeah. I guess I can do it."

"We all need a little luck." Billy popped out of the chair. "You'll be leaving for Fort Lauderdale day after tomorrow. The Seminole Paradise Casino. I'll have my people watching, so don't worry about anything untoward. You will be closely watched. I'll give Jack the details. He can tell you all about it."

He walked away briskly, but then he turned and pointed at Jo. "I got it! *Big Brother All-Stars.* The seventh season. You remember, Clayton?"

Clayton said, maybe, he wasn't sure.

"Come on, man! Erica. The tall bitch with the big rack. She played the game real sneaky."

"Oh, yeah," said Clayton. "Yeah, I can see it."

The Seminole Paradise Hard Rock Hotel and Casino was a hell of a mouthful for what amounted to your basic two-hundred-dollar-per-room Florida hotel complete with fountain display and an assortment of clubs and bars notable for the indifferent quality of their cuisine and the bad taste evident in their decor. Particularly annoying was Pangaea, a club decorated with "authentic tribal artifacts" that likely had been purchased from a prop supply company. The entire complex was a surfeit of fakes. Fake breasts, fake smiles, fake youth, fake people. Why anyone would choose such a place to put a dent in their credit cards, I'll never know— maybe it offered them the illusion that they were losing fake money.

We went down to the casino early the same afternoon we checked in, and Pellerin nabbed a chair at one of the poker tables. I watched for a while to ascertain whether he was winning—he was—and went for a stroll. I wanted to see how far my leash would stretch. There were several men hanging about who might be Billy's people and I was interested to learn if any of them would follow me. I also wanted to get clear of the situation and gain some perspective on things. Once I reached the entrance to the grounds, I turned right and walked along the edge of the highway, working up a sweat in the hot sun, until I came to a strip mall with about twenty-five or thirty shops, the majority of them closed. It was Sunday in the real world.

A Baskin-Robbins caught my eye. The featured flavors were banana daiquiri and sangria. Sangria, for fuck's sake! I bought two scoops of vanilla by way of protesting the lapsed integrity of ice cream flavors and ate it sitting on the curb. I tried to problem-solve, but all I did was churn up mud from the bottom of my brain. The assignment that had been forced upon us—upon Pellerin—was to attract the interest of a wealthy developer named Frank Ruddle, an excellent poker player who frequented the Seminole Paradise. Pellerin's job was to play sloppy over the course of a couple of weeks. That way he would set himself up as a mark and Ruddle would invite him to the big cash game held each month at his Lauderdale home. According to Billy's scenario, once Ruddle went bust, he would feel compelled to open his vault in order to obtain more cash. At this point Billy's people would move in on the game. He wanted something from that vault. I thought it might be more of a trophy than anything of actual value, and that his real goal was purely personal. The plan was paper-thin and smacked of Billy at his most profligate. There were a dozen holes in it, a hundred ways it could go wrong, but Billy was willing to spend our lives for the chance to gain a petty victory. Had the aim of the exercise been to secure the item at any cost, it could have been far more easily achieved. That he was willing to squander an asset with (if Jo were to be believed) unlimited potential was classic late-period Billy Pitch. If we failed, it was no skin off his butt. He'd wait for his next opportunity and while away the hours throwing Tanqueray parties for his fellow reality-show addicts. And if we succeeded, he might decide that his victory would not be secure so long as we were alive. I saw a couple of outs, but the odds of them working were not good.

Across from the mall lay a vacant lot overgrown with weeds, sprinkled with scrub palmetto, and adjoining it was another, larger lot that had been cleared for construction, the future site of LuRay Condominiums—so read a sign picturing a peppy senior citizen couple who seemed pleased as all get out that they would soon be living next door to a casino where they could blow their retirement in a single evening. Farther along was a cluster of tiny redneck dwellings set among diseased-looking palms. Squatty frame houses with shingle roofs and window-unit air conditioners and front yards littered with sun-bleached Big Wheels and swing sets. They looked deserted, but each of them harbored, I imagined, a vast corpulent entity with dyed hair and swollen ankles, who survived on a diet of game shows and carbohydrates, and went outside once a day to check the sky for signs of the Rapture. Now and then a car zipped past and, less frequently, one pulled into the mall and disgorged a porky Florida Cracker family desirous of some Burger King or a couple of bare-midriffed Britney Spears clones in search of emergency eye liner.

This dose of reality caused the mud to settle, the sediment to wash from my thoughts, but clarity did not improve my prospects. I tossed my trash into a bin. Zombie hold 'em players and doe-eyed ladies who were a little damaged . . . I wanted that crap out of my head, I wanted things back the way they had been. Small Time. That was me. Yet I was content with my small-time life. I was adept at it, I was pleased with my general lack of ambition. Tentatively, I gave the trash bin a kick. It quivered in fear, and that inspired me to unload on it. The bin rolled out into the parking lot and I kept on kicking it. I crushed its plastic ribs, I flattened it and squeezed out its soggy paper-and-crumpled-plastic guts. Inside the Baskin-Robbins, people stared but didn't appear terribly alarmed. They were accustomed to such displays. Heat drove men insane in these parts. The manager took a stand by the door, ready to defend his tubs of flavored goo, but the moment passed when I might have stormed his glassed-in fortress and engendered the headline Five Dead In Baskin-Robbins Spree Killing—Louisiana Native Charged In Crime. I strode out to the highway, fueled by a thin, poisonous anger, and was nearly struck by a speeding Corvette that veered onto the shoulder. Dizzy with adrenaline, I gazed off along the road. Despite the vegetation, I felt I was on the edge of a desert. Weeds stirred in a fitful breeze. One day the Great Sky Monkey, sated with banana daiquiri ice cream, would drop down from the Heavenly Banyan Tree to use the place for toilet paper. I tried to calm myself, but everywhere I cast my eye I saw omens and portents and outright promises of doom. I saw a wine bottle shattered into a spray of diamonds on the asphalt, I saw a gray-haired man poking his cane feebly at a dead palm frond, I saw a sweaty twelve-year-old girl with a mean, sexy face pedaling her bicycle full tilt toward me, and I saw a black car with smoked windows idling beside a dumpster under the killing white glare of the sun.

*F*rank Ruddle looked like an empty leather gym bag. He had recently lost a great deal of weight, something he proclaimed loudly and often, and his skin had not tightened sufficiently to compensate. Forty-something; with thinning blond hair and a store-bought orange tan and a salesman's jaunty manner; these attributes—if attributes they were—had been counterbalanced by dewlaps, jowls and an overall lack of muscle tone. His outfits always included some cranberry article of clothing. A tie, a pair of slacks, a shirt. I assumed this was his lucky color, for it was not a flattering one, serving to accent his unhealthiness. At the tables, prior to making a bold play, he was in the habit of kissing a large diamond signet ring. He appeared to have taken a shine to Pellerin, perhaps in part because Pellerin was an even unhealthier specimen than he, and, when sitting at the same table, he would applaud Pellerin's victories, including those won at his expense, with enthusiasm.

"Damn!" he would say, and give an admiring shake of the head. "I didn't see that coming."

Pellerin, in heads-up play, let Ruddle win the lion's share of the pots and took his losses with poor grace. Watching him hustle Ruddle was like watching a wolf toy with a house pet, and I might have felt sorry for the man if I had been in a position to be sympathetic.

We had been at Seminole Paradise ten days before Ruddle baited his hook. As Pellerin and I were entering the casino in the early afternoon, he intercepted us and invited us for lunch at the hotel's fake Irish pub, McSorely's, a place with sawdust on the floor, something of an anomaly, as I understood it, among fake Irish pubs. Pellerin was in a foul mood, but when he saw the waiter approaching, a freckly, red-headed college-age kid costumed as a leprechaun, he busted out laughing and thereafter made sport of him throughout the meal. The delight he took from baiting the kid perplexed Ruddle, but he didn't let it stand in the way of his agenda. He buttered Pellerin up and down both sides, telling him what a marvelous player he was, revisiting a hand he had won the night before, remarking on its brilliant disposition. Then he said, "You know, I'm having some people over this weekend for a game. I'd be proud if you could join us."

Pellerin knocked back the dregs of his third margarita. "We're going to head on to Miami, I think. See what I can shake loose from the casinos down there."

Ruddle looked annoyed by this rebuff, but he pressed on. "I sure wish you'd change your mind. There'll be a ton of dead money in the game."

"Yeah?" Pellerin winked at me. "Some of it yours, no doubt."

Ruddle laughed politely. "I'll try not to disappoint you," he said.

"How much money we talking here?"

"There's a five hundred thousand dollar buy-in."

Pellerin sucked on a tooth. "You trying to hustle me, Frank? I mean, you seen me play. You know I'm good, but you must think you're better."

"I'm confident I can play with you," Ruddle said.

Pellerin guffawed.

"I beg your pardon?" said Ruddle.

"I once knew a rooster thought it could run for president 'til it met up with a hatchet."

Ruddle's smile quivered at the corners.

"Shit, Frank! I'm just joshing you." Pellerin lifted his empty glass to summon the leprechaun. "This is a cash game, right?"

"Of course."

"What sort of security you got? I'm not about to bring a wad of cash to a game doesn't have adequate security."

"I can assure you my security's more than adequate," said Ruddle tensely.

"Yeah, well. Going by how security's run at the Seminole, your idea of adequate might be a piggybank with a busted lock. I'll send Jack over to check things out. If he says it's cool, we'll gamble."

I sent Ruddle a silent message that said, See what I have to put up with, but he didn't respond and dug into his steak viciously, as if it were the liver of his ancient enemy.

Somehow we made it through lunch. I pushed the small talk. Movies, the weather... Ruddle offered curt responses and Pellerin sucked down margaritas, stared out the window and doodled on a napkin. After Ruddle had paid the check, I steered Pellerin outside and, to punish him, dragged him on a brisk walk about the pool. He complained that his legs were hurting and I said, "We need to get you in shape. That game could go all night."

I walked him until he had sweated out his liquid lunch, then allowed him to collapse at a poolside table not far from the lifeguard's chair. They must have treated the water earlier that day, because the chlorine reek was strong. In the pool, a huge sun-dazzled aquamarine with a waterfall slide at its nether end, packs of kids cavorted under their parents' less-than-watchful eyes, bikini girls and speedo boys preened for one another. Close at hand, an elderly woman in a one-piece glumly paddled along the edge, her upper body supported by a flotation device in the form of a polka-dotted snail. The atmosphere was of amiable chatter, shrieks, and splashings. A honey-blond waitress in shorts and an overstrained tank top ambled over from the service bar, but I brushed her off.

"You got a plan?" Pellerin asked out of the blue.

"A plan? Sure," I said. "First Poland, then the world."

"If you don't, we need to start thinking about one."

I cocked an eye toward him, then looked away.

"That's why I played Ruddle like I did," Pellerin said. "So you could get a line on his security."

"We do what Billy tells us," I said. "That's our safest bet."

Three boys ran past, one trying to snap the others with a towel; the lifeguard whistled them down.

"I did have a thought," I said. "I thought we could tell Ruddle what Billy's up to and hope he can protect us. But that's a short-term solution at best. Billy's still going to be a problem."

"I like it. It buys us time."

"If Ruddle goes for it. He might not. I'm not sure how well he knows Billy. He might be tight with him, and he might decide to give him a call."

A plump, pale, middle-aged man wearing a fishing hat and bathing trunks, holding a parasol drink, negotiated the stairs at the shallow end of the pool, stood and sipped in thigh-deep water.

"I'll check out Ruddle's security. It may give me an idea." I put my hands flat on the table and prepared to stand. "We should look in on Jo before you start playing."

Pellerin's lips thinned. "To hell with her."

"You two got a problem?"

"She lied to me."

"Everyone fibs now and again."

"She lied about something pretty crucial."

I suspected that Jo had told him he hadn't always been Josey Pellerin. "Mind if I ask what?"

"Yeah," he said. "I mind."

I watched him out of the corner of my eye. His features relaxed from their belligerent expression and he appeared to be tracking the progress of something through the air. I asked what he was looking at, half-expecting him to claim that he had discovered a microscopic planet with an erratic orbit, but he said, "A gnat." Then he laughed. "A gnat with a fucking aura."

"You see that shit all the time?"

"Auras? Yeah. Weirder stuff than that."

"Like what?"

"Shadows." He fumbled in his pocket and fished out a wad of bills, napkins, gum wrappers—there must have been thirty or forty hundreds in with the debris; he selected a twenty, tossed the rest on the table and hailed the blond waitress. "Margarita rocks," he told her. "Salt."

"Better slow down," I said. "If you're going to play poker, that is."

"You kidding me? I need a handicap to play with those old ladies."

I let my thoughts wander, vaguely mindful of the activity in the pool, speculating on the rate of skin cancers among the patrons of the Seminole Paradise, reflecting on the fact that I had not seen a single Seminole during our stay, if one omitted the grotesque statue of Osceola in the lobby, fashioned from a shiny yellowish brown material—petrified Cheese Whiz was my best guess. The waitress set Pellerin's margarita down on the table; her eyes snagged on the cash strewn across it. She offered Pellerin his change and he told her to keep it. He tilted his head, squinted at her name tag, and said, "Is waitressing your regular job, Tammy, or just something you do on the side?"

Tammy didn't know how to take this. She flashed her teeth, struck a pose that accentuated her breasts and said, "I'm sorry?"

"Reason I ask," said Pellerin, "I wonder if you ever done any hostessing? I'm throwing a party up in my suite tonight. Around ten o'clock. And I was hoping to get a couple of girls to help me host it. You know the drill. Take care of the guests. See that everyone's got a drink. You'd be doing me a huge

Dead Money

favor." He reached into his other pocket, peeled what looked to be about a grand off his roll and held it out to her. "That's a down payment."

A light switched on in Tammy's brain and she re-evaluated Pellerin. "So how many guests are we talking about?" she asked.

"I'm the only one you'd have to worry about." Pellerin gave a lizardly smile. "But I can be a real chore."

"Why, I think we can probably handle it." Tammy accepted the bills, folded them, stashed them next to her heart. "Around ten, you say?"

"I'm in the Everglades Suite," said Pellerin. "Wear something negligible. And one more thing, darling. It'd be nice if your friend was a Latina. Maybe a Cuban girl. On the slender side. Maybe her name could be . . . Thomasina?"

"Why, isn't that a coincidence! That's my best friend's name!" Tammy turned and twitched her cute butt. "See ya tonight."

As she sashayed off, Pellerin slurped down half his margarita and sighed. "Ain't freedom grand?"

"What was that bullshit?" I said. "You're in the Everglades Suite?"

"Three nights from now, we could be lying in a landfill," he said. "I booked myself a suite and I'm going to have me a party."

"This isn't wise," I said. "Suppose she gets a look at your eyes?"

"Did you get a load of the brain on that girl? I could tell her I was down in the Amazon and got stung by electric bees, she'd be fine with it."

I wasn't too sure about that, but then I was distracted from worry by thinking about Jo all alone in Room 1138.

"Yeah, boy!" said Pellerin, and grinned—he'd been watching me. "What they say is true. Every cloud has a silver lining."

I made no response.

"Hell, if Jocundra don't do it for you," he said, "I'm sure Tammy and Thomasina wouldn't mind accommodating another guest."

"That's all right."

"On second thought, I believe you're the kind of guy who needs that old emotion lotion to really get off."

"Shut your hole, okay?"

Pellerin finished his margarita, signaled Tammy for another. I was through cautioning him about his drinking. Maybe he'd drop dead. That would let us off the hook. More people had jumped into the pool—it looked like a sparkling blue bowl of human head soup. There came a loud screech that resolved into "The Pina Colada Song" piped in over speakers attached to the surrounding palms. I was half-angry, though I couldn't have told you at what, and that damn song exacerbated my mood. Tammy brought the margarita and engaged in playful banter with Pellerin.

"Does your friend want a friend?" she asked. "Because I bet I could fix him up."

"Naw, he's got a friend," said Pellerin. "The trouble is, she ain't treating him all that friendly."

"Aw! Well, if he needs a friendly-ier friend, you let me know, hear?"

I shut my eyes and squeezed the arms of my chair, exerting myself in an attempt to suppress a shout. Eventually I relaxed and my mind snapped back into on-duty mode. "What kind of shadows?" I asked Pellerin.

He gazed at me blankly. "Huh?"

"You said you were seeing shadows. What kind?"

"You're starting to sound like Jocundra, man."

"What, is it a big secret?"

He licked salt off the rim of his glass. "I don't guess they're shadows, really. They're these black shapes, like a man, but they don't have any faces. Sometimes they have lights inside them. Shifting lights. They kind of flow together."

I laughed. "Sounds like a lava lamp?"

"Everybody's got one," he said. "But it's not an aura. It's more substantial. I see patterns, too. Like . . ." He poked around in the pile of money and trash on the table and plucked out a napkin bearing the McSorely's logo. "Like this here. The whole thing creeps me out."

On the napkin were several sketches of what appeared to be ironwork designs: *veves*. I asked why it creeped him out.

"When we were on the island," Pellerin went on, "I found these books on voodoo. And while I was leafing through them, I saw that same design. It's used in the practice of voodoo. Called a *veve*. That there's the *veve* of Ogoun Badagris, the voodoo god of war. And this . . ." He pointed to a second sketch. "This one's Ogoun in his aspect as the god of fire. I get that one a lot." He paused and then said, "You know anything about it?"

I had no doubt that he could read me if I lied and, although it was my instinct to lie, I didn't see any reason to hide things from him anymore; yet I didn't want to freak him out, either.

"Jo told me she had another patient who saw this same sort of pattern," I said.

"What else she tell you?"

"She said he did some great things before . . ."

"Before he died, right?"

"Yeah."

There ensued a silence, during which I noticed that the song playing over the speakers was now "Margaritaville".

"She told me he got to where he could cure the sick," I said.

He stared at me. "Fuck."

"Let's get through the weekend, then you can worry about it," I said.

"Easy for you to say."

"It's a lot to process, I give you that. But you can't . . ."

"I knew she was holding back, but . . . man!" He picked up his drink, put it back down. "You know, I don't much fucking care if we get through the weekend."

"I care," I said, but he appeared not to hear me, gazing out across the pool toward the hedge of palms and shrubbery that hid the concrete block wall that separated Seminole Paradise from a Circuit City store.

"You ever have the feeling you're on the verge of understanding everything?" he said. "That if you could see things a tad clearer, you'd have the big picture in view? I mean the *Big Picture*. How it all fits together. That's where I'm at. But I'm also getting this feeling I don't fucking want to see the big picture, that it's about ten shades darker than the picture I already got." He chewed on that a second, then heaved up to his feet. "I'm going to the casino."

"Wait a second!" I said as he walked away.

I busied myself plucking the hundreds out of the mess we'd made on the table, and I pressed the clutter of bills into his hands. He seemed startled by the money, as if it were an unexpected bonus, but then he stepped to the edge of the glittering pool and said in a loud voice, "Hey! Here you go, you lucky people!" and tossed the money into the air.

There couldn't have been more than four or five thousand dollars, but for the furore it caused, it might have been a million. As the bills fluttered down, people surged through the water after them; others sprawled on the tiles in their mad scramble to dive into the pool. Children were elbowed aside, the elderly were at risk. A buff young lad surfaced with a joyous expression, clutching a fistful of bills, and was immediately hauled under by a bikini girl and her boyfriend, their faces aglow with greed. The water was lashed into a froth as by sharks in a feeding frenzy. Terrified screams replaced the prettier shrieks that had attended roughhousing and dunkings. One man dragged a woman from the melee and sought to give her mouth-to mouth, whereupon she kicked him in the groin. The lifeguard's umbrella toppled into the water. He shouted incoherent orders over his mike. This served to increase the chaos. He began blowing his whistle over and over, an irate clown with his cheeks puffed and a nose covered in sun block.

Pellerin was laughing as I pulled him away from the pool, and he was still laughing when I shoved him through the double glass doors of the hotel. I adopted a threatening pose, intending to lecture him, and he made an effort to stifle his laughter; but then I started laughing, too, and his mirth redoubled. We stood wheezing and giggling in the lobby, giddy as teenage girls, drawing hostile stares from the guests waiting in line at Reception, enduring the drudgery of check-in. At the time I assumed that we were laughing at two different things, or at different aspects of the same thing, but now I'm not so sure.

That picture of Pellerin laughing by the side of the pool, bills fluttering out above the water . . . it emerges from the smoke of memory like a painted dream, like one of those images that come just before a commercial break in a television drama, when the action freezes and the colors are altered by a laboratory process. Though it seems unreal, the rest—by comparison—seems in retrospect less than unreal, a dusting of atoms, whispers, and suggestions of hue that we must arrange into a story in order to lend body to this central moment. Yet the stories we create are invariably inaccurate and the central moments we choose to remember change us as much or more as we change them, and so, in truth, my memories are no more "real" than Josey Pellerin's, although they have, as Jo would put it, more foundation . . . But I was saying, that picture of Pellerin beside the pool stayed with me because, I believe, it was the first time I had acknowledged him as a man and not a freak. And when I went to see him late the next morning, it was motivated more by curiosity over how he'd made out with Tammy and Thomasina than by caretaker concerns.

The door to the suite had been left ajar. I sneaked a look inside and, seeing no one around, eased into the foyer. The living room was empty, an air-conditioned vacancy of earth tones and overstuffed furniture, with potted palms and a photomural of the Everglades attempting a naturalistic touch. Everything was very neat. Magazines centered on the coffee table; no empty glasses or bottles. On the sideboard, a welcome basket of fruit, wine, and cheese was still clenched in shrinkwrap. I proceeded down the hall and came to an open door. Wearing a terrycloth bathrobe and sunglasses, Pellerin sat beside the rumpled bed, his feet propped on a table covered with a linen cloth and laden with dishes and metal dish covers, drinking champagne out of a bottle and eating a slice of pizza, looking out the window at the overcast. In the bed, partly covered by the sheets, a brown-skinned girl lay on her belly, black hair fanned across her face. Thomasina. There was nary a sign of Tammy, though the bed was king-sized and she might well have been buried beneath the covers. I knocked and he beckoned me to come on in. A big scorch mark on the wall behind his head, about the size of a serving tray, caught my notice. I asked what had happened and he told me that Tammy had shot an aerosol spray through a lit cigarette lighter, producing a flamethrower effect.

"You know those sons-of-bitches wouldn't let me order in a pizza last night," he said. "Is that bullshit or what? I had to bribe the bellboy." He pointed to a Domino's box on the floor—it held two slices fettered with strings of congealed cheese—and told me to help myself.

I declined, sat opposite him, and he asked what time it was.

"Around eleven." I picked up a plastic pill bottle from the table. The label read:

R. Saloman

Viagra 50 mg.
1 tablet as needed.

"Who's R. Saloman?" I asked.

"Beats me. Friend of the bellboy, maybe. The kid's a walking pharmacy." Pellerin scratched his chest. "Want some room service?"

"I'm okay."

"How about some coffee? Sure, you want some coffee."

He reached for the phone, ordered coffee and sweet rolls. Thomasina stirred but did not wake.

"Where's Tammy?" I asked.

"In the head? Or she might have gone home. We were doing shots last night and she got sick."

"You trying to kill yourself, man? Maybe you haven't noticed, but you're not in the best of shape."

Pellerin had a swig of champagne. "You my fairy godmother now?"

"I'm just being solicitous of your health."

"Because that was Jocundra's job, and I shit-canned her."

"Look, don't get the idea you're in charge here. You're not in charge."

"Oh, I'm far from having that idea. We all know who's in charge."

Jocundra's voice called from the living room. "Josey!"

"In here, darling!" He gave me a wink. "This ought to be good."

Seconds later, Jocundra materialized in the doorway, dressed in jeans and a man's pinstriped dress shirt with the sleeves neatly rolled up. Her eyes stuck on Thomasina, then went to me and Pellerin. "I need to talk to you. I'll come back."

"Don't be that way," said Pellerin. "We're all pals. Sit with us. We got coffee coming."

She had another glance at Thomasina, then came to the table and took the chair between me and Pellerin.

"I spoke to management," she said. "They're not going to kick us out, but you're banned from the pool area."

"Damn!" said Pellerin. "And here I was dying for a swim."

Jocundra started to speak, likely to reprimand him, but thought better of it. An edgy quiet closed in around us.

"You know they got a couple of live gators in that pond in the courtyard? That's why there's a fence around it." Pellerin shook his head in mock amazement. "They don't never show themselves. Can't say as I blame them."

Another stretch of quiet.

"I'm going over to Ruddle's house later to see what I can see," I said. "It's right on the water. That might be good for us. It's a potential avenue of escape if things go south."

There would probably have been another interval of silence, if not for Tammy who, wearing a towel turbaned around her hair and nothing else, entered the room, said, "Oops!", and tippy-toed to the bed, slipping in under the covers next to Thomasina. She sat up, shook out her hair, and said to me, "Is this your friend? She's so pretty!"

"Hey, babe!" Pellegrin said. "I thought you went home."

"I was making myself sweet for you," said Tammy in a little-girl voice.

"I'll be in my room," said Jocundra.

"Why you acting this way?" Pellerin caught her wrist. "Like you been wronged or something. If anyone's been wronged, it's me. Sit down and be polite. There's no reason we can't act like friends."

Tammy, baffled, gestured at me and said to Pellerin, "I thought she was *his* friend."

Jocundra twisted free and walked out. I caught up to her in the living room. "Hey, slow down," I said, blocking the door to the suite.

She folded her arms and lowered her head, shielding her eyes with one hand, as if close to tears. "Let me by!"

"All right." I moved aside, inviting her to leave. "You're not helping him by behaving like this. You're not helping me, you're not helping yourself. But go ahead. Take a break. I'll handle things. Just try and pull yourself together by Saturday night."

She stood a moment, then walked over to a sofa, stood another moment and sat down.

"Why're you getting so bent out of shape?" I dropped into a chair. "I thought you didn't have a strong connection with this guy."

"I don't!"

"Then why . . ."

"Because I *couldn't* make a connection with him. It's my fault he's alone."

"He's not exactly alone," I reminded her.

"You know it's not the same. He needs someone with him who understands what he's going through."

With two people breathing in it, the room seemed almost airless, like a room in a Motel 6 with bolted-shut plastic windows. I thought about yanking back the drapes and opening the glass door onto the balcony, but I couldn't muster the energy.

"He's not exercising," Jocundra said. "He's not taking his meds."

"Maybe you should have slept with him."

"I tried once, but . . . I couldn't. And that's your fault."

I was about to ask her why it was my fault—I knew why, but I wanted to hear her say it—when Pellerin limped into the room.

"I've been taking my meds. And I'm not a fool." He lowered himself into a chair, smirking at us. "You crazy kids! Why don't you run away and get hitched?"

Jo's startled expression waned; she folded her hands in her lap and bowed her head, like Anne Boleyn awaiting the inevitable.

"It's no big thing," said Pellerin. "Really. So how about we ditch the soap opera and move on?"

"I'm worried about you," Jo said.

"Fine. Worry about me," said Pellerin. "But don't get all fucked up behind it."

The doorbell bonged and a man's voice called out, "Room service."

"I'll get it," I said.

I prevented the room service guy from entering, but he peered over my shoulder as I signed for the coffee and rolls. After I had poured coffee for me and Jo, Pellerin asked if I'd see whether the girls wanted anything, so I walked back to the bedroom to check and found Tammy and Thomasina engaged in activity that would have made the White Goddess blush. I returned to the living room and, in response to Pellerin's inquiring look, said, "They're good."

"We were thinking," Jo said, "that we should have a Plan B."

I joined her on the sofa, tore open a package of Sweet 'n Low and dumped the contents into my coffee. "I didn't realize we had a Plan A."

"Confessing to Ruddle," said Pellerin.

"That's our plan? Okay." I stirred the coffee. "Maybe we could create a disturbance. Get away in the confusion. I don't know."

Pellerin said, "You're not exactly an expert criminal, are you?"

"I'm not a criminal at all. I arrange things, I put people together. It's a gray area."

"He's an entrepreneur." Jo smiled at me as if to cut the sting of what she'd said.

A shift in alignment seemed to have occurred—judging by that remark, she had repositioned herself closer to Pellerin than to me. I wondered if she were aware of this. A cruel comment came to mind, but I chose not to make it.

"We could cause a major earthquake, and I doubt it would help," I said. "Josey can walk pretty good, but I expect running's going to be called for and he's not up to that."

Even the coffee sucked at Seminole Paradise—I set my cup down. Pellerin fiddled with the sash of his robe and Jo clinked a spoon against her cup, tapping out a nervous rhythm.

"What about the stuff I saw you doing on the island?" I asked Pellerin. "The night we had that dust-up on the beach, you were doing things with the water. Pushing waves around."

A hunted expression flashed across his face, and I had the thought that he might be hiding something. "I can do a few parlor tricks," he said.

"What's your best one?" I asked. "Give us a demonstration."

"All right." He leaned over the table and put a napkin in an ashtray. "Sometimes I can do it, but other times . . . not so much."

He concentrated on the napkin, wiggled his fingers like a guitar player lightly fingering the strings. After about twenty, thirty seconds, smoke began to trickle up from the napkin, followed by a tiny flame. He snuffed it out with a spoon. Jo made a speech-like noise, but didn't follow up.

"That's my biggie," he said, leaning back. "If we had another month, I might could do something more impressive. But . . . " He shrugged, then said to Jo, "If we come through this, I want you to tell me about Ogoun Badagris. How that relates to me."

She nodded.

"You know, that might have possibilities," I said. "If you could start an electrical fire, we . . ."

"I don't want to talk about this anymore," he said. "After you get back from Ruddle's, we'll talk then."

"I'll tell you now if you want," Jo said. "About Ogoun. It won't take too long."

Pellerin suddenly appeared tired, pale and hollow-cheeked, slumping in his chair, but he said, "Yeah, why don't you?"

I was tired, too. Tired of talking, tired of the Seminole Paradise, tired of whatever game Jo was playing, tired of listening to my own thoughts. I told them I was off to Ruddle's place and would return later that afternoon. On my way out, I heard a hissing from down the hallway. Tammy, wearing bra and panties, waved to me and retreated toward the bedroom, stopping near the door.

"Is your friend going to stay?" she asked in a stage whisper.

"For a while."

She frowned. "Well, I don't know."

"You don't know what?"

"We didn't bargain on a four-way, especially with another woman."

"You got something against women? It didn't look like you did."

Tammy didn't catch my drift and I told her what I had witnessed.

"That's different," she said primly.

"Would more money help?"

She perked up. "Money always helps."

"I'm going out now, but I'll take care of you. I promise?"

"Okay!" She stood on tip-toe and kissed my cheek.

"One more thing," I said. "Jo's kind of shy, but once you start her up, she's a tigress."

"I bet." Tammy shivered with delight. "Those long legs!"

"So in a few minutes why don't you . . . maybe the both of you. Why don't you go out there and warm her up? She really loves intimate touching. You know what I mean? She likes to be fondled. She may object at first, but stay with it and she'll melt. I'll get you your money. Deal?"

"Deal! Don't worry. We'll get her going."

"I'm sure you will," I said.

The one salient thing I learned at Ruddle's was that a pier extended out about a hundred feet into the water from a strip of beach, and at the end of the pier was moored a sleek white Chris Craft that had been set up for sports fishing—the keys to the boat, the *Mystery Girl*, were kept in a small room off the kitchen that also contained the controls to the security system. The house itself was a post card. Big and white and ultramodern, it looked like the Chris Craft's birth mother. An Olympic-sized pool fronted the beach, tennis courts were off to the side. The grounds were a small nation of landscaped palms and airbrushed lawn, its borders defined by a decorous electric fence topped with razor wire and guarded by a pink gatehouse with a uniform on duty. There was a plaque on the gate announcing that the whole shebang was called The Sea Ranch, but it would have been more apt if it had been named The Sea What I Got.

Ruddle's son showed me around—a blond super-preppie with a Cracker accent that had acquired a New Englander gloss. During our brief time together he said both "y'all" and "wicked haahd," as if he hadn't decided which act suited him best. He was impatient to get back to his tanned, perfect girlfriend, an aspiring young coke whore clearly high on more than life. She sat by the pool, listening to reggae, painting faces on her toenails, and flashed me an addled smile that gave me a contact high. I made sure to ask the kid a slew of inane questions ("Is that door sealed with a double gromit?" "What kind of infrared package does that sensor use?"), delaying and stalling in order to annoy him until, growing desperate, he gave me the run of the house and scurried back to her side.

The card room could be isolated from the remainder of the house. It had no windows and soundproofed walls, a bar, and, against the rear wall, three trophy cases celebrating Ruddle's skill at poker. The place of honor was held by a ring won at a World Series of Poker circuit tournament in Tunica, Mississippi. It was flanked by several photographs of Ruddle with poker notables, Phil Ivey and Chris "Jesus" Ferguson and the like, who were apparently among those he had defeated. I was inspecting the table, an elegance of teak and emerald felt lit by a hanging lamp, when a lean, long-haired, thirtyish man in cut-offs walked in, holding an apple, and asked in a Eurotrash accent what I was doing. I told him I was casing the joint.

"No, no!" He wagged a finger at me. "This is not good . . . the drugs."

I explained that "casing the joint" meant I was looking the house over, seeing whether it would be possible to burglarize it.

He took a bite of his apple and, after chewing, said, "I am Torsten. And you are?"

I thought he had misunderstood me again, but when I had introduced myself, he said, "You have chosen a bad time. There will be many here this weekend. Many guards, many guests."

"How many guards?" I asked.

"Perhaps five . . . six." He fingered the edge of the table. "This is excellent work."

"Are you a friend of the family?"

"Yes, of course. Torsten is everyone's friend." He strolled around the table, trailing a hand across the felt, and said, "Now I must go. I wish you will have success with your crime."

Later that afternoon as I was preparing to leave, sitting in my rental car and making some notes, I spotted him outside the house. He was carrying a Weed Whacker, yelling at an older man who was pruning bushes, speaking without a trace of an accent, cussing in purest American. There might be, I thought, a lesson to be drawn from this incident, but I decided that puzzling it out wasn't worth the effort. While driving back to the hotel, I noticed that a motorcyclist in a helmet with a tinted faceplate was traveling at a sedate rate of speed and keeping behind me. Whenever I slowed, he dropped back or switched lanes, and when I parked in the hotel lot, he placed a call on his cell phone. Aggravated and wanting to convey that feeling, I walked toward him, but he kicked over the engine and sped off before I could get near.

A Do Not Disturb card was affixed to the doorknob of the Everglades Suite, so I went down to 1138. Jo, who had been napping, let me in and went into the bathroom to wash her face. I sat at her table and put my feet up. She came back out and lay down on the bed, turned to face me. After I'd briefed her on what I had learned, she said softly, "I'm glad you're back."

"I'm glad you're glad," I said glibly, wondering at the intimacy implied by her tone.

She shut her eyes and I thought for a moment she had drifted off. "I'm afraid," she said.

"Yeah. Me, too."

"You don't act afraid."

"If I let myself think about Saturday, I get to shaking in my boots." I leaned toward her, resting my elbows on my knees. "We got to tough it out."

"I'm not feeling very tough."

I said something neutral and she reached out her hand, inviting me to take it. She caressed my wrist with her fingertip. Holding her hand while sitting on the edge of the chair grew awkward, and I moved to the bed. She curled up against me. I stroked her hair, murmured an assurance, but that seemed insufficient, so I kicked off my shoes and lay down, wrapping my arms around her from behind.

"I'm sorry," she said.

"For what?"

"For how I behaved on the island. For this morning. You must think I'm a terrible tease. But when I see Josey like that, I feel I should comfort him, even though . . ."

"What?"

She shook her head. "Nothing."

"Say."

Her eyes teared; she pressed my hand against her breast. "It's not him I want to comfort. You know that."

I told her not to cry.

She drew a deep breath, steadying herself. "That's how I was brought up," she said. "I was taught to deny what I wanted, that I had to let it come second to what everyone else wanted."

"It's okay."

"No! It's not! I watched my mother wither away taking care of my daddy, his brothers, of every stray that wandered by. She could scarcely let a second pass without doing something for him. I swore I wouldn't be like her. But I'm exactly like her."

I came to realize that we were less having a conversation than engaging in a litany: she, the priestess, delivering the oration, and I, the acolyte, offering appropriate responses. And as we continued this ritual of confession and assurance, the words served to focus me on the hollow of her throat, the pale skin below her collarbone, the lace trim of a brassiere peeking out between the buttons of her shirt, until the only things in the world were the sound of her voice and the particulars of her body. For all it mattered, she could have been reciting a butcher's list or reading from a manual on automotive maintenance.

"Feeling that way screwed up almost every relationship I ever had," she said. "Because I *didn't* feel that way. Not at heart . . . not really. It was just a rule I couldn't break. I resented men for making me obey the rule, but they didn't enforce it. I did. I couldn't simply be with them, I couldn't enjoy them. And now I don't care about rules, I finally don't care, and it's too late."

I told her it wasn't too late, we'd pull through somehow.

Dominus vobiscum,

Et cum spiritus tuo.

Tears slipped along the almost imperceptible lines beside her eyes. I propped myself up on an elbow, intending to invoke some further optimistic cliché, wanting to make certain that she had taken it to heart. Lying half-beneath me, searching my face, her expression grew strangely grave, and then her tongue flicked out to taste my mouth, her hips arched against mine. The solicitude, the tenderness I felt . . . all that was peeled away to reveal a more urgent affinity, and I tore at her clothing, fumbling with buttons, buckle, snaps, rough with her in my hurry. She cried out in abandon, as if suffering the pain of her broken principles. Cities of thought crumbled, my awareness of our circumstance dissolved, and a last snatch of bleak self-commentary captioned my desire—I saw in my mind's eye the image of a red burning thing in a fiery sky, not a true sun but a great shear of light in which was embedded an indistinct shape, like that of a bird flying sideways or a woman's genital smile, and beneath it a low, smoldering wreckage that stretched from horizon to horizon, in which the shadows of men crouched and scuttered and fled with hands clamped to their ears so as to muffle the echoes of an apocalyptic pronouncement.

We spent that night and most of the next day in 1138. Every so often I would run up and check on Pellerin, but my concern was perfunctory. We stayed in bed through the afternoon and, late in the day, as Jo drowsed beside me, I analyzed what had happened and how we had ended up like this, who had said what and who had done what. Our mutual approach seemed to have been thoroughly crude and awkward, but I thought that, if examined closely, all the axiomatic beams that supported us, the scheme and structure of every being, could be perceived as equally crude and awkward . . . yet those scraps of physical and emotional poetry of which we were capable could transform the rest into an architecture of Doric elegance and simplicity. The romantic character of the idea cut against my grain, but I couldn't deny it. One touch of her skin could make sense out of stupidity and put the world in right order.

About seven o'clock, simply because we felt we should do something else with the day, we walked down to the strip mall, to the Baskin-Robbins, and sat by the window in the frosty air conditioning. I had two scoops of vanilla; she had a butterscotch sundae. We ate while the high school girls back of the counter listened to the same Fiona Apple song again and again, arguing over the content of the lyrics as if they espoused an abstruse dialectic. Jo and I talked, or rather I talked and she questioned me about my childhood. I told her my father had been a saxophone player in New Orleans and that my mother had run off when I was seven, leaving me in his care. Jo remarked that this must have been hard on me, and I said, "He wasn't much of a dad. I spent a lot of time running the streets. He was primarily concerned with dope and women, but when he was in the mood, he could be fun. He taught me to play sax and guitar, and made up songs for me and got me to learn them. I could have done worse."

"Do you remember the songs?"

"Bits and pieces."

"Let's hear one!"

After considerable persuasion, I tapped out a rhythm on the tabletop and sang in a whispery voice:

"I said, Hey, hey! Devil get away!
Get a move on, boy . . .

I'll lay the saint's ray on ya.
Shake a calabash skull,
Make the sign of the jay . . .
Don't you give me no trouble,
or as sure as you're born,
I'll make you jump now, Satan,
'cause I got your shinbone."

"They most of them were like that one," I said. "The old man was a bear for religion. He'd haul me down to the temple once or twice a week and have me anointed with some remedy or another."

"I can picture you singing that when you were a little boy," she said. "You must have been cute."

In the darkened parking lot, I saw the black car I had noticed a few days earlier, the occupants invisible behind smoked glass. The sight banished my nostalgia. I asked Jo what she had told Pellerin the previous day when she talked to him about Ogoun Badagris.

"I told him about Donnell," she said.

"About the big copper *veve* and all?"

"Yes." She licked the bottom of her spoon.

"How about your theory? About the Ezawa process being an analog of possession. You tell him about that?"

"I couldn't lie to him anymore."

"What'd he say?"

"He was depressed. I told him if we got out of this situation, he'd live a long time. Long enough to understand everything that was happening to him. That depressed him even more. He said that didn't motivate him to want to live that long. I tried to cheer him up, but . . ." She pinned me with a stern look. "Did you sic those girls on me?"

"What girls?" I asked innocently.

"You know which ones."

"I was pissed at you. I'm over it now, but I was seriously pissed."

"Then you would have been delighted by my reaction." She dabbed at her lips with a napkin. "Once they came in, that was it for the conversation."

"So y'all had some fun, did you?"

"Maybe," she said, drawing out the first syllable of the word, giving it a playful reading. "I thought the dark-haired girl was very attractive. You never know, do you, when love will strike?"

"Is that right?"

"Mm-hmm. Think I should have gotten her number?"

"We could invite her on the honeymoon, if you want."

"Is that what we're having? A honeymoon?"

"It might have to do for one," I said.

Not long afterward, we left the Baskin-Robbins and, as we crossed the lot, I noticed a motorcyclist, the same one, judging by his bike, who had tailed me the day before. He was parked about ten slots down from the black car. I thought Billy must be getting paranoid, now that he was close to his goal, and had doubled up on security. We walked along the shoulder through the warm black night. Moths whirled under the arc lamps like scraps of pale ash. Jo's shampoo overbore the bitter scents of the roadside weeds. She slipped a hand into mine and by that simple gesture charged me with confidence. Despite the broken paths we had traveled to reach this night, this sorry patch of earth, I believed we had arrived at our appointed place.

There was some talk that we should approach Ruddle prior to the game, but I convinced Pellerin and Jo that the wisest course was to wait until we had a better idea of the connection between Ruddle and Billy Pitch. We held a strategy session before the limo picked us up, but since our strategy was basically to throw ourselves on Ruddle's mercy, the meeting was more-or-less a pep rally. Pellerin, however, was beyond pepping up. As Jo and I led the cheers, he glumly flipped through channels on the TV and, instead of his usual pre-game ritual of slamming drinks, sipped bottled water.

During the drive, Pellerin sat with a suitcase full of cash between his legs, flipping the handle back and forth, creating a repetitive clicking noise that I found irritating. I rested my eyes on Jo. She had on the black cocktail dress that she wore the first time I saw her. Whenever she caught me looking, her smile flickered on, but would quickly dissolve and she would return to gazing out the window. I managed to sustain my confidence by rehearsing what I intended to say to Ruddle. But as we pulled past the gatehouse and the lights of that enormous house floated up against the dark, like a spaceship waiting to take on abductees, I felt a tightness in my throat and, the second we stepped through the door, I realized that Plan A was out the window and, probably, Plan B as well. Standing with a group of middle-aged-to-elderly men at the entrance to the living room, wearing what looked to be powder blue lounging pajamas, was Billy Pitch. Clayton was not in evidence, but close by Billy's shoulder stood a lanky individual with a prominent Adam's apple and close-cropped gray hair and a cold, angular hillbilly face. I recognized him from New Orleans—Alan Goess, a contract killer. Clayton, I assumed, was too showy an item for Billy to take on a trip. Seven or eight young men in private security uniforms waited off to one side, watching their elders with neutral expressions, but contempt was evident in their body language.

Ruddle steered Pellerin away and introduced him to the other players, who were dressed in clothes that appeared to have been bought from the same Palm Beach catalogue. Clad in burgundy, olive, nectarine, coral, aqua, and plum, they bore a passing resemblance to migratory birds from different flocks gathered around a feeder. He introduced Billy as an old friend, not a player.

"Not a *poker* player, anyway," said Billy, giving Pellerin's hand a three-fingered shake.

Goess's eyes licked Jo head to toe. She didn't seem as anxious as I would have thought, or else she kept her anxiety contained. With Goess in the picture, my best guess was that Billy planned to humiliate Ruddle, then kill him. Whatever his plans, the odds against our surviving the evening had lengthened. I tried to think of an out, but nothing came to me. Ruddle shepherded us across the living room, a considerable acreage with a high ceiling, carpeted in a swirly blue pattern that was interrupted now and again by a sofa grouping or a stainless steel abstract sculpture—it reminded me of the showroom of an upscale car dealer, minus the cars. I wanted to cut Pellerin out of the herd and tell him about Goess, but the opportunity did not arise.

A dealer had been brought in for the occasion, a motherly brunette carrying some extra pounds, dressed in a tuxedo shirt and slacks; a thin, sleek Cubano was behind the bar, dispensing drinks with minimal comment. Some of the men seemed to have a prior relationship with the dealer; they cracked jokes at her expense, addressing her as Kim. Goess and Billy took chairs on opposite sides of the central trophy case, separating themselves from each other, and from Jo and I, who sat in the corner, with Pellerin facing us at the table. Once everyone was settled and a few last pleasantries observed, Kim said, "The game is Texas Hold 'em, gentlemen. No Limit. The buy-in is five hundred thousand. Play will run until eight AM, unless an extension is agreed upon. If you go bust, you can make a second buy-in, but not a third."

The buy-ins commenced, cash being traded for chips. The cash was placed in a lockbox and then wheeled off on a luggage cart by two of Ruddle's employees. This done, Kim dealt the first hand.

For the better part of an hour, some chips passed back and forth, but no serious damage was done and the men bantered amiably between hands, telling dumb stories about one another and chortling, huh huh huh, like apes at a grunt festival. As best I could judge, there were two dangerous players apart from Ruddle and Pellerin—a portly man with heavy bags under his eyes by the name of Carl, who rarely spoke other than to raise or check or call, and an ex-jock type with an Alabama accent, his muscles running to fat, whom everybody called Buster and treated with great deference, laughing loudly and long at his anecdotes, though they were none too funny. The remaining four were dead money, working their cards without discernable stratagem or skill.

"We can gossip and trade antes all night," said Ruddle, "but I call that a ladies' bridge tournament, not a poker game."

"I didn't notice you stepping up, Frank," said Pellerin. "You been betting like you playing with your mama's pin money."

The table shared a chuckle.

Ruddle took it good-naturedly, but there was an edge to his smile and I knew he couldn't wait to hurt Pellerin.

Truthfully, my mind was not on the game, but on Billy and Goess. The transfer of the lockbox to the vault made it clear that Billy's true interest did not lie in that direction. My uneasiness intensified and it must have showed, because Jo gave my hand a squeeze. The play remained less than aggressive until, several hands later, Pellerin check-raised Ruddle's bet after the flop by twenty thousand.

"I bid five clubs," he said, causing another outburst of laughter.

Having watched him play every day at the Seminole Paradise, I knew this was a move he had been setting up ever since he arrived in Florida. He'd backed off a lot of players with it in the casino and it usually signified a bluff, something of which Ruddle would be aware. Now, I thought, he might have a hand. The flop was the four of spades, the seven of spades, and the seven of clubs. Pellerin bet another twenty thousand. From the way Ruddle had bet before the flop, I figured him to be holding a second pair, probably queens or better. If Pellerin wasn't bluffing, he might have a third seven. Ruddle, after thinking it over, called the raise. Everyone else got out of the way. The turn card was the queen of hearts. Pellerin pushed out thirty thousand in chips.

"You got the nuts?" Ruddle asked him.

"There's one way to find out," said Pellerin.

Ruddle riffled a stack of chips and finally called. "Now we're playing poker," he said.

The river card was the eight of spades. With four spades face up, both men had the possibility of a flush draw.

"I hate to do this to our gracious host, but I'm all in," Pellerin said.

"Call," said Ruddle. He didn't wait for Pellerin to show his hand—he slapped his hole cards down on the table. Ace of diamonds and ace of spades. He had made an ace-high flush.

"You got the high flush, all right." Pellerin turned over his cards. "But mine's all in a row."

His hole cards were the five and six of spades, filling an eight-high straight flush.

The other players responded with shocked "Damns!" and "Holy craps!" Having lost close to half a million on the turn of a card, when there were only a couple of hands that could have beaten him, four sevens or a gutshot straight flush, Ruddle was speechless. Pellerin had been lucky, but he had played the hand so that if the cards were friendly, he was in position to take advantage.

"If you'd re-raised on the turn, I would have folded. Shit, all I had was a draw." Pellerin began to stack his winnings. "Who was it said Hold Em's a science, but No Limit is an art? I must be one hell of an artist." He waved at the bartender. "Jack Black on the rocks. A double."

I expected Billy to be angry that Pellerin had moved on Ruddle so early in the evening, and I scrunched down so I could see him through the glass of the trophy case. He was sitting placidly, as if watching an episode of *The Amazing Race,* but I detected a little steam in the way his neck was bowed. Jo caught my eye and we exchanged a disconcerted vibe.

"Yes sir," Pellerin said expansively. "You might have whupped a bunch of Leroys and Jim Bobs down in Tunica, but this here's a different world, Frank."

Ruddle stood and, walking stiffly, left the room. Some of the other gamblers followed him, doubtless to commiserate over the bad beat. Kim called for a short break, and Billy stepped over to me and whispered, "What's he doing?"

"I'll find out," I said.

Billy's nose was an inch from my face—I could smell his breath mints. "I want the bastard to suffer! You tell him that!"

He went to join the commiserators. I pulled Pellerin aside and told him Billy was upset.

"He'll get his pound of flesh," said Pellerin. "This'll make it easier to manage the game. Ruddle will play tight for a while, and that gives me time to clear out the garbage."

"Don't do anything stupid," I whispered. "The guy in the camel blazer's a hired killer. I know him from New Orleans. Alan Goess."

"Is he? No lie?" His eyes flicked toward Goess and he smiled. "Hey, guy!" he said to Goess. "How they hanging?"

For a split-second, the real Alan Goess came out from behind his rattlesnake deadboy guise, and I got a hint of his underlying madness; then the curtain closed and he said, "I'm doing well. So are you, from the looks of things."

"Looks can be deceiving," said Pellerin. "Yea, I am a troubled soul, but a firm believer in the Light and the Resurrection. How about yourself?"

"'Fraid not," said Goess. "I've never yet seen anyone come back."

"You just think you haven't," Pellerin said, and would have said more, but I hustled him out of the room and told him not to screw around with Goess.

"I got it under control, boss," he said. "I know exactly what I'm doing."

In the living room, Billy was having a chat with Carl, and Buster had cornered Jo. The other players were huddled up around Ruddle, patting him on the back, saying that Pellerin had been lucky, encouraging him to get back in the game. I gazed out the window toward the *Mystery Girl*, floating serene and white under the dock lights, impossibly distant.

Ruddle had had more chips than Pellerin, so the beat hadn't wiped him out; but he didn't have enough left to compete and he made a second buy-in of a quarter-million. The game resumed, albeit with a less convivial atmosphere. The room, small already, seemed to have shrunk and the men sat hunched and quietly tense under the hanging lamp. Conversation was at a minimum . . . except for Pellerin. He drank heavily and whenever he won a pot he'd offer up a disparaging comment, engaging the ire of one and all. After taking forty grand off Buster, he said, "Where'd you learn poker, old son? From some guy named Puddin' in the jock dorm?"

Buster said, "Why don't you shut up and play cards?"

This notion was seconded by some of the others.

"In case you didn't notice, I'm playing cards," said Pellerin. "Damned if I can figure out what you're playing."

When Buster won a pot at his expense, he said, "Jesus must love a hillbilly fool."

I had to admire Pellerin. Though he had a distinct advantage in the game, it took great skill to manipulate the fortunes of six other poker players. Ruddle gradually built his stack, winning back the majority of the chips he had lost. His mood grew sunnier and he began to joke around with the table, but when involved in a hand with Pellerin, he was barely civil, speaking brusquely if at all. By one o'clock, two lesser players had been driven out and another was teetering on the brink, down a quarter of a million, pushing in antes and mucking his cards hand-after-hand. At three-thirty, Buster decided to cut his losses and withdrew.

"Thanks for the contribution, Busted . . . I mean, Buster," said Pellerin, grinning hugely. "We going to miss you, sure enough."

Kim called for another break and everyone made for a buffet that had been set-up in the living room. Billy gave me a thumbs-up before heading over to the food. Standing apart from the rest, I told Jo about Goess and said that we had better do something soon or else I didn't like our chances.

"I thought we were going to wait until the last minute," she said.

"Far as I can see, this is the last minute."

She seemed amazingly calm. "I have go to the restroom. Just wait, okay? Don't do anything."

I watched her cross the living room, her long legs working the dress, hips rolling under the silky fabric, and then went back into the card room, where Pellerin was playing with his chips.

"If you've got something in mind," I said, "now might be the time to try it."

"Right now?"

"Whenever you see an opening."

He nodded. "All right. Y'all be ready. I'll give you a warning beforehand." He picked up a stack of chips and let them dribble through his fingers. "Life ain't never as sweet as it appears," he said.

"What that supposed to mean?"

"Just my personal philosophy."

"Fuck a bunch of personal philosophy. Get your mind right! Okay? When it comes time, I'll handle Goess."

"You take care of Billy. Leave Goess to me."

"You think you up to it?"

"It's a done deal," he said.

"What are you going to do?"

He spread the deck of cards face-up on the table and started nudging out the painted cards with the tip of his forefinger.

"Tell me!" I said.

"I believe I may have to violate his personal space," said Pellerin.

I would have inquired of him further, but people began to wander back into the card room, carrying plates of food. Ruddle, Kim and Carl took their places at the table. Jo patted my arm and gave me a steady look that said everything's okay, but it was not okay and she knew it . . . unless she had slipped gears and gone to Jesus. Billy, Goess, and a straggler came in. I sought to make eye contact with Billy, but he stared straight ahead. The game resumed three-handed, with Carl winning a decent pot. Pellerin made his bets blind, not bothering to check his cards, tossing in chips until after the flop, and then folding. As Kim was about to deal a second hand, he stood up and said, "Gentlemen. And ladies. Before we begin what promises to be an exhilarating conclusion to the evening, I'd like to propose a toast."

He lifted his glass. With his left hand, I noticed. His right hand was afflicted with a palsy, the fingers making movements that, though they were spasmodic, at the same time seemed strangely deft.

"Frank," Pellerin went on. "You have my deepest gratitude for hosting this lovely occasion. I'd love to stick around and pluck your feathers, but . . . duty calls. I want to thank you all for being so patient with my abusive personality. Which, I should say, is not entirely my own. It comes to you courtesy of the folks at Darden, where your good health is our good business."

"Are you through?" Ruddle asked.

"In a minute." Pellerin's voice acquired a sarcastic veneer. "To Miz Jocundra Verret. For her ceaseless and unyielding devotion. You'll always be my precious sunflower. And to Jack Lamb, who—sad to say—is probably the closest thing to a friend I have in this world. What are friends for if not to fuck over each other? Huh, Jack?"

"Sit your ass down," said Carl. "You're drunk."

"True enough." Pellerin gestured with his glass, sloshing liquor across the table. "But I'm not done yet."

Billy gave a squawk and leaped from his chair, backing away from Goess. I leaned forward and had a look. Goess's eyes bulged, his hands gripped the arms of the chair, his face was red, glistening with sweat, and his neck was corded. He began to shake, as if in the grip of a convulsion.

"To Mister Alan Goess, who's about to burst into flames!" Pellerin raised his glass high. "And let's not forget Billy Pitch, at whose behest I came here tonight. I hear you like those reality shows, Billy. Are you digging on this one?"

The Cuban bartender had seen enough—he ran from the room. Buster started toward Goess, perhaps thinking he could render assistance, and

Pellerin said, "Y'all keep back, now. Combustion's liable to be sudden. Truth is, I suspect he's already dead."

"It's a trick," said Carl. "The guy's faking it."

Pellerin whipped off his sunglasses. "What you think, Tubby? Am I faking this, too?"

Green flashes were plainly visible in his eyes.

Ruddle threw himself back from the table. "Jesus!"

"Not hardly." Pellerin laughed. "You folks familiar with voodoo? No? Better prepare yourself, then. Because voodoo is most definitely in the house."

Everyone in the room was frozen for a long moment, their attention divided between Goess and Pellerin. Goess's skin blistered, the blisters bursting, leaking a clear serum, and then there came a soft *whumpf*, a big pillowy sound, and he began to burn. Pale yellow flames wreathed his body, licking up and releasing an oily smoke. I smelled him cooking. Kim screamed, and people were shouting, crowding together in the doorway, seeking to escape. Billy dipped a hand into his voluminous hip pocket. I grabbed his shoulder, spun him about, and drove my fist into his prunish face, knocking him into a trophy case, shattering the glass. His mouth was bleeding, his scalp was lacerated, but he was still conscious, still trying to extricate something from his pocket. I kicked him in the gut, again in the head, and bent over his inert body, fumbled in the pocket and removed a switchblade and a platinum-and-diamond money clip that pinched a thick fold of bills. The clip was probably worth more than the bills. With millions resting in Ruddle's vault, I felt stupid mugging him for chump change. Jo's hands fluttered about my face. She said something about listening to reason, about waiting, but I was too adrenalized to listen and too anxious to wait. I gave Billy a couple of more kicks that wedged him under the wreckage of the trophy case, and then, shoving Jo ahead of me, glancing back at Goess, who sat sedately now, blackening in the midst of his pyre, I went out into the living room.

Ruddle's security was nowhere to be seen, but Ruddle, Kim, and the rest were bunched together against the picture window, their egress blocked by tracks of waist-high flame that crisscrossed the blue carpet, dividing the room into dozens of neat diamond-shaped sections. It was designer arson, the fire laid out in such a precise pattern, it could have been the work of a performance artist with a gift for pyrotechnics. Beside a burning sofa from which smoke billowed, Pellerin appeared to be orchestrating the flames, conducting their swift, uncanny progress with clever movements of his fingers, sending trains of fire scooting across the floor, adding to his design. I recalled the scorch mark on his bedroom wall. Along with everyone else in this lunatic circumstance, Pellerin had been holding something back. I thought if you could see the entirety of the pattern he was creating, it would be identical to one of the *veves* he had sketched on the napkin that day by the pool. I maneuvered as close to him as I dared and shouted his name. He ignored me, continuing to paint his masterpiece. The fire crackled, snacking on the rug, gnawing on the furniture, yet the noise wasn't sufficiently loud to drown out the cries of Ruddle and his guests. Some were egging on Buster and another guy, who were preparing to pick up a sofa and ram it against the window. I shouted again—again Pellerin ignored me. Bursts of small arms fire, like popcorn popping, sounded from the front of the house.

Billy's people, I told myself.

"Did you hear that?" Jo clutched my arm.

I bellowed at Pellerin. He looked at me from, I'd estimate, twenty-five feet away, and it was not a human look. His features were strained, his lips drawn back, stretched in a delirious expression, part leer and part delighted grin. That's how it seemed, that he had been made happy beyond human measure, transported by the perception of some unnatural pleasure, as if the fire were for him a form of release. I was frightened of him, yet I felt a connection, some emotional tether, and I was afraid *for* him as well. I urged him to come with us, to make a try for the boat. He stared as if he didn't recognize me, and then his smile lost its inhuman wideness.

"Come on, man!" I said. "Let's go!"

He shook his head. "No way."

"What the hell are you doing? You're going to die here!"

His smile dimmed and I thought his resolve was weakening, that he would break through the fences of flame separating us and join us in flight; but all he did was stand there. Behind me, I heard an explosive crash as the window gave way; the gunfire grew louder.

"Listen!" I said. "That's Billy's men out there! You want them to catch you?"

"That ain't Billy! Don't you believe it!" He pointed at Jo. "Ask her!"

Despite the high ceiling, smoke was beginning to fill the room, drifting down around us, and Jo was bent over, coughing.

"This shit isn't working for me." Pellerin seemed to be talking mostly to himself. "It's just not acceptable."

I understood what he meant, but I entreated him once more to come with us. He shook his head again, an emphatic no. Turning his attention to the fire, he performed a series of complex gestures. The latticework of flames surrounding us appeared to bend away from his fingers and a path opened, leading toward the kitchen. The heat was growing intolerable—I had no choice but to abandon him. My arm around Jo's waist, I started along the path, but she panicked, fighting against me, scratching my face and slapping the side of my head. I hit her on the point of the jaw, picked her up in a fireman's carry as she sagged, and broke into a stumbling run.

The sky was graying as I emerged from the house and staggered across the lawn; the *Mystery Girl* lurched in my vision with each step, appearing to recede at first, as though I were on a treadmill that kept carrying me backwards. The small arms fire had intensified—at least a dozen weapons were involved. I had no idea what was happening, and not much of an idea where I was going. If the boat had gas, I thought I would head north and search for the entrance to the intercoastal waterway, try and make it to Tampa where I had friends. But if Billy had survived, Tampa would not be safe and I didn't know where to go. Not New Orleans, that was for sure. I could have kicked myself for not shooting the scummy little weasel when I had the chance.

The planks resounded to my footsteps as I pounded along the dock, and the smells of creosote and brine hit me like smelling salts. When I reached the *Mystery Girl*, I laid Jo in the stern. She moaned, but didn't wake. I climbed the ladder to the pilot deck, keyed the ignition, and was exultant when the engine turned over. The needle on the fuel gauge swung up to register an almost-full tank. I pulled away from the dock and opened up the throttle. There was a light chop on the water close to shore, but farther out, beyond the sandbar, the surface was smooth and glassy, with gentle swells.

Crumbling banks of fog blanketed the sea ahead. Once inside them we'd be safe for a while. I wondered what had gotten into Pellerin, whether it was Ogoun Badagris or simply a madness attaching to having been brought back to life by bacteria that infested your brain and let you use more of it. Maybe there wasn't any difference between the two conditions. Jo's first slow-burner had gone out in much the same way, in the midst of a huge *veve,* so you were led to conclude that some pathology was involved . . . and yet it might be the pathology of a god trapped in a human body. I remembered how he'd smiled, leering at his fiery work, and how that smile had planed seamlessly down into a human expression, as if the man he was had merely been the god diminished by the limitations of the flesh.

I cleared my mind of ontological speculation and focused on practical matters, but when I tried to think what we were going to do once we reached Tampa, it was like trying to walk on black ice and I wound up staring at the flat gray sea, listening to the pitch of the engine. I zoned out and began to think about Pellerin again. Formless thoughts, the kind you have when you're puzzled by something to the point that you can't even come up with a question to ask and are reduced to searching the database, hoping that some fact will provoke one.

I had all but forgotten about Jo and when she called out to me, I turned toward the sound of her voice, full of concern. She came scrambling up the ladder and, once she had solid footing, she told me to cut the engines, having to shout to make herself heard. The wind lashed her hair about, and she held it in place with one hand.

"Are you crazy?" I gestured at the fog bank. "Once we're into the fog, we'll be okay."

"We'll never get away! If I thought we could, I'd go with you. You know that, don't you?"

"You are going with me," I said. "What's the problem?"

She didn't answer, and I glanced over at her. She had moved away from me and was standing with her legs apart, aiming a small automatic with a silver finish. A .28 caliber Barretta. With that black cocktail dress on, she might have stepped out of a Bond movie. She had to be wearing a thigh holster. The unreality of it all tickled me and I couldn't repress a laugh.

"Where'd you get that thing?" I asked her. "Out of a cereal box?"

She fired, and a bullet dug a furrow in the control console an inch from my hand.

I recoiled from the console. "Christ!"

"I'm sorry," she said.

She looked sorry. Her make-up was mussed. The heat of the fire had caused her to sweat, and sweat had dragged a mascara shadow from the corner of her eye, simulating a tear. She told me again to cut the engines, and this time I complied. The boat lifted on a light swell. I heard the faint cries of seagulls—they sounded like the baying of tiny, trebly hounds. I heard another noise, then. Two dark blue helicopters were approaching from the south.

"Who the hell is that?" I shouted.

"Calm down. Please! This is . . ." The wind drifted hair across her face; she brushed it aside and said weakly, "It's the only way. They're relentless, they keep coming after you."

"You did this? You told them where we were?"

"They always knew! They never went away! Don't you get it?"

"You knew the whole time? Why didn't you tell me?"

"I didn't know. Not for sure, not at first. And what good would it have done? You didn't listen to Doctor Crain."

"I would have listened to you," I said.

One of the helicopters positioned itself off the port side of the *Mystery Girl;* the side door had been slid back and someone in harness sat in the

opening. I couldn't see what he was doing. The other helicopter hovered above the boat. A gilt script D was painted on the nacelle.

"I love you, Jack," Jo said.

"Yeah, uh-huh."

"I do! Back at the hotel . . . they contacted me. They were going to step in, but I convinced them to keep the experiment going."

"The experiment. This was an experiment?"

"I told them we might learn more about Josey if he went through with the game. Maybe that was wrong of me, but I wanted some time with you."

I was unable to line up all the trash she'd told me about her mother, how it had warped her, with her capacity for betrayal. Yet what she had said smacked of a childish willfulness and a clinical dispatch that, I realized, functioned as a tag-team in her personality. Until that moment, I had not understood how dangerous these qualities made her.

"I can lose them in the fog," I said.

"You can't. You don't know them."

"I'm damn well going to try. You think they'll let me go after what I've seen? They just wiped out twenty people!"

"I'm sure they didn't kill them all."

"Oh . . . well. Fuck! That's all right, then."

I punched in the ignition; the engine sputtered and caught, rumbling smoothly.

"Don't, Jack! Please!"

"I'm fucking dead if they catch me. Do you understand? I am dead!"

The barrel of the automatic wavered.

"You're not going to shoot me," I said.

I pushed the throttle forward. Jo said again, "Don't," and I felt a blow to my back, a wash of pain. I was out of it for a while, and when I was able to gather my senses, I found myself lying on the deck, with my head jammed up against the base of the control console. I knew I'd been shot, but it felt like the bullet had come from something larger than a .28. The guy in the harness, maybe. I was hurting some, but a numb feeling was setting in. It was a chore to concentrate. My thoughts kept slipping away. Jo knelt beside me. I locked on to her face. Looking at her steadied me. "Did you . . . " I said. "Did you shoot . . . ?"

"Don't talk," she said.

Silhouetted against the gray sky, a man was being lowered from the helicopter overhead, along with a metal case that dangled from a hook beside him. It seemed as big as a coffin. The sight confused me visually, and in other ways as well. I closed my eyes against it.

Jo laid a hand on my cheek. The touch cooled the embers of my anger, my disappointment with her, and I was overwhelmed with sentiment. Bits of memory surfaced, whirled, dissolved. She lay down on the deck beside me. She became my sky. Her face hanging above me blotted out the chopper and the man descending.

"I'll take care of you, I promise," she said.

Her brown eyes were all that was holding me. A gurgling came from inside my chest. She started raving, then. Getting angry, swearing vengeance, weeping. It was like she thought I'd passed out, like I wasn't there. Half of it, I didn't understand. She said they would regret what they'd made her do, she'd make certain I remembered everything, and I would help her make them pay. I didn't recognize her, she was so possessed by pain and fury. She laid her head on my chest. I wanted to tell her the weight was oppressive, but I couldn't form the words. The lengths of her hair were drowning me. Her voice, the helicopter rotors, and the fading light merged into a gray tumult, an incoherence.

"Jack . . ."

. . . *Jack* . . .

A jolt, as of electricity, to the back of my neck.

Jack . . . Jack Lamb . . .

My eyelids fluttered open.

A gray ocean surrounded me, picked out by vague shapes.

Jack Lamb . . . Jack . . .

Another jolt, more intense than the first. I tried to move, but I was very weak and I succeeded only in turning my head. Someone passed across my field of vision, accompanied by a perfumey scent. Wanting to catch their notice, I made a scratchy noise in my throat. The effort caused me to pass out.

Jack . . .

"Jack? Are you awake?" A woman's voice.

"Yeah," I said, my tongue thick, throat raw.

Something was inserted between my lips and a cool liquid soothed the rawness. My chest hurt. My whole body hurt.

"How's that? Better?" The voice had a familiar ring.

"I can't see," I said. "Everything's a blur."

"The doctor says you'll be seeing fine in a few days."

I asked for more water and, after I had drunk, I said, "I know you . . . don't I?"

"Of course. Jocundra . . . Jo." A pause. "Your partner. We live together. Don't you remember?"

"I think. Yeah."

"You've been through a terrible ordeal. Your memory will be hazy for a while."

"What happened to me?"

"You were shot. The important thing is, you're going to be fine."

"Who shot me? Why . . . what happened?"

"I'll tell you soon. I promise. You don't need the stress now."

"I want to know who shot me!"

"You have to trust me," she said, placing a hand on my chest. "There's psychological damage as well as physical. We have to go cautiously. I'll tell you when you're strong enough. Won't you trust me 'til then?"

I asked her to come closer.

Something swam toward me through the gray. I made out a crimson mouth and enormous brown eyes. Gradually, the separate features resolved into a face that, though blurred, was indisputably open and lovely.

"You're beautiful," I said.

"Thank you." A pause. "It's been a while since you told me that."

Her face withdrew. I couldn't find her in the murk. Anxious, I called out.

"I'm here," she said. "I'm just getting something."

"What?"

"Cream to rub on your chest and shoulders. It'll make you feel better."

She sat on the bed—I felt the mattress indent—and she began massaging me. Each caress gave me a shock, albeit gentler than the ones I had felt initially. Soft hands spread the cream across my chest and I began to relax, to feel repentant that I had neglected her. I offered apology for doing so, saying that I must have been preoccupied.

Her lips brushed my forehead. "It's okay. Actually, I'm hopeful . . ."

"Hopeful? About what?"

"It's nothing."

"No, tell me."

"I'm hoping some good will come of all this," she said. "We've been having our problems lately. And I hope this time we spend together, while you recuperate, it'll make you remember how much I love you."

I groped for her hand, found it. We stayed like that a while, our fingers mixing together. A white shape melted up from the grayness. I strained to identify it and realized it was her breast sheathed in white cloth.

"I'm up here," she said, laughter in her voice, and leaned closer so I could see her face again. "Do you feel up to answering a few questions? The doctor said I should test your memory. So we can learn if there's been any significant loss."

"Yeah, okay. I'm feeling more together now."

I heard papers rustling and asked what she was doing.

"They gave me some questions to ask. I can't find them." More rustling. "Here they are. The first one's a gimmee. Do you recall your name?"

"Jack," I said confidently. "Jack Lamb."

"And what do you do? Your profession?"

I opened my mouth, ready to spit out the answer. When nothing came to me, I panicked. I probed around in the gray nothing that seemed to have settled over my brain, beginning to get desperate. She touched the inside of my wrist, a touch that left a trail of sparkling sensation on my skin, and told me not to force it. And then I saw the answer, saw it as clearly as I might see a shining coin stuck in silt at the bottom of a well, the first of a horde of memories waiting to be unearthed, a treasure of anecdote and event.

Firmly, and with a degree of pride as befitted my station, I said, "I'm a financier."

DINNER AT BALDASSARO'S

Though she herself was not beautiful, Giacinta had a beautiful sneeze. Scarcely more than a musical sniff, it seemed to restate the cadence of her name and was followed, in short order, by a giggle as she wiped a residue of white powder from the rims of her nostrils. She was thick-waisted, heavy in the thighs, with an undershot chin and breasts no bigger than onions. But her eyes were shots of dark rum, her pale olive skin held the polish of youth, and her thin face had a desperately merry quality. For all her flaws, I considered her quite a prize.

"This . . ." She scowled dramatically and pointed to the little heap of cocaine on the mirror in her lap. "No good! But I like! I like too much!" She made to hand me the mirror and a straw—the same she had used—and adopted a mischievous look designed to tempt me. I declined temptation and, in faltering Italian, explained that drugs were not beneficial to my health.

"*Salute*," she said, correcting me—I had used the Spanish word for health, *salud*. Her eyes flicked across my body, as if inspecting me for signs of frailty. "*Va bene.*"

She dipped her head again to the mirror, face obscured by the fall of her chestnut hair.

We were sitting in the offices of the Villa Ruggieri, where Giacinta worked as a receptionist and I had taken a suite. A showplace in the eighteenth century, its high-ceilinged rooms and muraled walls reverberating with the strains of archlute and cello, by the early twenty-first it had matured into a seedy relic of the Late Baroque, a hotel whose best two weeks came during the annual chile pepper festival (just ended), when all the shops of Diamante, the Calabrian seaside village it overlooked, featured fanciful decorations in their windows contrived of chile peppers, and tourists promenaded along the Via Poseidone wearing chile pepper T-shirts and chile pepper hats. Now in October, both the hotel and the village were in the process of shutting their doors, and, that evening, as Giacinta and I walked down the cliff trail and along a narrow, meandering street, we encountered only a few shopgirls hurrying home.

We stopped at a sidewalk café on the corner of the Via Fiume and the Via Poseidone, where we were to meet Giacinta's friend, Allessandra, for a drink before going to dinner. Incapable of other than the most primitive conversation, we endured an awkward silence of considerable length. She studied the wine list, wrinkling her nose as if responding to the various bouquets, and I examined the mural adorning the facade of the building across the street—it depicted several Renaissance children, elegantly clothed, chasing each other about the columns of a room in a palace, all done in sepia tones. There were hundreds of murals in Diamante. At least half a dozen were visible off along the block. I was mildly curious regarding the reason underlying such a proliferation, but I did not inquire about them, having no wish to endure a labored explanation couched in fractured English, with table objects used for demonstration purposes. The night air was growing cool. Giacinta threw on a light sweater over her yellow summer dress. She smiled anxiously at me, and I smiled in return.

Allessandra, who arrived twenty minutes late, was a willowy brunette who had spent a great deal of time and money at the hair salon to achieve a fabulously tousled and frosted look. She wore a leather mini that showed off her long legs and enormous gold hoop earrings through which, it seemed, a toy poodle could have jumped. She bussed Giacinta on the cheek, lit a cigarette with scarcely an interruption to her rapid-fire chatter, and began to interrogate me as might an anxious mother on the occasion of her daughter's prom, asking first how old I was.

"I'm forty," I told her.

"Gia is twenty-six," she said.

"It's a lovely age."

Giacinta looked to Allessandra, and Allessandra translated, apparently accurately, for Giacinta ducked her eyes and blushed.

"Are forty and twenty-six incompatible?" I asked. Allessandra failed to grasp the word *incompatible*, so I presented her with alternatives. "Unsuitable? Ill-matched?"

"No, no! I was pointing out that for you, Gia is much less, uh . . . sophisticated."

"Ah! I see."

Giacinta wanted to know what was being said, but Allessandra told her to wait and asked my occupation.

"I do some travel writing," I said.

"For the magazines?"

"Books, mainly. I own a travel agency with offices in Rome, Paris, London, New York . . . and elsewhere. The business more-or-less runs itself, and I've been at loose ends the past few years. So I've taken up writing."

Allessandra paused to translate. Her perfume overwhelmed the less aggressive aura of Giacinta's scent. Within the café, under a bilious yellow bulb, two waiters in white shirts and aprons were playing backgammon at the bar, while the bombastic pop stylings of Zucchero leaked into the street, seeming to empurple the air. The lights along the Via Poseidone marked the curve of the shore, otherwise the darkened coastline would have been all but indistinguishable from the sea. Two elderly men in caps and bulky jackets strolled along the sea wall; one threw his right arm over the other's shoulder and, making repetitive forceful gestures with his right hand, appeared to be offering advice.

"Maybe," Allessandra said, "you write the article about Diamante?"

"No, I'm here to meet some friends. We try to get together every year somewhere in Europe. This year it happens to be Diamante." I leaned forward and touched Allessandra's cigarette pack, resting by her elbow. "May I?"

"Of course."

"I quit years ago, but I still get the urge on occasion." I lit up and exhaled a plume of smoke that a breeze swept toward the sea wall. "I'm meeting my friends for dinner tonight. At Baldassaro's. They're all bringing someone, and . . . well, I didn't want to come alone. I thought Giacinta would make a charming dinner companion."

Hearing her name, Giacinta again asked for a translation and, following a brief exchange, Allessandra said, "There is a thing I don't understand, Mister . . . You . . . "

"Taylor," I said. "Please."

"Very well. Taylor." She stressed the T with a flick of her tongue, crossed her legs and lit another cigarette. "You are a man of wealth, of experience. And very handsome. Many beautiful women would be happy to take dinner with you. Especially at a place of elegance like Baldassaro's. So why have you choosed this one?"

I had a sip of wine. "I assumed that Giacinta invited you for drinks so she could ask questions through you and make a judgment on my character. But this is your question, isn't it?"

Allessandra made a wry shape with her mouth and gave the slightest of nods.

"Perhaps you would care to go to dinner with me?"

"Another night . . ." She gave her hair a toss. "It's possible."

A Vespa with a pair of young men astride passed along the street—I allowed the angry rip of the engine to fade before continuing.

"You're a beautiful woman, Allessandra. I'm sure any man would be delighted to have you as a companion. However, I'm looking for a certain type of beauty. Beauty that falls short of the ideal. Innocence that's been corrupted, but only just. A woman who's been slighted by the world, perhaps treated roughly, yet maintains a belief in romantic possibility."

Giacinta, seeming to recognize that Allessandra was flirting with me, plucked at her friend's sleeve. Her purpose in having me meet Allessandra had less to do with ascertaining my good character than with showing me off, and now she was afraid that she had made a mistake.

Allessandra told her to wait a second and said, "Your picture of . . . What you say about the woman . . . uh . . . "

"Description. Is that the word you're looking for?"

"Yes. Your description . . . it fits every woman."

"Yes, but Giacinta possesses this quality in a way you do not. If I were to send her to a spa, have experts counsel her on matters of diet and exercise, perhaps get some work done to her chin, her breasts, she'd be very much the kind of woman you are. As it is, she's the absolute embodiment of the quality I'm seeking. Her body and mind flavored by a precise degree of sadness."

Allessandra's frown took the measure of some poignant indelicacy, as if she detected a bad smell. "It seems you are a connoisseur, a . . . I don't know how to say. Your feeling for Gia is not . . ." She snapped her fingers in frustration.

"You're suggesting that my appreciation of Giacinta's charms may be perverse? Like a preference for dwarves or the morbidly obese? Why don't you tell her that?"

Once again Allessandra had to hold off Giacinta's demand that she be filled in, saying forcefully, *"Aspetta!"*

"I'm attracted to plain women," I said. "Physical beauty bores me. I'm talking about what's generally considered beautiful. And now that beauty's become affordable . . ." I made a disparaging noise. "That qualifies me as jaded, not perverse. Still, it may be a phase I'm going through. Tomorrow night, for instance, I may feel differently."

For a second or two, Allessandra looked puzzled. Then she shook her finger at me in mock chastisement and laughed. "You fool with me!" she said. "I know!"

She turned to her friend and delivered herself of a lengthy pronouncement detailing our conversation or, more likely, a fictive version of it, darting sideways glances at me as if to affirm an unstated complicity. Judging by Giacinta's tremulous smile, I suspected Allessandra was informing her that I'd been attracted to her mental and spiritual qualities, that she could consider herself safe while in my company, and that she could expect nothing more threatening to her virtue than a fine meal at Baldassaro's—in sum, diminishing the importance of the evening, so that when I asked Allessandra out, something both women were certain I would do, Giacinta would not be so distressed.

Shortly afterward, Allessandra took her leave, seizing the opportunity of a perfunctory embrace to slip her business card into my jacket pocket, and, once she had rounded the corner, an act preceded by a wave, coquettishly fluttering her fingers, Giacinta's mood grew instantly sullen and uncommunicative. I caressed her forearm, asked if she was all right, and she shook her head, refusing to look at me. "Giacinta," I said softly, making the name into a form of adoration, and held her hand, pressing my lips to the inside of her wrist, to the rapid pulse beating there, the smell of blood and lemons. With palpable reluctance, she swung about to face me and, after I laid my hand along her cheek, letting her lean into it, only then did she relent and favor me with a wan smile.

*T*oward the southern extremity of the Via Poseidone, an ancient stone causeway extended several hundred yards out into the sea, connecting the mainland with a small island, almost invisible against the night sky, picked out by the lights of Baldassaro's. In addition to a four-star restaurant, the island was home to some nondescript Roman ruins that attracted a few tourists, but no one had lived there for over a century, thus it was ideal for our meeting. The causeway itself, however, was populated by a number of young couples who had come for a twilight stroll and stayed to exploit the anonymity of the dark. Every few yards we passed a shadowy couple locked in an embrace or whispering with their heads together. I had slipped a drug into Giacinta's wine back at the café, a hypnotic designed to lower inhibitions, and, upon finding an unoccupied stretch of railing, when I suggested we take our ease along it, she raised no objection. Perhaps she would have raised none in any case. If she had, I could have persuaded her with a mental nudge; but I never have liked manipulating them in that way—it tends to damage them and it might have cost me some effort. These Italian girls, whether due to Catholic fear or fleshly anxiety, were capable of reconstituting their virginity at a moment's notice. And so I trusted the drug to liberate her from such impediments.

We gazed out across the Mediterranean, lying flat beneath a salting of dim stars. I asked Giacinta to talk, telling her I liked the sound of her voice, although I understood little of what she said (a message that required some considerable time to convey, due to its relative complexity). She hesitated, but I urged her on and soon she started in reciting poetry like a schoolgirl regurgitating memorized verses on cue. After three poems she faltered, but then began speaking rapidly in a husky tone of voice. To my amusement, I recognized several vulgar words, words such as *"pompino"* and *"cazzo"*, that I had learned from a woman in Bologna. I put my right hand on the join of her waist and hip, and her breath caught; she half-turned so that my hand slid up onto her rib cage, very near the swell of her breast. Her voice thickened and her speech became peppered with crudities, particular emphasis being laid on terms like *". . . mi fica . . ."* and *". . . mi culo . . ."* and so forth, references to portions of her anatomy upon which, I assumed, she wished me to lavish attention.

I was delighted to play a game with her, with someone so similar to and yet so vastly different from the women with whom I was accustomed to playing a more involving game. I kissed her, tasting wine and licorice from her tongue. My hand engulfed a breast, squeezing it a trifle hard, perhaps, for I felt her mouth slacken momentarily. I lifted her by the waist, boosted her up to sit upon the stone railing, and pushed her skirt up around her hips. She protested, of course, pushing feebly at my chest and saying, *"No, Taylor! Non in questo!"* But the distinction between passion and its counterfeit had blurred for us both. I fingered her panties to one side and, finding her ready, entered her. She clung to my shoulders, gasping with each thrust. I forced her to lie back, suspending her over the drop—twenty feet, I reckoned it. All that prevented her from falling was our genital union and my hands supporting her waist. She cried out . . . not loudly. Modesty was still a concern. She did not want to be caught, yet she needed this validation so desperately, this romantic violence in the service of her self-image, that she was willing to risk her reputation, not to mention her life, and entrust herself to a stranger's whim.

"Non preoccupe, Giacinta," I said, and then repeated it. She gradually relaxed. Her head drooped, her arms dangled toward the dark water. Gleaming palely in the ambient light, her face was serene, enraptured, lips parted, slitted eyes directed to heaven, to a pattern of stars that exhibited the workings of a divine intellect and transformed our rutting into a mating of angels. God knows what fantasies populated her head! Perhaps she saw herself as a goddess suffering a vile martyrdom, or as a twenty-first century Leda. I gave passing thought to the notion of letting her fall, but though I am not known for my generosity of spirit, neither am I the cruelest of my

kind, and I must admit to having some trivial affection for every creature who shares with us their inch of time. Yet the scent of her despair and desperation, the fact that she was surrendering herself in the faint hope that her ardor might persuade me to love her, to sweep her up into a moneyed life, one wherein she could afford the procedures I had mentioned to Allessandra, those that would make her uninteresting to me—all this yielded a fine perfume that stirred my emotions to such an extent, I believed I loved her more purely than those who had previously used her, and it occurred to me that I might want to keep her around for the winter, that I might, for my own amusement, if nothing else, grant some of her wishes.

Afterward she brushed stone dust off her dress and cleaned herself with a tissue, casting furtive glances at lovers less bold than we; and when she was done with her toilette, she rested her head on my chest, as if sheltering there. I tipped her face toward mine and kissed her brow, an affectionate gesture unalloyed by irony. A worry line creased that kissed brow. She pushed me away and began berating me—that much was evident from her tone, but she spoke too rapidly for me to catch a single word until I heard "... *profillatico*..." The poor girl was rebuking me for not having worn a condom, a fact to which she had just awakened. I could have eased her fears on this score, but in the spirit of the scene I acted out my own concern, expressing that I had been swept away by passion, pledging that everything would be all right, that together we would find our way whether or not a little troglodyte had started its journey lifewards in her belly. At length I made myself understood and, mollified, she allowed me to guide her toward Baldassaro's. We had scarcely gone ten paces when she quickened her step, allowing the hint of a smile to touch her lips, and latched onto my arm with a proprietary grasp.

It was the last night of the season but one at Baldassaro's and we had rented the entire restaurant for a party of nine. A waiter led Giacinta and me through the main dining area and along a corridor to a large room, where a table had been set with a white linen cloth, crystal, and gold utensils. The cream-colored walls bore a mural of Roman galleys engaged in battle with a fleet of sleeker ships manned by soldiers with Persian-style beards. At one end of the room were French doors that opened onto a balcony overlooking the water. Jenay, a brunette this year, resplendent in a blue business suit tailored to accentuate her statuesque figure, smelling of flowers, greeted me with a kiss and introduced her companion, a German furniture salesman named Vid, a pop-eyed little monster in a houndstooth jacket who might have been her pet frog. When I introduced Giacinta, Vid performed a jaunty bow and Jenay whispered to me in the Old Tongue, "She's exquisite! I'm certain you'll win this year."

"What were you going for?" I asked her. "Comic relief?"

"I thought I'd give the rest of you a fighting chance."

"Just because you won last year doesn't mean . . ."

"I've won the last two out of three," said Jenay with mock indignation. "And it should have been three in a row."

"What language are you speaking?" Vid asked. "It's familiar, but I can't place it."

"It's an archaic French dialect," I said. "From the Aquitaine region."

"We belonged to one of those secret societies in college," said Jenay. "Learning it was required for membership."

"Aquitaine," said Vid. "I would have thought farther west. It reminds me of Basque."

"My, you're quite the linguist, aren't you? But then . . ." Jenay made suggestive play with her tongue and smiled. "I suppose I already knew that."

Vid, I swear before God, puffed out his chest, like a male bird fanning its plumage, and explained that in his undergraduate days, he had studied the French language and its origins; a family crisis had forced him to give up his studies.

"May I have some wine?" Giacinta looked at me crossly—she was feeling left out.

I hastened to serve her, also pouring Vid a glass, which he downed in a gulp, and the four of us began talking about Diamante, the only subject with which Giacinta seemed conversant. The town's many murals, she told us, were the result of a contest held each year—artists were invited from all over the world to paint a wall and the best of their work became part of Diamante's permanent exhibition.

Next to arrive was Elaine, also a brunette, more slender than Jenay, her perfume more subtle, with darker hair and piercing blue eyes, her pale, classical features rendered saintly by a cowled evening gown of a shimmering beige fabric. She had in tow a leather-jacketed street hustler named Daniele, his chiseled chin inked with stubble, who challenged me with a stare and otherwise exhibited a cool indifference that doubtless accorded with the personal style of some cinematic tough guy. Both Jenay and I took the position that Daniele was far too handsome and self-assured. Elaine defended her choice by saying that his pathos was inherent to his fate, which was so precisely demarked as to be obvious, but Jenay reminded her that, pitiful though Daniele was, our contest was judged on appearances and behavior, not potential.

"What do you expect?" said Elaine. "I only had a few hours to find someone."

"You could have arrived sooner," said Jenay. "Everything is always so last-minute with you."

Elaine made a dismissive noise.

"No, really," said Jenay. "It's tiresome. You've never taken your responsibility seriously."

"This hardly qualifies as a responsibility." Elaine pushed back her cowl and I saw that she had left a white streak in her hair. "This is a pig party. It cheapens us. Though I must say . . ." Coquettishly, she touched my chest. "Yours is wonderful! Where you did find her?"

"She found me," I said. "She more-or-less fell into my lap."

Elaine smiled. "Repeatedly, no doubt."

I had grown weary of Lucan's dramatic entrances, as had we all, this mostly a reaction to his overabundant personality, which was redolent of a gay *maitre de*; yet I must confess that I also anticipated them. Music preceded him, piped in over hidden speakers: Verdi's *March from Aida*. Next came Professor Rappenglueck, Lucan's lover for a term, now reduced to a familiar, and a guest at our dinners for nearly thirty years: a diminutive man, once handsome, his looks severely diminished by age and a slovenliness attributable to mental deterioration. He shuffled forward, gray and shrunken, like a piece of fruit left too long in the icebox, mumbling as he came, absently stroking his beard, and stood at the end of the dinner table, his voice increasing in volume and waxing lectoral, addressing the empty chairs as if they were a vast assembly, holding forth in an erratic fashion on the subject of Cro-Magnon sky maps in the caves of El Castillo.

". . . the Northern Crown," he was saying. "Remarkable in its accuracy. Of course, these maps are not the greatest . . . the greatest secret of El Castillo."

The professor fell silent in mid-ramble, and Lucan stepped into the doorway, his white hair combed back from his face and glowing like a flame, lending him a leonine aspect. He swirled his opera cape with a magician's flair, as if making himself reappear after an occult disappearance, then bowed to each of us in turn, reached into the corridor and drew forth not a rabbit, but a rabbity, stoop-shouldered girl. Liliana (so Lucan introduced her) was at least six feet tall, no older than eighteen or nineteen, with dark circles under her eyes, possessed of a morose expression and a flat chest that seemed hollowed due to her posture and loose-fitting blouse. Everything about her testified that here was a girl who had contemplated (and perhaps attempted) suicide more than once, and was likely to do so again, possibly before the evening was over. A distinct threat to Giacinta in our competition, but one I was confident that she would withstand, for although Liliana's presentation offered a complex palette of disaster, she was long of limb and doe-eyed, and neither bad skin nor poor posture nor the attrition caused her flesh by the poisons of depression hid the fact that she was a real beauty who, but for the indifference of chance, might have been walking a runway in Milan. Lucan, who had not spoken a word other than her name, presented her to Giacinta with an ornate gesture, and Liliana put out her hand.

"We've met," Giacinta said, and turned away, ostensibly to select an appetizer from the table; but the insult was clear.

Liliana snatched back her hand and held it clenched at her waist, looking crushed. I suspected, if given the opportunity, she would brood over this slight the rest of the evening and later memorialize it with a cutting or some other form of self-punishment.

Lucan winked at me and said, "I'll bet those two become a lot friendlier before the night is done."

"If you say so."

"Oh, I absolutely do." Lucan removed his cape, folded it over the back of a chair. "It's a natural pairing, you see. Liliana has gotten the better of this one"—he indicated Giacinta—"in an affair of the heart. Nothing else could have provoked such a reaction. It's our duty to heal the breach between them." He lifted a glass of wine, held it to the light to judge the color. "Lovely little town, don't you think? Have you seen the murals?"

"A few."

"Liliana took me on a tour this afternoon," he said. "Really spectacular, some of them. But I feel they need a centerpiece, something monumental to provide them with an overall context."

"Talk English!" Giacinta slapped my arm, demonstrating once again her shrewish side, a flaw she hastened to cover by conveying her frustration with being unable to understand what I was saying. She wanted to understand, she said, because . . . well, I understood, didn't I? She gazed up at me adoringly. Lucan rolled his eyes and, taking Liliana's arm, escorted her to the table.

At dinner, the four guests were seated all on one side of the table, Vid and Daniele bracketing Liliana and Giacinta; our side had a similar arrangement, Elaine and Jenay separating me and Lucan. By the time the seafood course had been served, Vid and Daniele were sneaking glances at one another over the top of the women's heads, and Liliana was casting shy looks at Giacinta, who was grumpily toying with her shrimp risotto. They struck up a conversation during the main course, an excellent veal marsala, and, when next I noticed, while the waiters cleared away the dishes, the women were chatting amiably, as if there had never been the slightest bitterness between them—it was clear that someone had influenced Giacinta to be receptive to Liliana. Recognizing this, I was incensed. An overreaction, perhaps, but I had grown fond of Giacinta and felt protective of her.

"Now that Taylor has overcome his reluctance for the game, we can proceed," said Lucan, dropping back into the Old Tongue. "I'd like first . . ."

"It's not reluctance," I said. "I simply find it jejune, this business of having guests at our dinners."

Lucan arched an eyebrow. "Yet Giacinta carries your scent. You had sex

Dinner At Baldassaro's

with her. You had sex with the one you brought last time . . . and the time before that. You enjoy that part of it."

"I'm prone to the same perversity as the rest of you," I said. "I fuck them because they're there to be fucked. Because their helplessness encourages me in some fundamental way. However, I don't make a big deal about it. And more to the point, I haven't used my influence on her tonight." I pointed to Giacinta, who, unaware of our attention, was leaning toward Liliana, touching her forearm as she spoke. "This is someone else's work."

"Why, that's damned impolite!" Lucan said, not trying to hide his smile. "Interfering with another man's . . . what shall we call it? Dinner date? Catch of the Day? A cross between the two, I'd reckon. It verges on the criminal."

"I know it was you, Lucan," I said. "You've always abused your authority, even in trivial matters."

"Very well! I admit it!" With a theatrical display, Lucan made as if to bare his chest so it might more readily accept my blade. "I'm the guilty one! The poor creatures looked so lonely, I felt compelled to give them a push."

"Whatever," I said.

"You don't need my permission," Lucan continued, "to return them to something approximating their former state. But you'll be denying them pleasure, and there's so little pleasure in their lives."

I refused to look at him. "Degrade them however you wish. I won't take part in it."

"Let me make sure I understand you," Lucan said. "It's not our behavior in general you're objecting to; it's the formalization of that behavior. Yes?"

"That's it basically," I said. "Though we might do well to examine the entire range of our relationships with them. It seems we're not doing ourselves much good by . . ."

"Must we always have this conversation!" Jenay threw down her fork in disgust. "You or Elaine trot out the same tired argument every time. It's become as much a part of our dinners as Rappenglueck."

At the sound of his name, the professor began mumbling—Lucan hushed him with a snap of his fingers.

"Are you insane?" I said to Jenay. "We never have this conversation. Each time we start to have it, you complain how tedious it's become. I was thinking about this the other night. We haven't done more than touch on the subject since Torremolinos, and that was nearly sixty years ago."

"Is there anything new to say?" Jenay attempted to make the question rhetorical by framing it in an indifferent tone.

"I don't know! Is there?" I put down my napkin and stood, stepping around to the opposite side of the table, walking behind the guests, who took incidental note of me, but not so as to subtract from their attentiveness to one another. "Let's find out. Does anyone have anything new to add to the conversation that we never have?"

"We've tried to help them—that hasn't worked," said Elaine. "And they've thwarted our best efforts at destroying them."

"That goes without saying . . . though it's been centuries since we made a concerted effort in that regard," said Jenay. "They're like roaches in their perseverance."

"We don't have the strength of will we once had. I'm sure that's due in part to my leadership, but I won't accept all the blame." Lucan shook his head ruefully. "I wish you could have known Furio. If ever a man was suited for a time . . . ."

"My mother knew him," said Jenay. "In fact, he sent a gift on the occasion of my birth."

"Furio was perfectly suited for the Dark Ages," Lucan went on. "He was as decisive as an ax, and as pitiless. When it came time for his release, he . . ."

"We know," said Elaine with heavy sarcasm. "It woke volcanoes, knocked down walls a hundred miles away, and created a symphony in the process."

"You've never attended a release," Lucan said. "If you had, you might not be so disrespectful."

Elaine wrinkled her nose in distaste. "Nobody I know would be so vulgar as to perform such a ritual. It makes you wonder at the sensibilities of our ancestors. The pyrotechnic release of one's life energy to entertain a crowd of drunks. It's . . ." She cast about for an appropriate word. "Primitive!"

"Being primitive has its uses," said Jenay. "There's a reason for the persistence of these cultural relics."

"That's how it's come to be viewed," said Lucan. "A cultural relic. I prefer to see it as something more vital. When Furio knew death was upon him, he gathered his friends so they might witness the vigor of his passing and celebrate the potency of his days."

"For all his potency, he failed to destroy the humans," I said.

Lucan scowled. "The *animals*. They outbred the plague. That's all. The one thing they do well is breed."

"They outbred us, to be sure. If we hadn't found our little French thistle, we'd have gone the way of the wooly mammoth." I paused, tamping down my annoyance with Lucan. "Yet if they hadn't outbred us, if it were a choice we'd been presented, a trade-off, giving up procreative dominance in exchange for long life and the enhancement of our mental gifts, who here would have it otherwise? We should view our survival as a gift, not a privilege. They *earned* their right to survive. They . . ."

Lucan snorted. "Next you'll be telling us their survival is God's will."

"My problem is," Elaine said, "I don't enjoy it anymore."

"Enjoy what?" Jenay asked impatiently.

"Exploiting them." Elaine half-turned to her. "Taylor's right. This ritual dominance, this antiquated behavior, colors our lives. It's a debased practice, no different from a release. And I don't like how it makes me feel."

"How *does* it make you feel?" asked Jenay, archly.

"Taylor's not right!" Lucan said. "Not in the way you mean, at any rate."

"Uneasy." Elaine met Jenay's challenging stare. "Uncertain of myself. You know."

"I'm sure I *don't* know," said Jenay.

I saw that Liliana had let her head fall back, exposing the arch of her throat, and Giacinta was pressing her lips to it, feathering her tongue along a vein that showed beneath the skin. The sight infuriated me.

"This is ridiculous!" I said. "The entire conversation."

"You insisted on having it." Jenay signaled to a waiter that he could remove her plate.

"We're not having the conversation I wanted. Far from it." I paced to the end of the table. "Look. We've established that we can't exterminate them, not without killing ourselves in the process. Now, despite our best efforts to save them, they're on the verge of destroying themselves . . . and us.

We're the superior beings. Can't we come up with a scenario other than one that involves mere containment or their destruction?"

Without bothering to excuse themselves, a silent communion having been reached, Vid and Daniele left the table and, soon after, the room. His expression bemused, Lucan started to speak, but I cut him off and said, "We have to examine the possibility that our intervention is stimulating their urge toward self-destruction."

"Not this again," said Jenay.

"Yes, we've mentioned it," I said. "But always as a drollery. We need to take it seriously. If these dinners have any purpose, they remind us how easily we can damage them. One touch and they start to come apart. Look at their leaders, the ones whom we've influenced most frequently. They're pathetic. The majority of them can't even muster coherent speech."

"Pish-posh," said Lucan.

"Look at Rappenglueck," I said.

The professor lifted his head and belched, and Lucan said, "Let's not make this personal, shall we? The thing is, our affairs are inextricably mingled with theirs. We can't afford to take the chance that Taylor may not be right." He pointed at the door. "Someone should check on the boys. Elaine?"

Elaine lowered her head. "Somebody else go."

Lucan turned to Jenay.

"They're just off to have sex," she said.

"We don't want that, do we? Not with the staff still here. And the manager. Why complicate things?"

"Oh, all right. I'm sick of this blather, anyway." Jenay stood, adjusted the fit of her jacket, and strode from the room.

"You have a point, Lucan. We can't change course abruptly," Elaine said. "At the same time, we shouldn't be overcautious. We've been acting within narrow parameters. Too narrow, if you ask me. We've been trying to maintain the status quo. It's like trying to stop a two-ton boulder from rolling downhill by jamming a doorstop beneath it. Given we're stuck with the situation, what I'm suggesting is, let's change what we can safely change and see what happens. This, the dinners, is one area in which we can experiment."

"That's not all you're suggesting." Lucan pretended to be concerned with shooting his cuffs. "What you're suggesting has larger implications."

"I realize that," Elaine said. "Changing our attitude toward them during these dinners may have a ripple effect. Perhaps it'll engender cultural change and one day we may find ourselves in partnership with them. As things stand, we only weaken ourselves with this kind of interaction."

"Partnership," Lucan said. "You mean, reveal ourselves to them?"

"Not right away," she said. "Eventually, perhaps. We're not so different from them, after all. Our superiority is based on a plant, for heaven's sake. An accident of biology."

"And we're not certain that the thistle can't be of benefit to them," I said. "We've only done the most primitive of experiments in that regard. It's quite possible . . ."

"You're talking about our enemy." Lucan enunciated his words precisely, as if speaking to a child. "Surely you comprehend that much. Our natural enemy. They very nearly destroyed us. We're at war with them. How can you forget?"

"When's the last time we took a casualty in that war?" I asked. "They're more our victims than enemies. Our governance of them sets the model for terrorism. We've become invisible, yet if we lift a finger, the earth shakes. As for our nature, I'd like to think we've risen above it."

Jenay re-entered the room. "They're fine," she said as she sat down. She glanced along the table. "Did I miss anything?"

Lucan gave a limp wave, as if commenting on the hopelessness of our impasse. "Taylor was saying he thinks we've risen above our natures in respect to the animals. I won't bother detailing how incredibly stupid I find that presumption." Then, addressing me: "If we reveal ourselves, you know what will happen."

"It would be nasty," I said. "No doubt. But if we prepare the way, who knows? And if worst comes to worst and there's a war, we'll win it."

Lucan studied me, as if weighing what I had said, but then he brought his hand down on the table, giving everyone a start . . . except for Giacinta and Liliana, who remained intent upon one another. "This is absurd! It's like listening to children prattling on about their favorite puppy."

"If you'll just listen—" I began.

"No." Lucan came to his feet. "I won't waste any more time with this shit. If Elaine and Jenay want to discuss . . ."

"Leave me out of it," said Jenay.

"If they want to discuss it, do it another day. As eldest, I determine the agenda for this meeting. It's time we got down to business."

Vid and Daniele wandered back into the room and stopped by the door. Daniele's mouth was agape and there was spittle on his chin; Vid's lips moved silently.

"Damn it!" Elaine spun about to confront Jenay. "You didn't have to ruin them!"

Jenay took in the scene by the door. She gave an amused sniff. "Sorry."

Elaine clenched her fists. "If you think I'm going to clean up after you . . ."

"Be quiet!" Lucan shouted it. "Jenay. Get them seated. And you . . ." He glared at me. "Sit. We've got work to do."

Jenay herded Vid and Daniele toward the table and, after returning Lucan's glare, I sat. Lucan refreshed his wine glass and said, "State the concerns of the clans you represent."

"China," said Jenay. "China, China, and China."

"Agreed, the question of China troubles us," said Elaine. "Iran remains an issue. And Africa."

"Africa?" Lucan laughed derisively. "That's not a problem. Taylor?"

"We'd like to accelerate the imposition of an overtly Fascist government in the United States," I said. "We need stricter immigration controls, surveillance policies. And we need those things now. The timetable that's been established is, in our view, dangerously slow. They've got so many black agencies within their government, no one knows what the other is doing, and I'm not certain we know. We have to get a handle on that immediately."

"Skyler Means will take care of it," he said. "I have complete confidence in him."

"Means and his people are stretched too thin," I said. "We're all stretched too thin. Cracks are starting to show, especially in the States."

"All right," he said. "We'll discuss it. Is that all?"

"For the moment."

"Isn't that odd? I'm not hearing anything about a redefinition of our relationship with the animals." Lucan built a church-and-steeple with his fingers. "We'll begin with China. I believe it's time to consider another thinning of the herd."

It was past eleven before we concluded our business. The waiters brought in the cheese cart; the manager put in an appearance, thanked us for our business, and then they withdrew. Vid and Daniele occupied one end of the table, carrying on a faltering conversation that, judging by what I heard, made sense only to them. At the other end, Lucan sat with the professor, prompting him in his ceaseless lecture, rewarding him now and again with a wedge of cheese. Their political differences set aside for the moment, Elaine and Jenay chatted and laughed by the door, while Giacinta had followed Liliana out onto the balcony. She had unbuttoned Liliana's blouse and they were embracing.

We had that night made significant decisions that would affect millions of lives, but I was more interested in Giacinta's well-being, in repairing the damage Lucan had done, than I was with assessing my evening's work, second-guessing the compromises I had made and weighing them out against what I had won. Goaded by Lucan's tampering, encouraged by Jenay-and-Elaine's validation of my choice, but mainly due to the thrust of my own peculiar tastes, I had developed an affection for Giacinta during the brief span of our relationship and I felt no small jealousy toward Liliana—though Giacinta's attraction for her was a contrivance, a falsity, mine for Gia was equally false, equally contrived, and the only way I could deny this was to steer her away from Liliana and immerse both of us in an illusion I created. But manipulating a human mind is like entering a room filled with mist and fashioned of fragile crystal, and you must step carefully or else you will break everything. Restoring a mind is still more difficult—it was nothing I could accomplish without a degree of concentration difficult to achieve at Baldassaro's. And so, deciding that repairs would have to wait until we were back at the Villa Ruggieri, I went to refill my wine glass, coming within earshot of Lucan and the professor.

"One might reasonably conjecture," Professor Rappenglueck was saying, staring at the cheese cart, "that the great turns in human history were accomplished by force of arms, by inventions that caused society to evolve, and so forth. Who could imagine . . ." His features twisted as he sought to complete the sentence.

"Come on, Rappy." Lucan waggled a wedge of gouda in front of the professor. "'That for all intents and purposes . . .'"

"Who could imagine," the professor went on, "that for all intents and purposes our history ended in the mid-Paleolithic with the discovery by Cro-Magnon man that a variety of starthistle, when attacked by *rhinocyllus conicus* . . ."

"'. . . yielded a chemical,'" Lucan prompted.

". . . a chemical. . ." The professor licked his lips. ". . . that slowed the rate of . . ."

Lucan clicked his tongue in annoyance and fed Rappanglueck the cheese.

I pulled back a chair and sat, stretching out my legs. "Doesn't your pet mouse know any other tricks?"

"It's a synaptic response," Lucan said absently. "He senses the importance of these gatherings, and he tends to think he's back in Geneva, giving the address he prepared for the IGY conference."

"The one you prevented him from giving," I said. "By destroying him."

Lucan's face hardened, yet he refused to rise to the bait. He cut another wedge from the wheel of gouda. The professor was still nibbling on the previous wedge, yellow crumbs in his beard; he chewed faster on seeing the fresh wedge.

"A year ago," said Lucan wistfully, "he could have recited entire paragraphs. Now he can barely get through a sentence. He's falling apart." He fed the professor the second wedge, stroked his hair, and spoke to him as though to a precious child. "But you were almost famous, weren't you, Rappy? You might have been as famous as Newton or Leakey."

"Tell me. Do you still fuck him?" I asked, repulsed by Lucan's display of intimacy.

"You know, I think I'll answer your question. One day the information may come in handy." Lucan resettled in his chair. "At home, Rappy's almost his old self some days. On those days, sometimes the illusion of wholeness suffices and we're affectionate with one another. Is there anything more you'd care to know?"

The professor made a complaining noise; he had finished his gouda.

"No," I said. "I think I've got the picture."

"You really are an astonishing fool!" Lucan hacked at the cheese. "For someone who became a clan leader in so short a time, you have the most appalling blindness. You can't see yourself at all."

"And you can, I suppose?"

"See you? Oh, yes. The fact is, I've always recognized your potential. One day you'll be my successor, and I have the highest of hopes for your term. If a cure for your blindness is found, that is." He tipped his head to the side. "Would it surprise you to learn that I espoused attitudes similar to yours when I was young? Regarding the animals, I mean."

"I'd be more surprised if you didn't make that claim," I said. "The elderly are prone to react that way when confronted with the logic of the future. 'Ah, yes!' they say. 'Once I thought as you, but experience has cured me of such enthusiasms.'"

Lucan fed another wedge to the professor. "Forget it."

"Wait! Aren't you going to tell me? I'm dying to hear. Let me think. What would you say?" I sat beside Lucan, affecting the pose of someone in deep study. "When you were younger, you were afire with possibility. You had a vision of the world based upon trust, upon accords, not on the hard-won wisdom of your elders. The long centuries armored you against such foolishness, but in your dotage you took a lover from among the animals. You'd had many such lovers, but this one . . . he was special. A professor who had stumbled across the secret of our primacy, of our very existence. After you were forced to destroy him, you continued to love him. Of course, it wasn't altogether love you felt. Part of your emotional commitment was a tribute to the youthful philosophies you once embraced. It may be you understood now that they were not so foolish, after all. But it was too late in life, your position was such that you couldn't publicly espouse them. So in a sense, your love became an emblem that demonstrated you bore the gene of caring. The taint of the animals, our cousins, whom we detest and love . . . it's a crutch we have to carry. We must proclaim it, wear it like a lapel pin in order to testify that, though we assault them with

AIDS, with endless warfare, with pollutants to which we are immune, we *love* our deficient cousins. What a tragedy we're forced to poison them like rats!" I leaned back, crossed my legs. "Perhaps one day even someone as blind as I may come to adopt this posture."

"One day," said Lucan distantly. "Even you."

It was unlike him to be so docile—he had always been fierce in his arguments. He went back to grooming Rappenglueck, cleaning the crumbs from his beard. In hopes, perhaps, of receiving more cheese, the professor said, "On the shoulder of the buffalo, if you'll note the slide, there is a pattern of dots."

"It's all right, Rappy," Lucan said.

The professor tried again. "Unlike similar patterns in the other paintings, this does not represent a constellation, but the starthistle. Its position relative to the Northern Crown, appearing directly over the bull's shoulder, leads me . . . leads . . ."

"That reminds me," I said. "We haven't discussed the project."

"There's nothing to discuss." Lucan wiped Rappenglueck's lips. "No progress."

"We were told to expect a breakthrough."

"Do you really believe we'll abandon them? That we'll just slip off through some sidereal door and leave them to heaven?"

I was shocked to notice that tears had collected in Lucan's eyes . . . so shocked that I failed to respond.

"There'll be no breakthrough," Lucan went on. "The science is there, but there's no will for a breakthrough. If we inadvertently stumble upon one, we'll only use it as a last resort."

". . . leads me to suspect," the professor said triumphantly, "that Cro-Magnon man associated the thistle in a most specific way with the stars of the Northern Crown."

Lucan patted his hand.

"Am I to infer from what you say that the project staff is slacking?" I asked. "Because if that's . . ."

"Not at all. I'm saying we're bound by the patterns of the past. We're enslaved by our natures. Our hatred of the animals, our love for them . . . it's the same emotion. That's why our only recourse is extermination. We're capable of killing something we love, but abandon it? Never." Lucan made a show of cracking his knuckles. "Our ambivalence toward them has caused our current troubles. Over the millennia, it's developed into a weakness. A terrible weakness. We need something to rouse us from our stupor."

"I've heard this song far too many times," I said. "I'm sick of listening to it."

"Oh, I understand. Really, I do. You need a lesson to drive it home. I don't know if I'm the one to teach you, but tonight I'll teach you at least one small lesson. You'll learn that mercy is more of an indulgence than a grace."

"What are you talking about?"

"For one thing, your companion for the evening. Giacinta." Lucan had completed the professor's toilette and now he set about adjusting the knot of Rappanglueck's tie. "I'm afraid I left her in a rather delicate condition. As it stands, she'll likely live out her years in excellent mental health. But any further interference with her mind, if you attempt, let's say, to sway her from her passion for Liliana . . . They're so flimsy. She won't be able to withstand another alteration. You'll spend the rest of her life trying to restore her. Not the happiest of choices, as you can see." He put a hand on the professor's shoulder. "You could kill her. That would be the simplest course. I can tell you're smitten and I know that makes things difficult. But it would spare you a lot of grief."

Furious, I wanted to strike him, and I would have done so had we been elsewhere, engaged in less public business. I made for the balcony, intending to ascertain the extent of the damage he had done to Gia.

"Oh, Taylor!" he called.

I looked back to where he sat plucking at Rappenglueck's clothing.

"My compliments on your choice of a companion." Here Lucan offered a final florid gesture, one of such ornate, ironic precision, it seemed a summing up of the evening. "As eldest, it's my pleasure to declare Giacinta the winner of our competition. She, more than anyone I've seen in recent years, embodies the frailty and strength of the human weed. You have my sincere congratulations."

⁕ ⁕ ⁕

I shooed Liliana away from the balcony, closed the French doors after her, and examined Giacinta. It was as Lucan had said. Having been altered, the stability of her mind, of that crystal, mist-filled room, had been compromised and any further alteration would cause the walls to crack, only a little at first, but the cracks would spread, leading inexorably to collapse; yet I found myself altering her even before I had decided to do so, obeying an impulse I was unable to resist. Steeped in her thoughts, discernable as might be glints and movements, the dartings of fish in a murky bowl, I could not abide the notion that her passion, the focused product of all that indistinct energy, be directed toward anyone aside from myself for an instant longer. When I pulled back from her, I felt drenched, dripping with her, droplets of pure need, her sweet yearnings, her sour greed, her sullen ambition, her tangy lust, her bloody hungers. Her face, tilted up toward me, was once again adoring, heartbreakingly plain. But absent was that accent of desperation. My restoration having been clumsier by necessity than Lucan's alteration, I knew I would never again glimpse the original Gia.

My good-byes were perfunctory and once out on the Via Poseidone, I hailed a taxi and had the driver convey us to the Villa Ruggiere. Giacinta giggled and clung to me as we rode the ancient elevator up to my suite, where, in an immense teak bed with sheets marbled by moonlight, dappled with shadow, beneath a high frescoed ceiling, and under the regard of pale torturers and poisoners and assorted monsters of the ruling class who glowered from decaying tapestries on the walls, their rich velvets and silks reduced to a brownish ferment by the centuries, I made love to her, wanting as much of her as I could gather before she began to decline. After she had fallen asleep, I put on a shirt and trousers, went into the sitting room and lay down upon a sofa. I thought briefly of the evening, of the business we had done, and then I thought of Gia and what I intended to do about her.

She was irretrievably broken and thus unattainable, at least in her original form, the form that had initially attracted me, and I saw the trap into which I was about to walk, entering into a relationship that could be no more than a heterosexual copy of Lucan's with Professor Rappenglueck. However, her unattainability was half her charm. Love in all its forms, I supposed—love between the animals, between us, love between the sub-species—followed a similar development, beginning with a flirtatious glance, a dash of pheromones, thereafter progressing to doting looks, then to sex, and at every step along the way a decision was involved: you decided to take the first step, to walk the next step farther; you contrived the illusion that this was it for you, this was the ultimate; and once past its peak moment, you decided whether you wanted to stick around for the tragedy, whether that suited your notion of love, whether you were going to attempt to create the illusion of unconditional love, to believe that there was more to love than your contrivance of it, that it was not your creation but a powerful universal force that swept us along. These little dramas in which we cast ourselves so as to inspire our lives, to give us reason to persevere . . . They would be amusing if not for the fact that, no matter how often our faith is proven unwarranted, we believe in them.

The cynicism of these thoughts and their underlying naïvete should have been sufficient to persuade me to rid myself of Giacinta. They seemed proof of her negative effect upon me. Yet I continued to debate the matter. An enormous face, counterfeited by shadows and the visible portions of a fresco, stared down at me from the ceiling, and I was contemplating that face, thinking it superior in design to the sylvan scene actually depicted, when I heard a chthonic rumbling, followed by a tremor that shook the building for more than a minute, toppling a clock from the mantel, sending ashtrays scampering across tabletops, overturning a chair, bouncing me onto the floor. I staggered up, knowing at once what had happened, having a clear perception of it, though I tried to persuade myself that I must be wrong, and hurried into the bedroom. Gia was still on the bed, poised on all-fours, her eyes wide with fright. I convinced her to lie back, gentled her, and told her she would be all right if she stayed in the suite, but that I had to go.

"Please!" She put her arms about my neck. "You take me."

"I can't," I said. "Wait here. Two hours. I'll come back in two hours. I promise."

My cell phone rang. Elaine. I switched it on and said, "Yes, I know."

"I can't believe the son-of-a-bitch . . ."

"Have you called Rome?"

"No, I thought you . . ."

"Call Rome. Now. Tell them to send helicopters. We have some in Palermo. Seal off the area. You coordinate from the hotel. Have you heard from Jenay?"

"No. Shouldn't you coordinate?"

"That's your job now."

Following a silence, she said tremulously, "I guess it is."

"Find out which satellites are passing over southern Italy and blind them. Knock them down if you have to."

"God, what a mess!"

"Call Rome. I'll get back to you."

Gia renewed her pleading after I switched off, but once again I rebuffed her.

"Stay. Here you be secure," I told her in fractured Italian. "*Due oras.* Okay?"

She put on a sad face, but she drew the blankets up to her neck. "Okay."

I kissed her and backed from the room, reassuring her with a smile. Then, not trusting the elevator, I raced down the stairs, ignoring the hotel guests and staff that I encountered, and descended the hill into the ruins of Diamante.

There was a tremendous amount of dust in the air. It coated my tongue, the membranes of my nostrils, got into my eyes. In the upper reaches of the town, the buildings were some of them intact, others partially demolished, yet I saw no one on the streets and I assumed Lucan's release must have killed everyone in an instant. His mental signature, which had been palpable at the hotel, boiled like steam from the wreckage, overwhelming all other sensory impressions. My cell phone rang. It was Elaine again. She told me the helicopters were on their way, the satellites had been dealt with, and our operatives within the Italian government were busy attempting to defuse the situation. As I listened, I began to feel the weight of my new responsibilities.

"Where are you?" she asked and, when I told her, she said, "I'm on top of the hotel. Wait until you see the waterfront. We're going to play hell cleaning it up."

"Call Skyler Means. Find out how much the Americans know. They're certain to have picked up something on satellite. Tell him to do whatever he has to."

I told her to continue checking in with me and switched off.

Shortly after Elaine's call, I found the body of a young woman lying under some bricks, but I did not pause to examine her, nor did I allow her death to disturb me—there were many dead that night, and I had no time to ponder my emotional state. As I descended through the town, the devastation increased. Buildings were flattened and the rubble in the winding street provided a surreal accent to the scene. Portions of Diamante's murals lay everywhere. Here a chunk of stucco bearing the pointillist rendering of an elephant's foot; here a sunrise broken into five sections; here a child's arm, a little dog trotting, a piece of a carousel, the bell of a tuba; half a Madonna's face was intact—the other half was pitted and unrecognizable. It was as if the pretty shell of the world had been blown apart to reveal its true disastrous nature.

Because of the extent of the destruction, I was able to see the waterfront long before I reached the Via Poseidone. The sea wall and the causeway had been obliterated, and, surrounding the islet on which Baldassaro's was situated, the water had been transformed into glass or something like, and the glass twisted into hundreds of tortured, translucent shapes, some diminutive, others towering thirty feet into the air, gleaming in the moonlight. The island itself was burning with a strangely steady, reddish flame, marking Lucan's grave and that of his lover. From where I stood, the entirety of the scene resembled an enormous, complicated blossom with a fiery stamen and irregular stiff petals.

The burning came to me as a faint windy sound. I was too far off to discern what the translucent shapes were, but when I stepped out onto the Via Poseidone, I realized they were heroic figures, none of them complete, yet all the more heroic for their lack of completion. Had they been finished figures, correct in every detail, they would have looked cartoonish; unfinished, mired in webs of glass, leaping out of glass waves, trying to shrug off glassy shrouds, charged with moonlight, like silver blood flowing through their limbs, they seemed more what Lucan would have had in mind: ancient warriors, both succumbing to and struggling to break free of the moonstruck glass that gave them substance. How long, I wondered, must he have trained himself in order to produce so complex a result at the moment of release? Decades, I reckoned. And I had no doubt that he had achieved his intent—the imagery and its incompleteness spoke to his obsession with the old days, to his belief that we had repressed our warrior instincts, restrained them beneath a decadent veneer. Confronted with the visible expression of those beliefs, I was moved a ways toward agreement with them.

I walked toward that barbaric sculpture garden, to the crumbling verge of the Via Poseidone, and examined a figure with a half-formed face and flowing hair, the muscular torso straining, with a two-handed grip on a club. As I inspected it from various angles, light glided back and forth inside it like the shiftings of a spirit level, bringing up bits of detail. Hulking just beyond, one of the larger figures appeared to be effortfully rising from a crouch, its head lowered, using a spear to push itself up, weighed down by a glass robe. I was about to call Elaine, thinking to modify my previous orders, when I spotted Jenay off along the street, standing beneath the immense figure of a woman depicted in the act of slashing at an invisible enemy with a knife. She was approximately a hundred feet away, anonymous at that distance, but it could only be Jenay. I hailed her and, as I approached, I saw that she had changed into jeans and a short jacket. Her hair was loose about her shoulders; she wore no make-up. She might have been the sister of the sculpted woman, who was also buxom, her wide hips flowing up from a glassy wave. They shared the same calm expression.

"Did you see it?" she asked as I came up. "The light he made?"

I told her I had been otherwise occupied.

"It was magnificent," she said. "He ruled the sky for nearly a minute."

Her poised demeanor and admiring tone aroused my suspicions. "You knew," I said.

"A few years back, he told me he wanted to die with Rappy. He only had about fifty years left, he thought, but he was emotionally spent. He said he was contemplating a release."

"And you knew he would do it tonight."

"I didn't *know*. Perhaps I suspected. He didn't seem himself."

I tried to turn her, wanting to search her face for signs of a lie, but she knocked my hand aside.

"You watched for the light," I said. "You must have known."

"I wasn't watching, I happened to be looking out the window," she said defiantly; then she put a hand to her forehead and blew out a breath, as if trying to steady herself. "Perhaps I knew."

"You should have told me, even if it were only a suspicion." Agitatedly, I opened and closed my cell phone several times. "He's left us a hell of mess."

"Is that all you take from it?" She shot me a hard look.

"I don't have time to appreciate Lucan's artistry now that I'm in command."

"Are you . . . in command? We'll see."

"You're challenging my authority?"

"If I'm challenging anything, it's your willingness to exercise authority."

"So you are challenging me. Do you want to formalize the challenge?"

"Not at this point," she said.

She glanced up at the sculpture and I, too, glanced up—the flame of the burning island brightened, and the fall of the woman's hair glowed redly. Jenay strolled off a couple of paces, her attention gathered by a smaller figure, a bearded, transparent, ax-wielding barbarian. The cell phone made a chilly noise in the empty street. I switched on and, keeping an eye on Jenay, said, "Yes."

"I can't reach Skyler," said Elaine.

"Try him in New York."

"I've tried all his numbers. Everybody's tried. The whole network is down. We haven't been able to reach any of our people on the east coast. It's Rome's opinion we've been compromised."

"That's obvious." I came a step toward Jenay. "What action do they recommend?"

"They recommend we go to a war level," said Elaine.

"Not yet." I closed to within arm's length of Jenay. "Go to Bronze . . . but tell them to go to Iron if they don't hear from me every half-hour. And tell the helicopters to fucking clean-up and get us out of here. If the Americans are going to react locally, it'll take a while, but there's no point running a risk. Jenay and I are down by the water, about seventy-five yards north of where the causeway used to stand."

"This is no coincidence," said Elaine. "Lucan and Skyler, both the same night."

"No," I said. "It's no coincidence."

Jenay's face betrayed, I thought, an almost undetectable trace of amusement. I shaped the words, You knew, with my mouth and said to Elaine, "Tell Palermo to prepare a nuke. We may be able to pass Diamante off as some sort of terrorist incident. I doubt it, but it's worth a try."

"What's happening?" Jenay asked as I switched off.

"Don't treat me like an idiot. You know very well what's happening."

She was silent a moment. "Lucan's forced your hand."

I chose not to reply.

"It follows that he would," she said. "Once he made his personal decision, he wouldn't have let the opportunity pass. And if the Americans are involved . . . Are we facing war?"

I folded my arms, scarcely able to contain my anger.

"You have to tell me," she said.

"If you want to continue with your pretense, call Elaine," I said. "She'll fill you in."

Jenay put her hands on her hips. "I realize you'd like to think of me as an element of a conspiracy, but there's no conspiracy. You're our leader now. People are going to watch you, they'll judge you by your actions. If I hesitate to give you my absolute approval, you shouldn't assume that's due to a conspiracy."

"Judge all you want. I won't be pressured or coerced any further. I've been maneuvered into a bad situation, but I may not do what Lucan wanted."

"What Lucan wanted was for someone to take decisive action. Action he couldn't bring himself to take, except in the way he did. He was well aware of his weaknesses. He used to tell me you were our hope. He saw in you a leader capable of making the kinds of decisions that we needed." Jenay touched my forearm. "Whatever he's done, he did it in part for you."

"This? This selfish, indulgent act? This treason? Yes, I can see that."

"Don't be obtuse! However you perceive it now, it's an opportunity to prove that Lucan was on the mark about you."

"Right. He created this fucking disaster just to make my leadership skills bloom." I went nose-to-nose with her. "He's killed Skyler! And probably hundreds more! Once they were taken, I'm certain Skyler and his people did what was necessary to preserve our position. But that they *were* taken, an entire network, it implies the Americans have a means of defeating our mental control. Skyler's people may not all be dead; a few may be in rooms somewhere spilling our secrets."

"Well, then. You have your work cut out for you." She said this flatly, as if to suggest it proved her point.

"Once this gets sorted out," I said, "if it can be sorted out, I promise there'll be an investigation."

Jenay shrugged. "And you'll have my full support."

A searchlight swept over the nearby figures, bringing them to flashing life, and a helicopter descended out of the night, its rotors swirling the dust that lay everywhere and making conversation a chore. Jenay and I moved apart, waiting for it to land.

From directly overhead, the burning island and its immediate surround looked even more like a blossom. I thought of those gigantic Sumatran flowers. Corpseflowers. The helicopter veered inland, and we began passing over the darkened Calabrian hills. My headset crackled. The pilots' helmets were silhouetted against the lights of the control array. Beside me, Jenay gazed out the window as I plotted the next days. Sleeper cells would have to be activated throughout the United States. Hundreds of individuals would be terminated, dozens of hard targets neutralized. I could feel the constrictions that Lucan had devised closing in around me, limiting the scope of my actions, enforcing a restructuring of my attitudes, leaving me to orchestrate the parameters of a new and improved holocaust. Thanks to him, we were entering a dangerous phase of history, one in which we would be more visible, thus more imperiled, than at any time since the Iron Age. This enlisted my paranoia and I imagined, not for the first time, that—unbeknownst to us—another group was monitoring our activities, and, above them, another group, and another, and so on and so forth. The universe as terrorist. Conspiracies of angels and demons. God the infinite suicide bomber.

"I've got Palermo on," said the co-pilot. "The package is ready for delivery."

"Have we reached a safe distance?" I asked.

"Yes."

"Patch them through to me."

I hadn't had a moment to think of Giacinta since rushing out of the hotel. I wondered if she had gone back to sleep, or if she had disobeyed my admonition and was wandering the streets, terrified and confused by the destruction of her home. The image troubled me, but at heart I was indifferent to her fate. Lucan's actions had nipped that passion in the bud and stripped from me all but the thinnest veneer of sentiment. I wished things were different, that I could indulge in mercy, that I could wound myself with love or its imitation, that I had time for such games, but that wish was subsumed by the eagerness we feel at the onset of war. The desire to wield power, to destroy, to win—they were the enticements of a more involving game. Yet as I gave the order that would erase Diamante from the maps of the world, I nourished a twinge of regret, I savored it, I stored it away in memory for whatever use I might one day find for it. Though we were flying away from the town, the flash, when it came, was visible as a reflection in the helicopter's plastic canopy. It held for several seconds, considerably less long than the light of Lucan's release, then swiftly faded. Jenay sighed—in satisfaction, I believed. She rested her hand atop mine, and we continued north toward Rome.

ABIMAGIQUE

She's the girl with the Halloween hair. The Morticia Addams Cut, dyed jet black, with asymmetrical streaks of orange. She's twenty-four, twenty-five. A child-woman, you imagine, who dotes on books about famous poisoners and has several of the more painful piercings. Typical Goth material. But once you get past the hair, the vintage dress, the pearl ring shaped like a bulbous spider, the tattoos on the backs of her hands (a vampire's skull, a human heart), and the extreme make-up, you notice that her face has a maternal sensuality and softness that seem too unguarded to be part of the modern world.

Most weekdays she has lunch at this little teriyaki place just off the Ave on 45th, in the University District of Seattle. She usually sits at a table where Bill Gates once ate, an occasion memorialized by a framed Polaroid of the great man on the wall above it, and she always orders the Number Three (Veggie Special) and a bottle of water, and reads while she eats (trade paperbacks as a rule), except when it's raining—then she stares out the window, absently forking up bites of food. This suggests she might be native to the region, because people born in the Pacific Northwest don't generally view the rain as depressing; they're more likely to accept it as a comforting veil drawn across the world, one that encourages contemplation.

No one hits on her, and that surprises you. Some guys are doubtless put off by her personal style (which you suspect is less a statement of cultural disaffection than a disguise), and some will assume she's a ball-buster and that any approach could trigger a barrage of insult. Yet others wouldn't be so easily dissuaded. She's a beautiful woman—no, a *lovely* woman; lovely being a word more evocative of her antique quality. Her breasts, always displayed to advantage, are large and milky white, *zoftig*, like the breasts of models painted by Titian and Raphael, and the remainder of her body conforms to this unfashionable standard of voluptuousness. There must be a special atmosphere around her, you think. An envelope of force that keeps her space inviolate. One way or the other, you understand she's not a girl who can be easily acquired. You can't just walk up to her and say, Mind if I sit here?, or, If you're going to break my heart, do it now, because later it'll be too painful, or, Didn't I see you at the Crocodile Club last Saturday?, and talk about the cool bands you've both seen and then ask for her number, and by then you'll have gone past the need for conversation (it's really more of an animal preliminary), and you'll either wind up in bed together or you won't. Though you desire the same thing that guys who use such uninspired openings desire, you recognize that if you are going to reach that night, that bed, you'll first have to desire everything about her. You'll have to fall in love, succumb to her, so when you introduce yourself, employing no greater wit than that typically employed by anyone else your age, your introduction will be supported by a depth of emotion, a weight of knowledge, and by then you will have discovered that conversation is rarely a trivial matter for her—a moral conviction underlies her words—and you'll have learned she works with the handicapped as a massage therapist and lives alone in a frame house on a fir-lined street in Fremont, and that her eyes are green as bottle glass under strong sunlight, and that she's called Abi, which is short for Abimagique.

Of course no one would name their daughter Abimagique. It's a self-chosen name, a name that, when you first heard it, caused you to harbor derisive thoughts, to imagine her the victim of some Wiccan delusion, and this appears to be more-or-less the case. On the walls of her house hang classic representations of the angels; Tibetan and Native American masks; curious constructions of dried vegetable matter and silk ribbon; ankhs, crosses, backwards 7s, and other symbols less readily identifiable. Long strings of beads—silver and amber, topaz and lapis lazuli—drape the bedroom mirror, carving reflections into slices; herbal sachets that yield peculiar odors are strewn everywhere; scraps of paper bearing inscriptions hand-inked in a Tolkienesque script are tucked beneath pillows, in the backs of drawers, under potted plants, inside tins and jars, many of these featuring a backwards 7. After you've been friends with her for a month (you've insinuated yourself into her life as a client, seeking treatment for back problems you suffered in an automobile accident years before), you realize that these arcana don't announce her character, they merely reflect it; they're natural expressions, like sprays of foliage from a central trunk. When she talks about God, gods, spirits, ghosts, miracles, monsters, the magic of animals, of plants, the circles of Hell, the potency of angels, the entirety of the mystic landscape she inhabits, she expresses herself neither defensively nor assertively, but with a calm certainty that inspires you to argument. You want to debunk her beliefs not because you're such a huge fan of empirical truth or because you're so locked in to your science-geek grad-school thing, but rather because a vague male reason demands it. She refuses to argue, she merely submits there may be some things you're not yet aware of, and that's not something you can argue, though you try.

Just past the turn of the year, you become lovers. Rain falls intermittently and the firs enclosing Abi's house lend the pewter light a greenish undersea opacity in which her skin glows. You discover a backwards 7 tattooed on the inside of her right thigh, close to her sex; you trace the blue ink with a finger, puzzle over it a moment, then make gentle play with her genital piercing. She tells you that she loves you, but her tone is oddly dispassionate and, once you're inside her, though you experience the ferocity of desire, your feelings seem muted by a tranquil energy you recognize as uniquely hers, as if you've penetrated that protective envelope you sensed, that atmosphere, and now it surrounds you. You're lulled, cradled by her acceptance. It's like you're adrift on the undulations of a tide, not moved by female sinew and bone. But the instant before you come, she breaks the languid rhythm of your lovemaking; she places her hands on the small of your back and presses down hard with her fingertips, manipulating the nerves and muscles there. Electricity snaps along your spine, heat floods your brain. You cry out from spasms of sensation so violent, they take you to the brink of unconsciousness. Once you recover, you ask with a degree of anger (because it hurt), but with a greater degree of wonderment (because you've never experienced such an intricate orgasm), what the hell was it that she did to you?

"It's a massage technique," she says. "Didn't you enjoy it?"

You start to say "no"—you're accustomed to having more control in bed than, in retrospect, it appears you had, and you're annoyed. "I would have enjoyed it a hell of a lot more if you hadn't sprung it on me," you tell her.

"That doesn't say much for your sense of spontaneity." She fixes you with her green gaze. You're startled by how specifically it communicates her disappointment; you suspect that her emotions may be more deeply held, more genuine than your own, and thus easier to read. Whether true or not, the thought that it might be increases your annoyance; but then she cuddles against you, her softness a distraction, and says, "I won't do it anymore if you don't want."

You're coming to understand that's how things work in your relationship, and how they probably always will work—she cedes control to you when control is no longer an issue.

Days, weeks, months fly past, and you move in with her, but what you know about her never gets much more detailed than the fact that she likes teriyaki. Oh, there are things you discover through observation and experience. Things about her character, her quirks. She believes the world will end in a series of cataclysms for which we should prepare. She loves the rain and likes to run out into it without an umbrella, sometimes without clothes. She keeps a large aquarium filled with water, with a pump that gurgles loudly, but no fish—she explains that she hasn't found the right kind to put in it, but enjoys the sound made by the pump, so having fish is unimportant. She eats a weird vegetarian diet, flavored with herbs grown in a garden at the side of the house, that you also must eat (though you supplement it with burgers you sneak after classes or while at work in the microbiology lab). She has the habit of calling you "angel," a term she also applies to taxi drivers and restaurant workers, random people, and when you ask why she does this, she says that some people are descended from angels—she recognizes them by their aura—and she's just acknowledging them as such. She practices Tantric magic, sexual magic, a discipline you're coming to appreciate, being a direct beneficiary of it. But her history, the plain truth of her, remains elusive. She says her parents died when she was young and she was brought up ". . . all over the place . . ." in foster homes, but she pushes the subject aside so quickly, you have the idea that it may be standing-in for a more unpleasant truth. She doesn't appear to have any friends, but claims to have a few and promises you'll meet them soon. As far as you're concerned, the fewer friends, the better. Your fascination has grown to the level of obsession and you want to monopolize her time. Trying to explain how you feel to your best friend, Gerald, you're reduced to cliché and hyperbole, and say that she's redefined your view of women.

At twenty-four, Gerald's a full year older than you, yet he still wears his baseball cap backwards and acts like an idiot. He tells everyone he's in a band (he's not), shares an apartment with a lipstick lesbian whom he claims is his girlfriend (she's obviously not), and is employed as a barista, manning the coffee cart outside the University Book Store. Nevertheless, you maintain the illusion, held since you attended high school together, that his opinion has value. He slams an espresso shot, wipes his mouth and shudders as if in reaction to raw whiskey.

"Yeah?" he says. "She a trannie?"

You tell him that the qualities you perceive as flaws in other women, Abi possesses as strengths. Her skill at manipulation, for instance. You never feel used, you say, when she manages to get her way by manipulating you, because there's always something in it for you, and also because she performs the act with such subtlety, it's as if she elevates it beyond criticism. And that has allowed you to see that the art of manipulation in the female is pure and necessary, as essential to her well-being as body mass and muscle to a male.

You understand that you're talking utter bullshit. You're trying to convey Abi, all of her, by describing, ineptly, one aspect of her, and that can't be done. Gerald isn't listening, anyway; he's leafing through a skateboard magazine.

"Dude, is she hot?" he asks.

"Why don't you tell me? You want to meet her?"

"'Cause if she's hot . . ." Gerald swats at you with his magazine and grins. "None of that other shit matters."

Gerald's partner, a white guy who's too cool to talk—he nods, he grunts, he gestures—and has nasty-looking blonde dreadlocks that have been dipped in blue dye, takes over at the cart and you drive to Abi's house in Gerald's shitbox. It's raining steadily by the time you arrive and Abi is out gathering herbs in the garden. Her T-shirt's plastered to her body, reminding you of an old Italian flick in which Sophia Loren wandered around for half the movie wearing a ragged, soaked-though dress. You park across the street, point Abi out to Gerald, and the two of you sit and watch for a minute. Her curves accentuated by wet black cloth, Abi looks nothing if not hot.

"I don't get it," says Gerald. "She's a plumper, dude. I didn't know you're into plumpers."

You gape at him.

Gerald turns his eyes toward Abi once again. "She's got some potential, okay? But seriously, man. Way she is now . . . I mean, she's built like your mom. What's your mom now? Forty-five, forty-six? If Abi-whatever is this big at twenty-five, time she's forty-five, she's gonna be like one of those freaks they have to cut through the roof to lift 'em outa their bedroom."

"Fuck off!!"

"No, really. I'm trying to help you out, okay?"

"No, really! Fuck off!"

"Hey, man! Since you been with this chick, she's got you so whipped, it's like you're not even the same guy. You're all fucking oh-I-love-her-so-much-she's-such-a-big-fat-goddess. You should hear yourself. You got me thinking about doing an intervention."

Gerald has adopted an earnest expression that doesn't quite cover up his underlying attitude, which you perceive now to be one of jealousy—you haven't been spending much time with him since you hooked up with Abi and he's taken it personally.

"I'm serious," he says. "I'm thinking about it."

"You're being a real asshole, y'know."

"You're the asshole! Letting this cow lead you around by the dick!"

You open the door and Gerald, angry now, says "Carole, man. She was hot. I can't figure why you broke up with her. But this one, she's got a butt on her looks like a bagful of oatmeal. Maybe you got a thing for chicks who look like your mom."

You jump out of the car, slam the door.

"Maybe you got a thing for your mom?" Gerald shouts. "Little Oedipal thing? Maybe that's why you're so into Miss Piggy!"

He says "edible" for "Oedipal." You tell yourself it's time you put high school behind you. Gerald's trapped in a universe of Tool concerts, stoner weekends at Rockaway Beach and raves in some scuzzy warehouse with underage girls on Ecstasy, whereas you have moved on. Steaming, you flip him off as he pulls away from the curb, shouting something about ". . . fat bitch!"

Abi stands at the edge of the garden, her fingers black from grubbing in the dirt, and there's a smudge on her chin, too, where she's wiped her face; strands of wet hair cling to her pale cheeks. She looks like a sexy vampire fresh from a dirt nap. "Hey, angel," she says, and asks who was the guy in the car and you say, "Just this assbag." From the way she kisses you, a promise of more and better to come, you imagine that she must have heard some of what Gerald had to say and the kiss is your reward for defending her.

Gerald's dismissal of Abi, however, has planted a seed and in the weeks that follow you spend a good deal of time wondering if your entire experience with her has been the product of a newly manifested perversion. The suspicion that your feelings might be unhealthy or somehow unreliable causes you to notice things about her that are less than ideal and you become aware that she's far from the perfect woman you described. Her refusal to talk about personal affairs now strikes you as pathological. While she'll go on at length, say, about the relationship between astrology and electro-magnetism, or the role of angels in human affairs, she's reluctant to speak of anything regarding your relationship. This frustrates you—it's like you've switched roles with her, like you're the sensitive woman and she's the uncommunicative guy. Equally frustrating is her tendency to talk about the end of the world as though it's already occurred. Because of this, it's impossible to make plans more than a couple of weeks in advance without prefacing the discussion by saying, "If we're still around . . ." or something of the sort; otherwise she'll point out the omission and maneuver the conversation onto a different track. Her passion for the rain seems demented, cracked, fetishistic; her diet gives you gas. Perhaps the most problematic of her flaws is a lack of empathy.

Crossing a Safeway parking lot with her one evening, you encounter a deaf couple having an argument, a man and a woman of late middle age, reeking of alcohol, wearing soiled down jackets and baseball caps. Instead of making delicate, quick speech with their hands, they jab at one another with fists and fingers, gesticulating wildly, their fury all the more intense for its silence. Abi laughs and says disdainfully, "From a distance you'd think they were Italian."

    Taken by itself, it's not an important failure. But it opens a door that's difficult to close and you're persuaded to believe that what appeared to indicate an insensitivity goes much deeper: Abi is contemptuous of everyone and, though you're getting the best part of her, the kisses, the smiles, the sex, you conclude that her passion for you must be counterfeit and what you have assumed to be gentle teasing in regard to the movies you like, the books you read, your favorite foods, everything, has always borne the stamp of contempt . . . and yet you refuse to accept this as true. Your ego won't permit it, nor will logic. If she feels nothing for you, why hook up with you? You decide you must be missing something. She displays such a narrow range of emotions, perhaps you're overlooking some nuance that distinguishes her disdain from her affection. You can't quite accept that, either (you're not sure which are less trustworthy, your judgments or her emotional responses), but it makes a good fallback position.

    One night, coming home late from lab, you round the corner onto your block and spot Abi standing in the doorway, dressed in her green silk robe, talking to two figures on the porch—they're partially silhouetted by the light issuing from inside the house and are wearing purple sweatshirts with the hoods up. You can't tell much about them, but you assume them to be men since they're considerably taller than Abi. Startled, because this is the first time you've seen her speak to anyone except busboys and waiters and the like, you slip behind a fir trunk across the street and spy on them. You can't hear what's being said, but every so often, over the ambient noise, you catch a fragment of a gruff voice. Abi stands with her arms folded; the men's hands are at their sides. Solicitors, you think. You get lots of Greenpeace people in the neighborhood, Secretaries For A Better Tomorrow, that sort of thing, most of whom Abi rebuffs, pissing them off by saying it's too late to save the planet their way. But that notion takes a hit when one of the men puts his hand on Abi's shoulder, a gesture you interpret as affirming, as if he's saying, Be strong or something similar. With that, the men trot down the steps and walk briskly away. As they pass beneath the streetlight, you notice their sweatshirts are identical, each bearing letters that spell out Washington Huskies Athletic Department. Their jeans and running shoes, also identical, look to be brand new, but the light shows nothing of their cowled faces. Abi gazes after them and, with a sharp glance in your direction, goes inside and shuts the door.

"I saw you lurking," she says as you enter and toss your pack on the sofa.

"I wasn't lurking."

"Do you always hide behind a tree before you come in?"

"I was surprised you had company."

"Well, if you'd acted normally, I could have introduced you."

"You should have called me over."

"I didn't want to interfere with your lurking."

She passes into the kitchen and you follow, watching her ass roll under the green silk.

"Who were they?" you ask.

"Just some friends. Mike and Rem Gregory. You'd like them." She peers inside the refrigerator.

"Rem? Like rapid eye movement? Like the band?"

She moves a Tupperware container aside. "I think it's short for something."

"So are they twins?"

She frowns at you over her shoulder. "No. Why would you say that?"

"Because they dress alike. You don't see a whole lot of that these days . . . adults dressing alike."

She takes out a bottle of water. "They're eccentric, but they're angels, really. I'll have them over to dinner some night."

"That's cool. Maybe next week sometime."

"They stopped by on their way out of town. I'm not sure when they're getting back."

"Yeah, well, let's do it for real. I'm looking forward to meeting them."

"For God's sake, stop it!" Abi gives an inarticulate yell and throws the bottle at you. Thankfully, it's plastic and her aim is off. "You're always picking at me! You're always prying and sneaking around!"

"What do you mean? I'm not sneaking around!"

"What do call hiding behind a tree? Then you stroll in asking all these questions about Mike and Rem."

"Are you insane? I was making conversation. I don't give a fuck about your fucking friends!"

Abi stares coldly at you; she takes off her pearl spider ring and sets it on the edge of the sink.

You laugh. "What . . . you gonna take a swing at me?"

"I'm insane, I'm liable to do anything."

"Calm down, all right?"

Without further warning, she hurls herself at you, scratching, clawing at your face, and slams you back into the stove. You cover up, but a fingernail clips you near the eye; you feel wetness on your cheek and push her away. She reels off-balance and goes staggering through a door that leads into a hallway. Her robe fallen open; breasts swaying; panting; hair in disarray; she looks like the poster girl for a bad acid trip. She rushes you again. This time you control her wrists, spin her around and the two of you go dancing across the kitchen. Momentum carries you out into the hallway, where you manage to pin her against the wall. She tries a knee that you block by flattening her with your body.

"Calm the fuck down!" you shout.

She snaps at you, snagging your lower lip. She struggles to break free, but gives it up after a few seconds. She slumps, her face empties.

"You okay?" You relax your grip slightly, and she tries to head butt you. "Goddamn it!" With your right hand, you clamp both her wrists above her head, and put your left hand at her throat to restrain her.

"Want to rough me up?" She lets out a peal of laughter that would not sound out of place echoing down the corridor of an asylum. "Come on! Rough me up!!"

"What the hell's wrong with you?"

"Can't you handle it?" She grinds her pelvis against you. "Come on, bitch!"

"Take it easy!"

She snaps at you again, but less fiercely, more a love bite, and keeps saying, half under her breath, "Come on, come on!", taunting you, turning the fight into animalistic foreplay. You're bleeding from the corner of your eye and from your lip, but you go with the moment and drag her into the bedroom, shove her down onto the bed. She raises her knees, opens to you, laughing now, and soon you're going at it like beasts.

You expect her to apologize afterward, but she merely inspects your wounds, says "You'll live," and then gets out of bed and slips on her robe.

You watch her searching for the sash. "Can I ask a question without setting you off?"

She finds the sash, ties it, sits on the bed. "Sure."

"Why do you get so defensive?"

"It's not defensiveness, it's I'm irritated. You do pry a lot. And that hiding-back-of-a-tree thing was just stupid."

"Maybe so, but you totally overreacted."

A shrug. "Didn't you have fun?"

"Fun? At the end I did. It wasn't much fun earlier."

"I enjoyed every minute."

It takes you a moment to absorb this. "You mean you weren't angry?"

"I was angry . . . but not that angry. I thought letting the anger out would be a healthy exercise."

She's a wholly different woman than she was a half-hour before. The way she's sitting there, fussing with the end of her sash, giving off a cheerful, self-possessed vibe. It's difficult to picture her shrieking, infuriated . . . though not so difficult as once it was.

"So you were . . ." You grope for the right word. "Acting out? We could've gotten hurt."

"I have complete confidence that you're my physical superior. I knew you wouldn't hurt me."

"You hurt me."

She makes a wry face. "Oh, yeah. You're scarred for life."

You tell her you don't see how going straight from minor disagreement to a violent confrontation is going to do other than muddy the waters.

"Do you feel muddied?" she asks. "I don't. I feel perfectly clear. And we went from a disagreement to violence to sex. You left out the sex." She stands, cinches the sash tighter. "Life is the reasoned exercise of passion. When it's not, it's death."

You're becoming accustomed to her use of homespun aphorisms, but still it tends to piss you off, as do the lectures that invariably follow. But you're too worn out by the reasoned exercise of passion to do other than listen.

"People today are like tigers who've forgotten how to be tigers," she says, moving toward the door. "Which explains why everything's so fucked. We have to teach ourselves to be tigers together. That's how we'll last. I realize I haven't been forthcoming with you, and I realize that makes you crazy, because you're the inquisitive type. We have to push back the limits slowly, gradually reveal our natures. You'll learn everything about me in time. And about yourself. Until then we need to snarl and claw on occasion, and let sex heal us." She pauses in the doorway, gives her sash a final tug. "Want something to eat?"

Each Friday you catch an early bus to the U District and prepare for your 11 o'clock seminar in one of the coffee shops along the Ave. One morning in late May, while you're poring over an article on protozoan genomes amid conversational clutter and the smells of exotic grinds, a little man stops beside your table, bracing on his cane. He's got snappish blue eyes edged by crowsfeet and deep lines bracketing his mouth and unkempt reddish-brown hair and beard that make it seem he's peering at you through a hedge. It's an odd face, an old young face like a leprechaun's. Hard to put an age to him. He could be in his late twenties or, just as easily, in his forties. He has on scruffy jeans and a denim jacket covered in patches that celebrate Jimi Hendrix, marijuana, Peter Tosh, and a sampling of leftist political causes. His torso is twisted—there appears to be something wrong with his spine. With a labored movement, he lowers himself into the chair opposite, draws a deep breath and releases it unsteadily.

"So you're her latest," he says; then he cocks his head and says in an altogether different voice, a reedy British voice, "Latest what?, you might ask. Lover? That would be the obvious assumption." He leans forward, pushing into your space. "Perhaps he's referring to something else. Something more sinister, eh?"

You're accustomed to being approached by whack jobs—the U District is their natural habitat—and experience has taught you to be brusque. Yet in this instance, you're pretty sure that "she" refers to Abi and you ask him what he's talking about.

"About Abimagique." He stares at you intently. "Your fat whore. Are you aware you're sleeping with a fucking monster?"

"Watch your mouth."

"It cost me a lot of pain to come here today, man. You need to hear this."

You begin stowing books and papers in your pack.

"My name's Richard Reiner," he says, and tries to connect with your eyes—you look away, make a pretense of signaling the waitress. Maybe he knows Abi, but he's still a whack job.

You tell him your name's Carl, thinking it would be unwise to tell this madman your actual name. His face tightens, he swallows dry. Managing his pain, you suppose.

"I met her five years ago," he says. "She wasn't my type, but there was something about her. You know what I mean. Once you hook up with her, it's like an addiction."

You say, "Yeah," to keep him moving along, certain that his experience with Abi—if, indeed, he had one—could have nothing in common with yours, though his reference to addiction strikes a chord.

"She lived in the same house, wore the same clothes. Looked the same. Nothing ever changes for her. Anyway, I moved in with her. Just like you."

"How do you know that? About me moving in?"

"Because I been checking you out, *Carl*," he says, giving the name a sardonic emphasis. "You want to be Carl, that's fine with me. But don't think . . ."

You zip up the backpack, scrape back your chair.

"Hey! Where you going?" Reiner grips your forearm, but you shake him off. You've heard enough to validate your judgment. The guy's a flake, possibly a dangerous stalker.

"The thing she does when you fuck," he says. "The thing with your lower back? You don't want to let her do that anymore."

That surprises you. Angry at Abi for using that trick, one you've come to relish, with another man, and angry at Reiner for forcing you to confront what seems, against ordinary logic, an intimate betrayal on her part, you ask, "Why not?"

"She'll turn you into a cripple, man. Before she did it to me, my spine wasn't a fucking corkscrew. I could walk more than ten steps without having to stop. That shit she makes you eat . . . all that fucking seaweed and algae and herbs. I think that's tied with it. I think it makes you susceptible. Or maybe there's drugs in it and that's how she keeps you under control." He grabs your arm again as you try to stand. "It's the truth!! I was her first . . ."

The waitress materializes and you order another Americano, tell her you'll pick it up at the counter. She asks Reiner what he's having and he says impatiently, "Nothing, okay?" and glares at her until she walks away. "I was the first," he goes on. "But she's done it to six other guys. There might be more, for all I know. Here . . ." He two-fingers a piece of paper from his shirt pocket and pushes it toward you. You unfold the paper and look at the six names and addresses written thereon. One, belonging to someone named Phil Minz, sticks in your mind, because it's in a building where you used to live.

"She must have fucked it up with me," Reiner says. "Punched the wrong buttons. Or maybe she just needed more practice, because the others are all in wheelchairs."

"I have a class," you say.

"You're not hearing me!" Reiner slaps the table, frustrated. "I used to be into it, man. Way she'd slip her hands down there and start poking around. I was like all . . ." He puts on a show of panting rapidly, like a dog. "I couldn't wait for her to set me off. And then this one day, it was like she hits me with the A-bomb. I was fucking drooling. In a stupor. Jesus couldn't have made me feel any better. The next morning, I was all seized up. Not like I am now. It got worse over a period of about six weeks. But she did it to me. The doctors, they can't say what happened. When I tell 'em, they don't come right out and laugh, but . . . ." Reiner leans back and rests his cane across his knees. "You're not laughing. You know what I'm talking about."

His manner seems rational, though what he's telling you does not. Yet you've had a recurrence of back trouble since you and Abi became lovers, and you've been blaming it on too much sex. "Why would she do that?" you ask. "Even if she could . . . which I'm not buying."

"You want to understand her motivations, ask her. I thought maybe she'd messed up with me. Y'know, like it was some kind of dangerous technique and she went too far. But six other guys, that tells me different."

You stand and shoulder your pack.

"C'mon, man! Talk to her! If it's bullshit, what's the fuck's the harm in talking?"

The waitress pops back over and cautions you to keep it down or you'll have to leave.

"I'm leaving," you say.

Reiner struggles to his feet. "You want to end up like this . . . or worse? Do you?"

You make silent apology to the waitress, slip her a couple of dollars.

"What do you think I'm doing here?" says Reiner as you head for the door. "I'm trying to break you two up? I want to spare you from suffering my fate? I'm crazy but well-intentioned? Fuck you! I want you to make the bitch pay! After that you can fucking die!"

That night before making love, lying with Abi in bed, you tell her about Reiner and show her the list of addresses. Her silence makes you feel contrite, as if you're confessing, as if you're guilty for having listened to Reiner. When you're done, when she says, "I'm sorry," it's like she's bestowing a benediction.

"What're you sorry for?" you ask. "Some whacko running around saying shit? I shouldn't even have told you."

"You needed to tell me," she says. "Otherwise I couldn't clear things up."

"You don't have to clear anything up. I only told you because I thought you'd want to know."

She shifts closer, a breast nudging your arm. "Richard was a client. He's right about one thing. I did make a mistake with him, I got too involved. When I broke it off, I tried to maintain the friendship, but . . . I should have seen how psychologically damaged he was. He became irrational. He accused me of making him worse. Now he's taken it a step further."

You rush to assure her everything's cool, you didn't give what Reiner said any weight, but she goes on as if she hasn't heard.

"The diet," she says. "I'm trying to keep us healthy. I realize it's not what you're used to, but . . . I don't know. I can try fixing you a separate meal. I won't cook meat, though. I don't even want it in the house. If you need meat, you'll have to get it somewhere else. This . . ." She reaches behind her and fumbles for the list. "These are some of my current clients. They are in wheelchairs, but all of my clients are incapacitated in some way. I'm not sure how he got their names. Perhaps he followed me." She lets the scrap of paper fall between you. "If you don't want me to manipulate your back when we make love, I understand."

"No, I mean, if you want to, it's all right." You're eager to compensate for the weakness you've shown, for half-believing a lunatic, for injuring her.

"I do it to increase our pleasure. To hurry you, so you'll come when I do. I like it when we finish together."

"I do, too."

"Yeah?"

"Yeah."

You kiss, you apologize for doubting her, she apologizes for getting mad, you say you didn't notice, her anger as mild as her passion, and you kiss again, a deeper kiss. Soon you're moving together and the shadows crouched in the corners, the hum and gurgle of the pump on the empty aquarium, the candle flames on the night table flickering . . . you're aware of these things as extensions of her. They're her shadows, her flames, her humid breath. Even you are in process of becoming her, an immersion in another human being such as you've never known before, and when her hands slide down to the small of your back, her touch tentative, you encourage her, you submit to her. Afterward, dim with pleasure, you recall what Reiner said, how he didn't notice any ill effects until the next day. But you're secure in the moment and, holding Abi spoon style, you indulge in one of those passages that come to lovers during which they ask questions that seek to annotate their relationship, trivial questions like, When did you know? and What did you feel then? and When was the first time you looked at me . . . I mean really looked? You find yourself asking what was it that attracted her to you? She says it wasn't anything specific. But you insist, you say, "There must've been something you noticed first."

"Your eyes," she says. "Your beautiful blue eyes. I'd like to have babies with those eyes."

This being the first mention ever of babies, you're a little uneasy, but you decide she's speaking more-or-less in the abstract.

"Yeah," you say, trying to sound on the positive side of neutral. "That'd be nice someday."

She makes a forlorn noise and says, "I don't know if there'll be time."

After puzzling over the comment, you realize it probably refers to her sense of foreboding about an imminent doomsday. You've begun to think that her obsession with the end of the world is responsible for her emotional detachment and that she doesn't allow herself to become exuberant about anything, because she sees the inevitable downside. You don't know what to tell her, so you hold her more tightly. Ten or fifteen seconds flow past and she says, "I don't believe you understand how serious things are."

You're astonished that she wants to get into this now, that she's willing to trash the afterglow in order to pound on the lectern and talk about the death of nations. You start to say as much, but she cuts you off.

"No, listen! It's very important that you listen," she says. "Our future depends on it."

You tell her, grumpily, to go ahead.

"I know you think I'm a nut . . ."

"That's not true."

"Yes, it is." She disengages from you, rolls onto her back and locks you with her eyes. "You humor me. You love me in spite of it. But you think I'm nuts. That's all right. I'm used to it. And I realize nothing I say now is going to change things. But I want you to try, hard as you can, to give me the benefit of the doubt."

"Of course I will. You know . . ."

She puts a finger to your lips. "Just listen. I want you to try to accept that I know certain things, things you don't know. And I want you to try to accept that this knowledge has an important application. You won't be able to do it right away, but I want you to try in any case, because there's going to come a moment when you'll have to trust me. And if you don't, everything we've working toward will be destroyed."

"I'm . . . What am I supposed to trust you about?"

"Everything. You'll have to place your trust in me completely. Do you think you can do that? No matter how things look? I think you can. I think we have that kind of potential."

"It sounds like you're talking about something dangerous."

"Love's dangerous," she says. "And these are dangerous times to be in love. Do you believe that?"

How can you disbelieve such a melodramatic challenge, with her eyes boring into you and her breath heating your skin?

"Promise you'll always remember this conversation," she goes on. "If you do, if you can remember us, the way we are this minute, everything will be all right."

The pump gurgles loudly, the hum cycles down, and the damp smell of the firs is carried inward on a breeze

"Do you trust me?" you ask.

"I'm trying to."

"Then why not tell me what's up? And this stuff about you knowing things I don't . . . what do you know? What's the situation going to be when I have to trust you completely?"

"I think for us," she says, "trust has to be like when we make love. It has to come together, you giving your trust and me giving mine, at the moment when we want it the most."

You're uncertain of the metaphor, but you think you understand what she means.

"Promise me," she demands, pressing her body against you.

Though you're no longer clear as to what you're promising, you promise. She clasps your head in both her hands and looks at you for a long time, searching below the surface glints and gleams for whatever hides in you from ordinary light. At last, apparently satisfied, she pulls you close and tells you all the things she wants you to do to her, whispering them sweetly, almost demurely, as if concerned that God and his angels might overhear.

Over the summer, you give up hamburgers. You've become so accustomed to Abi's food that even the smell of a burger makes you nauseous. It's a small thing to have given up—you've never been so happy. The way things are going, if you and Abi were traditional types, you'd be renting out a church and looking into rings. You run into Reiner occasionally and whenever he tries to accost you, you sprint away, leaving him to yell some madness about Abi in your wake. One day in the fall, you're coming back from a meeting with your thesis committee, a distinctly unpleasant meeting, your work's been slipping badly, and Reiner limps from the doorway of a used CD store directly into your path. Your temper flares and you push him back into the doorway and tell him to keep the fuck away from you or you'll bring in the cops.

His laughter has an unsound ring. "You can't threaten a dead man."

You become aware again of your surroundings, of passers-by slowing their pace and staring, of two long-haired guys inside the CD store who appear ready to intervene, to rescue the cripple, and you take a step back.

"Those addresses I gave you . . . you never checked them out, did you?" Reiner asks. "You haven't done anything."

You start to turn away, but he grabs a handful of your jacket and hangs on. "What'll it cost you to check 'em out? Just check out one of 'em!"

"They're her clients, man!"

"She made them her clients! She crippled them."

You twist free of his grasp.

"You still have the addresses?" Reiner asks.

You tell him you do, you'll check them out, and hurry off.

"Didn't she even leave you one ball?" he shouts.

The scrap of paper bearing the addresses is long gone, but you still remember the one, the building you used to live in, and a month later, walking past that building, you have a what-the-hell moment and stop to inspect the directory. Phil Minz, 1F. Once inside, you walk down a corridor past apartments A through E, and catch sight of a harried-looking gray-haired man wearing a coverall coming out of F, preparing to lock the door. You inquire of him and he tells you that Minz moved out last week. They took him, he thinks, to a clinic somewhere. Maybe in California. He's only now getting around to inspecting the place.

"The apartment's available?" you ask.

"Yeah, but I won't be showing it until after it's cleaned."

"Can I take a look?"

He hesitates.

"You know how hard it is to find an apartment this close to the campus," you tell him. "Let me take a quick look?"

A beat-up sofa in the living room, some paper trash on the floor. The back room is empty but for a queen-sized bed stripped of covers and, on a counter recessed in the wall, an aquarium filled with greenish water, pump gurgling, empty of fish.

"Guy left his fish tank behind," the super says unnecessarily.

"What kind of fish did he have?" You peer into the tank, searching for signs of habitation, for algae, fish grunge, food debris. Thoughtful of them to clean a tank that was going to be abandoned.

"Hell, I don't know." The super joins you at the tank and for a second you're both peering into it, like curious giants into a tiny lifeless sea. "I never had to come into the apartment when he was here."

The presence of an empty fish tank is an odd coincidence, but you doubt it's other than that. It's conceivable that Abi thought the sound of the pump might soothe her patient, and it's more likely that she had nothing whatsoever to do with it, that there were fish in the tank and someone did a cleaning. You promise yourself that you won't let Reiner undermine your feelings anymore. Abi's flaws aren't mysterious or sinister. They're human flaws and if they have an underlying explanation, it must have something to do with her past, with whatever secret she's keeping. She says that someday she'll tell you about it. Someday when the two of you are closer.

"Closer? We've been together for months," you say. "What's it going to take?"

"You don't think we can be closer? I do, I believe we've got a miles to go."

The way she deflects your question with half a compliment, half a criticism, implying that the relationship has room to grow and at the same time telling you it's imperfect—you understand she has the ability to outflank you, that she can switch subjects or turn a conversation into a guilt trip, and you'll fall into her trap every time. It make you crazy. She plays this game so much better than you, it would be pointless to keep pressing her. But you press her anyway and, a few weeks before Thanksgiving, exasperated, she says, "Let's get through the holidays, all right? Then we'll have a talk."

You're not sure what's going to be so difficult about getting through the holidays, since they're the same for her as other days—she attends neither parties nor religious services, and invites no one over to the house. Yet you don't care. At least there's a firm date set for clearing up the mystery.

*E*ither you're crippled, lying in Minz's bed, Apartment 1F, staring at the aquarium, empty of water, or you're dreaming that you're crippled—whichever, it's more vivid than you want it to be. Your vision is blurry and your thoughts are muddled by meds that aren't doing their job. The least movement triggers intense pain in your lower back; your spine feels brittle. Abi, naked and hugely pregnant, is standing next to the bed. You call out to her—you're dying of thirst, you require different meds—but she doesn't even twitch. She's a lifelike statue to which a neatly trimmed strip of pubic hair, nipple rings and a genital piercing, glinting silver in its rosy cleft, have been applied. Hands resting on her swollen belly, staring into nowhere. Yet despite her silence and immobility, she seems to have a more genuine reality than the rest of the room. She dims and brightens as if, somewhere out of view, thick curtains are blowing in and out, each billow altering the light. Her breasts, delicately clawed by stretch marks, milk-heavy, nipples distended, areola darkened and warped into oval irregularities, seem more the emblem of her pregnancy than her belly. Their taut skin has a waxy sheen. You imagine a bowlful of them, Still Life With Humongous Tits, on the night table by the bed, placed there for your nourishment, like those wax confections from childhood made to resemble pop bottles and holding flavored syrup.

You gaze at the ceiling, seeking solace in the patterns that melt up from the wormy patterns of paint, but they yield a medieval imagery that's not in the least consoling: a solitary hooded rider shouldering a scythe, mounted on a skeleton horse; a reclining giant, propped on his side, examining a gaping wound in his belly from which tiny men and women dressed in medieval fashion are escaping; a man with a stylized crescent moon for a head and a red lolling tongue. You close your eyes, hoping for someone to come, and before long two men in purple hooded sweatshirts wheel a big-screen TV into the room, plug it in, and toss the remote on the bed. You assume them to be Mike and Rem, Abi's friends, but you're frightened of them. They're much taller than you thought, both almost seven feet, and their faces are shadowed, indistinct . . . and that's not a product of your blurry vision. It's as if their features are being manufactured out of the dark stuff that's in flux beneath their hoods. Once they finish with the TV, they lift Abi—she remains rigid, hands clamped onto her belly, legs straight, like a mannequin—and stand her next to the aquarium. One presses a spot on the small of her back and her belly opens like a Chinese puzzle, two panels with interlocking teeth that fit together perfectly, their joins invisible to the eye. Inside is a many-galloned bottle full of greenish water. This they remove and empty into the aquarium; they switch on the pump. Then they close up Abi's belly and carry her into the front room, handling her more easily now that she's lighter. You've watched all this transpire in a state of shock, but now, horrified, you struggle to get to your feet. That failing, you rack your brain for a means of escape. After a while, having nothing better to do, you hit the power button on the remote.

The men bring you food. Cookies, potato chips, sandwiches, ice cream. They also bring meds and provide you with a wheelchair. Desperation fades beneath an onslaught of calories, drugs, and soap operas. Now and then you try to come up with a plan, but you can't walk and the men, who station themselves in the front room, check on you frequently, so you can't shout or wave out a window or toss down messages into the parking lot. You begin to tell time by what's on TV. It's half past *The Amazing Race* or a quarter to the *Guiding Light*. You drowse, eat, fall asleep watching a movie on the SciFi Channel, eat, wake to *Sportscenter*, develop an interest in *Law and Order* reruns, in celebrity. You think Oprah's a beast no matter how many pounds she loses; and you decide that although Donald Trump serves the Evil One, he's just an enormously powerful nerd; you hope the blond girl wins on *American Idol* and you can't wait for the new season of *Battlestar Galactica*. You speculate that it might be possible to conduct a conversation upon any subject by limiting yourself to the career of John Travolta as a metaphorical construction. The only things that undergo a change in your environment are your weight—you're getting fat—and the aquarium, in which a number of white sporelike things, perhaps a hundred of them, are floating.

The appearance of the spores, if that's what they are, causes a renewal of desperation. Since they were bred in water removed from Abi's belly, you're forced to accept that they well may be her children . . . and yours. This notion kindles dread in you and, when next they bring food, you beg one of the men for help. His head swivels toward you and for an instant the lineaments of a disfigured face surface from the turbulent flow of dark matter. He makes a noise like static heard underwater, a faint seething, and leaves you quaking and alone amid a pile of fried fruit pies and doughnuts and potato chips . . . Maui Sweet Onion chips, you see on picking up the bag. Excellent!

Your fear abates the next day, your attention captivated by an *X-Files* marathon, and it abates still more when you realize that the number of spores has diminished. Some of them are turning into tadpoles that eat the remaining spores. Once the spores are gone, a process that occupies about two weeks, the tadpoles begin to eat each other, until finally a single white fish, the exact shade of white as Abi's skin, circulates in the tank. Mike and Rem feed it daily and it grows fatter and more active while you fatten and grow sluggish. You become accustomed to its presence. That it may be your child amuses you. Boy or girl?, you wonder. You decide it's a boy and name your son Gerald. Despite your amusement, there's a horrific tinge to these thoughts, but the men have increased the strength of your meds and you can't take anything seriously.

You sleep most of the days, waked by an internal alarm clock in time to catch your favorite shows, and when you manage to think at all, you think about Abi. You miss her. Not the inhuman Abi, the vessel you filled, but the Abi you imagined her to be. You miss her so very much that you weep at the slightest emotional cue. You remember the good times, kissing in the rain, making love, listening to her disparage diners in restaurants, passers-by, people on TV. . . you even miss the massage technique that left you a cripple. You take to watching the Lifetime Movie Channel because it enlists these same emotions, and you sob in sympathy with the plight of battered wives, rape victims, girls on the run from lustful dads, women with deceitful lovers and abducted children.

One morning you wake to discover that Gerald's not in his tank. A large damp spot stains the carpeting beneath the tank, and a trail of wetness leads toward the foot of your bed. You try to sit up, wanting to learn if Gerald's still alive, but Mike and Rem have increased your meds again—you can barely lift your head. You shout out to them, you want them to save Gerald, to restore him to the tank, but no one responds. They haven't been in to check on you for two days now and Gerald must be starving. No wonder he hurled himself onto the floor. The bedspread tightens convulsively down by your feet, as if it's being tugged, and the next thing you know, Gerald heaves up onto the bottom of the bed. His fins have developed into primitive hands, and he's half-wriggling, half-hauling himself along, moving past your ankle. He's even bigger than you thought, he must weigh nearly three pounds. His face is an obscene caricature of the human, a squashed, round, dolorous face gashed by a wide mouth that sports rows of barracuda-like teeth. A chill apprehension steals over you. With another heave, he succeeds in flopping up onto your pelvis, where he snoots at the spread overlying your genitals. His glabrous skin shows a tracery of blue subcutaneous veins, like Abi's breasts. He has your eyes . . .

As absurd as this nightmare is, as explicable in terms of its imagery, it unnerves you. You can't get it out of your head. The next morning, newly suspicious, you go through Abi's address book and copy down the names of her male clients. It's not that you believe she intends you harm, you tell yourself. You're the one with a problem. It's your ambivalence toward her that's causing you to pursue these fantasies. You did the same thing more-or-less with Carole, suspecting her of cheating on you, then dumping her before she could. By making a thorough investigation, you're certain you'll be able to defuse your suspicions and defang your nightmares.

You dedicate the weeks after Thanksgiving to checking out Abi's clients. Your master's thesis is circling the drain, but you hope that by cutting classes following a vacation holiday, you can build the grounds for an excuse, an emotional crisis, illness in the family, something, and perhaps your committee will be lenient. You don't much care one way or the other, though. The relationship is what's important. Five of Abi's clients have moved away, including Phil Minz. With the others, you pretend to be taking a survey for a study designed to improve handicapped services. Those you interview during the first week have all been injured prior to meeting Abi and have discernable reasons for their disability, whether disease or accident or congenital defect. Your investigation doesn't seem to be leading anywhere and you think you must be coming down with something. Your energy's depleted, you're running a mild fever, and you're having trouble concentrating. To top things off, Reiner has re-entered your life, popping up here and there in the U District and shouting profane threats then hurrying away. Two or three more days, you decide. After that, you'll pack it in.

On Tuesday of the second week, you interview one Nathan Sessions, a muscular black guy with a spinal injury who's three years older than you. He opens the door wearing gym shorts and a gray T-shirt, a pair of dumbbells resting on his lap, and asks if you would mind talking in his bedroom? He's been exercising and would like to lie down. As he precedes you in his wheelchair, you observe a backwards 7 tattooed at the base of his neck and, when you enter the bedroom, you see an aquarium set on a table, almost obscured behind stacks of books, pump gurgling merrily. No fish. Books are scattered about the room, on the floor, in chairs. The pile on the chair beside the bed, which you clear in order to sit, consists of works treating with the nature of time. A sheet of paper falls out of one; on it, the word "Bottom" and, depended beneath it, a list of numbers that appear to be longitudes and latitudes. You ask him about it, and he takes the paper, peers at it, shakes his head, and says, "I had a geography class last semester. Must be some old notes or something."

With practiced agility and a notable lack of effort, Sessions transitions between the chair and his bed, settles himself, and cheerfully tells you to fire away. After a battery of inessential questions, you ask how he came by his disability. He says it's a degenerative condition that relates to an injury he suffered on the wrestling team back in high school, and was later exacerbated when he was "messing around." His attitude strikes you as buoyant and energized—you remark that he seems extraordinarily well-adjusted compared to others you've interviewed.

"Why shouldn't I be?" he says. "I'm more alive now than I ever was. I can't begin to tell you how much my life's improved."

"What do you mean? How's it improved?"

"Before I was paralyzed, I was bored with my life . . . though I didn't understand it that way. Not so I could say it. I wasn't interested in the world, except for the pleasure it could give me. Now I'm interested in things. Passionately interested. There's not enough time in the day. I suppose my attitude's partly compensatory. I'm determined not to get depressed."

This seems right out of the Abimagique textbook of new age morality, and you wonder if Sessions actually feels that way or if he's been drinking the Kool Aid. You wonder also if that's a meaningful distinction.

"There must be some things you miss," you say.

"If I sit and think about it . . . sure. I don't like being in crowds anymore. Can't see over people. Things like that. But I don't worry about that shit. I've got too much else going on."

Employing as much sensitivity as possible, you ask about sex.

Sessions fold his arms and gives you a cool stare. "Isn't that outside the scope of your survey?"

"Not really. I'm hoping to get a complete profile on everyone I interview. That way, when I analyze it, I'll be dealing with more than just statistics. If you prefer not to answer . . ."

"No, it's fine. I'm fully functional."

You pretend to make a note. "Isn't that unusual with spinal injuries?"

Sessions starts to respond, pauses, and then says, "My massage therapist, she . . ."

It seems that he's debating whether or not he wants to touch upon the subject of his therapist. You wait for him to continue.

"Okay," says Sessions. "My therapist . . . we had a thing, you know. She did stuff to my body, man, that you wouldn't believe. With her knowledge of muscles and the chakras, you know. She really got me off. Especially when she did this thing with my back. It was incredible. So one morning after we had sex, I woke up with bad pain in my back and I couldn't move my legs. My doctor said it would have happened eventually, anyway. But what she did probably accelerated the deterioration. I was pissed, man. Full of negativity. But Abi, my therapist, she wouldn't let me cop an attitude. She brought me back physically and mentally. She helped me with my diet, my rehab."

"She must have had a lot of guilt."

"With Abi . . . she's not easy to figure out. But I never tripped on her about what happened, you know. I was the one begging her to do her thing, so it's on me."

It appears that Sessions has said all he intends to about the subject and you're having difficulty framing a question that will start him up again, one that won't give away your position—you're not sure about Sessions's disposition toward Abi. It's possible he's her complicitor, though to think that would be quintessential paranoia, and the question arises, complicit in what?

"That's a cool tattoo on your neck," you say. "The backwards seven."

"It not a seven, it's a letter in the Hebrew alphabet. I had it done when I was with Abi. She's got one like it."

"Does it stand for anything?"

"It's got something to do with angels." Sessions shifts uneasily, flicks a glance at the door, as if expecting someone.

"Seems like this woman's been a big influence on every part of your life."

"Oh, yeah. Abi's unique. If I told you some of the stuff she can do . . . Man!"

"Like for instance?"

"That's okay," says Sessions. "You can live without hearing it. I'll tell you this much. She made me realize that we can change our destinies. Abi's all about destiny. Hers, mine . . . everyone's. She's trying to change the world, and I think she just might do it."

"How's she going to change it?"

"By changing the planet's dharma."

It's a rote answer, glibly stated, and you don't know how to respond; you shuffle your papers, pretending to be searching for something. "So you're not with her anymore?"

"We're doing a project together, but we're not . . . like we were." A distracted expression comes over Sessions's face. "Listen, I need to get working here."

"You mean work on the project?" Grasping at straws, you pick up one of the books you cleared off the seat. "Does it have anything to do with time?"

Sessions swings himself back into his chair and precedes you toward the door, obviously eager to have you gone. "That's right, man. There's never enough of it. We need to make some more."

The Hebrew letter tattooed on Sessions's neck and Abi's thigh is *Chof.* As far as you can determine, there's no connection whatsoever between this letter and the various hierarchies of angels, but while searching the internet for such a connection, you happen across a webpage entitled Fallen Angels, a section devoted to a group of such angels known as the Grigori, also known as the Watchers. According to the page, they looked like men, only larger, and were appointed by God to be the shepherds of mankind, there to instruct and lend a helping hand when necessary, but never to interfere in the course of human development. Sort of like that Federation rule, the Prime Directive, that Captain Kirk used to break every other episode of *Star Trek.* The Grigori, too, broke the Prime Directive by teaching mankind the forbidden sciences of astrology, divination, herb craft, and magic (the very disciplines, you note, in which Abi claims proficiency). To compound their sin, they began to lust after human women, to cohabit and have children with them. For this, they were banished from Heaven. Two of the princes of the Grigori were the angels Michael and Remiel.

Mike and Rem Gregory.

Abi's friends, the purple sweatshirt non-twins.

. . . they're angels, really . . .

You wish you hadn't stumbled across the webpage; you don't want conjecture about angels, or any peripheral matter, cluttering up your head and interfering with your ability to make judgments, now the essential circumstance that's confusing you has been revealed. Though Reiner and Sessions corroborate each other's story to an extent, the stories have different outcomes. Sessions may have been under pressure to tell you what he did—that could explain his haste in getting rid of you; but his anxiety could be also be chalked up to boredom or, as he indicated, to time considerations. Whatever, the bottom line is clear. Either you're misinterpreting a series of coincidences, or Abi is serially fucking and crippling clients for purposes unknown, purposes that may involve the complicity of angels and will, if Sessions is to be believed, affect all of mankind.

After interviewing everyone on Abi's client list, you conclude that if Reiner is correct in his assertion, if she's crippled six other men aside from him, five of them must be the five who have moved away from Seattle, because—except for Sessions—none of the rest qualify. Accepting Reiner's thesis that he was Abi's mistake, those five men plus Sessions plus you equals seven, the same number as Abi's tattoo... yet according to Sessions, it's not a backwards seven, it's *Chof,* thus the number seven is irrelevant. Maybe it's both a seven and a Hebrew letter. Maybe an upside-down L, too. You can't fit all the details into a single theory. Angels, sevens and Hebrew letters, time, empty aquariums, Abi transforming men into cripples, the end of the world, etc.—you consider the possibility that one or more of the details may be extraneous, and if you removed it from the mix, the rest would cohere. That's the crux of your problem. Your witnesses are unreliable. Reiner's vituperation and Sessions's nervous evangelism equally nourish your capacity for doubt and serve to cast everything you yourself have witnessed in a shaky light. You can't tell how much to keep of what they've said and how much to throw away. Confronting Abi won't provide an answer. She'll only dissemble, or she'll speak the truth and you'll mistake it for dissembling.

You finally come down with whatever it is you've been coming down with and are dog-sick for two weeks, debilitated for several days thereafter. Abi nurses you through the illness, a consolation for which you're slavishly grateful, but your gratitude is tempered by the dreams that accompany your fever. In their basic architecture, they're similar to the dream you had about your son, the fish—you're crippled, bedridden, but instead of occupying an apartment, you're in Abi's house. From those fundamentals, the dreams diverge wildly in character and have different endings, some ordinary, some dire, some ecstatic, some perplexing. Especially memorable is a dream in which Abi proves to be a mental patient escaped from an asylum in the future, and has come back to the twenty-first century to save the planet, but bungles the job. In one, she assumes the role of an alien, a member of an invasion force bent on destroying the environment; in another, she's a sexual demoness, a spirit named Lilith devoted to torturing young men; in another yet, she's a Gaian incarnation with noble intentions and extraordinary powers. In the remaining two dreams (there are six in all, seven if you count the one with the fish) she's the Abi with whom you're familiar, a human female. In the first of these, she makes your life hellish with her psychotic fits, eventually setting fire to the house and incinerating you both; in the second, she nurses you back to health, you walk again, and the two of you embark upon a life of accomplishment and good works.

The dreams are exceptionally vivid and too organized to be typical expressions of your subconscious, but you don't concern yourself with them until they begin showing up in rerun, variants of each repeating night after night (except for the nightmare about the fish, which never resurfaces). The most significant variant elements are the endings: the dream about the time traveler, for instance, ended badly the first time, but ends well in rerun. The aquarium, Rem and Mike, and other facets of your life with Abi figure in all of them to one degree or another. You wonder if Abi's responsible for the dreams, if she's gotten into your head that deeply. But then you imagine that you may be on the wrong track altogether. Suppose you and she are at the center of a cosmic hiccup, an eddy in time, a branch poking up from the surface, disordering the flow, that must be cleared before the temporal stream can resume its customary race? The way the dreams are circulating in your head lends a physical resonance to this idea and you have the sense that you've given up your destiny to a game of musical chairs; when the music stops, you'll be stuck with one of six possibilities. In essence, if not in actuality, you'll wind up with a well-intended madwoman from the future, an ordinary psychotic, a seeker after truth, an alien, a sexual predator, or a goddess. It's ridiculous, you think. Yet each of these roles signifies a color you have assigned to Abi's character at some point or another, and you can't avoid the feeling that one of your dreams will come true.

You understand that you should put some distance between yourself and Abi, that the relationship has become entirely too unrealistic—in your head, anyway—and you should tell her that you need some time apart; but the thing is, aside from the fact that you love her, this has all come to seem normal, this world of mystic possibility, of dreams and portents, of secrets and Tantric orgasm. You're dizzy with it, yet you don't mind being dizzy, you've come to enjoy the spins, the drama, the meta-fictional weirdness. As is the case with Abi's food, you've adapted to her ways and you don't believe you can function without them. It could be simply that you've gone too far—or are too far gone—to jump ship. You're in a canoe going over a falls, right at the edge, and it makes no sense to start swimming now.

*T*he day after Christmas, 2004. You wake early, before first light and, leaving a note for Abi, who's still asleep, you go for a walk. You intend it to be a short walk, but the day dawns clear and crisp, a rare sun break in the gloom of winter, and you keep on walking until you reach the U District. Around 8:30, you're idling along the Ave, browsing store windows, and there's hardly any traffic, pedestrian or otherwise, but suddenly there's Reiner, recognizable by his cane, his crookedness, standing on the opposite side of the street about a half block away. In reflex, you start down a side street, but decide that this would be a good time to deal with him, with nobody about. As you draw abreast of him, he stares at you grimly, but doesn't speak or try to approach. Though easier to live with than his curses, his silent regard is disconcerting, and you suspect that he sees some new crookedness in you that has made you not worth hassling.

You call Abi, but she's not up or not answering; you step into a chapati place, recently opened, and order the Mandalay Combo, watch patches of ice melting on the asphalt outside. Once you've eaten, you call Abi again—she's still not answering—and head home, keeping to the sunny side of the street. By the time you reach the house, it's gotten cloudy and colder. You hear the TV muttering in the bedroom as you enter. Abi's sitting in the chair by the window, still wearing her robe, watching CNN. "I tried to call," you say, and fling yourself down onto the bed. On the screen, in a tropical setting, people are weeping, being consoled, digging into a wreckage of palm litter and concrete. You ask what happened and Abi says it was a tsunami.

"A tidal wave?"

"Yes."

She makes it clear that she's in no mood to talk. The screen shows a replay of the wave, caught on tourist video, striking a Thai resort; then a pulsing red dot in the Indian Ocean with little cartoon waves radiating away from it to strike the coasts of Sri Lanka, India, Thailand, Indonesia. The death toll, it's estimated, may rise into the hundreds of thousands. A commercial for L'Oreal intercuts the news and you try once again to talk with Abi, but she flounces out of the room, goes to stand by the kitchen sink, staring out the window into the back yard. Her shields are up, maximum power, and she's sealed inside her envelope of intimacy-rejecting force. Though you follow her, you don't say a word. You sit at the kitchen table and wait for her to speak.

"I knew this would happen," she says without turning from the window.

With anyone else, you would offer comforting platitudes, but she takes these natural disasters personally; platitudes would only provoke her.

"I didn't know it would be today." Her voice catches. "Over the holidays . . . yeah. But I didn't expect it today."

You stretch out your legs, enlace your hands behind your head.

"Aren't you going to say anything?" She whirls on you, her face full of strain, spoiling for a fight, needing to vent the frustration and pain she feels. You no longer doubt that she feels it. She has this general empathy, this overweening concern for the species, though she seems to lack empathy in the specific; you remain dubious as to its authenticity, thinking that she may be like a Method actress, submerged in her role.

"What can I say? This is so huge, you can't feel it. Maybe *you* can, but it's tough for me. I walk in and see a little red dot on the TV and cartoony wave symbols striking map countries. It might as well be a hundred thousand cartoon people are dead." You shake your head, as if sadly bewildered. "I think there's something that protects most people from feeling so much death. A basic indifference that kicks in when it's needed. You don't seem to have that protection."

Practice makes perfect. Whether or not it's bullshit, you've said exactly the right thing; perhaps you even halfway believe it. Mollified, she sits beside you and caresses your arm. "I'm sorry," she says. "You know how I get."

You shrug. "It's okay."

She draws circles on your arm with a finger. "I have to start making things ready."

"Things?"

"Me, mostly. I have to prepare myself."

You've got a feeling of prickly numbness in your left foot, sciatic damage from the old car accident, and you react to this with a noise that, it appears, she assumes to be a sign of disapproval.

Exasperated, she says, "Do you remember the conversation we had months ago? I told you I wanted you to accept that I knew some things you didn't?"

"Yeah."

"I knew this would happen in late two-thousand-and-four. I didn't know what form it would take, but I knew where, more-or-less, and I knew it would involve water. In two-thousand-and-eight there'll be a second cataclysmic event. Much worse than this. In Latin America, I think. It'll involve the earth. Maybe a quake . . . I'm not sure. From that point on, there'll be a string of disasters, all coming close together. In two-thousand-twelve . . . it ends."

"The disasters end?"

"Everything ends. I can't explain it. I could make up a story that would present an explanation, but no matter how hard I tried to be truthful, it would be so far off the mark, it might as well be a lie. I could tell you I've seen it happen, but how I've seen it, it's too diffuse to explain. What you said about me not being protected like most people? That's more accurate than you know. I've exposed myself to a force that . . . " She clicks her teeth in frustration. "If I could explain it to anyone, I'd explain it to everyone. All I can do at this point is try to remedy it."

"This remedy," you say, recalling Sessions and his books. "Does it have anything to do with time?"

"Yes, partly. And the Tantra . . . and other things." She gives you a sharp look. "How did you know?"

You're tempted to lie, but can't come up with one that would be persuasive. "I talked to Nathan Sessions."

"Nathan? How did you . . . ?" She breaks off. "You looked at my client list."

"I needed to know what was going on. You wouldn't tell me, so . . . yeah."

"What did Nathan tell you?"

You're astounded that she's not furious. You report the conversation, as best you can recall it.

"I should have trusted you," she says. "If I had, you might not know much more, but you'd be more grounded in the ritual."

"Us having sex, you mean? That's part of it?"

"An important part. Your body's the launching pad that makes everything I'm going to do possible."

You don't particularly like being characterized as a launching pad, but you let it pass. "Then do I have to prepare, too?"

"I'm going to fix a special tea that'll help you be more receptive."

"It'll get me in the mood, huh?"

She smiles at your joke, takes a pause, and then says, "You're worried about a mistake, but I won't make one. I won't hurt you."

"You've made mistakes before?"

"Things haven't always gone the way I wanted them to, but I didn't know as much as I do now. You'll be safe, I promise." She worries her lower lip. "I can't walk you through this. There's too much for you to learn and I don't have time to teach you. What I need now is for you to trust me."

"Okay, but . . ."

She sits up straight, hands in her lap, face neutral, her pre-annoyance pose. "What?"

"I still don't get why you can't explain it better."

"I don't know what more to tell you. I've given you the basics. I could give you some specifics, but without any context they'd be meaningless. If I told you there's a power out there that hates mankind, that derives pleasure from tormenting and torturing us, deceiving us, fooling us so completely that millions, maybe billions of people worship it, and now it's tired of us and it's getting ready to close the show . . . would that help?"

"It sounds like you're talking about God."

"It's got lots of names. That's one of them, for sure. Legion's another. But what's that tell you?"

"You're saying God, the creator-of-the-universe God, he made all this just so he could have someone to screw with?"

"I don't pretend to understand its motives, and that's probably an oversimplification, but that's how it seems. If you look at the world, anyone rational would conclude that God's the ultimate villain. Cruel and uncaring. Vicious, whimsical. Trouble is, God's got this great PR department. Anytime anyone jumps up and says that, thousands of idiots start preaching about you've got to have faith, mysterious ways, his master plan, all that crap. You've got to trust in God, they say. So what if he sponsors rape, usury, genocide, cancer? You can't see his real intentions, they say. You can't know him. You just have to trust him. What I'm saying is this. You *can* know God, you can learn to see him, to detect his hand in things. And once you do, you discover that your original impression of indifference and cruelty, that was the correct one. And once you reach that point, you begin to be able to understand how to thwart him." Abi rests her hand atop yours. "Does that help?"

You think it has helped, but now that she's stopped talking, now that her words have become merely words in your head, without her conviction to back them up, they seem generic, lacking solid foundation.

"The disasters," you say. "You're going to stop them? Just you?"

"My friends and I. It's a coordinated action. We've been preparing for this a long time."

"Mike and Rem?"

"Among others."

Sleet begins falling, sounding like a series of little slaps against the tarpaper roof, slimy drops oozing down the panes like the thick crystalline blood of some magical creature—a translucent angel, a hazy gray gargoyle—who's been crouched up there for years. Abi studies the tattoo on the back of her hand, waiting for you to say something, but not pressuring you—it's a conversational habit the two of you have developed, these bursts of dialogue that border on argument, followed by silences during which an accord is reached. The room seems colder and smaller than when you entered, as if it's settled around you, revealed its mystical drab, the secret order of second-hand refrigerators and chipped coffee cups; the air is aswarm with tickings and small hums, and out in the wild world, the horn of a Chevy Suburban or a Volvo, three quick blasts, gives voice to urgency or impatience. You have a feeling of great sobriety, the sense of an enclosing moment.

"I trust you," you say.

*F*or the next seven days, the house reeks of bitter incense and herbal candles that Abi's had custom made—tall candles placed at the four corners of your bed, sallow in hue, with dark thready stuff embedded in the wax. The overall scent reminds you of a Paris outdoor market (which you visited one undergrad summer), but damper and more cloying. Abi speaks rarely, but you gather she's purifying herself for a ritual that must be performed soon. She sits naked on the bed, meditating for hours, and when she's not in bed, she's bent over the kitchen table, scribbling symbols on scraps of paper, which she will burn later in the special candles, as if she's writing cheat sheets for a supernatural exam; or she's taking baths in hot water so dense with herbs, a greenish brown matte is left in the tub after it drains. Twice a day, she asks you to fuck her Yab-Yum style, with you sitting in as close to a Lotus position as you can manage and her facing you, astride you, scarcely moving. During these encounters, her eyes roll back, the whites visible beneath half-lowered lids, and at such moments you appreciate the strangeness of her sexuality, its eerie mix of the sublime and the sensual; but you mainly appreciate her power. It's like you've embraced a dynamo. She throbs and shivers, undergoes surges of heat and tremor. Even after you've disengaged, you feel her energies coursing around you.

You no longer doubt that she has the power to cripple you (okay, maybe there's a little doubt), and while you can't quite wrap your head around the whys and wherefores, how a union of crippled men and friendly, kicked-out-of-the-club angels and Tantric witches is going to be of much help to the world in its hour of need, you've gone a ways toward conceding that she and her pals might have the power to avert a planetary disaster, or at least to minimize it. The issue of trust . . . well, you understand that trust isn't really at issue. You've been drawn into unnavigable waters, committed yourself to Abi's deep, and you have no choice except to let her steer. If it eventuates that you've opened yourself to a particularly vile form of torment, if Abi turns out to be a psychotic, or the embodiment of a demoness, or a more ordinary crippler of men, a deluded Goth chick who's wrong about everything, you'll have to deal with that. And you will. You'll find a way. You won't be anybody's chump. With that settled in your mind, you give up your pursuit of answers and live as happily as you can in the green house—it seems to have gone green from the fresh charge of her vitality, so much so that you half-expect the furniture to put forth sprigs of leaves and blossoms—and assist Abi by fielding her phone calls.

The first four days of Abi's purification, you catch twenty, thirty calls a day, all announcing themselves by giving their first name and the call's point of origin. This is Frannie from San Diego, Ted from Vero Beach, Rene from Medelin, Jonathan from Perth, Lisa from San Francisco, Terry from Madison, Pat from London, Syd from Duluth, Pauline from Chapel Hill, Jean-Daniel from Nantes, Lamon from Paris ("Kentucky, dude . . ."), Patrice from Diamante, Juana from Taxco, and so on. They don't need to speak to Abi, they say. Just mention they called. Most sound young. Since the phone hardly ever rings under normal circumstances, you assume these folks are the mystic warriors of her alliance signaling that they're ready to rock n' roll. Your personal favorite is Mauve from Oberlin, whose voice is such a fey, wispy instrument, you imagine a pixie hovering beside the receiver, and that two other pixies have helped her lift a pencil that dwarfs them to punch in the number. There's Marko from Volgograd (baritone)—you picture a bullfrog the size of a compact car wearing a tattered pro-Satan T-shirt. Ving from Chiang Mai (lisping tenor) becomes a gecko in a spandex body stocking. Anne from Mataplan (grating contralto) you morph into a Sasquatch transvestite. You become downright chatty with some of the callers—making light of what's happening helps dispel your nervousness. On the fifth and sixth days you receive far fewer calls, but you get one that, albeit brief, achieves the opposite effect.

"Hello."

"This is Rem . . . from Olympia." A hoarse voice that sounds squeezed-out, as if he's been gutshot or has a great weight on his chest and, unable to use his diaphragm, it's an effort to speak. He may have, as well, a slight accent.

"Abi can't come to the phone. Take a message?"

"Tell her . . . I called."

Like, "Tell her . . ." Gasp, shudder, gasp. ". . . I called."

"Hey, Rem?"

A grunt that may have been a mangled, "Yeah."

"They say the eagle flies on Friday."

Silence, then: "I don't . . . understand."

"It's the password, guy. You're supposed to say, 'I have yet to feel its shadow.'"

"Abi told us . . . you had an . . . inelegant sense of humor."

"She did, huh? She used that word? Inelegant?"

A round of heavy breathing, then: "Fool."

The seventh morning, Abi makes a few calls of her own; she cautions you that tonight, should you wake and find her still involved in the ritual, you're not to interfere, you're to keep clear until she tells you otherwise. She pounds home this point until she's sure you grasped it, then retreats into seclusion. You try to study, but give up after an hour and veg out on the living room sofa, alternately napping and catching up on your comic book reading. It's late afternoon, already dark outside, and you're deep into Alan Moore's collected *Promethea,* when Abi emerges from the bedroom, goes into the kitchen, and fixes you a cup of herb tea. You take a sip. The taste is horrid. You ask what's in it, but Abi's not communicating. She's withdrawn, pulled back inside herself; she urges you to drink it all and returns to the bedroom, leaving you to contemplate a cupful of brackish liquid with pieces of brown vegetable matter floating on the surface. You know it's a drug—nothing else could taste that bad—but you drink it. At heart, no matter how much evidence there is to the contrary, you can't accept any of this. Teen witches versus the Apocalypse. It's just not happening. The only part to which you lend the slightest credence is the possibility that your back will get screwed up and, at this juncture, that's not enough to do more than give you pause.

An hour, two hours, or twenty minutes later, you're not sure, your sense of time has been wrecked, and you're not sure about anything, especially your decision to drink the tea. You've passed through a period of sweats, intense physical discomfort, and major stomach pain, and now, though your head's not in a bad place, it's not a particularly good place, either. It seems you're sitting beside a fire, included in a circle of old half-naked men, who're talking in booming voices, in a language you don't understand, and you're terribly confused—you get that they're discussing you, that by being there you're making a kind of expiation, but you're confused by the flickering firelight, by noises in the vegetation beyond the light, by an inner unsteadiness. Furthering your confusion, this hallucination winks on and off, and, when it's off, you have a distorted view of the room, of yourself lying sweaty and disheveled on the sofa, tossing and turning. There's this relationship stuff about your mom, too. Scenes revisited from the past. Arguments, emotional confrontations, and the like, replayed at lightning speed, a fast-forward mind movie. Your dad's in some scenes, but he's a peripheral figure. It's all about your mom, really, and you're overwhelmed with sadness on realizing that these conflicts remain unresolved. And then you re-experience your first childhood memory. You're two or three, you still have blond hair, and you're playing on a hooked rug, the sunlight falling around you, and you're seeing yourself from a height, from your mom's perspective, through her eyes, her mind, and you feel love, the powerful bond between mother and child that can never be entirely broken . . . Suddenly you've left pain and confusion behind. You're in a small boat passing along a green river, bordered by low jungle. This is no ordinary river, you understand, but the river of time. A metaphor made visible by drugs and Tantric sex, a stand-in for the literal functioning of time, which—for reasons doubtless plain to Steven Hawking, but unclear to you—cannot be grasped by the human mind. Though it's a metaphor, it's an unusually accurate one. Its currents and eddies are representative of actual structures within the timestream and now, somehow, you've become separated from it . . . or not separate, exactly, but able to control your movements within its medium. How you know all this, you're not certain, but you suspect the old men of having imparted this knowledge. You sense them close by, but they're no longer participants in your life, merely observers. You find that you can switch off the hallucination at will, but the house is too cluttered for your tastes, too modern in its complexity, so you go with the flow of the green, green river, content to lie back, thinking long riverine thoughts, letting its serene currents carry you nowhere and everywhere the same . . .

And that's when Abi comes back into your world.

At first you assume she's a creature of hallucination, a river goddess, a spirit made flesh. She's painted her body with elaborate green designs, vines framing her face and spiraling round her breasts, columning her arms and legs, most profuse about her sex, as if it's her center or is central to the issue at hand. She is, without question, the most beautiful woman you've ever seen, the manifestation of a fabulous unearthly tropic. In a daze, you allow her to lead you into the bathroom, where she bathes you meticulously, using aromatic oils afterward to polish you, drying your erection with her hair, never speaking a word, and neither do you speak, not wanting to break the erotic spell she's weaving with her hands and tongue and breath. Her eyes, adorned with kohl, resemble caverns with green fires in their depths. You both smell of flowers. As she leads you from the bathroom, you notice that her back and buttocks also bear designs. Someone must have assisted her, they must have come to the house while you were going through your changes on the sofa. That doesn't trouble you. Nothing does. You're atop a chemical peak, too high above the world for trouble to reach.

In the bedroom, where candles are pointed with glittering flames, smoke ghosts thinly rising from them, the air disturbed by currents only you can see, you sit in the Lotus posture, achieving it easily, as if the tea has made you more flexible, and when Abi mounts you, when her weight descends, the gorgeous intimacy of your union seems to have rendered you both weightless and you're floating up from the green satin bedspread, levitating, nudged this way and that by impalpable eddies. Abi begins chanting softly, but with prayerful intensity, and the rushed rhythm of her words, impassioned utterances followed by turbulent silences, her breath shuddering out, it becomes your mutual rhythm, orchestrating miniscule squeezings and shiftings. Her eyes are wide open, all white, and you have the idea you're making love to an idol come to life, that she's possessed by a spirit too large to fit within her skin, compressed to the point of exploding. But the distance created by that thought closes quickly, and soon there is only her other body and yours, indistinguishable one from the other, trembling with energy, an engine harnessed to the task of salvation.

How long this goes on, you can't say. Hours, minutes, days... your time-sense is still wrecked and that strikes you as odd, because time is flowing all around the ship built of your two bodies, a green river carrying you everywhere and nowhere, its currents visible even when you shut your eyes, so real it seems you could lift your hand from Abi's waist and cause a splash that would disrupt its flow and destroy some yet unenvisioned future. She brings you to the verge of orgasm over and over again, but holds you from the brink, her chanting slowing, easing you down into your animal self, storing up power until it can no longer be contained and achieves maximum release. It's almost painful, this denial, but pleasure and pain are blended together, even as you and Abi are blended, and your mind admits only to delight. She kisses you, tongue of idol flicking forth to taste your soul, and her fingertips fit to ten familiar places along your spine. Your hands glove her breasts. You're enthralled by their softness, by her dress of vines, her white-eyed stare, her scarlet mouth and Halloween hair. It's a mental snapshot you'll keep forever... or wherever it is she's about to send you.

You're in and out of consciousness for a while. Mostly out. Your eyes open once and you see her standing at the foot of the bed, head bowed and arms upraised, like a diver preparing for her big finish, the air watery and rippling around her. Your dreams are muddled images and vignettes, nothing special, and when you wake, cracking an eye to see a faint lightening of the sky, thinking you haven't slept all that long, you realize that you've moved your legs. Not only have you moved your legs, you have no pain—your back's sore, but it's always a little bit sore in the morning, and you feel incredible. Strong and well-rested, as if you've slept for a week. You test your legs again and lie there for a minute, thankful that you're not crippled and that you didn't make a mistake in trusting Abi... which seems an upset, because what she did earlier, it felt as if your nervous system short-circuited. You swing your legs onto the floor and, keeping one hand on the headboard, afraid that you'll collapse, you stand and stomp your feet, bounce on your toes. All good. You pull on pants and a shirt, and go looking for Abi . . . and for food. In the kitchen, you cut a thick slice of bread, a hunk of cheese. You cram it in. Shit, you're hungry. You hope Abi's okay. It might be that you're going to have to buck her up. Boost her spirits. Because the chances are, all that Yab-Yum boogaloo abracadabra worked out to be was a great fuck. Chewing, you push open the door to the living room.

Abi is there.

Either you're still high, and why wouldn't you be? you only were out a couple of hours and the world's still as unstable as a mirage, flocked with pinpricks of actinic ligh t. . . either you're high or else you're still asleep and dreaming you're awake, because what you see can't be real, and yet you deal with it as if it is, you try and understand what's happening.

Let's say once again, metaphorically speaking, that time is a river, a green river consisting of separate and discernable currents, and that seven of these currents have pierced the walls of your living room, penetrating windows and walls, bookcases and doors, visible as six translucent scarves looping through the air, liquid spokes joined to a central scarf, which is much thicker than the rest, a column connecting ceiling to the floor. In sum, a vaguely treelike shape, an exotic anomaly among the thrift store furniture and cheap oriental rugs.

Let's further say that the water in those currents has been frozen, transformed into tiny ice particles, trillions of greenish particles, each the size of a dust mote, hovering in place . . . that's how you interpret what you're seeing. The metaphorical representation of time, or something to do with time—its underpinnings, its internal structures. Abi's encased in the central column, poised within it, her right arm lifted, looking as if she's about to pick a flower from a branch above her head. Naked, white-eyed, skin decorated with vines. She, too, appears frozen. And then, almost imperceptibly, she moves. The thumb and forefinger of her right hand rub together, as if she's selected one of the particles, pinched it loose from the rest and is rubbing it away between her fingertips. She makes a quarter-turn inside the column to face you, smiling a ghastly smile. Any smile might seem ghastly in relation to those white eyes, but it puts fear in your heart and you start to freak out.

Witch, you think, and take a step backward.

The smile grows more ghastly and gloating, stretched impossibly wide, and you think that the rubber, the latex or whatever, of the Abi costume she's been wearing will split, a great seam will open between her breasts, and the skinny demoness inside with shiny putrescent skin and black nails hard as horn will step forth.

Vile, unholy witch.

Enemy of God, the god whom you've never believed in, but in whom you now yearn to seek refuge.

Kali lacking her necklace of skulls would look no less fearsome, her face no more devoid of human qualities, and you can't help thinking that this is her nature revealed, this voodoo bitch in her green viney gaud. She's been waiting for this moment, waiting to show you, waiting to laugh at you. You reject the notion, but then she stretches forth her hand to you and you know she's about to cast a spell—she'll lure you close, snatch out your spine and brandish it aloft, a dripping bone spear to plunge into your heart, mash it into pudding, and then she'll slurp up your soul as it squirts from the torn flesh. Her vast life surrounds you, surrounds all things. She dwells in the timestream, a pearl spider god dances on her finger, and she is reaching out to slaughter whatever her hand encounters, be it a strand of DNA or a burning city whose flames she'll snuff out so as to inhale the fumes that ascend from its dying...

In your panic, and it's not even a full-on panic, because you don't entirely credit your senses and also because you recall what she said about not interfering... in your partial panic, then, you've forgotten that the kitchen door only swings one way, and when you turn and attempt to flee the room, you slam headfirst into its unyielding surface. The impact stuns you, sends you staggering sideways. You lose your balance, instinctively grope for something to hold yourself up. Your hand catches at the bookcase, the same pierced by one of the frozen currents of time, and, as you fall, your hand locks onto the edge of a shelf, pulling the whole thing down atop you. Digging out from beneath a cascade of trade paperbacks, you hear a tremendous crack, followed by an ear-splitting shredding noise. You come to one knee. Abi's staring at you, her eyes no longer rolled up into her head. The voodoo bitch of whom you were so terrified has been replaced by a frightened woman who realizes she has lost some crucial measure of control. Behind her, it looks as if something has bitten a chunk out of the corner of the room, creating a ragged hole that's as wide as a church door. The treelike shape, the green confluence of time, has lost its structural integrity, and its currents, unfrozen now, are washing past Abi, flooding through the hole and merging with a flux of darker stuff that appears to be flowing just beyond it. She's about to be washed out along with them, and she, too, is losing her structural integrity, her limbs elongating and bending in odd ways, as in a funhouse mirror—yet she's struggling to keep her feet, still reaching toward you, fingers splayed, silently imploring you to help. You have an instant to become aware of this, but before you can act, she's sucked back toward the hole, strikes her head on a broken board, and is gone. There's a scream, fainter than you'd expect, muted by some imponderable distance as she pinwheels away, her pale figure dwindling against the dark flow of . . . you don't know what it is, but it seems infinitely deep and, if you had to give it a name right now, you'd call it God.

You stand there, racked first by the beginnings of anguish, then by guilt (she told you not to interfere), then by disbelief. The tea, the drug she gave you . . . maybe this has all been a production of the drug. But the hole in the wall presents incontrovertible evidence against disbelief, stable and solid, its edges displaying strata of plaster and insulation undeniable in their authenticity; though the dark flux beyond it lacks a certain reality and may be, like the tree of green time, a metaphorical construction, the simplified rendering your mind has contrived to represent an unfathomable phenomenon.

Something is gathering in its depths, accumulating form from the void. A face, you think. It acquires detail, growing larger, swelling from the darkness, and, yes, it's definitely a face. Abi's face, pale and painted with vines. Improbable though it seems, she must have found a way to fight against the flow, she's forging upstream, coming back to the world. But the larger her face grows, the less you believe it. It's rippling, wavering, like the painting of a face borne upward on dark water, threatening to dissolve at any moment . . . and it's enormous. Close to the hole, all that's visible is its lower half, chin and lips, a bit of jawline, the point of her nose, and, drawing closer yet, it's reduced to a huge photo-real scarlet mouth that's pressed up against the hole.

The lips purse convulsively, making a squelching noise that puts you in mind of someone worrying at a sliver of meat stuck between their teeth. The mouth opens and an immense human tongue lolls forth, expelling the mass of bloody tissue, bone, and hair that rested upon its tip. This lands with a soggy thump and is, most assuredly, no metaphor. The pulped organs and macerated bone shards, they're Abi's remains. You recognize them by the orange streaks in her matted hair. Something breaks in you, and you run through the kitchen, out the back door, expecting God to swallow you and spit up your bones . . . but you don't care. If extinction's what it takes to wipe that image from your brain, let it come.

The cloudy sky is ancient water-damaged wallboard, the motionless firs are stage props, the dim rush of the freeway is a sound effect. It closely resembles the world you once knew, but now you've seen what lies behind it, you know it was never what it seemed. The black chow mix in the yard next door is going insane, barking and hurling itself to the end of its chain. You move to the opposite side of the house and sit, resting your head on your knees. Grief sets in. Or maybe grief comes later, and this is merely shock. You welcome it, whatever its name. You seek refuge in tears, in the hot weight lodged in your chest, the absence in your skull. You still can't believe what's happened and these physical proofs of loss are all you have to rely on. Abi warned you not to interfere and you fucked up, you blundered, you bungled her to death. Grief and guilt mixed together are too much to bear. Shivering from the cold, you get to your feet and walk stiffly to the kitchen door. You can't bring yourself to go inside and that's when the problem of what to do next surfaces from the moil of your thoughts. Call the police. Run away. Join a monastic order and devote yourself to good works. Off yourself. That's tempting, but you're not that kind of coward. Not yet. The chow takes up barking again, like barking is its fucking religion, and that drives you back inside.

The phone's ringing.

Could be it's your mom forgetting again what time it is in Seattle, or your neighbor calling to complain about how you upset his dog, or a friend who knows you wake up early. Whichever, it offers you temporary relief from being alone. You pick up the kitchen extension and say hello.

"Is Abi there?" The inimitable voice of Mauve, the pixie from Oberlin.

"No."

There follows a silence that she apparently doesn't intend to fill.

"Abi's . . ." you begin, but can't finish.

"Yes? Is she all right?"

Your voice catches. "Not really."

"What happened?"

Picking up the phone, you think, wasn't such a great idea. "I don't know you."

"Goddamn it! Tell me what happened!"

Hearing her curse is like hearing Tweety Bird getting salty with Sylvester—it's almost funny.

"Who are you?" you ask.

"Is Abi dead?"

It's a question you can't resist. "Yes."

A pause, and then: "Tell me what happened."

You glance up to the ceiling and, as if that flat white surface were a poignant reminder of Abi, or just by lifting your head you disturbed a frail emotional balance, you burst into tears.

"Do you know how many people died tonight?" Mauve asks. "Nobody gives a fuck how bad you feel. If you cared about her, tell me what happened. It's the only thing you can do for her now."

Haltingly, you tell her, you hold nothing back, and when you're done, in her teensy voice, like a diminutive hanging judge, she says, "She should have paralyzed you."

"I wish she had." Then, thinking about what Mauve said, you ask, "Why didn't she?"

"Because she loved you, because she doesn't like hurting people. Fucking jerk!" A second later she says, "I'm sorry. You don't deserve that. It's not your fault."

You don't want to deny that.

"I have a . . . " Mauve begins, but you break in: "You said some people died tonight. How many?"

"A lot."

"How many of them did I kill?"

"Don't concern yourself with that. What you need to do now. . . "

You laugh. "Don't concern myself?"

"You haven't got time for guilt. Bottom's got your scent now. It'll find you again, you can count on it."

Bottom, you say to yourself. Bottom dweller? Like *A Midsummer Night's Dream* Bottom? Then you recall the sheet of paper that fell out of Sessions's book. "What the hell is Bottom?"

After a second, she says, "*The* Bottom. Didn't Abi explain it to you?"

"No. What is it?"

"Jesus." After a pause she says, "You totally need protection. I want you to take the next plane you can catch to Cleveland."

The next plane. For a moment you're thinking astral plane, plane of existence.

"Call me after you've got a flight, and I'll meet it," Mauve says. "You have my number?"

You check caller ID. "Yeah."

"Get out of the house now. Don't pack. Don't . . . "

"What about Abi . . . her body?"

"You don't have time to worry about her. Just get out. You're not going to be safe 'til you're here."

"You can protect me?"

"Yes."

You've been flipping back and forth between despair and mild hysteria, but her saying this jams you up into full-blown hysteria. "Excuse me," you say. "But it looks to me like you're seriously fucking up here. There's these guys with twisted spines, people are getting swallowed and spat out. It's like you're playing things by ear, you know? That didn't work. Let's try this. Oops! Lost her! Well, you better come to Oberlin and we'll see what happens. How can you protect me when you don't know what the fuck you're doing?"

"Okay," Mauve says. "You have to keep it together or you're not going to make it. This is not something we trained for, you understand? We didn't study it in college. We found out something was happening that no one else noticed and there wasn't time to educate the public. No time to build a consensus. Got it? We were just suddenly in the middle of the shit. We've had to learn on the job."

"What's the Bottom?" you ask again. "Are you talking about God?"

"If you don't leave soon, you're going to find out. I'll explain when you get here. I can protect you. I may not always be able to, but I can protect you for a while."

"Why? Why would you?"

"Because Abi would want me to. And because you've become a resource. I need another partner and you've been prepared . . . at least to an extent."

The implication is that she intends to perform the ritual with you, or a similar ritual, and you tell her that you're not interested in having sex with her.

"I'm not going to be your lover," she says. "Don't worry about that. Look at it as a job. An awful duty that might keep you alive."

"So I'm supposed to come to Oberlin and what? Let you paralyze me?"

Angry, Mauve says, "I see why Abi didn't tell you much—she'd have been explaining herself all the time. If you can put aside your skepticism, I won't paralyze you. But if it needs to be done, you bet your ass I'll do it. You'll be taken care of, but you're not going to be walking for a while."

"How did your partner die?"

Silence.

"You had a partner, right? And something happened to him?" You wait for Mauve to comment and, when she does not, when all you hear from the receiver is silence, you ask, "Was it your fault or mine?"

"I'm done," she says crisply. "You have a choice. Get out of the house or die. Catch a plane, don't catch a plane. Absolutely up to you. I don't really care. Give me a call if you're coming."

The bus to the airport is about a third full. At first you sit in the back, far away from everyone, but then you think that if anything happens, if the freeway, for instance, bursts asunder and a giant claw thrusts up from the Bottom to snag the bus, you wouldn't stand a chance; so you move up to a seat with a window that pops out. Wearily, you rest your head against it. Transmitted through the glass, the sound of the tires on asphalt is amplified into a whiney high-pitched insect choir—like Alvin and the Chipmunks on helium—chanting *Abi Abimagique, Abi Abimagique, Abi Abimagique*, over and over. You don't need your loss pounded home and you sit up. It's funny, albeit not funny ha-ha, that you're off to Oberlin to hook up with a woman who sounds like no less a ball-buster than Abi, off into the same mystery, the same basic relationship, because you don't think Abi loved you, not in the way you loved her. And yet no matter how firm Mauve's expression to the contrary, the Tantra involves emotion. You and Mauve will have to arrive at some emotional accord, no matter how impossible that seems at the moment. Unless she's bringing you to Oberlin for the purpose of revenge, to wreck your health and torment you as payback for the people who died, one probably being her partner . . . you hate that word in context of relationships. It's no less redolent of inequality than wife or indentured servant; it merely omits the modifier. Managing partner, junior or senior partner, sex partner, and so on. It makes juiceless and dry the concept of a life together, and it presents the idea that handing over your heart to another animal for safekeeping involves a rational decision.

Those thoughts, irrelevant as they are, provide a short vacation from even bleaker thoughts—when you return from it, you find your head's in awful shape, full of tears, recriminations, regrets, and you rest it on the window glass again, preferring insect choirs commemorating your dead girlfriend to the alternative. The rhythm's changed ever so slightly:

. . . *Abimagique Abi Abi Abimagique Abi Abi* . . .

you kind of get into it, singing drowsily along under your breath, and that starts you thinking how she was when she wasn't all deranged about the cause, she could be so damn funny—she had this dry sense of humor you often mistook for insult and you didn't understand until later how clever what she said really was

. . . *Abimagique Abi Abi Abimagique* . . .

that time in the lab when you made love by the light of the Bunsen burners, she wandered about afterward in the dark, materializing as she passed by the flames like a voluptuous spook

. . . *Abimagique Abi Abi Abimagique Abi* . . .

you're not sure you want to fly to Cleveland, because what if it's a trap, what if it's all the Bottom now, what if God now owns everything except this one scrap of protoplasm, you, and the rest has been swallowed up and spat out and reconstituted as evil

. . . *Abimagique Abi Abi* . . .

you don't know anything, you have never known anything, and the chances are you never will, because here you are running off to meet this Stevie Nicks sound-alike who promises she'll explain everything later, who likely wears gypsy skirts and plays a mean tambourine, stands four feet eleven and fucks like a champ, a woman to whom you'll be no more than a dick, a launching pad

. . . *Abimagique Abi Abi* . . .

fuck it, you've had it with all the mystic claptrap, all the you-cannot-hope-to-understand-it-until-you-experience-it bullshit

. . . *Abimagique Abi Abi Abimagique Abi Abi* . . .

you're glad the bus is close to the exit that leads onto Airport Drive, it runs for miles past hotels shitty burger joints topless bars and if you decide you don't want to know how it ends, you can tell the driver to let you out anywhere

. . . *Abimagique Abi Abi Abimagique Abi* . . .

but who're you kidding, you're hooked through the gills, you'll fly to Oberlin, you'll have Mauve or, should you say, she'll once have you, because that's the only way you'll find out what happened and is happening, and even if what you find out is bad, painful, the end, well, at least you'll understand the reason why you went through all you did with

. . . *Abi Abimagique Abi Abi* . . .

you do know one thing, though it's certainly nothing cosmic—she's already unraveling in your memory, and part of the pain you feel comes from trying to hang on to her reality, and you'll keep trying to hang on until the pain is all you have left of her

. . . *Abimagique Abi* . . .

there should be permanent memorials in the mind, shrines with candles, enormous tombs stuffed with tastes and sights, cenotaphs and gigantic statuary, and not just these gauzy tatters of memory

Abimagique

   . . . Abi Abimagique . . .

and what does this say about you, about us, about the way we are as friends, children, lovers, about God and the Bottom and human nature, that when people die, all that seems to happen is they fall out of the dream we're having about the world

   . . . Abi Abi Abimagique . . .

THE LEPIDOPTERIST

I found this in a box of microcassettes recorded almost thirty years ago; on it I had written, "J. A. McCrae—the bar at Sandy Bay, Roatan." All I recall of the night was the wind off the water tearing the thatch, the generator thudding, people walking the moonless beach, their flashlights sawing the dark, and a wicked-looking barman with stiletto sideburns. McCrae himself was short, in his sixties, as wizened and brown as an apricot seed, and he was very drunk, his voice veering between a feeble whisper and a dramatic growl:

I'm goin to tell you bout a storm, cause it please me to do so. You cotch me in the tellin mood, and when John Anderson McCrae get in the tellin mood, ain't nobody on this little island better suited for the job. I been foolin with storms one way or the other since time first came to town, and this storm I goin to speak of, it ain't the biggest, it don't have the stiffest winds, but it bring a strange cargo to our shores.

Fetch me another Salvavida, Clifton . . . if the gentleman's willing. Thank you, sir. Thank you.

Now Mitch and Fifi were the worst of the hurricanes round these parts. And the worst of them come after the wind and rain. Ain't that right, Clifton? Ain't that always the case? Worst t'ing bout any storm is what come along afterwards. Mitch flattened this poor island. Must have kill four, five hundred people, and the most of them die in the weeks followin. Coxen Hole come t'rough all right, but there weren't scarcely a tree standing on this side. And Fifi . . . after Fifi there's people livin in nests, a few boards piled around them to keep out the crabs and a scrap of tin over they head. Millions of dollars in relief is just settin over in Teguz. Warehouses full. But don't none of it get to the island. Word have it this fella work for Walmart bought it off the military for ten cent on the dollar. I don't know what for sure he do with it, but I spect there be some Yankees payin for the same blankets and T-shirts and bottled water that they government givin away for free. I ain't blamin nothin on America, now. God Bless America! That's what I say. God Bless America! They gots the good intention to be sending aid in the first place. But the way t'ings look to some, these storms ain't nothin but an excuse to slip the generals a nice paycheck.

The mon don't want to hear bout your business, Clifton! Slide me down that bottle. I needs somet'ing to wash down with this beer. That's right, he payin! Don't you t'ink the mon can afford it? Well, then. Slide me that bottle.

Many of these Yankees that go rushing in on the heels of disaster, these so-called do-gooders, they all tryin to find something cheap enough they can steal it. Land, mostly. But rarely do it bode well for them. You take this mon bought up twenty thousand acres of jungle down around Trujillo right after Mitch. He cotching animals on it. Iguana, parrots, jaguar. Snakes. Whatever he cotch, he export to Europe. My nephew Jacob work for him, and he say the mon doing real good business, but he act like he the king of creation. Yellin and cursin everybody. Jacob tell him, you keep cursin these boys, one night they get to drinkin and come see you with they machete. The mon laugh at that. He ain't worry bout no machetes. He gots a big gun. Huh! We been havin funerals for big Yankee guns in Honduras since fore I were born.

This storm I'm talkin about, it were in the back time. 1925, '26. Somewhere long in there. Round the time United Fruit and Standard Fruit fight the Banana War over on the mainland. And it weren't no hurricane, it were a norther. Northers be worse than a hurricane in some ways. They can hang round a week and more, and they always starts with fog. The fog roll in like a ledge of gray smoke and sets til it almost solid. That's how you know a big norther's due. My daddy, he were what we call down here a wrecker. He out in the fury of the storm with he friends, and they be swingin they lanterns on the shore, trying to lure a ship onto the reef so they can grab the cargo. You don't want to be on the water durin a norther ceptin you got somet'ing the size of the Queen Mary under you. Many's the gun runner or tourist boat, or a turtler headin home from the Chinchorro Bank, gets heself lost in bad weather. And when they see the lantern, they makes for it in a hurry. Cause they desperate, you know. They bout to lose their lives. A light is hope to them, and they bear straight in onto the reef.

That night, the night of the storm, were the first time my daddy took me wreckin. I had no wish to be with him, but the mon fierce. He say, John, I needs you tonight and I hops to it or he lay me out cold. Times he drinkin and he feel a rage comin, he say, John, get under the table. I gets under the table quick, cause I know and he spy me when the rage upon him, nothin good can happen. So I stays low and out of he sight. I too little to stand with him. I born in the summer and never get no bigger than what you seein now.

We took our stand round St. Ant'ony's Key. There wasn't no resort back then. No dive shop, no bungalows. Just cashew trees, sea grape, palm. It were a good spot cause the reef close in to shore, and that old motor launch we use for boarding, it ain't goin to get too far in rough water. My daddy, he keep checkin' he pistol. That were how he did when t'ings were pressin him. He check he pistol and yell at ever'body to swing they lanterns. We only have the one pistol mongst the five of us. You might t'ink we needs more to take on an entire crew, but no matter how tough that crew be, they been t'rough hell, and if they any left alive, they ain't got much left in them, they can barely stand. One pistol more than enough to do the job. If it ain't, we gots our machetes.

The night wild, mon. Lord, that night wild. The bushes lashing and the palms tearin and the waves crashin so loud, you t'ink the world must have gone to spinnin faster. And dark . . . we can't see nothin cept what the lantern shine up. A piece of a wave, a frond slashin at your face. Even t'ough I wearin a poncho, I wet to the bone. I hear my daddy cry, Hold your lantern high, Bynum! Over to the left! He hollerin at Bynum Saint John, who were a fisherman fore he take up wreckin. Bynum the tallest of us. Six foot seven if he an inch. So when he hold he lantern high, it seem to me like a star fell low in the heavens. With the wind howlin and blood to come, I were afraid. I fix on that lantern, cause it the only steady t'ing in all that uncertainty, and it give me some comfort. Then my daddy shout again and I look to where the light shinin and that's when I see there's a yacht stuck on the reef.

Everybody's scramblin for the launch. They eager to get out to the reef fore the yacht start breakin up. But I were stricken. I don't want to see no killin and the yacht have a duppy look, way half its keel is ridin out of the water and its sails furled neat and not a soul on deck. Like it were set down on the rocks and have not come to this fate by ordinary means . . .

You t'ink you can tell this story better than me, Clifton? Then you can damn well quit interruptin! I don't care you heared Devlin Walker tell a story sound just like it. If Devlin tellin this story, he heared it from me. Devlin's daddy never were a wrecker. And even if dat de case, what a boy born with two left feet goin to do in the middle of a norther? He can't hardly get around and it dry.

Yes, sir! Two left feet. The mon born that way. Now Devlin, I admit, he good with a tale, but that due to the fact that he never done a day's work in he life. All he gots to do is set around collectin other folks' stories.

The Santa Caterina, that were the name on the yacht's bow . . . it were still sittin pretty by the time we reached it. But big waves is breakin over the stern, and it just a matter of minutes fore they get to chewin it up. I were the first over the rail, t'ough it were not of my doin. I t'ought I would stay with the launch, but my daddy lift me by the waist and I had no choice but to climb aboard. The yacht were tipped to starboard, the deck so wet, I go slidin across and fetch up against the opposite rail. I could feel the keel startin to slip. Then Bynum come over the rail, and Deaver Ebanks follow him. The sight of them steady me and I has a look round . . . and that's when I spy this white mon standing in the stern. He not swaying or nothin, and it were all I could do to keep my feet. He wearing a suit and tie and a funny kind of hat with a round top that were jammed down so low, all I seein of he face were he smile. That's right. The boat on the rocks and wreckers has boarded her, and he smilin. It were like a razor, that smile, all teeth and no good wishes. Cut the heart right out of me. The roar of the storm dwindle and I hear a ringin in my ears and it like I'm lookin at the world t'rough the wrong end of a telescope.

I'm t'inking he no a natural mon, that he have hexed me, but maybe I just scared, for Bynum run at him, waving he machete. The mon whip a pistol from he waist and shoot him dead. And he do the same for Deaver Ebanks. The shots don't hardly make a sound in all that wind. Now there's a box resting on deck beside the mon. I were lookin at it end-on, and I judged it to be a coffin. It were made of mahogany and carved up right pretty. It resemble the coffin the McNabbs send that Yankee who try to cut in on they business. What were he name, Clifton? I can't recollect. It were an Italian name.

Who the McNabbs? Hear that, Clifton? Who the McNabbs? Wellsir, you stay on the island for a time and you goin to know the McNabbs. The worst of them, White Man McNabb, he in jail up in Alabama, but the ones that remain is bad enough. They own that big resort out toward the east end, Pirate Cove. But most of they money derived from smugglin. Ain't an ounce of heroin or cocaine passes t'rough Roatan don't bear they mark. They don't appreciate people messin in their business, and when that Italian Yankee . . . Antonelli. That's he name. When this Antonelli move down from New York and gets to messin, they send him that coffin and not long after, he back in New York.

So this box I'm tellin you about, I realize it ain't no bigger than a hatbox when the man pick it up, and it can't weigh much—he totin it with the one hand. He step to the port rail and fire two shots toward the launch. I can't see where they strike. He beckon to me and t'ough I'm still scared I walk to him like he got me on a string. There's only my daddy in the launch. He gots a hand on the tiller and the other hand in the air, and he gun lyin in the bilge. Ain't no sign of Jerry Worthing—he the other man in our party. I'm guessin he gone under the water. The mon pass me the box and tell me to hold on tight with both hands. He lift me up and lower me into the launch, then scramble down after me. Then he gesture with he pistol and my daddy unhook us from the Santa Caterina and turn the launch toward shore. It look like he can't get over bein surprised at what have happened.

My daddy were a talker. Always gots somet'ing to say about nothin. But he don't say a word til after we home. Even then, he don't say much. We had us a shotgun shack back from the water, with coco palms and bananas all around, and once de mon have settled us in the front room, he ask me if

I good with knots. I say, I'm all right. So he tell me to lash my daddy to the chair. I goes to it, with him checkin the ropes now and again, and when I finish he pat me on the head. My daddy starin hateful at me, and I gots to admit I weren't all that unhappy with him being tied up. What you goin to do with us? he ask, and the mon tell him he ain't in no position to be askin nothin, considerin what he done.

The mon proceed to remove he hat and he coat, cause they wet t'rough. Shirt, shoes, and socks, too. He head shaved and he torso white as a fish belly, but he all muscle. Thick arms and chest. He take a chair, restin the pistol on his knee, and ask how old I am. I don't exactly know, I tell him, and my daddy say, He bout ten. Bout ten? the mon say. This boy's no more than eight! He actin' horrified, like he t'ink the worst t'ing a man can not know about heself is how old he is. He tell my daddy to shut up, cause he must not be no kind of father and he don't want to hear another peep out of him. I goes to fiddlin with the mon's hat. It hard, you know. Like it made of horn. The mon tell me it's a pith helmet and he would give it to me, cause I such a brave boy, but he need it to keep he head from burnin.

By the next morning, the storm have passed. Daddy's asleep in the chair when I wakes and the mon sitting at the table, eating salt pork and bananas. He offer me some and I joins him at the table. When Daddy come round, the mon don't offer him none, and that wake me to the fact that t'ings might not go good for us. See, I been t'inkin with a child's mind. The mon peared to have taken a shine to me and that somet'ing my daddy never done. So him takin a shine to me outweigh the killin he done. But the cool style he had of doing it . . . a mon that good at killin weren't nobody to trust.

After breakfast, he carry my daddy some water, then he gag him. He pick up that box and tell me to come with him, we goin for a walk. We head off into the hills, with him draggin me along. The box, I'm noticing, ain't solid. It gots tiny holes drilled into the wood. Pinholes. Must be a thousand of them. I ask what he keepin inside it, but he don't answer. That were his custom. Times he seem like an ordinary Yankee, but other times it like he in a trance and the most you goin to get out of him is dat dead mon's smile.

Twenty minutes after we set out, we arrives at this glade. A real pretty place, roofed with banana fronds and wild hibiscus everywhere. The mon cast he eye up and around, and make a satisfied noise. Then he kneel down and open the box. Out come fluttering dozens of moths . . . least I t'ink they moths. Later, when he in a talking mood, he tells me they's butterflies. Gray butterflies. And he a butterfly scientist. What you calls a lepidopterist.

The butterflies, now, they flutterin around he head, like they fraid to leave him. He sit crosslegged on the ground and pull out from he trousers a wood flute and start tootlin on it. That were a curious sight, he shirtless and piping away, wearin that pith helmet, and the butterflies fluttering round in the green shade. It were a curious melody he were playin, too. Thin, twistin in and out, never goin nowhere. The kind of t'ing you liable to hear over in Puerto Morales, where all them Hindus livin.

That's what I sayin. Hindus. The English brung them over last century to work the sugar plantations. They's settled along the Rio Dulce, most of them. But there some in Puerto Morales, too. That's how they always do, the English. When they go from a place, they always leavin t'ings behind they got no more use for. Remember after Fifi, Clifton? They left them bulldozers so we can rebuild the airport? And the Sponnish soldiers drive them into the hills and shoot at them for sport, then leave them to rust. Yeah, mon. Them Sponnish have the right idea. Damn airport, when they finally builds it, been the ruin of this island. The money it bring in don't never sift down to the poor folks, that for sure. We still poor and now we polluted with tourists and gots people like the McNabbs runnin t'ings.

By the time the mon finish playing, the butterflies has vanished into the canopy, and I gots that same feelin I have the night previous on the deck of the Santa Caterina. My ears ringing, everyt'ing have a distant look, and the mon have to steer me some on the walk back. We strop my daddy to the bed in the back room, so he more comfortable, and the mon sit in he chair, and I foolin with a ball I find on the beach. And that's how the days pass. Mornin, noon, and night we walks out to the glade and the mon play some more on he flute. But mainly we just sittin in the front room and doin nothin. I learn he name is Arthur Jessup and that he have carried the butterflies up from Panama and were on the way to La Ceiba when the storm cotch him. He tell me he have to allow the butterflies to spin their cocoons here on the island, cause he can't reach he place in Ceiba soon enough.

I t'ought it was caterpillars turned into butterflies, I says. Not the other way round.

These be unusual butterflies, he say. I don't know what else they be. Whether they the Devil's work or one of God's miracles, I cannot tell you. But it for certain they unusual butterflies.

My daddy didn't have no friends to speak of, now he men been shot dead, but there's this old woman, Maud Green, that look in on us now and then, cause she t'ink it the Christian t'ing to do. Daddy hate the sight of her, and he always hustle her out quick. But Mister Jessup invite her in and make over her like she a queen. He tell her he a missionary doctor and he after curin Daddy of a contagious disease. Butterfly fever, he call it, and gives me a wink. It a terrible affliction, he say. Your hair fall out, like mine, and don't never come back. The eye grow dim, and the pain . . . the pain excrutiatin. Maud Green cock her ear and hear Daddy strainin against the gag in the back room, moanin. He at heaven's gate, Mister Jessup say, but I believe, with the Lord's help, we can pull the mon back. He ask Maud to join him in prayin over Daddy and Maud say, I needs to carry this cashew fruit to my daughter, so I be pushing along, and we don't see no more of her after that. We has a couple of visitors the followin day who heared about the missionary doctor and wants some curin done. Mister Jessup tell them to bide they time. Won't be long, he say, fore my daddy back on he feet, and then he goin to take care of they ills. It occur to me, when these folks visitin, that I might say somet'ing bout my predicament or steal away, but I remembers Mister Jessup's skill with the pistol. It take a dead shot to pick a man off a launch when the sea bouncin her round like it were. And I fears for my daddy, too. He may not be no kind of father, but he all the parent I gots, what with my mama dying directly after I were born.

Must be the ninth, tenth day since Mister Jessup come to the island, and on that mornin, after he play he flute in the glade, he cut a long piece of bamboo and go to pokin the banana fronds overhead. He beat the fronds back and I see four cocoons hangin from the limbs of an aguacaste tree. They big, these cocoons. Each one big as a *matrimonio* (hammocks large enough to hold husband and wife). And they not white, but gray, with gray threads fraying off dem. Mister Jessup act real excited and, after we returned home, he say, Pears I'll be out of your hair in a day or two, son. I spect you be glad to see my backside goin down the road.

I don't know what to say, so I keeps quiet.

Yes sir, he say. You not goin to believe your eyes and you see what busts out of them cocoons. That subject been pressin on my mind, so I ask him what were goin to happen.

Just you wait, he say. But I tell you this much. The man ain't born can stand against what's in those cocoons. You goin to hear the name Arthur Jessup again, son. Mark my words. A few years from now, you be hearin that name mentioned in the same breath with presidents and kings.

I takes that to mean Mister Jessup believe he goin to have some power in the world. He a smart mon . . . least he do a fine job pretendin he smart. Still, I ain't too sure I hold with that. Bout half the time he act like somet'ing have power over him. Grinnin like a skull. Sittin and starin for hours, with a blink every now and then to let you know he alive. Pears to me somebody gots they hand on him. A garifuna witch, maybe. Maybe the butterfly duppy.

You want to hear duppy stories, Clifton be your man. When he a boy, he mama cotch sight of the hummingbird duppy hovering in a cashew tree, and ever after there's hummingbirds all around he house. Whether that a curse or a blessing, I leave for Clifton to say, but . . .

Oh, yeah. Everyt'ing gots a duppy. Sun gots a duppy. The moon, the wind, the coconut, the ant. Even Yankees gots they duppy. They gots a fierce duppy, a real big shot, but since they never lay eyes on it, it difficult for them to understand they ain't always in control.

Where you hail from in America, sir?

Florida? I been to Miami twice, and I here to testify that even Florida gots a duppy.

Evenin of the next day and we proceed to the glade. The cocoons, they busted open. There's gray strings spillin out of dem . . . remind me of old dried-up fish guts. But there's nothin to show what else have come forth. It don't seem to bother Mister Jessup none. He sit down in the weeds and get to playin he flute. He play for a while with no result, but long about twilight, a mon with long black hair slip from the margins of the glade and stand before us. He the palest mon I ever seen, and the prettiest. Prettier than most girls. Not much bigger than a girl, neither. He staring at us with these big gray eyes, and he make a whispery sound with he mouth and step toward me, but Mister Jessup hold up a hand to stay him. Then he goes to pipin on the flute again. Time he done, there three more of them standin in the glade. Two womens and one mon. All with black hair and pale skin. The mon look kind of sickly, and he skin gray in patches. They all of them has gray silky stuff clinging to their bodies, which they washes off once we back home. But you could see everyt'ing there were to see, and watchin that silky stuff slide about on the women's skin, it give me a tingle even t'ough I not old enough to be interested. And they faces . . . you live a thousand years, you never come across no faces like them. Little pointy chins and pouty lips and eyes bout to drink you up. Delicate faces. Wise faces. And yet I has the idea they ain't faces at all, but patterns like you finds on a butterfly's wing.

Mister Jessup herds them toward the shack at a rapid pace, cause he don't want nobody else seein them. They talking that whispery talk to one another, cept for the sickly mon. The others glidin along, they have this supple style of walkin, but it all he can do to stagger and stumble. When we reach the shack, he slump down against a wall, while the rest go to pokin around the front room, touchin and liftin pots and glasses, knifes and forks, the cow skull that prop open the window. I seen Japanese tourists do less pokin. Mister Jessup install heself in a chair and he watchin over them like a mon prideful of he children.

Few months in La Ceiba, little spit and polish, he say, and they be ready. What you t'ink, boy? Well, I don't know what to t'ink, but I allow they some right pretty girls.

Pretty? he say, and chuckle. Oh, yeah. They pretty and a piece more. They pretty like the Hope Diamond, like the Taj Mahal. They pretty all right.

I ask what he goin to do for the sick one and he say, Nothin I can do cept hope he improve. But I doubt he goin to come t'rough.

He had the right of that. Weren't a half-hour fore the mon slump over dead and straightaway we buries him out in back. There weren't hardly nothin to him. Judgin by the way Mister Jessup toss him about, he can't weigh ten pounds, and when I dig he up a few days later, all I finds is some strands of silk.

We watches the butterfly girls and the mon a bit longer, then Mister Jessup start braggin about what a clever mon he be, but I suspect he anxious about somet'ing. An anxious mon tend to lose control of he mouth, to take comfort from the sound of he voice. He say six months under he lamps, with the nutrients he goin to provide, and won't nobody be able to tell the difference between the butterflies and real folks. He say the world ain't ready for these three. They goin to cut a swath, they are. Can you imagine, he ask, these little ladies walkin in the halls of power on the arm of a senator or the president of a company? Or the mon in a queen's bedchamber? The secrets they'll come to know. They hands on the reigns of power. I can imagine it, boy. I know you can't. You a brave little soldier, but you ain't got the imagination God give a tick.

He run on in that vein, buildin heself a fancy future, sayin he might just take me along and show me how sweet the world be when you occupies a grand position in it. While he talkin, the women and the man keeps circulatin, movin round the shack, whispering and touchin, like they findin our world all strange and new. When they pass behind Mister Jessup, sometimes they touch the back of he neck and he freeze up for a moment and that peculiar smile flicker on; but then he go right on talking as if he don't notice. And I'm t'inkin these ain't no kind of butterflies. Mister Jessup may believe they is, he may think he know all about them. And maybe they like he say, a freak of nature. I ain't disallowin that be true in part. Yet when I recall he playin that flute, playing like them Hindus in Puerto Morales does when they sits on a satin pillow and summons colors from the air, I know, whether he do or not, that he be summonin somet'ing, too. He callin spirits to be born inside them cocoons. Cause, you see, these butterfly people, they ain't no babies been alive a few hours. That not how they act. They ware of too much. They hears a dog barkin in the distance, a coconut thumpin on the sand, and they alert to it. When they put they eye on you . . . I can't say how I knows this, but there somet'ing old about them, somet'ing older than the years of Mister Jessup and me and my daddy all added up together.

Eventually Mister Jessup reach a point in he fancifyin where he standin atop the world, decidin whether or not to let it spin, and that pear to satisfy him. He lead me back to where my daddy stropped down. Daddy he starin at me like he get loose, the island not goin to be big enough for me to hide in.

Don't you worry, boy, Mister Jessup say. He ain't goin to harm you none.

He slip Daddy's gag and inquire of him if the launch can make it to La Ceiba and the weather calm. Daddy reckon it can. Take most of a day, he figures.

Well, that's how we'll go, say Mister Jessup.

He puts a match to the kerosene lamp by the bed and brings the butterfly people in. Daddy gets to strugg180lin when he spies them. He callin on Jesus to save him from these devils, but Jesus must be havin the night off.

The light lend the butterfly people some color and that make them look more regular. But maybe I just accustomed to seein them, cause Daddy he thrash about harder and goes to yellin fierce. Then the one woman touch a hand gainst he cheek, and that calm him of an instant. Mister Jessup push me away from the bed, so I can't see much, just the three of them gatherin round my daddy and his legs stiffening and then relaxin as they touch he face.

I goes out in the front room and sits on the stoop, not knowin what else to do. There weren't no spirit in me to run. Where I goin to run to? Stay or go, it the same story. I either winds up beggin in Coxxen Hole or gettin pounded by my daddy. The lights of Wilton James' shack shining t'rough the palms, not a hundred feet away, but Wilton a drunk and he can't cure he own troubles, so what he goin to do for mine? I sits and toes the sand, and the world come to seem an easy place. Waves sloppin on the shingle and the moon, ridin almost full over a palm crown, look like it taken a faceful of buckshot. The wind carry a fresh smell and stir the sea grape growin beside the stoop.

Soon Mister Jessup call me in and direct me to a chair. Flanked by the butterfly people, my daddy leanin by the bedroom door. He keep passin a hand before his eyes, rubbin he brow. He don't say nothin, and that tell me they done somet'ing to him with they touches, cause a few minutes earlier he been dyin to curse me. Mister Jessup kneel beside the chair and say, We goin off to La Ceiba, boy. I know I say I'm takin you with me, but I can't be doin that. I gots too much to deal with and I havin to worry bout you on top of it. But you showed me somet'ing, you did. Boy young as you, faced with all this, you never shed a tear. Not one. So I'm goin to give you a present.

A present sound like a fine idea, and I don't let on that my daddy have beat the weepin out of me, or that I small for my age. I can't be certain, but I pretty sure I goin on eleven, t'ough I could not have told him the day I were born. But eleven or eight, either way I too young to recognize that any present given with that kind of misunderstandin ain't likely to please.

You a brave boy, say Mister Jessup. That's not always a good t'ing, not in these parts. I fraid you gonna wind up a wrecker like your daddy . . . or worse. You be gettin yourself killed fore you old enough to realize what livin is worth. So I'm goin to take away some of your courage.

He beckon to one of the women and she come forward with that glidin walk. I shrinks from her, but she smile and that smile smooth out my fear. It have an effect similar to Mister Jessup's pats-on-the-head. She swayin before me. It almost a dance she doin. And she hummin deep in she throat, the sound some of Daddy's girlfriends make after he climb atop them. Then she bendin close, bringin with her a sweet, dry scent, and she touch a finger to my cheek. The touch leave a little electric trail, like my cheek sparklin and sparkin both. Cept for that, I all over numb. She eye draw me in til that gray crystal all I seein. I so far in, pear the eye enormous and I floatin in front of it, bout the size of a mite. And what lookin back at me ain't no butterfly. The woman she may have a pleasin shape, but behind she eye there's another shape pressin forward, peekin into the world and yearnin to bust out the way the butterfly people busted out of they cocoon. I feels a pulse that ain't the measure of a beatin heart. It registerin an unnatural rhythm. And yet for all that, I drawn in deeper. I wants her to touch me again, I wants to see the true evil shape of her, and I reckon I'm smiling like Mister Jessup, with that same mixture of terror and delight.

When I rouse myself, the shack empty. I runs down to the beach and I spies the launch passin t'rough a break in the reef. Ain't no use yellin after them. They too far off, but I yells anyway, t'hough who I yellin to, my daddy or the butterfly girl, be a matter for conjecture. And then they swallowed up in the night. I stand there a time, hopin they turn back. It thirty miles and more to La Ceiba, and crossin that much water at night in a leaky launch, that a fearsome t'ing. I falls asleep on the sand waitin for them and in the mornin Fredo Jolly wake me when he drive his cows long the shore to they pasture.

My daddy return to the island a couple weeks later, but by then I over in Coxxen Hole, doin odd jobs and beggin, and he don't have the hold on me that once he did. He beat me, but I can tell he heart ain't in it, and he take up wreckin again, but he heart ain't in that, neither. He say he can't find no decent mens to help, but Sandy Bay and Punta Palmetto full of men do that kind of work. Pretty soon, three or four years, it were, I lose track of him, and I never hear of him again, not even on the day he die.

Mister Jessup have predicted I be hearin bout him in a few years, but it weren't a week after they leave, word come that a Yankee name of Jessup been found dead in La Ceiba, the top half of he head chopped off by a machete. There ain't no news of the butterfly people, but the feelin I gots, then and now, they still in the world, and maybe that's one reason the world how it is. Could be they bust out of they shapes and acquire another, one more reflectin of they nature. There no way of knowin. But one t'ing I do know. All my days, I never show a lick of ambition. I never took no risks, always playin it safe. If there a fight in an alley or riot in a bar, I gone, I out the door. The John Anderson McCrae you sees before you is the same I been every day of my life. Doin odd jobs and beggin. And once the years fill me up sufficient, tellin stories for the tourists. So if Mister Jessup make me a present, it were like most Yankee presents and take away more than it give. But that's a story been told a thousand times and it be told a thousand more. You won't cotch me blamin he for my troubles. God Bless America is what I say. Yankees gots they own brand of troubles, and who can say which is the worse.

Yes, sir. I believe I will have another.

Naw, that ain't what makin me sad. God knows, I been livin almost seventy years. That more than a mon can expect. Ain't no good in regrettin or wishin I had a million dollars or that I been to China and Brazil. One way or another, the world whittle a mon down to he proper size. That's what it done for Mister Jessup, that's what it done for me. It just tellin that story set me to rememberin the butterfly girl. How she look in the lantern light, pale and glowin, with hair so black, where it lie across she shoulder, it like an absence in the flesh. How it feel when she touch me and what that say to a mon, even to a boy. It say I knows you, the heart of you, and soon you goin to know bout me. It say I never stray from you, and I going to show you t'ings whose shadows are the glories of this world. Now here it is, all these years later, and I still longin for that touch.

DAGGER KEY

The seagull's wing
        divides the wave
   the lights of Swann's café
            grow dim . . .

. . . and morning comes to Cay Cuchillo, a dagger-shape of sand and rock off the coast of Belize, a few miles southwest of the Chinchorro Bank. Nine miles long, seven wide at the hilt. The gray sky is pinked in the east, bundles of mauve cloud reflecting the new sun. Venus low on the horizon.

Rollers break on the beach at Half Shell Bay, the waves sounding like a giant breathing in his sleep. Crossing the tidal margin, a ghost crab pauses in its creep as the thin edge of the water inches up to erase its tracks from the mucky sand. The fronds of a coco palm twitch; the round leaves of sea grape appear to spin in a sudden freshet. Hummingbirds hover beside the blossoms of a cashew tree.

Near the hilt of the dagger, shielded from the winds by a hill with a concave rock face, lie the white buildings of a resort. Treasure Cove. A skull-and-crossbones hangs limp above the office, a stucco faux-colonial that also encloses two luxury apartments and a bar-restaurant. It's set close against the hill and, among palms and jacaranda and flowering shrubs, bungalows are scattered beneath it along the curve of the beach. From the eastern end of the beach, a wooden pier extends into the water—moored to it are several sailboats and a cabin cruiser. Dark-skinned women in head wraps and blue uniform dresses mop the patio that abuts the beachside bar, a construction of poles and thatch. A radio plays softly. *Solo tu . . . siempre solo tu.* Astringents mask the smell of brine.

Swann's faces the Belizean coast, about two miles from the point of the dagger. It's a low, derelict building with a thatched roof, a packed sand floor, and boards painted red, green, black. A hill rises inland and clinging to its side, about halfway up, is a shanty with boards painted in identical colors. Inside the café, Fredo Galvez, a slender, small-boned man of middle years, is sweeping up broken glass from last night's riot with a twig broom. He wears a pair of ragged shorts and a T-shirt from which all but the word *Jesus* has been bleached. His features and coloration are a mix of Spanish and Indian, yet he has sharp blue eyes and his hair is crispy. Once he's finished with sweeping, he stows the broom in back of the bar and rights an overturned stool. He surveys his work and, satisfied, steps out onto the beach and lights a cigarette, stands looking at the sea, at the dark coastline melting up from the morning haze. The sun has not yet cleared the horizon and already the morning freshness is burning off.

Beside the café is a palm tree stripped of its fronds, its trunk shaped roughly like an L, growing more-or-less parallel to the ground for eight or nine feet, then shooting upwards. Fredo sits on the horizontal portion of the trunk to finish his smoke and plan his day. He has to fetch fuel for he generator, meat for the kitchen. They have enough rice and potatoes to get through the week. He spots a solitary figure off toward the point and, though he can't make her out, he recognizes her by her clothing—a white blouse and tan leggings—and by the thrill that passes across the base of his neck. It's been three years since she came to him, and he'd been hoping for at least three more. She's been up in the hills, keeping company with animal spirits and duppies, with the soul-shell of an old Caribe wizard.

"What you know, Annie?" He whispers the words; she could not possibly hear them, but she does. Neither can he hear her—the words tumble into his head somehow

Somebody's coming at you.

"A Yankee?"

Worse.

"What kind of worse we talking about?

You might have to dig me a hole.

They seem to mingle, the edges of two clouds interpenetrating, yet he has no real sense of her, no clue as to what sort of woman she is. She never lets him near, except when she wears him like a dress and then he can remember no more than bits and pieces. He knows her story, but it's only a story and has little personal context. The vague apprehension he has of her is fading and, though her image lingers, motionless on the beach, if he turns away for a second, if he even blinks, she'll be gone. He lowers his head, worried by what she has told him.

A bell ringing.

Armed with a long switch, William Jerome, a skinny black man, is driving five cows along the beach toward their grazing ground in the hills inland. As he comes abreast of the cafe, he sings out, "How's she going, Fredo?"

"You know, mon. It going and going."

The bell cow veers toward the water and William drives her back with a flick of his switch. "Damn," he says. "If I rule the day, it ain't going to get no hotter than this." He waves to Fredo and, as the herd picks up the pace, he breaks into a trot. Fredo sits a while, listening to the hiss of the surf, then he sighs, stands. He's got work to do.

*F*redo buys turtle meat, conch, and a stalk of bananas in the market at Dever's Landing, the island's sole town, a collection of shanties perched on thin posts against the storm tides, like drab long-legged birds carrying their nests on their backs, and, at the foot of a long concrete wharf, a dun-colored stucco building housing the police, the customs office, the bank. Tully Langdon, the man who runs the wharf, is late in rising, so Fredo has to wait for his gas. He sits on an empty oil drum, cooled by the salt breeze.

> A vulture,
> it might be carved
> of shadow or obsidian,
> black wings folded

atop a creosote-tarred piling,
turns its head

toward him and he crosses himself. Tully arrives and, once Fredo has accomplished his business, he catches a ride on the iceman's truck back to the café. At mid-morning, his wife Emily, a lean black woman in faded print dress and tennis shoes, walks down from the hillside shanty and joins him, their four-year-old, Leona, in tow. Their boys, Jenry and Palace, are at school. Leona plays about Emily's feet in the kitchen as she cuts the turtle meat into strips and pounds it soft. Shortly after noon, Wilton Barrios, thickset and yellow-skinned, acne scarring on his cheeks, comes in and plants himself at a table, the chair complaining beneath him. Heavy eyelids lend him a sleepy, sated look. He's one of the island's few prosperous citizens. Gold rings on his fingers, cell phone clipped to an alligator belt. He sold the land upon which the resort was built and, for the particular character of his prosperity, if for no other reason, he's not well liked.

"Got some nice turtle," Fredo tells him. "If you want, Emily fix you some conch salad, too."

Wilton grunts his approval and says, "I'll take fries with the turtle." He adjusts his belt beneath the overhang of his belly. "There's a white mon asking about you at Treasure Cove."

"That so?" Fredo carries Wilton a beer.

"Yeah, a German fella. The mon's crazy about pirates. 'Pears like he got an interest in talking to you. I tell him I'm going up your way for lunch, I got room for he and his woman in the Jeep. But he just grin and say, 'No, we going to walk. Walking be good for us.'" Wilton chuckles. "The sun duppy panting in the street, and he think it be good for them."

"When they coming?"

"I seen them toiling up the beach. They be along directly and they don't die first."

A battered truck pulls up outside and two laborers saunter in and sit as far away from Wilton as possible. They order beans and rice, beer. Wilton has almost finished eating and a squall is moving in from the northeast, leaden clouds sweeping over the island, when the German couple arrive. The man is fit and tanned, in his late thirties, dressed in shorts and a sweated through T-shirt, his blond hair pulled into a ponytail; the woman is similarly attired, but her hair is a silky platinum blond, and her skin is pale where her clothing has protected her, face and arms and legs sun-reddened, and she is soft, voluptuous to the point of caricature, with enormous breasts and a rear-end that nearly obscures the seat of the stool onto which she has collapsed. She has the look of an enormous doll, skin dappled with hectic patches, stuffed into garments that must have belonged to a smaller doll. A diamond plump as a cashew on her left hand signals wealth to the world. She orders a Pepsi, which Leona fetches, and, as the little girl gapes, astonished by her milky immensity, she presses the cold bottle to her neck and forehead, and gazes at the thatch, her eyes lidded and lips parted, as if spent by passionate demands.

Emily darts from the kitchen and snatches Leona back, and the man introduces himself as Alvin Klose (Klo-suh, he says) and asks if he is speaking to Fredo Galvez.

"That's my name, all right," Fredo says.

Klose divests himself of a small backpack, setting it atop the counter. The woman, whom he introduces as his wife, Selkie, asks if they have a ladies' room and Fredo tells her there's a place out back. Klose unzips the pack, extracts a notebook and pen, and says, "I hope you won't mind if I ask you some questions?"

"As things allow," says Fredo, gesturing at the tables.

"Yes . . . yes, of course. I understand you're busy." He stares at Fredo admiringly. "I want to ask you about Anne Bonny."

"Anne Bonny." Fredo pretends to reflect on the name. "Weren't that the Yankee girl got herself killed over on the mainland?"

"No, no. She was a privateer. A pirate."

"We don't tolerate no pirates on the cay."

"This was years ago," Klose said. "Hundreds of years. In the early eighteenth century."

"Anne Bonny." Fredo swipes at the counter with a rag. "Maybe I hear something about her. Yeah."

Wilton scrapes back his chair, heaves a sigh, comes over and drops his money onto the bar. He salutes Klose and says to Fredo, "I'll see you tomorrow." He calls back to the kitchen, "That some fine salad, Emily." As he makes for the door, thunder growls. He glances back, gives Fredo a wink, and says, "Right on!" The laborers, who have been talking quietly, laugh and one says to Fredo, on hearing the Jeep's engine turn over, "Now the mon think he Jesus."

"Last week he thinks he Bob Marley, so Jesus be a comedown," says Fredo.

John Bottomley and his son take stools at the bar. Fredo serves them beer and holds a brief conversation about fishing. Selkie, who looks paler for her experience of Swann's outhouse, retakes her seat and the couple begin whispering heatedly in German. Fredo's been around tourists enough to know that Selkie wants to go and Klose insists on staying. They break off their argument. Selkie stares at the wall with a frozen expression. Rain seethes on the thatch. Klose, his tone clenched, says, "We will have lunch now."

He orders the turtle and, after a second heated exchange, Selkie orders the conch salad.

Things get busy and, when next Fredo notices, the German couple are in a better mood. Selkie is drinking a beer. Klose says something that makes her smile, then turns his attention to Fredo, who is clearing their plates.

"Let me tell you a story, Mister Galvez," he says. "And afterward you can tell me if it sounds familiar."

"I guess I got time for a tale," says Fredo.

"It won't take long." Again, Klose opens his backpack and removes a paperback with a garish cover. "Anne Cormac," he says, leafing through the pages, "was a young Irishwoman, barely sixteen, who married a pirate named James Bonny. He carried her off to Nassau—in those days it was known as New Providence. There she engaged in an affair with the notorious pirate Calico Jack. Anne was of a violent disposition, adept as any man with a cutlass, and when Jack put to sea again, she went with him. Some say she disguised herself as a man, but according to members of the crew, she only dressed in men's clothing before a battle." Klose offers the paperback to Fredo, open to a central page. "Here. Have a look."

On the page is a sketch of Annie, a slender woman dressed in trousers and a loose-fitting ruffled shirt, a cutlass in one hand, a pistol in the other. Fredo has never had so precise an image of her and he studies it intently.

"Of course," Klose goes on, "I'm skipping over a great deal. Anne had many adventures prior to meeting Jack. Many affairs. Her husband James was deathly afraid of her. In fact, he had her arrested at one point by the Governor of New Providence, claiming that she would kill him if set free. But Anne had done the governor a favor, informing him of a plot against his life, and he refused to send her to the gallows. He said if Jack could not persuade James to accept a divorce-by-sale, Anne would be flogged and returned to her husband. She was incensed by the idea that she could be bought and sold like a cow. She and Jack made their escape not long after. They stole a sloop and returned to pirating."

"An early feminist, *nicht wahr?*" Selkie says, a sardonic edge to her voice, and asks for another beer.

"In a way, I suppose," says Klose.

As Fredo sets a fresh bottle on the counter, she places her hand atop his and says, "You must forgive Alvin. He is drunk with these pirate stories."

"Besotted," Klose says coldly. "I believe that is the word you want."

Selkie says something in German that Klose ignores. Thunder grumbles in the distance, the rain beats down harder. Outside, a vehicle pulls up, its engine dieseling.

"In the end," Klose continues, "Calico Jack and Anne were sentenced to hang in Jamaica, along with another female pirate, Mary Reade. She had joined Jack's crew as well, recruited from a ship that they captured. Anne seduced her, thinking she was man, and the two of them had an affair. Quite a passionate one, it's said. Eventually Jack was hanged and Mary was reported to have died of a fever in prison. But Anne did not hang. She disappeared. Now it is generally thought that her father, who was a wealthy lawyer, bought her freedom and conveyed her to a plantation that he owned in South Carolina, where she lived out her days under a false name. But this I do not believe. I believe she came to Cay Cuchillo."

Fredo affects nonchalance; he scratches his neck. "Nobody around here named Bonny."

Wilton re-enters, makes a show of shaking off rain. "Occurs to me you folks might want a ride back to the Cove. It's coming down fierce."

"That would be wonderful!" Selkie hops off her stool.

"She married," Klose says. "She changed her surname to that of her husband."

"Alvin!"

Klose casts her a bitter look, but begins to pack up his possessions. "The fact is," he says to Fredo, "I believe she married an ancestor of yours."

"You got your facts wrong there," Fredo says, moving off to help another customer. "Ain't no Yankees in this mon's family."

In the hillside shanty up from the bar, Fredo and Emily lie facing one another in a nylon hammock. Because wind is driving rain through the windows, they have put up the shutters and the air is close; the room is illuminated by the low yellow flame of a kerosene lamp that hangs on one of the posts to which the hammock is secured. Jenry and Palace are asleep in the next room. On a pallet to the side of the hammock, Leona makes a gurgling noise. The shanty shudders with a gust. Rain slashes against the boards.

"This weather harsh," Emily says.

"It likely clear by morning." Fredo presses against her and she laughs softly, pleased to feel his arousal.

"You want something? You got to work for it, then, 'cause I weary."

"I weary, too. All except this one part."

"That's the part usually gets it way, don't it?"

They kiss, his hand goes to her breast, and she makes a musical noise in the back of her throat. Her lined face looks older than her thirty-two years, yet despite three children, her body is still youthful, her breasts firm, and she likes having them fondled.

"Maybe you won't have to work so hard after all." She rests her knee on his hip and fits herself to him. "Mmmm," she says as he pushes inside. "Ohh . . . that's nice."

They set the hammock to swaying, but their lovemaking grows less insistent and soon they are content with merely being joined, sustaining their arousal by means of slight shifts in position.

"I had a visit from Annie today," he says.

"What she want?"

He tells her and she asks what he plans to do.

"I don't know," he says.

They move lazily together, hammock strings squeaking, and Emily says, "Think Annie warning us against the German?"

"The mon seem like a decent sort. It could be anybody."

After a brief let-up, the rain pounds harder, the shutters rattle and, taking his cue from the storm, Fredo thrusts heavily into Emily, but she clamps both her hands to his buttocks, holding him still.

"Show him the pictures," she says.

"The German fella?"

"You got to 'least show him. Find out how much money he willing to part with. And you know they got plenty. You see that stone his wife wearing?"

"We be taking a risk."

Emily pushes him away, breaking their union. "Every time Annie come visit, there risk and there opportunity. We taking a risk not to show him. I worried about the boys."

"The boys solid," he says. "They be fine."

"They not solid, they just young. But Jenry, he old enough he starting to understand that he don't have no future better than what he sees in front of him. He come home the other day acting all crazy and smelling of gas. You know what that mean. He sniffing red gas with that bunch hangs around the wharf."

"I speak to him."

"Speaking to him won't do no good. We got to give our children reason to hope."

She rolls up to her knees, a practiced maneuver that allows for the unsteadiness of the hammock, and comes astride him.

"You want Jenry to wind up like them wharf boys? Begging for pennies and falling out back of Tully's place?" She hisses in frustration. "That not my ambition. We got to do what we can for the children, no matter the risk."

Fredo tries to pull her hips down, seeking to enter her again, but she restrains him.

"You don't show him the pictures," she says, "I will."

Her ferocity seems to heat the room further and, confronted by such passion, weakened by desire, Fredo says, "All right. I'll take care of it."

"Tomorrow?"

"If you can manage the cafe . . . Yeah, I do it in the morning."

She braces with her right hand, reaches beneath her with the left and guides him inside. In the yellowed dimness, like light from another age, ancient light, she looks younger now, her face softer and less careworn. As she moves, touching herself, her breath quickening, a hoarse groan is dredged from Fredo's chest.

>   Lights break
>   behind his eyelids,
>   the serpent moon
>   uncoils
>   along his backbone,
>   a bamboo flute
>   shrieks in his ear

as Emily reaches her moment, collapsing atop his chest. They lie quietly, their breath subsiding, the hammock strings quivering. After a time she slips off him onto her side. She rests her head on his shoulder. "I know this hard for you," she says.

"Hard ain't the word for it."

"Well, hard or worse than hard, it's all we can do." She turns onto her back, gazes at the ceiling. "We gots to put things right for the family."

A muggy, windless morning, but Treasure Cove's dining room is cool, air-conditioned, furnished with Spanish Colonial-style tables and chairs, its whitewashed ceiling crossed by thick varnished beams. On the wall above the bar is a painted map of the island—Dagger Key, the legend reads (the Spanish name is inscribed in smaller letters and enclosed in parentheses beneath). The other walls are hung with flintlocks and cutlasses, replica work manufactured and given a patina of antiquity on the mainland. Sunlight tilts in through a big bay window overlooking the sea, leaving most of the room in shadow. Beside it, bumping against the glass, a pair of flies mate in mid-air, their buzzing unnaturally loud. Close to the horizon, a shrimper lies becalmed in an inch of dazzle.

Only three of the tables are occupied, one by a woman and her two small children, their piping voices shrill and demanding; another by an elderly couple peering at a guidebook, and the third by Wilton Barrios and a gray-haired man. He picks at a fruit plate and nods solemnly while Wilton talks. Fredo sits at the bar and Vinroy, the bartender, a handsome, young, energetic black man, serves him a cup of rich-smelling coffee.

"Can you tell me anything about this Klose fella that staying here?" Fredo asks.

"Klose," Vinroy says. "Yeah, the pirate mon. One thing I know, his wife ain't never going to be lonely. She catting around something crazy. Every time he go for a swim, she in here fooling with whoever on duty."

"You not tempted by that, now?"

"I tempted, all right." Vinroy rubs thumb and forefinger together. "Cash money, you know. She willing to pay, I willing to play."

"You going to lose your job, mon."

"Ain't lost it yet." Vinroy grins. "Tell the truth, I expect her husband be happy if someone take her off his hands."

Fredo sips his coffee. "How they fixed for money?"

Vinroy takes a stack of round glass ashtrays and begins distributing them. "He throw the cash around pretty good. Their diving gear real sweet." He aims an ashtray as might a shuffleboard player, slides it along the bar, gives it some body english, and snaps his fingers when it teeters at the end of the counter and stabilizes. "Divina, the girl who clean they suite, she say the wife got herself some fine clothes." He picks up a rag, swipes it along the bar. "They got a nice little motor boat with a cabin below decks and a wheel house. Klose tell me it were builded from a kit, you know. So I don't expect it worth that much. They come down along the coast from Cozumel. That's where he buy it. They planning to run the coast down to the Bay Islands."

Fredo removes a cigarette from a crumpled pack. "They early risers?"

"You ain't got long to wait. Mon come in every morning about this time. The woman like to sleep in." Vinroy checks his watch. "I got to go change. You all right on the coffee?"

"I could use some fire."

Vinroy reaches beneath the bar, flips him a packet of matches with a skull-and-crossbones on the flap, and goes out through the kitchen. Fredo lights the cigarette. His smoke uncoils bluely and his thoughts stretch out, less thoughts than they are appreciations of the coolness, the taste of the coffee, the play of light and shadow beneath the window.

> Skin a delicate mosaic,
>   inlay of viridian and jade,
>   a gekko freezes on the wall
>   waiting for an unwitting fly

and Klose enters the bar, a folded newspaper under his arm. He stops on seeing Fredo and comes over. "Mister Galvez!" He puts a hand lightly on Fredo's shoulder. "I didn't expect to find you here."

"Thought I'd hear the finish of that tale," says Fredo.

Klose hesitates, smiles. "Will you join me for breakfast?"

They relocate to a corner table and Vinroy, now dressed in white shorts and a navy polo shirt with Treasure Cove inscribed in white on the breast pocket, comes to take their order. Fredo asks for eight strips of bacon, well done, and a roll.

"So much meat," Klose says chidingly. "It's not healthy to eat meat so early in the morning."

"I have me some fritters earlier. I figure I wrap the bacon up for lunch."

Klose's smile falters as he digests, perhaps, the economic nuances that attach to Fredo's response.

"What you got to tell me about old Eduardo Galvez?" says Fredo. "The mon who marry Annie."

"You know about this?"

"Sure I know. It family business."

Klose appears stunned. "You are claiming to be Anne Bonny's descendant?"

"Yesterday you trying to pin it on me, and now you say I claiming it?"

"You denied the connection. I thought . . ."

"I don't like talking about Annie where other people can hear."

"But why? All this happened three hundred years ago."

"It still happening, mon. But I'll get to that." Fredo has a sip of coffee, finds it to have cooled. "You worked out some of the story; now I going to tell you the rest. Annie come to the island and she marry Eduardo Galvez some years after. But she did not come alone. That Mary Reade were with her. I know . . ." He holds up a hand to forestall an interruption. "They say she die in prison, but that were another woman did the dying. It were Mary that engineered the escape. She bribe someone high up with the promise of treasure. It ain't clear who. Someone she knew that were close to the governor, though . . ."

Fredo breaks off as Vinroy approaches with a tray, delivering bacon and rolls, granola, chopped banana, chunks of mango and papaya, a fresh jug of coffee.

"The plan were for Mary and Annie to take their share of the treasure and go to New Orleans," Fredo says once Vinroy is out of earshot. "But Mary . . ."

"The treasure was here?" asks Klose. "On Cay Cuchillo?"

He's excited, unmindful of his food, and Fredo feels more secure about telling him the rest.

"That's right," he says. "Calico Jack bury it here, and Mary use the knowledge to secure their freedom. They make sail from New Province-town to Cay Cuchillo and once they divide the treasure up, like I saying, they plan to find a boat what will carry them to New Orleans. But Mary decide she want to stay here. They have a big row about it, but in the end they build a café on the island and call it The Two Swans."

Wilton Barrios stands abruptly, knocking over his chair, and spits curses in Spanish. The gray-haired man looks up at him placidly and has a bite of melon.

"Maricon!" Wilton clenches his fists and appears ready to strike the man, but instead turns and stalks toward the door. On seeing Fredo and Klose, he takes a hitch in his stride and his furious expression abates as he goes out into the corridor, leaving the children gawking in his wake, the elderly couple whispering together, Vinroy shaking his head behind the bar.

As far as Klose is concerned, however, none of this might have happened. "The Two Swans," he said. "This is your cafe?"

"It been rebuilt more times than I can tally," says Fredo. "The boards rot, the winds blow it down . . . you know. Over the years, people drop the 'Two,' and then when the British write down the name for their records, they throw in an extra n and the change stick. But I guess you could say it more-or-less the same. It occupy the same ground, at least."

Fredo nibbles the end of a thick-cut strip of bacon. "Cay Cuchillo were a place where nobody care what two women do with one another, and that why Mary so strong for to stay here. For a while they happy, but Annie have a roving eye. She like men and other women, too. And come the day when she say she going to take her fair share of the treasure and leave. Mary beg her to stay, but once Annie have it in mind to do something, the weight of the world can be against her and she going to have her way. So Mary say, 'Go ahead, then. But the treasure ain't going nowhere.' She snatch up a cutlass and menace Annie. She not angry, she stricken by the thought of losing her love. But Annie's angry at being thwarted, and when she angry she a terror. She go at Mary with a dagger and stab her deep. Mary run out onto the beach, down toward the point from the café, and that's where Annie catch her. Mary pleading for her life. She tell Annie that she didn't mean nothing, she loves her. But Annie say, 'To hell with love, and to hell with you!' And she cut Mary down.

"When Annie realize what she have done, the spirit go right out of her. All her fierceness, all her joy in life, were spent with that one knife-stroke. She pass the days drinking and weeping. She don't care no more about New Orleans, about the café, about nothing—she might have drink herself to death if Eduardo Galvez didn't happen along. He prop her up, he help her to face things. She never come to love him, but she grateful to him and that's enough. She bear him three sons. The last of them, the one she died giving birth to, I of his line."

Vinroy saunters up, concerned that there's something wrong with the food, they haven't eaten a bite—Klose tells him, no, he was preoccupied, and shovels in a spoonful of granola as if to demonstrate his appetite.

"What all that fuss with Wilton?" Fredo asks.

"Some business. I don't know," says Vinroy, and nods toward the gray-haired man. "Wilton tell me he's an investor. 'Pear he got the good sense not to invest with Wilton."

"Yeah, mon," says Fredo as Vinroy walks off. "I hear that."

The dining room has begun to fill and Klose, taking cognizance of this, lowers his voice. "What happened to the treasure?" he asks.

Fredo reaches into his hip pocket, withdraws a grimy, much-folded piece of paper—stiff paper, like that used by artists—and lays it on the table. "This my family's fortune," he says. "If anybody hear of it, it could mean trouble for me."

Klose rests the fingertips of one hand on the paper, but Fredo also keeps his hand on the paper.

"You seen my place," says Fredo. "I better off than some, but I a poor mon nonetheless. Now you a rich mon. Maybe not king-rich, but rich enough you can help me out."

The German's face tightens as he realizes that money is to be the topic of conversation.

"I not going to try to sell you something you ain't interested in," Fredo continues. "If you don't want what I got, I no be bothering you again. But if you interested, remember this. You tell anyone what's on this paper, the deal is off. There's three items sketched on it. A cross, a cup, and a dagger. There's information written down about them. You can check it against the cargo manifest of the *Nuestra Senora de Alegria*, a Spanish galleon that were lost with all hands in these waters. The treasure ship sites online, they can tell you about it." He pushes back his chair and stands. "The dagger's not for sale, but I can let you have the cup or the cross."

Suspicion gone from his face, washed away by eagerness, Klose starts to unfold the paper, but Fredo restrains him and says, "Not here, mon! Not where anybody can see. Take it somewhere private."

Klose apologizes, then says, "May I show this to Selkie?"

"I'll be direct with you. From what I hear about your wife, she ain't the kind to trust with a secret."

Strain surfaces in Klose's voice. "I'm aware of my wife's proclivities, but where a matter of finance is concerned, you can count on her to be discreet."

"Well, that's up to you. But the same rule apply. She tell anyone, we ain't doing business."

Fredo tells him they'll talk early tomorrow and leaves Klose to his breakfast, intending to walk the beach to Dever's Landing. He cuts across the patio toward the water and notices two boats moored to the wharf: a sloop with a blue hull and a white cabin cruiser, the *Selkie*. As he's about to take a closer look, Wilton hails him and asks if he can use a ride. Minutes later, Fredo is hanging onto the roll bar of the Jeep as they lurch and rattle over the potholed road toward town, producing so loud a racket that Wilton has to shout to make himself heard.

"You got some business with that German fella?" he asks.

"He pay me a few dollars to tell him some lies. That's all."

Wilton appears to nod, though it may just be the bouncing of the Jeep.

"If it get any more that that, you let me know," says Wilton. "These Germans, they slick operators. You need someone looking out for you. Someone who can see you don't get took advantage of."

Fredo gazes at the dusty-leaved shrubs along the roadside, at palms with brown fronds and bunches of dried-out nuts, at the aquamarine sea that shows itself whenever the Jeep tops a rise. "No doubt," he says. "I be sure and consult with you first thing."

All through the day, doing chores and filling orders behind the bar, Fredo worries about whether he's doing the right thing. Annie thinks that dealing with Klose is worth the risk, that's apparent, though Fredo's not certain how much she actually thinks or what her process is. She may possess a thread of instinct or premonitory sense that causes her to seek him out, or it may be something unknowable that triggers her appearances. What worries him most is his family history. Once filling two deep chests, the treasure has dwindled over the course of the centuries to a cross, a chalice, and a dagger, and almost every transaction, every attempt to sell a piece or two, has been attended by abysmal luck, errors in judgment, drunkenness, and so forth. On occasion, a Galvez has realized some small profit from the sale of a ring or a golden place setting, but it seems that a curse has been laid upon the treasure and whenever a great profit is sought, tragedy results. Fredo believes that if a curse exists, it is one worked through the social fabric of the island. The way things are, the way they always have been, it's extremely problematic for someone poor, someone powerless, to sell an item of great value and come away with any money. Too many prying eyes, too many men with grasping, conniving natures. Impoverished men with hopes like his own; the police; government officials; gangsters and thugs; each looking for a glint of gold in the ordinary dirt of their lives. And should they catch sight of such a glint, they'll act without compunction.

The cross is a processional cross, 18 inches high, designed to be mounted on a wooden staff and held aloft by the acolyte preceding, in this case, the Archbishop of New Providence, for whom it was intended as a gift. Fashioned of yellow gold, exquisitely carved, and set with four diamonds of approximately forty karats and a ruby nearly twice that size. Also a gift meant for the Archbishop, the chalice is more resplendent yet, made of white gold and studded with emeralds and diamonds. By contrast, the dagger is nondescript, its hilt of horn chased with silver, but it has history on its side, having belonged to the fourth Marquis of Vallardo and been put to bloody use by both him and Annie. Fredo has held them in his hands several times, yet he has never once laid eyes upon them. Annie keeps her secrets close.

He sleeps poorly, ridden by dreams of a pale woman in a white blouse and brown leggings, and he rises before dawn to make the long walk into Dever's Landing, catching a ride from town with young Gentry Samuels, who delivers fresh bread to the resort. The eastern sky is touched with mauve when he arrives, and Fredo waits on a stool at the beachside bar until a red sliver of sun has crept up over the horizon and the lights come on inside Klose's bungalow, watching as

>
> an orb weaver,
> a galaxy of white spots
> speckling its black back,
> dangling from the thatch
> on a single strand of silk,
> lowers itself to within an inch
> of the countertop, then stalls
> as if wary of the wet ring
> left by a drunkard's glass . . .

and when it finally descends to the wooden surface, only then does he approach the bungalow and knock.

To his surprise, Selkie opens the door. She's wearing a frilly nightgown that extends from the slopes of her breasts to mid-thigh, and conceals nothing. Her pink areolae are visible through the sheer fabric, as is the dark suggestion of a pubic patch, at odds with her blond head. Fredo is put off by this casual display, but he also recalls what Vinroy said and wonders how it would be to lie with her. She seems less woman than a parfait of cream and strawberry, and he thinks that though the image she presents is arousing, she would not give him the pleasure of a real woman like Emily. He asks where her husband is.

"He is showering," Selkie says, sitting on the large overstuffed sofa that dominates the room, a harmony of white and pastel blues, except for the breakfast nook, decorated in sunnier colors. "Do not concern yourself with him. He is quite happy to remain in the bedroom while we are concluding our business."

"He not coming out, then?"

"Not unless we wish him to." Selkie pats the cushion beside her, indicating that he should sit, and, once he does, she scoots nearer so that their knees are almost touching. The musky scent of her perfume surrounds him, seeming to issue from the depths of her cleavage. She nods at the bedroom door. "Perhaps you would be more comfortable dealing with him?"

"I can handle it if you can."

"Oh, of this I am quite sure." She smiles coyly, the crimson bow of her mouth lengthening as if being strung, and gives his leg a pat. "The paper you gave Alvin . . . are you the one who made the sketches?"

He wrenches his eyes away from the milky valley between her breasts. "That were a friend of mine did the drawing."

"Your friend has had a peculiar education," she says. "He uses antiquated spelling. The double f instead of the s, for example. Did he perhaps copy the words from the cargo manifest?"

"I suppose," says Fredo.

"Were you not present when he made these sketches?"

Rattled, Fredo says, "What you want to know all this for?"

Dagger Key

"I am wishing only to satisfy my curiosity." She dismisses the subject with a wave of her hand. "To business, then. Your friend has noted the diamonds in the cross are weighing forty karats, and the ruby is . . . . " She casts about, as if searching for something. "*Scheisse!* My little book? Do you see it? It has a green cover."

"The ruby seventy-eight karats, if that's what you looking to know. The emeralds on the cup, now . . ."

"We have no interest in the cup. Too bulky. The cross is better because it lies flat."

Fredo shrugs.

"We will, of course, require to see it before we commit," Selkie continues. "Once we have made an assessment of its value, we will secure the funds."

"No, no! That's not how it going to be," Fredo says. "You gets the money, I brings the cross. You like what you see, then we make a trade and go our separate ways. And we do it quick. If the money not here tomorrow evening, say about seven-eight o'clock, it might as well never be here."

"But we must authenticate the cross . . . and the stones."

"Then best you learn about authenticating quick. Look here. When you see the thing, you going to know it old. And if you don't trust it, walk away. That's what I intends to do and the money ain't right."

Selkie looks at him without expression for a long moment. "How much do you want?"

"Fifty thousand dollars," he says. "Cash money."

Selkie starts to raise an objection, but Fredo says, "I ain't going to bargain with you. Fifty's what I need. Fifty in small bills. I can't get it from you, I'll get it somewheres else. For fifty, you stealing it. Any one of the stones worth a damn sight more than that, so I ain't going to listen about you ain't got it. If that the case, we got no use to talk further."

After a pause, Selkie says, "Fifty thousand. Yes. This I think we can manage, but it's good you do not ask for more. We will have to sell some things. And to transfer the money takes time. We cannot do this in less than two days."

Fredo doesn't like it, but after a brief internal debate, he agrees. "Two days, then. Not a minute longer."

He gathers himself, preparing to stand, and Selkie asks if he would like a drink. To seal the bargain, she says. She leans back, half-reclining on the sofa, and puts one slippered foot up on the cushion, opening her legs. A smile plays about the corners of her lips, and Fredo realizes that more than a drink is being offered. His eyes go to the bedroom door. It's cracked open and would afford anyone behind it an unobstructed view of the sofa.

"Please, Fredo. Stay for a drink . . . or two," Selkie says. "Alvin will not mind."

Angry that they think him a fool, or that he would willingly serve their perversity, he stands and says, "I'll take back my paper now."

"Your paper? I don't understand."

"The one with the sketch of the cross."

She makes a smacking sound with her lips, rises and goes to the breakfast table; she opens a drawer and extracts the folded paper, holds it out to him.

"I don't want no funny business when I bring the cross," he says. "I catch a sniff of anything wrong, and that be the end of it. You hear me?"

"No problem," Selkie says flatly.

He snatches the paper, avoiding the touch of her fingers.

"When will you bring it?" she asks.

"If I not here by ten that night, I not coming. But I see you in the morning, day after tomorrow, and give you instructions. Meet me in the bar for breakfast. Eight o'clock."

"So early!"

"I got things to do of the day."

She tips her head to the side, as if this new angle will allow her to see inside him. "Is the cross buried so deep, it will cost you a day to dig it up?"

"Not deep," he says, opening the door to admit the humid air, perfumed by a night-blooming cereus. "But deep enough that no man alive can find it."

The bank opens each morning at eight-thirty, and at eight-fifteen, Fredo is sitting across the street in a shanty bar known as John Wayne's, named for its owner, John Wayne Casterman, an elderly man with nut-brown skin and a wizened neck like a turtle's, his head nearly bald, a few tufts of cottony hair seeming to float above his scalp like clouds above a barren planet. The bar is accessed by a two-tiered stairway of rickety boards and rotting railings, and consists of a single room containing half-a-dozen tables and a makeshift counter of oil drums. Faded reggae posters advertising bands that no longer exist postage-stamp the weathered planking of the walls. John Wayne is perched on a stool behind the oil drums, humming to himself, reading a day-old newspaper, and Fredo sits by the door, nursing a warmish beer, watching the armed guards smoking in front of the bank, the passage of a Toyota pick-up, an old VW bus, a Hyundai truck carrying a load of concrete blocks. A young black woman, Jenny Bowen, in a tight skirt and a red tank top, balances a bowl covered in cheesecloth on her head, her walk an African elegance, serene and sensual. She pays no mind to the guards, who stare at her, whisper together, and laugh. Fredo remembers her as a little girl, when she skipped everywhere she went. Two pariah dogs engage in a snarling match, snapping at one another, until a bystander runs them off. The sun is a yellow glare in the east. Dust settles, rises from the dirt street, settles again.

Garnett Steadman, a man even older than John Wayne, hobbles into the bar, and, after a brief exchange with Fredo, How's Emily doing?, I spied your boy Jenry yesterday, etc, he takes a stool and talks fishing with John Wayne . . .

> . . . I bait the hook
>   with a chunk of barracuda,
>   and where I toss it in,
>   the sea go dark with mackerel.
>   The surface all lathered up around me
>   just like in the back time
>   when the fishing always good.
>   But not a one take a bite of that barra,
> and I had that duppy feeling,
>   cold in the middle of the day,
>   like the sun ain't truly hot,
>   like them fish ain't truly there . . .

A little after nine, a taxi stops in front of the bank, and Klose climbs out. He disappears inside the stucco building. Less than an hour later, he emerges from the bank and waits, nervously pacing, until a second taxi arrives to collect him. Fredo bids so long to Garnett and John Wayne, and begins the long walk home. Satisfied that things appear to be going the way he wants, he's anxious for the same reason. Annie has come to him three times before, none of which he recalls after a certain point. The first two occasions yielded neither profit nor loss, but the third time, after making a small profit from the sale of some coins, he had the idea that something bad happened. When he checked on the buyer the next morning, the man, a college professor from New Mexico, locked the door of his bungalow, refusing to admit him, and fled the island at the earliest opportunity. Now, with so much more at stake, dealing with untrustworthy people, he knows there's a potential for serious trouble.

"When Annie come, never try and thwart her," his father advised him. "You don't want her mad at you. She got your interests at heart, and 'cept you a big fool, like some of us has been, she bound to keep you safe. Whatever she do, that's on her, so don't wreck your soul worrying about it."

Sound advice, but Fredo is a less pragmatic soul than was his father and, since the old man died, he has learned he can't equate absence of guilt with innocence. He dreads these days when Annie's morality is imposed upon him, when he is at the disposition of a three hundred-year old spirit who, driven by a freakish sliver of blood loyalty, will go to any extreme on his behalf. As he walks the beach toward the café, he mutters prayers for himself and Emily, for Klose and Selkie, for anyone who may become involved. The words occupy his mind, but give him no comfort.

That afternoon, in the cool shade of the café, Fredo mopes about the place, drinking coffee and treating his customers dismissively. To avoid conversation, he takes a portable TV/VCR from beneath the counter, parks it at the end of the bar, and plays an old cassette of *Miami Vice* episodes, losing himself in gun battles and explosions, beautiful women, neon gleaming on the metal skins of expensive cars. Captivated by these images, three men join him at the bar and, when the tape ends, one of them, Philby Davis, says, "How about you put on some *Baywatch,* mon?," a notion seconded by the other customers. Fredo complies, and soon the women of *Baywatch* are jogging down the beach in their red Speedos, breasts asway in slow motion, while the ragged men of Dagger Key hoot and offer risqué comment.

"Look like that brown-haired gal going to catch ol' Pamela," says Philby. "But Pamela always edge her out by a nipple."

The others laugh and slap Philby's palm.

Fredo goes outside and sits on the palm trunk, wishing that he remembered to buy cigarettes. The sun is declining in the west, the light going orange. Waves pile in—the same wave, it appears, a low roller thinning to a frothy edge of water that races up the slope of the island to be absorbed by the sand. Shadows blur on the beach. Sand crabs burrow into silt at the tidal margin, leaving tiny airholes. Fredo imagines his thoughts are similar to theirs, a quiet, fretful paranoia.

Emily joins him on the palm trunk, places a hand on his back. "Why don't you go on up to the house?" she says. "You can send the boys down after dinner. They help me close."

Fredo nods. "Okay."

"What time you leaving?"

"I might go in tonight. These people got a boat. Little cabin cruiser. I need to make sure they don't go nowhere."

"How you going to do that?"

"Battery acid in they fuel. That way, if they want to test the motor, it going to start right up. But if they go to running, they won't run far. I slip out early in the morning and take care of it."

"You coming back home after that?"

"Maybe not. Maybe I find a spot up in the hills and sleep."

Emily looks doubtful.

"Don't worry. Nothing going to trouble me with Annie around."

She idly rubs his shoulder, appearing distant.

"What you thinking?" he asks.

"I'm hoping that Jenry and Palace don't have to bear this burden."

Resentment sparks in him, and he shifts away from her touch.

"Something wrong?" she asks.

"I wish you spare some of that hope for me."

"What you talking about?"

"You always thinking about the children. Seem like you got nothing left over."

She gapes at him, gets up and walks off a couple of paces, then turns back. "You must be crazy! I your wife, Fredo. I with you 'til the end. But I'm their mother, too. And you they father. You want them to have Annie with them all their days? Is that what you saying?"

Fredo says, "I expect Annie going to be with them one way or the other."

"Not and you sell these three pieces! Once the treasure gone, she gone."

"That's just what my daddy say."

"And his daddy before him, and his daddy's daddy. They all been saying that from the back time 'til now."

"Sometimes I feel that way, but just because a thing a tradition, that don't mean it true. Other times I think Annie never let go. She going to hold onto that dagger 'til the last days."

"Don't you be telling me that!"

"I can't help it. That's how I feel."

"No, don't be telling me that!" She confronts him, hands on hips. "You just vexed about Annie, and you pitying yourself. And you trying to get me to pity you. But you don't want that. The day I come to pity you, that's the day I stop loving you."

Shocked, he looks up at her.

"I'm serious," she says.

"I can't believe you say something like that, after all these years."

She drops to her knees in the sand, puts her hands on his knees. "Fredo, I just trying to get your attention. You know I love you, but there's days when it seem you got too much Jesus in your head."

"You going to start blaspheming now?"

"If that what it take to get you straight," she says. "Jesus don't have to live in this world. We do. Like it or not, when time tough, we gots to be hard, even if it sinful."

Fredo hangs his head and digs in the sand with the toe of his shoe, his thoughts circulating between the good sense of what she's said and his views on personal salvation.

"We counting on you to be hard, Fredo. The boys and Leona, we all counting on you." Emily sighs and pushes up to her feet. "I gots to go back in before Philby steal us blind."

"I'd pass through hell for this family," he says. "But I no want to get stuck there."

Emily's fingers brush his shoulder, startling him, and he glances up.

"Want me to wake you when I come in?" she asks. "Or I can sleep down with Leona."

In her face, beneath the worry and agitation, he finds what he has always found when she looks at him. "Yeah, wake me," he says. "I leave the lamp burning for you."

*P*alace is dribbling a soccer ball in front of the shanty, a skinnier, eleven-year-old Fredo, but with his mother's dark eyes, and Jenry, a well-built fifteen-year-old with Emily's African features and coloration, and his father's blue eyes, is lying in his parents' hammock, listening to dancehall on a battery-operated CD player. He's a strikingly handsome kid and he knows it. Seeing him, Fredo is tempted, as usual, to take him down a peg. He considers bringing up the gas-sniffing incident, but limits himself to saying, "Turn that mess off." Lately it has been difficult for Fredo to warm up to Jenry, and he's had the thought that his son may be growing into someone he does not much like; but Jenry is still a child, still salvageable, and Fredo understands that this is the reason he has to go with Annie, to fund that salvation. That both makes him feel more kindly disposed to Jenry and amplifies his resentment of the situation.

Jenry lets the CD play, then—just as his father is about to repeat his instruction; he's learned how to time these things—he switches it off and climbs from the hammock. He's wearing his school uniform, as is Palace. Short-sleeved white shirt, dark blue trousers and matching tie. He shoves his hands into his pockets and leans against the wall, the generic pose of the layabouts who hang around Tully's shop.

"Mama say you had a visit from Annie," he says in a challenging tone, as if daring Fredo to deny it.

"Change out of them clothes," says Fredo. "You got to keep them fresh for school."

Jenry loosens his tie. "I want to go with you."

Fredo grunts in amusement. "There a long walk between what you want and what going to happen."

Palace, the soccer ball under his arm, comes into the room, and Fredo tells him to change his clothes, saying he'll start supper going.

"Why can't I go with you?" Jenry asks, and Palace says happily, "Roxy Tidcombe already fix us sandwiches over the resort." He giggles. "Her cat purring for Jenry."

Jenry gives him a scornful look.

"Go on," says Fredo. "Change them clothes. Your mama's got enough to do without washing 'em every day."

He stretches out in the hammock and closes his eyes, listening to the boys bickering in the back room. Palace: "You the one tell me about Roxy!" Jenry: "Did I tell you to spread the news around, too?" Fredo's thoughts slow, but he does not sleep, hovering just above sleep's surface. A breeze pushes open the door, the rusting hinges squeak. Through the doorway, a narrow band of the sea appears to billow like a blue-green scarf drawn between earth and sky. Footsteps behind him, and Jenry steps into view. He asks again about Annie and Fredo, less irritable now, says, "Your mama needs you to help out while I gone. The time come soon enough you going to learn about Annie."

"How soon?"

Fredo swings his legs over the side of the hammock. "You remember that toy you wanted a few years back? That robot with its eyes light up and it shooting sparks?"

"That were six, seven years ago," Jenry says defensively. He's clad in a pair of shorts and has a cheap gold chain about his neck, the links showing like golden stitches against his black skin.

"We told you it were a piece of trash, but you had to have it. And once you get it, it fall apart in a week. The eyes don't light and the sparks burn your arm. Wanting to know Annie's like wanting to get your hands on that robot. Ain't no pleasure at the end of it."

"So you say. Maybe I feel different."

"What you want to argue with me for? Your mama need you—that all you gots to know." Fredo comes to his feet, stretches, then with a sudden movement grabs Jenry by the back of the neck and tickles him with his free hand. "What you going to do now, huh? How you going to argue with this?"

After a brief struggle, which veers between play and actual ferocity, Jenry breaks away. He seems about to smile, but instead glowers at Fredo.

"Back off with the attitude, mon," Fredo says. "Okay? I got a long night ahead of me, and maybe a long day to follow. I could stand a break."

Jenry's expression degrades into sullenness, and Fredo busies himself rummaging in the tool box that sits atop a dresser, searching for a large plastic syringe and a set of lockpicks.

"Roxy Tidcombe, huh?" he says. "That one pretty gal. She what we call back in my day pure glamity."

"She okay," Jenry says. "But she holding out on me."

Fredo grins at him over his shoulder. "And here I thought you grown into a grindsman."

"Seem like all she want to do is give me a car wash."

"Well, I wouldn't complain and I was you. Lots of girls that way at first. They afraid of catching a big belly."

"That how it were with you and mama?" Jenry asks sneeringly. "She give up her puni straightaway and you never get no car wash?"

> Something like anger,
>   but stronger,
> something of the old blood,
>   Annie's blood,
> surges through Fredo,
> and he has to close his eyes
>   against the sight of his son
>   until it has passed,
>   gripping the wooden handle
>   of the tool box
> so hard it cracks.

"Get on down to the café," he says. "You can ask your mama about the car wash and you got the courage. Take Palace with you."

"It Friday night, mon! I got better to do," Jenry says, and Palace, who has obviously been eavesdropping, comes to the door and says, "I ain't finish my schoolwork!"

"What kind of schoolwork they give you on a Friday night?" Fredo asks.

Palace glances away, a sure sign he's fishing around for a believable lie. "I got a book to read."

"Read it at the café," says Fredo. "Jenry can do your share of the chores. When you done with reading, then you can do his."

Both boys complain and he says, "I ain't going to tell you again."

He stands in the doorway, watching them walk down the hill. Emily's right, he thinks as his anger fades. Jenry may be already lost and Palace won't be far behind. Contemplating this, Fredo shakes his head ruefully and spits. As they reach the foot of the hill, Jenry shoves his brother, knocking him off his feet, and starts jogging along the road toward town.

A moonless night; thin clouds reduce what stars there are to a scatter of dim white points. Fredo steals along Treasure Cove's pier, his footsteps hidden by the slop of water against the pilings. The watchman is asleep on the beach in a cabana chair, his rifle resting across his knees. His dory is drawn up on the beach, the outboard tipped up out of the sand. A fresh creosote smell from the pier overwhelms all other odors. From its seaward end, the bungalows are almost indistinguishable in the dark— vague white shapes mounted against the hill, like lumps of mashed potatoes. Fredo climbs over the railing onto the deck of the cabin cruiser and locates the hatch covering the engine. Using a penlight to see, he picks the lock and slides off the cover. He draws battery acid into the syringe and squirts it into the fuel, repeating the process; then he slides the cover shut and locks it. The door to the cabin is open, and that astounds Fredo. These people must have no idea where they are, he tells himself. He disables the radio and makes a quick search, finding a flare gun and a revolver in a cabinet. He renders the flares unusable and, after emptying the revolver, decides it will be safest to drop it over the side. This done, he hurries along the pier, clambers into the rocks above the resort, and curls up on a ledge to sleep.

He wakes in bright daylight, worried that he's missed his appointment. Entering the bar, he spots Klose and Selkie sitting by the window, dirty dishes in front of them. They're dressed in shorts and tank tops, and Fredo thinks that they more resemble a brother and sister than a husband and wife. He threads his way among tables, drops into a chair across from them. With a petulant frown, Selkie says, "We thought you were not coming."

"I had some business, but I here now," Fredo says. "You have the money?"

"I will collect it from the bank this morning," Klose says. "And the cross?"

"I fixing to get it this afternoon."

"Then all is in order?"

"We got things to talk about, but I'll order me some breakfast first." Fredo gives Vinroy a wave. "You making out a damn sight better than me, so this on your tab."

"There is no guarantee of that," Selkie says with a degree of irritation. "We must smuggle the cross into Germany. We must find a trustworthy buyer. *Boah!* Too much can go wrong!"

"The poorer you are, the more you got those same problems. We both taking a gamble, but if you win, you crazy rich, mon. That cross, even and you sell it cut up for the stones and the gold, it worth millions. Like that English fella on TV used to say, you be having champagne dreams." Fredo makes a disgusted noise. "Me, maybe I get my kids off the island. Nothing much else going to change. But if I try to sell the cross for true value . . . and it my property, mon! It come down to me all the way from Annie." He slaps the table angrily. "If I asks for millions, you think I be getting it? Hell, no! You can't count to ten before I'm lying in a ditch somewhere with my throat slit and some bastard already rich rolling into his bank and everybody smiling upon him, saying, 'Have a chair, sir,' and 'Ain't you looking splendid this morning, sir,' all because he stole a poor man's property."

Having listened to this outburst, Klose seems abashed—he clears his throat and looks down at his coffee cup; but Selkie maintains her expression of sleek, sulky discontent. It's evident to Fredo now, if it hasn't been before, that she's the ruler of the marriage. It's also evident that her perversity colors the couple's actions. Klose is merely a drone and she's the one Annie will have to watch.

"What for you, Fredo?" Vinroy, looking crisp in his navy shirt and white shorts.

"Fry me up about ten of them little sausages and wrap 'em with some rolls. For now, let me have some hotcakes."

"Coffee?" Vinroy asks.

"Yeah, mon."

Vinroy inquires whether the German couple would like a refill of their coffee, and Selkie says, no, they have to be going. Vinroy stacks their dishes and, once he's gone, Klose says, "You said you would have instructions for us."

A wave of fatigue washes over Fredo. He sits up straight, blinks against the sunlight chuting through the glass. "I be at your place around nine o'clock. At eight-thirty, you sit down at the kitchen table and stay there. Don't make a move until I say so. Leave the door unlocked and the window shade open so I can peer in. Wear what you got on now. That way I can see you ain't carrying no weapon. Keep the money close by. I don't want you have to go into another room to fetch it."

"Would you like us to put our hands in the air?" Selkie lays the sarcasm on thick, but Fredo gives her question its due.

"Maybe, and I see something not right," he says. "Do what I say, everything go smooth. But let me tell you this much. You ain't dealing with no bobo tonight, so have a care."

After Selkie and Klose leave, Vinroy brings Fredo's food, the sausages and rolls wrapped in a tin foil packet. "I seen you scaling down the rocks earlier," he says. "What you doing way up there?"

"Wasting time," says Fredo. "I used to crawl up there when I a boy and spy on the water."

Vinroy looks perplexed. "What you expect to see?"

"Seen manta rays out past the reef."

"I ain't see no mantas for years."

"None left to see, I reckon."

Fredo spreads butter and blackberry jam on his hotcakes and cuts them into little bites. His thoughts turn to Selkie as he eats, but he pushes them aside and recalls

> a big shadow coasting
> through aquamarine water
> over white sand,
> rising explosively,
> hidden by spray,
> and then revealed for an instant,
> the great rubbery body aloft,
> strange monstrous beast
> flapping black wings of muscle,
> peering into unaccustomed light
> with eyes opposed like a hammerhead's,
> crashing down, making a splash
> like a depth charge,
> becoming once again
> a big shadow coasting
> through aquamarine water
> over white sand.

A young American couple sits at an adjoining table; they talk about mix ratios and the woman's new rebreather. Her hair is the color of a fresh honeycomb, bleached to straw in places by the sun. She has an easy laugh, health insurance, a future. For a change, Fredo is too preoccupied to envy her beautiful blond life. He ladles more preserves onto his plate, dips a bite of pancake in it, savoring the sweetness.

*L*ong ago, after the murder of Mary Reade, before Annie conceived her first child, she was in the habit of walking into the hills, carrying with her a bottle of rum. There she would sit in a secluded spot and drink herself blind, grieving, weeping, lamenting the sins of her young life. That spot, shadowed by banana trees and sabal palms, is near the top of Dagger Key's tallest hill, a weedy notch some twenty feet wide and twelve feet deep. Bromeliads, ferns and vines festoon walls of dark conglomerate rock; and, matting one section of wall, is a mass of vines that have been interwoven with dozens of cowrie shells, bits of ribbon and oddly shaped pieces of driftwood. Fredo doesn't know who tends the notch. It must be tended, he thinks. The ribbons must fade, the shells must fall away as the vines wither; yet the vines are always green, the shells white, and the ribbons unfaded whenever he comes. It seems unlikely that an islander would be responsible—most recognize the notch to be a duppy place and keep their distance. Many of those who have trespassed will testify to having night terrors for months after the fact and rarely return.

Maybe, Fredo thinks, it's Annie.

That was his father's view. The first time he brought Fredo to the notch, he voiced the opinion that the vines were tended either by Annie or the Caribe wizard whose spirit has befriended her—or, perhaps, served her—through the centuries.

Fredo arrives at the notch shortly past noon and begins drinking from a fifth of unrefined rum purchased at John Wayne's. Though not usually a drinking man, indulging in a beer now and then, he has been taught that he has to open himself to Annie, to attune himself to her drunken grief, her guilt and rage. He can't abide the taste of rum, but he forces the raw stuff down and soon grows bleary and addled. The sun veers across the sky when he looks up, and the fringe of vegetation that hides the notch from all but the most discerning eye appears to undulate with unseen currents.

>   Mired in a complicated
>   shadow of banana fronds,
>   he feels that he's being lowered
>   into a deep well,
>   a spiritual depth,
>   a hole bored into the bottom of the world
>   from the world below . . .

. . . and the more he drinks, the deeper he sinks, until it's as if he's at the end of a long tunnel, a place that the sun, although he sees it shining, cannot warm, and the wind, although it stirs the leaves around him, cannot reach. And it's then that he starts to sense Annie's presence and the presence of other spirits, too. The grass at his feet ripples with the passage of a snake duppy, the shade of a lizard, and the vine matte shakes itself as if some old ghost is shouldering on its cloak, the cowrie shells clacking together. The base of his neck prickles as Annie begins to settle over him, a cloud obscuring his soul. On the verge of passing out, he sees the vine matte shift forward, moving at the pace of a very old man taking hobbling steps. Something is dislodged from the matte, a bundle wrapped in a grimy sack, bulky, dropping with a clank onto the ground. Drool escapes the corner of Fredo's lips, eels onto his chin. His head lolls, his eyelids flutter and a thick, glutinous noise issues from his throat. He stretches a hand out toward the sack, wanting to touch his treasure, to see its golden glory... but a crunching in the brush stays him. A voice, Wilton Barrios' voice, says, "Fredo..." The remainder of his utterance is obliterated by Annie's fury, a fuming hiss, like fire drowning in rain, that swirls around Fredo, seeming to occupy a space both inside his head and without. In his confusion, he's inspired to struggle to his knees. Ignoring Wilton's booming, unintelligible speech, he pushes up to his feet, staggers, braces with one hand on the ground, inadvertently gripping a fist-sized rock, and then he straightens, swaying, half-possessed, blinking in sunlight that has suddenly grown too warm and too bright. The world steadies around him. The vine matte snaps back to its customary position against the rock face; the vegetation seethes with the ordinary actions of the wind. Wilton swims into focus, wearing a sweated-through Cuban-style shirt that's hiked up over the revolver stuck in his waistband, a confident look on his jaundiced, jowly face.

Effortfully, Fredo says, "Best you go from here, Wilton."

"Now what I want to do that for? You going to shoot me with that rock?" He draws the revolver, trains it on Fredo's chest, and nods at the sack. "This what you been hiding up here? Mon, you got to show me where you hide it. I been searching three years, ever since you put the fear of god in that professor, and I ain't never find it."

"You not going to steal my property, mon."

"I ain't going to do nothing but. Drunk as you is, think you stop me?" Again, he indicates the sack. "What you got in there? The professor say it a bag of pirate gold. You shouldn't have scared that mon so bad. He couldn't leave off talking, and him so angry with you."

The vine matte shifts, rattling its shells, but Wilton does not appear to have noticed. He sidles toward the sack, keeping an eye on Fredo, and picks it up. "Heavy," he says. "How much you got in here?"

When Fredo does not respond, Wilton says, "Tell you what. After I fix my problems, if there's anything left over, I split it with you."

Fredo grips the rock more tightly, trying to maintain consciousness and balance.

"You might wind up with more money that way than if you sell it on your own," says Wilton.

"Listen here!" Fredo slurs badly and the words come out *Liss' hyeer*. He's strangely concerned for Wilton's well-being and wants to tell him to get away, to run, because nothing good can happen to him in this place, and he's baffled by Wilton's attempt to smooth things over. Wilton knows that stealing a man's property, be it pirate treasure or an engine part, constitutes a blood crime on Dagger Key.

The vine matte shifts again, and this time Fredo sees that the vines are draped over the frame of a wizened black Caribe, a frail, bony old man, his face so withered and wrinkled, it appears inhuman, a crafty disguise contrived by a lizard or a spider. The wizard shakes his vines, clatters his shells. He capers, moving with unnatural agility, as if he's light as a thistle, adrift on a breeze, the clacking of the shells counterfeiting a dry cackle. Wilton sees him, too. The big man gives forth with a guttural cry, the sound of abject fear, and fires twice in the direction of the wizard . . . and Fredo, fueled by an anger not entirely his own, steps forward and, with all the force at his command, slams the rock against Wilton's head, catching him on the temple. As Wilton falls, Fredo is on him, striking again and again with animal ferocity. He feels the skull collapse, the cracking impact of rock on bone yielding to a soft, plush noise that brings to mind Emily pounding on turtle meat to tenderize it. In horror, he scrambles away from the body. One whole side of Wilton's face is covered in blood. A brown eye stares up at Fredo, the mouth open in awed regard, tongue lolling, and, overwhelmed by terror at his mortal sin, by drink, by things less nameable, he loses consciousness.

Flies,
tiny black emperors of nature,
gather to their work,
crawling black on red—

> their religious droning
> >adds a monastic note;
> a heretic beetle walks up the cooling tongue
> >into the damp cavity of the mouth,
> >>never to return,
> >losing its way amid the intricacies
> >>of the flesh,
> the garden of the flaccid organs.

>Twilight . . .

. . . and Annie wakes, stunned by a newly elaborate sense of the world, though not relishing it, not comfortable with the sudden wealth of impressions. She squats beside the body, reflecting on the uses of violence, remembering her violent life, arriving at a sketchy understanding of what has happened here, aligning her memories with Fredo's. She takes Wilton by the arms, drags him to the lip of the notch, pushes him over the edge with her foot and watches him roll away into the brush. Fredo's body does not suit her, but she approves of its strength. She picks up his gun, studies it briefly, then flings it after him. A gun has never been her weapon of choice. She goes to the sack, removes an object wrapped in rags of linen. She reaches deeper into the sack and brings forth a smaller object, which she unwraps. A dagger with a thin, double-edged blade, its hilt fashioned of horn, chased with filigrees of silver. *Mary.* She says the name to herself, tasting its bitter flavors. She tucks the dagger into Fredo's boot, carries the sack to the vine matte and thrusts it in among the vines, deeper than one would think it could be thrust—they writhe, seeming to welcome it, the shells clacking ever so slightly. Moved by the notion of a duty sacred to her, she bows her head and prays to the blur of memory in which God is concealed, asking that His blessings be not so dire as is His wont. And then she is off, making her way with a stride that might strike the eye as less purposeful than Fredo's, somewhat delicate and mincing, not quite a woman's walk, nor yet a man's.

						Inside the shadow
		of a fragrant jacaranda,
						the ground at her feet,
			carpeted by its lilac blossoms,
						Annie watches the window
								of the Germans' bungalow,
					her attention held by the woman—
			how she sits with one leg raised,
		her knee drawn up, foot braced on a rung
			of a wooden chair,
					and the other leg outflung,
								as if she were in her petticoats,
				her stink doused with perfume,
						reclining on a harlot's couch
										in New Providence.

Framed by the lighted rectangle of the window, the Germans' mood is easy to read. The man, Klose, is negligible. Weakness shines out of him. He fingers his wedding ring, plucks at his shirt, his anxiety displayed in every gesture. But Annie recognizes in the woman, Selkie, a strength akin to her own. The way she looks down at her breasts, inspecting the white cloth that covers them and flicking off a speck of imperfection, then restores her gaze to the window and smiles—like a woman who knows she's being watched and enjoys the experience. Another couple walks past, headed for the bar, and Annie steps deeper into the shadow. Once she is certain no one else is about, she enters the bungalow. The Germans stare at her expectantly; their eyes fall to the cloth bundle under her arm.

"Is that it?" Selkie half-stands, then sits back down.

Annie holds up her hand, cautioning them to stay put; she quicksteps into the bedroom, has a look around, then retreats into the outer room and lowers the window shade.

"There's no one else here," says Klose.

"Where's me brass?" asks Annie.

The Germans are confounded by the question, and Klose says, "What do you mean?"

"Me brass," says Annie impatiently. "The money."

Selkie says, "We will see the cross first."

Annie sets the bundle down on the edge of the table and steps back. The Germans come to their feet and Annie snaps at Klose, "You . . . sit! Let the bitch have a look!"

Klose retakes his seat and Selkie—in her greed, unmindful of having been referred to as "the bitch"—leans over the table, begins unwinding the linen rags, going carefully, as if what they cover were made of glass. She gasps when she glimpses the gold and, when the cross is revealed in its entirety, its surface worked with carvings of birds and fruit, leaves and vines, symbols of nature's abundance, the great ruby glowing like a heart, diamonds glinting coldly under the yellow light, it seems to Annie, as it always does, a pagan thing, an object of power . . . and Selkie, trailing her fingers over it, says in hushed tones, *"Ach, du meine Gute!"* She turns to Annie, apparently overcome, unable to speak, and, after hesitating a moment, she flings her arms about Annie's neck, presses her lips to Annie's mouth.

If Fredo were the recipient of that kiss, he would almost certainly push her away, but his soul has been tamped down into a quiet corner by Annie's cloudy presence, and it has been a very long time between kisses for Annie. The pressure of Selkie's breasts, her pliant lips, the intimate physicality of hips and loins . . . it's as though these sensations are restoring Annie's body. A phantom body, yet she feels it nonetheless. Her nipples ache with longing, her quim grows juicy. She cups Selkie's buttocks and pulls her closer, recalling another, firmer ass, and darts her tongue into Selkie's mouth . . .

>   the serpent-kissing,
>   soul-stealing, silk-skinned,
> female-fleshed demoness of lust,
>   licking pleasure from a woman's slit,
>   'til it yields lavish, thick-flowing treasure . . .
>
>   . . . Mary . . .

. . . and then she does push Selkie away, roughly, recognizing that she is not

Mary, but a whore who would get on all fours for a gentleman's mastiff if the purse were sufficient, or even were it not.

Klose is smiling, a crooked, febrile smile, and Selkie, flushed, wipes her mouth on the hem of her shirt with undue thoroughness, as if wanting to remove every trace of spittle, and Annie, her head spinning, dizzy from the kiss, no matter how false, once again demands her money.

"In the cabinet. The one on the left." Klose points to it. "Shall I get it for you?"

Annie eases around the table to the cabinet he's indicated. It's empty, but for a biscuit tin. She removes the tin, rests it on the counter and pries up the lid. Packets of bills inside, each bound with a band that states the value of the packet is five thousand dollars. She tells Selkie to sit, saying that she has to make a count. Selkie complies, still dabbing at her mouth, and, their backs to Annie, the two Germans fondle the cross as if it were a thing alive.

Annie counts one packet—as stated, it contains five thousand dollars. Counting the rest will be a chore, but she's determined not to be cheated. She counts three packets . . . or was it two? She's not sure. Three, she decides. She glances over at the Germans. Selkie looks at her and smiles, then goes back to admiring the cross; she whispers to Klose. Partway through the fourth packet, Annie loses the count and has to start over. She's muddleheaded—from the excitement, she thinks, and she tries to concentrate. Twenty, forty, sixty . . . sixty. She can't recall what comes next. A wave of lightheadedness seems to lift her and she realizes that something is wrong. She's unable to hold a thought in her head and two Selkies, both insubstantial, both wavering, are smiling at her. Klose says . . . Annie's unclear as to what he says. The words reverberate, seeming to overlap. And Selkie laughs, a giddy, high-pitched cascade of musical tones that serves to destabilize Annie further. Selkie parodies a kiss, her lips making a smacking noise, and laughs again.

The fat sow is mocking her, Annie realizes, and that recognition centers her, spurs her to act. Furious, she bends down, reaching for the dagger tucked in Fredo's boot. Blood rushes to her head. The linoleum tile of the kitchen floor confuses her. It's too close. It takes her several seconds before she understands that she has fallen. Her eye locks on the pattern, an abstract of yellow and gray, like gray swirls of cloud in a yellow sky. She strains to move, to stand, but succeeds only in stirring, her hand scrabbling, scratching at the tiles. Poison, she thinks. They've poisoned her somehow... and then she remembers the kiss, Selkie's scrupulous wiping of her mouth. Fury takes her again and she pushes up from the floor, but a foot planted between her shoulderblades flattens her. Their voices swoop and curvet above her, one high, one low, intermingling like two currents. Beneath her, gray clouds larded with white folds are racing in a yellow sky, running away toward the rim of the world, a flickering dimness toward which Annie, too, is borne...

            ... into an abyss
        painted with demons,
like the bole of that opium pipe
            Jack smoked—
he pointed them out to her.
This, the Demon of Black Rope Hell,
        And this one,
    the Demon of Unsavory Appetites.
You'd think he'd be fatter, wouldn't you?
        And here be
    the Demon of Lost Hope,
my favorite. How twisted and pale he is!
         An eye peering
    from each of the hundred sores
spotting his sour flesh. Pity the sinner
        who falls to him...

       Jack!
     Those demons now
         reaching out for her...

...and on the far side of that dimness, after a night of undetermined length, Annie discovers the clouds are no longer racing, the yellow sky is once again a floor, the demons stoppered up in their bottle. She comes to her knees, disoriented, head pounding, and becomes aware of the silence in the bungalow. She struggles to her feet, grabbing the counter for support, and makes her way to the bedroom. The closet's empty, all the hangers unused. Anger and distress fuel her. She's been dishonored, cheated, robbed of the pittance for which she sold the cross, and . . . As her head clears, her intent sharpens and she draws her dagger, holds it by her side as she goes out into the night. The moon hangs an insanely jolly, silver Jack o' Lantern grin amid countless stars and the beach gleams white, its silicates sparkling. No one is about. The cabin cruiser is gone. Annie walks to the end of the pier, gazing across the glittering sea toward Honduras. That was their plan: Honduras. But common sense tells her that they have changed their plan. They would choose to return to Mexico with their treasure, then to Germany. They'll be west of Cay Cuchillo, and not far. Not nearly far enough. An hour or two, no more.

"Stand easy!"

The watchman, coming along the pier, his antique rifle at the ready, shirttails belling in the breeze.

"That you, Fredo? What you doing here so late?"

In his fifties, already an old man from hard work and drink, the watchman's grizzled face relaxes from its stern expression as he approaches. An unsteadiness in his step, rum on his breath, he lowers the rifle. Beyond, the shadowy outline of his dory notches the beach.

"You been drinking?" he asks. "You such an early riser, I expect you must be drinking, you out this late."

"Which way did the Germans sail?" she asks.

"The Germans?"

"The cabin cruiser," Annie says. "A man and a woman."

"Oh, yeah. Now that a peculiar thing. They claim they off to Puerto Cortez, but far as I can tell, they headed for the Chinchorro Bank. They all turned around." A chuckle. "Hope they knows what they doing. A mon can come quickly to grief out there." He lays his hand on Annie's shoulder. "Let's have us a drink, Fredo. I got a bottle under my chair."

Without hesitation, Annie seizes the opportunity, drives the blade of the dagger deep into his abdomen, gives it a twist as she pulls it free. Before he can cry out, she yanks back his head, exposing his throat, and slashes him across the windpipe. The watchman falls, convulsing, and he is still convulsing when she wrenches off his belt and nudges his body off the pier. She hops down into the water, dragging the body under, holding her breath. Working blind, she secures him to a piling with the belt, leaving him among barnacles and tubeworms and crabs, all the little feeders for which he'll provide a delightful feast, floating beneath the pier at a depth that will hide him until any urgency attaching to his loss has been forgotten. She strikes out for the beach, swimming with a strong, confident stroke. She'll take the dory, go after Klose and his bitch. When she finds them, and find them she will, they'll wish the Devil had come in her stead.

*E*arly morning on the Chinchorro Bank. The sun burns a ragged hole through a pale blue, papery sky. A string of bone-white, lizard-haunted islands rises out of waters a thousand meters deep, the visible portion of a coral reef that stretches forty miles and more, from Belize into the waters off Quintana Roo. Fringed with mangrove, dabbed with spinach-colored vegetation, some of the islands bear living trees, but dead trees abound, their naked limbs hung with osprey nests. Overlying the reef, the sea is a patchwork of light and shadow, here dark over a bottom of yellow-green manatee grass, here a sun-dazzled expanse of aquamarine over white sand, dark again where a forest of feathery gorgonians overgrows a sloping shelf, brightening as Annie crosses a shallows above a bed of lettuce coral . . . She feels the slow, persistent beat of the coral's mind on the perimeters of her consciousness, watches the reef's traffic of angelfish and sergeant majors, tangs and jackknife, obeying the direction of that mind, flitting back and forth in schools, slaves to its unguessable purpose. She knows these waters, as much as they can be known. Ships out of Cartagena would ply north to Havana, then sail the western passage along the bank, and the *William* would lurk by Cay Lobo, picking off the weakest, though Annie would urge Jack to seek bigger prizes. She was ever hard on him. On the day he was taken to be hanged, she told him she was sorry to see him in chains and on his way to Deadman's Key, but if he'd been more of a man, put up more of a fight, he might have avoided that fate.

There's no sign of the *Selkie*. Perhaps, she thinks, she has miscalculated.

She should have sighted them by now, and she wonders if they were foolish enough to try the windward passage. If so, they may have gone down, down into a graveyard already populated by hundreds of ships, some sent there by Annie's hand. And yet she feels they're close by. Engineless, they wouldn't want to be caught out in the channel with weather coming and the cross on board; they would have allowed the boat to drift close to shore before trying to effect repairs. Leaden clouds are pushing in from the west, black brooms of rain sweeping the sea. She needs to find them before the squall hits.

> Sputter and pop
> of the dory's outboard.

> Annie cuts the motor and drifts.

> Winded silence.

It was a day like this she first met Jack. Clear, with a squall in the offing. In the market at New Providence. She carrying a basket, tarrying by a fishwife's stall, inspecting a fresh-caught bonita, and there he was, walking with his mates, like a lion among dogs, handsome in a tri-corner and an embroidered frock coat, a full head taller than the rest. In answer to her inquiry, the fishwife said, "Why that's Calico Jack, miss. The pirate." He was not much of a pirate, Annie learned. Too cautious by half. Cock like an Irish toothpick. Still, if he'd had a lion's heart, she would never have strayed . . . though Mary would have tested her loyalties, no matter the circumstance, teaching her the woman's way. The night Jack caught them at it, scissoring their quims in the sail locker, he made a show of outrage and wounded pride, but was intrigued by their display and let himself be drawn into a game of rub-and-tickle, seduced by shy looks and clever smiles. La, but that was a merry voyage! The crew rarely saw their captain abovedecks, and then only when they would anchor off the edge of the reef, lower a longboat and go fishing for shark, she and Jack and Mary, bait fish flopping in the bilge, their mineral reds and blues and yellows glistening like rare gemstones. The *William* might have sailed in circles and mutiny been muttered had not the first mate been a man of sober purpose and scant imagination.

God's light! Where are they?

Having reached the end of one cay, Annie restarts the motor and points the dory toward the next, about two hundred meters away. Then a dazzle hard by the tip of the island, as of the sun off a metal surface. She cuts the outboard and peers toward it, shielding her eyes. There. By that cove. An off-white shape against whiter sand. She unships the oars and begins to row. After thirty meters, she's certain it's the *Selkie*. She quits rowing and assesses the situation. Unless she waits until nightfall, it's unlikely she'll be able to catch them unawares, and she doesn't want to wait. She's been too long in the body. The tastes of this world are too rich, their joys too poignant. She's grown accustomed to being desireless and dreamless, the merest stripe of her old self. The memories circling her now, pecking and clawing at her brain . . . she yearns to have them fade, become as ephemeral as monsters in fog. Even the good ones have their attendant pains.

Her stomach growls. She wishes she hadn't ruined those sausages. Water seeped through a rip in the foil while she was stowing the watchman's body beneath the pier, making a soggy mess of the packet. She takes the dagger from her boot. Her best chance of approaching the *Selkie* without being noticed, she concludes, is to swim. She has a sailor's fear of the water, and of sharks, but she's dealt with that fear before. The sun strong on her back, she rows to within a hundred meters of the cabin cruiser, hoping the light chop is sufficiently busy to hide the dory, and drops the sea anchor. She shucks her boots and strips off her shirt, bites down on the dagger's blade and slips over the side. The water feels like a new, cool skin.

As she swims, rain needles the sea and the leading edge of the squall darkens the sky. Annie's less than twenty meters from the *Selkie,* when a figure in shorts appears in the stern. Klose. She stops swimming, keeping afloat by moving her arms. Klose appears to be staring directly at her, but gives no sign of alarm. He has a drink from a plastic bottle, then ducks down, going out of sight. He must be attempting repairs on the engine. She starts to swim again, dog-paddling, not wanting to make a splash, angling toward the bow. Music, faint and jangly, comes across the distance. On reaching the boat, she realizes the bow is too high—she'll have to board in the stern. She works her way around to the other side of the craft and hangs onto a projection. The music is cut off. Selkie calls out, asking a question in German. Klose's response, also in German, is curt. Annie waits for the music to resume, but it does not. There is only the slap of wavelets against the hull, the hiss of the rain, an occasional sound of metal on metal. She'll have to be quick.

She gathers herself, seeking in the stream of time a propitious moment, a moment that summons her, and then she launches herself from the water, jaws clamped tightly upon the dagger, clutching the rail; her feet find purchase and she vaults over it, landing in a half-crouch. Kneeling by the open hatch, wrench in hand, Klose turns toward her, his aghast, grease-smeared face a parody of shock. Annie stabs downward, but the blade is deflected by Klose's wrench. He calls to Selkie, tries to stand, but he's twisted around, thrown off-balance by the blow. She slips behind him, bars an arm about his neck, strangling his outcry, and hauls him erect; she bends him backward and drives the dagger into his side, excavating under the ribs with the blade. He stiffens, thrashes about, makes an effort to see her, as if hoping to engage her mercy with his eyes. She stabs again, quieting his struggles, though he pries at her arm, which is slick from his spittle. A third blow quiets him utterly. His fingers unpeel from her arm, the wrench falls, he slumps to the deck. The rain, coming down harder now, sluices away his blood before it can pool.

At the bottom of the companionway, the door to the cabin stand ajar. Selkie must have heard the commotion, and Annie waits for her to emerge, to call to her husband, to peek out.

The cabin cruiser rocks on the heavying chop.

Gusts of wind slanting the rain,
whitecaps pitching,

land and sea gone gray as death.

At length, alert for surprises, she creeps down the ladder, pushes open the door with the point of the dagger, and passes through the galley into the sleeping quarters. Selkie is lying on her belly in a bunk, one foot in the air, wearing a pair of opaque pink panties. She's leafing through a magazine, headphones over her ears. Annie's captivated by the shape of her leg, the curve of her back. So like Mary in her carefree attitude, yet entirely unlike her in form. Plush and soft where Mary was lean and muscular. Annie steps inside the cabin and undergoes a dislocation. It's as if she's standing in a ruder cabin with dark, ill-fitted boards and a port whose glass is warped and bespotted with birdlime. The vision dissolves and once again the windows are narrow, the walls paneled, the bunk carpentered out of some polished reddish wood. Yet the shade of that other cabin persists and she thinks it may be a sign of more significant persistence. She recalls a Hindu sailmaker aboard the *William* who told stories of souls passing from one flesh to another, stories that charmed her with their easy, airy logic and caused her to rethink the moral oversimplifications of the Christian creed (not that she was ever a zealot)—it seemed just that the character of one's life, as the sailmaker claimed, was a punishment for sins committed during a previous existence, that good be rewarded with perfect emptiness, that evil men be reborn as calves or suckling pigs, kings as chattels, and pirates as whores, all that was hard and strong in them made pliant and submissive.

Selkie turns onto her side and sees Annie. She registers the blood on his clothing. Her eyes drop to the dagger, sheathed in Klose's blood. A look of fright occupies her face. She presses back into the corner of the bunk, breasts nodding, one hand clutching the sheet, the other braced against the wall.

"The money," Annie says.

Tremulously, Selkie says, "In the galley. The cabinet under the sink. Please! Don't hurt me."

Annie half-turns, intending to investigate, but is struck by a more vivid dislocation—Mary, brown and naked, holding out her arms, inviting her into an embrace.

"Mary?" Annie says. "Is it you?"

She cannot believe it, yet neither can she deny the temptation toward belief—she wonders now if the things of herself she recognized in Selkie were intimations of Mary reborn in this harlot's flesh. They shared a soul, she and Mary, though Annie owned the stronger half of it.

"Mary?" she says again, and her heart beats faster, as if those two syllables keyed the racing of her blood.

Selkie's fear has been diluted by bewilderment, and Annie, uncertain herself, comes a step nearer.

"Do you not know me, Mary?" she asks. "It's Annie."

Bewilderment, again. And then a canniness shows itself in Selkie's expression. Hesitantly, she puts a hand to her temple, the gesture seeming to convey that she's experiencing an inner turmoil, that what Annie said has waked something inside her and provoked a fleeting recognition; yet it's such an artificial gesture, it fails to convince, and the look of dismay that accompanies it accents this failure.

"Annie?" she says. "I . . ."

She makes a second pass with her hand, the fingertips just touching her cheek. A feeble noise issues from her throat. It appears she's caught between grief and the memory of love, between her husband's blood and a fleeting glimpse of another time.

Annie realizes that Selkie must have heard the story of Dagger Key from Klose and, confronted by this dangerous man with her husband's blood on his knife, someone she must assume is deranged, she's attempting to play a tune he'll dance to—but that she's acting is no proof of anything. Mary was always quick-witted. It may be she's both acting and stirred by a memory.

Lowering the dagger, Annie sits down on the edge of the bunk, places her hand on Selkie's thigh. A tremor runs through the milky flesh, but Selkie does not freeze up, rather her expression grows dreamy and unfocused; her eyes drift to Annie's fingers, lying so near her quim. And Annie, possessed by yet another memory, re-envisioning the time when Mary first revealed herself and, lying back, let her knees fall apart to show Annie her rosy . . . Annie twigs aside the flimsy pink fabric and slides a finger along Selkie's lips. Already moist. She cannot be, Annie thinks, so good at playing a part that her body would not betray her.

Selkie's belly quakes, her hips bridge up off the mattress as Annie thrust two fingers inside her. The cabin shrinks around them. There is no corpse abovedecks, no history of betrayal. All that exists is the sounds of rain and wind, the rolling of the boat, the bunk. Lost amid the recollection of other days with the rain sawing and wind gusting hard, the *William* knocked about on a choppy sea, Annie cuts away the panties and lowers between Mary's legs, Selkie's legs, making play with tongue, teeth and lips, until Selkie's outcry lights the sexual darkness and her thighs clamp viselike to Annie's head. They lie quietly for a time. Annie rests her head on Selkie's belly, her mind thronged with contraries, the urge to have done with this fancy contending with the desire to linger, to make of the day an idyll, or more than a day. After three hundred years, she has earned a bit of freedom, has she not? She exults in the taste coating her tongue, the scent cloying her nostrils. Then Selkie, Mary . . . she shifts away and sits on her haunches. Tentatively, she fingers the top button of Annie's shorts and, when Annie doesn't object, she undoes the buttons and slides the shorts down past her hips. Annie's momentarily put off by the sight of a man's yard standing to attention between her thighs and, when Selkie takes it in her mouth, it seems unnatural to know a man's portion of pleasure. But in that milk-pale face she finds the lineaments of Mary's darker, angular face. She closes her eyes, holds tight to the dagger and recalls a fiercer delight.

In the afterglow of sex, Selkie cuddles, her arm flung across Annie's chest. She whispers, "Oh, Annie. It is you!" She, Selkie, claims to have been awakened by Annie, a process that began when she met him at the café. Met *her*, rather. It's all so confusing! When she touched her hand, she had this curious *frisson*, a sense of there having been something between them. Does he remember that moment? Did he feel it, too? Ever since, bits and pieces of memory have leaked into her head. And then the kiss . . . She's sorry about that. Alvin forced her to paint her lips with the drug. Of course, she was a willing complicitor. She hadn't recognized Annie yet. Not entirely. But when they kissed, that's when the memories really started to come. She can't recall much about their time together, mere fragments, but she will remember, she thinks, with Annie's help. And now, well, they'll sell the cross and then they'll travel, just as they always wanted. England and the Continent. Asia. Annie is charmed by this portrait of an ideal life and makes an affirmative noise, and Selkie, appearing to gain in confidence, prattles on about getting a little cottage somewhere, a home base. For the most part, Annie believes none of what Selkie says, yet she can't discount it utterly, because Selkie's physical reactions remind her so much of Mary's. When Annie toys with her nipples, she shivers and gives a little musical sound that's identical to the one Mary used to make. She thinks it strange that Selkie's pillowy breasts would respond the same way as Mary's, which were the size of onions. Yet all her soft cries and responses bear an astounding similarity to Mary's and, as a result, Annie allows herself to be seduced by Selkie's dream of the future, however calculated it may be. It's as if the cabin has been crammed with the invisible furniture of another life . . .

> . . . with bolts of silk,
> half-unrolled,
> gold coins spilled from a chest
> the size of a piglet,
> the sound of Jack pissing
> into a pewter jug,
> a tall mirror with an ebon frame
> reflecting the tumbled bed,
> two tousled female heads,
> and beyond,
> past the window frame,
> a dawn sky, a flotilla of lavender clouds . . .

> Annie lives among those clouds
> for a time.
> She breathes in spices,
> tastes a softer clime . . .

Then, shocked from that dream, perhaps by some ancient reflex, a sense of wrongness, a ghostly alarm given, or perhaps it's simply a matter of the overcast brightening, the squall lessening, the change in the weather alerting her to the need for action, she makes one of those abrupt decisions upon which her life has always turned. She leans over Selkie, who's half-asleep, and, using the point of the dagger, nicks the artery in the side of her neck. Selkie's eyes snap open. She clamps a hand to the wound to stifle the blood spray. She mouths a word: Annie. She pleads silently for a life that's spewing out between her fingers.

"Go," Annie says to her, retreating from the bunk. "Hurry from this world."

Selkie gurgles; her eyes widen further.

Annie's heart is numb, her spirit is numb. She leaves Selkie struggling on the bed, goes into the galley, looks in the cabinet and collects the biscuit tin; on the same shelf as the tin lies a bulky object wrapped in linen rags. She hesitates, then lets it lie. They've paid a sufficient price to carry it with them into eternity and, without the burden of the cross, Annie reckons that she's one step closer to extinction . . . and, mayhap, rebirth. Serve her right, it would, if she were to be Mary's victim in another existence. She snatches a hatchet from the wall and tests the edge—it will serve to scuttle the boat. She steps back into the sleeping quarters. Selkie's fingers are still pressed to the wound, her eyes are open, but judging by the blood pooling on the sheets, she is either dead or close to death. There's still a trace of color in her face. Annie studies her for a moment, feeling both regret and vindication. The voluptuous body on the bunk and the memory of Mary offer a dissonance and an affinity that she cannot resolve. It seems that she has been confronted by something approximating this odd imbalance in every relationship she's had.

"If you are Mary, God rest ye. We'll meet again someday," Annie says by way of farewell. "If you're not, you should remember it's ever a bad omen to sail on a vessel that bears your name."

*I*t's closer to morning than midnight when Fredo returns to Swann's Cafe, walking the beach from the pointed tip of the island. He's wearing a clean T-shirt and trousers that he knows must belong to Klose, and he has no memory of what happened aboard the *Selkie*. The biscuit tin under his arm, however, tells him that no good came that day to the German couple. And, too, he has a cloudy memory of a struggle with Wilton Barrios that will not come clear. High, thin clouds rush across the moon, reducing but not obscuring its radiance, and the wind blows steadily at his back as if pushing him toward home. When he reaches the L-shaped palm, he feels about in the sand for a key, finds it, and opens the door to the café. He digs with his hands in the packed sand behind the counter. Once the hole is deep enough, he places the biscuit tin in it, covers it with sand and stamps it smooth. Only then does he light a kerosene lamp. He sits at the counter, stares at the brightly painted boards for the longest time—they have the look of a puzzle that's been fitted together, but the puzzle in his mind is scattered and fathomless. Exhausted, he puts his head down on his elbows. He drifts toward sleep, but the thought of the murders he almost certainly has committed pricks him to alertness and he sits up straight. Immediately, he wants to rest his head again, but instead he takes the broom from behind the counter and begins to sweep. He has been sweeping for about fifteen minutes, losing himself in the task, when the door creaks, giving him a fright. Emily peeks in, her hair covered by a paisley scarf. He doesn't know what to say to her, so he lowers his head and takes an ineffectual swipe with the broom.

"Why you don't come home, Fredo?" she asks, slipping into the café. "You know I'm worrying about you."

"I just get back," he said. "I thought I do some cleaning."

She steps close, puts her hands on his waist. "You all right?"

He drops the broom and enfolds her in an embrace. Tears start from his eyes. They hold one another in silence, and then Emily pushes him away. "You hungry? I make you a sandwich if you want."

He sits again at the counter while she busies herself in the kitchen. A brownish stain on his thumbnail attracts his attention. He scrapes at it with a fingernail until it is gone. Through the kitchen door, he can see Emily's back—she's bent over the cutting board. "How the boys?" he asks.

"Palace, he act angry all the time you gone. That how he show he's worried, I expect. Jenry . . ." She makes a fretful noise with her tongue. "I don't know what to do about that boy." She glances at him over his shoulder. "You get the money?"

"Yeah. I bury it back of the counter."

"You have trouble getting it?"

He lets the question hang for a moment. "I gone for . . . what is it? Must be more than a day, and you ask me that? Damn right, I have me some trouble! There's blood on these hands. I don't remember nothing about it, but I know!"

Not moving a muscle, Emily stands with her head down, back bowed, hands on the cutting board.

"I know," says Fredo weakly.

Emily returns to her labors, but says nothing. She finishes the sandwiches and carries them to Fredo. Cheese, lettuce, avocado. And bacon.

"I got that bacon for you yesterday," she says. "I had to cook it up, or else it spoil."

Fredo nods his thanks, has a bite. The taste fuels his hunger—suddenly he's ravenous and wolfs down half a sandwich. Emily fetches him a warm Coke and he takes a swig.

"We going to give some of that money to the church," Emily says firmly.

Fredo swallows. "You think if we slip Jesus a little something extra, that make it right?"

"Don't talk that way to me! Don't make out it's only you gots to bear this burden! I bearing it, too. Difference is, I glad to bear it for the boys."

Fredo has another bite, chews. "Sorry."

"I don't need your sorry, I needs you to be a man."

"Ain't I proved that to you? You can't allow me to have a bad feeling about things?"

Emily comes around to his side of the counter, puts her arms around him and kisses his cheek. "We both of us on edge. Things going to go better now."

"This thing with Wilton," Fredo says. "I can't get it out of my head."

"What about Wilton?"

He relates his clouded memory of a struggle between he and Wilton up at the notch.

"I'm not going to waste tears over Wilton," says Emily. "If it happen, it were because he try and steal from us. The same with the Germans. Two days, Fredo. You gone two days. You know they must try and cheat you."

"True," he says.

"No matter her evil ways, Annie always protect this family. We in the clear—you can trust her to make certain of that. All that's left is for us to live with what she done." Emily cups his face in both her hands. "Together, we strong enough. It take some doing, but we'll manage."

The flickering light softens the iron of her expression. He seems to see down to her irresolute self and understands that she's as frightened as he of the mortal consequences of Annie's crimes. Oddly enough, that comforts him more than her assurances. He kisses the knuckles of her hands and sighs.

"If it up to me," he says, "I throw that damn cup into the sea. The dagger, too."

She pulls away, sits on a stool beside him. "Maybe we should take the money and leave the island behind. Maybe that be best for everyone."

"It's something to think about," he says. "But I too weary to make decisions now. We got time to work it through."

"Why don't you go on up and get some sleep? I finish with the cleaning."

"I ain't ready to sleep. You need anything from town?"

"Some fish would be nice. Maybe a barracuda head for a stew."

"Nothing else?"

"The usual. Bread, bananas . . . you know."

They settle back into their familiar roles, discussing the functioning of the café, the household, taking refuge in gentle talk that seems to rise up like smoke to conceal the strangeness of the past days, Emily laughing as Fredo tells her about Garnett Steadman, his story of how he saw a vast congregation of mackerel off the reef, and Fredo chuckling over Emily's gossip about Annabelle Lister and her several lovers.

Outside, the sky is purpling. Some of the stars have disappeared. A solitary wave crunches on the reef. The wind has all but died, an occasional breeze lifting a palm frond, causing a hibiscus blossom to nod. Crabs glide and scuttle across the beach, pausing in their race, hearkening to an indefinite signal. Somewhere inland, an engine sputters to life. Beneath the dock at Treasure Cove, the night watchman floats in murky water, tiny fish swimming in and out of his eyeless sockets. In the notch, the vine matte writhes, clacking its braided cowrie shells, and grows still. Fifty feet below, in a thicket of thorny shrubs, the corpse of Wilton Barrios has been rendered unrecognizable by dogs. Vultures soar on an aerial above hills that are starting to show green. The morning widens, the eastern sky is pinked. All the mysteries of Dagger Key are being obscured beneath the semblance of an ordinary day, buried in light. What's true remains unknown, what's false is abundantly clear. Fredo steps from the café, fires up a cigarette, and stares toward Belize. His exhalation suggests an expansive measure of relief. A pariah dog ambling along the edge of the water pauses to sniff at the still-pulsing body of a jellyfish.

    The seagull's wing
  divides the wave,
    the lights of Swann's Café
        grow dim . . .

STORY NOTES

Stars Seen Through Stone

I made my living for a decade as a rock musician, mostly in the Detroit area. Though many of my collaborators were excellent technicians, most of the musicians I played with were not terrific human beings. Speaking generally, they had enormous egos and the attention span of gerbils, and tended to sulk when their every whim wasn't being catered to. A case in point, I recall a rhythm guitar player who had been in a mood, unresponsive and scowling and occasionally belligerent. After a couple of weeks, he made his difficulty known to me, drawing me aside and asking in a surly tone, "How come you write all the songs?"

I was surprised, since he had never expressed any previous interest in writing, and I said, "I don't know, man. Why don't you write one?"

He was nonplussed by this, having expected me to argue for my creative primacy, but soon recovered and said that he would get right on it. I never heard any more about songwriting from him, but his mood improved immeasurably.

Minor problems of this sort were endemic, but from time to time they escalated. On one occasion, we were playing an outdoor concert in front of seven or eight thousand people, when the rhythm section fell apart behind me. I turned and discovered that the drummer and the keyboard player were having a fistfight on stage. All bands have these personality conflicts to one degree or another, but I would wager that most bands never had to deal with anyone like the man upon whom the character of Joe Stanky is modeled.

Not only are all the episodes concerning Stanky are solidly grounded in fact; I have underplayed the pain-in-the-ass that he actually was and omitted the most egregious of his malefactions for fear he would be perceived as unrealistic. For example, when he broke up with his inamorata, "Liz," Stanky, displaying a zeal and—I must say—a certain stick-to-it-iveness that he had never shown with the band, waited until she went home to visit her mother and proceeded to masturbate on all her possessions, paying especial attention to her books and records. He then fled the premises.

He was like a great, ugly child who had to be watched over, nurtured, punished, and fed. I was forced to see to his dental care. A trumpet player without teeth is scarcely an asset, and his teeth were in a state of dire neglect. Despite the fact that he made my life difficult for a couple of years, he was an immensely talented musician, and I was, like Vernon in the story, a fool for talent. Perhaps this was the root of my downfall in the music business. But I wasn't a complete fool—eventually I severed all ties with him. A few years later, I was chopping wood in front of my house, when I saw a penguin-like figure walking down the street toward me. A chill swept over me. As the figure drew near, I realized it was, indeed, Stanky. He came up, all smiles, exhibiting the body language of a dog who has been beaten, and began talking about "the good old days," what a great band we'd had, etc. He asked if I had a band currently and suggested that we should get together and play some music.

I had the ax in my hand, and perhaps I made some twitch that persuaded him I might be feeling murderous, for he quickly dropped that topic and, after fumbling around for a bit, he tried another tack, coming at the subject obliquely, and began telling me how he was a changed man due to his acceptance of Jesus Christ. I never saw him again after that day, but I kept expecting him, like a curse, to reappear.

And now, in this story, he has.

Emerald Street Expansions

I'm not much of a reader. I read a lot when I was a kid, but after I got to college I stopped for about fifteen years, partly because the way literature was taught put me off the good stuff. I still don't read as much now as I suppose I should. But once in a while I've gone on jags during which I read an author's entire output . . . or as much as I can tolerate. I read Foucault and Celine in this fashion, also Balzac and de Maupassant, Cendrars and Mallarmé and Genet, Proust and Michaud . . . It seems I have something of a passion for French writing. When I was sixteen or so, I read all of what remains of the work of Francois Villon and was struck by the lines:

> ". . . when I lie down at night,
> I have a great fear of falling."

I've been unable since to find the poem that contains those lines, so this story may be based on a misapprehension (though it's as likely that my attempt at finding it was desultory). Anyway, I was fascinated by Villon, who was a thief and a poet. I also fancied myself a poet and a criminal (though, in truth, I was far more criminal than poet, having been arrested for several minor offenses and having no published work), and I greatly admired Villon for his career flexibility. And so, later in life, I wrote this story for no other reason than to express that admiration and for the opportunity to do a pastiche of his style.

I should mention, because she will vilify me if I don't, that the aspect and character of Amorise is derived partly from Villon's poem, "The Testament," and partly from a friend of mine, Elle Mauruzak, who played in the Goth-punk band, The Hiss, and worked by day in what is fondly referred to by some Seattle-ites as the Ban Roll-on Building, due to its similarity in appearance to that product.

Limbo

I knew a guy in Detroit named Alkazoff who was a member of the Armenian Mafia, who were reputed to be behind most of the organized crime in the area. I first met him in this vast, dingy poolroom on Woodward Avenue, a major artery of Detroit, and, as we shared a common background in music and were equally matched as pool players, we wound up spending time together. We both were devotees of boxing and, since Alkazoff was connected, he could get great seats and would occasionally take me along. Sometimes we went to the fights in the company of his associates and on those occasions I felt like a chicken among foxes. I never *really* felt in danger among them, but Alkazoff had told me stories, carefully edited, about his life and I suspected that some of these men had figured in those stories and that there was blood on their hands. When I became a writer, I started a piece based on the stories that Alkazoff had told me, but I lost interest in the factual material and turned it into a story about a criminal hiding from other criminals, using Alkazoff as the protagonist.

The setting of the story, the town of Champion, the lake and the cabin, reflects a place in the Upper Peninsula of Michigan where my ex-wife and I spent a pleasant vacation one autumn. My most salient memory of the time (a memory I tried unsuccessfully to fit into "Limbo") is that one morning I dropped acid, took my National Steel guitar (a lovely old thing with a painting of a girl waterskiing on the back), and went into the woods to write songs. I found a sunny spot between two fallen trees that lay about thirty feet apart, and sat with my back against one and plunked away. It was incredibly peaceful there, with birds chittering, lots of little sounds, the sun warming my bones, and that peace infected me. I felt in absolute harmony with my environment, and perhaps I was, for soon birds and squirrels began hopping about me, coming close enough to touch. It was like a damn Disney movie. I smiled beatifically at them and made incidental music for the film. I'd been in this state for perhaps an hour when suddenly an animal popped up from behind the fallen tree opposite me, bracing with its forepaws on the trunk. I stared at it inquisitively, wondering what delightful forest creature had now been sent my way. It was, I'd estimate, about 40 pounds in weight, with a bear-like body and a head like a cross between those of a raccoon and a dog. It stared back at me for five or six seconds, and emitted a fierce, high-pitched growl, rather like the outcry of a tiny jaguar; then it disappeared behind the trunk and, apparently, went to tend other business. When I returned to the cabin that afternoon, I told the wife, a native of Michigan, about my day and described the animal to her and asked if she knew what it was.

"You're lucky it didn't tear you apart," she said, busy doing something at the sink. "That was a wolverine."

"No shit?"

She proceeded to tell me in brief about the ferocity of wolverines, relating an anecdote or two by way of illustration, and repeated, "You were lucky."

"Huh," I said.

Liar's House

"Liar's House" is one of several stories I've written about the dragon Griaule, (the first being "The Man Who Painted The Dragon Griaule") and there will be at least two more. The idea of Griaule occurred to me when I was stuck for something to write while attending the Clarion Workshop— I went out onto the campus of Michigan State University and sat under a tree and smoked a joint to jog my brain. I then wrote down in my notebook the words "big fucking dragon." I felt exceptionally clever. Big stuff, I thought, is cool.

The notion of an immense paralyzed dragon, more than a mile in length and seven hundred feet high, which dominates the world around him by means of its mental energies, seemed appropriate to the Reagan Administration; but even a paralyzed dragon must grow and change, and for this story I decided, during the course of writing it, that Griaule would want children—how then would he go about it? Well, who cares, really? I understand that Griaule is representative of Christ or Oprah or some other mythic figure, but we're talking about a bloody dragon here. However, in case you do care, such was—stated in question form—my idiot thesis.

I don't know what it is that brings me back to Griaule. I hate elves, wizards, halflings, and dragons with equal intensity. Maybe it's because I saw a list once of fictional dragons ordered by size and mine was the biggest. And the stories are fairly popular. It makes me think that I might make a career of this, writing stories about the biggest whatever. The biggest gopher, an aphid the size of a small planet, a gargantuan dust bunny. Anyway, the next story in the Griaule cycle or whatever it is will be "Beautiful Blood," which will be published by Night Shade Books in '08 and details certain unusual properties of the dragon's blood. And the last story, a short novel of approximately 60,000 words, will be entitled *The Grand Tour*, and will be included with the other stories, collected in a single volume.

Unlike the majority of my stuff, there's little autobiographical material in "Liar's House", the exception being that the sketch of the hotel's owner is based on one of my old landlords, a man who surely will have his own special boutique hell. God bless you, Mr. Weimer, wherever you are. When it comes time for you to pass, I'll be there with itching powder and a ball gag to make certain your last moments are a joy.

Dead Money

For a long time now, I've intended to revisit the materials of my first novel, *Green Eyes*, and the female protagonist of that novel, Jocundra Verret.

"Dead Money" is the result. I had wanted to put a poker game into the novel, but Terry Carr thought it would break the continuity of the narrative and I see now that, as was his habit, Terry was right.

Occasionally I play poker at a local card room. I never win much, never lose much, but I like the game and the environment, and I could easily lose a whole lot more if I let myself go. There's a guy who comes into the card room who sometimes uses a cane, sometimes not. I have no idea if he's a good player or bad, but he's the model for Josey Pellerin in the story. I've never exchanged a word with him, so I have no idea what he's about, but he looks cool in his black cowboy hat and shades, and I've imagined various sinister reasons for his condition.

Some relationships are like self-inflicted wounds. Jack's relationship with Jocundra is like that—he knows it's going to be bad for him, but he goes ahead in spite of that and, though he reads innumerable signs along the way directing him to desist, he continues pursuing it to the bitter end. Obviously, many people have this same propensity. For my part, show me a woman who's a psychological wreck and, better, doesn't know she's a wreck and, better yet, has a prescription for anti-depressants, a trouble-plagued, ongoing relationship, and bursts into tears every few minutes . . . hey, I'm there! I assume that this signals some sort of mental problem, but why fix it if it ain't broke? I'm considering having T-shirts printed that bear the legend, "You're Beautiful—Just Shoot Me Now", and business cards that say . . . Well, never mind.

Enough of matters sub-textual.

The Seminole Hard Rock Casino and Hotel in Hollywood, Florida is one of God's most egregious errors. I recommend you spend a night there if you ever get down South Florida way and are, like myself, an aficionado of the grotesque and love the smell of terminal despair. Perhaps the International Conference on the Fantastic could be moved there—it might liven things up. Judging by the chests of the waitresses, hostesses, and pros who populate the place, there must be a silicon mine nearby. Look too closely, you could lose an eye. Gaping old men with ghastly complexions teeter on the bar stools; old women with leathery tanned skin, heavy gold bracelets adorning their liver-spotted wrists, lounge by the pool like alligators who have put on a human guise, their cold eyes tracking the cabana boys. It is home to mutants of every imaginable stamp. Aliens could land on the grounds and people would believe it was a publicity stunt. After a while they'd embrace those nine-foot-tall green beans with eyes and fangs as part of their natural surroundings. Seriously, folks.

The Seminole Paradise. Check it out.

Dinner at Baldassaro's

My stories often begin life with, not an idea, but a phrase or a sentence, often not part of the opening, though in this instance it was. This particular sentence ("Giacinta had a beautiful sneeze.") originally was in a story set in present-day Havana, concerning a CIA agent recuperating from a broken hip in his Havana apartment, stoned on painkillers, who is alternately keeping tabs on the progress of an operation and remembering his days in the Canal Zone and a young brother-and-sister whom he caught gleaning the high-security dumpsite. That story has been stewing in my pot for many years, and I'm beginning to doubt it will ever be done; so I lifted the sentence and used it to open the present story.

I spent a few days in Diamante not too long ago directly following the town's chile pepper festival, a week during which the townspeople decorate everything, including themselves, with peppers, an event I was happy to avoid. I prefer to visit places in the off-season, when they let drop the disguise they have adopted for the tourist trade. While there, I had a dream in which the waters of the Tyrrhenian Sea were transformed overnight into a garden of heroic statuary. The story developed backward from that point and deals with one of my favorite recurring paranoid fantasies: I have always suspected (though I doubt it's true) that the world would not have gotten this fucked-up unless someone was orchestrating things toward that end.

There simply aren't enough Cro Magnon stories for my tastes. Let's leave it at that.

Abimagique

When I lived in Seattle, I sometimes took lunch in a little teriyaki place in the University District (Teriyaki Plus, near the corner of 45th and Roosevelt). It was notable for the fact that Bill Gates had eaten there, an event commemorated by a Polaroid of The World's Richest Nerd on the wall above one of the tables. Often I would find a zaftig woman with orange and black hair eating alone at one of the tables, reading a paperback. Despite being slightly overweight, she was quite attractive and I wondered why no one ever hit on her—the restaurant was frequented by students at the University of Washington, many of them males who targeted her with stares.

One afternoon I went home and wrote the paragraph that opens this story, except in the first person. It sat in my computer for several years, then, while I was recovering from a serious back injury, unable to write in other than short bursts, I opened the file and, on a whim, changed the paragraph to the second person. That inspired me to write a couple of pages. When I picked up the story a few months later, I quickly realized I was writing a novella in the second person, present tense, a difficult chore; but I thought, What the hell.

I made the narrator callow in the extreme so I could have him drift along cluelessly while the plot happened around him and at the end he'd be no more knowledgeable than, say, you or I would after an intense experience with a Tantric witch and her crippled minions that ended in her death. Human beings are lousy at figuring things out, yet their fictive creations are often brilliant at it, and this strikes me as highly unrealistic; thus I was striving for a kind of bungling naturalism in the character. Bungling naturalism being one of my strengths as a writer, I'm confident I succeeded.

The Lepidopterist

The island of Roatan off the Caribbean coast of Honduras is a place rife with storytellers. John Anderson McCrae, now deceased, was not among the best of them. The best I knew was Devlin Walker, who's mentioned in the story as having two left feet . . . which, in fact, he did. McCrae was always drunk and usually his stories became incoherent ramblings after he had a few. But he had a couple of interesting narrative twitches, not least among them the habit of exclaiming, "God Bless America!," whenever he thought he was losing his audience or preparatory to asking to be bought another drink. So I decided to use him as the narrator for this little political fable.

I originally approached McCrae because I wanted to ask him about Lee Christmas, an American railroad engineer who became, first, a general in the Honduran army and, second, a mercenary who played a major role in establishing the United Fruit Company, a man whom, according to my informants, McCrae had known as a boy. After ten or twelve beers, he took to acting out his story. When he talked about his childhood, telling how his father, a mean drunk, told him to get under the table, he got under the table to demonstrate how he'd obeyed, an exertion that caused him nearly to pass out. We (my brother-in-law and I) hauled him up and tried to get him talking again, but he was too far gone to do other than babble incoherently, punctuating his half-sentences with loud, "God Bless America!"s. This caused some unpleasantness with a group of Americans who were staying at a nearby resort and thought that he was putting them on. I imagine he was, in a way, putting all of us on. But McCrae's attitude toward Americans was not informed by hostility, rather by a gentle humor.

I realize I may have painted him as a colorful relic, a memory souvenir of the Caribbean, but that's not how I viewed him. He was a man who'd seen a lot. His father actually had been a wrecker, and he was afflicted by the fact that he had participated in his father's crimes, which included smuggling and gun-running. He knew a lot, too, and, had he been born to a better estate, who can say what he might have done.

The last time I saw him, he was scuttling from bar to bar in Coxxen Hole, the island's capital. I was impatient to be on my way, let him hustle me for a dollar, and hurried off. He yelled something after me, which I'm certain was a colorful island tribute, but I paid no attention—I was hurrying to meet someone; I can't recall who—and thus it is forever lost. When I returned to Coxxen Hole five years later, McCrae was dead and it was too late (if I ever had the necessary funds) to realize my dream for him. I wanted to buy a TV station and give him an hour in the seven PM slot, usually handed over to reruns, and a set dressed to resemble an island bar. I'd prime him with a six-pack and let him shout "God Bless America!" to his heart's content, using these exclamations as parentheses to enclose his wit and wisdom, gradually sinking into a stuporous condition and passing out just before the last commercial break. I think he'd be huge. No one would believe he wasn't the latest thinking man's comic. It'd be paradise for McCrae. He'd have guests to hustle, pretty girls at whom to leer, and he could afford a liver transplant. And I'm fairly sure that "God Bless America!" would become a catchphrase meaning, more-or-less, "You bet your ass!"

Dagger Key

I wanted to write an old-time pirate story, complete with ship-boardings and chases across the Spanish Main, but I hate doing research. I don't even like being close to more than a few books. Libraries put me to sleep. There must be some chemical given off by all those old books that has a soporific effect on me. The Internet helps, but even there, after a short while, I find myself drifting over to my message board, or I buy something online or visit a sports site . . . In short, I guess I'm lazy. So the problem was to write such a story, yet set in a time with which I was familiar.

When I was a boy, I'd read about Anne Bonny and her lover, Mary Reade, and I decided to write about Annie who, by all accounts, was more bloodthirsty than the men with whom she sailed. I hated to think that, as is commonly held, she wound up as Southern Belle in South Carolina, so I put her on a remote key off the coast of Belize (or in Fredo's head, depending on your interpretation of the story).

Fredo and Emily are based on a couple I met in Guyana fourteen years ago. They had, to my mind, the most equitable marriage I've ever been privy to. They were so reasonable with one another, I assumed that one or both had to be deeply twisted, if not insane, and I was intrigued by the idea that this marriage could be sustained by the lurid fantasy of a serialist or the violent nature of a family ghost.

I've long been an admirer of Peter Mathiessen, the author and naturalist, especially of his classic novel, *Far Tortuga*. In this story, I wanted to do homage to him and to the experimental typography of that novel. I wanted to go him one better and incorporate bits of poetry into the prose, because life along the Caribbean littoral strikes me as being intensely poetic in character due to a constant interaction with the natural world, and to the speech of those indigenous to the region, which can be scanned as poetry.

There are other, more significant reasons, of course, why I wrote the story, but this is the sort of thing I tell people who ask.